THE FIFTH FOREIGN LEGION

CONTAINS THREE FULL NOVELS

THE FIFTH FOREIGN LEGION

Contains Three Full Novels

ANDREW KEITH AND WILLIAM H. KEITH, JR.

NEW YORK TIMES BESTSELLING AUTHOR

WordFire Press
Colorado Springs, Colorado

Contents

BOOK ONE:
MARCH OR DIE

PROLOGUE

[M]orrison's Star]: Distance from Sol 112 light years ... Spectral class F7V; radius 1.252 Sol; mass 1.196 Sol; luminosity 2.548 Sol. Stellar Effective Temperature 6420°K ... Eight planets, one planetoid belt. The sole habitable world is the fourth planet, known as Hanuman ...

[IV Hanuman]: Orbital radius 1.25 AUs; eccentricity .0102; period 1.28 solar years (466.76 std. days) ... No natural satellites ...

Planetary mass 0.8 Terra; density 1.15 Terra (6.33 g/ cc); surface gravity 1.02 G. Radius 5658.14 kilometers; circumference 35,551.1 kilometers ... Total surface area 402,306,340 square kilometers ...

Hydrographic percentage 87% ... Atmospheric pressure 1.10 atm; composition oxygen/nitrogen. Oxygen content 24% ...

Planetary axial tilt 9°19'42.8". Rotation period 33 hours, 48 minutes, 7.8 seconds ...

[Planetography]: Hanuman is somewhat less active geologically than Terra.... The planetary terrain, however, is fairly rugged. Just over half the land surface is hill or mountain, with broad, level tracts of ground - coastal or upland plains comprising the rest of the land area. There is one major continent dominating the northern hemisphere, plus five smaller continents and scattered islands.... Tidal effects are minimal....

Equatorial temperatures average near 55°C, while polar temperatures rarely drop below freezing. Warm ocean currents keep coastal areas pleasant even above the Arctic Circle. Humans can live in regions north or south of the 55° latitude lines (particularly in the cooler uplands) … High mountain elevations are dangerous due to the high ultraviolet output of Morrison's Star.…

Temperature and humidity produce wide jungles in the equatorial regions, extending as far as the 60° latitude lines. Beyond these the climate moderates, with temperate forests, upland steppes, deserts …

[Biology]: Intelligent life first arose in the mid-latitude jungles, evolving originally from brachiating omnivore/ gatherer stock in a niche closely paralleling Terrestrial mangrove swamps.… Intelligence arose as a defense mechanism to counter a variety of predators.… The sophonts of Hanuman (they call themselves *kyendyp* in the language of the primary human-contacted nations) are bilaterally symmetrical, up-right bipeds, basically humanoid in gross appearance but differing sig-nificantly in detail. They are homeothermic, with leathery olive-green skin.… The average local stands roughly 1.25 meters in height. They are hairless but possess a ruff of short, quill-like spines around the neck. These normally lie flat against the skin but may stiffen in response to certain emotional stimuli (fear, anger, etc.). The movement of the ruff can be used as a gauge to their reactions.…

The *kyendyp* are full hermaphrodites, simultaneously possessing fully developed male and female sexual organs. Either partner in a sexual union can become pregnant, and any individual can bear and rear young. Children are born live and drink an analogue to milk secreted by the parent. Kyendyp languages have no terms or cases involving gender; the word adopted by humans to replace "he" or "she" is "ky.…"

[Civilization]: The *kyendyp* of the mid-latitude jungles never advanced out of the Stone Age. Those who left the jungles for the cooler uplands of the northern latitudes, however, found that their simple hunter-gatherer life-style was inappropriate.…

At the time of the Semti Conclave's surrender to the Terran Commonwealth a hundred years ago, the civilized *kyendyp* were still roughly equivalent to nineteenth-century Europe in technological achievement, though once the Semti influence was gone their development accelerated dramatically.… There are still large numbers of Stone-Age savages in the jungles, however, who are often exploited by more civilized groups as cheap labor.…

[Commonwealth Contact]: The first Terran settlement was at Fwynzei, an island leased to the Terrans by Vyujiid, which remains the

largest and most civilized of all *kyendyp* nations.... Penetration of
Vyujiid was achieved with little difficulty, thanks to the relatively
enlightened views of the local leaders.... The medicinal value of zyglyn
vines spurred commercial development, strongly sponsored by StelPhar
Industries, which uses processed zyglyn from Hanuman as a base for a
line of full-spectrum antivirals....

Excerpted from
*Leclerc's Guide to the Commonwealth Volume V:
The Devereaux/Neusachsen Region 34th Edition,*
published 2848 AD

Chapter One

We shall all know how to perish,
Following tradition.

—from "*Le Boudin*" Marching Song
of the French Foreign Legion

I can't really explain it." Captain Armand LaSalle made a gesture to encompass the banquet hall. "I just don't think we should trust these monkeys."

Howard Rayburn shrugged. "One hannie's pretty much like another," he said. His languid tone seemed out of character for a captain of the Fifth Foreign Legion. It reminded LaSalle of the pampered young officers of the regular Terran Army. "Why should this bunch be any different?"

LaSalle frowned. "That's just it. This bunch *is* different. When the Semti pulled out a hundred years ago, these little bastards were still primitives. Up to now we've been dealing with civilized hannies, but we can't just assume the same rules apply here."

"*Iy-jai wei sykai?*" A hannie—one of the short, olive-skinned humanoid sophonts native to Hanuman—held a tray before the two Legion officers. "What will you drink, masters?"

"*Iyuniy.*" LaSalle crossed his arms in the local gesture of negation to emphasize the refusal.

"Damn monkey gibberish," Rayburn said irritably. Touching a stud on his wristpiece computer, he said "Gimme wine, junior." The computer echoed his words in the kyendyp tongue of the locals. *"I iyyi diiegyi kytuj-jai."*

The ruff of quills around the hannie's neck stiffened. LaSalle wasn't sure if they were expressing fear or anger. Adchip orientation had left him with a good working knowledge of the languages and customs of the human-contacted regions of Hanuman, but translating the subtle nuances of a local's ruff movements was something few humans ever mastered. The alien might have been in awe of the human-sounding voice speaking from Rayburn's 'piece, or angry at the man's arrogance and disdain. Terran officers who let their computers translate for them instead of taking the trouble to learn local dialects or mores were all too common in the Commonwealth, though.

As Rayburn accepted a slender glass filled with the vile yellowish liquid that passed for wine on Hanuman and sipped it gingerly, LaSalle made a face, looking away. *Diiegyi* contained enough alcohol to satisfy any hard-drinking legionnaire, but its sour flavor was a taste LaSalle didn't like to think about.

The banquet hall was the largest reception room in the sprawling palace the locals called the Fortress of Heaven, the ceremonial capital of the realm of Dryienjaiyeel and the seat of power of the hereditary monarch, the *yzyeel* Jiraiy XII. Most of the throng of guests were members of the nobility of Dryienjaiyeel, the court, military lead-ership, and clergy of the realm. A few lighter-skinned natives moved among them with an air of confident superiority, merchants and diplomats visiting Dryienjaiyeel from Vyujiid, its more civilized neigh-bor to the north. The handful of humans from the Co-monwealth mission to Dryienjaiyeel stood out from the crowd like trees towering over the barren steppes of LaSalle's homeworld, Saint Pierre.

Hairless, with dry, wrinkled, leathery skin, the natives didn't look that much like Terran monkeys, but there were just enough similarities to make the epithet appropriate. The hannies were short and dark, with long arms and barrel chests, wearing colorful but scanty garb. It was hard to think of them as an industrialized civilization here in the barbaric splendor of their ancient royal city. Men like Rayburn came by their bigotry naturally. *We conquered the Semti; we made the Ubrenfars back down. The Terran Commonwealth stands head and shoulders over the rest....*

That kind of arrogance had killed a lot of good soldiers.

"Captain Rayburn?" The voice came from behind, speaking Terranglic with a soft, lilting accent. "Captain LaSalle?"

LaSalle turned to meet the new arrival, a lieutenant dressed like the other officers in the formal full-dress uniform of the Fifth Foreign Legion. The khaki jacket and trousers, blue cummerbund, archaic red and green epaulets, and black kepi were part of a tradition that stretched back over the centuries. Since the days before Mankind had left Mother Terra, legionnaires in similar garb had kept the peace in far-flung colonies. Five different legions serving different masters, different ends ... but always the same tradition of service, honor, and glory.

"What is it, Chiang?" Rayburn was asking.

"Sir, Mr. Leighton wanted me to remind you that it is almost time for the reception ceremony." Chiang blinked owlishly behind thick glasses. Rayburn's Executive Officer didn't look much like a soldier. He was typical of the officers Rayburn preferred for his company: Terran-born, gentlemanly, well-educated. For the officers, at least, Charlie Company was like a miniature Regular Army unit, a far cry from the typical mixed bag of the Legion. Whatever Rayburn, Chiang, and their platoon leaders might have done to warrant assignment to the frontiers, they seemed determined to maintain their own standards regardless of their surroundings.

LaSalle smiled faintly. He wondered if Charlie Company's fastidious officers liked outpost duty here in Dryienjaiyeel, in Hanuman's mid-latitude jungles where temperatures rarely dropped below 30°C and humidity, rain, and mud were worse enemies than any native.

"I guess we'd better go line up so the head monkey can play king," Rayburn said. He set his glass carelessly on a passing waiter's platter and straightened his tie. "Then maybe we can get out of this goddamned hothouse and back into cli-control. Coming, LaSalle?" Though Rayburn was nominally the junior captain, he managed to sound like an aristocrat ordering a servant.

That was inevitable any time you mixed Terran-born officers with men like LaSalle, colonials whose fathers and grandfathers had won their Citizenship the hard way, earning it in service to the Commonwealth. Anyone born on Terra or one of the other Member-worlds was a Citizen automatically, part of a long line of Citizens, and was apt to regard himself as superior to any mere colonial. LaSalle had suffered under the system since the first day he'd entered the army.

The two officers pushed their way through the throng, past native courtiers in elaborate ceremonial headdresses, minor functionaries whose clipped neck ruffs were tokens of their complete identification with their *yzyeel*, and soldiers whose trappings were an odd cross between the traditional and the starkly functional. LaSalle's eyes narrowed as he studied one such, a senior NCO in the Dryien army according to the facial dye that marked unit and rank around the soldier's muzzle. The native's complex harness and ornate daggers were traditional enough, but the short assault rifle and the pistol holster both showed signs of long, hard service. That was unusual; Dryienjaiyeel court troops were hardly ever employed in the field....

The NCO had the look of a trained soldier, too. LaSalle had seen enough nonhuman troops in his service with the Legion to recognize the universals that transcended species lines. Ky was a veteran, no mere ornamental court guard. Transferred for meritorious service in the *yzyeel's* ongoing war with the savages of the southern jungles? Maybe. But the sight brought back LaSalle's concern in full force.

"Ah, LaSalle, Rayburn. 'Bout time." Geoffrey T. Leighton, Commonwealth Envoy to the *yzyeel* of Dryienjaiyeel, was a big man with a booming, jovial voice. "It wouldn't do for the senior garrison officers to be out of place when The Excellent makes kys appearance, y'know."

"Yes, sir," LaSalle responded, but Leighton didn't seem to notice the answer. The diplomat's eyes had taken on a glassy, far-away look.

Listening to his implant, LaSalle thought with a twinge of jealousy. Back on Terra, tiny computer implants were all the rage among aristocrats and government functionaries. They filled the same role as LaSalle's wristpiece, but they were lodged directly in the user's brain. Implants gave their owners what amounted to instant access to any computer records or programs, total recall, automatic translation, near-telepathic communication with others wearing implant chips—a full range of functions without the bother of operating a primitive wristpiece.

"Ah, very good. Very good indeed." Leighton smiled as his eyes focused again on the two officers. "We've just received word from the harbor, gentlemen. Transport just set down in the bay with StelPhar's first consignment of equipment and technicians aboard. They'll hold meetings here before going out to the Enclave."

StelPhar Industries, Terra's largest importer of exotic pharmaceuticals, was the main reason for the Colonial Administration's interest in Dryienjaiyeel. For over thirty years the Commonwealth base at Fwynzei had been sufficient as Hanuman's main port and administrative center, handling a steady traffic in the planet's one valuable export commodity, the zyglyn vine. Processed zyglyn was a useful base for StelPhar's line of full-spectrum antiviral agents and commanded a high price Earthside. But zyglyn grew only in the hot, inhospitable mid-latitude jungles of Hanuman, and for just under a century StelPhar had been forced to depend on native traders to bring the vines from Dryienjaiyeel to Fwynzei.

Now, though, Leighton's patient months of negotiation with the *yzyeel* had yielded a new off-world enclave on Hanuman where Terran colonists would soon be settling to establish direct Commonwealth control over the harvest and shipment of zyglyn vines in much larger quantities than the native traders could hope to supply.

"So soon, sir?" LaSalle asked. "I thought we'd have at least another month before civilians settled in Monkeyville."

Leighton pursed his lips in disapproval. "The Enclave, Captain LaSalle, or Outpost D-2," he said irritably. "How many times do I have to tell you not to use that pejorative name in dealing with the kyen?"

"Sorry, sir," LaSalle answered. Everyone in the two companies of legionnaires employed in constructing and garrisoning the new Terran enclave referred to the complex as "Monkeyville," and to the Legion fort protecting it as "Fort Monkey." The diplomats, of course, were never happy at any hint of bigotry toward the natives and tended to become disdainful at the use of epithets like "hannie" or "monkey," or even the generic "loke" or "ale" in referring to the nonhuman inhabitants of Hanuman.

"As far as the schedule goes," Leighton continued as if LaSalle hadn't spoken, "I believe you reported last week that the Enclave is ready, didn't you?"

"The fort, the landing field, and the settlement buildings are, yes, sir," LaSalle replied. "But we've got more work to do on the inland roads, and I'm still not happy with the outer defenses."

"That work can continue after the StelPhar people settle in," Leighton told him. "After all, your legionnaires will need to find things to keep them employed while they maintain the garrison." Like most of his ilk, Leighton managed to convey massive disapproval in that simple word "legionnaires." The Colonial Administration needed the Legion to do the dirty jobs no one else would do, but that didn't mean they accepted the unit of misfits....

LaSalle pulled his chin thoughtfully. "Mr. Leighton, I don't think it's a good idea to bring in civilians this early," he said at last. All his misgivings seemed to surface at once. "We've had reports of Dryien troop movements into the area around Mon ... the Enclave for over a week now. Not to mention the reports we've been getting of military maneuvers on the northern frontier. And our native contacts have been hinting at some kind of trouble with the government. Not the *yzyeel*, but lower levels. Bureaucrats and military officials, those sorts."

"Unsubstantiated rumors," Leighton huffed.

"Maybe so, sir. But if they're not ..." LaSalle paused. "A lot of the locals out in the jungles are afraid of us. They think Terrans are some kind of demon come to rape the planet after casting out the Gods. I've even picked up stuff like that from the civilized ones here on the coast. Two companies aren't enough to garrison the Enclave against a heavy attack. More than a quarter of my men are brand-new recruits, and my Exec's just out of a Regular Army intel unit, with no combat experience." He glanced at Rayburn. "I'm sure Charlie Company's got the same sort of problems. If there's trouble, my men might not be able to protect civilians."

Leighton turned to Rayburn. "Do you agree with Captain LaSalle on this?"

The other captain grinned. "Hell, no, sir. Ain't no loke—er, native, sir—able to beat the Legion."

LaSalle interrupted. "All I'm asking for is more time, Mr. Leighton. Time to get the recruits shaped up and my Exec broke in ... time to firm up the outer perimeter of the Enclave. And time to find out if there's anything behind those rumors."

The envoy shook his head. "Nonsense. Captain. I can assure you that the *yzyeel's* government is entirely behind us. I'm certainly not going to put off StelPhar just because your legionnaires aren't spit-and-polish soldiers. If I waited for that, the Enclave would never be ready, y'know." He smiled, but there was steel in his eye.

Maybe the yzyeel *is behind us,* LaSalle thought. *Ky's happy as long as the offworlders keep sending pretty new toys to play with. But what about the plantation owners and merchants StelPhar's putting out of business? And what about the bureaucrats who won't be getting the tax revenues from the zyglyn trade any more?*

"If you're concerned about getting the construction work for your perimeter finished, I suggest you see Lieutenant Winters when you get back," Leighton went on. "Schedule your work through her office. Otherwise, I expect you to deal with your problems yourself, Captain." The diplomat turned away, cutting off further discussion.

LaSalle seethed inwardly. As usual, it looked like the Legion was getting the short end of the stick. *That's the way it always is,* he thought bitterly.

Around the banquet hall Terrans and hannies were jostling for position for the entrance of the *yzyeel.* LaSalle watched the courtiers as they argued over precedence. The Terran diplomats remained aloof; they *knew* they were superior to the natives. They moved among the native servants and guards as if the locals didn't exist.

There were quite a few guards in the hall—more than there had been a few minutes ago. Or was it just his imagination finding danger where none existed?

Movement near The Excellent's dais caught LaSalle's eye. A hannie in a particularly ornate harness was just entering the room, not the *yzyeel* but a high-ranking officer. LaSalle recognized ky: Zyzytig, the Dryien general whose office roughly corresponded to chief of staff. The general was in deep conversation with a taller figure swathed in a dark cloak. That angular, gaunt shape filled LaSalle with an instinctive loathing. *Semti! What's one of those ghouls doing here?*

A hundred years ago, the Semti had owned this part of space, before their defeat at the hands of the fledgling Terran Commonwealth and the destruction of their capital. Now the Commonwealth was expanding into the old Semti Conclave while the surviving Semti, their central government gone, submitted meekly to the conquerors. They were superb governors and xenopyschologists, useful mandarins in the Terran administration of the newly acquired territories, apparently eager to continue their work under their new masters without a thought for the war.

But a lot of people found it hard to trust them, LaSalle included. Maybe it was their scavenger ancestry, the foul breath and the hairless vulture skulls. Or perhaps it was their ancient culture and un-fathomable philosophy, which seemed to mock everything human under a mask of helpful service. Not *all* the Semti were friendly; stories of plots against the Commonwealth fomented by discontented Semti schemers surfaced time and again. They were too useful to dispense with, too dangerous to trust....

And one of them was here, in the court of The Excellent. When the Semti ruled Hanuman, they had been worshipped as gods in Dryienjaiyeel, while the Terrans who replaced them were cast as devils who had overthrown the natural order. A Semti agent could do a lot of mischief playing on old superstitions....

"Leighton," LaSalle began. "What's a—"

"Shh! The Excellent is coming." Leighton's voice was a reproving hiss.

Wide doors behind the dais swung slowly open to admit The Excellent, the *yzyeel* of Dryienjaiyeel, Brother of Heaven, Lord of the Eternal Mists, Champion of the Gods. Not quite a king, not quite a pope, the *yzyeel's* power was little short of absolute, but kys authority in the ordinary government was almost nonexistent.

Barely a meter tall, with a soft, innocent face, ky would not reach the age of maturity for another four standard years, but as *yzyeel* the young ruler commanded near-total obedience throughout Dryienjaiyeel. There had been other claimants, of course, when kys parent had died two years ago, and LaSalle had heard mutterings among the common hannies that the selection of Jiraiy XII had been a mistake, that the child-*yzyeel* was too enamored of the offworlders, too easily manipulated, tainted with the curse of the old gods....

The *yzyeel* paused at the front of the dais and Leighton, flanked by LaSalle and Rayburn, stepped forward to honor the young ruler. Each bowed in turn, rendering the ceremonial greeting: fingers clasped, thumbs crossed, palms outward, touching forehead, mouth, and throat. It was all correct, proper, but LaSalle thought he heard a stir in the crowd. Perhaps they resented the fact that the Terran envoy and his military leaders now took precedence over their native counterparts. Or was it something else, some ceremony or gesture Terran chip-training had left out?

A whipcrack sound filled the hall, a thunder LaSalle recognized instantly. *Gunshot!* Dark blood bubbled from the *yzyeel's* throat, oozing through kys ruff. The ruler swayed, staggered, fell. Gunfire erupted throughout the room.

LaSalle threw himself sideways, seeking the cover of a pillar. Leighton and Rayburn went down together as one of the heavy native assault guns sprayed the foot of the dais with full-auto fire. Another Terran, an economic attaché on Leighton's staff, fell to a savage hannie bayonet thrust. Someone was screaming. He wasn't sure if it was a Terran voice, or a native.

Clawing at the holster of his 10mm rocket pistol, LaSalle peered around the pillar at the chaos of the hall. Two hannie guards burst through a door a few meters to his left and opened fire at a trio of native soldiers running toward them, only to fall as autofire hammered from across the room. Two more Terrans fell beyond them—Lieutenant Chiang and Rowlands—the mission's linguistics expert. Near the rear of the hall a man in a Terran Army lieutenant's uniform urged one of the diplomats toward another door. A hannie raised kys gun …

LaSalle squeezed off a round, aiming at the soldier. The tiny 10mm rocket projectile left the barrel with a soft *swoosh* that grew louder as it gathered speed. His target went down in a bloody heap, and the two Terrans dived for safety. The lieutenant fired twice with a laser pistol, the shots making a crackle in the air that left a tang of ozone, but no visible flash. Behind the officer, the diplomat crouched low, eyes darting wildly from side to side.

The captain tried to cover the two, but answering fire from a dozen native rifles *pinged* off the pillar and the wall behind LaSalle. *If I had combat battledress I might have a chance,* he thought grimly. His dress uniform wasn't intended to stop bullets, even the primitive rounds they used on Hanuman.

He snapped off four quick shots and rolled to his left. If he could just reach the other two survivors, they might make it out together.

A pile driver blow to his chest staggered him, spinning him around. He coughed and gasped, feeling pain lance through his body. Then a second bullet hit him, and a third. His hand went numb and he dropped the rocket pistol with a clatter. LaSalle felt himself spinning, falling, hitting the unyielding tile floor. He tried to rise, but another shot slammed into his back.

LaSalle raised his head from the ground, squinting through the red haze of pain. Across the room the Terran lieutenant fired again, then spun backwards as autofire slammed into his chest. Then the civilian was kneeling over the fallen officer, scooping up the laser pistol and firing wildly.

Struggling to rise again, LaSalle felt his strength ebbing fast. A shadow fell across him. He rolled onto his back and found himself looking up at the stooped, gaunt, black-robed form of the Semti. The alien raised one arm slowly, and the tiny weapon concealed in his hand flared.

Agony seared deep in LaSalle's chest. Blackness closed around him, and he felt his life slipping away.

His last thought was of his home … the Legion.

Chapter Two

You legionnaires are soldiers in order to die, and I am sending you where you can die.

—General Francois de Negrier,
French Foreign Legion, 1883

Keep firing, dammit! Maintain your fire!" Lieutenant Colin Fraser staggered and swore silently as a bullet slammed into the plasteel chest plate of his battledress. He dropped to one knee behind an improvised barricade. "Trent! Where the hell is Dmowski with the heavy weapons?"

Gunnery Sergeant John Trent fired a burst from his FE-FEK kinetic energy assault rifle before answering. "He's on the way, L-T." He sounded strangely calm and unemotional, as if oblivious to the firefight raging around them. "Five more minutes." Trent raised his voice abruptly but lost none of his detached, professional manner. "Come on, Krueger, get with it! You've got grenades—use 'em!"

Fraser flipped down the light intensifier display on his helmet. Chaos reigned within Fort Monkey. Panic gripped him with icy fingers, but Fraser forced himself to follow Sergeant Trent's example and remain outwardly calm, in control. *The men are looking to you,* a stubborn inner voice reminded him. *You're in charge until Captain LaSalle gets back.*

If LaSalle was coming back. In the ten minutes since the first attack by Dryien troops, every effort to raise LaSalle and the diplomatic mission in the Fortress of Heaven had been answered by crackling static. And even if the captain was all right now, how was he supposed to reach Monkeyville in an unarmored staff car when what looked like half the *yzyeel's* army was trying to overrun the Legion garrison?

A native machine gun hammered from the top of the north wall, its muzzle flashes showing on LI as a strobing beacon in the gloom. Legionnaire Krueger raised his FEK and triggered a three-round burst of 1cm rocket grenades. They arrowed toward the target with a hiss, impacting in a neat pattern just below the stuttering MG. With a scream, the hannie soldier spun backwards over the parapet and out of sight, kys weapon tumbling to the ground inside the compound.

Two more bullets flattened themselves against Fraser's battledress in quick succession, one against his chest plate, the other on the duraweave material covering his left arm. The second one stung, and Fraser's heart beat faster.

The hannies were primitive by Legion standards. Their technology was roughly equivalent to mid-twentieth century Terrestrial standards, with weapons that would not have been out of place in either of the first two World Wars. Their equipment was eight centuries out of date even measured against the cast-offs that made up the bulk of Legion gear. It would take a lucky hit for conventional munitions to penetrate issue battledress, with or without plasteel armor plates augmenting the protection of the tough fatigue uniform. But sooner or later one of the hannies occupying the northeast tower was going to score that lucky hit—if not on Fraser, then on one of his men.

Even if the hannies were primitive, they outnumbered Bravo Company by at least ten to one. The legionnaires just couldn't afford to take casualties … *any* casualties.

"Sergeant!" Fraser tried without much success to make his orders sharp and crisp. "I want that tower cleared *now*. Those snipers are getting too good a view."

"On it, L-T," Trent responded. He sprinted down the defensive line in a half-crouch, bawling orders as he ran. "Recon lances! Time to earn your pay, you lazy buggers!"

Fraser's FEK whined on full auto, sending a stream of needle-thin slivers hurtling from the muzzle at over 10,000 meters per second with scarcely any recoil. He swung the rifle in a smooth arc, laying down fire across the ragged line of hannies at the foot of the north wall. This fight wasn't so much a battle as a slaughter, but there were a lot more native soldiers out there to replace the ones who fell.

The first attackers had burst in through the north gate, apparently admitted by one of the company's hannie servants or auxiliaries without raising an alarm. If Sergeant Trent had not been making the rounds of the barracks area when the first shots were fired ... Fraser didn't want to think about that. Alerted, with high-tech weaponry and uniforms virtually impervious to small arms, the legionnaires could beat the monkeys easily.

But the natives had the advantage of numbers ... and they were on their home turf, with supplies and reinforcements close at hand. The legionnaires couldn't even raise their captain. Or Charlie Company, scattered in outposts deeper in the Dryien jungles to the west. He glanced at his command/control/communications technician. *If only she would get through to someone....*

As if in answer to Fraser's unvoiced thoughts, the C^3 operator looked up from her field communications pack and grinned at Fraser. "I've got something, Lieutenant!"

"What is it, Garcia?" Fraser ducked down behind the barricade. Around them the other legionnaires kept firing.

"A transport lighter ... *Ganymede*." Angela Garcia made a quick adjustment to the console and handed Fraser a patch cord. "They're in the capital harbor."

He plugged the cord into a terminal on the side of his helmet, switched on his commlink, and spoke aloud. His throat mike picked up his words. "*Ganymede*, this is Alice One. Do you copy? Over."

"Alice One, *Ganymede*. Reading you five by five. Hold for Captain Garrett."

Static crackled on the line before a new voice cut in. "Alice One? What's your situation?"

Fraser winced as machine-gun fire rattled off the barricade. "*Ganymede*, we're under attack by an unknown number of native regulars. Nothing but infantry so far, no armor, air support, or heavy arty. At least not yet. We're holding our own, but ..." He trailed off.

"Roger that, Alice One," Garrett responded. "We've had trouble here, too. Native troops attacked our shore party about half an hour after we set down. We've also had reports from the Fortress of Heaven of a massacre of Terrans at the diplomatic reception. Those are unconfirmed, repeat, unconfirmed."

Fraser bit off a curse. A massacre ...

If it was true, then Captain LaSalle wouldn't be coming back. Fraser recoiled from the thought. For a long moment everything—the

Legion, the battle, the bullets slamming into the barricade in front of him—all seemed remote. He fought to get his whirling feelings back under control.

"Acknowledged, *Ganymede*," he said at last. "Have you had any orders from HQ?"

Garrett sounded grim. "They're ordering an evac, Alice One. We're checking for Terrans in town now. Then we're coming to pull you people out."

"Sounds good to me, *Ganymede*," Fraser said. "You have a timetable on that yet?"

"We've got a couple of hundred civilians to pull out here, Lieutenant," Garrett replied. "I'd say we'll be stuck here 'til morning, unless the lokes bring in artillery our hull can't handle. We'll keep you apprised." There was a pause, "*Ganymede*, out."

Evacuation. The word echoed in his mind.

Unless they drove back the hannie attack, though, an evac was going to be tough to manage. And the heavy weapons and the Legion's fire support vehicles still hadn't come up. *Damn it! Where the hell are they?*

Colin Fraser braced his FEK on the barricade and opened fire again. Right now, the legionnaires needed every rifle they could muster if they were going to hold off the hannie attack....

*   *   *

"Keep down, Honored," the native hissed. "Down!"

Lieutenant Kelly Ann Winters, Commonwealth Space Navy, nodded and hunkered lower behind the rocks, her fingers tightening around her LP-24 laser pistol. Hardly daring to breathe, she waited. Seconds dragged by.

The cluster of buildings that made up the Enclave Rezplex were lost in the darkness less than a kilometer behind her, but they remained a looming, half-felt presence, a grim reminder of danger. It was hard to keep memory at bay, to hold back the terror of the massacre there. All those people slaughtered ...

Kelly gripped the pistol harder, forcing the picture out of her mind. She couldn't give in now, or she'd end up like the others. Somehow she'd won free of the rezplex and onto the rugged slopes of the plateau. Above her, on the highest hill of the Enclave Heights, lay Fort Monkey. Safety ... she hoped.

"Azjai-kyir zheein sykai," the native said at last. "They are gone, Honored. We must move before another patrol comes."

Nodding reluctantly, Kelly rose to a half-crouch and followed the native. Ky was right; they had to keep moving. But every instinct rebelled at leaving cover. That rocky outcropping hadn't offered much protection for a human, but it was better than nothing.

The native moved rapidly, barely pausing to check for signs of Dryien troops. *Can I really trust one of them?* After the horror of the native attack, it was hard to see the hannie as a friend. *But ky did save me from the soldiers. Why?*

Maybe it was safest to accept the native as an ally. If ky hadn't been friendly, ky wouldn't have helped Kelly in the first place. The local, a native servant working for a Terran xenobotonist, had spotted the native troops as they crept into the rezplex, overheard their officer ordering the Terran demons slaughtered. Kys employer was in the capital tonight, at the banquet being thrown in the Fortress of Heaven. It had taken time for the servant to locate another Terran to warn Kelly … and by that time the shooting had started.

She'd been able to escape in the first moments of the attack. With the native's help, she'd evaded the soldiers in the streets of Monkeyville and the patrols beyond. Ky seemed to like the Terrans … or perhaps ky hated the soldiers more.

The little servant made an unlikely ally. She didn't even know kys name.

"Hykwai! Hykwai!"

Kelly dropped and rolled as the shouts echoed behind her. Autofire rattled, the bullets passing over her head. Acting more by instinct than training, Kelly opened fire. The LP-24 pulsed once, the invisible shot burning a hole through the throat of the closest hannie soldier. Three more were still on their feet, shooting wildly.

The natives, their eyes adapted to Hanuman's bright F7V star, were ill suited for night fighting. *I'm not much better,* Kelly thought, firing twice more and rolling to one side so the natives wouldn't locate her position. *I'm supposed to be an engineer, not a combat soldier!*

Her next two shots missed, but the sixth caught another hannie in the leg. The soldier screamed, firing a long burst as ky fell. Behind Kelly there was another cry. The two remaining soldiers rushed forward, sweeping the ground with autofire. A bullet plucked at her uniform as she rolled to the left and fired again, catching one of the attackers square in the chest. An unpleasant smell of burning flesh stung her nostrils.

She fought down her nausea and squeezed off another shot. The laser pulsed again, then died. Empty … and she didn't have a fresh cell.

And the native soldier was still on kys feet still firing randomly. If she didn't act fast, the whole Dryien army would be here soon, and she'd never escape.

Kelly screamed as autofire probed toward her. Then she lay still, moaning softly.

The soldier advanced slowly. She watched as the hannie's figure emerged from the gloom, kys weapon pointed straight at her. Her heart beat faster. If the native decided to be thorough, she was dead….

She stopped moaning and tried to keep still. What would the native do?

The soldier stood over her, prodded her once with the barrel of kys autorifle. With a quick motion she grabbed the rifle with both hands, pulling the soldier down on top of her. The rifle rolled free. Kelly lashed out with her forearm, trying to crush the native's windpipe. Pain lanced through her arm.

The neck ruff! Those sharp quills were like dozens of tiny knives. The soldier sprang back as she cried out, drawing a long knife with a lightning motion. Ky leapt to the attack again, but her foot arced sideways and caught the soldier in the back of the leg. Kelly rolled as the native fell, still trying to slash at her with the heavy blade.

Something hard and metallic tripped her as she tried to scramble to her feet. The hannie rose slowly, deliberately, weighing the knife in one hand as ky stalked her. Kelly's hands groped on the wet ground, closed on the rifle …

With a screech, the hannie charged. The alien weapon was heavy, awkward. She fumbled for the trigger, but the unfamiliar design balked her. Kelly swung the rifle wildly and caught the hannie's knife arm. There was a sickening crack of breaking bone, and the native screeched as ky dropped the knife. Kelly swung again … again …

The native fell, blood oozing from kys head. She backed away, feeling sick.

There was a moan in the darkness. "Honored … Honored …"

Kelly rushed to help. Her native ally was huddled in the grass, clutching a wounded leg in both hands. She shied away at the sight of more blood, then forced herself to act. Dropping to one knee, she tore a strip of cloth from the sleeve of her uniform jacket and bound the wound.

"Leave me, Honored …" the native gasped, weak.

"Forget it," Kelly answered in Terranglic. She glanced away, straining all her senses to detect signs of more hannie soldiers approaching. There wasn't much time. "I'll carry you," she told the native in kyendyp. "But you'll have to guide me."

Her arm still hurt from the soldier's quills, but Kelly ignored the pain. *I have to work fast. We can't stay here.*

*   *   *

Gunnery Sergeant Trent peered over the top of the low drainage ditch and pointed. "Braxton, your lance on the left. Clear the top of the wall and *keep* it clear. Got it?" He didn't wait for Corporal Braxton's nod. "Strauss, your boys'll go up to the ladder under Braxton's cover fire. Secure the tower. Pascali's lance stays at the bottom of the ladder to keep the hannies busy. Any questions?"

The three corporals shook their heads.

"Right. Get your boys and girls together and get ready to move." Trent continued to scan the north wall as they crawled off to join their lances. The eerie green images on his IR readout seemed oblivious to the legionnaires in the trench. They'd worked their way along it from the barricade in silence and were now poised less than twenty meters from the ladder that led to the northwest observation tower … and the hannie snipers.

He had fifteen legionnaires against … how many? It looked like there were fifty or sixty hannies fanning out along this stretch of the wall, and probably more coming fast. *Pretty good odds,* Trent thought. With surprise, and with their high-tech weapons, the three recon lances would cut through the locals easily. *As long as they don't start bringing up the heavy stuff,* he added grimly.

As if in response, a deep-throated *wham-WHAM* shook the compound. A two-meter section of the wall collapsed inward in a shower of loose masonry. One hannie soldier was buried in the tumbling debris; another, dodging the danger behind, ran directly into a stream of FEK fire and was flung back against the rubble, screaming. The explosions showered dust and debris over Trent.

Behind the dying native, a squat shape clanked slowly forward on broad treads, the barrel of its fixed-mount 8cm cannon poking through the hole, questing, searching. The self-propelled gun was primitive and ungainly by Legion standards, but its shells could turn the tide against Bravo Company.

Tanks breaking through the wall, he thought. *Hell, that's* all *we need.*

But the noise and confusion could be turned to good advantage. "Go! Go! Go!" he yelled, waving the legionnaires forward. They rose from the ditch with a yell and rushed forward. Trent fired his FEK as he ran, sending needle-sharp slivers slicing into the natives on full-auto. Nearby, Legionnaire Rydell dropped to one knee and raised his Whitney-Sykes HPLR-55. The laser rifle pulsed invisibly, but a hannie at the top of the wall screamed and toppled over backwards. Laser rifles weren't as common in the Legion as they were in regular Commonwealth Army units, but Legion snipers like Rydell made every one count.

Trent reached the ladder first and fired upward, catching a native soldier who was having trouble with rungs spaced too far apart for kys compact body. The hannie lost kys grip and fell in an untidy heap near Trent's feet. He ignored the twisted body and sought out new targets among the natives swarming through the opening behind the lumbering SPG thirty meters away. More soldiers from Pascali's and Strauss's lances joined him under the looming shadow of the tower.

"Get your people moving, Strauss!" Trent shouted. "The rest of you spread out and cause trouble. You boys know how to do that, don't you?"

Corporal Helmut Strauss, a burly native of Neusachsen with a bushy blonde mustache, grunted acknowledgement. "Ve climb," he said harshly. He spoke Terranglic, like every soldier in the Legion, but eight years in the service hadn't softened his accent much. "You, nube, first."

Trent hid a smile. As long as there were NCOs in the Legion, the nubes—the raw recruits—would always get ridden the hardest. Strauss's victim, a kid who looked no older than sixteen, slung his FEK and started climbing the ladder. Darkness quickly swallowed his black, chameleon fatigues.

The sergeant turned his attention back to the problem at hand. While Strauss and his lance climbed, the rest of Trent's men had to occupy the hannies ... without drawing too much attention from the self-propelled gun that was slowly forcing its way into the compound. Trent switched from infrared to light-intensification vision and signalled to Corporal Pascali. *Move out.*

Pascali's lance fanned out in a loose arc around the base of the tower, weapons probing the darkness. Trent caught movement on the wall to the left on his LI display, dropped sideways and rolled, triggering a short burst on his FEK as the barrel came into line. Behind him, he heard the whine of Legionnaire Cole's weapon. A chorus of shouts and screams answered, then the stutter of native autoweapons returning fire.

Bullets ricocheted off the base of the tower and raised gouts of dust around Trent's feet. He fired again, a long burst this time, then shifted to a quick spread of grenades. The ripple of explosions along the top of the wall illuminated the hannies better, and he fired again.

"Look out, Sarge!" Cole yelled. The legionnaire knocked the sergeant down, sending him sprawling in the dirt. As he fell, Trent saw a hannie stepping from the shadows behind the vehicle. The native was balancing a heavy tube on one shoulder, one of the primitive rocket launchers the Legion referred to as blunderbusses. Flame spat from both ends of the tube and the rocket leapt across the compound. Too late, Cole tried to roll aside. The rocket caught him in the back, tearing through plasteel and duraweave cloth before it exploded. Sickened, Trent turned away from the bloody remains and flipped his FEK to full-auto. The launch tube rolled under the treads of the tank as the local's face and throat were shredded by dozens of needle-thin metal shards.

Trent crawled to where Cole had fallen. There wasn't much left of the legionnaire who had saved the sergeant's life. *You are soldiers in order to die.* The saying had been part of Legion tradition for centuries. It seemed grimly appropriate now, an epitaph for Legionnaire First Class Arthur Cole ... or whatever his *real* name had been, before he'd sought the anonymity of the Legion.

The sergeant reloaded his FEK and fired again; smiling grimly as hannie soldiers took refuge behind the bulk of their big vehicle.

Then the smile faded as the clash of changing gears and clattering treads deepened, and the vehicle began to turn. The cannon barrel was swinging slowly, relentlessly toward Trent....

CHAPTER THREE

Don't trust any legionnaire who tells you he has no fear.

> —Colonel Fernand Maire,
> French Foreign Legion, 1918

egionnaire Third Class John Grant paused three meters from the top of the ladder and took a deep, careful breath—"tasting the air," his brother might have called it, back in the days when they ran together in the back streets of Old London.

"John Grant" wasn't his real name, of course. He no longer answered to his real name, and Old London was no longer his home. The memories of the good times, before Billy was killed, seemed distant now, but as he clung to the ladder and steeled himself for his next move he could almost see himself back on Terra. The long climb, the need for absolute silence and perfect timing, all brought back that last caper where Billy had died. For a moment, it was as if the trial, the sentence condemning him to lose his citizenship and serve five years in the Legion to get it back, the long hours of tortuous training on Devereaux, all were part of some dream. He almost expected to look down and see Billy's cheerful grin gleaming in the darkness below his feet.

But below him was Vrurrth, the hulking Second Class Legionnaire from Gwyrr. *What's that stupid SOB Strauss doing sending the Gwyrran up here? Silence, finesse ... that's what we need. Not brute strength.*

Carefully, he drew his combat dagger from its leg sheath and tested its weight in his hand. In the old days, he'd knocked over some fancy rezplexes, but though he might have been a criminal he had never been a killer. Now he had to use his old skills for a new, grisly purpose. *Well, Slick,* he told himself, using the nickname Billy had given him so long ago. *This is it!*

Keeping the knife firmly gripped in his left hand, Slick started climbing again, every move smooth, silent. The ladder came up to an open trap door on the bottom of the tower floor, and there was no one in sight above it. Cautiously, Slick raised his head above the level of the floor and scanned his surroundings. One ale soldier ... two ... three. All of them were at the parapet, firing down into the compound below. Slick allowed himself a smile. *A kid could pull this one off.*

There was a metal-on-metal clatter just below, and the nearest hannie soldier cocked kys head and started to turn. *Damn Gwyrran monster!* Slick thought angrily. He gathered his strength and sprang through the opening, his knife blade flashing in the dark. The hannie gurgled and slumped, lifeless. The *clang* of kys rifle on the floor made the other two natives swing around. One of them loosed a shot that skimmed above Slick's helmet.

He rolled to one side, fumbling with the sling of his FEK. Adrenaline pumped through his veins. At this range, those native rifles could penetrate duraweave, and Slick wasn't wearing any plasteel armor over his fatigues. *Speed over protection, that's what you wanted* ... The hannie fired again, and Slick reeled backward. Blood flowed freely from a ragged gash in his shoulder, and raw pain throbbed down his left arm.

The other hannie thumbed the selector switch on kys weapon, brought it up ... and reeled, a dozen dark blossoms of blood opening in kys chest and stomach. The second soldier collapsed over the body of the first. The high-pitched *whir* of Vrurrth's FEK died away.

"Nube fights, does not ready." The Gwyrran's grin revealed his sharp-pointed carnivore teeth. "The haste is danger. Death." He clambered slowly through the trap door, eyes roving warily around the platform.

"Dammit, I could've taken 'em all if you hadn't made a noise!" Slick exploded. "You almost got me killed!"

Legionnaire Dmitri Rostov, the lance's demo expert, was next up the ladder. "Save the fighting for the bad guys, nube," he advised. "We're supposed to be a team."

Slick turned away, unslinging his FEK and surveying the compound. *Yeah, a team,* he thought bitterly. *I can take care of myself, as long as my so-called team leaves me alone.* He fought back anger. *I can take care of myself!*

* * *

Trent scrambled to his feet, eyes darting left and right. The self-propelled gun was lumbering toward him now. The main gun remained silent, but the heavy machine guns mounted on each side of the sloping hull chattered as the vehicle slowly advanced. The sergeant dived for the cover of a man-sized chunk of rubble as the 15mm bullets tracked across the ground.

Corporal Pascali dropped into a crouch beside him, raising her FEK and triggering the grenade launcher. The rocket grenade exploded just above the right-hand tread but did not penetrate. Pascali fired again, with the same result.

Damn! We need something heavier....

Hannie soldiers swarmed through the opening the tank had made, and more natives were rising from cover where they had been pinned down by fire from the main perimeter. Trent scanned the improvised barricade where the company had dug in. Their firing was slacking off now. What was the lieutenant doing over there?

"Fall back, Pascali!" he ordered sharply. "I'll cover you!"

She seemed about to argue, then nodded grimly. As Trent fired, the corporal sprinted back toward the base of the tower, shouting orders to the rest of her lance.

The SPG roared, and a fireball erupted near the west wall. Still firing, Trent lurched to his feet and followed Pascali. Machine-gun fire probed toward him. Something slammed into his leg, knocking him off balance. He fell and rolled, then crawled desperately for cover. The enemy cannon roared again. The explosion burst barely ten meters away from Trent, and dirt showered over him from the blast. Someone—a legionnaire, from the sound of the voice—was screaming now.

If the lieutenant doesn't get it together, we've all had it!

Trent slid into a drainage ditch and checked his throbbing leg. No blood, no signs of a serious wound. His duraweave fatigues had stopped the hannie bullet, but he'd have a bruise and a limp for a while ... assuming he lived through the battle.

He pulled himself up against the side of the ditch and braced his FEK against his shoulder. Death rumbled toward him on broad, clattering tracks.

* * *

Colin Fraser slapped a fresh clip into his FEK as he listened to the tinny voice in his earphones. "Repeat that last, Sergeant," he ordered sharply.

Platoon Sergeant Persson was breathing hard. "Don't know how many there are, Lieutenant, but they've got us pinned!" he answered. "And there're booby traps everywhere! I lost ten men in the motor pool alone, and Dmowski says he lost a couple when the armory door blew up in their faces!"

"God *damn*!" Fraser ground his teeth in helpless rage. "Can't you do anything, Sarge?"

"Lieutenant, half my people aren't even armed!" Persson said. He sounded angry. "We can't get past those booby traps while we're dodging snipers, and I can't clear the snipers with a handful of pistols and a couple of FEKs!"

Fraser looked up, over the barricade. There was another self-propelled gun starting through the hole in the north wall. Without heavy weapons or the fire support vehicles in the motor pool building, Bravo Company didn't stand a chance against those hannie tanks. If Persson couldn't handle it alone....

"All right, Sergeant. Hang tight. I'm sending help." He cut the comm channel and looked around him. "Bartlow!"

"Here, sir." Subaltern Vincent Bartlow looked terrified. He was the youngest of Bravo Company's platoon leaders, Fraser remembered, and this was his first time in action. *Welcome to the club, kid,* he thought.

Fraser jerked his head at the line of soldiers manning the barricade. "Round up your platoon, Sub," he ordered. "There are hannies around the armory and the motor pool! Get over there and shred 'em. Got it?"

"Yes, sir." Bartlow bit his lip uncertainly.

Fraser ignored the man's hesitation. "And get your weapons lances armed, for God's sake. We need something better than popguns if we're going to take on tanks!" The subaltern nodded.

"Move it!" Fraser snapped. The subaltern flinched and backed away, shouting for his platoon sergeant. Fraser turned back to contemplate the breach in the north wall. The self-propelled gun had turned and was moving toward the northwest tower. Trent and his recon troops had stirred up trouble there, relieving the pressure on the main perimeter and knocking out the snipers in the tower. They couldn't hold out long, though; sixteen legionnaires wouldn't stand off a tank and the rocket-armed hannie troops who were pouring into the compound behind the vehicle.

Without heavy weapons on the firing line all they could do was pick off the hannies who were too stupid to take cover. The legionnaires from the company's six weapons lances were supposed to be drawing their gear from the armory. Until they came, Bravo Company's chances looked grim....

* * *

Gunnery Sergeant Trent grunted and slid deeper into the ditch as his second clip ran dry. *What does it take to discourage these bloody monkeys?* he wondered as he slapped his last 100-round clip into place in the receiver of the FEK. The hannie regulars were taking heavy casualties, but it didn't seem to be hurting their morale. They just kept on coming, pouring through the hole in the wall. With rubble and the tank for cover, they were getting enough troops into the compound to pose a serious threat to the legionnaires defending the perimeter.

A rocket like the one that had killed Cole streaked over the trench, then another. The self-propelled gun spoke again. Trent crouched low in the ditch, playing a waiting game.

Trent's lances didn't stand a chance on their own. At this point there was only one way to turn the tide....

A hannie soldier jumped and landed barely two meters away, holding one of the short, stocky, native autorifles with a determined grip. Trent triggered a short FEK burst that sent the soldier spinning sideways to collapse in the trickle of water at the bottom of the ditch. Two more hannies appeared at the top, firing wildly. A round *pinged* off the plasteel legpiece just below his left kneecap. His finger tightened on the trigger three times as he pumped needles into the natives.

More hannies were reaching the ditch now. Many were oblivious to the legionnaire, their rifles chattering and barking as the soldiers plunged straight ahead. Trent killed two more natives before they could take a more deadly interest in him. Then he saw the target he'd been waiting for.

Popping to his feet, the sergeant sprayed FEK fire on full-auto into a clump of locals. Ignoring their ululating screams, Trent sprang forward before any others could react. He kicked a dead hannie aside and scooped up the blood-soaked blunderbuss that had been pinned underneath the body.

As he raised the tube awkwardly to one shoulder, Trent struggled to recall the adchip briefings on native weaponry. *That* switch was the safety ... and *that* one controlled the primitive electronic sight. Ignoring the sighting system, Trent lined up on the slow-moving vehicle and yanked back on the trigger. The rocket ignited and *whooshed* away, trailing flame.

Without waiting to watch the shot, Trent ducked and rolled for the cover of the ditch. As he landed at the bottom, the roar of the explosion drowned out the jabbering cries of the natives. His light intensifiers blanked out for an instant, then adjusted.

Raising himself cautiously to the lip of the ditch, Trent peered over the top. A smile tugged at the corners of his mouth as he surveyed his handiwork. Smoke trailed upward from the hole near the bottom of the vehicle's forward chassis, just over the left-hand tread. The tank was turning again, trying to line up on the company perimeter, but the left tread was flopping loose. The vehicle was still dangerous, but it wasn't going anywhere. The hannies were wavering now as they realized their most potent weapon was damaged.

"Come on, Sarge!" someone yelled behind him. Two FEKs on full-auto hosed across the hannies. From above, on the tower platform, more Legion rifles joined in. A hatch on the tank opened, and a squat local started to climb out, only to be knocked down by a shot from the legionnaires on the tower.

Trent realized his own FEK was gone, lost in the scramble for the alien rocket launcher. Drawing his 10mm PLF rocket pistol, he ran toward Pascali and Legionnaire Reinhardt.

We shook 'em, he told himself as he dived behind the corner of the tower next to Corporal Pascali. *We shook 'em ... but they haven't broke yet.*

* * *

Legionnaire Spiro Karatsolis crouched low, sheltering behind the corner of the fort's tiny chapel, and peered cautiously around the neoplast wall toward the much larger structure that housed the Fort Monkey motor pool.

The dead body of Legionnaire Vance sprawled between the two buildings was a grim reminder of the effectiveness of the unseen native snipers who had the unit pinned. Half the man's head was gone, thanks to a high-caliber hannie bullet.

Karatsolis hefted the FEK in his hands. Compared to the turret-mounted plasma cannon of his beloved Sabertooth fire-support vehicle, the infantry weapon was a popgun. But it would have to do.

"Last chance to back out, man," Corporal Selim Bashar said behind him.

"Yeah, sure." Karatsolis took another look at Vance. "Let's do it."

They had worked their way this far forward of the rest of the legionnaires of the transport platoon without drawing fire. If they could just make it the rest of the way....

Even one FSV would make the difference, both here and up on the north end of the fort. He'd heard Sergeant Persson calling for assistance from the lieutenant, but even if help was on the way those hannie snipers were too well hidden for infantry to root out quickly. But a Sabertooth wasn't vulnerable to sniper fire.

Bashar slapped him on the back. "Ready," he said tersely. The swarthy Sabertooth driver wasn't armed, but he carried a satchel of tools slung over one shoulder. If Karatsolis could cover him long enough for the Turk to reach the motor pool, Bashar would deal with the booby traps they'd discovered before. Or at least that was the plan.

Karatsolis rolled out from behind the corner, his finger tightening on the trigger of the FEK. The weapon whined, spraying needles at the south wall. He paused a moment, and a native rifle raised a gout of dust at his feet. Throwing himself sideways, he fired at what he estimated was the source of the shot. He shouted as he fired. "Move! Move, Bashar!"

The Turk bounded across the compound at a dead run, zigzagging to avoid the sniper bullets. He dove, rolled, and came up next to the motor pool door, flashing Karatsolis a quick thumbs up. Another bullet missed his head by inches. The Greek gunner swung his FEK and squeezed off another long burst, and was rewarded by a scream. A hannie body tumbled from behind the cover of a ventilator housing on top of the armory across the road from the motor pool, landing heavily on the ground below.

Now that he had one of their hiding places spotted, Karatsolis switched from needle rounds to 1cm grenades and fired a quick three-round burst at the housing. *That should discourage anyone who's still up there,* he thought as the explosions lit up the compound with a brief false dawn.

He took advantage of the distraction to run, firing randomly again as he crossed to Bashar's side. The Turk was hunkered down beside the door studying a tripwire that ran almost unseen in the dirt.

"Not bad shooting for a goatherd," the corporal commented coolly as he located the mine the tripwire ran to and disarmed it by jamming a screwdriver into the firing mechanism.

"You do all right yourself, Bashar … for a rug merchant." They both came from New Cyprus and kept up a long-standing feud over the merit of Karatsolis's farm-boy origins versus the city background Bashar had grown up with.

Bashar grinned and gestured at the door. Karatsolis kicked it in, FEK at the ready, half-expecting an explosion or a fusillade of shots to meet him.

The lights came up automatically as the sensors detected the two legionnaires. Inside, the ranked Legion vehicles waited, neatly parked in their workbays, ready for action. His heart leapt at the sight of the old, battle-scarred Sabertooth in Bay Five. Though in theory, maggers— transport platoon crews—were interchangeable among vehicles, there was still a tendency for specific crewmen to become attached to individual vehicles. Bashar and Karatsolis regarded that FSV as their own. They'd christened it *Angel of Death* and lavished as much attention on the ancient veteran as some men did on a mistress.

Lying quiescent in the workbay, the Sabertooth didn't look very threatening. The flat manta-ray shape with its sleek bubble turret was half-hidden by a clutter of tools, workbenches, and spare parts. But once it was powered up, with magrep modules for lift and four General Dynamics ground-effect turbofans for thrust, the Sabertooth would become a living thing, as deadly as the carnivore on Medea that had given the vehicle class its name.

Side by side, the two legionnaires ran to the FSV, eager to come to grips with the enemy.

* * *

Zydryie Wyzyeet steadied kys bolt-action sniper's rifle and scanned the Demon Fort in search of targets. Ky was having trouble getting used to the new nightscope that registered differences in temperature rather than light. It was a new device, issued only to the most elite units of the Dryien army, and this was kys first chance to use it in the field. The fuzzy, greenish images it showed were mostly dead bodies or pat‑ ches of vegetation; none of the offworld demons were showing them‑ selves now. Since the two humans had reached the big building they used to shelter their vehicles, no others had ventured into the open.

Two humans surely couldn't do much even if they penetrated the booby traps outside the building. Still, Wyzyeet cursed silently. Kys superior wasn't known for tolerance, and kys failure to stop the two demons might result in Wyzyeet's demotion from the ranks of the Soldiers of the Eternal Mists. Only the very best of Dryien's soldiery could aspire to serve in the elite commando unit. Aided by agents among the native servants employed by the demons, the commandos had penetrated the fort in perfect silence, set their traps, and prepared their ambush. Cut off from their armory and their vehicles, the offworlders would be easy prey for the main assault.

Wyzyeet felt uneasy. Those two humans had made it past the snipers. Their vehicles were certainly powerful....

Raw sound hammered at kys ears, and an explosion of blinding light made Wyzyeet duck down involuntarily. Kys night vision was gone, but when the *zydryie* looked back into the compound ky could see the demon vehicle clearly enough.

It was broad and flat, with a sleek bubble turret that mounted a menacing weapon some said was magical, plus missile launchers mounted on either side of the hull. And it *floated,* as if held up by an unseen force. Huge fans roared under the body of the machine, but Wyzyeet knew of no fan that could hold up so monstrous a weight.

The vehicle floated a few *kwyin* above the ground, scarcely higher than a full-grown *kyen.* It pivoted slowly in place like a beast questing for a scent.

Ky remembered the stories other soldiers told of the demonic devices that could see a kyen in total darkness ... or through solid walls. Devices that made the night-scope like a child's toy by comparison.

These were the demons who had cast down the Ancient Gods and shattered their great Sky Fortress.

Wyzyeet's hands shook. Ky hesitated, torn between duty and fear.

Then the great cannon on the demon vehicle's turret flared once, a searing pulse of light and heat. Wyzyeet never even felt the ball of superheated plasma that consumed kys body and a three-meter section of the south wall.

Chapter Four

An officer knows inside a week if he clicks or doesn't click in the Legion.

—Major Fernand Maire,
French Foreign Legion, 1918

Kelly Winters cringed at the sound of gunfire from the top of the slope, the crack and chatter of native weapons mingled with the high-pitched whines of old-style FEK gauss rifles. The fighting up there sounded fierce … and it sounded like the legionnaires in the garrison were badly outnumbered.

Crouching low behind a clump of twisted, thorny bushes, she lowered the injured native to the ground and checked kys pulse. *You should have known there'd be no safety up in the fort,* she told herself bitterly. *Damned legionnaires.*

Why had the Commonwealth sent legionnaires to garrison the Enclave, anyway? Everybody knew they were nothing but malcontents and troublemakers—everybody who wasn't dazzled by the "romance" of the Foreign Legion, that is. She'd been forced to use them as her primary construction crew in putting together the Enclave, the landing strip, and the fort itself, and the road net that connected the Enclave with the capital and the inland zyglyn plantations. Slovenly, disrespectful, equipped with outdated gear and attitudes to match, the legionnaires weren't much good for peacetime work. From the sound of it they weren't doing much better at fighting, either.

But she didn't have much choice. The locals were in complete control in the rezplex, and she'd seen a patrol heading for the landing field an hour earlier. The legionnaires at the fort were still putting up a struggle, at least.

And both she and the native needed medical attention. Her injured native ally had passed out soon after she'd administered first aid and had been drifting in and out of consciousness ever since. She bit her lip as she examined the blood-soaked bandages on the native's leg. Infections were easy to come by in Hanuman's mid-latitude regions. Without competent medical aid and a dose of regen therapy, the little alien would probably lose the limb. *If either of us live that long,* she thought grimly.

Underneath makeshift bandages, her arm still throbbed where the hannie soldier's neck quills had opened half a dozen deep, painful stab wounds. Now that she was reasonably safe, the adrenaline wasn't pumping any more, and she felt sick and exhausted. She wanted to close her eyes, to sleep.

But she knew that sleep would just bring back the memories. The massacre ... the hannie soldier dying under the smashing blows of kys own rifle, killed by her own hand. Her own hand....

No. She couldn't let herself remember. Not yet.

It took a major effort to focus on her surroundings again. A glow from downslope relieved the darkness ... Monkeyville was burning. At least it gave her enough light to examine the hillside.

Were the shots above coming closer?

She froze in place as several small, dark shapes scrambled down the hill, heedless of their surroundings. They were hannies, soldiers by the look of them, but only one was armed. As she watched ky threw away the weapon, then suddenly toppled, kys torso erupting in a spray of blood and flesh and metal slivers. The native twitched a few times as ky hit the ground, then lay still.

"Come on, lads!" a human voice cried out in Terranglic. "We've got the little bastards on the run! Let's get 'em!"

A legionnaire ran past her position, still shooting at the fleeing natives. In the glow of the burning rezplex, Kelly could see him clearly. His uniform matched the darkened hillside but seemed to shimmer a little where the firelight hit it. Plasteel body armor covered his arms, legs, and chest over his duraweave coverall, and his bulky helmet was made of the same material. Armor, equipment, even his FEK had the scarred, battered look of gear that had either been badly maintained or seen long, harsh duty.

Another man appeared and fired at the fugitives, apparently oblivious to the fact that they were unarmed now.

"I'm glad to see you can fight *someone,* soldier," she said harshly. "Next time try for some of the dangerous ones. You know, the ones who can shoot back."

The soldiers reacted instantly to the noise, pivoting toward her with weapons held ready. "Hold your fire!" she called. "I'm a Terran ... a Navy officer."

A corporal appeared out of the shadow, studying her closely. His watchful expression didn't waver. "Lieutenant Winters, isn't it?"

Kelly nodded.

"I'm Corporal LeMay," he said. "How many with you?"

"Just a native," she said, trying to match his brisk, professional manner. "I don't know if anyone else managed to get out...."

He cut her off with a curt gesture. "Never mind the details, Lieutenant," he told her crisply. "No telling how much time we have before they re-form."

"What about the hannie, Corp?" one of the legionnaires asked, pointing to her injured ally.

"Leave it. Don't have no orders about lokes."

"Belay that, mister," Kelly snapped. She wasn't going to abandon the native to the mercies of the Dryien army. "Ky helped me escape. Bring ky with us."

The corporal looked stubborn, then shrugged. "If you say so, Lieutenant," he said resignedly. "Kraisri, get the hannie. Ma'am, we'd better get back to the fort."

Kelly took a step, suddenly conscious of the weakness in her knees, of the sweat dripping down her face and neck, of the pounding throb in her wounded arm. Her arm ... it felt swollen under the bandages.

"LeMay...?" She tried to speak, but her tongue felt swollen. Breathing was difficult, as though unseen hands were closing about her throat. "LeMay ..."

The ground swept up and collided with her face. From a very great distance, she could hear LeMay calling her name.

Then there was only darkness.

* * *

The noise of the turbofans was music, a triumphant fanfare that put fresh life into the beleaguered legionnaires at the barricade. Colin Fraser found himself grinning from sheer relief as he opened fire once again.

The scarred hull of a Sabertooth shot past, the flare of light from its plasma cannon illuminating the name painted on the side of the turret: *Angel of Death*. The FSV was living up to the name as the plasma gun and the hull-mounted CEK chaingun swept the north wall. A second native tank that had squeezed through the hole created by the first took a plasma round square in the front, leaving a wide hole surrounded by half-melted armor right over the driver's compartment.

Nearby, an M-786 Sandray APC grounded with a roar of braking fans, the rear troop ramp dropping as it set down. Grim looking legionnaires filed out at a trot. First came Corporal Dmowski, carrying a Fafnir rocket launcher, while the next two, armored head to toe in plasteel, cradled onager plasma rifles in their arms. Other soldiers followed. Bartlow's platoon was still on the south side of the compound, mopping up the hannie commandoes, but at last Fraser had the heavy weapons units who could turn the tide. And the vehicles, two Sabertooth FSVs and four Sandrays armed with CEKs.

Now maybe we can teach those monkeys a lesson about fighting the Legion. Fraser allowed himself another grim smile. He clicked to his command channel. "First and Second Platoons, attack on my signal!"

"First Platoon confirms," Subaltern Fairfax said over the commlink.

"Second Platoon, acknowledged." That was Subaltern Watanabe, the soft-spoken native of the Japanese colony on Pacifica.

Fraser peered over the top of the barricade one more time, then clicked to another comm channel. "Sergeant Trent! Are you there, Trent?"

"I'm here, L-T," the sergeant's voice responded promptly. Trent sounded out of breath, preoccupied.

"Time to show the lokes some firepower, Gunny. How're your people doing?"

"Three down from First Platoon Recon." There was a pause. "With all due respect, L-T, I wonder if you could stop talking and start shooting? Those little bastards are still trying to get at us."

Fraser smiled in spite of himself. Would anything shake Trent's unflappable style? "Acknowledged, Gunny." He keyed in the command channel again. "Now!"

The explosion and the impossibly bright flare of plasma rounds blanked out Fraser's LI display for a second, until his helmet electronics could compensate for the glare. All six of the company's armored onager gunners were sweeping the north side of the compound with their plasma rifles, and the effects were devastating. As Fraser's vision returned, he could see hannie soldiers throwing down their weapons and fleeing for safety. Onager and FEK fire pursued them.

The whine of FEKs mingled with the deeper-throated hum of the MEK lance-support weapons as the rest of the legionnaires surged forward across the barricade, firing as they charged. A few shots rang out in answer but quickly fell silent.

And then, suddenly, it was over. The compound was quiet, the night peaceful again, as if the battle had never been.

Lieutenant Colin Fraser listened to the silence. The attack was over ... or was it? Something had caused the Dryien army to turn on the Legion. Until that *something* was dealt with, the legionnaires would still be in danger.

The silence seemed somehow more threatening than the fury of the battle.

*   *   *

Slick winced as Dmitri Rostov probed at his shoulder. "Careful, for God's sake!"

Rostov grinned. "You deserve it, nube," he said. He came from the Russian-settled frontier world of Novy Krimski, but he spoke flawless Terranglic. "That was a damn fool stunt you pulled, trying to take those ales with a knife."

He didn't answer. He was tired, his arm hurt, and the last thing he needed was another lecture on teamwork.

When the judge had passed sentence on him for trying to break into the freighter and stow away on the London/Orbit shuttle, Slick had been almost relieved. The Fifth Foreign Legion—what youngster didn't spin romantic dreams of serving in the company of those tough outcasts in their distant off-planet outposts? He'd talked Billy into the caper to get away from Terra's swarming beehive cities, out into the Colonies where life was exciting. The Legion shouldn't have been punishment at all! The idea of serving with the misfits, the ad-venturers ... The chance to be *part* of something, and not always on the outside ... it should have been a dream come true.

But he was quick to discover the bitter truth behind the romance.

From the moment he'd arrived for training at the main Legion depot on Devereaux, Slick had been miserable. The NCOs were either sadists or martinets, while most of the other legionnaires were con-cerned with proving how tough they were. Dreams of camaraderie were quickly overshadowed by the realities of being an easy target, a nube, someone to cuff or humiliate or ignore. But they still expected him to be part of the team.

I'll show them I don't need their team, Slick thought. A planet like Hanuman didn't offer the disgruntled legionnaire any place to try desertion. His only alternative was to win some respect, to show that he could make it on his own.

"All right," Rostov went on after a long silence. "Far as I can tell it's a clean wound, and nothing's broken. Strauss'll probably hurt you worse next time he decides you need an obedience lesson."

Slick nodded curtly. "Thanks, Rostov," he said.

"Just doing my job, nube," the other legionnaire replied cheerfully. He lowered his voice again. "And listen, kid ... what you did was stupid, but it took guts. You're all right ... in a kind of a dim, thick-skulled sort of way. Know what I mean?"

Rostov packed up the first aid kit, whistling happily. Pulling on his fatigue jacket carefully, he looked over the tower parapet. The hannies were gone now, scattered by the furious Legion counterattack.

I'm still alive. The realization was only starting to sink in. *I'm alive....*

And Rostov seemed friendlier, more willing to accept him. Maybe he really could fit in.

Maybe.

*   *   *

"So I guess we have our orders." Lieutenant Colin Fraser leaned forward over the desk. It felt wrong to be sitting in Captain LaSalle's chair, presiding over the company staff meeting. But the word from the capital was positive: LaSalle was dead. Right or wrong, Fraser was in command now.

It wasn't fair. He'd been attached to the Legion less than two months, on Hanuman with Bravo Company barely a week. He still didn't understand these outcasts, these misfits who seemed determined to close ranks and go their own way and tell the whole universe to be damned. They were strangers to him, more alien than the hannies. How was he supposed to make combat decisions that risked the lives of these men?

He glanced around the office. Gunnery Sergeant Trent and all three platoon leaders were present. So were the company's four warrant officers, the specialists whose authority lay outside the regular chain of command. This one room held the entire surviving command staff of Demi-Battalion Alice, the Legion's garrison in Dryienjaiyeel—for the next few hours, at least.

"Commandant Isayev has confirmed the evac order," Fraser went on. "The transport lighter *Ganymede* will be here by dawn. Come noon, we'll be back in Fwynzei, safe and sound. We have to be ready to pull out by then. Doctor Ramirez, what's the medical situation?"

WO/4 Eduardo Ramirez raised his head tiredly. The doctor was best known in camp for his capacity for alcohol consumption, but he had been hard at work since the beginning of the Dryien attack three hours before and hadn't taken a drink in the entire time. He looked, Fraser thought, more like one of the patients than the unit's medical specialist. "Battle injuries all treated, sir," he mumbled almost inaudibly. "Nothing very severe. Almost anything that got through armor killed the target."

"God rest their souls," WO/4 Fitzpatrick added softly. Father Michael Fitzpatrick—he was known to one and all within Bravo Company as "the Padre"—was the unit's chaplain. He was a Catholic from Freehold, one of the colonies that had been cut off from contact with Terra during the Shadow Centuries. Although his brand of Catholicism didn't recognize the primacy of Rome, it was a popular religion in the Colonies. At least half of Bravo Company was made up of Catholics of one kind or another, and the Padre served their spiritual needs as well as any conventional Vatican-backed priest.

"Good." Fraser looked over at the platoon leaders. "Tighten perimeter security for the rest of the night, gentlemen. No repeats of tonight's little performance. I want this evac to go smoothly."

"We'll do our best, sir," Fairfax said. Bartlow nodded agreement.

"Are we giving up on the people in town, and on Charlie Company, sir?" Watanabe asked.

"There's nobody left in the capital to give up on." Donald Hamilton, the WO/4 responsible for native affairs and intelligence, tapped the arm of his chair nervously. "*Ganymede* rescued a couple of eyewitnesses to the massacre in the Fortress of Heaven. Everybody else is dead. Including Captain LaSalle. I gather *Ganymede*'s going to make a couple more search sweeps overnight, but it doesn't look good."

Fraser nodded slowly. "We have to mag out, Subaltern. There's been no word from Charlie Company, and with more hannies moving in around the base of the plateau it won't be easy to send anyone out."

"The lieutenant's right," Trent said bluntly. "Hell, how long could a platoon-sized outpost last if they got hit the way we did?"

"We could probably run a search from the lighter," WO/4 Hendrik Vandergraff, the unit's science and technology analyst, suggested. "They can't do much to us once we're aboard, and we could scout around for radio sources."

"Maybe," Trent said. "Don't think I'd like to tangle with the whole Dryien air force, though. Those cargo-mods they drive might not be much, but they could damage a transport. Now if we had an assault boat—"

"We don't," Fraser said. "If there's a chance to locate other survivors, we will, but the commandant wants us to pull out of here and back to Fwynzei intact. We don't risk Bravo Company on the off chance there's a couple of other Terrans still blundering around out in the jungle. Got it?"

"Yes, sir," Vandergraff said. Fraser thought he heard Trent say something like "The Legion takes care of its own" under his breath, but he ignored the sergeant.

"Last thing," Fraser went on. "Hamilton, you're supposed to be an expert on our hannie friends. Any special recommendations?"

"Don't underestimate them," he said curtly. After a moment, he added, "Sir. They're a potent threat even if they don't have our weapons and armor." He paused again. "Specific things to consider … hmmm. First, maintain a tight watch tonight, and have the off-duty platoons sleep with weapons ready so we don't get caught with the heavy stuff in the armory again. Keep all the armed vehicles deployed around the compound. And for God's sake make sure there aren't any locals inside the fort!"

Fraser nodded thoughtfully. "All right, let's get things rolling. One platoon on watch, the others packing up or getting some rest. See Gunny for a schedule. I want to be ready for the lighter when it gets here."

"And ready for the hannies, too. I bet we'll see them first." Trent added, rising. He made it sound like a casual social call, not another bloody assault.

"That's a bet I won't touch, Gunny," Fraser said quietly. He looked away. *I don't understand these people. I don't belong with the Legion. Not as Exec … certainly not in command.*

He thought of Trent, so self-assured, so dedicated to his soldier's life. A warrior born and bred. A legionnaire.

I just don't belong.

* * *

"Idiots! Fools!" Zyzyiig slammed a fist down on the table. "How could two regiments be driven back by a handful?"

Shavvataaars, the Semti Chief Advisor to the Throne of the Eternal Mists, spoke with a whispering, sibilant hiss, pausing frequently as he struggled with kyendyp vowel-sounds. "That journey is done now; it cannot be retraced. The demons are trapped in their jungle lair, where your troops may still destroy them all. But you cannot afford delay, my dear *Asjyai.* Their transport ship may fly them all to safety, and you cannot afford to allow the Terrans to regroup and mount a counterthrust against you here. They must learn that Dryienjaiyeel is not safe for their kind."

It was galling to have success so near, yet still hanging undecided, a ripe jungle fruit just out of reach on a high tree limb. The youthful usurper, Jiraiy, was dead, and with the child the offworlder demons who had led ky from the ways of the Ancients. The army was in total control here in the Fortress of Heaven, and the process of rooting out the false *yzyeel's* supporters in the capital was going smoothly. By morning, the new *yzyeel,* Zyzyiig's chosen candidate, would be secure on the Throne of the Eternal Mists.

But the offworlder skyship floating in the harbor remained intact, until artillery or armor could be summoned to the capital from the outlying provinces. And the demon soldiers, the offworlder *Foreign Legion,* were still holding out. But two full regiments were already in place below the offworlder fortress, and two more crack armored units were on the way. The three smaller camps where the interlopers had settled in the deep jungle were gone now, two of them overrun, the third evacuated. That would free up another regiment, but it surely would not be needed.

"You are sure the demons will withdraw?" Zyzyiig asked. "Might they send help to their garrison instead?"

"They cannot," Shavvataaars replied. "Their strength is not that great, and their attention will soon be elsewhere. Nothing shall stand in the path of the Great Journey. But the Time of Cleansing cannot begin until the demons have been cast out."

Dryienjaiyeel would be free of the offworlders, of the northern merchants, of everyone who exploited the zyglyn trade and interfered with the savages of the deep jungles. And the People of the Mists could return to their own ways again under the protection of the Ancients, Shavvataaars and his sibs.

Yes ... yes, the Cleansing will soon be complete.

"Best if I go to command the assault in person," Zyzyiig said. "Then there will be no mistakes."

The Semti's rasping voice sounded worried now. "That is not wise, my Companion of the Journey. Such will only delay the moment of decision, perhaps aiding the demons to evade their fate."

Zyzyiig crossed arms firmly. "My decision is made, Honored One. I will lead the troops into battle and see these *legionnaires* crushed as the mists melt away in the morning sun."

Chapter Five

Most legionnaires have nothing to lose and life itself is not held very dear.

—Legionnaire Adolphe Cooper,
French Foreign Legion, 1933

Gunnery Sergeant Trent peered cautiously over the embankment of the slit trench. "What've you got, Pascali?"

"Heat sources there," Corporal Pascali replied, pointing. "And there ... there ... down there. Goddamned big ones, Sarge."

Trent switched to his IR helmet display. In the eerie green light of the infrared screen, the bright plumes of heat stood out like brilliant stars on a dark night. "Hmmm ... power plants. Vehicle engines. Looks like our monkey friends aren't settling for half-measures this time."

Sunrise was still almost an hour away, but a pre-dawn glow was already suffusing the eastern sky. Hanuman's rotation period was close to thirty-four standard hours long, and everything—day, night, twilight—seemed to stretch out endlessly.

The trouble was, the hot, moist climate made heavy morning mists inevitable. A thick fog clung to the lower slopes of the Monkeyville plateau, masking the jungle ... and the native troops assembled there. Visibility was better around the Enclave itself, but not by much. Even infrared was obscured to some extent.

Perfect conditions for an attack, Trent thought. He keyed in his radio to the command frequency. "Alice One, this is Guardian."

"On line, Guardian," Legionnaire Garcia replied promptly. "Go ahead."

"I've got four confirmed heat sources on the north road. Probably vehicles. Better tell L-T the monkeys are on the warpath again."

"'Firm. Wait one." Static crackled as long seconds passed. Then Garcia's voice came back on the channel. "Acknowledged, Guardian. Lieutenant says to come back inside and take charge of the main perimeter. Strauss and Braxton will reinforce the trenches."

"On my way." As Trent cut the channel, an alarm siren wailed behind him, inside Fort Monkey.

Those vehicles were climbing the main road from the north-western valley. No doubt there were more behind them, and enemy troops filtering through the jungle and up the slopes to support the armor. It looked like the long-expected hannie attack was finally grinding forward.

"They want me inside," he said crisply. "Pascali, take charge out here. L-T's sending the other two recon lances, and I'll get you a couple of heavy weapons for support. Don't fire until they're right on top of you. We want to sucker as many of the little bastards as we can."

Pascali nodded. "We'll nail 'em, Sarge," she said confidently. She and Reinhardt were the only survivors from her recon lance, but two legionnaires from one of the First Platoon's rifle lances had been drafted to join them on guard. They looked ready to wipe out the hannie army without any help at all from the rest of the company.

He slapped the top of her helmet and scrambled out of the trench.

The trenches had been Subaltern Watanabe's idea. With most of the native troops gathered on the northwest side of the plateau, and the only decent road running straight up into Fort Monkey from the north, it seemed likely that the main threat would be to that side—the same area they'd attacked the previous night. Two slit trenches on either side of the road and thirty meters from the north gate would be a nasty surprise to hannies who thought they knew the terrain. Trent smiled. Watanabe was shaping up into a real legionnaire—tough and cunning.

Of course, there was always the chance the hannies would try to bypass the main route. They had troops on all sides of the fort, but getting tracked vehicles across the rugged ground surrounding the plateau would be quite a challenge. It looked like they were going to take the easy route, and they'd pay for that.

He crossed the road and headed for the hole the hannies had blasted in the north wall on their first attack. Bravo Company's second

FSV was grounded in the opening. Despite the alarm siren, Legionnaire Ignaczak was still lounging in the open turret hatch, eating from a ra-pack while he studied a pornographic magazine.

"Button up, Zak," Trent called. "We've got company coming, so put that shit away and get ready."

"We'll kick ass, Sarge," the gunner replied. He stuffed the magazine into his fatigue jacket and sealed it up. Taking a last mouthful from the ra-pack, Ignaczak crumpled the package and tossed it carelessly into the compound behind the Sabertooth.

"Better go after it, Zak!" another legionnaire called from the parapet above. "That's a week in cells for littering!"

"Yeah?" Ignaczak shouted back. "Then what do those monkeys get for knockin' down the wall last night?"

"Well, shitfire, Zak," the other man answered, patting his FE-MEK barrel and grinning. "They're not in the Legion. I guess we'll either send 'em home without their dinners or shoot 'em. How 'bout it, Sarge?"

"New directive from the Colonial Office, Gates," Trent responded. "We're supposed to make them go to camp sanitation lectures."

"That's cruel, Sarge," Gates said, shaking his head and laughing. "Real cruel. We'd better just put 'em out of their misery."

Trent laughed and broke into a trot across the parade ground. The banter was a good sign; the legionnaires were ready for a fight.

And a fight, Trent reflected as he watched Bravo Company boiling out of the fort's barracks buildings, was exactly what they were likely to get.

* * *

"Go! Go! Go!" The corporal's voice was hoarse with excitement.

Slick jumped into the trench, wincing as the motion jarred his bruised ribs. DuPont climbed in after him, taking care not to bump his laser rifle. Though the Whitney-Sykes HPLR-55 was rugged enough to be the standard infantry weapon of most Terran Army light infantry units, the Legion snipers who used the laser rifle were inclined to handle them with exaggerated caution. The least little flaw in the alignment of the crystals could spoil the Legion's reputation for fielding the best snipers in the Commonwealth Defense Forces.

Rostov and Vrurrth were last, and paused to pull the chameleon tarp into place. Except for narrow gaps along the front of the trench, the tarp completely covered the legionnaires' position. The microcircuitry worked into the weave of the cloth would analyze the reflective qualities of nearby terrain and adjust the tarp's colors accordingly. The same principle was used in duraweave battledress coveralls and made the cloth—and anything it covered—a nearly perfect match for most backgrounds.

Across the road Braxton's lance was already in place beside Pascali's improvised unit. Thirteen legionnaires awaited the hannie army, joking, swearing, laughing ... Thirteen legionnaires, and Slick.

As he chambered a round in his FEK and poised the rifle on the rim of the trench, Slick found himself recoiling from the others. Overnight he'd had his baptism of fire, his first exposure to the realities of battle. But he still felt totally out of place here. Rostov had started to make him feel welcome, but these legionnaires were still almost as alien as the monkeys creeping through the mist.

Fear gnawed at his stomach. The trench was constricting, like a box ... or a coffin. *No room for stealth this time,* he thought. *What the hell am I doing here?*

*   *   *

"Ganymede, Ganymede, this is Alice One," Fraser said into the handset of his C^3 unit. He was hunched over the computer map table in the front compartment of an M-786C, the command variant of the Legion's ubiquitous Sandray APC. "Say again your ETA, *Ganymede.*"

"Alice One, *Ganymede.*" Captain Garrett sounded tired, irritated. "ETA is thirteen, I say again, one-three, mikes. What's your situation, Alice One, over?"

"Ganymede, I have hostiles advancing on the north wall," Fraser responded. "I can't cover the fort and the landing field, too."

The captain's voice took on an even sharper edge.

"Well, you're the one who knows the score. How do you want to play it, Alice One?"

Fraser released the transmit key and looked down at the computer-generated map of the compound. Bravo Company was already mustered on the perimeter, ready to meet the hannie attack. The command APC was near the center of the compound, together with a handful of other Sandrays, ready to deploy as needed. He glanced at Legionnaire Garcia, who sat at one of the other C^3 terminals monitoring reports from the rest of the unit.

They could wave off the transport until the natives were driven off, but Fraser didn't like the idea of more delays. It had taken all night to get the ship to Monkeyville, and that had given the hannie army time to muster for a big push. What if the hannies just kept throwing troops at the legionnaires all day? If numbers finally overpowered Bravo Company, they'd want *Ganymede* down and waiting to dust them off in a hurry.

But if she set down at the Enclave's landing field south of the fort, *Ganymede* would be exposed, vulnerable to any attack mounted from the southeast through the deserted civilian facilities of the Enclave. A pair of Sandray APCs were sufficient to keep an eye out for patrols working along that side of the plateau, but they couldn't cover the landing field. And Bravo Company just didn't have the men to spare to cover the landing field in the middle of an enemy attack.

There was one other solution....

"*Ganymede*, Alice One," he said at last, keying in the handset again. "Can you put down in the open space on the east side of the fort? Over."

"Wait one," the captain answered crisply. Fraser could visualize him calling up the computer files on Monkeyville to cross-check sizes and distances. "Alice One, that's affirmative."

"Then that's the drill, Captain. That'll keep you under my guns."

"And away from the natives, I hope," he said. "This bucket wasn't designed to play around in a hot L-Z, Lieutenant. We're not armed, and even that primmie stuff the monkeys have is enough to put a hole in the old girl."

"I hear you, Captain," Fraser said. "We'll do our best for you. Alice One, out."

He replaced the handset. Fraser examined the map again. *Did I make the right decision?* he wondered. *Damn it! I wish LaSalle was here.*

But LaSalle was dead, and if his men didn't hold the hannies on the perimeter there would be a lot of legionnaires joining the captain before dawn came.

And whatever happened, it would be Colin Fraser's responsibility.

"Assault column in position, *Asjyai*," the radio operator said.

* * *

The army command post was a ramshackle hut in a small jungle clearing near the base of the Demon Plateau. It was crowded with radio equipment and the big table where topographic maps of the area were spread out to accommodate tactical planning. There wasn't much room left over for personnel, so most of Zyzyiig's staff waited outside for orders. The arrangement had advantages; ky could think and plan better with fewer underlings clamoring for their leader's attention.

Zyzyiig stroked kys muzzle slowly. "What about the turning column?"

"*Jyiedry* Ghyzyeen reports it will be ready to attack in another five *dwyk, Asjyai*," ky replied. "The terrain to the east is very difficult for the armored vehicles."

"Tell Ghyzyeen I want action, not excuses," Zyzyiig growled. "They must be ready to strike just as soon as the enemy is fully engaged."

"Yes, Honored."

Behind them, Shavvataaars stirred. "You would do well not to underestimate the offworld demons," he whispered. "They will detect your maneuver."

"I handle this *my* way!" Zyzyiig snapped. Ky glanced back at the Semti, suddenly aware of who and what ky was speaking to. Zyzyiig was a civilized kyen, far too sophisticated to believe that the Semti were really the Ancient Gods of Dryien myth. But they were an old and powerful race, long-lived, wise ... and vital allies. "Honored One," ky continued, "I have planned this carefully. Two attacks on the ground will keep the demons off-balance. Armored vehicles can kill them. So can rockets, and we have issued launchers to soldiers in both columns."

"Many of your soldiers will complete their journeys," Shavvataaars said. "The demons will not be caught by surprise this time."

"I know, Honored One. But if we can keep the enemy occupied on the ground, our last surprise will have a chance of getting through." Zyzyiig smiled grimly. Ky turned again to face the radio operator. "Order the assault column to attack!"

*　*　*

"Here they come! Get ready!"

Slick tightened his grip on the FEK and fought the temptation to fire. Green shapes glowed against a darker green backdrop on his IR display: heat sources, the larger, brighter ones hannie vehicles, the smaller but more numerous ones individual native soldiers creeping forward to the attack. It was quiet, except for the distant clank of vehicle treads. The enemy movement was slow and cautious. Were they expecting the legionnaires to spring a trap, or was the fog hampering their advance? Probably the latter, since hannie IR gear was still scarce in Dryienjaiyeel's army....

"Wait for the onagers to fire, *mes amis*." Platoon Sergeant Henri Fontaine was in command in the trenches now. Second Platoon's senior NCO had joined the three recon lances with two heavy weapons units, bringing the total strength of the advanced force to twenty-four men—nearly a quarter of Bravo Company's strength. There was a lot of firepower here ... but would it be enough against the weight of the hannie attack? "Steady ... pick your targets...."

A burst of native machine-gun fire erupted from the left, loud in the pre-dawn stillness. More hannies joined in the firing, accompanied by a chorus of shouts. Slick couldn't make out what they were yelling, but from the way the gunfire fell silent he guessed the monkey officers or non-coms were trying to get control over nervous troops.

It helped to think of the enemy soldiers as being just as nervous as he was. Slick shifted his FEK, lining up on the closest heat source. The closest troops were no more than twenty meters from the con-cealed trenches now. The vehicles were still lagging behind the in-fantry, hindered as much by the rugged terrain as by the visibility. When would Fontaine give the order to fire? Couldn't he see how *close* the monkeys were?

The onager gunner next to Slick chambered a round with an audible *cha*-CHUNK. Clad from head to toe in plasteel armor, with a modified helmet that covered his entire face and contained sophisticated sighting gear that slaved the aim of his plasma gun to the movement of his eyes, Legionnaire Childers was the very image of the ultimate high-tech soldier. The man's weapon shifted minutely in its ConRig harness as Childers lined up on his target, one of the vehicles lumbering up the main road.

"Onagers ..." The tension was plain in Fontaine's voice. "Ready ... fire!"

Childers squeezed the trigger. Slick blinked back tears as a blinding flash of raw light and heat surged from the barrel of the onager and hurtled toward its target trailing a visible streak like some impossibly straight bolt of lightning. The French who had first developed the plasma weapon had called it the *fusil d'onage*, or "storm rifle." Seeing it in action, Slick didn't think the label was strong enough.

All around him, the rest of the defenders were shooting now as legionnaires threw back the tarps to improve their fields of fire. Corporal Dmowski had the other onager in action over in Pascali's trench, and the two plasma rifles kept up a measured, accurate fire. Kinetic energy rifles whined, while the deep-throated hum of a pair of heavier MEKs droned a deadly harmony. The hannie line faltered under the weight of a barrage equal to what a regiment of their own troops might have poured out.

Slick fired, then ducked down involuntarily as a native anti-tank rocket leapt from a blunderbuss launcher toward him. The rocket passed over the trench, exploding harmlessly near the base of the fort's north wall. When he peered over the rim of the trench again, Slick saw that one of the vehicle heat sources was now much brighter. Raked by multiple onager hits, a hannie tank was on fire.

The scene reminded him of the carnage inside the fort after the first assault ... had it only been a few hours go? There were dead hannies everywhere, but more were advancing to take their places. He fired at them mechanically, hardly caring if he scored a hit or not. The deadly hail of Legion firepower would mow them all down long before they could be a threat.

Another rocket skimmed above the trench, much lower than the first. Again Slick couldn't help ducking, though he knew the thing was only really a threat if it scored a direct hit. Even without plasteel, his uniform would keep out most shrapnel and ordinary bullets, and this morning Slick had added plasteel plates over his chest and back. In this kind of fight, armor counted more than freedom of movement.

"Come on, nube!" DuPont grabbed his uniform collar and hauled Slick to his feet. "Get with it!"

"Incoming! Incoming!" Rostov yelled. Something screamed overhead and exploded behind them, showering the trench in dirt.

"What the hell?" DuPont shouted. "I didn't see any of the tanks firing!"

"That wasn't a tank," Childers said, firing his onager again. "Too big. Must've been one of their big howitzers, down in the jungle somewhere."

"Who's sighting for it?" DuPont asked wildly. All his bravado had fled. "Where are the bastards calling in the fire, dammit?"

"Steady, *mon brave*," Fontaine's voice cut in smoothly on the radio circuit. "Keep the line clear. I'll see what the lieutenant wants us to do."

Slick fired a spread of grenades, more by reflex than design. He felt trapped in the narrow confines of the trench, trapped and helpless under the fall of those shells. Not even full plasteel body armor would save the defenders once the enemy artillery found the range....

* * *

"Lieutenant! Sergeant Fontaine reports the natives are calling in arty."

"Damn!" Fraser turned in his seat to face Legionnaire Garcia. He had hoped that the poor jungle roads would make it impossible for the hannies to bring up heavy guns. The natives didn't have much in their arsenal capable of breaking the Legion defenses, but artillery was definitely a threat. "What size guns?"

Garcia shook her head. "He's not sure, Lieutenant. One-oh-eights ... maybe one-twenty-ones."

Fraser looked down at the map table. "All right. Order Fontaine to pull back ... heavy weapons first. That'll buy us some time."

"Yes, sir." She turned back to the radio.

Fraser swiveled his seat to face a control console. The command version of the Sandray lacked the weaponry of the ordinary APC model, substituting a satellite dish for the usual turret arrangement. It did, however, mount something the other M-786s lacked: a launch rack for surveillance drones. His fingers danced over the controls, programming one to search out the enemy artillery.

First they had to know what they were dealing with. Then the legionnaires would take steps to counter the threat.

* * *

Another shell arced toward the defenders. It fell short this time, the explosion ripping through a clump of hannies in an improvised foxhole thirty meters from Slick.

"Goddamn it!" DuPont shouted, "They're bracketing us!"

"Once they get the range ..." Rostov said. His voice was cold and flat.

"All right! Listen up!" Fontaine broke through the clatter. "The lieutenant knows what's going on. Weapons lances, fall back to the main gate. Recon lances, cover them. On my mark ... move!"

Rostov was helping Childers scramble out of the trench, while farther down the line Childers's lancemate, Legionnaire Hsu, was already running for the fort wall, the elongated tube of a Fafnir missile launcher slung over one shoulder. There was a renewed volley of FEK fire from the trenches as the recon lances laid down covering fire. Slick opened up at a hannie soldier fifty meters away, saw the tiny native spin backward and fall....

"Incoming!" The call came again, this time from Strauss. There was another screech as a howitzer shell rose from the jungle fog, streaking heavenward, then arcing over and down, plummeting straight toward the trench. Slick stared up at it in horror, unable to react at all, unable to move, to think, even to scream....

Chapter Six

The goal of a Legionnaire is the supreme adventure of combat at the end of which is either victory or death.

—Colonel Pierre Jeanpierre,
French Foreign Legion, 1958

Grid coordinates five-seven by one-zero-nine," Fraser said, reading the display underneath the video monitor that was re-laying the view from the surveillance drone. "Six targets. Computer IDs them as one-twenty-one mike-mike field guns. Recognition named Hellhound."

"Five-seven by one-zero-niner," Trent's voice answered over the comm channel. "Six targets, ID Hellhound. Copy."

"Confirmed," Fraser said. "Pound 'em flat, Gunny."

"Count on it, L-T," the sergeant responded. "Count on it."

"All right, Zak," Trent shouted. "Let 'em have it!"

Trent thought he could hear the distant *crump* of the hannie guns loosing a full barrage now that they had their target bracketed. He was crouched beside the Sabertooth parked in the gap in the north wall. The sounds of fire from the trenches were slacking as the defenders pulled back. If those guns weren't silenced fast....

Beside him the Sabertooth seemed to vibrate as one of the two Grendel missiles left its launch rack with an ear-splitting roar. The second Grendel followed moments later, riding a column of smoke and fire.

Trent hit his comm switch. "Fafnirs ... lock target profiles and fire!"

Corporal Toshiro Ikeda nodded and aimed his Fafnir rocket launcher skyward. "You heard the man," he said. His fingers danced over the tiny keyboard that controlled the rig, programming in silhouette and IR signature data. "Ready ..."

The corporal stabbed the launch button savagely, and the missile leapt from the tube with a roar like a wounded beast. Moments later, three more missiles followed. The man-portable Fafnir rocket launchers used programmable guidance computers to recognize preselected targets. They were ideal for tracking down unseen enemies, though their warheads were smaller than the vehicle-mounted Grendels.

"Missiles running ... running ..." Legionnaire Ignaczak's voice droned in Trent's earphones. His two Grendels, unlike the Fafnirs, were set for controlled tele-guided flight; after the Fafnirs found their targets, the Grendels could smash whatever was left of the hannie battery. "I've got one ... two hits. Three. Three down, Sarge! Sending in the big boys now!"

"Fafnirs!" Trent called. "Fire another spread ... just to make sure."

As the missiles leapt into the air Trent allowed himself a smile. The hannies wouldn't be trying *that* little trick again!

* * *

The explosion erupted less than ten meters away. Slick staggered under the force of the shock wave, dropping his FEK in the mud at the bottom of the trench. His helmet protected his ears from the force of the blast, but he could feel blood trickling from his nose. Sluggishly, he pulled himself up, surprised to find that he was still in one piece.

"Childers is down!" Rostov yelled.

"Help him, nube," Strauss ordered harshly. "The rest of you keep firing!"

Shaking his head to clear the ringing in his ears, Slick started to clamber out of the trench. The ground seemed to be swaying under his feet. Then he saw Childers.

The armored legionnaire was sprawled on the ground a few meters away, close to the shell crater. The man's left leg was twisted around at an impossible angle, broken.

Blood spurted from the stump of his right leg. The legionnaire's foot, still sheathed in plasteel, lay nearby. Slick stared at the sight, unable to move, unable even to look away. Nausea twisted inside him.

"Help him, kid!" Rostov's voice sounded far away.

Slick sank to his knees, clawing at his helmet, and pulled it free barely in time. Vomit clogged his nose and throat.

"Goddamned nube!" he heard Strauss curse. "Vrurrth, help Childers. Rostov, get the nube out of here!"

Gasping for air, Slick saw the big Gwyrran crouch next to the fallen onager gunner. Vrurrth's massive fingers were surprisingly deft as he stripped away plasteel leg armor and tied off a tourniquet above the man's wound. Gently, he lifted Childers, armor, weapon, and all, hoisting the fallen legionnaire over one huge shoulder and sprinting for the cover of the fort.

"Come on, kid, move it!" Rostov said, pulling Slick to his feet and shoving him in the same direction. There was a far-off scream of more incoming shells as the rest of the legionnaires retreated, firing back to discourage the hannies from pursuing too close. Rostov caught Slick as he tripped and staggered, urging him on again. Nearby, another legionnaire fell, his back ripped open by a hannie rocket.

Slick closed his eyes, trying to block out the scene, but the horror wouldn't go away.

* * *

The warning light on the computer-generated battle map strobed urgently. Fraser stared down at it in sinking despair. *Not now, damn it!* he thought. Panic threatened to overwhelm him. *Not* there!

He fought for control. The light indicated that something had set off the fort's remote sensors on the east side of the compound. As he watched, the computer identified the intruders and displayed symbols on the map ... native infantry and armor pushing over the rough terrain toward the east wall.

And the lighter was only minutes away from landing on that side of the fort ... the place *he'd* pronounced safe. *Damn those hannie bastards!*

"Garcia!" he snapped. "Get *Ganymede* on the line. Instruct her not to land until she gets confirmation." Without waiting for her acknowledgement Fraser keyed in his private line to Trent. "Gunny, there's trouble on the east side of the fort. Computer says we've got at least a company of monkey infantry with eight tanks coming up. Get some men over there and turn those bastards back. We've got to secure the area for the transport to land."

Trent's reply was calm and measured. "I'll take care of it, L-T." Was there a rebuke in his voice? "Permission to use Bashar's Sabertooth?"

"Anything you need, Gunny," Fraser told him, trying to suppress his uncertainty. "Just clear that area!"

"Lieutenant!"

"What is it, Garcia?" He tried to sound calm, in control.

"*Ganymede* reports a flight of primmie aircraft. Bearing three-four-seven. Heavy stuff … bombers, maybe."

As if we didn't have enough trouble! Fraser nodded wearily. "Acknowledge."

Artillery, flanking columns, bombers … what next? And when would Bravo Company finally run out of resources to deal with whatever the hannies were going to come up with?

Fraser stared down at the map. It looked like the legionnaires were running out of time … and luck.

*　*　*

"It's huge, *Asjyai*! Huge!"

Zyzyiig's neck ruff stirred in anger. *The offworlders and their demon technology!* First they had crippled the artillery battery the troops had hauled so laboriously over mud-choked roads to support their attack. Now, it seemed, one of their huge air vessels was in the sky over their fort. If this craft mounted weapons like the ones their soldiers used….

"Be not so ready to give in to defeat, *Asjyai*," Shavvataaars whispered behind him. It was as if the Semti was reading his mind. The thought sent a chill up Zyzyiig's spine. Perhaps the legends were true….

"The vessel your soldiers describe is of the type the demons refer to as Camerone-class," the Semti continued. "It is a transport, un-armed, ill-armored. They never intended such craft for operations in a combat area."

"Then …" Hope was rekindling in kys heart.

"The vessel is no threat to your soldiers," Shavvataaars confirmed the unspoken statement. "They need not fear. The Cleansing may continue unhindered."

Zyzyiig smiled, reaching for kys radio. Perhaps there was time after all.

*　*　*

The wall burst inward in a roiling cloud of smoke and splintered masonry. Sergeant Trent fired a spray of grenades into the opening before the dust could settle. "Pour it on, boys! Let 'em know you're here!"

Beside him, Legionnaire Fiorello squeezed off a plasma bolt from his onager. The flare as it found a target backlit the smoke, giving the scene an eerie, hellish quality. Other legionnaires of Third Platoon added in their firepower, and hannie screams testified to their accuracy.

A tank gun barked, sending a shell whistling through the opening. It struck the back of a supply hut thirty meters behind Trent. Machine guns hammered.

The first hannie tank rumbled through the new gap in the east wall, firing again as it came. This time, the shell found its mark, an MEK gunner crouched behind an improvised barricade of upturned cargo-mods. Fiorello's onager flashed again, tearing a hole in the tank's front chassis armor. The vehicle ground forward, followed by another. Hannie troops charged out of the smoke firing rockets and screaming defiance.

With a whine of strained turbofans a Legion Sandray shot past, slewing sideways in front of Trent's position. The APC's gun chattered, spraying death. Natives scrambled for cover or fell, torn by dozens of needle shards. The lead tank fired again, but the Sandray's composite-laminate armor absorbed the impact easily. A second Sandray appeared from the left of Trent's defensive line, pumping high-volume autofire into the hannies. The gap in the east wall was a seething cauldron no infantry soldier could survive.

Farther down the line, a second explosion opened a new hole. As another hannie tank crashed through the debris, Corporal Bashar's Sabertooth opened fire. The turret-mounted plasma cannon illuminated the battlefield like a brief, false dawn. Superheated metal smashed into the hannie tank, vaporizing the vehicle's gun mount and leaving the chassis a twisted, smoking hulk.

"Score one for the cavalry!" someone shouted.

Fiorello's third shot exploded right over the lead tank's engine compartment, tearing a hole through armor plating and complex machinery. The vehicle rolled to a stop as smoke poured from the gash, a thick, oil-blackened cloud. The second tank smashed into it, pushing the cripple aside.

Bashar's Sabertooth pivoted on its fans, ready to make the kill....

"Sabertooth One, this is Alice One. Break off and await new orders!" Garcia's voice sounded urgent over Trent's headphones.

"Confirmed," Bashar replied blandly. The FSV continued its turn without firing.

"Goddamn it!" Trent roared. "What the hell do you think you're doing, Garcia?"

"Lieutenant's orders," Garcia replied. "He wants the Sabertooth redeployed."

Trent thought about overriding the order. With the FSV on the east wall, there was no way the enemy would manage a breakthrough. Without it ... well, the onagers would still keep their tanks at bay. But Fraser had promised him the Sabertooth for support....

"We've got enemy aircraft inbound, Sarge," Garcia said quietly. She seemed to be reading his mind. "And Sabertooth Two's got troubles on the north wall. We need Bashar for anti-air."

"Right," Trent said at last. "We'll make do here."

He raised his FEK to fire another burst of grenades.

We'll make do ... unless they've got more surprises for us....

* * *

"Six bogies, bearing now three-three-niner, speed five hundred, altitude five-five-zero, range nine hundred, closing." The lieutenant's voice sounded tinny in Legionnaire Spiro Karatsolis's ear. "Tentative ID is native propeller-driven bombers, recognition code Boomerang. Repeat this is a tentative ID only."

"Roger, Alice One," Karatsolis replied. He ran his fingers over his tracking board, slaving his computer to the feed from the command van. Data readouts flashed confirmation of Fraser's verbal information. "Receiving your input. Ready to fire."

"Just be goddamned careful of the transport!" Fraser snapped.

Corporal Bashar glanced up and back from the Sabertooth's controls. "Sounds like the lieutenant's getting jumpy, huh?"

"That's what they pay him for, Bashar," the gunner responded with a grin. "Officers worry ... we just pull the trigger and collect the bounty."

As Bashar guided the FSV past the barracks, Karatsolis programmed the two Grendels. "Fire on the rail!" he warned, hitting the launch buttons in quick succession. Bashar compensated for the recoil so smoothly that the Sabertooth barely rocked.

Monitors flashed on above the Grendel control console, giving Karatsolis a warhead's eye view of the missiles' flight paths. The *Gany-*

mede filled the two screens as it circled to the northwest of the fort. Karatsolis smiled and gripped a joystick. Those hannie bombers would get the surprise of a lifetime, and thanks to the transport they'd barely have time to see it coming.

The view on the screens lurched and plunged as the two missiles dived together, dropping under the lighter, then up … up … Karatsolis disengaged the teleguidance and switched to heat-seeking mode, making sure the transport's IFF code was registering. The lead Grendel locked on an enemy bomber. The second started to follow, but the legionnaire overrode and the missile selected the second high-est signature to home in on. An instant later, the two screens flared and went blank almost as one. Two of the six targets went dead on the Sabertooth's fire-control board.

"Two down!" he yelled.

"Two for the goatherd," Bashar agreed. "Kind of reminds me of that time on Ossian. Remember?"

Karatsolis swung his chair to operate the turret controls. "Tracking!" he shouted, ignoring Bashar's comment. The turret rotated smoothly. In front of him, another monitor lit up to display sighting data for the Sabertooth's powerful onager cannon. The legionnaire raised the plasma gun skyward, probing for targets. His left hand called up the feed from Fraser's computers and superimposed the information on the aiming display.

The bombers had split up. One pair was dropping low, while the others climbed, angling behind and over *Ganymede*. The transport lighter screened the second pair….

He dropped the barrel so that one of the low-flying bombers was centered in the video monitor. A few quick keystrokes locked the target image into the computer and slaved the turret to the aircraft's motion. "Clear!" he called, and Bashar fired up the turbofans again. The turret swung under computer control as the Sabertooth moved, keeping the image of the aircraft locked on the screen. Seconds later, crosshairs lit up over the target in red, and Karatsolis squeezed the trigger that fired the onager cannon.

The noise was deafening, the heat almost unbearable as the cannon fired, flinging a packet of raw plasma at the target. The superheated metal lanced toward the airplane like summer lightning, and in an instant the target was gone, vaporized.

"Tracking!" he repeated, and even before Bashar had halted the vehicle he was already starting to line up for the second shot. This bomber had no more chance than the other. The plasma bolt found its mark and destroyed the aircraft before the crew knew what had hit them.

But where were the other two…?

"Bashar! Move around … give me a better angle!" The last two aircraft were still masked by the lighter. They'd be close enough to drop their loads soon….

Damn! Ganymede *was still in the way. Damn! Damn!*

* * *

Wyzzeer Gyeddiig pulled back on the yoke and pushed all four throttles forward, feeling the *Fwyryeel* bomber shudder as its nose came up and the four props revved to three-quarters power. So far the demons below hadn't fired on kys plane, but it was only a matter of time. If their lightning weapons didn't find a mark, their tame servant-rockets would. Ky had watched four of the six aircraft in Flight Predator knocked out of the sky by the devil weapons. So far only luck had protected the two survivors … luck, and the screening bulk of the demon skycraft lumbering in a slow circle above the Demon Plateau.

Zeeraij Dreeyg, kys copilot, pointed downward. The ground battle was still raging around the demon fort. Flight Predator was supposed to deliver the knockout blow that would break the offworlders, but with two aircraft left and certain destruction awaiting them if they ventured too close, how could they hope to carry out the mission? Without a powerful strike, and soon, the ground attack was sure to fail. Those demon weapons were as deadly on the ground as they were to aircraft….

Lightning leapt from ground to sky, engulfing the other bomber in fire. Gyeddiig fought the controls to keep the aircraft stable as the shock wave buffeted them. They were alone now.

"We're not going to make it," Dreeyg said softly. "Even if we turn back and get clear, the *Asjyai* will have our ruffs."

"Not that there's much hope of getting clear," Gyeddiig commented. Ky banked the aircraft. The huge bulk of the alien air ship loomed ahead.

The *Asjyai* had told them these demon craft were powerless, unarmed, and so far this one certainly hadn't fired. It was moving slowly, like a dirigible but without visible propellers. Would it be as vulnerable as a dirigible?

If they couldn't strike a blow against the demons on the ground, couldn't they at least damage the sky vessel? Its fall might discourage the demons, disrupt their defense of the fort below....

Grimly, Gyeddiig adjusted the bomber's course and switched on the intercom. "Bombardier ... arm all weapons."

Dreeyg was looking at the pilot with wide, horrified eyes. "You're not—?"

"Bombs armed, *Wyzzeer*," the bombardier reported. Gyeddiig pushed the throttles to full. "Ancients and Eternal Mists!" ky shouted. The bomber plunged toward its helpless target.

Chapter Seven

People grow old quickly here. Yesterday, they were baptizing us—today they're giving us the last rites.

> —Legionnaire Forster's dying words,
> French Foreign Legion, April 1908

My God, Fraser, we've been hit!"

The words brought Fraser out of his seat. "*Ganymede*! What's your condition?"

Over the open comm channel he could hear Captain Garret shouting orders while other voices babbled in the background. He caught the phrase "drives failing ... crash ..." but little else. Fraser rushed to the rear of the APC, calling for the driver to drop the ramp.

Outside, he gaped at the scene. *Ganymede* hung suspended over the east side of the camp, less than a hundred meters off the ground. Smoke and flame billowed from her stern section, where the hull was twisted and crumpled around a wide gash. As Fraser watched, the stern sank visibly. The ship stirred, lifting slightly, turning; for a long moment, it looked as if the crew was regaining control over the damaged giant.

Then she faltered again as the main repulsion fields failed. The ship dropped.

The ground shook at the impact, and a sound like a hundred thunderclaps washed over the fort. Dust and smoke obscured the scene, but as it thinned Fraser could see the transport's broken hull lying astride the remains of the east wall. Flames were rising from the wreck. Something exploded, sending a fireball mushrooming back into the sky. Mingled with the roar of flames, the screams of the wounded—human and native alike—were a nightmare sound.

Fraser realized that he wasn't alone. A cluster of onlookers had gathered nearby, at the door to the medical hut. Like him, they all seemed stunned by the crash, shocked into immobility.

He forced himself to tear his mind away from the horror. "Don't just gawk!" he yelled. "Get over there. *Help* those poor bastards! Come on, Doc! Move!"

Ramirez snapped out of his paralysis and pushed the others to work—the Padre to round up medical supplies, the other two warrant officers to round up vehicles. A bulky Sandray rigged for engineering work stirred from the ground, its bulldozer blade dropping down into the ready position in front of the driver's cab.

Fraser turned, glancing into the command van's darkened interior. "Garcia! I'll be at the crash site!"

The C^3 tech shook her head. "You can't, Lieutenant!"

"Damn it, don't argue with me!" He stopped himself. Garcia was right. Whatever he wanted, he still had an obligation to the unit. Reluctantly, he turned his back on the chaos outside. "All right. Tell Ramirez … tell him to save as many as he can…."

He sank into his seat, drained. The transport crew … Third Platoon … Sergeant Trent … He shuddered, picturing the butcher's bill.

And the battle wasn't over.

*　*　*

"Sarge! Come on, Sarge, wake up!"

Gunnery Sergeant Trent groaned and opened his eyes. He was lying in the dirt behind a tumble of cargomods, half buried by dirt and debris. Somewhere nearby, close enough for him to feel the heat and hear the crackle, a fire was burning. His leg hurt, the same leg he'd twisted before. Blood trickled down his forehead and dripped in the dirt.

Legionnaire Krueger was kneeling beside him, his face grimy but determined. "Come on, Sarge!"

"Enough, Krueger," Trent growled. He raised himself to his hands and knees and looked around. "What the bloody hell happened?"

"The transport, Sarge. It crashed." Krueger looked away. "It just crashed...."

The lighter lay like a broken toy across the ruined east wall. The ship's tail rested on a flattened, twisted pile of wreckage that had been one of the hannie tanks. Hull plates had fallen away over much of the length of the vessel, exposing the ship's interior in a dozen or more places. Smoke boiled suddenly out of one of the holes as explosions rippled inside the wreck.

Trent started to rise. Something in front of him caught his attention ... Legionnaire Fiorello, his body cut nearly in two by a jagged piece of hull plating. It had sliced clean through the soldier's plasteel bodysuit.

Two meters to the left and it would have caught Trent instead.

"What are our casualties, Krueger?" he asked, shaking his head to clear it.

Krueger shrugged. "Sergeant Qazi and Mr. Bartlow are okay, Sarge. And I saw a couple of the other guys moving around a minute ago. The two seven-eighty-sixes were right under that thing when it hit...."

The medical APC was racing towards them, followed by a gaggle of other vehicles. Trent picked up his FEK and started to meet them, favoring his sore leg.

Someone was moaning softly, the sound almost drowned out by the roar of the fires. Another one alive....

How many had survived? How many? The question was a searing pain deep within him, a knife in his gut.

Every legionnaire's death would twist that knife deeper.

* * *

"Retreating! What do you mean, retreating?" Zyzyiig smashed a tight-clenched fist against the table. "They will continue the attack, by the Ancients!"

"*Asjyai*, Regiment Godshammer has lost all but two tanks," the radio operator protested. "The demon sky vessel crushed them when it fell. More than a hundred soldiers were lost ... and that does not include the ones killed in the fighting!"

Zyzyiig whirled, neck ruff puffed out full. "Say the wrong word and you will be the next casualty, *Zydryie!*"

The radio operator crossed arms. "I ... I am sorry, Honored," ky said, subdued. "But ... the flank column is already in full retreat. How can we rally them now?"

"Call for my car," Zyzyiig ordered. "I will go there and *personally* see to them."

"Y-yes, Honored One." The *Zydryie* turned back to kys radio gear.

"Do not allow your anger to deflect you from the path of success, my Companion," Shavvataaars said softly, intercepting the *Asjyai.*

"Demons take you!" Zyzyiig spat. "Get out of my way!"

"The moment is not ripe to complete this journey," the Semti insisted. "You cannot force your soldiers to act against their natures, and for the instant their nature demands retreat. Recovery."

"You said yourself that we must not waste time in overrunning these demons," Zyzyiig said. "Now you say we should wait?"

"The moment has changed. An attack in the night might have broken them. Before the fall of their vessel, they might still have been overcome. Now, though, your troops lack the will for victory."

"What of the demons? Their skycraft crashed! They must be demoralized...."

The Semti spread his thin, long-fingered hands. "Indeed they will be, my Companion. The difference is that time will help your soldiers to recover their courage. According to my sources, that transport was the only one the Terrans had available to remove these legionnaires. They are trapped here. And time will only serve to sap their strength, as their knowledge of these facts ripens."

Zyzyiig stepped back. "You are sure of this?"

"Very sure, my Companion of the Journey. As always, time withers all opposition. Now they are trapped. Your army can destroy the demons at leisure...."

Zyzyiig paused, pondering the alien's words. "Cancel the order for my car," ky said at last. "Pass the word to disengage. We will let the demons live ... for now."

*   *   *

The command APC grounded with a shudder as the magnetic fields collapsed, its rear ramp already opening. Fraser climbed out slowly, afraid of what he might find.

Most of the fires around the crashed transport had gone out, extinguished by fire-fighting foam or smothered under dirt piled high by the bulldozer blades of the Legion construction vehicles. One of those was still at work near the stern of the wreck, pushing crumpled hull plating aside so a party of legionnaires could reach wounded crewmen trapped inside.

Close by the command van, the medical APC was parked in the center of a circle of wounded men. There was no sign of Doctor Ramirez; presumably he was in the tiny field surgery inside the vehicle. Legion medics moved among the wounded, performing triage. Other soldiers carried stretchers to waiting APCs to take wounded men back to the fort's medical hut.

Not far away, Father Fitzpatrick knelt beside one casualty, his hands sketching the cross in the air as his lips moved in prayer. Last rites … how many times had the Padre administered them today?

At least the hannies had pulled back long enough to give the legionnaires time to look after the wounded … and the dead.

Sergeant Trent was crouched over a piece of wreckage a few meters beyond. As Fraser came up beside him, Trent looked up.

Fraser cleared his throat. "What's the situation, Gunny?"

Trent answered. "It isn't good, L-T," he said softly. "Best count so far is twenty dead out of Third Platoon … most of them in the crash. Six more seriously wounded."

"God!" Fraser looked away. "Two thirds of the platoon…."

"Yeah." A shadow seemed to cross Trent's face. "Six dead from First and Second Platoons in the fighting on the north perimeter. We lost two onagers and a Fafnir launcher … two Sandrays and their drivers, too."

"What about *Ganymede?*"

"We've pulled fifteen wounded off," the sergeant replied. "Most of them pretty bad. When she hit, she set off ammo and fossil fuel aboard the vehicles under her … and she was carrying ammo in her hold, too." He shook his head. "I'm surprised anyone lived through it."

"God … and all those refugees aboard …" Fraser remembered Captain Garrett saying there were two hundred Commonwealth citizens in the capital for *Ganymede* to pull out. Two hundred civilians crammed into the vessel's troop bays … "Did any of the bridge crew make it?"

Trent shook his head. "No. No ship's officers at all. A couple of corpsmen, the rest ordinary shiphands."

"Well …" Fraser wasn't sure what to say next. "Well, keep at it as long as you think it's practical, Gunny. We … can't afford to keep too many men tied up for too long, though. The hannies could still try again."

"Yes, sir." Trent paused. "What's the word from Battalion, L-T?"

"Out of touch," Fraser replied. "Next sat pass is seventy minutes."

The sergeant frowned. "Let's hope they move faster getting us out this time. All we'd need is for the monkeys to come up with another surprise or two."

"I hear you, Gunny." He hesitated, looking at him. Trent had been a tower of strength since the first hannie attack. Even though exhaustion was plainly written in every line of his face, the man was still going on. "Look, Gunny … thanks. Thanks for everything you've done today. We wouldn't have made it … *I* wouldn't have made it without your help."

Trent shrugged. "It's what we're trained for, L-T," he said simply.

"Yeah." Fraser looked back at the smouldering wreckage again, feeling inadequate. Trent's unflappable calm was something he'd never understand, much less live up to. *How can I lead these people when I don't even know what makes them tick?* "Carry on, Gunny. I'll be in HQ if you need me."

Trent saluted stiffly and limped away.

Walking back toward the command van, Fraser tried to shut out the sights and sounds around him. So many people killed….

It's what we're trained for. The words haunted him. *I wasn't trained for this! I shouldn't have tried to bring the ship into the fort. They're dead … and I killed them.*

I wasn't trained for this!

* * *

Slick leaned on his shovel and mopped sweat from his forehead. Although his fatigues were climate-conditioned, the heat and humidity were enough to keep his bare head damp even when he wasn't working. Shoveling dirt into sandbags to fill in the gaps remaining in the east wall after the engineering vans had finished clearing the debris was hard, sweaty work.

Less than an hour had passed since the end of the battle, but it was still vivid in his mind. In a way, the heavy labor was welcome; it kept him from thinking too much about the fighting. He knew the image of Childers, one leg gone below the knee, bleeding to death before his eyes, would haunt him for the rest of his life. Childers was dead despite Vrurrth's first aid. *Maybe if I hadn't frozen....*

"Back to vork, nube!" Strauss shouted. Slick grunted and dug the shovel into the dirt again. It was almost good to have the corporal shouting at him. At least that was better than being ignored.

For a while, after last night, Slick had thought he was gaining a measure of acceptance. Now the rest of the lance, even Rostov, seemed barely willing to acknowledge that he existed.

They think I'm a coward, Slick thought bitterly. *Maybe they're right....*

That was something he didn't like to admit to himself.

Growing up on the streets in Old London ... there hadn't been much room for cowards there. Slick and Billy had lived by their wits from the day their parents had died in that rezplex fire. Twelve years old, with a younger brother to look after, living on whatever they could beg or steal ... Slick had always seen himself as a survivor, not a coward. He'd been scared a time or two, but he'd always kept on going.

Except the night Billy died, of course....

If he had reacted faster, perhaps he could have kept Billy from falling. Or, today, he might have saved Childers. *Maybe I am a coward.*

A coward would never win acceptance among the legionnaires. Someone like DuPont could get scared under an artillery barrage and still fight. But being too paralyzed by fear to keep a man from dying ... that was unforgivable.

Slick dropped the shovel and dragged the full sandbag into place, conscious of the way Rostov and DuPont turned away as he came close. All his life he'd been looking for some place where he could be a part of something larger, like the Red Brethren, or the Legion. Or a family. The Brethren had turned him out because he hadn't been willing to kill a man.

Now the Legion was closing ranks against him because he hadn't saved one.

At least the first time Billy had been there. This time there was no one to turn to.

He had never felt so totally alone.

*   *   *

"Lancelot, this is Alice One," Fraser said. "Lancelot, do you copy, over?"

Fraser was alone in the communications shack. He had ordered Garcia to grab a few minutes of sack time, and Trent and the subalterns were still out supervising the repairs to the perimeter. With the orbital communication satellite overhead, he had transmitted a full report to Battalion HQ. Now all he needed was some kind of response, some word of what would come next.

"Alice One, Lancelot." The voice was crusty with more than just static. Commandant Viktor Sergeivich Isayev, senior officer of Third Battalion, First Light Infantry Regiment of the Fifth Foreign Legion, sounded stiff and formal. "Copy your last transmission."

Fraser waited expectantly, hoping Isayev would continue. But the comm channel gave him nothing but static. "Lancelot, request further instructions," he said at last. "When can we expect another evac mission, over?"

There was another long pause before the commandant replied. "Alice One, there will be no evac. Repeat, no evac." Isayev's voice softened. "Lieutenant Fraser, *Ganymede* was the only ship we had available for you. *Magenta*'s in for repairs, and *Ankh'Qwar* left two days ago for the systerm to rendezvous with the carriership *Seneca*. I couldn't get you a ship in less than a week, Fraser ... even if the resident-general would allow it."

"Sir?"

"The resident-general is concerned that the situation in Dryienjaiyeel might spread. He's issued orders restricting Commonwealth forces to Fwynzei until further notice." The commandant paused. "There's no way he'll risk more men, Fraser. I'm sorry."

"Then what are our orders, Commandant?" Fraser fought to keep his tone level.

"It's your discretion, Fraser," Isayev replied. "If you think you can hold out until we can get you relief, do so ... but I can't tell you how long that will be. Otherwise ... you know the score better than I do, son."

"Yes, sir." Fraser swallowed. "I understand."

"Just remember that you're in the Legion now, Fraser. Remember Camerone. And Devereaux."

"Are you telling me to hold on here to the last man, Commandant?"

Isayev coughed. "What you do with those men is your decision, Fraser. Just make sure whatever they do brings credit to the Legion. If you stand, then stand with courage. If you die, do it with honor."

"We'll do our best, Commandant," Fraser said slowly.

"I know you will, Fraser. Lancelot out."

Fraser's hand was shaking as he replaced the handset. Bravo Company had been abandoned.

Chapter Eight

I could not expose them, as an officer of the Legion, to such a dishonorable solution.

—General Pierre Koenig,
French Foreign Legion, 1942

So there's the situation," Fraser finished grimly. "We're on our own."

The headquarters building was full for this meeting. Fraser sat behind LaSalle's desk, with Garcia nearby to operate the computer in case they needed reference material or other data. All three of Bravo Company's subalterns were there, together with their platoon sergeants. Watanabe had one arm in a sling, while Platoon Sergeant Fontaine wore a bandage on his head that gave him a piratical air. A fourth platoon sergeant, Persson, represented the transport platoon; his unit's officer, Subaltern Lawton, had been at one of the Charlie Company outposts when the crisis began.

The unit's four warrant officers were clustered together in one corner. Ramirez looked exhausted. The Padre seemed more discouraged than tired, with a look of despair Fraser thought he could understand easily enough. Fitzpatrick had watched too many men die today.

Gunnery Sergeant Trent rounded out the gathering.

"Well, the damage to the east wall can't be repaired in less than two days," Trent said. "But we've plowed up dirt to block the worst gaps, with some sandbags thrown in where we could. It's not what I'd call defensible, but at least the monkeys won't get in too easily."

"I'm more concerned about the remote sensors," WO/4 Vandergraff put in. "The crash knocked out a good chunk of the east-side perimeter, and I don't have enough in stores to replace them all. That's going to be a weak spot until we can cannibalize enough spares out of other electronics."

"Sensors aren't all we're short on," Trent added. "We've got a good mix of supplies, but a few more battles like what we did this morning'll eat up our ammo faster'n anything. If the hannies keep launching attacks on us—"

"They will," WO/4 Hamilton, the native affairs specialist, said. "Depend on it, they will. We're becoming a symbol to them. If they're trying to oust the Commonwealth, our presence here will goad them into more attacks."

"If so," Trent continued, shooting an irritated look at Hamilton, "I think we could run into some pretty serious supply problems. We can handle two or three more pitched fights ... but as long as they can keep coming, time's on their side."

"Shouldn't we try to get Battalion to change their minds?" Ramirez spread his hands. "I mean, they can't be *serious* about leaving us on our own, can they?"

Sergeant Fontaine snorted derisively. "Another civilian heard from!" he muttered. The words were loud enough, though, for everyone to hear.

"What was that, Sergeant?" Fraser asked softly.

Fontaine met his look with an icy stare. "Any legionnaire knows the only thing we can count on is getting screwed by the damned civs!" Qazi, Third Platoon's senior NCO, nodded agreement.

"That's enough, Sergeant," Fraser said dangerously.

"If it was up to Commandant Isayev, there wouldn't be a problem," Trent put in. "The Legion takes care of its own. It's when the politicians get involved that we get the short end of the stick...."

"What about negotiating with the locals?" Vandergraff suggested. "Surely we could strike some kind of deal. Even if we had to surrender, it would be better than sitting here waiting to be slaughtered."

"Surrender, hell!" Sergeant Fontaine said.

"Legionnaires don't surrender," Karl Persson added.

Fraser opened his mouth to speak, but Hamilton beat him to it. "It just won't work," he said quietly. "You all heard what happened in the capital last night. We can't negotiate with them."

"But if we open a dialogue...."

"If the hannies wanted to talk surrender with us, don't you think they would have given us the option before now?" He shook his head. "Haven't you heard the way they refer to us among themselves? We're demons ... and this thing is turning into some kind of Holy War to get rid of us. They don't want us as prisoners. They want us dead."

"There can't be any question of surrender," Fraser agreed, nodding. "As for making a deal ... they're the ones that started this. With all due respect, Padre, turning the other cheek isn't going to get us very far. If they want to offer some kind of solution ... we'll see. But I think Mr. Hamilton is right. The only kind of settlement the monkeys are looking for is one we aren't going to like at all."

"Then what's left, Lieutenant?" Subaltern Bartlow asked.

It was Trent who answered. "We can't stay here and we can't give up," he said. "Looks to me like our best bet is to try to pull out."

"You're the one who said we can't get an evac," Fairfax said.

"So we do it ourselves," Trent answered. "Overland."

There was an explosion of comment from around the room. "Overland?" Fairfax began. "How—"

"We're surrounded up here," Bartlow was saying. "We're trapped—"

"Do you have any idea...?" Vandergraff said.

Fraser held up his hand. "One at a time!"

"You're talking about a march of nearly fifteen hundred kilometers to reach Fwynzei," Vandergraff persisted after the others had fallen silent. "Through Hanuman jungles and across the Raizhee Mountains ... some of the worst terrain on the planet. That'll take a hell of a lot longer than waiting here for another transport."

"*And* we'd be crossing hostile territory," Fairfax added. "Their army isn't going to sit still and let us go marching out, you know."

"Once we break contact, we'll be home free," Trent insisted. "Even if we have to fight once or twice, our ammo stocks'll be good for it. That's better than what we'll have if we try to fight it out here."

"It's still a hell of a long way," Persson pointed out. "Hauling the wounded, I don't know if we'll have enough vehicles to mount everybody. There won't be any room for error, at least. It'll slow us down if we have to move at a marching pace."

"We'll still move faster than the lokes, though," Qazi said. "We can let the men rest aboard the APCs while the column keeps moving."

Hamilton nodded. "The Dryiens aren't fully mechanized, anyway. That tracked junk they use isn't cut out for long-distance jungle movement, while our MSVs can handle damn near anything we're likely to pass through. Hannies on foot'll fall behind pretty quick, so all we'll really have to worry about are the garrison troops between here and the border. The worst problem is Zhairhee, right below the pass to Fwynzei. There've been reports of a troop buildup there. 'Maneuvers,' the monkey staff calls it."

"What about supplies?" Fairfax asked. "Can we even make it that far?"

"That's your department, Ham," Trent prompted. Sergeant Qazi doubled up his duties as a platoon sergeant with the responsibility for Bravo Company's logistics.

Qazi stroked his pencil moustache thoughtfully. "We've got more stuff here than we can carry in the two supply vans," he said. "If we cut down our troop capacity some more, we can stock up pretty good. Say a month's worth … six weeks with rationing."

"That's cutting it tight," Fontaine said. "Fifteen hundred kilometers of rugged ground in six weeks…."

"We can supplement our food from local sources," Vandergraff admitted grudgingly. "Biochemistry's compatible … there'd be some vitamin deficiencies, but those won't start hurting anybody in six weeks."

Fraser had deliberately kept quiet while the discussion unfolded, taking in everything. It sounded like Sergeant Trent's idea would work … but the task was daunting at best. "I guess we don't have a lot of options," he said at last. "Gunny, looks like your scheme's the only one we've got."

Trent shrugged. "It's the only one that has a chance of getting anybody out alive, L-T," he said. "Like they say, 'March or Die.' Don't get me wrong. This ain't gonna be a picnic. We'll lose a lot of men … and there's no guarantee we'll make it at all."

"It still sounds better than any other options I've heard," Fraser replied. "All right … I want you people to start sizing up the job. We need to be sure we can handle this once we get going. There won't be time to turn back later." He looked around the room, studying them. Not everyone was convinced, but they all looked more hopeful now that they had something to shoot for. "You each have your own responsibilities. Coordinate through Gunny Trent. I want a report in six hours. Understood?"

* * *

"Okay, let's run over what we've got," Trent said at last.

He had appropriated the command APC; its computer terminals were tied in to the company HQ network, and it offered him privacy to go over the unit's options. Ramirez, Qazi, Persson, and Legionnaire Garcia were with him.

"The vehicles we have left give us a lift capacity of 194 men," Persson said, consulting his wristpiece. "That's assuming no wounded … and no extra space for supplies or equipment."

"We'll lose some space to litters for the casualties," Trent said. "What do you need, Doc?"

Ramirez consulted his wristpiece computer. "We have twenty-seven wounded. If we stack the litters, I can make do with … hmmm. Looks like I'll need the medical van, an APC, and something else … say one of the engineering rigs. We'll need to mount extra fittings to hold stretchers, but that shouldn't be too hard."

"Good." Trent looked at Qazi. "What about the supplies, Mohammed?"

"If we strip the place, and I think we'd better, I'll need a hell of a lot of space to carry it all," the Arab sergeant replied. "For starters, let's talk about throwing everybody but the crews out of both supply vans, both fabrication vans, and one of the APCs. That *might* do the job … but I'd be happier with a couple of the engineering vans carrying supplies instead of troops, too."

"There's a problem," Persson put in. "Three of the engineering rigs are in pretty bad shape. They were pulled for maintenance last week, but Battalion never sent the parts to repair them. They'll break down inside of a couple of days."

"So if we take two for supplies and one for the Doc …" Trent trailed off.

"We can mount everyone in the company," Persson finished. "But just barely. We'll have ten guys clinging to the outside of APCs or crammed in where there ain't room. First time we have a breakdown, we're slowed to marching pace."

"That's better than I thought it would be," Qazi said. "Hell, we'll all ride out!"

"There's gonna be breakdowns, Ham," Persson said. "We're talking about loading up a lot of high-tech MSVs and pushing them to the limit with nothing but field maintenance. We'll be lucky if half those puppies make it to the border."

"It's still worth trying," Trent said. "With everybody mounted, we'll be able to break contact with our buddies down there in the jungle and put some distance between us and the Dryien army."

"Yeah," Persson said. "Maybe ..."

"What's the matter, Swede?" Qazi asked. "It checks out, doesn't it?"

Persson grunted. "Sure. But everything's riding on the Exec. He ain't a Legion man, know what I mean? Too much of the old officer-and-gentleman about him ... not much in the guts department."

"Knock it off, Swede," Trent growled. "I don't want to hear that kind of talk!"

"Ah, hell, Johnnie, you know I'm just tellin' it like it is! The way I heard it, he screwed up on his last assignment and got transferred to the Legion 'cause he had friends in high places to keep him from being court martialed!"

"And *I* heard he got reassigned because of some political mess," Qazi added. "If he's screwed up in that kind of peacetime shit...."

"I said *knock it off!*" Trent repeated harshly. "L-T can hack it, as long as you screw-ups do your jobs!"

"But, Johnnie ..."

"I mean it, Swede! Things are gonna be tough enough without you trying to second-guess the L-T, so just lay off! He's doin' all right ... and he'll get us out."

Qazi and Persson nodded reluctantly. "If you say so, Sarge," the Arab said.

"I do. Now let's finish up." Trent turned away, making a pretense of studying his 'piece. The two sergeants didn't have the whole story on Fraser's transfer to the Legion, but they had parts of it right. The lieutenant's previous CO was the man blamed for sending the faulty intelligence reports that had led to the loss of two battalions of Commonwealth Regulars on Fenris. From what Trent had heard, it was Fraser's testimony that had damned the man at his court martial ... but he had some influential friends. Not powerful enough to save the officer, but with sufficient pull to ruin Fraser's career. The lieutenant was given the "opportunity" of serving in the Colonial Army ... and like so many officers under a cloud had wound up in the Legion.

Fraser wasn't trained as a combat officer, and he was out of his element here. Trent was sure of it. But the sergeant wouldn't allow that kind of talk to spread, for fear of what it might do to the unit's morale. He'd make sure the lieutenant didn't screw up.

Or he'd die trying.

* * *

"Lieutenant Winters? I hope I'm not disturbing you."

Kelly Winters looked up from the laptop terminal across her knees. "What is it?"

The young officer in the Legion lieutenant's uniform looked tired and worried. "I'm Fraser. Acting CO of this post. Doctor Ramirez said you'd asked to see me."

They'd brought her unconscious to the fort's tiny hospital, where the unit's doctor had treated her for anaphylactic shock. Apparently she'd had a strong reaction to the alien proteins of the hannie soldier's quills. She'd spent some time in a regen chamber, dead to the world, but after the *Ganymede* crash they'd pulled her out to make room for some casualties who needed far more treatment. For the most part, Ramirez and his assistants had ignored her since, except as strictly necessary.

She was going stir-crazy from lack of news. Just what was happening outside the cramped confines of the small storeroom they'd converted into a private room for her?

"You're in charge? I thought Captain LaSalle was—"

"Captain LaSalle was in the capital when the hannies turned nasty. He's officially listed as missing, but ..." Fraser spread his hands. "I'm afraid you're stuck with me."

She studied him. He wasn't anything like the unit's old Exec, a worn-out lieutenant whose only real love was the bottle. Fraser looked like a competent, ambitious young officer on his way up in his profession. What was he doing with the Legion?

"I wanted to find out about evac plans, Lieutenant," she said at length. "After what happened with *Ganymede* ..."

He shook his head. "There won't be another ship, Lieutenant. HQ won't authorize it. We're preparing for an overland withdrawal now."

"Overland! We're a thousand kilometers from friendly territory!"

"Fifteen hundred," he corrected dryly. "But we can't stay here. The Dryiens will get us sooner or later unless we break contact."

Kelly didn't answer. The prospect of crossing an entire continent … Could legionnaires do it? Or would they fall apart as soon as the going got tough?

"Doctor Ramirez assures me you'll be able to travel," he said after a long pause. "We'll make you as comfortable as possible, but I can't guarantee the accommodations will be very pleasant."

"Don't worry about me, Lieutenant," she said sharply. "I can take care of myself all right."

"That I don't doubt," Fraser answered. "You were the only one to get out of Monkeyville alive. That took some doing."

"What about the native? I thought ky—"

"Oh, right. Myaighee, I think the doctor said kys name was." Fraser smiled reassuringly. "Your loke friend's well enough, under the circumstances. Still in regen, I guess."

She sank back on the bed, relieved. Fraser wasn't so different from the other legionnaires after all. Not even enough compassion to think about a native who'd risked so much to help the Terrans. "Just make sure ky is treated well, Lieutenant. My loke friend is a damned sight more a hero than any of your so-called soldiers."

Fraser raised an eyebrow, then nodded. "I see. I'll be sure the doctor does everything possible. Good day, Lieutenant Winters." He spun on his heel and left the room.

*　*　*

"Sounds good," Fraser said, nodding approval. "With everyone mounted, we'll make good time."

The entire staff was assembled again to go over the final details of Sergeant Trent's proposed overland withdrawal. Fraser had tried to keep his face unreadable as he listened to the sergeant's report. His doubts about his own abilities were only reinforced by the slim resources at their command.

Right now Bravo Company had only 106 officers and men available, plus Kelly Winters. There were twenty-seven wounded to be cared for. And while Trent's report was encouraging in suggesting they could leave the fort mounted, their assortment of available vehicles was none too reassuring. There were only two Sabertooth FSVs at Monkeyville, plus a total of nineteen Sandray APCs of various types. The four standard carriers designed to hold two full lances each were the only ones mounting kinetic energy cannons, and two of them were going to be carrying supplies or casualties instead of troops. Each of the other vans was designed to carry only one lance plus specialized equipment: computer and comm gear for the command model, mobile workshops and parts stores for the two fabrication vans, and so on. Only the nine engineering vans—three of them apparently broken down beyond repair—mounted weaponry, and that only low-powered lasers designed for felling trees or fusing tunnel walls, not combat armaments.

All in all, it would be a delicate balance, and Fraser wasn't happy at relying on such slim resources to make the long journey north. Not that they had any choice.

"All right, get the men ready to move out," he said. "We'll break out of here tomorrow morning."

"Just how the hell *are* we getting out, Lieutenant?" Subaltern Bartlow asked hesitantly. "I mean, the lokes really have us in a bag up here. How do we break out?"

"We blast a hole and go through," Fairfax said. "Simple enough."

"We'll take casualties, though," Watanabe said thoughtfully. "This time *they'll* have the defensive positions ... and we can't afford to waste our ammo on one battle."

"Yeah," Fraser agreed. He looked down at his desk. Tactics weren't his specialty, but some kind of tactical trick would help them. "We need surprise ... a diversion ..."

Trent looked thoughtful. "If you'll let me have Garcia and Tran for a few hours, L-T, I think I might have just the trick you're looking for...."

Chapter Nine

Bah! No bunch of [deleted] savages can stand against the Legion!

—Colonel Wilhelm Lichtenauer
following the Battle of Concorde Station,
Second Foreign Legion, 2191

Angela Garcia wiped sweat from her forehead and silently cursed the fault in the climate-control circuits of her uniform. Less than an hour after dawn the temperature was already close to 30°C and climbing steadily. The humidity-laden mist seemed to wrap tight around her.

She was hunched over Bravo Company's portable C^3 unit in an improvised foxhole at the edge of the *Ganymede* crash site overlooking the eastern edge of the Monkeyville plateau. Legionnaire Tran and Gunnery Sergeant Trent crouched on either side of her, the sergeant scanning the fog-shrouded landscape with his IR scope while Tran helped Garcia set up the terminal for the task ahead.

"Anything, Sergeant?" she asked softly.

"Not yet, Garcia," he replied. "Second and Third recon lances are in position … but there's no sign of the bad guys yet."

"Damn." Garcia bit her lip and squinted up through the mist. The fierce heat of Morrison's Star would soon burn away the morning fog, and once that happened the chance for surprise would be gone. "Maybe we should we call it off, Sarge."

Trent spat expressively. "Give it a few more minutes, Garcia," he said. "We'll find a few witnesses soon."

"All right, Sergeant. You're the boss."

Garcia looked back down at the computer terminal and checked the settings again, more for something to do than because there was any need for another run-through. She wondered how Fraser was managing without either of his C^3 technicians to help coordinate the main body's escape.

He had wanted to take charge of the diversion personally, but Trent's arguments against it were too strong. The company needed him on the spot if and when the enemy took the bait and gave him his opening to lead the main body out of the fort. So Fraser was stuck in his command van, waiting for the signal to move out, while Trent super-vised the operation that was supposed to give him the chance he needed.

Tran cocked his head sideways and said something too softly for Garcia to hear, speaking into his throat mike. The junior C^3 tech flipped a control on the terminal pack and looked up at Sergeant Trent. "Second recon lance has something, Sarge," he said. His finger moved over the computer-generated map display. "Hannie patrol ... *here*, moving south. Just outside the sensor line, and acting like they know it's there."

Trent pulled his chin thoughtfully. "Didn't think the little bastards knew about 'em," he said. "Well, let's give them a show, Garcia!"

Her fingers danced over the terminal controls.

*   *   *

Zydryie Kiijyeed held up a hand to stop the column and cocked kys head, listening to the morning mists.

The sounds coming from the heights above were demon-spawned, not a part of the natural voice of the mists at all. Ky had heard that sound before. It was the noise made by the demon float-tanks when they moved. Ky had been a common soldier on city security duty when a parade of their float-tanks passed through the capital streets back when the demon army first arrived in Dryienjaiyeel.

Here, surrounded by jungle and mist, the sound took on new terror for Kiijyeed. Everyone in kys unit was talking about the terrible vengeance wrought by the guns the demon vehicles mounted. The casualties taken by Regiment Godshammer even before the skyship had fallen ... Immortal Ancients! How could ordinary mortals fight such demon weapons?

The help the Ancient was giving the army seemed paltry by comparison with the power of that weaponry. It was good to be able to locate the devices that helped the demons track the Dryien troops around the perimeter of their fortress, but what did that really do to protect them from danger?

Especially now. It sounded as if the demons were sending their vehicles *this* way, toward kys patrol. The *Asjyai* had warned that the demons might attempt to break out from their plateau to wreak vengeance on the countryside. Could they be seeking out the trail Regiment Godshammer had used to bring up the tanks used in yesterday's attack? This side of the perimeter was weakly held at best.

Kiijyeed signalled to kys radio operator. Headquarters had to be informed....

The noise grew suddenly louder as a huge, flat-bodied shape burst out of the mists only a few *kwyin* away. Kiijyeed recoiled instinctively, dropping the radio handset and snatching at kys submachine gun. The alien APC roared past as if the driver hadn't seen the patrol. Behind it, a second shape thundered through the fog.

Throwing kyself to the ground, Kiijyeed scrabbled for the radio handset again. This was surely the breakout attempt the *Asjyai* was waiting for. Troops had to be shifted to block the demons before they broke through the lines and spread over the countryside, harrying, destroying....

As ky gripped the handset the radio operator flopped sideways in the dirt, half of kys face burnt away silently, invisibly, by some unseen demon weapon. Kiijyeed fought down terror as ky opened the radio channel.

"This is patrol three! Patrol three! The demons are attacking! Sector four ... demon attack!"

The sinister whine of demon *effeekaa* rifles seemed to come from everywhere. Two more of kys soldiers died almost instantly, while a third was screaming horribly and clutching at the stump of kys arm, cut off at the wrist by the hail of demon bullets.

"Patrol three under attack by demons! They are breaking out...!"

Kiijyeed hardly even felt the needles that pierced kys body in a dozen places. The handset dropped from nerveless fingers as ky died, still gasping out kys last warning....

* * *

"Cease fire! Cease fire!"

Corporal Strauss's words grated harshly in Slick's earphones. He dropped behind a fallen tree, FEK at the ready, and scanned his surroundings on IR. None of the hannie soldiers was moving any more. It had been a perfect ambush, short and sharp. Dark shapes rose out of the mist around the killing field.

"Report!" That was Sergeant Trent, speaking on the general comm channel.

"Red Lance," Strauss replied. "All clear here. Patrol eliminated. No casualties."

"Same for Blue Lance," Corporal Braxton added. The two full-strength recon lances had been responsible for the ambush, while Pascali's understrength unit remained in reserve. Trent had directed the legionnaires into position hard on the heels of the decoy vehicles. The timing had been perfect—after the hannie patrol had sighted the three engineering vans, they'd been given just enough time to report the movement to their HQ before being silenced. If all went according to plan, the natives would shift forces to investigate. And the more they shifted, the easier the *real* breakout would be.

"Very good," Trent said. "All right, Red and Blue … get moving. Position number two. Spread out and start planting your Galahads. Rostov, Cunningham, start unloading your gear and setting the charges. Get moving, people!"

"You vill help Rostov, nube," Strauss ordered curtly.

Slick followed the two demolitions experts as they headed for the nearest of the three engineering vehicles, now grounded a few meters beyond the ambush site.

The vehicle certainly looked convincing, Slick thought, as he moved up alongside it. With the engineering fittings stripped away and the laser turret disguised by a little sheet metal and some ingenious camouflage paint, the engineering van looked a lot like an ordinary Sandray troop carrier. With luck, it would convince frightened hannies that the main weight of the Terran breakout was coming through the east perimeter.

In fact the three vehicles were being remotely controlled by Legionnaire Garcia. As a computer and electronics expert, Garcia knew enough about programming to preset simple autopiloting instructions in the onboard computers and then use a C^3 terminal to transmit updated orders as needed. With the recon lances deployed to spot the enemy and provide a little on-site firepower, the legionnaires could manage a convincing simulation of a breakout attempt—convincing enough, everyone hoped, to fool the natives, at least.

Rostov opened the rear door, revealing a stack of cargomods inside. Bravo Company had been well-provided with PX-90 explosives and detpack programmable detonators for use in their engineering work. Now the demolitions gear would serve a more lethal purpose, supplementing the unit's assortment of M46 Galahad antipersonnel mines in a defensive perimeter that should help protect Trent's diversionary force when the hannies arrived in force.

With a scowl, Rostov tossed the first case of explosives to Slick. Although he knew the explosives were completely safe unless equipped with suitably programmed detonators, he still flinched involuntarily as he caught it. Rostov's eyes were full of contempt as he turned away to pick up another cargomod.

They all think I'm a coward. The words had become a litany echoing through his mind. Slick tried to push the thought away, deny it, reject it ... but it kept coming back.

If the diversion worked the way it was supposed to, the full weight of the hannie army would be pushing this way soon. Part of him shrank from the thought of another fight. Another part, though, welcomed the prospect.

He wasn't going to run from combat this time. When the battle began, Slick would be in the thick of it.

They wouldn't call him a coward then.

∗　∗　∗

"Good ... good ... come a little left now." Colin Fraser studied the video image carefully, noting the movement of vehicles and men. "Steady on that view."

"Got it, Lieutenant," WO/4 Vandergraff acknowledged.

"What do you make of it, Mr. Hamilton?" Fraser asked the other warrant officer.

Hamilton leaned forward to look over his shoulder at the view relayed from the drone hovering low over the main hannie camp. "They're moving, all right. Looks like our monkey buddies are falling for it."

Fraser stood up, ducking to avoid the low roof of the command van. "Take over here, Mr. Hamilton," he said. "Let me know when they're committed."

"Yes, sir." Hamilton slid into the chair beside Vandergraff.

Moving forward, Fraser stuck his head into the driver's cab. Platoon Sergeant Persson looked up from the control board.

"Everything ready?" Fraser asked.

"Looks like it, sir," Persson replied. "All the 'rays are loaded up. Bashar and Mason have the FSVs in position."

"Good. We'll mag out as soon as the monkeys are busy with Gunny Trent's little show."

Fraser could hardly control the excitement rising inside him. Now there was finally a chance to *act*, instead of just sitting and waiting. Sergeant Trent's arguments had been convincing … but he still wished he had insisted on taking charge of the diversion. It was frustrating to sit back in the safety of the fort, waiting and worrying while others risked everything. Getting them out after the rest of the company was clear of the fort was going to be dicey.

But Trent was right. His responsibility was to the whole unit....

In the back of the command van, Legionnaire Hengist and the Padre were waiting in silence. Fraser caught the Padre's eye from the compartment door.

"Know any blessings for a mag-out, Padre?" he asked, keeping his tone light.

Fitzpatrick raised his hand in benediction. "May the Good Lord bless and keep this mag-out …" he intoned solemnly, "moving just as fast as possible."

Hengist laughed. "Think He's looking out for us, Padre?"

"Of course, my son," the priest responded "God watches and cherishes the very worst sinners. I can't think of anyone He loves more than the Legion."

Fraser turned away, smiling again. He hoped God *was* watching over them. In the next few hours they'd need all the help they could get.

* * *

Slick tamped wet dirt down around the cylindrical base of his last Galahad mine, then flipped open the plasteel lid covering the arming controls and touched the pressure pad labelled "TEST." A green light glowed briefly as the mine's sensor array went through a brief diagnostic check. At the same moment Slick heard the tone in his earpiece that indicated his helmet's IFF system was operating. Any legionnaire with a working transponder could walk through the minefield without fear ... but once the Galahad was armed, any other living thing that passed within ten meters of the deadly little cylinder would trigger it. The open-topped tube contained ten separate egg-shaped bomblets. Each time the mine's computer brain registered a valid target and no nearby friendly forces, one of those bombs would be hurled into the air where it would explode, showering the area with a hail of lethal shrapnel.

Satisfied, Slick armed the mine. Between Rostov's explosive charges and the pattern of Galahads, the hundred-meter stretch in front of the position Trent had designated as the main line of defense was now a death zone. The hannies would have to take this route—it was the only one suitable for their vehicles on the whole east side of Monkeyville. Anyway, in a few more minutes the engineering vans would be back in action, drawing the enemy's attention again.

He stood up and picked his way up a steep slope toward the location Strauss had chosen for him. The corporal had assigned Slick a spot on the end of the Red Lance line, probably to keep him on the periphery of the action in case he froze up again. But Slick wasn't planning to be left out. He'd show Strauss ... he'd show them all.

As he settled behind one of the stunted, twisted trees typical of Hanuman's jungle growth, Slick felt rather than heard a distant vibration. He'd finished his work just in time. Hannie vehicles were coming.

Slick checked his FEK's battery charge and ammo counter, then flipped down his helmet display screen and called up the map Garcia was transmitting over the C^3 net from Trent's observation post. Pascali's lance was out ahead of the main line, scouting out the enemy as they headed for the diversionary force. Red symbols crawled across the screen, creeping slowly toward the thin blue line that represented Bravo Company's forlorn hope.

* * *

"Yeah, L-T, six to eight tanks, maybe a hundred infantry. They'll be on top of our mines in about ten minutes." Trent smiled wolfishly. "Looks like they got our invitation!"

"Just about what we were looking for, Gunny." Static crackled around Fraser's reply. "The drones are showing a lot of activity on this end. They've started shifting most of their boys your way. If we hit 'em hard, we'll break through without much trouble."

"Roger that," Trent said. He glanced over at the C^3 display. Garcia was peering at a video image relayed from the lead decoy vehicle while she entered new commands to the autopilot through the keyboard. "We'll let 'em know we're here, L-T. Don't make a move until we've got the buggers' attention."

Fraser's reply sounded stiff. "We'll keep to the plan, Gunny. You just make sure you get disengaged in time."

"Don't worry about that!" Trent said. "We're not sticking around here any longer than we have to!"

"Roger. Alice One, clear."

"Guardian clear." Trent turned his attention to the battle map on his helmet display. The hannies were moving up steadily....

"All right, Garcia," he said softly. "Time to bait the trap."

$$* \quad * \quad *$$

The morning mists were all but gone now, broken up by the heat as Morrison's Star rose higher above the horizon. *That's one advantage gone,* Slick thought. *Let's hope our other surprises make up for it.*

His display map showed the hannie forces closing in, less than half a kilometer away now. The jungle hid the enemy, but Pascali's lance was still tracking their advance ... and the three decoy vehicles remained in front of them, continuing to simulate the movement of a larger Terran force trying to get past the native lines. Periodically Slick heard cannonfire as native tanks challenged the empty APCs. The last few shots had been close ... *really* close....

With a roar of turbofans, one of the engineering vehicles burst from the tree line in full retreat, crossing the minefield at top speed. The Galahads ignored the friendly target, and the charges Rostov and Cunningham had placed were rigged for radio-controlled detonation. Any observer would have assumed that field was safe to cross.

The APC moved straight across the open ground and up the gentlest part of the slope. The sound of the fans died and the vehicle stopped moving, resting on its magnetic suspension near the crest of the hill. Then, slowly, the fields collapsed and the Sandray settled to the ground, hull-down behind the shelter of the rising ground. The turret, though, remained visible. Slick could see Corporal Pascali climbing down off the back of the vehicle. Trent had ordered the scouts to hitch rides aboard the computer-controlled vehicles so they could join the defenders along the perimeter.

Then the second and third APCs appeared almost together, farther down the line of trees, weaving past obstacles before they revved up to make the final run across the open ground. Somewhere back in the jungle another tank gun coughed. An explosion raised a gout of thick black mud from a pool of stagnant water a few meters ahead of one of the Sandrays. Legionnaire Reinhardt, lying on top of the flat manta-ray shape and facing the jungle, squeezed off an FEK burst.

Slick braced his weapon on the improvised barricade in front of him and tried to keep his breathing regular. *This is it!*

A squat, massive metallic shape crashed through the trees below him, clanking into the clearing with the implacable momentum of a juggernaut. Around the tank, hannie foot soldiers were fanning out into a loose skirmish line. An officer with a gaudily-painted muzzle jabbered orders, gesticulating wildly as ky urged the troops forward.

Movement to his right made Slick shift his head. Another party of native infantry was emerging from the tree line. Most were armed with blunderbuss rocket launchers or bulky heavy machine guns, but they were moving fast considering their loads. Slick drew in a quick, sharp breath.

These natives were ignoring the easy route up the slope. They were moving straight up the most difficult part of the hill, well clear of the minefield and the defending legionnaires.

Despite the difficult terrain and the burdens they were carrying, those hannie soldiers would be behind the Legion line in another few minutes, and those weapons they were carrying were a lot more dangerous to the Terran troops than the standard enemy longarms.

The trappers were about to be trapped....

Chapter Ten

What matters is the action, the combat which places you on a different plane from the rest of the herd.

—Colonel Pierre Jeanpierre,
French Foreign Legion, 1958

 green light on the C^3 terminal lit up, and Garcia smiled in satisfaction. The final program was in place; the three diversionary vehicles were committed.

"It's set," she told Trent.

Trent nodded acknowledgement. The engineering vans had stopped maneuvering. Now they were deployed in a loose defensive line, and their drilling lasers were programmed to fire on command. That, in combination with the explosives Rostov and Cunningham had planted, would keep the hannies busy for a while.

She frowned at the terminal video display, watching the images relayed from the middle vehicle. This remote-controlled battle was like a distant, unreal game, a dreamchipper's fantasy. No, not even that ... a dreamer's visions *seemed* real enough while he was under.

Garcia wondered how the soldiers down on the perimeter were feeling. This would be all too real for them.

Her screen showed a native tank advancing slowly into the minefield with hannie soldiers fanned out around it. She tracked the hannie vehicle, calling up a set of crosshairs and centering them over the target. Something moved to one side of the scene; a small, oblong something that rose a meter off the ground and exploded in a glittering shower of metal fragments. A pair of hannies went down with blood welling from wounds in their chests and arms.

"Now!" she called. Her finger stabbed the remote firing control, and red light bathed the front of the tank. The last battle of Monkeyville had begun.

* * *

The bursting Galahad down in the minefield made Slick duck and turn. The flanking party had driven all thought of the main body out of his mind.

Down below, hannies were gibbering and running. The nearest tank glowed red under the intense light of the laser focused on it from one of the engineering vans. Although their lasers were not intended as combat weapons, they had the power to fell trees and fuse tunnel walls … and a few seconds was enough to superheat the target's armor. The front chassis just above the main gun dripped and melted. An instant later something inside exploded, raining debris over the panicked native soldiers. Farther down the line, one of Rostov's PX-90 charges went off directly under a lighter tank, ripping open the bottom of the AFV.

Slick jerked his attention back to the flanking party. They had heard the explosions too, but a spur of the hill blocked their line of sight. An officer or NCO was urging them on, pointing wildly at the top of the slope and screeching rapid-fire orders—or maybe invective—and physically pushing one laden soldier from behind. It looked so much like something Corporal Strauss might have done that Slick smiled.

But what to do about them? Slick considered calling for help, then rejected the thought. *They think I'm a coward already....*

If he needed help handling a few lokes, they'd be sure of his cowardice. He had to act by himself. That was the only way to win back their respect.

As he rose from his hiding place and sprinted a zigzag course for the top of the hill, Slick was surprised at just how important winning their respect had become.

* * *

The command van lurched once as Legionnaire Hengist swerved to avoid an obstacle. Colin Fraser braced himself against the doorframe and peered over the driver's shoulder at the monitor showing the vehicle's path ahead. "Rev her up, Hengist," he ordered. "Persson, pass the word. Show a few revs."

The van shuddered once as the fans whined louder. Suspended on magnetic fields and driven by two powerful turbofans, the vehicle began to glide forward, gathering speed. Fraser braced himself against the motion and looked over the driver's shoulder at the video display from the vehicle's forward cameras. Ahead of them, Corporal Weston's supply van was surging forward.

Fraser raised his voice over the noise of the fans. "The path forks off about a half a klick ahead, sergeant. Tell your drivers to be ready to turn."

"Yes, sir."

Hengist swerved again, this time to avoid the smoking remains of a hannie self-propelled gun on the right side of the road. Bashar's Sabertooth had literally opened the trail for the rest, cutting through the unprepared hannie outposts before they realized the legionnaires were even coming. With most of the enemy's strength and attention focused on the diversionary force, Bravo Company's breakout was running smoothly.

But they couldn't stay on the main northwest road for very long. The jungle was too thick down in the lowlands to allow the Legion vehicles any freedom of movement, and the drones had shown another large hannie mechanized column farther down the road pressing hard to join the siege of Monkeyville. Bravo Company couldn't afford to let itself be trapped between the reinforcements and the bulk of the native army, which wouldn't stay distracted too much longer....

One trail did break off from the main road, winding north into deeper jungle. They had to secure that fork in the road and hold it until Trent's rearguard could be extracted. That would be the most dangerous part of the entire plan.

Persson pointed to the flashing map display between the driver and passenger seats in the cab. "Bashar's up to the fork, Lieutenant!" he shouted. "He reports all clear."

"Right," Fraser replied. "Pass the word. Get the APCs off the road!"

Without waiting for a reply he turned back into the command center, staggering as the van sideslipped, then sinking gratefully into a chair next to Vandergraff. He took control of one of the drones and steered it northwest. Time to find out how long they'd have to get Trent out....

* * *

Slick dropped to his belly and lay still, hardly breathing. The chameleon coating on his fatigues and armor faded from the grey-brown of the rocky slope to a mottled yellow-green as sensors embedded in the uniform read his surroundings and the suit's miniature computer transmitted the appropriate electrical impulses through the climate-control mesh that triggered the color change. In the tall grass at the top of the hill, Slick would be nearly invisible.

Below him the ten hannie troopers were still climbing, but more slowly now. The exertion was probably starting to get to them, Slick thought. Hanuman's natives were strong for their small size and tough, capable of surprising feats of endurance, but yomping that heavy gear up the steep hillside must surely have taken a toll by now.

The first local appeared less than five meters away. Ky was carrying a blunderbuss rocket launcher and several reloads. The weapon seemed impossibly large for the native, but after a few seconds rest the soldier was moving again, crossing the flat hilltop and scanning the battlefield below with a clumsy-looking optical imager. More troops followed ... three more blunderbusses, a pair of HMGs, then two soldiers with ordinary native-issue rifles, belts of ammo draped over their shoulders and chests, and folded tripods slung across their backs. They joined the HMG gunners and started setting up the weapons in commanding positions overlooking the valley.

The officer and another soldier were last up. A shout from the first trooper made the leader hasten to kys side, where the two hannies jabbered together with frequent gesticulations. Slick thought he heard the native word that meant "devil". He remained motionless, his mind racing. The natives were too spread out. So far they hadn't offered a target he could take out all at once. There wasn't much time....

The first native was raising the blunderbuss and training it on the ridgeline below. Slick tensed, hesitated. Ky was aiming about where DuPont had been posted with his sniping laser. He had to act, despite the danger.

He rolled into a crouch and brought the FEK up, spraying caseless kinetic energy rounds into the soldier with the blunderbuss, and the officer. The trooper's fingers tightened convulsively on the weapon's trigger as ky fell, and a rocket roared from the tube. Officer and soldier collapsed in a bloody pile, and Slick swiveled his rifle toward the nearest of the machine-gun teams.

Needles slashed into the natives at 10,000 mps, flinging them backward as they tried to wrestle their weapon into line. The gunner sprawled against a rock in an untidy heap; kys loader balanced for a moment on the crest of the slope before tumbling out of sight. A blunderbuss roared and Slick felt the heat as the rocket passed inches from his head. He kept on firing, and three more hannies went down.

The FEK clicked and whirred, the hundred-round magazine empty. Rising to his feet, Slick cursed and shifted to his grenade launcher, firing a stream of 1cm projectiles into the second hannie machine-gun position. The gunner's scream was cut short as one of the warheads struck soft flesh and exploded, tearing the soldier in half. Slick didn't have time to react to the sight.

Something smashed across his back. The fatigues absorbed some of the blow, but it still knocked Slick to his knees, and the FEK spun out of his hands into the tall grass. The native swung kys rifle butt again, but Slick rolled with the blow and caught the weapon in both hands, pulling hard. The native, already off-balance, staggered and let go. An instant later ky was on him, long fingers extended to grope for Slick's neck.

An explosion a few meters away showered them with dirt, and the native's attention wavered. Slick drove his fist into the hannie's stomach and the soldier rolled off him, hitting the ground hard. In a flash, his other hand closed around the knife in his boot-top. A quick upward stroke finished the hannie before ky could recover.

A second explosion made Slick stagger as he rose. He shook his head to clear it, realizing dimly that the blasts were from Legion rifle grenades, not hannie weapons. The hannies were all down, dead or dying.

"Cease firing! Cease firing!" he screamed into his radio. He flipped down his helmet display to try to get a fix on whoever was firing. "Rostov, this is Grant! I'm on the hill you're firing at! Cease fire!"

The last explosion raised a shower of rock splinters from a nearby boulder. Slick's map display went dark as a rock the size of his fist slammed into his helmet.

Then a different kind of darkness engulfed him.

* * *

"Damn!" Angela Garcia swore softly as the video image on her screen blacked out. "That's two down."

She shifted the pickup to receive from the number three van. The hannies had backed off from the minefield, but their tanks were concentrating heavy fire on the Legion APCs from the edge of the jungle. The Sandrays were well-armored by native standards, but they couldn't stand up to the punishment of a head-to-head slugging match with main battle tanks. She fired the APC laser at the closest target, but the driver quickly dropped the tank into reverse and backed into the trees before the beam could do more than scorch the chassis armor. The hannies might be primitive, but they weren't stupid. They'd learned how to deal with APCs.

And their troops were getting wary of the minefield now. The locals might not have the technology to produce mines with multiple war-heads, but they'd grasped the concept quickly enough. There were reports of flanking parties trying to turn either flank of the defensive line. As they found the direct route blocked, they'd be pushing more troops to the sides.

"Corporal Pascali reports three casualties," Tran was telling Trent. "One dead in her lance ... another in Braxton's. And one of Strauss's men is wounded. Damn fool went off on his own without telling anyone and took friendly fire out on the flank. Rostov and Vrurrth are marking the pickup now."

"All right. Pull back by teams to the next position." Trent frowned. "Damn! I was hoping we'd hold 'em longer there." He paused, then shook his head. "The hell with it. All right, get 'em moving!"

Garcia turned back to the terminal and started programming the retreat orders into the vehicle's autopilot.

*   *   *

"*Asjyai! Asjyai!* The demons have broken out of the fort on the northwest side!"

"What?" *Asjyai* Zyzyiig whirled to face the panting messenger by the tent flap. "What are you talking about?"

"It's true, Honored! Many of their floating demon-cars, and heretic soldiers with them!" The messenger flinched under Zyzyiig's stare. "They destroyed our tanks and scattered the troops along the road! The demons are between us and the Regiment Fearmongers!"

Beside Zyzyiig, the Semti stirred. "I told you not to send so many to respond to that first report," Shavvataaars said. "These legionnaires are more resourceful than you believed ... or more ruthless. Expending part of their force in a false breakout called for considerable courage. The Terran demons rarely show such understanding of the needs of war. Their commander is one I would wish to Journey with...."

"He won't live long enough for your Journeys!" Zyzyiig snapped. The demons were getting away! He turned to the radio opera tor. "Order Fearmongers and our reserves to converge on them!"

"Honored ... it will take an hour to launch the attack!" the messenger protested. "And the demons control another way out!"

"You will not catch them, *Asjyai*," Shavvataaars said calmly. "Their vehicles are too fast for you."

Furious, Zyzyiig rounded on the Semti. "This is *your* fault! You said we had them where we wanted them, that they could not escape!"

"I also said that patience was the greatest of all wisdom," the Semti replied coldly. "Had you been less eager, you might have had sufficient forces assembled to meet this attack."

Zyzyiig felt kys neck ruff rippling. Taking a deep breath, ky forced the anger back. "If we cannot stop the main force, we can at least crush this diversion. Order the Regiment Deathshead to press the attack!"

"Vengeance will gain you nothing," Shavvataaars said. "You would do better to regroup in case these legionnaires do not remain in flight. They could still cause much damage, left unwatched."

"You want me to call off this attack, too? I won't do it." Zyzyiig spat. "Ancient or not, you have interfered with my command once too often. You have your preparations to make to the north, Shavvataaars. I suggest you get to them, and leave the demons here to me!"

* * *

"Keep your head down, Garcia!" Sergeant Trent fired an FEK burst and glanced at the C^3 technician. She was crouched behind a rock, her FEK held ready.

The last engineering van had fallen prey to hannie tank guns almost half an hour back, and the legionnaires were on their own now. The three recon lances, less four dead and two wounded, were holding a narrow perimeter around Trent's original observation post. The natives were pressing their attack more fiercely than ever, flinging in troops and vehicles with careless disregard for casualties. Apparently they didn't realize, or perhaps didn't care, that this wasn't the real breakout force. The monkeys seemed determined to destroy Trent's force no matter what.

That was bad ... very bad. The plan had counted on hannie pressure letting up as soon as they realized that Bravo Company was trying to escape. Maybe the diversion had worked *too* well.

"Tran! Give me the command channel!"

He nodded acknowledgement and passed him the handset. Now that it wasn't being used as a remote control for vehicles, the portable C^3 terminal was on his back again. Garcia lifted her FEK and fired as Trent started broadcasting.

"Alice One, Alice One, this is Guardian. Abort rescue! Repeat, abort rescue!" Trent swallowed once, fighting off despair. The rearguard had counted on him....

"Guardian, Alice One," Fraser's static-crusted voice came back. "Negative! Rescue unit on the way. Hold out ... three more minutes."

"Damn it, L-T, they'll be charging into the middle of half the Dryien army! The monkeys know how to knock out our APCs! Abort the op, for God's sake!"

Corporal Bashar's voice came on the line. "Not a chance, Sarge! Ain't no primmie bastard can hit *my* baby. Anyway, you still owe me twenty sols from that poker game last week!"

Trent swore. "You can't collect if you're dead, Bashar! Call it off!"

"Shut up and let me rescue you, Sarge!" The line went dead.

Trent replaced the handset and peered cautiously around the rock. Thirty meters away a hannie tank was lumbering slowly forward across bare, rocky ground. Suddenly a grey-brown figure lunged out of the cover of a rockslide and leapt on top of the vehicle, poking his FEK into the open hatch. Corporal Strauss's finger tightened on the grenade launcher trigger, sending a stream of small but powerful rifle grenades into the low-slung vehicle. Smoke and flame gouted from the hatch and the driver's slit as Strauss jumped clear, hosing a squad of hannie infantry with autofire as he ran for cover.

Farther away another hannie tank fired once. Then the sleek shape of a Grendel missile skimmed over the ridge beyond the vehicle. It seemed to pause for an instant like a hound casting for a scent, then plunged downward into the tank.

The explosion hadn't subsided when the Sabertooth topped the rise, fans revving at full speed. Legionnaire Karatsolis guided the plasma gun to bear on another target and fired. The Sabertooth pivoted on its fans, maintaining a steady barrage. Behind it, a Sandray appeared, its CEK chattering as it passed through a cluster of hannie troops.

"Recon lances! Let's savkey! Go! Go! Go!" Trent realized he was shouting into the radio. So much for his image of unflappable calm.

The legionnaires were scrambling from their defensive positions, laying down their own covering fire to augment the heavier guns on the two vehicles. Trent watched as Legionnaire Rostov helped Grant, who had recovered enough to walk, into the back of the Sandray. The rest of the recon troopers quickly climbed aboard and the APC skittered sideways to make room for the Sabertooth. As it touched down, Trent was already urging Tran into motion. He sprinted across the open ground and reached the rear door while the ramp was still dropping.

Garcia was next. A hannie machine gun opened up, and slugs slammed into the legionnaire's legs. She stumbled and fell.

Trent fired a three-round grenade burst at the machine-gun nest and leapt from cover. He barely paused to help Garcia up, half-carrying her. It looked like her uniform had stopped the bullets, but he knew the kinetic energy of those hits would still have been enough to hurt, maybe even cause a fracture. She gritted her teeth. "Thanks, Sarge," she gasped as he pushed her into the back of the Sabertooth. Tran helped her up and stretched her out on one of the troop benches, rolling up the trouser leg to examine the injury. Trent slapped the ramp button and sank onto the other bench, exhausted.

With a roar, the Sabertooth lurched forward, the plasma gun still firing wildly.

Trent could hardly believe they'd managed to escape.

CHAPTER ELEVEN

—traditional slogan, Fourth Foreign Legion, c. 2650

It's no good, lieutenant. It'd take a week in a repbay and a list of spare parts as long as a Toeljuk's tentacles to get this baby running again."

Colin Fraser frowned. "You said these carriers were working, Sergeant."

"They were, Lieutenant," Persson replied patiently. "As of the last check-up ... and before you tried to take them through the jungle."

Bravo Company's vehicles were clustered in a large clearing surrounded by jungle. Monkeyville was nearly two hundred kilometers behind them now, and there had been little sign of pursuit. Legionnaire Ignaczak had shot down a hannie fighter plane pacing the column in the first hour of the retreat, but beyond that it looked as if they'd broken contact cleanly.

The trail they'd followed north away from the main road had been a good escape route, but an hour after leaving the main road Fraser ordered the column to turn east into the jungle. At that time the decision had seemed valid enough. The trail emerged from the rain forest and rejoined the main road net halfway between the capital, Jyeezjai, and Dryien's second largest city, and Fraser wasn't about to lead Bravo Company into that kind of danger again so soon. And the possibility of more aerial harassment while they remained on the open trail was something he had to consider as well. The two Sabertooth FSVs could knock down aircraft easily enough, but a really large-scale attack might be more than they could handle, especially given the restricted fields of fire on the jungle road.

Now, though, it seemed that his decision had been wrong.

"These Sandrays ain't built to go bouncin' off trees," Persson continued as if to emphasize Fraser's gloomy thoughts. "You can't use them as battering rams without expecting to take some damage."

"All right, Sergeant, you've made your point. How long will it take to transfer the supplies to another APC?"

"Maybe an hour, Lieutenant." Persson paused. "A couple of hours if we do things right and strip the beast."

"Strip it?"

"Yeah ... pull out the electronics and the magrep modules, break down the fans for spare parts, that sort of thing."

Fraser studied the damaged vehicle. It was one of the two cargo vans, stocked with food, ammo, and other gear. One of its fans had been knocked out, another damaged, and it was sagging on one side from a magrep module failure. He felt his fists tighten at his sides. A breakdown this early in the long journey was a bad sign. This would be enough to force some of the legionnaires to ride on the outside of other vehicles or travel on foot ... and that would slow the column down.

Forcing himself to relax, he nodded. "All right. Do it the right way, Sergeant. But I'm holding you to that two hours. Don't do anything that'll end up taking longer."

"Yes, sir." Persson turned away, shouting for Corporal Weston.

Specialists in the transport platoon were cross-trained in mechanical maintenance and repair; Persson's men would be able to handle the salvage work on their own. But transferring supplies from the supply vehicle into another Sandray would go faster with some extra help. Fraser sought out Sergeant Qazi and told him to round up a work detail, then headed back to the command van. Trent met him by the ramp.

"L-T, Garcia's got something on the radio," the sergeant said.

Legionnaire Garcia had suffered a sprained ankle and some bad bruising on her legs, but she was back on duty at the van's C^3 console. Trent seemed little the worse for wear, but Fraser thought the man looked exhausted. After the fighting outside Monkeyville, that wasn't surprising.

"What is it, Gunny?"

Trent shook his head. "Can't be sure, L-T. There's a lot of static, and the signal's pretty weak to begin with. But it's on the platoon net assigned to Charlie Company, and a couple of clear spots sounded like human voices."

Fraser locked eyes with Trent, startled. If some of Charlie Company had escaped after all...! "Did you try to raise them?"

"Garcia gave it a go, L-T, but there wasn't an answer. She says they're probably using helmet sets, and the range is just too long. All we're getting is stray stuff, nothing coherent."

"Yeah ... or our hannie friends are using recordings." Fraser looked away.

"Shit, L-T, you're not going to ignore them, are you?" Trent looked angry. "We can't just leave them!"

"God, Gunny ... I don't know!" Fraser suddenly felt dizzy, weak. One crisis after another, decision after decision ... and a wrong choice at any turn could kill them all. "I just don't know!"

"I could take out another patrol ..." Trent was swaying with fatigue as he spoke.

"Forget it, Gunny," Fraser told him. "You've done enough for one day." He paused, wrestling with his doubts. "All right. Pass the word to Watanabe to get his platoon ready to move out—but leave the recon lance out of it. Mount them on one of the APCs, a Sabertooth, and one of the engineering vans. Uh ... better have a couple of the other vehicles ready in case we do find survivors."

"You're putting Watanabe in charge, then? Good choice...."

"I'll take command myself, Gunny. If this is a trap, I'm not sending in any of those kids while I sit on my butt back here. Tell Fairfax he's in charge if I don't come back. And get the column moving again in two hours whether or not we've reported in. We'll catch up."

"L-T, I don't think—"

"That's an order, Gunny!" Fraser interrupted with more force than he'd intended. Now that he'd made the decision, he was impatient to go through with it.

Trent drew himself to attention and saluted. "Yes, sir."

Fraser watched the sergeant as he left in search of Subaltern Wata-nabe. So many wrong decisions already ... would this one go wrong, too?

He didn't want to think of what would happen to Bravo Company if it did.

* * *

"How'd we get stuck with this detail, anyhow? Didn't we do enough already?"

Slick grunted, ignoring Legionnaire Rostov's complaining as he manhandled another box of supplies down the damaged cargo van's ramp. The effort made his head throb, but he was glad to be working. Sitting in an APC while it lurched and swerved through the jungle had made his head hurt just as much, and there hadn't been any way to take his mind off it.

Vrurrth picked up Slick's box at the bottom of the ramp as if it was packed with feathers. "The fight, the work," the alien rumbled, looking at Rostov. "The duties make us Legion."

"Easy for you to say, big guy," Rostov told him. "You'd think a fifty-klick hike was a nice way to rest. *I'm* tired."

"Could be worse," Slick ventured. "We might have had to go with the rest of the platoon on that run the lieutenant ordered."

Rostov grinned. "Hell, at least I could get some sleep sitting on my ass in an APC!" He wrestled another box out of the stack and across the floor of the van. Slick took over at the top of the ramp. "It's a good thing we're not going, all the same. Corp'd probably tie you up and leave you in the back of the 'ray if we went out on another op."

Slick felt himself flushing. Since waking up after the fight on the hilltop, he had been starting to feel accepted again. No one was likely to doubt his courage now, not after he'd taken on ten hannies alone! But underneath Rostov's bantering tone he thought he detected a hint of genuine warning.

"What're you talking about? Don't tell me he's still after me for that shit in the trench!"

"I'm talking about this morning, kid. That stunt you pulled was enough to get you a couple of weeks in cells. If—"

"Stunt? I saved the lance! Maybe the whole goddamned battle, for Chrissake!"

Rostov straightened up from the box in front of him. "You really don't get it, do you, kid?"

"Get what? Why—"

"Look, you may have saved some lives this morning ..."

"*May* have! There was a blunderbuss aimed right at DuPont—"

"Shut up, kid! I'm trying to help you." Rostov pulled out a slender Medean cigarette and lit it. "Like I was saying, you might have saved some lives out there. But the *way* you did it was stupid … criminal, even. Did it ever occur to you to warn somebody about the monkeys?"

"Yeah, right," Slick responded sourly. "With everybody already saying I'm a coward, I'm gonna call for help. No thanks, man."

"Call for *help*! How about you call to report and *ask* for some orders? Hell, what are they teaching you nubes these days, anyway?"

"I used initiative," Slick said firmly. Inside, though, Rostov's words hit home.

"You wouldn't know initiative if it sat up and bit you on the nose, nube. You were thinking with your pride, not your brains. For God's sake, kid, I damn near snuffed you today 'cause I didn't know you were up there. And where the hell would we have been if they'd killed you, huh? You *report* what you see and you *follow orders*." Rostov spread his hands. "Get with the program, Grant. In the Legion we look after our own. That means we think about our buddies before we think about ourselves … and we don't go hogging the glory and risking everything the way you did!"

"That's real great advice, Rostov," Slick said, angry. "Real great. Maybe if I thought I *had* some 'buddies' around here I'd buy all this teamwork crap I keep hearing. Every move I make gets me nothing but grief. If it isn't from Strauss or from one of you guys, it's from one of the sergeants—or from Gunny Trent. I'm not a part of your team, and I don't think I ever will be!"

"Not with that attitude you won't, kid," Rostov said bluntly. "You'll be accepted by the Legion just as soon as you show you're really a legionnaire, not before. As long as you keep playing games, though, don't expect anybody to think you're anything but a dumb nube."

"Enough talk!" Corporal Strauss shouted from outside. "Get back to vork!"

Slick turned back to the nearest box and started shoving it down the ramp, attacking it with some of the fury seething inside of him. Rostov was right about the mistakes he'd made in the fight with the hannies, but the rest…! The harder he tried to understand the Legion, the worse things got. It wasn't like he had volunteered; the court had forced him to join. And it seemed as if there was no way he'd ever fit in on *their* terms.

All he could do, he decided, was survive.

* * *

"Can't you push this thing any faster, Mason?" Fraser asked irritably as the Sabertooth slowed down to swing wide around another tight-packed clump of trees.

Sergeant Paul Mason didn't even raise his head from the monitor screen in front of him. "Not unless you want to tear the guts out of her, Lieutenant," he said gruffly. He had the sound of a man protecting a child.

"Survey map says it thins out in another few klicks, sir," Legionnaire Tran said from behind Fraser. He was filling in for Garcia, since she was still recovering from her injury, and what he lacked in technical expertise he made up for in enthusiasm. "We can make better time there."

Mason grunted. "Yeah. Maybe."

It had been a frustrating two-hour trek. Following the line of the radio signal Garcia had picked up, the three Legion vehicles had travelled deep into the jungle. Fraser had been tempted to turn back when it became clear that they weren't heading for any of the three Charlie Company outposts, but his conscience wouldn't allow him to act until he was sure. They'd been delayed repeatedly by the dense jungle growth. In places the short, twisted trees were so tightly intertwined that they seemed like a single organism. Patches like that were impenetrable to men and machines alike, and the only option was to change course and seek an easier way around the obstacle. With Mason worried that the Sabertooth and the two APCs might suffer the same kind of damage as the crippled supply van, they were forced to proceed at a painfully slow pace.

Fraser had been thinking of the detachment as a "flying column." The phrase rang in his mind like a feeble joke now.

By now the main body would be moving again, and each passing hour would widen the gap between them. It would cost more precious time if they had to stop so Fraser's party could catch up ... but the alternative, keeping the tiny Legion force divided in the heart of a hostile country, was unthinkable.

Another choice gone wrong....

"I'm getting something, Lieutenant," Tran said suddenly. He was holding a headphone to one ear. "Sounds like ... yeah, that's Russo. Charlie Company's command C^3 tech. I think they're under attack!"

Fraser took the headphones and slipped them over his ears. Static made the signal ragged.

"...get the damned Fafnirs over on the left ... too late!"

"That's firm ... bastards moving up the road ..."

"Sub's been hit! Tell Baker to get a medic down here...! Where's the Sarge? He's in charge now!"

Handing the phones back to Tran, Fraser looked down at the C^3 terminal balanced on the legionnaire's knees. "Do you have a line on them?"

"Yes, sir. And Garcia's feeding us a second line from the command van. Looks like they're right about ... here." The terminal's map display showed two lines intersecting at a point about twenty kilometers away. Tran touched a stud and a detail map replaced the first. Fraser bent forward to examine it.

The lines touched at an open area labelled "Shelton's Head." It was at least 110 kilometers from any of the three outposts where Charlie Company's platoons had been stationed ... more like 200 klicks from the site of the company HQ, where Russo would have been stationed.

"What have you got on this place, Tran?" he asked, pointing to the name.

Tran called to the data from the computer. "It's a zyglyn plantation, Lieutenant," the Viet legionnaire said. "Head of the trail. Surveyed by a free-lancer working for StelPhar by the name of Shelton ... ten years back. Seems Shelton and his wife struck a private deal with some of the local growers and settled there after he retired. It was Shelton who convinced StelPhar to open the trail from Monkeyville up to his place."

Fraser nodded slowly. "So ... if they got cut off from Monkeyville, some of the people from Charlie Company might have holed up with this Shelton."

"Looks that way, sir," Tran agreed.

Fraser studied the map again. "On the other hand, it still could be a trap. We don't have any proof that those signals are coming in live. They might have been recorded."

"Maybe so, sir," the legionnaire said. "But if they pulled back here, it would explain why the Sarge couldn't raise them when he did his recon the other night."

"Maybe so." Fraser frowned. "Damn! I wish we had the command van so we weren't going in blind. Drones'd be real handy right about now."

"Won't take long to call for one, Lieutenant," Tran told him. "Let me get Garcia for you."

He hadn't been thinking in terms of help from the main body … hadn't been thinking at all, in fact. Of course Garcia could send drones in to scout out the area; flying high over the jungle they'd be over Shelton's Head by the time his slow-moving vehicles made it overland.

Fraser clenched his fists. He couldn't afford to lose track of his assets like that. Not if he wanted to keep his men alive.

"All right, Tran. Get on it." He turned back toward the driver's cab. "You have the coords, Mason? Then rev it as much as you can. If those signals are the real thing, we've got men in trouble out there."

It felt good to have a clear course of action for a change. Fraser almost smiled as he strapped himself back into a seat and braced himself against the motion as the Sabertooth increased speed.

But the smile didn't quite come. He was all too aware of how little he really knew about commanding men in battle. And this time he didn't have Sergeant Trent to help him if he got in trouble.

This time, Fraser was on his own.

Chapter Twelve

The Third Company of the First Battalion is dead, but it did enough that in speaking of it one could say "It had nothing but good soldiers."

—Sergeant Evariste Berg in his report on Camerone,
French Foreign Legion, 1863

They're alive! Look, Lieutenant, those're humans down there!"

Fraser leaned closer to peer at Tran's video display. The shapes caught in the drone's cameras were unmistakable. He watched an armored soldier carrying an onager run across the open ground from the plantation building toward an odd-looking blockhouse. No ... not a blockhouse, the turret of a Sabertooth FSV. Someone had heaped dirt over the front and sides of the hull, leaving the turret with its lethal-looking plasma cannon free. The onager gunner stopped and fired, then ducked into the vehicle's rear hatch.

There were survivors from Charlie Company after all.

"Tell Garcia to circle wider. Let's get an idea of what they're up against."

"Yes, sir." Tran glanced at him. "Uh ... do you want me to raise Charlie Company, too?"

Fraser hesitated before replying. "No. We don't want to risk tipping off the bad guys that we're this close. If we can hit them by surprise, we might have better luck nailing the bastards."

Tran nodded and put through the call to Garcia.

The view on the monitor widened and blurred as the drone gathered speed, rising. Within moments it stabilized again, and Fraser could study a wider view of the battlefield.

It looked like Charlie Company had given a good account of itself in the fighting so far. Their hannie opponents were mostly infantry, with a small number of light tanks in support. From what Fraser could gather from the drone's camera views and computer interpretation of the images from the command van, the natives were not as well equipped as the ones who had attacked Fort Monkey. Charlie Company had taken casualties, and plenty of them—the best estimate from the computers put the Legion losses at roughly fifty percent—but most of those had probably been due to surprise and early weight of numbers rather than superior firepower. The Commonwealth defenders seemed to be holding their own now against a native force that had lost a lot of soldiers ... and a lot of cohesion as well.

One good blow could crack the enemy wide open....

"Right," Fraser said at last. The three vehicles were grounded less than two kilometers from the plantation by the time he'd put together a battle plan that looked like it would work. Watanabe and Platoon Sergeant Fontaine had joined him in the Sabertooth after deploying their platoon to watch the perimeter around the temporary camp. "Let's get moving before any stray monkeys find out we're in the neighborhood."

As he outlined his plan to the others, Fraser suppressed his own worries. The situation was straightforward enough, and the Legion held all the cards in this hand.

But, deep down, doubt gnawed at his self-confidence, and Colin Fraser couldn't shake the fear that he might be leading these men to their deaths.

* * *

Platoon Sergeant Ghirghik flicked his tail back and forth irritably. "How bad is it?"

Terranglic wasn't as well suited to conveying the full range of his anger as his native Khajrenf, but the three humans in the plantation office took a step back as he spoke. Of course, humans were often nervous around members of the Iridescent Race, even an outcaste like Ghirghik. He often wondered how they would react if confronted by one of the true Ubrenfars, a high-caste Drakhmirg or a Zhanghi warrior.

Had his father not dishonored the Line with cowardice at the battle of Jirghan, he would have been a Zhanghi himself. Instead he had fled his own kind, ending up among the humans. Once he would have called them "weakling humans" as any Zhanghi might have done, but twenty cycles serving in their Foreign Legion had taught Ghirghik that not all humans were weak. Some might almost have been Warriors themselves.

Now they would face their end like true Warriors, here on the planet they called Hanuman.

"We're down to less than two magazines per man, Sarge," Corporal Johnson said. "There's only one Grendel left, and maybe ten Fafnirs. If they all work."

Ghirghik touched his forehead, then gave the human equivalent of the gesture and nodded his head. Among his own kind, the gesture would have been degrading, but humans seemed unable or unwilling to learn any body language but their own. "Go on."

"Connie's starting to run low on juice, and I don't think we can get the powerplant going again," Johnson continued. Connie was Charlie Company's nickname for the Sabertooth FSV they'd managed to salvage from the chaos of the first hannie surprise attack. One of their tanks had put a round through her engine, and despite the best efforts of their lone mechanic, Legionnaire Brecht, their makeshift repairs kept giving way. The vehicle was now a pillbox on the southern perimeter around Shelton's Head, but on battery power it wouldn't be useful for long. "We've only got enough for five or six more shots, at best."

"Not good," Ghirghik said. "What about the men?"

"There's fifty-three guys still on their feet, Sarge," Legionnaire Delandry replied. She was one of the last two medics left with the unit. Although Ghirghik normally had nothing but contempt for the whole idea of medics, he respected the human woman's courage. He had watched her drag an injured comrade out of a trench and across fifty meters of open ground under heavy fire. It still struck him as foolish to rescue casualties—a Zhanghi warrior would have fought until he died, regardless of wounds—but that didn't detract from Delandry's personal bravery. "That's including walking wounded. We've got five more who're in pretty bad shape, including Subaltern Lawton."

That human had been another surprise. Ghirghik had naturally assumed that the commander of the transport platoon would be like most of his caste—a mechanic and a teamster, not a Warrior. But after the native surprise attacks took out the officers of each separate platoon, it was Lawton who had pulled them together and led them out. Ghirghik hoped the man would recover enough to face his death as a Warrior should, with a weapon in his hands and an enemy in his sights.

Sergeant Baker, the third human, cleared his throat. "What are we going to try, Sarge?" he asked. "If we keep sitting here, they'll take us sooner or later. Once the ammo runs out …" He trailed off.

"Are you suggesting we surrender?" Ghirghik showed his teeth in disapproval. Very few humans were likely to misinterpret *that* gesture as one of their "smiles."

"N-no, Sarge," Baker said. "But … well, what the hell do we do?"

"We fight. If we have to, we die." Ghirghik flicked his tail again. "At least we will die as Warriors!"

The door to the office burst open. Legionnaire Russo, the C^3 operator, stood framed in the door, his face a grim mask. "We got troubles, Sarge. Hassan's spotted movement down the main road. Tanks and infantry."

Ghirghik nodded. "Time to fight," he said. "Get the men ready. Johnson, put a lance out in the jungle on either side of the compound in case they try another flank attack like last night."

"Okay, Sarge." Johnson and Delandry hurried out of the room.

Ghirghik intercepted Baker before he could leave, closing one massive hand over the human's collar. "There will be no surrenders, Baker," he told the man in a low, even voice. "Do not dishonor this unit."

He released the sergeant and followed him out of the room. Outside, gunfire and explosions heralded the native attack.

Now Legion and Zhanghi alike would see that Ghirghik could face battle as well as any true Warrior.

* * *

Fraser drew his FE-PLF rocket pistol and chambered a round. "Almost time, Sergeant," he said.

Platoon Sergeant Fontaine nodded and made a hand signal: *Prepare to attack.* The legionnaires of Corporal Radescu's lance stirred in the undergrowth, checking weapons one last time, shifting to better vantage points, selecting targets.

Next to Fraser, Legionnaire Tran bent over his C^3 terminal, watching the twin displays that showed the drone's eye view of the battlefield and the computer-generated map depicting terrain and positions. Watanabe's understrength platoon was deployed in a scattered skirmish line along the west side of the main road into the beleaguered plantation. Farther down the trail, near Shelton's Head, gunfire interspersed with larger explosions echoed as the native attack got under way. Timing was crucial. He had to wait until the hannies were fully committed without giving them a chance to overrun Charlie Company.

Tension knotted his stomach, and even with his uniform's climate controls Fraser was sweating. This time, he would be leading his men in person instead of watching and directing from safety. Every man would be needed for this fight. He reminded himself that he'd been in the same position during that first hannie attack on Fort Monkey. It wasn't like this was his first time in battle.

But that time he hadn't been given time to think. He'd reacted to the enemy, moving to counter threats as they occurred. This battle, though, would be different. If he failed to anticipate something, the whole attack could go wrong. Men could die ... *he* could die ... all because of what he decided.

"Goddamn!" Tran said beside him. "Lieutenant, Charlie Company's Sabertooths stopped firing."

"Hit?"

"I don't think so ... my guess is they're low on power."

"Without that plasma cannon, those guys are sharv meat," Fontaine said. "They can hold the hannies for a while with onagers and Fafnirs, but not long...."

"They've fired a Grendel!" Tran said. "Looks like ... yeah, the racks are empty. They're leaving the Sabertooth now. Falling back toward the plantation buildings."

"Lieutenant ..." Fontaine's voice was low but urgent.

Fraser clicked on the radio command channel. "Go! Go!"

He was up and running with the words. Fontaine rushed past him, firing his FEK at the nearest knot of hannie soldiers as he ran. Radescu's legionnaires were in motion as well.

The hannies barely had time to react. Needles tore through the native soldiers before they even realized they were under attack. A few tried to run, but none lasted more than a few meters. Then the firing stopped. There were no more targets here.

Fraser hadn't fired a single shot.

"Right!" Fraser said over the comm circuit. "Mason, start your run. Dmowski! Get your lance into position! Everybody else form on Watanabe. Move!"

The plan was proceeding smoothly so far. Over a stretch of nearly 500 meters the platoon had knocked out the native troops moving up in support of the attack on Shelton's Head. Now Dmowski's heavy weapons lance would block one end of the trail, delaying monkey reinforcements while the rest of the platoon swung around to take the attackers in the rear. Mason's three vehicles, meanwhile, would support the infantry attack and then break into the plantation compound to pull out the besieged legionnaires from Charlie Company.

"Sergeant Fontaine, take Radescu's lance and support Dmowski," Fraser ordered. "I'll join the subaltern for the main attack."

The Frenchman saluted crisply. Fraser turned east and moved out at a trot, with Tran close behind.

Maybe everything would work after all....

* * *

Ghirghik knelt over the body of Legionnaire O'Neil and pried the Fafnir missile launcher from the human's dead fingers. Neither the soldier's headless body nor the machine-gun fire slamming into his own torso armor distracted the Ubrenfar NCO as he double-checked the weapon calmly, trained it on the nearest native tank, and ran through the targeting sequence. The missile leapt from the launch tube as if eager to do battle.

As the rocket exploded just over the driver's slit, Ghirghik bared his teeth in defiance. *I am Zhanghi! I am Warrior!*

"Come on, Sarge! We'll cover you!" Corporal Johnson was shouting from the door of the nearest of the plantation buildings. He had an MEK cradled in his arms. Its harsh, grating hum sounded in counter-point to the whine of nearby FEKs when Johnson fired.

Ghirghik checked O'Neil's pack hastily, but there were no Fafnir warheads left. He threw the useless launch tube in the direction of the enemy and unslung his own kinetic energy rifle. Firing a ragged burst, he sprinted for the door, ignoring enemy bullets.

"Report!" he snapped as Johnson closed the door behind him.

Russo looked up from his C^3 terminal. "Two more dead ... I guess it's three with O'Neil. Delandry says the monkeys are getting close to the med hut. She doesn't know how much longer her gang'll hold out."

"Baker's down to less than half a clip per man," Johnson added. "Hell, I'm about ready to start throwing rocks myself."

"I'm on my last Fafnir round," somebody else said.

"Hey, Sarge," Russo broke in. "I'm gettin' some funny signals on the terminal. Like input from a relay...."

"Never mind that," Ghirghik ordered sharply. "Get your weapon."

"What're we doing, Sarge?" Johnson asked.

"We will attack," Ghirghik told him. "Break out into the jungle. Pass the word: take any native weapons or ammo you find on the way out."

"That's suicide!" Legionnaire Griesch said loudly.

"A few of us will make it out," Ghirghik said. "The rest ... better to die like Warriors than skulk here."

Johnson showed his teeth. It took a moment for Ghirghik to realize the human was grinning in agreement, not arguing with his orders. "I'm with you, Sarge," he said. "Come on, you apes! Let's give 'em hell for the Legion!"

*　*　*

"Legionnaires!"

Fraser took up the battle cry along with the others as they burst out of the jungle in the rear of the hannie attackers. A detached part of him wondered at the transformation in Subaltern Watanabe, normally so diffident and quiet, but now shouting and waving his FEK with an enthusiasm to match any common soldier's.

Not far away, Legionnaire Hsu dropped to one knee and fired a Fafnir missile at a hannie light tank. The warhead struck the vehicle at the juncture between hull and turret, sent a gout of flame and smoke spiralling skyward. An FEK whined somewhere, and a knot of native soldiers toppled in an untidy clump.

This end of the wide plantation clearing was thick with hannies mustering for the assault against Charlie Company. The buildings where the legionnaires had taken refuge were not visible, nor could the sounds of that more distant struggle be heard over the din of the firefight here, but that fighting was playing a key role in Fraser's battle plan. Caught by the Legion attack from an unexpected direction, the natives were completely unprepared. Despite their superior numbers, Watanabe's understrength platoon was handling them easily.

He wondered how Charlie Company was managing in the meantime. Fraser had kept firmly to his decision not to contact the survivors or use any frequencies they might monitor to preserve surprise right up to the moment of the attack. Since the locals had demonstrated their ability to locate Legion remote sensors he had developed a hearty respect for their capabilities. And Kelly Winters had mentioned seeing a Semti working with the hannie general who seemed to have launched the coup. If so, the natives had access to information and equipment outside their own technological capacity.... It had seemed best to let Charlie Company act and react without the knowledge of the relief force, just to minimize the chance of giving something away too early.

Apparently the gamble had paid off. If the enemy was monitoring Legion communications, they weren't listening to any of the channels Bravo Company was using, and they hadn't been ready for the attack. In a few more minutes, it would be time to let Charlie Company know the cavalry had arrived.

Hsu fired another Fafnir as a hannie tank pivoted. This shot wasn't quite as good. It tore a gouge in the hull armor along the left side but didn't keep the tank from finishing the turn. The vehicle lurched forward on clattering treads while a hull-mounted machine gun hammered at the legionnaires. Hsu fell under the deadly hail, blood seeping from a half a dozen wounds in his arms and stomach where the high-caliber bullets had pierced the duraweave uniform.

Legionnaire Tran snatched up the Fafnir launcher and moved closer. For a horrified instant Fraser stood frozen, watching the turret track toward the legionnaire. With a roar the tank gun fired, hosing Tran with a stream of flame. The legionnaire screamed, dropping the Fafnir, as the fire engulfed him.

The flamethrower tank shifted aim and fired again, narrowly missing Watanabe and another soldier a few meters to the right of Fraser's position.

Fans raced as the Sabertooth appeared in the clearing. The Legion vehicle swerved easily into the path of the flames, its armor proof against the fire. Ignaczak's plasma gun locked on and fired, and an instant later the tank exploded with a curiously flat, dull thud. The blast knocked Fraser flat. He had a brief impression of a pillar of smoke and flame spouting high in the air, raining burning debris across the clearing. A chunk of armor drifted lazily above it all, spinning end for end, hanging for a long moment before falling back to the ground. A hannie trapped under another piece of the vehicle was screaming.

Fraser rose unsteadily, afraid of what the explosion might have done to his men. But the legionnaires were on their feet already, pushing forward across the smouldering field as the remaining hannies wavered. Here and there natives threw away their weapons and fled for the safety of the jungle. Others died where they stood.

Then the firefight—perhaps the entire battle—was over.

CHAPTER THIRTEEN

What are you complaining about? I'm creating glory for you.

> —Colonel Pierre Jeanpierre,
> French Foreign Legion, March 1958

A glorious tactic, Lieutenant Fraser! Glorious!"

Fraser tried to conceal his unease as he regarded the Ubrenfar sergeant. The saurian's scaled, heavily-muscled body was marked by dozens of gashes, cuts and patches of missing scales but Ghirghik had spurned any offer of first aid. When Fraser's men had finally cut their way through to the survivors from Charlie Company, the big alien had been standing in the center of a ring of hannie dead, FEK dry of grenades and needle rounds alike, wielding a blade like an oversized kukri and singing a discordant Ubrenfar battle song.

Ghirghik had seemed disappointed that he hadn't died gloriously at the height of the battle, but his praise for Fraser's attack on the hannie rear had been unstinting.

Not that everyone agreed with the sergeant. Not even Fraser.

The hannies were gone, dispersed by the sudden onslaught of the legionnaires. But the butcher's bill at Shelton's Head made the triumph seem hollow. Seventy legionnaires had withdrawn to the plantation after the initial hannie attacks. Of the forty-six still alive when Fraser's men reached Ghirghik, over half were wounded—ten of them seriously. Subalterns Jacquinot and Lawton had died, and the two vehicles the legionnaires had brought out were both useless hulks now. Fraser's force had lost five dead and three wounded as well.

It didn't sound that bad ... except that every casualty suffered in these remote jungles was irreplaceable. And when primitive hannie soldiers could kill so many high-tech Commonwealth troops, even at the cost of hundreds of their own kind, the Terran victory was a Pyrrhic one at best.

"Goddamn it, Lieutenant, why didn't you let us *know*?" That was Sergeant Baker. He'd lost his helmet, and a hannie rifle butt had cut a deep gash across his forehead in hand-to-hand fighting around the plantation buildings. The heavy bandage over it gave the man a distinctly piratical appearance. "We could have held out long enough if we'd known you were coming! Instead of charging the monkeys...."

The Ubrenfar snorted derisively. "It was brilliant," he said. The afternoon sun lancing through the windows glinted off his scales as his tail twitched. "Using us to focus their attention, then hitting them from behind before they could react...!"

Fraser looked away. He *had* used Charlie Company, used them as a diversion for his attack. At the time it had seemed clever.

Now, though, he was ashamed. The Ubrenfar's praise was salt in the wound. Everyone knew their callous disregard for life, their ruthlessness in battle.

So much for clever tactics, he told himself bitterly. *More lives wasted. Another mistake....*

Watanabe cleared his throat. "Lieutenant, last report from Garcia says we've got bad guys gathering down the road. Shouldn't I be getting the men ready to saddle up?"

Fraser nodded slowly. "Do it, Sub. Wounded get first call on the APCs."

The subaltern saluted. "Yes, sir. I'll have Legionnaire Russo take over Tran's C^3 duties, if that's all right with you."

"Yeah. Fine." Tran's death was still fresh in his mind. Russo had been Captain Rayburn's C^3 specialist in Charlie Company and had come through the fighting unscathed. He'd make a good replacement for Tran.

Watanabe hurried out of the plantation office, shouting for Sergeant Fontaine. Fraser stared after him, ignoring the others in the room. The subaltern was right. They had to get moving, before the hannie army could reform and launch a fresh attack.

Right now, all he could do here was bury his mistakes, together with the dead, and keep moving. It was the only chance of survival the legionnaires had left.

*　*　*

Shavvataaars, Third Talon of the Everlasting Race, squinted in the harsh light slanting through the window of the Excellent's private audience chamber and drew his hood lower over his eyes. *An eternity's curse on this place,* he thought. Hot, humid, painfully bright under the glare of its F-class star, this world the Terrans called Hanuman wasn't far removed from the ancient Semti religious concept of hell.

Not that any rational being would believe such ideas. The Semti had too long manipulated the religious beliefs of others to set any stock in the mythologies of their own ancestors. But the teachings were a part of the Ancient Lore, treasured, tended, preserved. There were times when Shavvataaars looked around this inhospitable world and recoiled in horror from a scene from Journey's End.

But Hanuman represented a chance to reverse the temporary ascendance of the chaotic Terran barbarians and their Commonwealth. Somehow, unthinkable as it had been, their juvenile vigor had won them a victory over the Conclave. The destruction of Kiassaa, the Conclave's artificial capital, had thrown Semti administration into chaos and opened the way for the barbarian takeover. Yet the moment would pass, and in time the Eternal Race would resume its rightful place as guardian and arbiter of the immature species—the Terrans among them. The proper pressure applied now, here, would create the conditions that would bring the ephemerals tumbling down as quickly as they had first risen.

Assuming, of course, that the other ephemerals, the primitives of these hellish swamps and jungles, could be guided to do their part.

At the moment, that assumption was questionable.

"Another demon trick!" *Asjyai* Zyzyiig smashed kys fist on the table. The native officer was using the ceremonial hall as a personal office, having relegated the new *yzyeel* to virtual captivity in a well-guarded wing of the Fortress of Heaven. "Another slaughter! You told me the demons would lose heart, would be easy to destroy, and look where it led! They escaped their fortress, and now they have rescued the other survivors. And hundreds of kyendyp killed in each fight!"

Shavvataaars regarded the other patiently. Zyzyiig's own interference had been responsible for most of the mishaps so far, but of course it would be impolitic to say as much. The Great Journey, the plan his superiors had dubbed "Twilight Prowler" required the native's continued cooperation, at least until the embers of anti-Terran sentiment had been fanned into an all-consuming blaze. Dryienjaiyeel was a primitive country, barbaric even by Terran standards, but it had a place in Twilight Prowler that could not be ignored.

"The demons have indeed proved more resourceful than we might have hoped for," the Semti replied in even, thoughtful tones. "But remember, my Companion, that they have already suffered a grave setback at your hands. Otherwise, they would not be fleeing overland."

"Fleeing!" Zyzyiig bared kys teeth. "They attack as they please, go where they want to go. Is this flight?"

"Yet they are plainly travelling northward, toward the border. A long and difficult journey to undertake save in desperation, when a single transport could carry their entire band to safety in minutes. Our calculations have proven correct in that much, at least. These legionnaires have been abandoned. Time will wear them down, time and the deep jungles. When next your soldiers encounter them, you will surely triumph. You must exercise patience in this."

"I am tired of hearing your speeches on patience!" Zyzyiig flared. "Your 'advice' and your 'assistance' have been nothing but speeches!"

Shavvataaars did not answer. This was always the danger in trying to work too closely with barbarian allies. It was easy to guide a species on a desired path through subtle manipulation over a span of centuries, very hard indeed to apply direct control for some fleeting, short-term goal. Ephemerals lost patience so easily, and their haste created situations where a slow and measured response was impossible. But the success of the Cleansing depended on Zyzyiig and kys followers. Without ephemerals as tools, the Eternal Race was no match for the barbarians. Not yet.

"Well?" The *Asjyai* was growing less self-assured as Shavvataaars remained silent. Zyzyiig's grandparents had worshipped the Semti as gods. For all kys bluster, the native's superstitions weren't far below the surface. "Don't you have anything to say ... Honored?"

Shavvataaars studied Zyzyiig from under the recesses of the dark hood. The native was growing harder to control with each defeat inflicted by the Terrans. Perhaps it would be best to let matters in Dryienjaiyeel play themselves out and devote his own attentions to the wider aspects of Twilight Prowler. The events set in motion here could not be turned aside even if the legionnaires continued to elude Zyzyiig ... but it would be wise to develop other aspects of the plan in case the *Asjyai's* growing unreliability became a threat.

Yes ... that was the road to follow now.

"It is clear to me, my Companion, that you have no further need of my advice," Shavvataaars told ky smoothly. "My job here is done. You can complete the Cleansing without further guidance."

Zyzyiig looked stricken. "But—"

"I have other tasks I must attend to, *Asjyai*," he continued. "Focus your efforts on blocking the escape of the demon refugees ... until I send you word. When we are ready to complete this Journey, you and your army will have a vital part to play. Be ready."

The Semti turned away before Zyzyiig could reply. Shavvataaars felt a cold thrill of satisfaction as he left the audience chamber. *Twilight Prowler moves forward. Soon enough I will be able to leave this hellworld ....*

* * *

Colin Fraser climbed the ramp into the command van with a feeling of relief. Two long days of maneuvering, dodging hannie patrols through the dense lowland jungles, was over at last. Demi-Battalion Alice—or at least the hundred and seventy-odd survivors of the two Legion companies—had reunited, ready to make the final push for the frontier.

It sounded simple put this way. But the "final push" still had to cover over a thousand kilometers before the legionnaires could cross the mountains and leave Dryienjaiyeel ... and a lot could happen in the meantime.

Legionnaire Garcia looked up as Fraser ducked his head to enter the C^3 compartment. "Good to have you back, sir," she said.

He nodded curtly. "Thanks. Didn't think we'd make it for a while there."

It had been a near-run thing. They'd been a little too successful in rescuing the Charlie Company survivors: there just hadn't been enough room on the three Legion vehicles to transport them all. The retreat from Shelton's Head had been limited to a speed not faster than the slowest marching soldier. And with so many walking wounded, that had been a snail's pace indeed.

In fact, the natives would probably have cut them off entirely if Trent hadn't persuaded Subaltern Fairfax to turn the main body around and hold open an escape route for Fraser's men. There hadn't been much real fighting, but the action had cost them four Grendel missiles ... and precious marching time.

Fraser still wasn't sure if he wanted to thank Gunny Trent for saving them, or chew him out for making Fairfax put the main body at risk. The sergeant's dedication to Legion tradition, to the idea that the Legion always looked out for its own, didn't seem quite so admirable when it put so many lives on the line.

Then again, by that reasoning he should have passed Charlie Company by....

That was exactly the kind of decision Fraser didn't want to face again.

He settled into his seat at the computer console. "What's the feed from the drones, Garcia?" he asked.

The map screen lit up. "It looks clear to the northeast, lieutenant," the C^3 tech said. "But Sergeant Trent figures there must be hannie units trying to close it off by now, probably moving up outside our scouting range. Do you want me to extend the perimeter any?"

Fraser shook his head. "Not yet. We'll assume Gunny's instincts are right. I don't want to risk the drone. We only have two more left, and they have to last us all the way to the border."

She nodded. "If the lokes are out there...."

"We'll find them as soon as they do come in range. Meantime, all we can do is get our asses in gear and get moving."

He leaned back in the seat and closed his eyes. With one vehicle out of action and the men from Charlie Company added to the column, it really was going to be a matter of marching. The vehicles could carry supplies and wounded, and they could rotate fit men aboard some of the APCs so the march could continue virtually nonstop, but the pace would still be slow. Too slow, he thought bitterly. Terran troops were used to crossing continents in a matter of hours aboard transport ships. Now the hannies were probably going to be able to move faster than the legionnaires.

"We'll move out in an hour, Garcia," he said at last. "But we'll have to get organized first. I want Trent and the subs in here right away. Sergeant Ghirghik, too."

Survival would depend more on hard marching than on fighting, but the legionnaires had to be ready for both. That meant integrating

Charlie Company into the rest of the unit before they moved out. One more delay to deal with.

He only hoped they could afford it.

*   *   *

Far from fair Terra, from family and home,
Far from embraces of those that we love,
Marches the Legion, the damned, all alone,
Under a strange sky with strange stars above.

The slow, mournful song was more dirge than marching music, and it seemed to emphasize Slick's mood. His FEK was a heavy weight on his shoulder, and each step seemed harder than the last. There was still another hour before the next scheduled halt, after which the lance was supposed to have a four-hour shift aboard one of the APCs. He hoped he could hold out until then.

Even in training on Devereaux, the Legion hadn't marched this much. For three days now, since the lieutenant's return with the survivors from Charlie Company, their longest halt had been no more than an hour. The legionnaires marched in shifts, ate or slept aboard the carriers, and took turns on point, flank, or rearguard, watching out for hannie attacks. There'd been enough of those, too. Slick could still visualize the enemy ambush two days back, when Corporal LeMay fell into the concealed pit and the rest of the flank party, Slick included, had held off a swarm of screaming hannies who seemed to materialize out of the jungle from every direction at once.

They'd pulled LeMay out of the pit afterwards, but the sharpened stakes had gone right through his duraweave coverall. He was one of four men dead in that clash, left behind in the jungle as the column pressed on.

And still they marched. And sang. The Foreign Legion had a tradition that stretched all the way back to Old Earth of marching to a slow beat of 88 paces per minute. The somber beat was matched by the songs, depressing melodies about loneliness, nostalgia, and the whims of politicians.

Back on Devereaux, Slick had once been punished by an NCO for some minor infraction by being forced to parade all night in full battle kit, singing the entire time at the top of his lungs. He was beginning to recall the incident with fondness. At least then he'd known it would end when morning came.

A hand gave him a savage cuff from behind. "Come on, nube! Sing!" It was Strauss, seemingly unaffected by the hours of marching. "I haf my eye on you. Understand?"

"Yes, Corporal," Slick answered meekly. Any other response was likely to get him another cuff.

Strauss gave him one anyway. "You are lucky ve are too busy for punishment, nube. But I vill remember." The corporal moved down the line to talk with Vrurrth.

"Looks like trouble with the Corp, kid," Rostov whispered. "Maybe you'll get lucky and buy it before he comes up with something nasty, huh?"

"Maybe he'll buy it," Slick muttered.

Rostov laughed. "Fat chance, kid. Ain't no bullet taking out the Corp. They're too scared of him!"

Slick didn't answer. He was sick of Rostov, sick of all his lance-mates with their rough and ready humor and their air of superiority over the poor helpless nube. Sick of Strauss and his punishments ... sick of the Legion.

He'd heard once that as many as a third of all legionnaires deserted before their term of enlistment was up. If they ever made it back to civilization, Slick was determined to try it as well. He didn't belong in the Legion, and he wasn't going to stay any longer than he had to.

The endless march went on.

Chapter Fourteen

—General Francois de Negrier,
French Foreign Legion, 1881

'm sorry, Fraser, but there's nothing new to report on this end. The resident-general still won't release any transport."

Fraser nodded wearily. He hadn't really expected any change in policy. He talked to Battalion daily, and the word was always the same. "I understand, Commandant. But I have to tell you that things here aren't going very smoothly."

That was understatement. Just over a week had passed since the demi-battalion had reunited after the rescue of the Charlie Company survivors, and in that time they'd reduced the distance to Fwynzei by less than five hundred kilometers. The actual distance the legionnaires had covered was much greater, of course, but the twists and turns forced on them by terrain and enemy pursuit had caused them to make wide, time-consuming detours.

Supplies were becoming a problem, too. The extra mouths they had to feed now, and the unexpectedly slow pace of the march, had thrown off all their careful planning.

"If we keep on going as we've been," Fraser continued aloud, "I'm not sure how well our supplies will hold out. Yesterday we raided a prim-mie village, but I'm not sure if that's going to be wise in the long run."

"How so?" Commandant Isayev demanded.

"The farther north we get, the fewer villages we'll find, sir," Fraser replied carefully. "Up near the frontier is where the Dryiens have been building all those model settlements, and they'll be a hell of a lot better defended than anything the savages have. Every foraging expedition costs us time and could cost me men as well. If we go up against a strong defense, we could lose everything."

Fraser looked away from the communications terminal for a moment. There was another reason he didn't like foraging, but it wasn't something he could talk about. The memory of the hannie village in flames, the stench of fire and death, was still fresh. The jungle savages just wanted to be left alone, but now the legionnaires were carrying the fight to them. It was necessary to keep the unit going, but Fraser hated the one-sided killing of primitives who couldn't defend themselves.

"Do what you can, Lieutenant," Isayev said gruffly. "I'll keep trying to get some kind of relief mission organized on this end, but I can't say it looks too likely now. Not the way things have been going."

"Sir?"

"The carriership *Seneca* is a week overdue at the systerm, Fraser. It's probably nothing—some politician or bureaucrat probably ordered him to wait for a VIP or something—but it's enough to throw a murphy into our works here. The resident-general's hoping to divert some troops slated for the garrison on Enkidu. That's why *Ankh'Qwar* isn't home yet; she's still waiting at the systerm."

"More troops, sir? To retaliate on the Dryiens?"

"Partly," Isayev admitted. "But in the past few days we've had indications of trouble in Vyujiid, too. There was a riot in the Imperial City yesterday. Our intel people think there could be a rebellion brewing up here. If so, we're going to need every man we can get just to protect Commonwealth interests north of the frontier. Even if we get more men, Fraser, I'm not sure how much help we'll be able to spare. Even the transports are likely to stay busy ferrying garrison troops back and forth to trouble spots. The Navy's not going to want to risk a repeat of *Ganymede* when every ship's going to be essential."

"Yes, sir," Fraser said. "I see their point of view. It's just not a very comfortable one personally."

"At this point, I'd say you've made the best possible choice. If you can get the demi-battalion out of Dryienjaiyeel on your own, you'll have done everyone a good turn. You were smart to pull out of Fort Monkey when you did."

"Thank you, sir. But I still wish we didn't have to get past Zhair-hee."

Isayev nodded. "I've seen the satellite photos. I don't know if that buildup's there just for your benefit, or to forestall any retaliation from here, but there's a lot of activity between you and the frontier. You'll just have to dodge it as best you can … unless I can organize some kind of help in the meantime."

"Yes, sir," he said again.

"Stay in touch, Fraser," Isayev told him. "I know it feels like we've abandoned you … hell, the resident-general and his flunkies would like to. But you're part of the Legion, and the Legion takes care of its own. Good luck, Lieutenant. Lancelot clear."

"Alice, ending transmission." Fraser leaned back in his seat and stared at the blank screen for a long time. If the Commandant was right about trouble elsewhere on Hanuman, the chance of assistance was smaller than ever. The Legion really was on its own.

All they could do now was press on, knock off as many kilometers as they could … and pray they didn't run into something they couldn't handle.

*　*　*

Kelly Winters lowered herself wearily onto a log and sighed gratefully. After two hours of marching, any chance to sit down, even for just a few minutes, was a welcome relief to aching feet. Everyone in the column took a turn marching, except for the seriously wounded casualties aboard the ambulance vans. She'd spent an entire shift a few days back beside Father Fitzpatrick, and yesterday she'd spotted Lieutenant Fraser and his electronics tech at the head of the column.

Somehow it seemed right. The legionnaires, for all their mismatched backgrounds and ill-mannered behavior, seemed to respond to that sort of sacrifice. Kelly was even beginning to detect some signs of thawing towards her.

Once she would have put that down to being one of a handful of women among a preponderance of men. The Legion ran about ten-to-one in favor of males, and the proportion was about that in the demi-battalion now.

But she doubted sex had much to do with anyone's attitude by this time. Dirty, smelly, her uniform unwashed and caked in jungle mud, her hair cut short after she'd tangled it in a thorny clump of *küzaij* vines, Kelly had never felt so totally asexual in her life. And she was exhausted, completely exhausted. For all their superior airs, the legionnaires were feeling the fatigue almost as much as she was. Lust wasn't nearly as high on anyone's list as a good night's sleep.

Or a shower. Kelly wanted a shower even more than sleep.

She looked up as roaring turbofans drowned out the sounds of the jungle. An engineering van glided past, raising whitecaps on the sluggish, muddy water of the river that had stalled the column's progress. Without the obstacle they wouldn't have called a halt this early in the day, so in a way it was a welcome sight. But it also represented more lost time, more chances for the pursuit to catch up again.

Myaighee had told her it was the upper reach of the Jyikeezh River, main artery of a drainage basin the computers said was larger than the Amazon on Terra. Even this far from the sea, the Jyikeezh was broad and slow-moving, deep enough to be a serious obstacle to troops on foot. There were supposed to be some easier crossing points a few dozen kilometers upstream, but rumor had it Gunny Trent had persuaded Lieutenant Fraser to cross here to throw the enemy off the scent.

That sounded like Trent. Calculating, competent, but a manipulator. Why Lieutenant Fraser let him dominate the unit was beyond her.

Clever though this maneuver might be, it was still causing trouble. With too many legionnaires for the available vehicles already, and two Sandrays and a Sabertooth detached on a combination scouting run and foraging expedition, getting troops and supplies across was taking time. A long time.

The engineering vehicle grounded thirty meters away and dropped its rear ramp. Some legionnaires nearby started gathering stacks of supplies and manhandling them toward the vehicle. Despite her feelings about the Legion, Kelly had to admit the men seemed ready enough to work. It felt wrong to be sitting back when others were busy, but Sergeant Trent had already made it clear that the best thing she could do to help was stay out of the way.

That went for Myaighee, too. The little alien had finally been released from regen treatment. Like everyone else, ky alternated between marching and riding. With no one of kys own race for company, Myaighee spent a lot of time with Kelly.

It seemed strange, but she frequently felt she had more in common with the alien than with the legionnaires.

One of the legionnaires staggered and dropped his load before he could reach the APC. Someone laughed loudly.

Then the man was screaming, writhing on the ground and clutching at his leg. Kelly was up and running at once, reacting without conscious thought. She dropped to one knee beside the man.

His lower leg from boot-top to knee was covered by some kind of soft, pulsing tissue. "Medic! Someone get a medic!" she yelled, groping for the first aid kit on the man's web gear. He was still screaming, and his face was a mask of anguish.

She prodded the creature wrapped around his calf with a stick. It seemed to tighten its grip, and the soldier screamed again.

"Don't touch it, ma'am," someone said behind her.

Kelly looked up in surprise at the fresh-faced legionnaire. He seemed vaguely familiar.... Her eyes focused on the caduceus insignia on his shoulder, and memory clicked into place. Legionnaire Donovan was a medic in First Platoon, and had tended her back in Fort Monkey. He didn't look much like a medic, with his grimy fatigues and the battle rifle slung over his shoulder. Like all specialists in the Legion, Donovan was a soldier first and a medic second.

"Spineleech," Donovan added grimly. Kelly backed away and let him take her place.

"Poisonous?" Kelly asked.

"Might as well be," Donovan said as he began fumbling in his pouch. "Alien proteins. Causes massive anaphylaxis. Damn. He's going into shock already...."

The soldier was shaking spasmodically as the medic slipped a plastic airway down his throat. Kelly could see the swelling in the man's face, the mottled discoloration, could hear the thick rasp of his breath. Working quickly, Donovan produced a laser cutter and began to work on the pulsing tissue mass enveloping the injured man's leg. There was sizzle of burning flesh, the stink of charred meat. Then the thing relaxed its grip and dropped off in two pieces.

Kelly saw the gripping surface of the creature, a mass of sucker disks and needle-slim quills still dripping blood. The legionnaire was convulsing now, bucking under the grip of two other soldiers who tried to hold him down as the medic pressed a hypospray against his neck. He tried to scream and made a strangled sound against the airway.

"Call Doc," Donovan told one of the legionnaires. "Gates'll need a litter. And someone check around the bank to see if there are any more of those ugly bastards. Look for holes right near the edge of the water. Watch yourselves! They're damned fast!"

"Will he be all right?" Kelly asked.

Donovan turned bleak eyes on her, then shook his head. "He's suffering from a massive allergic reaction. When they get hit this bad, regen just isn't fast enough. Best we can do is keep him under until …"

Kelly shuddered and turned away, remembering her own brush with anaphylactic shock. It was horrifying being unable to do anything but watch the boy die. What was his name? Gates.

She walked away in a daze. Just another day in the jungle. Another young kid dead.

It always seemed to be the kids who bought it, the nubes. The old vets seemed indestructible, like they could take any hardship and keep right on going. They were too smart to let their guard down and too cunning to be outmatched by anything … or anyone.

She sat down on the same log and stared wearily at the slow-moving water. These legionnaires were something outside her experience, and they were making her take a long, hard look at everything she'd believed in. She still resented many of them—Sergeant Trent, for instance, with his patronizing "leave it to someone who can do the job" attitude. For most of these soldiers, if you weren't a legionnaire you just didn't count, and that was galling.

And yet these same men and women weren't just braggarts. They really were capable of incredible efforts. It was hard to picture a Commonwealth Marine doing any more than these troops, and the Marines were supposed to be the best of the Commonwealth Regulars. On the march, the legionnaires were tough. And in battle … in battle, they seemed unstoppable.

Kelly Winters was surprised to realize just how much she admired them.

*　*　*

The *Angel of Death* floated motionless in the center of a hannie village, a high-tech dragon in the midst of primitive mud huts. Flames crackled from the nearest of the ruined structures, testament to the determination of the savage natives who had defended it. A grizzled hannie missing most of the quills of ky's ruff had set fire to the hut while one of the legionnaires had been inside.

Now the hannie was dead, the legionnaire was smeared with burngel, and the pitiful building burned.

Spiro Karatsolis snapped the MEK support weapon into place on a pintle mount next to the turret hatch and scanned the village with a practiced eye. Using the onager cannon against primitives would have been akin to using a SAM against a bothersome fly, but the MEK would serve to cover the troops on the ground in case any of the natives mustered up the courage to attack again.

Around the floating FSV, legionnaires moved quickly, purposefully, rounding up supplies to load on the engineering van hovering near the edge of the river.

Three raids in four days ... Karatsolis was beginning to hate these foraging runs. These hannie villagers weren't the real enemy, but they were hostile to just about anything that moved through the jungle, so raiding them was the only way to secure supplies short of hunting and gathering on the march.

But it didn't make the job any more palatable.

Karatsolis had seen it all. He was working on his second hitch in the Colonial Army, with a tidy little nest egg in the Battalion Bank and every prospect of making corporal when this tour was up. He'd have made it long since if it hadn't been for that time he'd tried to desert back on Tanais. When he retired, he'd go back to New Cyprus and buy himself a farm. Or perhaps he'd settle on Thoth. That had been a nice world, not spoiled by developers. Maybe that girl—what was her name? Elena?—was still looking for someone to marry.

Meanwhile, he was a legionnaire, and a good one at that. Shooting savages wasn't his idea of a good fight, but if that was what had to be done, he'd do it.

"Hey, Spear, don't doze off on us, man!" Bashar called. The Turk had his own hatch unbuttoned. "Remember that time you fell asleep and the Gwyrran rebel made a break for it?"

"I got him, didn't I?" Karatsolis responded. "Anyway, I wasn't asleep. I was just checking to see if *you* were on the ball. Which you weren't."

Bashar snorted. "Sure. That's your story, and you stick to it."

"This ain't much like Gwyrr, though," Karatsolis went on. "Too fucking hot."

"Hot, cold, who cares? Just another planet full of ales." Bashar spat over the side of the Sabertooth.

"Better watch it, Bashar," Karatsolis warned. He pointed across the village at Sergeant Ghirghik. The big Ubrenfar was in command of the raiding party, which consisted of the Sabertooth, the engineering van, and a standard Sandray troop carrier, with three lances from the unit's newly-formed Fourth Platoon. Ghirghik had been made platoon leader.

That was only right. The new platoon was mostly made up of survivors from Charlie Company and would respond better to Ghirghik than to any leader the lieutenant might have appointed from Bravo Company.

But the Ubrenfar made Karatsolis uneasy. It was hard to think of an Ubrenfar as an ally, even in the Legion where there were very few planets and races that *weren't* represented one way or another.

"Ah, don't sweat it, Spear," Bashar said. "Hell, I heard old Ghirghik swearing about the damned ales himself last night! He's—"

Bashar was cut off by the sudden *whoosh* of a missile swooping just meters away from the Sabertooth, followed by the thunder of an explosion as it hit a nearby hut. Someone screamed; another voice shouted for a medic.

"Goddamn!" Karatsolis swore, dropping into the turret and sealing the hatch behind him. "That wasn't any hannie rocket!"

The whole Sabertooth seemed to quiver and come alive as Bashar powered up the turbofans. "Whatever the hell it was, it's after us!" the Turk replied.

The FSV pivoted smoothly and shot toward the trees to the west. Bashar's hull-mounted CEK sprayed round after round of kinetic energy fire into the jungle while Karatsolis activated his turret controls and chambered a round in the plasma cannon.

Neither man spoke, but Karatsolis knew Bashar was thinking the same thing he was. Another missile could lance out of those trees at any moment. If it did, the *Angel* might not be able to take it.

The FSV crashed between two squat, greyish-orange trees, still firing. A video pickup showed Karatsolis a handful of hannies in Dryien army uniforms running away from the oncoming vehicle. One of them threw away something bulky as ky fled.

He checked his sensor arrays. Nothing on the MAD … no sign of vehicles of any kind. He unbuttoned the turret and raised himself through the hatch again, taking a grip on the MEK's trigger and swinging the weapon to track the fugitives. The weapon hummed, and needle slivers sliced through air, vegetation, and hannie flesh.

The whole battle had taken only seconds.

The Ubrenfar sergeant deployed a lance to scout the perimeter for further signs of the enemy, but they turned up no evidence of other troops in the area. Corporal Johnson, however, brought back one trophy from the search.

"What the hell is this thing?" Bashar asked as they examined it together back in the center of the village.

The Ubrenfar turned it over in his hands. It was a bulky tube, too big for most hannies to carry easily, with a simple control box near one end and a fold-out eyepiece for targeting.

"It's about fifty years ahead of anything the monkeys have, that's for sure," Karatsolis said quietly. "The missile that bugger fired was a fire-and-forget job, and the hannies don't have anything like that. We're just lucky the little bastard rushed the shot."

"Looks like Gwyrran manufacture to me," Corporal Johnson added. "I saw a lot of their old military-issue stuff when I was on Gwyrr, and this is a lot like it."

Ghirghik pointed to a line of angular markings below the controls. "I know this writing," he said slowly. "We captured many weapons when we rose against the Semti. This is their language."

"Semti?" Bashar frowned. "What do those ghouls have to do with this?"

"Makes sense," Karatsolis said. "The Gwyrrans were their favorite combat troops before the Conclave fell. And they were worshipped by the hannies. Looks like some of them still have access to an armory somewhere."

"There's no proof the Semti are helping the monkeys...." Bashar trailed off.

"Remember the way the hannies got past the remote sensors back at the fort? I think the Dryiens are getting some high-powered help." Karatsolis looked at the Ubrenfar.

Ghirghik nodded slowly. "We must report this to the lieutenant. If it is true...."

If it was true, Karatsolis thought, then the Legion might end up facing a hell of a lot more than it could handle.

Chapter Fifteen

Only soldiers like these could endure, with undiminished discipline, the sniping, shelling, and casualties which are their daily lot.

—from a press report on the Legion peacekeepers in Beirut, French Foreign Legion, 1983

Lieutenant? Wake up, Lieutenant. They need you in C-cubed."

Fraser's eyes focused slowly on the Padre's face. Fatigue dragged at every muscle, and his whole body ached. He remembered an instructor at the Academy telling him once that a real soldier could grab a few minutes sleep anywhere, but a cramped passenger seat in a moving Sandray didn't make much of a bed.

"What is it, Father?" he asked, stifling a yawn.

"Targets, Lieutenant. Looks like a squadron of aircraft inbound from the direction of the capital. Mr. Bartlow has been tracking them. Best computer estimate is that they're ground-attack planes carrying some pretty heavy bomb loads."

He came fully awake with that. The battle at the fort had proved the legionnaires could deal with native aircraft ... but images of *Ganymede* lingered, a brutal reminder of what the enemy could do if any of their planes slipped through the Terran defenses.

They'd left the river behind two days before, continuing the march north. Although they'd avoided further contact with ground forces, a drone from the command van had spotted a force of Dryien troops mounted on tracked personnel carriers trailing the rearguard. The report from Sergeant Ghirghik of possible high-tech weapons in hannie hands had been enough to make Fraser worry about further contact. Add the almost tangible presence of Zhairhee, the garrison city now no more than three hundred kilometers to the northeast....

It hadn't been easy to get to sleep despite his fatigue. These incoming aircraft made the unit's prospects that much more bleak.

Legionnaire Russo and Subaltern Bartlow were huddled close over one of the video displays when Fraser entered the C^3 compartment. Warrant Officer Hamilton was at another terminal.

"Confirming now," Hamilton said without looking up. "Tornado tactical support aircraft. Prop-driven. One pilot. External bomb racks and twin HMGs."

"How many have we got on the screen?" Fraser asked.

Bartlow straightened up with a look of relief. "Twelve, sir," he said. "We've got the drone pacing them now."

"Pacing them?" Fraser bit back a curse. "Russo, set the drone on a search sweep. Let's see if they've got anything else out there."

Charlie Company's C^3 tech glanced at Bartlow and nodded. "Already programmed, sir." His fingers danced over the keyboard.

"Bartlow, get on the comm panel and alert the unit. Disperse the vehicles and have the men go to ground. And tell the Sabertooth crews to get some Grendels in the air."

"Number One Sabertooth is down to four missiles, Lieutenant," Hamilton reminded him.

"I know, Mr. Hamilton," Fraser snapped. "But we can't just ignore those bastards and hope they'll go away."

"Fafnirs'll take 'em down, sir," Russo said.

Fraser nodded. "Right. Deploy the weapon's lances. But get some Grendels flying, too ... just in case. Mr. Hamilton, try to ID the base those planes came out of and give me an idea of where else the hannies might try an airstrike from."

He took Bartlow's place at the command console as the others responded to the flurry of orders. Unlike his subordinates, he had noth-ing to do now but watch the screen and the cluster of moving lights that represented the enemy.

And worry.

* * *

Legionnaire Spiro Karatsolis closed his fingers around the joystick that controlled the Grendels in the air. "That's it, baby," he said softly. "Easy ... easy ... yeah! There! Eight ... ten ... twelve of the bastards."

Bashar's voice was loud in his headphones. "Sabertooth One has targets. Repeat, Sabertooth One has target acquisition."

"Roger that," Russo replied. "Stay with them."

"What's he think I'm going to do? Shell a clump of trees?" Karatsolis adjusted the missile's course to center the native planes in the video monitor. The four Grendels were loitering over the rear of the Legion column, slaved together so that all of them responded to one joystick, using superheated air sucked through maneuvering thrusters to maintain station.

"Nah," Bashar shot back. "He's just afraid you spot a sheep and lose interest in fighting. Love at first sight, or something." The Turk dropped the bantering tone abruptly. "Fafnirs in the air."

Karatsolis checked his sensor display. "Got 'em," he said. "Tracking ... targets are breaking formation."

The native aircraft dropped out of their tight welded-wing grouping, scattering. On the sensor display the pattern of moving traces swirled in a confusing dance, targets, rockets, and Grendel missiles dodging and weaving together.

"Damn!" That was Legionnaire Ignaczak in the second Sabertooth. "Looks like they're learning. I read two planes playing decoy for the others. What do you think, Spear?"

"Concur," Karatsolis replied tersely. His fingers were running over the terminal keyboard, programming new instructions. Two hundred meters above the forest floor and two kilometers away, the four Grendel missiles responded to the new commands. Their thrusters revectored to channel the air streams aft, and rocket burners cut in to add more speed. Like the hannie planes, the Grendels dropped out of formation, no longer slaved to a common controller. Each had a separate target now among the native aircraft that had not received attention from any of the Fafnirs. At the same time, Karatsolis knew, Ignaczak would be setting up similar programs for Sabertooth Two's five Grendels.

"Targets locked in," Ignaczak reported. "Missiles running."

"That'll teach the primmie bastards not to mess with the Legion," Bashar said.

"New targets! New targets!" That was Russo, a nervous edge in his voice. "Another flight. Coordinates feeding now!"

"Goddamn!" Ignaczak shouted. "Where'd the buggers come from?"

Karatsolis checked the computer feed with a sinking feeling. "Hedgehopped in on us," he said. The coordinates told the story. While the first hannie flight made its approach openly, more aircraft had circled wide, skimming just above treetop level, unobserved by Legion sensors. "Those primmie bastards know what they're doing, Bashar."

"Fafnirs, prepare new fire mission," Russo was saying. "Sabertooths, report status."

"Sabertooth One dry," Karatsolis reported.

"Number two, four missiles left," Ignaczak added. "Plotting fire program."

"Wait one."

On his screen, Karatsolis saw the first lights winking out as the Legion missiles found their targets. Usually a successful strike gave him a lift, an almost sexual release. This time it left him cold.

The monkeys had outmaneuvered the Legion. What else were the hannies planning to throw at them?

Fraser stared at the tactical screen, his stomach a hard knot. The second hannie attack wave was bearing down on the Legion column from the east. That second attack group had probably come from Zhairhee, skimming in at treetop level to avoid detection as long as possible. With missile reloads running low, it was going to take every bit of luck the Terrans could muster to meet the new threat.

They were already banking too heavily on luck as it was. The drone's search sweep had brought the enemy formation in view with bare minutes to spare.

Damn! If Bartlow had set up the search sweep right away...! But Bartlow had made a natural mistake. He was inexperienced.

Anyway, blaming the kid wouldn't change things. Fraser was CO, not Bartlow, and in the end it was Fraser who was really responsible.

"Fafnirs have fired, sir," Russo announced. The traces appeared on the monitor at almost the same moment.

Hamilton leaned over the back of Fraser's chair. "They're breaking formation again," he said, pointing. "Somebody in that bunch of monkeys has been going to school, Lieutenant. That kind of wild weasel maneuver would only be useful against high-tech weapons. The lokes never had to deal with homing missiles before."

Fraser glanced up at him. "Sounds like Ghirghik was right, then. Do you think there might be Semti behind this?"

"Could be. The monkeys are getting tips on how to handle our technology from somewhere. They knew enough to dodge the remote sensors around the Enclave ... and they didn't seem very frightened of *Ganymede*. Like they knew she was unarmed."

"Yeah." Fraser stared at the screen a moment longer. "Russo, tell Sabertooth Two to launch Grendels."

"It won't be enough," Hamilton said quietly.

"I know. But we have to cut down the odds somehow." He scowled. The trees here were thick enough to make maneuvering difficult. Could a Sabertooth swing around and bring down the intruders with plasma fire? That had worked in Fort Monkey ... but there had been room to move there. The jungle canopy would make it hard to track the aircraft, too ... though it might also give the Legion vehicles some cover.

Cut down the odds....

"Tell Sabertooth One to circle to the east side of the column and give us some cover fire," he ordered. "And get some more Fafnirs up, for God's sake!"

Russo shot him a worried look. Fraser took a deep breath, fighting for calm. He knew there was a panicky edge to his voice, and he had to get it under control. The unit needed a leader.

The unit needed *him*.

* * *

Zeeraij Kyindhee yanked hard on the control stick and the agile *Aghyiir* fighter-bomber climbed and banked, its overstrained engine screeching in protest. Kyindhee blinked as a brilliant flare of light engulfed squadron-leader Wyjlin's aircraft. Turbulence from the explosion made the *Aghyiir* buck like a maddened *zymlat*.

Kyindhee steadied the aircraft and adjusted course. Glancing up to the top of the cockpit canopy, ky took note of the digital readout on the face of the tiny black box fastened there in a hastily improvised mounting. The alien devices had only been installed a few days before as part of the *Asjyai's* program for driving out the demon Terrans. Rumor in the barracks claimed that the devices had been smuggled into Dryienjaiyeel by the Ancients themselves.

Kyindhee could well believe it. The device was like some kind of magic, able to locate a target from a great distance and guide kys plane toward it even when jungle obscured the view. And it would, so kys superiors said, gauge the aircraft's speed, range, and bearing precisely to tell the pilot the exact moment to release the bomb load slung on each wing.

A magical device, like having a co-pilot or a bombardier on board ... but without the extra weight and loss of maneuverability larger crews entailed.

The instructions called for the pilot to lock out signals from other, extraneous targets before commencing the final bomb run, to keep the device from becoming confused. Kyindhee reached up and touched the stud at the bottom of the box and watched the numbers flash in a brilliant shade of amber.

Ky pushed the stick all the way forward, and the fighter-bomber dipped low toward the jungle below. Kyindhee's left hand hovered over the bomb release as the pilot watched the countdown.

Four ... three ... two ... one ...

Kys finger jabbed the button, and twin 48-*yüz* bombs tumbled from the bomb rack.

A plasma flare consumed Kyindhee's aircraft three seconds later.

*   *   *

"Bomb release! Get clear! They targeted us!" Fraser barely had time to react to Hamilton's shout before the first blast rocked the command van. The shock threw him against the rear wall, knocking the wind out of him. He staggered, bracing himself against the door leading back into the troop compartment.

Hamilton and Russo were on their feet now, struggling to maintain their balance as the uneven motion of the APC continued. The C^3 technician pushed Fraser through the door as the second explosion went off.

This time the hit was much closer, tearing through the armor of the front left side of the vehicle. Fraser had a confused impression of screams from the driver's cab.

Hamilton lurched against him, his mouth wide in mingled pain and astonishment. A trickle of blood ran down his chin as the warrant officer sagged to the metal floor plates.

A shard of metal the size of a regulation bayonet protruded from Hamilton's back just above his heart.

Fraser stared numbly at the dying man until Russo took him by the arm and hurried him through the rear ramp door.

*   *   *

Legionnaire Karatsolis heard the servomotors whine in protest as the Sabertooth's turret spun in search of a new target. "I've lost the feed from command!" he shouted.

"Yeah." Bashar's voice sounded calm, almost flat, in his headphones. "Looks like they took a hit. Switch to onboard sensors."

"What'd'ya think I'm doing, man?" Karatsolis squinted at his targeting screen, trying not to think of what would happen if Lieutenant Fraser was dead. The lieutenant hadn't been much of a replacement for Captain LaSalle so far, but the alternative wasn't pleasant—three subalterns or a Navy combat engineer.

Demi-Battalion Alice needed a leader with some kind of experience ... even if he was still learning, like the lieutenant. At least Fraser had started to understand his job.

This deep in hostile territory, they couldn't afford to start breaking in a new commander. Not again.

"Look alive, Spear!" Legionnaire Ignaczak's voice was static-crusted. "Multiple targets headin' your way!"

He noted the blips at almost the same moment and smiled grimly as one faded out, smashed by plasma cannon fire from Ignaczak's FSV-2. "Hammer 'em, Zak!"

He swiveled the turret again, letting off a string of rapid-fire bursts from his own gun. Each shot filled the turret with noise, the metal-on-metal clang as the solid steel round slammed into the chamber, counterpointing the raw noise of the ammo being superheated and then flung from the barrel by intense gauss fields, so hot it made the very air screech with its passage. Another hannie plane vanished from the screen. In his mind's eye, Karatsolis could visualize the plasma fireball engulfing a fragile native aircraft.

A cluster of smaller blips detached themselves from the main targets at the same instant. The plasma cannon thundered twice more as he tried to center on the arcing bombs, but though another enemy plane vanished the deadly ordnance escaped his fire.

"Rev us up, Bashar!" he yelled. "Let's get the hell out of here!"

He fired again, the noise of the shot drowning out the whining fans as Bashar banked the FSV and accelerated. Karatsolis braced himself against the motion and stabbed the button controlling the turret motors again.

Then the Sabertooth rocked and swayed with a sickening lurch. Karatsolis was slammed back into his seat by the force of the motion.

"Hang on to your lunch, Spear!" Bashar called.

The legionnaire was about to shout a properly wisecracking reply when another blast caught the fast-moving vehicle from behind, slewing the FSV sideways. His head cracked hard against a projecting bit of hardware. Dazed, Karatsolis tried to clear his blurred vision. A warm trickle of blood ran down behind his left ear.

The pitch of the fans changed again just as a third explosion shook the Sabertooth.

"I can't hold her!" Bashar yelled, all trace of his earlier calm gone. "We'll—"

The FSV rammed into something hard and came to a shuddering halt. Even from the turret Karatsolis could tell that the Sabertooth had lost a magrep module in the crash. The front of the vehicle was tilting crazily to the right where the magnetic suspension had collapsed. The *Angel of Death* was listing like a boat taking on water from a hole in the bow.

"Bashar?" He felt groggy, disoriented.

Silence ... then a groan from the driver's cab.

And a crackle of shorting electrical systems, a tang of ozone in the stale air of the vehicle.

Hurriedly he punched the release on his seat harness and dropped through the hatch from the turret into the cramped center section of the chassis. His head was throbbing where he'd hit it, but Karatsolis ignored the pain and forced his eyes to focus as he squeezed past the heavy machinery that drove the turret and into the driver's cab.

Sparks leapt from a half-dozen places on the control panel. He wrestled a portable extinguisher from the rack behind Bashar and sprayed fire-retardant foam on the damaged panels, then unsnapped the driver's harness. Bashar groaned again, but didn't move. There was a gash over his eye.

Karatsolis jabbed at the hatch release button, but the clash of grinding gears told him the mechanism was damaged. With a savage curse he reached up for the manual control lever. It took every ounce of strength to free it, and the effort made his head spin. Somewhere in the back of his mind a tiny voice was screaming, urging him to get clear before the hannies dropped more bombs on the helpless Sabertooth.

But he wasn't going to abandon Bashar.

All at once the lever unlocked and the hatch beside Bashar's seat sprang open a few centimeters. Karatsolis braced against it and pushed, and it reluctantly swung up and back. Breathing hard, the legionnaire pushed the Turk through the hatch, then followed. A choking cloud of smoke made him gag.

Then he was clear of the wrecked FSV, inhaling deep breaths of hot, humid, but blessedly clean air. Bashar groaned again and tried to sit up.

"What the hell...?" the corporal asked groggily.

Karatsolis knelt beside him. "I always knew you slept through MOS school," he said, trying to maintain the traditional banter. "Look what you did to the *Angel,* city boy!"

The FSV's front and right side were burnt and pitted where the first near miss had caught it. With the magrep module out, the vehicle was canted steeply, the rear still floating on magnetic suspension, but half the front smashed up against an embankment.

"Medic!" A legionnaire was shouting as he appeared beside the two FSV crewmen. "Hey, Watts! Two wounded over here!"

Karatsolis raised a cautious hand to the side of his head. It came away sticky with blood. He stared at it for a long moment.

Somehow the loss of the *Angel of Death* was the worst wound by far.

* * *

Fraser waved away Dr. Ramirez impatiently. "I'm all right, Doctor," he snapped. "See to the ones who really need your help."

Ramirez gave a reluctant nod and turned away. The Padre trailed after him with a mournful look that spoke volumes. Father Fitzpatrick would be administering the last rites many more times this day.

"What's the damage, Gunny?" Fraser asked Trent. The sergeant had arrived as if from nowhere moments after Russo, Fraser, and the other survivors from the command van had staggered out through the rear ramp door. Even Trent looked shaken.

"Three vehicles out, L-T," Trent said. "The command van, of course. One of the FSVs ... and one of the vans carrying the wounded took a direct hit, too." A spasm of pain crossed the sergeant's face.

"Damn ..." Fraser looked away. "How many casualties?"

"We're still checking, L-T. Except for the wounded, not too many. Bashar and Karatsolis got out of the *Angel* after she was hit, and luckily the weapons squad had already dismounted before the hannies hit us."

"How the devil did the bastards hit us that hard?" Fraser demanded, more to himself than to Trent. "That primmie junk shouldn't have done this much damage!"

"Probably some kind of simple targeting computer," Trent replied. "The planes that released their bombs knew exactly when to turn 'em loose."

"But they didn't get their licks in cheap," Kelly Winters added from behind the sergeant. "The other Sabertooth knocked out the rest of their planes before they could make another pass or cut and run."

"Yeah." Trent spat expressively. "I'll bet we killed every plane they had that was rigged with those damn computers."

"Let's hope so, Gunny," Fraser replied wearily. "Because another attack like that one could finish us off for sure."

Chapter Sixteen

Their graves mark the sites of each night's halt.

—Captain Roulet writing of the Madagascar campaign, French
Foreign Legion, 1895

"**Y**ea, though I walk through the valley of the shadow of death, I will fear no evil: for thou art with me; thy rod and thy staff they comfort me."

Lieutenant Colin Fraser shifted uncomfortably as the Padre read the psalm. The assembled legionnaires filled the clearing, but the silence was broken only by Fitzpatrick's soft, lilting voice as they paid their last respects to the comrades who had lost their lives in the hannie bomb strike.

Fraser stole a glance at the shrouded forms lined up at the edge of the mass grave the company had prepared. Fifteen men had died in the attack. He had hardly known any of them, and the realization made him feel guilty.

Donald Hamilton, for instance … the young warrant officer had probably saved Fraser himself from the metal shard that killed him. It was only afterwards that Fraser had heard Hamilton's friend, Vandergraff, telling Fitzpatrick about the man's hopes and dreams. Hamilton had volunteered for duty with the Legion right out of college, planning to get a tour on the frontiers under his belt before trading in his Specialist's Warrant for a regular officer's commission. Apparently the man had been regarded as a prime candidate for rapid promotion within the Commonwealth Army intelligence staff, the same department Fraser himself had once been assigned to.

Or Platoon Sergeant Persson, who had been in the command van's forward compartment alongside the driver, Hengist, when the explosion tore through the front of the vehicle. "Swede" Persson's confidential records showed that he had volunteered for the Legion as an alternative to being sent to a penal battalion after killing three civilians in a drunken brawl in a Triton Systerm dive. Persson had been disagreeable, unpopular ... but a good soldier. A good legionnaire.

One man looking to the future, the other fleeing from the past. The Legion had been a home to both. And the rest of the dead were just as much of a mixed bag: the sentry who had been stabbed half a dozen times in the throat and chest during the first native attack on Fort Monkey ... the legionnaire from Charlie Company who lost an arm in the fighting around Shelton's Head ... the Navy man injured in the *Ganymede* crash. Death had claimed them all here on this remote world.

Fitzpatrick had closed his Bible now, but the burial service was still going on. Fraser wondered how many more times he would have to witness funerals like this one before Demi-Battalion Alice reached safety at last. Ten percent casualties from this one bomb attack....

And close to a thousand kilometers to go before they reached the frontier.

He felt the weight of his burden as the unit's commander like a tangible thing pressing on his shoulders. Those men had died, and as their leader he bore the responsibility for their deaths.

What could I have done differently? he asked himself bitterly. *What can I do differently the next time, to keep these men alive?*

They had a long march ahead of them, and Fraser knew there was sure to be a next time.

What he didn't know was whether he would be able to see this journey through to the end.

* * *

Slick felt the tension in the crowd as the Padre sketched out the Cross and signed for the assembly to bow their heads in prayer. He went through the motions of the ceremony, but inside he was wishing they would finish the funeral quickly.

The sight of those bodies in the pit brought back too many memories of battle and fear.

Unlike the weapons lances, Slick's unit had not been ordered to dismount during the attack. The lance had been rotated aboard the FSV crewed by Ignaczak and Sergeant Mason for a rest shift just an hour before the attack. They had ridden out the entire action in the cramped confines, deafened by the screeching plasma gun. For Slick, it had been the most terrifying combat of all, trapped in a metallic coffin and unable to take any active role in his own defense.

Somehow, *somehow* he had come through it all without breaking down. But the memory haunted him now as he thought of all those men killed when their vehicles had taken direct hits.

"In the name of the Father, and the Son, and the Holy Spirit, Amen," the Padre intoned at last with another quick sketching of the Cross.

Gunnery Sergeant Trent was stepping forward almost immediately. "Listen up! Pay your respects however you have to, but then get back to your details! I want you apes ready to mag out by 1800 hours." There was a rumble from the ranks. Trent scanned them with weary eyes. "That's 1800 hours *standard,* for those of you who were planning to make any excuses. Dismissed!"

The sergeant turned away to talk with the lieutenant and his staff as legionnaires began to disperse. Slick started to turn away, then checked the motion as Dmitri Rostov pushed past him toward the pit. The older legionnaire joined a queue, bending to pick up a handful of dirt. Curious, Slick followed him.

The line was a long one, filing slowly past the mass grave. As each man passed, he threw some dirt on the bodies. But they were mostly keeping some, too, tucking it in pockets or pouches. Near the head of the column, Corporal Strauss was opening a small vial already half full of varicolored soil and adding a little more from his hand.

"What're they doing, Rostov?" Slick asked softly. "What's with the dirt?"

Rostov looked at him with a surprised expression. "You never—?" Then he nodded. "Oh, yeah, you're still a nube. Look, kid, don't ask dumb questions if you don't like people thinking you're dumb, right?"

The line moved forward a meter or so in silence before Rostov spoke again. "It's tradition, kid. You help to bury the guys you can't take back, and you keep some of the dirt. It's how we help our buddies on their way to the Last March, y'know? Brings good luck."

"Ah, come on, Rostov," Slick said. "Don't tell me you believe in good luck charms! What kind of jerkwater planet do you come from, anyhow?"

Rostov flared. "Watch your mouth, nube!" He paused, visibly calming down. "Look, like I said, it's tradition. Legion tradition, not something from Novy Krimski. Call it what you want, but a lot of people believe in it. And it's not for some damned nube to say whether or not it's right. You get my signal, kid?"

"Yeah, sure, Rostov ... sure." Slick looked away. "It just seems kind of funny, that's all. It's not like any of those guys were part of our platoon. Or was one of them some kinda buddy of yours?"

"They're *all* my 'buddies,' nube. And yours, except you don't seem to understand it." He spat. "The Legion looks after its own. Doesn't matter if a guy's a total stranger or your tentmate for the last ten years. He's your buddy ... your comrade. And a part of the only family you've got!"

Slick had a sudden image of Billy's face as he'd seen it last, but pushed it out of his mind. How could Rostov compare some dead legionnaire with his own flesh and blood?

But he'd already angered Rostov enough. He wouldn't argue it further.

Behind them a guttural voice rumbled. "You should listen, nube."

It was Ghirghik, the Ubrenfar sergeant from Charlie Company. The huge, scaled saurian still made Slick nervous. How could you trust an Ubrenfar to be a Terran soldier?

Rostov didn't seem to share his feelings. "He's just a nube, Sarge," he said with a grin. "You should know by now that nubes don't listen."

"If they did, you Terrans would be better Warriors," Ghirghik replied. "Your Legion almost understands ... but fools like this one weaken your spirit." The Ubrenfar rounded on Slick again. "Honor your comrades, young one. The Warrior who fights without the respect of his own fights a lost battle from the beginning."

"Is that something your people teach?" Rostov asked.

The Ubrenfar showed a menacing number of teeth and gave a rumbling chuckle. "Actually, one of your lancemates shared it with me, though not in quite those words. Vrurrth. But it is very close to what our Warriors would say, if they were given to philosophy."

Rostov laughed. "I guess Warriors are a lot alike everywhere, Sarge."

"It is not something for laughter, Rostov." The Ubrenfar bent down to pick up a clod of dirt. "My people do not believe in this 'luck' you Terrans hold so dear, Rostov. But I hope none here will mind if I honor these men as you do." He shot an angry glare at Slick. "Even if some of their own kind will not."

Slick turned away before Rostov could reply.

*   *   *

Kelly Winters touched the center of the small disk clinging just behind Myaighee's ear. It came away on her finger, and the alien blinked several times.

"The ... magic is so strange," Myaighee said slowly in Terranglic. "Like a dream...."

She smiled. "It isn't magic, Myaighee. Just technology. Do you feel all right?"

The native gave a tentative nod, Terran-style. Ky was progressing well with the adchip lessons, learning Terranglic and some of the more basic Terran customs. Kelly had borrowed the chips from Father Fitzpatrick soon after Myaighee's release from the medical unit. If the native was going to travel with the Legion, it only made sense to teach ky the language. Even the rare legionnaire who bothered to study the language didn't always remember—or particularly care—that the locals wouldn't automatically understand Terranglic.

Besides, it gave Myaighee a purpose, something to keep the native from brooding about the things ky had lost.

The hannie looked longingly at the chip in Kelly's hand. She frowned and returned it to its carrying case. "That's it for today," she told ky. "I think you've had enough."

Most sentient lifeforms encountered by the Commonwealth could use adchips with remarkably little adaptation; only a radically alien intelligence was incapable of taking the direct subconscious feed and translating it into symbols the brain could comprehend. But adchip addiction was a problem in many species, and from what she had seen so far Kelly was fairly sure the *kyendyp* were particularly susceptible. An adchip could be a useful learning tool, or it could be programmed to deliver many kinds of entertainment, from role-playing games to sports to the kind of pornographic experiences most people on Terra thought of when they talked about "the adchip problem." But in any form the chip's induced dreams were a powerful lure, offering an escape from reality. Back on Earth, adchip addiction was a major social problem, exacerbated by the essentially idle welfare society that high technology and virtually unlimited resources had spawned among Terra's billions.

Kelly wasn't about to let Myaighee fall into the adchip trap. Ky had problems enough without getting lost in Dreamland.

The native was recovering from kys wounds well enough, but there were psychological scars ky might never get over. Myaighee had given up everything—home, family, kys very culture—to help Kelly escape. The native had fastened on her as kys only real friend, and she could not ignore kys need. She owed the alien her life.

But it couldn't go on like this much longer. Even though she didn't have any real job she could perform on the march, it wasn't a good idea for her to spend every waking moment helping Myaighee cope. It wasn't fair to the native to make ky so dependent upon her and her alone.

The alien had to be given something more, something to hold on to.

She had taken the matter up with Lieutenant Fraser a few days back. If he could find useful work for Myaighee to do …

"Lieutenant Winters? I hope we're not interrupting anything?"

She looked up to find Fraser behind her, with Sergeant Trent and Legionnaire Garcia. Kelly smiled. "Not at all, Lieutenant. I was just wrapping up with Myaighee here."

Fraser nodded vaguely at the native. *"Zhyinin as-wai nyijyük?"*

Myaighee replied in Terranglic. "Yes, Honored … sir. The doctor says … full recovery." Ky looked at Kelly. "Is that right?"

She nodded, hiding a smile at Fraser's ill-concealed surprise. "Something wrong, Lieutenant?"

"No. The other way around, in fact. I've been thinking about the suggestion you made the other day about finding our … guest here something to do. Sergeant Trent had some suggestions I thought we should talk over."

She glanced at Trent. He met her gaze with shuttered eyes. He probably had talked Fraser out of it, and the lieutenant was just looking for an easy way to let her down.

"I was skeptical when you first brought it up," Fraser went on. "But the sergeant here thinks now that Myaighee here can help us more than I thought."

It took several seconds for the words to sink in. Trent actually *agreed* with the suggestion?

Before she could react, Myaighee was already speaking. "Help,

Honored?" ky asked.

"That's right," Fraser said. "You see, one of the men we lost in the attack this morning was an expert advisor on your people. He gave me advice about the technical abilities of your army, about the people and politics we have to deal with. I'd like you to do the same."

"Honored ... sir, I know little about ... military. Only what I know from militia training. Very little. And technology ..." The alien crossed kys arms, the hannie *no*.

"Maybe not," Trent said. "But you must know something about politics. Even if all you have is gossip, what you know could help us."

"And we need every edge we can get," Fraser said. He glanced at Kelly. "Maybe we're asking too much, though. If you'd feel like you were betraying your people ..."

The alien crossed arms again. "It was the *Asjyai* who betrayed us," ky said bitterly. "Ky killed the *yzyeel*. Attacked the Terrans who had come in friendship."

"Then you'll help us?" Kelly asked.

Myaighee looked at her with grim, determined eyes. "Yes. Yes ... I will help." Ky hesitated, studying Fraser with the same bleak expression. "And I thank you, Honored. Lieutenant Fraser. I do not know if my help will be of value, but at least it will let me *fight back*. Thank you."

"Legionnaire Garcia will take you in hand," Fraser said. "I will want to talk with you some more later."

Garcia gestured to the native. With a single glance back at Kelly, Myaighee followed.

"Thank you, Lieutenant," Kelly said, interrupting his reverie. "And you, Sergeant. Myaighee needs this."

Fraser nodded absently. "We've got to use *all* our resources, Lieutenant." He gave Trent an odd glance and paused, apparently thinking about something completely unrelated. Finally he looked back up at her and continued. "How are you getting along, Lieutenant?"

She shrugged and gave a rueful grin. "Bored to tears, Lieutenant. And now I guess I don't even have social work to keep me busy."

"Well, I'm not sure what I can give you to do. Not much call for combat engineers out here ... not unless we can get some building supplies."

"I understand that, Lieutenant," she said. Inwardly, though, she felt empty, useless. Even Myaighee had more to contribute then she did. It surprised her to find out just how much she *wanted* to be able to help the legionnaires.

"I'm sure Miss Winters could be very useful helping Doc and the Padre with the wounded," Trent said blandly.

Fraser nodded vaguely. "Anything you can do is appreciated, Lieutenant. Meanwhile, just stick with it. We'll get clear yet."

She bit back an angry comment about nursing and women's work. It was true. Her skills weren't that useful out here. She was an outsider, not part of the Legion, and there wasn't much she could contribute apart from menial work.

At least it was *something*. "Maybe I should see if they need any help getting ready now," she said slowly. "The Padre said they lost a lot of medical supplies when the APC was hit." She stood up. "Unless you need me for something else, Lieutenant?"

"Not right now, Lieutenant," Fraser said.

She turned away, more unsure of her feelings than ever.

* * *

Fraser watched the Navy officer leave without really seeing her. The bomber attack had unsettled him, sapped what little confidence he had left, and it was hard to focus on anything beyond the certainty that the Legion's luck was sure to run out sooner or later. At each turn they had escaped total disaster … but the costs were mounting, and so were the odds against them.

Hamilton's death couldn't have come at a worse time. As they drew closer to the hannie garrison town of Zhairhee, his insights on the capabilities of the enemy would have been invaluable. Now he was dead. What kind of replacement would Kelly's alien make?

It was hard to see what good ky could really do. Certainly Myaighee lacked Hamilton's training and experience, his day-to-day study of Hanuman's cultures, technology, and politics. This palace servant … what could ky do?

But Trent seemed to think it was a good idea. "First rule of dealin' with the natives, L-T," he had said when he came to present the idea right after the funeral. "A local always understands local conditions best. Why else do you think Battalion keeps a dozen natives on *their* intel staff?"

Fraser still wasn't sure … but if Trent liked the idea, it was probably a good one. More and more Fraser was coming to realize that he needed to lean on a veteran like Trent if he was going to pull off the rest of the long march out of Dryienjaiyeel. If Trent said a native would make a good advisor, that was good enough for Colin Fraser.

Alone with Trent now, Fraser sat on a log and gestured for the sergeant to join him. "Are you sure about pushing out of here so fast, Gunny?" he asked quietly.

"Aren't you, L-T?" Trent looked surprised.

"Just ... having some second thoughts, that's all." He leaned forward. "Shouldn't we be salvaging what we can from the three wrecks? We did before."

"L-T, those bombers hurt us bad. If the hannies have any more of those things, we're in deep shit and no mistake."

"You said they didn't."

"I said they *probably* didn't," Trent corrected him. "'Probably' doesn't cut it in the field. The only thing you can be sure about is what you see and hear for yourself, L-T. If we have a chance to find out I'm wrong, it'll be too damned late for all of us."

Fraser nodded slowly. "I see your point. But if they've got more planes, they can still catch us on the march."

"Right now, sir, the only thing we can do is to *keep moving*. No matter what, we've got to keep ahead of their troops. That means we don't hold back for bombers, or patrols, or whole regiments. 'Cause if we let them catch us, we can kiss our chances of seeing home again goodbye."

"There's still Zhairhee," Fraser pointed out. "Hamilton said they were building up their forces around there."

Trent looked grim. "I know. We're just going to have to count on speed and surprise to get us past them."

"Look, Gunny ... I don't want to milk a dead sharv, but wouldn't it be a good idea to strip what we can off the command van? Try to get it running again, even? The recon drones would sure help us later on. And if we leave the van, we leave the sat link. Last time I talked to Battalion, Commandant Isayev said they were trying to bring in some extra troops. If we could wait it out, they might get a ship in here to lift us out. But only if they know where we are, what we're doing. I don't like being out of touch with HQ."

"It's your decision, L-T," Trent told him. "But do you really think the resident-general's going to risk another ship for us? We've got to proceed as if we're not getting any help. And I think every minute we're not on the march increases our risk of being caught about ten times over."

Fraser shrugged. "You're the expert, Gunny," he said at last. "Hell, you're running this show anyway."

Trent drew back. "Hang on, L-T! This is still your decision to make. If you want to strip the vehicles ..."

"Calm down, Gunny." Fraser spread his hands. "They told me in OCS to listen to what my top sergeant had to say. So ... I'm listening. We keep to the schedule."

Trent seemed to want to say more, so Fraser forestalled him. "Better make sure everybody *else* is sticking to it, too, Gunny. Report to me at 1700 hours."

"Yessir," Trent responded reluctantly.

As the sergeant left, Fraser leaned back, feeling better than he had since the bombing raid had started ... was it only this morning? As long as Trent was by his side, the burden of running the unit wouldn't push him under. Sergeant Trent was the man who could get them to safety.

If anyone could.

Chapter Seventeen

If hell falls on him, the legionnaire keeps marching.

—Lt. Colonel Magrin-Verneret,
French Foreign Legion, 1940

The terrain in the Zhairhee valley seemed to leap toward him as Fraser switched his helmet controls to the image intensification setting. With his left hand, he carefully dialed the magnification knob on the side of his faceplate until the digital setting of the unit's HUD read *x500*.

"Not much of a city," he said quietly.

Trent stirred beside him. "It's enough, L-T. Believe me, it's enough."

They were pressed flat against a steep rocky outcropping on a hilltop ledge overlooking the valley from the south. The little native, Myaighee, was crouched beside Trent, examining the scene through a pair of native-made binoculars they'd captured in a skirmish three days before. Four legionnaires from Pascali's recon lance provided unobtrusive security around the hilltop, their camouflage suits blending into the grey-orange background. Out of sight almost five kilometers away, back where the jungle cover was still thick enough to provide concealment from prying eyes, the rest of the survivors of Demi-Battalion Alice awaited their return in the unit's latest temporary camp.

Fraser studied the terrain spread out below the position. The valley was broad and level, fed by two rivers which wound down from the

Raizhee mountains and joined together just under the low rise which held the hannie city.

Much of the plain was inundated here. Myaighee had told them that this area was noted for *ylyn* farming, and Fraser could see hannies wading through the knee-deep water tending the *ylyn* paddies. A few of the large, shaggy beasts of burden the natives called *zymlats* were visible as well.

The paddies were crisscrossed by an elaborate pattern of dikes and causeways, some little more than makeshift barricades, but others supporting multi-lane highways that connected Zhairhee to the outside world. The city rose above it all like an island in the midst of a shallow sea.

Beyond the valley, no more than seventy kilometers away, the jagged peaks of the Raizhee Mountains formed a spectacular backdrop to the scene. They were steep and forbidding, higher and more treacherous than Terra's Alps. But high above Zhairhee the narrow notch of a pass was visible. Beyond lay friendly Vyujiid … and Fwynzei, the Commonwealth enclave.

Safety …

But only if the legionnaires could get past the daunting obstacle that was Zhairhee.

It had taken nearly three weeks for the unit to reach this milestone after the bombing attack, a long time for a trip of a thousand kilometers as measured on their maps. But every step of that long march had been through rugged, untamed terrain, jungles and foothills and, most recently, the wide expanse of the Jyeindyein swamp. Fraser reckoned they had covered more than two thousand klicks all told as they dodged enemy units and skirted impassable terrain in search of a reasonably safe route north.

Through it all their pursuers had never been far behind. Skirmishes with patrols had become an almost daily affair for a time, and reconnaissance planes dogged every twist and turn of their route. By taking to the swamp route they had finally left the hannie army behind; primitive tracked and wheeled vehicles simply couldn't follow magrep APCs through such terrain. By overloading the Sandrays and improvising harnesses so some of the men could strap themselves to the hulls of the carriers they'd managed to move everyone in one jump, but the extra weight made the APCs sluggish and unmaneuverable … and the legionnaires couldn't travel far in such an awkward position.

At least no further bombing attacks had been attempted during the passage of the marshes. Fraser still shuddered at the thought of the casualties they could have taken if the overloaded Sandrays had received the same kind of treatment as the lost command van.

Still, it hadn't been easy. Battle, fatigue, and mishaps on the march had reduced the unit to no more than 110 effectives, with thirty-three more too seriously wounded to march or fight. Four more vehicles had gone as well, two of them engineering vans that had just given up the ghost, the third a fabrication van taken out of action by a hannie tank in one of the running skirmishes before they had reached the swamp. The fourth, one of the precious troop carriers, had been damaged in the marsh itself after a clinging vine-like plant had fouled the fans and burned out the main rotor bearings. They were still using the APC to carry supplies. Since its magnetic suspension system was still functioning, it could be towed … but, again, it slowed the pace.

Had it not been for the knowledge that friendly territory was so close now, the survivors probably couldn't have kept on marching at all.

But there was still Zhairhee, and the disquieting reports from the first scouting party that had led Fraser and Trent to reconnoiter the valley in person.

"Take a look over there, L-T," Trent said, touching his arm. "Bearing 354. Just beyond the airfield."

Fraser shifted his view until the HUD gave the right bearing. There was a small prop-driven aircraft touching down on one of the runways, but that wasn't what Trent had been drawing attention to. What was it…?

There. Fraser's intake of breath was sharp, audible.

Just coming into view on the largest of the roads leading northward from Zhairhee a column of vehicles was rumbling slowly out of town. They were boxy, slow, mounted on wide tracks and painted a uniform greyish-orange. Fraser started counting but quickly gave up.

All-terrain transports of the Dryien army … at least enough to be carrying a full regiment. And making their way north, toward the pass. Toward the border.

"Corporal Braxton was right, then," Fraser said softly. He was sweating, and it wasn't all from the humid 30°C noontime heat.

Trent nodded. "He said three regiments went out of there yesterday … one of them armor. One more now. Good God, L-T, how many of the bastards are they sending up there, anyway?"

"More than we can break through, Gunny," he said. "Could they really be piling that many troops up there just to keep us hemmed in?"

"Doesn't make much sense, L-T," Trent replied. "I've been reading the survey reports on that pass. It's too narrow for that many troops to be used effectively. Hell, a couple of companies could hold that sucker against an army for a day or two. Four regiments would just get in each other's way."

"Hmmm. Unless ..." Fraser trailed off, watching the creeping vehicles on his II viewer.

"What is it, L-T?"

Fraser raised his faceplate and looked at the sergeant. "I'm just spinning this off the top of my head, Gunny, so bear with me. The hannies in these parts suddenly got the urge to throw out all the foreign demons, right? Killed the captain and all the diplomats they could lay their hands on, then went after us."

"Yeah." Trent lifted his own faceplate and spat expressively.

"Now we know the hannies have been getting some high-tech help, like info on our sensors and some kind of targeting gizmo. Probably Semti help, if that missile launcher Ghirghik brought in means anything."

Trent gave a slow nod. "Looks like some of our Semti buddies aren't so happy with us after all."

"Well, those ghouls would know that kicking us out of Dryienjaiyeel would just be temporary. Even if they'd wiped us out, you can bet a couple regiments will be heading south to let our monkey friends know that you don't just turn down a Commonwealth trading deal ... or kill off legionnaires. Hell, Isayev'd be leading a punitive expedition this way now if the resident-general would let him off his leash!"

"So you think ... what? That the Dryiens have something bigger in mind?" Trent frowned for a moment. Then his face went white. "Not an attack on Fwynzei, L-T?"

"Why not? It's not that far north of the pass. Push through fast enough, and the hannies just might roll over the city before the garrison could react. The commandant's got less than half a battalion of legionnaires and a regiment or two of native troops. Everything else is spread out in local garrisons. Hit hard and fast and the hannies could at least lay siege to the port, keep out anything short of an assault ship."

"Yeah, but they couldn't keep our boys out forever, L-T. And the Semti would know it."

"Mounting punitive raids to punish Zyzyiig for his little massacre is one thing. But if we have to fight the whole goddamned planet … it'd throw a murphy into our plans for this entire sector, Gunny." Fraser stabbed his finger at the enemy column. "That's an invasion force, and they're headed for Fwynzei. I'd bet my life on it."

Trent grunted. "Not a bet I'd take right now, L-T."

Myaighee shifted uneasily. "Lieutenant," ky put in softly. The native's English had improved with further language lessons, and ky wore the rank insignia of a legionnaire third class on the improvised torso armor Sergeant Forbes had assembled in the unit's surviving fabrication van. "I do not know if this information means anything, but I have been studying the unit crests on those tracks."

"They mean something special?" Trent asked.

"My … father? Yes, my father's sibling served in that unit many years ago. It is the Regiment Miststalkers. A very good unit, Lieutenant Fraser."

"Yes? So?" Fraser couldn't mask the impatience he felt.

"The unit has always been stationed at the town of Ghynjyik near the head of the Jyikeezh delta, Lieutenant. On the eastern coast. The Miststalkers are light infantry, trained to operate in the jungle s and marshes against the primitives of the inland regions." The alien trailed off, looking at Trent. "I don't know all the English words yet, Sergeant Trent. But they are very highly skilled soldiers, trained in rapid strikes, raids, operations against superior numbers …"

"Commandos," Trent said.

"That is one of the words I wanted!" Myaighee agreed. "Commandos. But the very best commandos. One of the most respected units in the army!"

"Elite troops, L-T," Trent said. "And way the hell off their regular stomping grounds. Would they bring in a unit like that to hunt for us, do you think?"

"If they were desperate enough, maybe," Fraser said without conviction. "But I think it clinches the invasion theory."

"Yeah." Trent flipped down the faceplate again and adjusted his image intensifier. "Yeah, a major mobilization on the frontier. Elite light infantry would be damned useful trying to overrun Fwynzei's defences. I think you're right on this one, L-T. Question is, what the hell do we do about it?"

"Damned if I know, Gunny," Fraser said. "But whatever we do, we've got to do it fast. Otherwise there might not be a way out even if we do get across the border."

* * *

The roar of the props diminished to a sigh as the aircraft rolled to a halt. *Asjyai* Zyzyiig unstrapped kyself awkwardly, waving away an eager staff officer who tried to help with the unfamiliar harness. Near the rear of the plane the crew chief was already unclamping the hatch.

With kys staff trailing behind, Zyzyiig stalked slowly to the opening. The wind blowing into the aircraft was uncomfortably cool, not at all like the pleasant climate of the capital. Of course Zhairhee was far more pleasant than the uplands north of the mountains, where the army was marching. It still made a distasteful contrast to the comforts of the Fortress of Heaven, though.

But with the final stages of the campaign against the offworlders beginning, it was essential for Zyzyiig to be close at hand to exercise personal control over kys troops. Otherwise, some local field commander might be in a position to claim more than kys share of the credit and threaten the fragile structure of Dryienjaiyeel's new government.

Workers were wheeling a ladder into place below the hatch. As ky had ordered, there was no ceremony being attached to the *Asjyai's* arrival. The invasion schedule must not be needlessly disrupted … and the Terrans, now that they were getting their first reports of the assault across the pass, must not have their attention drawn to unusual visits by VIPs.

Anyway, the last reports had placed the refugees from the demon Foreign Legion only a few days march to the south, in the Jyeindyein region. Best not to tempt fate. After the ill-fated bombing raid, ky had a healthy respect for what those legionnaires could do against air power.

Zyzyiig suppressed a shudder at the sight of the tall figure swathed in black robes standing near the ladder. So Shavvataaars was back from his mysterious errands.

The *Asjyai* hoped that this time the Semti would have something more concrete to give than vague warnings and obscure philosophy. Ky knew the alien would have something to say about the continued survival of the Legion. Not that they mattered now. They could never reach their friends with the Army Demonslayer between them and their compatriots at Fwynzei. Once the demons had been swept away there, the legionnaires would fall into kys hands like *ylyn* at a harvest.

Ky descended the ladder slowly, with all the dignity ky could muster. *Indjyeek* Dwyiiel, the commander of the Zhairhee garrison, stepped forward to greet Zyzyiig. From the set of the general's neck ruff, it was plain ky was agitated.

"*Asjyai* ... welcome to—"

Zyzyiig cut the officer off with crossed arms. "Never mind the pleasantries, Dwyiiel. I want a full staff meeting in one hour. And why in the name of the Eternal Mists was Regiment Blooddrinkers turned back to the south?"

"We ... we had reports of the demons moving through the marshes, Honored," the luckless commander stammered. "I thought—"

"You are not equipped to think, Dwyiiel. There are other units moving up from the capital who are tasked to deal with the demons. Regiment Blooddrinkers is needed beyond the mountains to exploit success in the attack on Fwynzei, but for that they must *cross the mountains*. Your bungling may have delayed our attack, and that could cost us this campaign." Ky looked around the ranks of junior officers around Dwyiiel. "You. You are Executive Officer of this base?"

"Yes, Honored."

"Wrong. You are commander of this base. Make sure Blooddrinkers return as soon as possible. And assign this fool to them. Ky will make an excellent scout, since ky is so good at thinking and planning."

"Yes, Honored."

Ky turned away to meet Shavvataaars as he approached. "Welcome, my Companion," the Semti whispered. As they talked, they walked together away from the cluster of officers. It would not do to have junior staffers know too much about the deeper layers of the campaign against the Terrans. "I see you are truly taking command of the situation here."

Zyzyiig studied the hooded face suspiciously. "If you are about to voice your disapproval, save your breath. I will brook no interference in my handling of my troops *this* time."

"On the contrary, Honored *Asjyai*," Shavvataaars demurred. "I am in complete agreement. The final phase of the Cleansing is at hand, and if we are to finish our burrow and set out traps, we must act swiftly and with decision."

"Then everything is prepared?"

"Everything. You will have had the reports on our agents' efforts at the pass, I believe. The traitors made sure the Vyujiid garrison offered no resistance to your lead column. There is a strong blockhouse near the head of the pass which was easily secured."

Zyzyiig made an impatient gesture. "Speak of the future, not the past, Honored."

"Very well, my Companion. Events in Vyujiid have proceeded satisfactorily. The merchants, the farmers, many of the common people are ready to throw off the demon yoke. By trying to circumvent the traditional trade routes, the demons proved the lie in their words of prosperity and social equality."

"Can we expect support in Vyujiid, then?"

"Perhaps not immediately," Shavvataaars admitted. "The demons are still regarded with great awe by the superstitious. When it is seen that they are not invincible, that they can be wounded and killed like any common mortal, then you will see support. The fall of Fwynzei will surely trigger a mass rising against the demons and their lackeys in the Imperial Government."

"If Fwynzei falls," Zyzyiig said, letting kys fears show through for a moment. "Much depends on overwhelming their garrison. Surely they have had time to detect our muster, to prepare for our attack?"

"Time they have had, my Companion, but not enough. Their garrison was not that strong to begin with—a mere battalion of their Foreign Legion, and a few regiments of native auxiliaries. Many of their units have been assigned to serve elsewhere, away from Fwynzei."

"And have these not been summoned to return?"

Shavvataaars gave a breathy, satisfied sigh. "Our sympathizers have caused many problems in the outlying garrison towns. Sabotage. Agitation. Bombings and threats of bombings. In most cases, the Terrans have not dared withdraw their garrisons, for fear it would turn the Imperial government against them. It was on their pledge of supporting the old order that the demons won the aid of Vyujiid's aristocracy, after all."

"Then perhaps we have time to prepare things further, draw off more of their strength?"

Shavvataaars replied with crossed arms. "I fear not, my Companion. Three transports carrying reinforcements are en route to the planet as we speak. I am afraid that this was one moment when fortune did not favor our plans. Their resident-general managed to divert these troops from a carriership that happened to be passing through the systerm on the way to Enkidu. Three battalions of assault troops ... a dangerous opponent. We must act before they arrive. It is a matter of days."

"Then we have to call it off!" Zyzyiig said. Ky lowered kys voice as ky realized the staff officers were looking at them curiously. "There is no margin for error ... no way to keep them from counterattacking, whatever we do at Fwynzei!"

"Now is the time of decision, *Asjyai*," Shavvataaars whispered coldly. "We must move quickly, yes, though haste is not normally wise. But the rewards if we are successful...."

"And do you have a plan to keep them from counterattacking as soon as they arrive?"

"More than one plan, my impatient Companion. More than one." Shavvataaars drew close enough for Zyzyiig to feel his foul breath on kys face. "First, these troops were not equipped to mount unsupported assaults. They are unlikely to attempt a landing in the face of opposition, remembering what your army did to the transport that tried to evacuate the demons from their enclave in the south. If they lose Fwynzei as a base, they are likely to wait in orbit until fresh ships, assault ships, can arrive. That will take many cycles, many long cycles, in which we may consolidate our hold here."

"It still sounds like a dangerous gamble...."

"Second, and far more important, you will soon have an ally with nearly the power of the Terrans and their Commonwealth. You have heard of the Ubrenfars?"

"Yes ... yes, I remember some Terran boasting over a banquet once. The Terrans outbluffed the Ubrenfars in a dispute some years ago and prevented them from encroaching into this region." Zyzyiig's neck ruff bristled. "Are these the allies you offer me? They have lost to the demons once already."

"I have been in touch with ... contacts among the Ubrenfars, my Companion. There are two of their warships in this system now. They will not act unless this world can speak with a single voice to plead for their protection, but once they hear such a voice, their government is prepared to support you here. The Terrans are unlikely to risk a war over this one planet. This time they will be the ones who will back down."

"And we exchange one set of masters for another?"

"I think not. The Ubrenfars seek only to humiliate the Terrans, to

resume their rightful place as a Great Power in this region. Your independence will be protected, no more … unless your people want more."

"So if we take Fwynzei …"

"The risings will begin in Vyujiid. And your nation in combination
with the Empire can call upon Ubrenfar support. The Terran transports
might never reach orbit, if our attack is swift enough. And decisive
enough."

"So it all comes down to a single throw of the dice, eh?"

"The Great Journey has been that since the first moments of the
coup, my Companion. Any mistake could cost all. But success …
success will spell the end of the demons on your world, and the effects
could spread outward to bring down their entire Commonwealth. But
we cannot have that success without making your gambler's throw."

Zyzyiig didn't answer the Semti. Instead, ky turned abruptly back to
face the staff officers. "Where is my car? I need to get to headquarters
now. Now! We must finish the preparations and launch the attack
immediately!"

*　*　*

Behind Zyzyiig, Shavvataaars felt a cold flush of satisfaction. The
Great Journey was rushing toward completion. Twilight Prowler would
soon be in motion.

He thought of what he had told the alien. It was the truth—as far as
it went.

But of course Zyzyiig did not need to know that success or failure
on Hanuman mattered very little to the overall plan. Once Fwynzei fell
and the rebellion began in Vyujiid, it mattered little whether the Terrans
abandoned the planet and suffered humiliation, or invested vast time
and energy reconquering the planet and exterminating the *Asjyai* and all
kys followers. Either result would set back the Commonwealth and
bring the return of the Semti to power one step closer.

Just let Fwynzei fall, and Twilight Prowler would be a complete
success, no matter what came afterwards.

CHAPTER EIGHTEEN

With or without helmet, death knows when it is your turn.

—Lt. Colonel Dmitri Amilakvari,
French Foreign Legion, June, 1942

This is it, people, so make sure everyone's set. All platoons, report readiness."

Fraser looked around the cramped interior of the engineering van that was now serving as the unit's command vehicle. It was much more cramped than the old one, with lower overheads and more massive bracing throughout. These rigs were meant for brute force construction work, not headquarters duties.

Beside him Legionnaire Garcia balanced her unfolded C^3 unit on her knees, with Russo on the other side of her helping as well as he could. Across the dim compartment WO/4 Vandergraff and Kelly Winters looked on helplessly. Myaighee, kys eyes wide, was crouched in one corner. Excited or afraid? Fraser didn't know the little alien well enough to be sure.

"First Platoon, ready," Fairfax's clipped, precise voice was the first to reply over his headphones.

"Second Platoon, set," Watanabe chimed in. The young Pacifican subaltern sounded calm and in control. He had been a tower of strength throughout the march.

"Fourth Platoon is ready." That was Sergeant Baker, nominally second in command of the provisional unit formed around the survivors of Charlie Company. Sergeant Ghirghik, along with Gunny Trent, had been assigned a special role in this operation, leaving Baker to run the platoon. Fraser didn't know much about the man, but he had decided to keep a familiar NCO in charge of the outfit.

"Third Platoon. Wait one." That was Sergeant Qazi, acting platoon leader since Subaltern Bartlow had stepped on a hannie land mine near the edge of the swamp. Bartlow was in a regen unit aboard the medical van. If they could get him to a civilized hospital facility, he might be able to walk again some day. "Third Platoon ready, Lieutenant. We've cut loose the damaged Sandray."

"Guardian ready, Alice One," Trent's voice added a moment later.

"All units," Fraser said. "Move out on my signal. Guardian, switch to channel two-nine."

"Two-niner, confirmed."

He nodded to Garcia, and there was a crackle in his headphones as she tuned in the private channel reserved for contact with the senior NCO. "Last chance for recommendations, Gunny," he said. "After this we don't get any time for new plans."

"Can't recommend anything when I don't know what we're up against, L-T. This is one where all we can do is wing it." Trent sounded tired. Fraser tried to imagine what it was like for the Gunnery Sergeant. He was strapped onto the outside of the unit's remaining FSV, his armor clipped to a ring hastily welded into the vehicle's hull the night before. It would be crowded on the back of the Sabertooth, with ten soldiers riding with him. But Trent had insisted that he needed to be outside, where he could see what was going on for himself.

"We could still send out a recon unit. Try to scout out the lay of the land, maybe knock out some of the bad guys before we make our move."

"It would be damned risky, L-T, like I said before. One slip-up and we've lost the only chance we've got."

Twenty hours had passed since Fraser and Trent had watched the column of hannie soldiers winding out of Zhairhee. Now, hidden in darkness, the Legion unit was poised near the edge of the jungle ten kilometers northeast of the city, as close to the road through the pass as they could get without breaking cover. The move had been carried out cautiously so as not to reveal the off-world presence to the patrols that were thick in the valley. Luckily, most of the Dryien attention was directed north, through the pass.

But that would change soon enough. Watanabe had gone out on patrol with one section of his platoon earlier in the evening and brought back word that there were fresh hannie troops skirting the edge of the swamp south of their last camp. The pursuers were beginning to catch up at last.

Trent had come up with this last-ditch escape plan, of course. They had already overloaded the vehicles once before, for the passage of the marshes. They could do it again tonight, counting on surprise, speed, and superior maneuverability to get them past the hannies in Zhairhee before the enemy had a chance to react.

That would probably work, Fraser conceded. It was what would happen later that worried him.

There were surely hannie troops higher up, in the pass itself … and a whole army on the other side of the mountains. Could the legionnaires break through to safety against those odds? Or could they reach a defensible spot and hold out until help arrived.

If there was any help available. Fwynzei might be a burned-out ruin by now.

"Understood, Gunny," he said at last. "But it still sounds like the cafarde to me."

"The bug's not biting me, L-T," Trent replied with a chuckle. *Le cafarde*—literally "the cockroach"—had been a part of Legion life since the pre-starflight days when the Foreign Legion was still French. Legionnaires went mad from *le cafarde*, deserting, running wild, committing suicide. "Anyway, we have to try. There are legionnaires in Fwynzei, and we can't let them down."

"Then it's settled. Switching frequencies." Fraser waited as Garcia adjusted the commlink. "All units, ready to move out."

He saw Russo speaking into another microphone, and seconds later the van was filled with the hum of the fans beginning to rev up. As the magrep fields built, the vehicle swayed slightly.

Adrenaline pumped through his veins. *This is it!*

* * *

The Sabertooth rose slowly on balanced magnetic fields, its fans roaring as the FSV gathered speed. Gunnery Sergeant Trent double-checked his harness one last time.

Beside him Legionnaire Karatsolis nudged Corporal Bashar. "Never saw the view from the outside of one of these babies," he said. "Makes a change, doesn't it, Bashar?"

Bashar spat over the side. "Just so Zak remembers we're out here. You cannon jockeys like to play with the turret controls too much."

Some of the other legionnaires clinging to the hull laughed, but Trent saw a few of them looking up nervously at the looming bulk of the turret.

"Hey, Corp," someone said. "Is it too late to tear up those re-enlistment papers I signed last month?"

Corporal Pascali chuckled. "All you gotta do is get to Fwynzei, Reuss. They probably lost your papers down in Personnel and are just waiting to get you in to fill out a new set."

Trent tuned out the chatter and tried to scan the terrain ahead. He knew a lot of noncoms, especially from the Commonwealth Regulars, who wouldn't tolerate talking in the ranks under conditions like these. But it kept up morale and helped the others keep their minds off what might happen in the next few hours … the next few minutes, even.

Anyway, these were legionnaires. Regular Army standards hardly applied to *them*.

The streamlined bulk of APC Number Two flashed past the FSV. Trent squinted at it through light intensifiers. Ghirghik, the Ubrenfar platoon sergeant, was crouched just behind the vehicle's CEK turret. A mix of legionnaires from recon and heavy weapons lances were clustered around him.

These two vehicles and forty-one soldiers were the vanguard of the column, the all-important strike force that would smash through the enemy defenses so the rest of the company could pass. They had been deliberately overloaded, but the troops they were carrying were the best equipped for the kind of fighting they'd be doing. It had to be hit-and-run tactics this time around: smash through anything in the way and keep going, no matter what. These two lead vehicles were a little slower than the rest, but they'd taken a good head start. As they cleared the way, the rest of the column would catch up and push on.

Or so everyone hoped. It wouldn't take much to derail the plan entirely, and once the legionnaires were bogged down the game would be over.

Almost side-by-side now, the two Legion vehicles raced over the dark, misty surface of the *ylyn* paddies. That was one advantage they had, at least. Any native transportation fast enough to keep up with them would be limited to the network of causeways and roads, while the legionnaires could cross the waterlogged fields at will.

But the rising ground on the upper end of the valley funnelled everything into the one north-south road that wound up toward the pass above. That was critical. They could reach the road by way of the relatively safe paddies, but once they were on that road they'd be almost as badly hemmed in by the rugged terrain as the natives.

That was why surprise was so essential. They couldn't allow the hannies to prepare.

He spared a glance over his shoulder. The rest of the Legion APCs were breaking from the cover of the jungle now. Ten left, aside from the two in the vanguard, and three of those probably wouldn't make it all the way to the top of the pass. They'd lost half their strength over the course of the march, and the men and machines that were left were near the breaking point.

Trent hoped Lieutenant Fraser wouldn't hesitate when the battle started. If Trent's men ran into trouble, the lieutenant's natural instinct would be to try to support them. That would be fatal.

The Legion looks after its own. Maybe Fraser had learned the lesson too well. But there were more legionnaires on the other side of those mountains, and it was just possible Bravo Company could still help *them*—provided Fraser kept his priorities straight.

He looked ahead again. The main road was much closer now. They might make it all the way out of the valley undetected....

As if to mock the hopeful thought, a piercing wail lifted from the direction of Zhairhee, shattering the night. An alarm siren.

They'd been spotted.

*　*　*

The shriek of the alarm siren interrupted *Asjyai* Zyzyiig as ky was debriefing the pilots who had been flying reconnaissance beyond the pass throughout the previous afternoon. The noise made kys ruff bristle. What could be happening at this late hour that would make the guards sound the alarm?

Fear gripped kys bowels. Could it be a demon attack? Had Shavvataaars been wrong in his estimate of when their reinforcements would arrive?

An aide rushed into the conference room ky had appropriated for planning. "*Asjyai!* The sentries on the northern perimeter report demon vehicles crossing the farmlands!"

It was true! Ky slammed a fist against the table. "Why weren't they spotted sooner?"

"They ... they were hidden, *Asjyai*," the junior officer stammered. "In the jungle. They must have approached under cover."

"What about our air defences? Do you mean they can move at will over the mountains and not be seen?"

The aide stared at Zyzyiig uncomprehending. "But ... but *Asjyai* ... these did not cross the mountains! They are the demons from the south, the ones who escaped."

The legionnaires! Zyzyiig turned a baleful stare on kys subordinate. "Am I one of the Ancients, to know your mind without speech? Never mind. Are you sure of this?"

"Y-yes, *Asjyai*," the officer replied. "One of their vehicles was recognized. It has the markings of the unit from the Demon Plateau. There is one less vehicle than our last intelligence report estimated, but ..."

"Enough! I will join you in the command center shortly. Meantime, order the Regiment Blooddrinkers to resume march immediately, and turn out the garrison." Ky could barely suppress the fury building within. *Their damned Foreign Legion again! What would it take to stop them?* "And pass the word to all checkpoints to be ready. I want them stopped—stopped, do you understand me?—no matter what it costs! Before they escape again!"

* * *

Spiro Karatsolis hefted the bulk of the FE-MEK and checked his magazine. It felt strange to be strapped to the hull of the speeding Sabertooth instead of cocooned within the armored security of the turret.

At least he'd acquired a decent weapon. The MEK had belonged to Legionnaire Verdura, but he had been stung by a spineleech crossing the marshes. Before he'd died he'd given his weapon to Karatsolis and his armor to Bashar, who shared his short, squat built. Verdura had been a magger once, before getting busted and transferred to an infantry outfit. He'd understood how Karatsolis and Bashar felt.

The Sabertooth's fans changed in pitch as the FSV nosed over the embankment onto the broad causeway that carried the north-south road over the *ylyn* paddies. Up ahead there were brilliant points of light strobing in the darkness marking hannie gunners. A bullet *pinged* against the front of the turret.

Bashar returned fire with a short burst from his FEK. Then the Turk switched from needle rounds to his grenade launcher, and a ripple of explosions lit up the ragged line of natives ahead.

"Easy on the grenades, Bashar," Corporal Howell admonished. "Make 'em last."

They had plenty of ammo for their Gauss weaponry; it was easy enough to fabricate the metallic slivers in the workshop van. But grenades were running short after the weeks of skirmishing.

"Fireball!" Sergeant Trent shouted.

Karatsolis reacted quickly, cutting in the polarizer in his helmet display. A moment later, Trent fired his rocket pistol into the air. The projectile rose quickly and burst, briefly turning night into day. For the legionnaires, prepared by his warning, the flare was a momentary incon-venience. Hopefully the hannies would find it much more of a handicap.

The Sabertooth's plasma cannon pulsed with an ear-tearing shriek of searing air and another blinding flash of light. Karatsolis, crouched on the other side of the turret, could still feel the heat of the shot washing past him. A hannie machine-gun nest up ahead vanished in flame and smoke.

"Pour it on!" Trent called.

Legionnaires braced against hull and harnesses and began to fire as the FSV raced toward the hannies. Karatsolis swung the MEK in a wide arc, the trigger held down to fire continuously. The flare was beginning to fade now, but he could still see the natives running, twisting, falling under the onslaught. One hannie with a bulky weapon, possibly one of their blunderbuss rocket launchers, was lifted from the ground and hurled backward five meters by the MEK fire. Ky toppled over the edge of the causeway with a splash.

For the first time since losing the *Angel* Karatsolis felt alive. After the long days of marching and evading and hiding, the pure rush of adrenaline was a welcome relief from the boredom that so often bred *le cafarde*. A legionnaire lived for battle.

Now they were rushing past the enemy troops, hurtling toward the rising ground of the pass. He had a confused glimpse of scattering hannie infantry being mowed down by the withering fire from the two vanguard vehicles, of a native tracked APC with smoke boiling from a hole where an onager had sliced through its armor. Then there were no more targets to fire at.

Karatsolis heard a complaining *click-click-click* sound that stopped as he released the trigger. Only then did he realize that he had burned up the entire five-hundred-round drum.

It had taken less than half a minute from the time Trent had fired the flare.

As he replaced the spent drum, he saw the Sandray carrying Sergeant Ghirghik's part of the vanguard pull past the Sabertooth. A couple of legionnaires waved nonchalantly. Bashar was waving back, and some of the men were cheering.

Karatsolis peered over the top of the turret and felt the enthusiasm of the first, easy victory ebbing. Up ahead, the hannies were preparing a more elaborate welcome.

The last of a double line of squat tracked vehicles was slowly taking up position blocking the road. He scanned the terrain with a sinking feeling. The hannie who had arranged this roadblock knew kys stuff, all right. On either side of the road fast-rising slopes would hamper the Terran APCs as much as any of the local vehicles. They would have to go through that barrier ... and Karatsolis wasn't sure they could break through this time.

$*\quad*\quad*$

Slick clung to his harness straps and tried to keep his head down as the APC gathered more speed. Around him his lancemates and some of the other soldiers clinging to the manta shape of the vehicle were keeping up a desultory fire against the hannies behind the barricade, but Slick's rifle remained unused at his side.

The Ubrenfar sergeant was scanning the barricade through his LI display. "Full revs, Singh!" he called to the Sandray's driver. "We have to get through those tracks!"

Nearby, Legionnaire DuPont raised his head for a quick look. "Come on, Sarge! You don't think we can make it in one piece, do you? Those carriers look *heavy*."

"Ve haf to try," Strauss said heavily.

"All right, listen up!" Ghirghik said harshly. "I do not know if the Sandray can take it or not, but we are going to break that barricade no matter what! It is the only way the others will have a chance to reach the pass!"

A blinding flare of light seared past them as the Sabertooth opened fire on the barricade from behind and to the left. Slick glanced back. Beyond the FSV the other vehicles were beginning to climb onto the causeway.

"Remember," Ghirghik continued. "If the APC cannot go on, dismount. Try to get aboard the other vehicles as they break through. You will have only one chance. The column will not stop if you are left behind."

"And meanwhile, keep those hannie bastards from forming up," Corporal Braxton, the leader of the Third Platoon's recon lance, added sharply. "We've got a lot of buddies counting on us this time."

Slick closed his eyes. They all sounded so coldblooded. How could they talk about it so calmly?

There was a distant hammer of machine-gun fire, the terrifying sound of bullets rattling off the hull. DuPont rose to take a shot with his laser rifle but never finished the motion. He jerked back against the harness with half his face torn away below the visor of his helmet. The rifle spun lazily end over end, hitting the pavement far behind the speeding vehicle. Sickened, Slick turned his head.

The Sandray slammed into the barricade with a bone-wrenching force that stunned Slick. He was only vaguely aware of the sounds of gunfire, of screams and shouted orders and the jibbering calls of the enemy.

"Come on, nube! Cut yourself loose!" That was Rostov, shaking him. "Move it or you'll miss the shuttle, kid!"

His hands fumbled at the harness snaps as he tried to clear his head. The strap came free and Slick half jumped, half slid to the pavement. The APC had smashed all the way through, pushing two bulky native carriers out of line. Now it hung in the air, bow down, one fan still whining as it pushed the vehicle uselessly against one of the enemy tracks. The rear ramp was down, and members of Dmowski's weapons lance were already scrambling out even as the rear magrep modules failed and the Sandray collapsed to the ground with a crash.

Another enemy vehicle erupted in fire as the Sabertooth's plasma cannon pulsed. Then the FSV brushed past the burning hulk, widening the gap. Hands reached down to help legionnaires scramble aboard. Slick saw Corporal Braxton make it up, shouting encouragement to the others as the FSV plowed ahead.

A hannie appeared from out of nowhere, kys rifle blazing. Bullets slammed into Slick's chest armor, and he staggered back. He brought his FEK up and squeezed the trigger. The native's scream seemed to go on and on.

Rostov dropped to one knee beside him and fired a three-round grenade burst into the open rear door of the nearest hannie track. Flame shot from the hatch, and Slick could hear Rostov's satisfied grunt over his headphones. Then the demo expert fired again, and again.

The fourth time he pointed the weapon, nothing happened. Rostov cursed at the empty magazine and shifted back to needle ammo.

"Here comes the lieutenant!" someone shouted. Slick looked up in time to see the line of fast-moving Sandrays racing toward the breach in the barricade. He started forward to join the cluster of legionnaires. Something soft caught his foot and he tripped. For an agonizing, long moment he spun around, desperately trying to keep his balance. A shooting pain in his right leg made him twist again. Then he fell, sprawling painfully on the road.

The first vehicle barely slowed as it came through, but several legionnaires managed to scramble aboard. The wind from its roaring fans was hot as it went past Slick. Groaning, he got to his knees. There was blood all over one leg, and his foot and ankle hurt, but the blood was thinner, lighter in color than it should have been. It took long seconds for Slick to realize that the blood had come from the body of the hannie soldier he'd tripped over. His own leg throbbed but seemed intact. Meanwhile, two more vehicles shot past.

He got up carefully, trying not to put any weight on the injured limb, then limped toward the breach awkwardly. Slick saw Rostov and Strauss clinging to the side of the medical van as it passed him. Rostov shouted something he couldn't make out. Only a few more APCs to go....

He tried to hurry, and that sent him sprawling again. Suddenly strong arms were lifting him, holding him, urging him forward while supporting his weight. The rough, dry, scaly hide, almost black with glistening highlights in this darkness, could only be Ghirghik's.

"Help him!" the Ubrenfar shouted. Slick felt himself being half-pushed, half-thrown. More hands closed around his dangling harness straps and his outstretched hands, hauling him aboard the engineering van. Legionnaire Vrurrth held on to him while someone else hooked his harness to a nearby ring.

"Ghirghik!" Slick gasped. "Where—?"

"He didn't make it," a legionnaire said quietly.

Slick looked back. There were no more vehicles behind this one … only a single dinosaurian figure towering above a swarm of hannie soldiers, wielding his broad-bladed knife as he howled a discordant battle song.

Chapter Nineteen

The mountain barred our way. The order was given to pass, nevertheless. The Legion carried it out.

—Inscription at the Foum-Zabel tunnel, Morocco French Foreign Legion, 1928

Two kilometers below the crest of the Zhairhee Pass, the Legion APCs clustered under the sheer rock face of a hundred-meter cliff. Legionnaires unstrapped their harnesses and dismounted to stretch weary muscles but kept their weapons close at hand and their senses alert for danger.

Inside Fraser's improvised command van, worried faces studied a holographic map of the pass.

"I don't see any other way, L-T," Trent was saying. "We can't just bull our way through, the way we did down below."

"I agree," Fraser answered, studying the glowing image. "With the blockhouse sitting there at the very narrowest point, and that sharp jog just beyond, we'd be dead meat. As soon as a Sandray slowed down to take the curve those bastards could nail it."

"Right," Trent said, nodding. "And don't forget they could have more of those missile launchers like Ghirghik found. Or tanks. I'm afraid the only way we're getting through is to try a fast sneak. Over the cliffs and down with the recon lances. Grab the blockhouse and we've got a fighting chance of getting through."

"Timing'll be damned tight, though," Fraser pointed out. "You know they'll be ordering troops up from Zhairhee soon enough. If they catch us here before you have the blockhouse secured …"

Kelly Winters spoke up from the other side of the compartment. "You could try to slow them down, Lieutenant. Some demo charges on the cliff would bring down enough debris to block the pass for days."

Trent scowled. "No way," he said bluntly.

"Why not, Sergeant?" she asked stubbornly. "Look, I may not know much about infantry tactics, but I'm a trained sapper. I know what a good dose of PX-90 up on that cliff will do."

"I'm not disputing it, ma'am," Trent said patiently. "But we don't have time to do that kind of demo work. Their lead elements will be knocking on our door here in an hour or two."

"Can you pull off your op that fast, Gunny?" Fraser asked.

Trent shrugged. "I'd better. Just to make sure, though, set the Sabertooth at the rear of the column and have Zak take a few potshots down the road. I guarantee those monkeys'll think twice before they push too hard."

Kelly seemed about to say something, then stopped. Fraser glanced at her. "If the blockhouse can't be taken, we might have to try the lieutenant's idea."

"Better hope you don't have to, L-T," Trent answered sourly. "'Cause if we get trapped up here we're in a hell of a lot of trouble."

"Sarge, if a couple of Sandrays tried to get past the blockhouse about the time you were ready to make your move, wouldn't that help the odds a little?" Sergeant Mason, senior NCO of the transport section since the death of Swede Persson, leaned forward and spoke for the first time. "Maybe that would give you the edge you need to take 'em."

Trent looked at him. "Yeah, but it would be suicide for whoever was aboard them. We don't have time for the kind of remote-control games Garcia and I pulled back at Fort Monkey."

"You won't find no shortage of volunteers, Sarge. Just say the word."

"Wait a minute," Fraser said, holding up his hand. "I'm not asking anybody to run that kind of risk…."

"Let's face it, L-T," Trent replied. "Right now we're *all* running a risk here. And Mason's right about getting an edge out of it. Our hannie friends up there will be expecting somebody to try to break past 'em. I kind of like to give an enemy just what he's expecting …

only not quite the way he's expecting it. That way the bad guys usually get to die happy."

There were chuckles around the map. Fraser looked away for a long moment.

"All right," he said at last. "If you think it's worth the risk, Gunny." He turned to Mason. "Pick the two Sandrays least likely to make it out of the mountains. Volunteer drivers for each. *Volunteers,* though, got it? None of this 'you just volunteered for the job' crap."

"Yessir," Mason said.

"All right, gentlemen," Fraser went on. "Let's get this thing into orbit, shall we?"

* * *

Slick winced as the doctor's fingers probed around the swelling over his injured ankle. Ramirez gave a satisfied nod.

"A sprain, nothing worse," he said. "It will clear up in a day or two if you keep this on it."

"This" was a tube 12 centimeters long which the doctor was clamping over Slick's leg as he continued. "Keep the regen cast on until the diagnostic light turns green," he said. "It will give you the support you need for limited movement, and it will stimulate the healing process. Don't try running or anything really strenuous for a while, though."

Slick nodded, gritting his teeth a little as Ramirez adjusted the fit. The regen cast began to hum, and Slick could feel a warm, tingling feeling spreading over his ankle and foot.

"Here's a light duty chit," Ramirez finished, handing him a small chip-reader. The doctor straightened up. "See me if there's any problem with the cast."

As the doctor left, Corporal Strauss advanced on Slick. "So, nube. Light duty, eh? You vill not be making the raid with us, then. Just as good."

Before Slick could react the corporal had turned his back, dismissing him entirely.

The lance was gathered around the supply van, working in the illumination thrown by a single red-glowing battle lantern. Since Gunnery Sergeant Trent had passed the order to get ready for an attack on the blockhouse further up the pass, the three recon units had been kitting up with climbing gear and extra weaponry. Slick had watched it all with a sense of detachment, unreality. The events at the hannie roadblock still filled his thoughts.

Rostov paused near him, a climbing rope and a field pack loaded with pitons slung over his shoulders. The demo expert looked keyed up, as nervous as Slick had ever seen him.

"Looks like you're well out of it, kid," he said. "Wish I'd been smart enough to trip over a corpse or something."

"I thought you liked all the commando stuff, Rostov," Slick said.

"Yeah, well ... climbing cliffs and launching suicide attacks aren't my idea of soft duty, kid. Vrurrth's, maybe, but not mine."

Someone from Braxton's lance laughed. "Come on, Rostov, don't go soft on us now!"

The laughter fell silent as Gunnery Sergeant Trent approached. "All right, you goldbricks, time to get moving. Pascali, you got my stuff?"

"Right here, Sarge," the corporal responded. She passed Trent a harness and a coil of line.

"Let's move out. First man at the top gets a bottle of Novykrim vodka at the Fwynzei Rec Room on me."

"Oh, great," Rostov said. "So now we gotta make sure we make it to Fwynzei *and* get you there in one piece, too!"

"I didn't just drop out of FTL yesterday, Rostov," Trent replied with a grin. "Now move out!"

Slick watched them moving away, his emotions a jumble of uncertainty and confusion.

I should have died back there, he thought. *I would* have died, *if Ghirghik hadn't saved me.*

Why had the Ubrenfar sacrificed himself to get Slick aboard the last APC? Ghirghik had been openly contemptuous of Slick the last time they'd talked, back at the funeral service. *He wasn't even human, but he died saving me....*

The Legion looks after its own. Doesn't matter if a guy's a total stranger or your tentmate for the last ten years. He's your buddy ... your comrade. And a part of the only family you've got! Rostov had said that, back at the funeral. For the first time Slick was beginning to understand it ... to believe it. The way Rostov did. And Ghirghik.

His eyes focused through his light intensifiers on the recon lances as they started their ascent. He glanced down at his foot, feeling frustrated.

He should have been up there with them ... with the rest of the team....

* * *

Gunnery Sergeant Trent pulled himself over the edge of the cliff and rose to a half-crouch, scanning his surroundings through the LI setting of his helmet display. The top of the ridge was stark and rugged. Nothing grew there. This high in Hanuman's mountains, the high energy output from Morrison's Star was lethal to all but the hardiest life forms. Travelers could pass through the region in relative safety, but a long stay at high elevations was definitely not advisable.

That was the reason the Imperial Army of Vyujiid had built most of their frontier post in the Zhairhee Pass underground, in a network of caverns extending far back into the cliff walls that closed in around the pass itself. The blockhouse that barred the Legion's path was only the tip of the iceberg; the caves held storehouses, barracks, and armories that could support an entire regiment of hannie troops for a month or more without resupply.

Somehow the Dryiens had overrun the strongpoint. If they were still there in strength, the three recon lances would have to hold them in place long enough to squeeze the rest of the Legion through the pass. More likely, though, the garrison would be fairly small. The enemy would need every soldier for the drive on Fwynzei.

Trent dropped behind a boulder overlooking the central valley and turned on his image intensifiers. The scene leapt toward him.

There was a lot of activity down there. Soldiers were erecting barricades and maneuvering heavy anti-tank weapons into position to guard the south end of the pass. Raising his wristpiece, Trent ordered a quick tactical evaluation. In seconds, the computer fed the information straight to his visor HUD. The valley was a little less than five kilometers from end to end. There was roughly a company deploying to defend the position, with no sign of additional troops lurking in the caves. About what he'd figured. Rough, but not impossible … as long as the legionnaires held onto surprise.

Three depleted lances against a company … ten men taking on over a hundred. *Typical Legion odds,* Trent thought grimly.

Corporal Pascali dropped beside him and studied the pass. She pointed to the cliff, then held up a coil of line.

He nodded wearily. *I'm getting too damned old to be playing these games,* he told himself as he checked the valley one last time. It had been ten years since he'd last served as part of a recon lance.

But he still had a few moves these youngsters wouldn't expect.

Trent touched the communicator control, two light taps. He wasn't taking any risks with making noise, not now. But the drivers Mason had selected would know what the signal meant.

The countdown had started. In five more minutes the battle would begin.

* * *

Corporal Frank Weston watched the seconds ticking away on the countdown clock and smiled coldly. *Not long now....*

It seemed like more than six years since a man named Franklin West had come home to find his family dead after the quake that virtually destroyed the colony on far-off New Paradise. If he'd only been *home* instead of out drinking that night, maybe Kathy and Caroline wouldn't have been killed. Or at least he might have died with them, instead of having to live with the memory of what he'd lost that night.

But he'd been drunk, and his wife and daughter had died, and with the colony in ruins and every cent he'd ever saved lost with the farm, Franklin West had decided he was better off dead.

The Foreign Legion had sent him where he could die.

Most of his pay—what he didn't lose drinking or gambling—went to Kathy's family, anonymously. It wouldn't bring back the daughter he'd taken from them, or the granddaughter, but it was the only way he could face himself in the mirror every morning. Some day his fate would finally catch up with him, and his Legion benefits would go to Kathy's family as well. And Franklin West, now Frank Weston, would be at peace.

The countdown clock reached zero and Weston switched on the turbofans. He'd drawn the unarmed supply van, which had been running on good thoughts and makeshift repairs for days now. Singh had an engineering van, with a laser that no longer worked and a bow mag-rep module that was on the verge of complete failure.

He wondered idly what had made Singh volunteer for the mission. No one asked another legionnaire why he joined, but everyone wondered. Singh was tough and wiry, a natural with a knife. Speculation in the platoon put him down as a murderer hiding in the Legion to escape his crimes.

In a way that was a lot like Weston.

"All right, Decoy," Sergeant Mason's voice crackled in Weston's ears. "Mag out!"

The supply van seemed reluctant to lift, as if it knew what awaited it at the top of the pass. A work detail had hastily unloaded the battered vehicle while the recon lances made their climb. It had been almost empty anyway, except for a lot of plundered hannie food and a few spare parts that wouldn't be that useful, anyway. With Fwynzei less than a hundred kilometers away there wasn't much need for large supply stockpiles any more.

Weston urged the throttle forward and the APC gathered speed. Singh's vehicle fell in behind, and the two decoys began to climb the pass.

Faster ... faster ... Sergeant Mason had made it clear that he wanted the decoys to draw maximum attention. Weston grinned to himself. The way the fans were acting up, the supply van could probably simulate a whole regiment.

Then the van swept around a rocky outcropping and over the crest of the rise. Searchlights stabbed down at the hurtling Sandray from a dozen places, and the familiar rattle of monkey machine-gun fire shattered the night.

Seconds seemed to drag out like long minutes as the Sandray hurtled across the floor of the valley. Weston had time to note the defenses, to see the barricade and the blockhouse and the looming bulk of a tank. From the cliffside above the blockhouse, he made out the subdued flicker of a laser firing into the hannies, its beam revealed by the dust that had been kicked up by the heavy equipment moving on the valley floor. The attack was starting, right on schedule.

The tank gun fired. The shell narrowly missed, and the explosion rained rocks and dirt on Singh's APC as it followed Weston into the enclosed valley.

He smiled again. That tank could spell trouble even if Trent's attack went down smoothly. There was one last thing he could do....

Weston steered straight for the tank. He didn't see the hannie soldier at the door of the blockhouse who wrestled a weapon far too large for kys small body into line, or the missile that swooped across the pass.

It hit the APC squarely above the driver's cab, on the left side, killing Frank Weston instantly. But it was too late to completely stop the hurtling juggernaut, and moments later the native tank was engulfed in flame.

Franklin West had found his peace in the middle of fire and fury.

* * *

"Nail the little bastards!" Trent shouted, spraying FEK fire across the nearest cluster of hannie soldiers.

The surprise had been perfect, with the legionnaires moving into position on the floor of the valley just as the two decoy vehicles stirred up the natives at their barricade. In the confusion, the first few bursts from the three recon lances had gone largely unnoticed.

The collision between the lead APC and the native tank had sent a pillar of fire into the night sky, blinding the defenders. The legionnaires, their vision protected by the polarization on their helmet feeds, had been able to take maximum advantage.

But by the time the second Sandray was destroyed by three offworld missiles, the hannies were beginning to realize their danger.

A native swung a bulky heavy-caliber machine gun toward Trent. Bullets tracked across the rock wall of the cliff, and Trent ducked and rolled under the firing line. In the seconds it took the gunner to shift the weapon back again, Trent switched to grenades and fired a single round. It was dead on target. The machine gun fell silent.

Close by, Corporal Braxton was maintaining a steady stream of fire at the barricade, pinning at least ten monkeys. Suddenly Braxton turned, but not soon enough. A hannie with a blunderbuss opened fire, and the primitive rocket caught the lance leader squarely in the stomach. Trent returned fire and the native went down. He swung the FEK back to catch the hannies Braxton had been keeping pinned as they tried to take advantage of the distraction. Most of them fell. A pair sprinted for the nearest cave mouth, only to go down as two bright streaks of coherent light flashed in rapid succession through the dust and smoke. Legionnaire Doug Rydell gave Trent a quick thumb's up and turned his laser rifle on another target.

Another hannie vehicle clanked slowly around the bend from the north end of the pass, a tracked APC this time with an HMG in a cupola mount on the top of the passenger compartment. The hannie gunner looked up in surprise as Legionnaire Vrurrth leapt onto the hull from the rocks above. The massive Gwyrran hands closed on the soldier's windpipe, lifting the luckless alien right out of the cupola and tossing ky aside like an unwanted rag. Then Vrurrth pointed his FEK into the open hatch and pumped several grenades into the vehicle. He jumped clear as the opening belched flame and the track ground to a halt.

Down by the blockhouse, Rostov and Cunningham slapped demo charges on either side of the door, ducked back, and triggered them. Firing through roiling smoke, they quickly cleared the building of native troops.

Then the fighting was over, with the remaining hannies streaming north out of the pass.

Trent slung his FEK and crossed the road to the blockhouse. Rostov met him beside the ruined door. "All secure inside, Sarge."

"Good. Signal the L-T."

Trent surveyed the battleground with a frown. They'd cleared the pass easily enough—perhaps too easily. He only hoped the column could win clear of the pass before the jaws of the trap sprang shut around them.

*   *   *

Fraser leaned over the driver's seat of the engineering van and squinted at the forward video display. The Sandray was at the head of the column, picking its way through the ruined native barricade. Somewhere toward the rear of the line the Sabertooth spoke, hurtling another plasma round into the hannie troops advancing from Zhairhee. The onager cannon had already torn up the road enough to block vehicles for a while, and there weren't many monkeys back there willing to brave the demonic weapon.

He saw Trent waving as the APC moved slowly toward the bend. The sergeant looked tired but cocky.

Trent had a right to be cocky. With ten legionnaires he had taken on over a hundred. Two dead and one wounded wasn't a bad price to pay for a victory like that.

Minutes passed as the column started down the Vyujiid side of the pass. They wouldn't have to keep on facing overwhelming odds on their own much longer....

"Holy shit...!" Legionnaire DiMarco, the driver, cut the fans. The vehicle floated at the crest of the hill overlooking the northern end of the pass. Vyujiid ... the end of the long march.

Except that the valley was filled with soldiers and vehicles. It was a huge camp, stretching as far as the video cameras could scan.

The hannie army hadn't moved on for Fwynzei. It was right here, squarely across their only escape route.

The legionnaires were trapped.

Chapter Twenty

If they're going to let the Legion die, then it will die bravely.

—Colonel Joseph Conrad,
French Foreign Legion, 1837

Lancelot, Lancelot, this is Alice One. Do you copy?" Fraser had to fight hard to keep from betraying his fears. "Lancelot, please respond. Over."

The legionnaires had deployed around the top of the pass, occupying the blockhouse and many of the positions the hannies had given up to Trent. That had been almost two hours ago. Fortunately, the Dryien reaction had been sluggish. The forces on the south side of the frontier were still cowed by the pounding they'd taken from the Sabertooth's plasma cannon; the regiments to the north seemed to be in disarray, perhaps because they were out of touch with their leadership in Zhairhee, or possibly due to the exaggerated accounts the refugees from the pass battle had no doubt been giving of Legion strength and intentions.

How much longer the legionnaires could count on being left alone was anybody's guess.

"Lancelot, this is Alice One. Respond, please. Over." Fraser bit off a curse. They *had* to raise the garrison at Fwynzei.

While Trent and the platoon leaders took charge of organizing some kind of defense, Legionnaires Russo and Garcia had climbed the cliffs to rig up a directional relay unit that would put them back in contact with Fwynzei. So far, though, they weren't having much luck.

"Alice, this is Lancelot." The voice on the commlink was ragged with static, but Fraser could also hear the suspicion in those cold, impersonal tones. "Transmit authentication codes."

He keyed in the computer and let out a sigh. Finally! He'd been on the verge of giving up.

The computers on each end of the line compared electronic notes, verifying that each transmitter was genuine and setting up a coded, scrambled circuit. A few seconds later, the radio operator from Fwynzei spoke again.

"Alice, Lancelot. Hold for Commandant Isayev."

Minutes went by this time before the commandant's gruff voice took over. "Fraser? Good God, man, we thought you'd bought it. Where the hell are you?"

Fraser swallowed once and tried to sound calm, professional. "Sir, the demi-battalion has reached the top of the Zhairhee Pass. We have driven back a force approximately one company in strength and now hold the blockhouse and the rest of the central valley. We have encountered elements of the Dryien Army, approximately two divisions, blocking the north end of the pass between the mountains and Fwynzei."

"We know about 'em," Isayev replied. "They had sympathizers in the Imperial Army who helped them take the pass in the first place. They drove back the Seventh Imperial Division yesterday and engaged a battalion of our native auxiliaries."

"It is our belief, Commandant, that they are making an attempt on Fwynzei as part of the anti-Terran movement that started with the coup and the attack on Monkeyville."

Isayev chuckled. "Well, it's nice to see that our junior officers have a better grasp on things than the Colonial Office. The resident-general spent most of the last two days trying to set up a meeting to, uh, 'mediate the dispute between two sovereign nations.' It wasn't until a couple of batteries of monkey artillery started shelling Govern-ment House that he finally got it through his thick head that they were after *us*."

Fraser looked up as Garcia came into the blockhouse, and gave her a thumb's up. "Commandant, we're stuck up here. We've got hannies on each side of the pass, and I'm down to under a hundred effectives. What's the chance of getting an evac from up here?"

"Wait one." There was a long pause before Isayev came back on. "Alice One, if you can hold out up there for forty-eight hours I think we'll be able to get you some relief."

"Forty-eight hours?" Fraser couldn't hold back his pent-up emotions any longer. "Do you have any idea what you're asking?"

"I know it's rough, Fraser," Isayev said, ignoring the outburst. "But in two days we should be able to deploy three battalions of Commonwealth Marines to the surface. They're en route from the system now, off *Seneca*. And if you're holding the pass, some of them can ground right there and take over for you."

"Sir—"

"As long as there is a unit up there, Fraser, the Dryiens on this side of the mountains are cut off. No supplies ... damned little contact with their HQ, unless they use aircraft to relay orders. The longer you hold out up there, the better our chances of keeping them out of Fwynzei. And if we can put the Marines down to take over from you, so much the better. I wouldn't want to try to retake that pass with unarmed transport lighters, and that's all we've got for now."

Fraser didn't reply for several seconds. Could they really hold out for two days? Or would the Marines arrive to find the legionnaires dead, overwhelmed by superior numbers?

But unless they could keep the pass blocked, Fwynzei was in danger.

The Legion looks out for its own. Zhairhee Pass could keep the hannies from getting at the rest of the battalion.

"Lancelot, instructions understood. Forty-eight hours until pickup."

Isayev let out a sigh on the other end of the commlink. "We're counting on you, Colin. If anybody has the guts to pull this off, it's your boys. You marched this far ... all you have to do now is sit still and shoot, eh?"

"Just don't be late, Commandant," Fraser said softly. "Just don't be late."

*   *   *

Karatsolis cursed as the MEK ran dry again. Ducking behind the shelter of a wrecked Legion Sandray, he slapped the release switch and fitted another drum over the receiver. After this one, there were only two more magazines for the weapon, unless someone brought him a fresh supply soon.

It had been a grueling test of endurance, this past forty hours, far worse than anything the legionnaires had faced on the march. Holding on to the precarious positions at either end of the pass had stretched the survivors of demi-battalion Alice to the limit and beyond. But they were still holding fast, and it was only eight hours now until the promised relief was supposed to arrive.

Karatsolis glanced over at Corporal Bashar. The Turk had a bloodstained bandage wrapped around his left arm where shrapnel from a hannie fragmentation grenade had scored a hit, but he was still fighting. A lot of the legionnaires had picked up light wounds in the course of six successive hannie attacks, although Karatsolis was still unmarked. Sergeant Baker, acting leader of the battered Fourth Platoon, was in charge of this part of the northern end of the pass despite the fact that he'd lost the use of both legs. Legionnaire Delandry had propped him up behind a boulder and applied regen casts to both legs, and Baker remained at his post.

That had been two assaults back. Luckily, the hannie regiments on the north side of the pass were still having trouble organizing their attacks efficiently, or the legionnaires wouldn't have held them this long. They seemed to be running low on supplies, and even lower on effective leadership. Word passed from Battalion HQ in Fwynzei suggested that a lot of hannie units had been purged of their old officers, with politically reliable coup supporters placed in charge of some of the units only days before the attack.

The monkeys were fighting well enough, but their morale was low. Stand up to them, and they broke despite their tremendous advantage in numbers.

Karatsolis had heard that things were different on the south side of the pass, nearly five kilometers away, where First and Second Platoons were trying to hold back troops out of Zhairhee. The assaults had taken time to get rolling down there because of the damage done to the causeway by Ignaczak's plasma cannon on the night of the first battle. Engineering vehicles had cleared the rubble by late afternoon of the next day, however, and since then the attacks had been mounting in frequency and determination. They had the leadership they needed down there ... but most of the troops were poor-quality garrison units.

The Legion had been lucky. They could last the few remaining hours until pickup ... but it would be close. Damned close. Casualties were starting to mount, and not just wounds. Two guys from Fourth

Platoon had bought it only an hour ago when a hannie aircraft strafed the road, and Subaltern Fairfax had been killed by a mortar round during a native assault on the south end of the pass.

"Hey, Spear," Bashar called, firing an FEK burst to discourage a cluster of hannie soldiers a few hundred meters down the road. "What'd'ya think? These hannies any better than those buggers we were up against back on Loki?"

Karatsolis braced the MEK and sprayed needle rounds at another enemy squad as it tried to work its way past the remains of a burning hannie track. "Hell, no! Those bastards had decent weapons. Not like that crap the monkeys are using."

Bashar held his fire for a moment, searching for targets. "Yeah, but these guys are persistent, you gotta give 'em that. On Loki, you only had to knock the buggers silly once or twice. These hannies don't ever seem to learn!" As if to emphasize the point, he produced a native hand grenade and tossed it down the pass with a nonchalant flourish. The legionnaires had found plenty of native weapons in the underground armories, and most of the legionnaires were carrying grenades again. Not as good as an FEK's rocket grenades, perhaps, but very effective at discouraging unwanted visitors.

Even better, they'd recovered a number of heavier weapons, including ten of the high-tech missile launchers like the ones that had taken out the two decoy vehicles during the first attack. Those had been very useful in keeping the enemy tanks and tracks at bay.

Karatsolis stopped firing and peered cautiously over the smoke-blackened wreck. The enemy was pulling back again.

Another victory ... for the moment.

* * *

"Called off? The assault was *called off?*" *Asjyai* Zyzyiig hit the map table hard enough to knock over a stack of markers. An aide hastened to clean up the loose counters and try to put the map right again.

Zyzyiig ignored ky. "What in the name of the Eternal Mists does that fool think ky is doing? There are two divisions on the north side ... the Terran demons have less than a company! Far less!"

"But, *Asjyai*," an officer quavered. "The demons have all the advantages of position. And their magic weapons. And our forces are in disorder, out of supply, and out of contact for most of the time. It is very hard—"

"Demons take you!" Zyzyiig shouted, kys neck ruff going stiff. "Demons take all cretins who can't show a little initiative!"

"Perhaps, my Companion, you have not considered the benefits of drawing back and truly organizing a single assault," Shavvataaars offered from the back of the map room. "Instead of throwing forces in piecemeal, a single coordinated thrust launched from both your forces simultaneously would certainly break the resistance of your enemies at the top of the pass."

Zyzyiig glared at the Semti, breathing hard. That cold whisper, so calm and calculating ... ky was beginning to hate the very sight and sound of the Ancient One.

But this time the advice was good. So far, the attacks had been organized hastily, with the assumption that a handful of demons couldn't possibly hold against the overwhelming numbers they faced. Yet time and time again their weapons knocked the assaults back.

What was needed was a final, all-out effort. That would break the legionnaires. Then the army could push on for Fwynzei and a final reckoning with the offworld interlopers.

Slowly, anger ebbed as ky turned the beginnings of a plan over in kys mind. "Yes ... yes, that is the answer," ky said at last. The softly spoken words seemed to make the officers more nervous than kys earlier shouts. "Get a squadron in the air," ky ordered one of the officers. "Enough aircraft to be *sure* of getting across the mountains." Demon missiles out of Fwynzei had been taking a high toll against Dryien aircraft, making it even harder to stay in touch with the invading army.

"Yes, Honored," the staff officer responded.

"Order an assault for ... call it two hours after dawn. Miststalkers to lead the advance."

"Yes, Honored," ky repeated.

Zyzyiig turned to another officer. "Pass the word to Blooddrinkers to be ready to resume the attack at the same time," ky ordered. Zyzyiig paused. "No, wait ... I will go myself. Order me a staff car. I will *personally* make sure Blooddrinkers do their job right this time!"

"*Asjyai* ... is that wise?" someone asked.

"Are you questioning my judgement?" ky thundered back. "This attack is too important to entrust to these time-servers and nay-sayers! I will command the attack! Submit final plans to me by dawn! Meeting dismissed!"

As the officers hurried to leave the room, Zyzyiig turned to Shavvataaars. "Do you wish to join me?"

Shavvataaars crossed arms. "I do not think my presence would be particularly useful, my Companion. I will remain here until you have broken through."

Zyzyiig showed kys teeth. "You do that, my Companion," ky said mockingly. "And I shall open the road to Fwynzei! No matter what it costs!"

*   *   *

Kelly Winters felt useless as she sat in the corner of the blockhouse. Outside the distant *crump* of artillery was louder and more frequent. The others in the building—Fraser, Trent, Garcia, and Russo—were staying busy, monitoring communications, fielding reports, and trying to decide on the best employment for a limited number of troops. Since dawn, it had become obvious that the hannies were gearing up for a major new attack. The question now was whether it would come before or after the Marines could deploy to take over the defense of the pass.

She had offered help to Ramirez, but the doctor and the Padre had things under control in the tunnel where the wounded had been shifted the day before. The medical van had been pressed into service as a regular APC ... until a hannie missile had taken it out on the south road overnight. Hannie artillery and air attacks had left only three vehicles in working order. One, the Sabertooth, was still deployed on the south end of the line, suppressing enemy movements. The other two were parked near the blockhouse now. Members of the three recon lances, Fraser's only remaining reserve, were busy loading them up with supplies and fresh needle ammo. Two wounded legionnaires were using gear cannibalized from the fabrication van to crank out ammunition, but it was being used up almost as fast as they could produce it.

There was no place for her in the desperate work of defense. All she could do was sit and wait, hoping that the Marines would arrive soon to put an end to the nightmare. The Marines! How often she'd wished they would swoop in to the rescue as the Legion column straggled northward.

They couldn't be any tougher than these legionnaires, but at least they'd be fresh. How the legionnaires kept fighting was beyond her.

Even little Myaighee had gone out there, equipped with hannie weapons from the armory. Ky had volunteered to carry messages along the Legion positions on the north side of the pass. Myaighee's small build made the alien an ideal runner. The soldiers on the line had adopted ky as a sort of mascot.

She'd considered volunteering to take a rifle and go out there herself, but she knew what Trent would say. She was no combat soldier.

"Lieutenant?" Garcia held up a handset for Fraser. "Subaltern Watanabe on the line."

Fraser hardly look up from the holomap over Russo's C^3 pack. "On speakers, Garcia."

Watanabe's voice, usually so calm and placid, was edged with something close to panic. "HQ, they've taken out the Sabertooth! The hannies're coming up the road and we don't have anything to hold them!"

Trent jumped in before Fraser could reply. "Are you sure the FSV's out of action? Not just damaged?"

"God, Sarge, they put a missile right into the turret while she was firing! The gauss field collapsed while the round was still in the barrel, man! Half the front end's melted to slag!"

"Madre de Dios," Garcia muttered. Fraser and Trent were both looking sick. Mason and Ignaczak couldn't have lived through something like that.

"Come in, HQ? What the hell are your orders?"

Trent and Fraser exchanged looks, and the sergeant killed the audio channel. "L-T, we've gotta reinforce them. Maybe send a couple of missile launchers down there. It won't make up for the Sabertooth...."

"We're stretched goddamned thin already, Gunny," Fraser said. He jerked a thumb toward the soldiers loading ammo outside. "You sure it's time to send in the last reserves?"

"No ... we need to get that ammo up to the front. Damn it, if only we had a few more people." Trent glanced around the room. His eyes lit on Kelly. "You," he said curtly. "You can handle a commlink, can't you?"

Kelly nodded, ignoring the sergeant's abrupt manner.

"Russo and Garcia can handle launchers, L-T. If we put her on the radio, we can free these two up to do some fighting."

Fraser looked uncertain. "Putting technicians on the line...."

"They're legionnaires first, L-T, and every legionnaire's an infantryman before anything else. I'll take charge down there, if you want...."

"Watanabe can handle it, Gunny," Fraser said sharply. "I need you here. Garcia, Russo, draw some launchers and get down to the south barricade. Take Braxton's lance off the loading detail ... and any stragglers you meet on your way down. Miss Winters ..." He gestured at the C^3 equipment.

Trent already had the circuit to Watanabe open again as she reached the table.

"Watanabe, hold on," Fraser was saying. "I'm sending you a couple of rocket launchers. Hold the bastards as long as you can before you give up any ground."

The subaltern seemed calmer when he responded. "Affirmative, HQ. We'll do what we can."

Kelly put on a set of headphones to monitor communications as Fraser and Trent returned to the holomap.

"Way I see it, L-T, if the transports don't get here soon, we're going to have to start thinking about last ditch schemes." Trent stabbed a finger at the map. "These caves could be a real godsend if we could just find a way to camouflage them a little better...."

A voice on the headphones made Kelly straighten up. "I see them!" someone was yelling.

"It's the friggin' Navy!" someone else shouted.

"Damn, I never thought I'd be glad to see those truck drivers!"

"Lieutenant!" Kelly called out. "We've got a visual on transports."

"About time," Trent said. "Have they requested landing info?"

Kelly cocked her head, listening as she ran the commlink through a channel search. "Nothing, sergeant. Nothing ..."

"What the hell are they doing?" she heard on the radio.

Legionnaire Donovan appeared at the shattered door, supporting Warrant Officer Vandergraff. Kelly gasped as she saw the science specialist. He'd lost his helmet, and his face was a mask of blood. Donovan stopped, staring at the sky. "Hey, Lieutenant, the Navy transport's not stopping! It's magging out!"

Fraser and Trent rushed outside. Kelly could see them through the blasted door, heard Trent's curse. "Goddamned Navy bastards. They're heading too far south."

"Lieutenant," Fraser said, swinging around to look inside at Kelly. "Raise those transports. Now!"

She switched to the standard ground-to-ship channel. "Navy transports, this is Alice One. Transports, do you copy? Over."

"Alice One. *Tuyen Quang*. We copy five by five."

Fraser was beside her, his face flushed with anger. He took the handset. "*Tuyen Quang*, this is Fraser, commanding Alice One. What the devil are you people playing at up there? I was told you'd be landing here to relieve my people."

There was a crackle of static. Then another voice answered. "Fraser, this is Colonel Reginald Smythe-Henderson, commanding the Provisional Marine Assault Regiment. Your orders are to hold as long as possible. Relief will arrive if and when it can be spared."

"With respect, Colonel," Fraser came back angrily. "With respect, my people can't hold on much longer. Commandant Isayev assured me—"

"Commandant Isayev is not in command of this operation, Fraser," the colonel broke in, "*I* am. Under the authority of the resident-general. We are launching an assault on the enemy supply depot at Zhairhee to relieve the threat to Fwynzei once and for all. Your unit forms a key part of this operation. Once we've secured an LZ and have the enemy on the run, we'll be able to spare ships to evac you. Until then, carry out your orders. Smythe-Henderson out!"

The silence in the blockhouse was broken only by the sound of hannie field guns. They were getting closer.

*　*　*

Lieutenant Commander Charles Wingate looked across the bridge of the lighter *Tuyen Quang* at the stiff, rigid figure of Colonel Smythe-Henderson. The Marine officer was studying a terrain map. He seemed to have put the radio exchange with Alice One entirely out of his thoughts.

As CO of the lighter, Wingate had participated in the planning sessions where the colonel and his staff decided on the attack on Zhairhee. It had sounded like a good scheme, using the legionnaires to draw the enemy's attention away from the critical area so the Marines could hit them hard and fast around their key supply nexus.

At the time, Wingate had admired the courage of the legionnaires who had volunteered to hold the pass in the face of such overwhelming odds. Now he was beginning to realize the truth.

"Colonel?" Wingate asked tentatively. "Colonel, shouldn't we do something to help those men down there?"

"What men, Wingate?" Sykes-Hamilton seemed genuinely confused. "What, you mean those Legion people?"

"Yes, sir. It sounds like they were expecting us to support them directly."

"We're not doing things by half-measures, Wingate," the colonel replied gruffly. "This op'll smash most of the Dryien army in one blow. That's better than Isayev's damned-fool relief mission!"

"I know, sir, but aren't you expecting too much of them?"

"They're dead men already, Wingate. You saw the recon views — the hannies are hitting them with everything this time. I'm not throwing away a chance to knock out the whole damned monkey army for dead men. While the hannies are busy with them, I'm winning this campaign."

The colonel looked back at the scrolling map. "Anyway," he said quietly, dismissively. "It's not like we're losing real soldiers. They're only legionnaires."

CHAPTER TWENTY-ONE

These are not men, but devils!

—Colonel Francisco de Paula-Milan, Mexican Army Speaking
of the defenders at Camerone,
French Foreign Legion, 30 April 1863

Kelly stared at the C^3 unit in disbelief. How could the Navy just abandon them?

Beside her, Fraser was clenching his fists, his face white. "He lied to me," he said softly, as if to himself. "Isayev lied to me!"

"Or someone lied to him," Trent said. He seemed to be handling it better. "Let's face it, L-T, the Legion's always been considered expendable. Put all the malcontents and bad apples in one unit, then give 'em the jobs you wouldn't give anybody else. That's the way it's been done for as long as there's been a Legion!" Fraser stared down at the holomap. Behind them, Vandergraff moaned as Legionnaire Donovan headed for the barracks tunnel Ramirez was using as a hospital.

"Hold on, uh ... Donovan," Fraser said suddenly. "Vandergraff ... how is he?"

"Shell sent a cloud of rock chips into his face, Lieutenant," Donovan replied. "I've given him a dose of analoke for the pain."

"Vandergraff ... did you find out anything before you were hit?" Fraser asked. The science specialist had been sent with a lance to scout

out the top of the cliff face overlooking the southern side of the pass. Kelly glanced over at Trent. It had been her idea to bring it down originally, but it hadn't been until Trent reminded him of it that Fraser had consented to check it out.

"I'm … I'm not sure, sir," Vandergraff said weakly. "Looked … possible, but I didn't have much time … not much of a geologist, anyway. Or explosives man."

"All right, Vandergraff," Fraser said. "You did your best. Donovan, get him to Doc."

Trent was looking at the work party around the two APCs. "I'll take Rostov to check it out, L-T," he said. "Should've done it that way in the first place." He looked angry. "Cunningham's our only other demo man, and he's with Braxton's lance. No time to get him back now. Damn!"

Fraser rubbed the bridge of his nose. "Take everyone who can be spared from getting those supplies forward, Gunny," he said at last. "Bringing down that rockslide's our only chance now."

"Let me come, too," Kelly put in. "Since you don't have Cunningham."

Trent shook his head. "You should stay here. You can help best by running C-cubed."

"Damn it, Sergeant," she exploded, angry at his patronizing tone. "I'm an engineer, not a commtech. I know explosives … and I know stress points. Digging techniques. This is what I was trained for. Let me do my job, for God's sake!"

Trent took a step back, assessing her with a long steady gaze. "I'm sorry, Lieutenant," he said in a subdued tone. "I didn't mean any insult."

"Take her, Gunny," Fraser said. He hesitated. "Perhaps I should go too …"

"No, sir," Trent said firmly. "There's no sense in a commander taking foolish risks. Your place is here, giving orders. Not screwing around on the front lines and letting the rest of the battle go to hell."

He looked at Trent. "My decisions haven't been much good without your advice, Gunny," he said softly.

"Nonsense, L-T … with all due respect." Trent grinned. "You've got everything you need … inside. All you need is the confidence to use it." He turned to Kelly. "Come on, Miss Winters. We've got some fireworks to set off."

Kelly followed him out of the blockhouse, listening to him shout for Strauss and Pascali.

She found herself wondering how anyone could cast aside men like these.

Slick looked up as Sergeant Trent and the Navy lieutenant crossed the paved expanse between the blockhouse and the mouth of the main tunnel.

"Looks like trouble," Rostov said quietly beside him. "Any time the Sarge starts looking for a recon lance …"

Slick hid a smile. Whenever Trent wanted something hard done, it was the recon lances who got the job. And Trent was usually right among them.

The regen cast was still on his leg, but there was very little pain now. He'd joined in the work detail when the recon units were pulled off the lines at dawn, and no one had said anything. It felt good to be contributing … like he really was part of the team now.

"All right, you goldbricks," Trent said loudly. "Time you got back into the war. Pascali, Strauss, I want your lances with me. Lieutenant Winters thinks she can bring down part of that damned cliff over there and block the monkey advance."

Slick bit his lip, worried. Warrant Officer Vandergraff and Dmowski's weapons lance had gone up there soon after dawn with the same idea. He'd seen Vandergraff and the medic. It sounded like a dangerous mission.

"Want me to take my bag of tricks along, Sarge?" Rostov asked cheerfully.

"No, Rostov," Trent said sarcastically. "I was figuring you'd bring down the rocks by showing them your ugly face!"

There was laughter. Trent held up his hand and went on. "Every man draw a pack of PX-90 in addition to regular kit. You won't need climbing gear this time. Vandergraff found a tunnel that comes out near where we're heading. Corporal Johnson, your lance stays here. Finish loading and get this ammo to the front lines ASAP. Then come back here. You're still in reserve until the L-T says different. Got it?"

"Yeah, Sarge," Johnson said.

"Oh, yeah. Don't forget to use the chameleon tarps on the Sandrays this time. Might make 'em a little harder to spot." Trent paused. "All right, get moving!"

"You vill stay here, nube," Strauss said. "Help load. Light duty gets you off of another mission, eh?"

Slick turned to face the stocky corporal. "If it's all the same to you, Corp," he said evenly, "I'll stay with the lance. The foot's not bothering me much now. I can fight."

The corporal started to say something, then stopped and gave him a curt nod. "Good. Draw your gear."

For a long moment, Slick stared at him. It had almost seemed like there was a note of pride in Strauss's voice.

Rostov slapped him on the back. "Come on, Grant. Let's get you kitted up."

Slick followed him, his surprise and confusion stronger than ever.

It was the first time anyone in the lance had called him by name.

*　　*　　*

Fraser sat in the blockhouse staring at the holomap, alone with his fears.

Trent's unit had started for the top of the ridge a half an hour before, and the two APCs had finished loading and headed for the front a few minutes later. Now, except for the chatter on the commlink from the two ends of the pass, it was as if he'd been isolated from everyone, friend and enemy alike.

We can't hold out without relief, he thought bitterly. *Damn the Navy … damn Isayev. How could they let these men die?*

It would take a miracle to save the legionnaires now. Even if Trent managed to blast enough rock to block the south pass, it was only a matter of time until the inevitable breakthrough.

The legionnaires would die … and for what? Would they really buy enough time for the Marines to mop up Zhairhee? He'd seen the city, its defenses. The Marines would need more than a few hours to win a victory there.

And the legionnaires didn't have hours.

"HQ … HQ, this is Leader Four." The voice on the commlink sounded strained. A man at the breaking point. Fraser remembered the voice. Sergeant Baker had been wounded, but he refused to leave his post in command of Fourth Platoon. All he would say about his choice was "I owe it to Sergeant Ghirghik."

"Fraser here," he said, keying in the channel. "Go ahead."

"HQ … we've got another wave heading out your way. Light infantry. Our hannie says they're the Miststalkers, whatever the hell that means."

He remembered the conversation during the recon of Zhairhee. The Miststalkers were the elite commandos. They wouldn't be turned aside as easily as past attackers.

From things Myaighee had said later, after the recon, he suspected the Miststalkers were likely to use the same sort of tactics Trent had used to grab the pass in the first place. Once the hannies stopped focusing on the pass and started climbing the ridges, the legionnaires would be finished for sure.

"Any estimates on their speed, Sergeant Baker?" he asked, surprised at how calm his voice stayed.

"They're moving cautiously, sir. Maybe an hour before they hit our lines ... unless they can't take the firepower and turn back."

"Don't count on it, Sergeant," Fraser said. "I'll see what I can do. Keep me posted. Fraser out."

I'll see what I can do. The phrase was empty. There was nothing he *could* do. The hannies were finally going to break through. They could expect to have their two forces united in another hour or two.

They could expect it....

He remembered Trent's words the night they'd come up the pass. "I kind of like to give an enemy just what he's expecting ... only not quite the way he's expecting it."

Was there a way to use their advantage, to take them by surprise?

Before the transports had gone over, Trent had been talking about a last-ditch plan. Something about the tunnels. They could withdraw into the tunnels, of course, but that would only delay the inevitable. And once they pulled back, there'd be nothing to keep the hannies from using the pass to stop the Marine landing ... or to renew the drive on Fwynzei.

What would Trent do? *If only I had him here to help me plan....*

But Trent was busy with his own problems now. It was up to Fraser to come up with the answer this time.

They had to find a way to draw the enemy into a trap ... to keep the legionnaires out of harm's way long enough to get the Miststalkers onto a decent killing ground. If the commandos met no resistance, they probably wouldn't deploy on the ridgetops.

The tunnels would be useful only if they could be blocked or camouflaged.

Fans whirred outside as one of the APCs touched down. Corporal Johnson scrambled out and started toward the blockhouse. His uniform was a dusty grey-brown, to match the rocky cliffs around him.

Like the tarp that half-covered the APC.

Fraser stood up slowly, the idea finally jelling in his mind. There might be a way to stop the hannies after all … at least for a little while longer.

* * *

"*Asjyai!* We have spotted more demons on the ridge. Up there!"

Zyzyiig followed the soldier's gesture. Far up on the cliff, a few tall figures moved. Ky couldn't tell what they were doing.

"If they have any of their magic weapons, they could fire on us from there," the commander of the Blooddrinkers observed. "Perhaps we should pull back …"

"No withdrawal!" Zyzyiig screamed. "Not until we've destroyed them! Order the regiment to attack again. Once we are past the shoulder of the ridge, their weapons cannot touch us! Attack!"

The officer nodded to an aide. "What shall we do about them in the meantime, Honored?" ky asked carefully.

"Artillery will discourage them," Zyzyiig said, regaining control. "Turn the clifftop into dust if you have to."

"Yes, Honored."

The enemy lines were weakening now that their lone tank had been silenced. Soon the demons would give way, and the pass would be clear.

Soon …

* * *

Alarm sirens shattered the air. Shavvataaars crossed to a window of the headquarters building and trained a pocket-sized image intensifier on the moving dots circling slowly over the valley. The image swam into clear view. A Terran transport lighter … two … three. The Commonwealth reinforcements had arrived.

There was still a chance of victory, but it was growing more slender with each passing moment. Shavvataaars tucked the magnifier into a pocket of his black robes and pondered for long minutes. Then, slowly, he turned from the window and crossed the room, his decision made.

It was time to leave the Dryiens to the hands of Fate. All he needed to do now was see that they mounted one last attack, to cover his escape from this wretched planet.

"Officer," he whispered as he opened the door. A Dryien staff officer looked up, hastily made a gesture of respect to the Ancient.

"Officer, three demon sky ships are approaching. If you have a stock of portable missile launchers available, you may yet drive them off. But you must act quickly."

The Dryien repeated the respectful salute and turned to kys radio equipment.

Shavvataaars felt the cold chill of satisfaction. This was one time that haste would pay off ... at least for him.

*   *   *

Lieutenant Commander Wingate scanned the instrument readouts one last time and gave a nod to his Exec, Lieutenant Greene. "Make it 'Landing Stations,' Number One," he ordered crisply.

"Landing Stations, aye aye," Greene replied. The transport shuddered once and began to settle toward the water-covered surface of the *ylyn* paddy. Wingate glanced at Colonel Smythe-Henderson. The Marines would have a soggy time of it crossing that muck. *Glad I'm a Navy man, and not some miserable mudfoot,* he thought.

It was a daring move, grounding three light transports so close to an enemy garrison town. But the bulk of their fighting forces were concentrated around the pass. The hannies wouldn't catch him the way they'd caught *Ganymede.*

The ship shuddered again and the noise of the drives faded. "Down and safe," Greene reported. "Troop doors opening ..."

"Targets! Targets!" abridge crewman shouted. "Multiple missiles. They have a lock on us!"

"Countermeasures!" Wingate snapped.

"No good ..." Greene looked up from his console. "No good, Skipper! I'm reading twelve missiles. They're going to—"

The Semti warheads tore through the bow of the transport, wrecking the bridge and spraying shrapnel through the forward troop bay. Over a hundred spacers and Marines died in the explosion, including Wingate and the Marine Colonel. It took Major Alvarez, the next in line of command, nearly an hour to restore order and reorganize the attack on Zhairhee.

Meanwhile, as the first column of smoke and fire coiled skyward from the stricken ship across the farmlands, the black-robed figure of the Semti agent watching from the edge of a causeway gave a cold, almost human nod.

* * *

"Incoming! Incoming!"

Kelly barely looked up as Corporal Pascali shouted the warning. They were so close to finishing. So close …

It had taken nearly an hour to get into position and get started setting the charges. The tunnel Vandergraff had found was part of the fortifications of the pass, leading from the valley floor not far from the still-smouldering wreck of the Sabertooth on the southern perimeter up to the very top of the south ridge. Stairs had been cut in the worst places, making it easy enough to haul the explosives up. They'd found some extra help near the top, Corporal Dmowski and three of the legionnaires from his weapons platoon. The two onagers in the unit were proving useful for carving holes in the rock where charges could be placed.

The first explosion was no more than fifty meters away, and Kelly worked faster. Two more detpacks to program and they'd be done.

"Come on, Lieutenant!" Trent shouted. "Get under cover, for God's sake!"

"Two more!" she shouted back.

Kelly sprinted to the next charge and dropped to one knee, checking the detpack carefully before she started to program it. Motion to her right made her glance up. It was Rostov, at the last of the PX-90 charges. He grinned and flashed her a thumb's up.

More shells shrieked overhead, a doomsday sound that made Kelly want to run. She forced herself to keep at it. A few last adjustments, and the ready light glowed.

Another blast, closer this time, showered her with dirt and splinters of rock. It made her think of Vandergraff. She grabbed her pack and started to run for the tunnel mouth, crouching low.

A giant's fist slammed into her from behind, accompanied by an ear-shattering roar. She fell, banging her head. Her ears were ringing, and it took an effort of will just to focus on her surroundings and sit up.

Trent was shouting something, but she was having trouble hearing. Slowly she shook her head, trying to clear the fog, then winced as it throbbed in pain.

The sergeant ran toward her, as if in slow motion.

Then another explosion, barely ten meters from Trent. He was flung forward by the force of the blast, and lay still.

Rostov was beside her, lifting her up. "Can you move?" His voice was distant through the pain in her head. She gave a nod. "Then come on!"

He supported her, but she pushed him away. "Get the sergeant!" she shouted. "I can make it!"

Rostov nodded and ran to Trent's side. Somehow, she made it back to where the others were waiting, clustered near the mouth of the tunnel.

The legionnaire had to carry Trent back. Inside the cave, he lowered the sergeant to the floor. The other legionnaires pressed close, their faces sharing the same apprehension.

Feeling a little better, Kelly knelt beside Rostov to check Trent's pulse. It was thready, but strong enough. The sergeant's eyes opened, focusing slowly on Kelly.

"Glad ... you made it ..." he whispered weakly. "It's all ... up to you now ..."

He lost consciousness.

Outside, the shells were still falling, but they hardly registered. She held the sergeant's wrist in one hand, staring down at him.

He was right. It really was up to her now.

*　*　*

"They're falling back! The demons are falling back!"

The call swept through the ranks of the Regiment Blooddrinkers. Zyzyiig climbed to the top of a track and waved kys command baton in the air. "To the top!" ky shouted. "Forward to victory! Forward!"

Other voices took up his call, and soldiers surged up the road eagerly. Engines roared as the armored vehicles lurched into motion.

It was an unstoppable tide. Success at last, despite hundreds of soldiers dead and wounded. The demons had fought like cornered beasts, but at last the Dryien army had broken their defenses. *Ky* had broken them.

"Honored! Honored, an urgent message from Zhairhee!"

"Forget Zhairhee," ky snapped at the aide who was waving from the ground.

"But Honored! They—"

"Forget them! Press on! We will take the demons!"

Chapter Twenty-Two

I have a rendezvous with Death at some disputed barricade.

—Legionnaire Alan Seeger,
French Foreign Legion, 1916

Kelly Winters straightened up from beside Trent and gestured at the hulking Gwyrran near the tunnel mouth. "Bring the sergeant. We've got to get back from here so I can set off the charges." She picked up his rifle and slung it over one shoulder. He'd want it back.

"The hannies are breaking through down below!" Corporal Pascali called from further down the tunnel. "Watanabe's falling back on the blockhouse!"

"We'll be trapped up here!" one of Dmowski's men said.

"Just head for the other end and worry about it when we get there," Kelly ordered. "Rostov, you get the relay in place?"

"Yes, ma'am," the demo expert said. They needed a radio relay near the mouth of the tunnel so they could transmit the detonation signal. Rostov had left it to help finish wiring the detpacks. She hoped he hadn't missed something.

A glance at his determined features reassured her. Rostov came across as a joker with a wry sense of humor, but she could recognize competence when she saw it.

None of these legionnaires would miss anything important. Even the youngster, the one with the regen cast on one leg, looked ready for anything.

"Move out!" she ordered.

The climb down seemed even longer than the trip to the top. Finally, only a few meters from the lower entrance, she held up her hand to signal a stop. Pascali's lance was already lurking in the shadows by the mouth of the cave. Sounds of native gunfire were all too close. If the monkeys decided to lob a grenade in here now....

She pulled out a remote control and armed all the charges. "This is it," she said aloud and saw an answering nod from Rostov.

Her finger closed on the detonation switch. Thunder rolled endlessly from the ridgetop above them.

* * *

The track's gears ground as it steered past the rocky outcropping and started up the incline toward the crest of the pass. Zyzyiig was still on top of the vehicle, where the soldiers could see their *Asjyai.* Ky basked in the moment.

The demons couldn't hamper the Cleansing any more. Even Shavvataaars could not dispute kys victory this time.

Almost directly overhead there was a brilliant ripple of flashes and a thunder that seemed to echo on and on. The noise drowned out the sounds of the engines, the cheers of the soldiers. Heads swiveled upward, and terror seemed to spread over every face at once.

Zyzyiig followed their gaze and felt kys spines stiffen in fear.

No ... it was not possible. Not at the very moment of victory!

With a rumble that grew stronger instead of weaker, tons of rock and dirt slid free of the cliff face.

Zyzyiig never felt the impact.

* * *

The ground shook until it seemed the tunnel was sure to collapse, and Slick dropped to his knees. Dust and loose earth showered the party. The rumble of the explosions and the falling rock outside lasted for a long time.

Then it was over. Slick could hear someone choking on the dust, and somehow the familiar sound was enough to make everything seem normal again.

Outside, the gunfire had stopped.

"The hannies are still out there," Pascali said. "A hell of a lot of them. But they seem to be confused. I think the blast must've done the job!"

Lieutenant Winters pushed past Slick and peered through the tunnel mouth. She was clutching Sergeant Trent's FEK in one hand. "They won't stay surprised long. Another couple of minutes and they're going to start getting mad!" Her teeth gleamed bright in the darkness of the cavern. "Well, what are you apes waiting for? Let's show those little monkey bastards what the Legion can do!"

She sprang from the cave mouth, leveling the FEK and spraying fire at the nearest knot of hannie soldiers. In an instant the rest of the legionnaires were surging after her, Slick among them.

Natives whirled to face the sudden onslaught but died where they stood. Slick dropped to one knee behind a boulder and switched to full autofire, listing to the whine of the gauss fields as they hurled burst after burst of flechette rounds. One hannie pointed an SMG straight at him, then toppled backward, torso shredding under the impact of dozens of needle rounds.

The surprise didn't last long. A hannie track made an awkward, clanking turn and rumbled toward the tunnel mouth, the cupola-mounted machine gun on top chattering death. Bullets slammed into the rock centimeters from Slick's head, making him duck back for cover. He rose up again to fire at the gunner.

The FEK whirred ... out of ammo. His grenade magazine was empty, too.

Corporal Dmowski trotted past him, looking like a miniature tank himself in the head-to-foot plasteel armor he wore to protect himself from the heat of his onager. Dmowski's plasma rifle spoke twice in quick succession, and the plasma rounds punched through the cupola armor as if it was tissue paper. The hannie screamed and slumped sideways.

A native with one of their awkward-looking blunderbuss rocket launchers dived around the side of the track and fired. The rocket dipped low, skimming only centimeters from the ground. It caught Dmowski in the left leg. The corporal went down with blood spraying from the shattered stump of his leg.

For an instant, Slick had an image of Childers, the gunner who'd fallen the same way in the battle for the trenches outside Fort Monkey. He started forward ...

Strauss pushed him aside and ran to Dmowski's side, dropping his FEK as he ran and groping for the first aid kit at his belt.

The hannie with the blunderbuss raised kys weapon again, then pitched over as Kelly Winters fired from the far side of the tunnel. The other onager gunner, Chundra, hit the driver's compartment of the track.

Slick groped for a fresh magazine, but he was out. Cursing, he looked around again. Another armored vehicle was stopped dead in the road fifty meters past the wrecked track, but its turret was still working. The barrel of the big 138mm smoothbore cannon swung slowly across the battlefield, lining up with the tunnel mouth.

Chundra fired again, missed. Slick tried to scream a warning as a hatch banged open on the top of the track, but before the words came out a pair of monkeys had leapt on Chundra, slashing at him with knives. Despite his armor, Chundra was helpless. Slick saw blood where one of the hannies found a weakened joint.

Strauss started to drag Dmowski back toward the shelter of the rock. Slick leapt to help him.

A native rifle barked, seemingly right in his ear. Slick dived and rolled as the hannie soldier fired again from close range. The native must have used the cliff wall itself for cover.

The bullets passed so close Slick could feel their hot wind across his cheek. A second later, the hannie was down. Behind him Slick heard Rostov's yell. "Grant! The Corp's hit!"

He turned. Corporal Strauss was sprawled backward over Dmowski's body, unmoving. Slick crawled to him.

The corporal's eyes were wide, staring sightlessly at the sky. Red stained the front of his coverall, just above the chest armor. The bullet had caught him low in the neck. There was nothing Slick could do for him.

His probing fingers touched a broken length of chain around Strauss's neck. Slick drew it out. At the end dangled a small vial filled with dirt.

The dirt of all the dozens of worlds where Corporal Helmut Strauss had lost comrades fighting for the Legion mingled together in one small container.

Slick stared at the talisman, the battle suddenly far away.

* * *

"Sir, Subaltern Watanabe on the line."

"Thanks, Griesch." Fraser plugged in the lead from the C^3 pack to his helmet. "Alice One. Go ahead, Leader Two."

"HQ, we're falling back on the blockhouse," Watanabe said breathlessly. "There were just too damned many of them. I'm sorry, sir...."

Fraser looked around the cramped, darkened confines of the cave he shared with ten legionnaires. When the explosion down by the south pass had gone off, he'd thought the pressure would be off Watanabe. Apparently he'd assumed too much.

"Understood," he said grimly. "Are you in contact with Sergeant Trent's team?"

"Negative, HQ," Watanabe answered. There was a pause, the sound of gunfire over the radio. "The tunnel to the top of the cliff is cut off now, L-T. There's a hell of a lot of hannies between us and them. Even if they're alive, they're probably too heavily engaged to report."

Fraser didn't answer right away. Just as his plan was starting to look like it might work ...

"Sir," Watanabe went on. "Sarge blocked the pass. There were just too many hannies already through for us to stop. I'm down to maybe twenty men here. If I just had some reinforcements, we could still break these bastards. They're shaky from being cut off."

At least Trent's party had cut the pass. *Damn! If Watanabe had only held a few minutes longer....*

The Miststalkers were still advancing carefully, but they'd be past the old perimeter positions in another five minutes if they continued at their present rate. All the legionnaires had withdrawn from the pass now, taking shelter in several tunnels and caves above the northern side of the pass. Everything was carefully prepared for the hannies. This could ruin the entire plan.

Or would it? If the troops facing Watanabe were as shaky as he claimed ...

"Listen to me, Sub," he said slowly. "Stop trying to hold the hannies on your end. Pull back out of their way. Defend yourself if you have to, but give them an easy way through the pass."

"Sir? Won't that drop them in your laps?"

Fraser grinned. "That's precisely what I'm hoping, Sub. When I give the word, close in behind them with everything you've got left."

"Affirmative, HQ. We'll do our best."

"I know you will, Sub. Fraser clear."

He was already trying to hand the Miststalkers the appearance of an easy victory. What could clinch it better than to see their friends from the south already surging through the pass?

He bit his lip and looked at the handful of legionnaires around him. If he miscalculated, a few more hannies wouldn't make much difference, anyway.

* * *

The roar of an explosion yanked Slick back to reality. He dropped Strauss's vial and threw himself flat as the cliff wall above the tunnel erupted in a shower of rock and flying dirt. Over the sound of the battle he heard Rostov's voice shouting "Get clear! Get clear of the tunnel!"

The native tank rumbled closer, the barrel of its cannon depressing for another shot. With Dmowski dead and Chundra still trying to shake off the hannies slashing and stabbing at him, there was nothing left that could stop that armored beast.

Nothing left to save the unit....

Something bulky and angular prodded Slick's thigh. His hand closed around it. Dmowski's onager, still linked to the gunner by its ConRig targeting harness.

Slick looked up at the tank. Nothing left.

Fumbling with the unfamiliar fittings of the weapon, Slick unhooked the cable that tied the onager to Dmowski's helmet, then freed the harness clasps and raised the awkward plasma rifle. He remembered the lectures on onagers in training back on Devereaux.

They were designed to be used with an aiming system tied to the movement of the operator's eyes, but a plasma rifle could be used without the ConRig, especially against a target as big as a tank.

Of course, the heat buildup of the weapon was enough to badly burn an unarmed man, but the first few shots wouldn't be too bad ...

And the legionnaires needed him now. Slick wasn't going to let the team down. Not this time.

He braced the weapon as well as he could and touched the firing stud. Heat washed over his hands and arms, and the onager bucked wildly.

Without waiting to see the effect of the shot he fired again ... and again.

Pain seared him, but Slick hardly noticed it. He squinted through the heat shimmer, saw the tank's turret leaking smoke. A machine gun flashed from the hull and he fired one more time.

Then the real pain hit, agony shooting up his arms. The onager fell, and Slick sagged to the ground.

Through a haze of shock Slick made out Rostov bending over him, heard the demo man's voice as if from kilometers away. "Don't worry, Grant. You got the bastards. The rest are running …"

"Not … not Grant," Slick whispered.

"Don't try to talk, Grant," someone else said.

"Not Grant …" he repeated. It was important … vital that he tell them. "Slick … call me Slick.…"

He wanted his family to know his name.

* * *

Fraser lifted the edge of the tarp carefully and peered through. The vanguard of the native force was already well past the cave, close to the gap where the valley widened at the top of the pass. In another minute, the hannies would be at the blockhouse … and it would be time to spring the trap.

He only hoped he had set it right. The way Sergeant Trent would have.

The natives passing by now were drawn up in a close formation, like a column on a parade march. That much had gone well, at least. The vanguard had advanced in a loose skirmishing formation, moving from cover to cover, ready for the first sign of resistance. When none had materialized, though, their vigilance had started to relax.

No doubt the slackening sounds of battle from the south were giving them some confidence. They probably imagined that the demons had already been overcome by the troops from Zhairhee.

Give them what they expect … but not the way they expect it. He hoped he'd be able to tell Trent how he'd put those words into practice. If either of them was alive after today.

Even if they savaged the Miststalkers, there were still a lot of hannies on the north side of the mountains, and after this battle Fraser knew his battered legionnaires wouldn't be able to fight again. But at least they'd bloody the enemy's elite before they went down.

Maybe the last stand of Bravo Company in the Zhairhee Pass would go down in the annals alongside such Legion hallmarks as Camerone and Ganymede and Devereaux ... lost causes that still shed luster on the Legion.

These men deserved to be remembered in such company.

"Alice One, this is Lookout." That was Myaighee's voice in his headphones. The little alien had volunteered for the most hazardous job of all. Lying sprawled in an uncomfortable position near the final barricade, with gear scavenged from a dead Dryien soldier and kys hair matted with blood from a cut Legionnaire Donovan had made in kys scalp. Myaighee was pretending to be a casualty so that Fraser's men would have a spotter in position to watch the enemy's progress into the valley.

Ky would be in almost as much danger from friendly fire as from the Dryiens when the shooting started, but Myaighee hadn't flinched. "I am the only one who can be safe, Honored," ky had said. "One of your men might be bayoneted ... just to be sure he was dead."

"Lookout, go ahead."

"A soldier is approaching the blockhouse ... two of them now." There was a pause. Myaighee's voice crackled with excitement as ky spoke again. "I see more soldiers coming from the south! They are coming! Miststalkers have seen them!"

Through the heavy material of the tarp, Fraser could hear the unearthly cheering, the enthusiasm. He nodded to Corporal Johnson. "Now!"

Johnson stabbed at the remote control in his hand savagely.

Out in the valley, the last twenty Galahad antipersonnel mines in the company's arsenal went off almost as one—not just a single round at a time, but all the charges in quick succession.

Legionnaire Griesch ripped away the tarp and the rest poured out into the morning sunlight, their FEKs spitting death.

Fraser's weapon swung easily in his arms, tracking across the dense-packed mass of enemy troops. The confusion was complete. Some of them were still cheering, still trying to press forward in a rush to meet their friends from the south. Others, reacting faster, tried to find their assailants, but too late. From half a dozen tunnel mouths the legionnaires charged, the whine of their guns echoing in the pass like a swarm of enraged insects.

And hannies died from their deadly stings.

"Hammer them! Hammer them!" Fraser looked up to see the big Greek from New Cyprus, Karatsolis, wielding an MEK with the same glee he'd once reserved for his Sabertooth's plasma cannon. The man's crewmate, Corporal Bashar, waved a hand over his head and urged a handful of legionnaires to the attack.

They weren't just firing from cover this time. The legionnaires rushed forward, eager to get to grips with the enemy. And that compounded the confusion, as Fraser had hoped. The hannies were killing almost as many of their own soldiers as the legionnaires were bringing down with FEK fire.

Baker, the sergeant with the injured legs, shouted to two of his men. They dragged him forward and helped him set up behind a boulder. He tossed a native grenade into a cluster of hannies, then another. He yelled a harsh battle cry he could only have learned from the Ubrenfar, Ghirghik. A hannie bullet took him in the face, pitching him back, but another legionnaire killed the native and snatched up the grenades. The fighting went on.

And farther up the pass, beyond the killing field where the Galahads had torn through the front ranks of the hannies forces, more shouts announced the coming of Watanabe's men.

The hannies wavered. Good as they were, the Miststalkers weren't prepared for this onslaught. Some fought and died. Many more broke, throwing away weapons and equipment and running back down the pass.

Those who could escape the wrath of the Legion.

Terran figures topped the crest of the hill…. Watanabe, slender and pale, grinning and flashing a "V-for-Victory" sign. Garcia, her helmet gone, her dark hair streaming in the breeze, carrying a native blunderbuss. Kelly Winters and a handful of the recon troops from Trent's force. More legionnaires closed in behind them, even Ramirez and the Padre, unlikely soldiers with FEKs and grenades tucked into their pockets and dangling from their belts.

The Legion had held.

Johnson caught his arm. "Lieutenant! Listen!"

He pulled off his helmet to hear better. Sounds of gunfire rose from the bottom of the north pass, carried on the wind. Gunfire, heavy machinery, shouting … and something else …

"Goddamn!" Griesch said. "Not another monkey attack!"

"We can't hold them this time," Johnson said. "No ammo left."

"We've got our knives," Bashar put in grimly.

"Wait!" Fraser held up his hand. "Quiet!"

He strained his ears, and a smile spread over his face. "Don't you hear it? The music?"

Some of them were looking at him as if he'd lost his mind, but Karatsolis was smiling now too. He'd heard the mournful fanfare drifting on the breeze.

"Le Boudin" … the age-old marching song of the Foreign Legion.

* * *

Shavvataaars tightened his harness and slapped the automated launch sequence control on the courier ship's main console. Drives cycled, and the ship stirred with barely a whisper of sound.

The boat lifted off, out of the concealment of an *ylyn* paddy east of Zhairhee, and hurtled skyward.

Below, on the surface of the planet the Terrans called Hanuman, Twilight Prowler lay in disarray. The ephemerals had failed.

From the moment Zyzyiig allowed kyself to be killed, the Great Journey had gone wrong. Nothing could put it back together now. The rising in Vyujiid, the Ubrenfar intervention … lost now, with the failure to defeat the Terrans and their Foreign Legion.

At least Hanuman would tie up extra resources, troops the Commonwealth had wanted on Enkidu and elsewhere on the frontier. And Shavvataaars was free. He would leave this hellworld behind and take passage with the Ubrenfar warships when their carriership returned for them.

Shavvataaars was patient as only a Semti could be. He would wait … and he would plan.

And some day he would see the Terrans defeated.

* * *

The command van grounded beside the blockhouse with a triumphant flourish of roaring fans and a swirl of dust. The rear door opened slowly, as if with a conscious sense of drama.

Fraser drew himself to attention and saluted Commandant Isayev as he stepped onto the ramp, holding the pose until the older officer returned it crisply.

The Fwynzei garrison had attacked the Dryiens in force, catching them off-guard at the height of the Miststalker assault. Already disorganized, with morale low from successive reverses at the pass, their supply situation worsening and their leadership out of touch with the headquarters in Zhairhee, the hannie army north of the mountains had fallen apart at the first touch of the Commonwealth counterthrust.

Now, an hour after that desperate last fight, Bravo Company was being relieved.

Isayev's eyes wandered over the valley, still littered with bodies and abandoned equipment. They came to rest on the shrunken ranks of Fraser's command, no more than fifty men and women still on their feet after the savage day's fighting. There were more alive, of course, the ones already being loaded aboard medical vans for the trip to Fwynzei. Like Gunnery Sergeant Trent, and Myaighee, the native.

But the unit had suffered over seventy percent casualties since the first attack on Fort Monkey. The survivors were ragged scarecrows, hardly able to walk.

Yet they stood in ranks proudly, soldiers of the Legion to the last.

"A good job, Fraser," Isayev said slowly. "A damned good job. You've done the Legion proud."

"Not me, Commandant," he said. He gestured at the others. "They're the ones who did it."

The commandant didn't seem to hear him. "That bastard Smythe-Henderson ordered us to sit tight, stay on the defensive. Said he'd relieve you. But we couldn't just sit still when we heard him changing the plans." His eyes locked with Fraser's. "I just wish we could have broken through sooner."

Fraser shook his head. "It didn't matter, Commandant. I think they all knew you'd come, somehow. They knew the Legion would take care of its own."

EPILOGUE

It's our captain who remembers us, and counts his dead.

> —Captain de Borelli, Tuyen Quang,
> French Foreign Legion, 1885

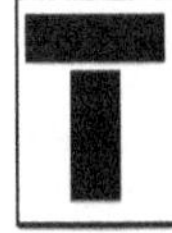

The streets of Fwynzei were a riot of color as the parade made its way down the streets toward the Commonwealth Spaceport. Hannies and humans mingled in an enthusiastic throng, shouting encouragement and tossing flowers.

At the rear of the long column of soldiers and Marines, marching to the slow beat of eighty-eight paces per minute, came the soldiers of the Third Battalion, First Light Infantry Regiment of the Fifth Foreign Legion. And leading the legionnaires, in the position of honor, marched Bravo Company.

Captain Colin Fraser stood next to Commandant Isayev on the review stand, watching the parade march past. His stiff dress uniform with black kepi and heavy epaulets felt heavy and uncomfortable; he would have preferred the issue battledress he'd worn through the long march from Fort Monkey. But the people of Fwynzei demanded a show from the soldiers setting out to restore order in Dryienjaiyeel.

In the three months since the Battle of Zhairhee Pass the Dryiens had fallen into virtual anarchy, with coups and countercoups and a state verging on civil war. With the arrival of fresh Colonial Army troops aboard the Carriership *Nestor*, the Commonwealth was ready at last to return to the war-torn country.

Fort Monkey would be reoccupied and expanded ... and it was only proper that soldiers of the Foreign Legion—soldiers of Bravo Company—should be among those who led the return.

And Colin Fraser, still hardly daring to believe his promotion and confirmation as commander of the unit, would be leading them on this new campaign.

From the reviewing stand he could see their faces. Most were unfamiliar, fresh drafts from Devereaux to bring the unit back up to strength. But there were plenty he recognized, too.

Gunnery Sergeant Trent, for instance, recovered from a long battery of regen treatments and looking as stolid and unemotional as ever ... and Subaltern Watanabe, who sported a ragged scar over one eye and a decoration for bravery on his breast.

He caught sight of Second Platoon's recon lance, the towering Gwyrran Vrurrth, the fresh-faced young legionnaire second class named Grant, and Dmitri Rostov, sporting corporal's stripes on his dun-colored uniform. And Myaighee, now a legionnaire third class in the same lance. Ky had enlisted even knowing that Dryienjaiyeel might be safe to return to as a civilian. The alien had adopted the Legion as a home.

As had Kelly Winters. After the battle, she had come to him for advice; the way the Navy had abandoned them at the pass had convinced her that it was no place for her. Now Kelly Ann Winters, CSN, was listed as dead in the fighting ... but Ann Kelly, Warrant Officer Fourth Class, would be accompanying the Legion as an expert on combat engineering. It was a bit of deception Fraser—and Isayev— had been glad to connive in. The Legion looked after its own, and Kelly had proven herself as much a legionnaire as any of them.

The last of Bravo Company went by, followed by the rest of the newly-designated Demi-Battalion Beatrice. Fraser turned to the commandant and saluted sharply.

"Permission to join my unit, sir?"

"Permission granted, Captain Fraser," Isayev replied, returning the salute.

Fraser gestured to Legionnaire Garcia. "Let's go."

An open-topped floatcar hovered on magrep fields behind the stand, waiting for him. Legionnaire Karatsolis held the door open for Fraser and Garcia, then slid into the passenger seat next to Corporal

Bashar. Their full dress uniforms were perfectly tailored, impeccably clean, but the men look just the same as ever.

They were legionnaires first … always.

And Captain Colin Fraser was one of them.

BOOK TWO:
HONOR AND
FIDELITY

PROLOGUE

Soldi Rochemont: Distance from Sol 138 light-years ... Spectral class G1V; radius 1.006 Sol; mass 1.02 Sol; lumin-osity 1.102 Sol. Stellar Effective Temperature 5900°K ... Four planets, one planetoid belt. There is only one habitable world, the innermost, designated "Polypheme"....

I Polypheme: Orbital radius 0.90 AUs; eccentricity .0136; period 0.845 solar years (308.8 std. days) ... One natural satellite, Non-homme, mass 0.004 Terra; density 0.6 Terra (3.3 g/cc); orbital radius 130,269 kms; period 5.16 std. days (123.8 hours) ... an airless, waterless body notable only for its significant tidal effects on Polypheme ...

Planetary mass 1.1 Terra; density 0.85 Terra (4.675 g/cc); surface gravity 0.93 G. Radius 6950.4 kilometers; circumference 43,670.54 kilometers ... Total surface area 607,054,524 square kilometers ...

Hydrographic percentage 82 % ... Atmospheric pressure 0.9 atm; composition oxygen/nitrogen. Oxygen content 18% ...

Planetary axial tilt 17°40'57.4". Rotation period 46 hours, 14 minutes, 28.9 seconds....

Planetography: Polypheme's close satellite produces tidal stresses which have shaped many facets of planetary development. The planet is more seismically active than Terra, with a consequently more rugged surface.... There are ten continents.... Tides cause broad coastal tracts to be regularly inundated and then exposed....

Equatorial temperatures have been recorded as high as 45°C.... Polar temperatures rarely rise above freezing but are too warm to produce permanent ice packs.... There is a moderating influence exerted on the planet by the oceans, and humans find the climate tolerable outside the tropics.

The low planetary density is indicative of a general lack of worth-while ore deposits, but there is an unusually high concen-tration of minerals in the planetary oceans, possibly caused by widespread undersea volcanic activity. By Commonwealth standards Poly-pheme is poor, and were it not for the twin interests of scientists studying tidal effects and miners lured by the high mineral content of the seas Polypheme might well have been ignored....

Although the usual variety in terrain and ecology is present on Polypheme, of greatest interest are the many adaptations to the tidal conditions.... The tidal plains have become home to many species uniquely evolved for this strange environ, including the planet's sapient race....

Biology: Intelligent life arose in the tidal flats, in a species originally adapted to a dual existence built around the ebb and flow of the tides.... Equally at home as swimmers or clinging by sucker-like appendages to rocks exposed on the flood plains, this species found intelligence useful both to cope with the fast-changing conditions of their unique ecological niche and to handle certain swimming predators. The latter further spurred adaptation to a dry-land environment....

The sophonts of Polypheme, the *drooroukh*, are a bilaterally symmetrical, bimodal race with four limbs all equally well adapted as hands, feet, or fins as circumstances warrant. A highly soph-isticated pseudogill system can extract oxygen from air or water with equal proficiency, with membranes in the gill outlets serving as speech organs. They generally stand upright on land but can move on all fours very quickly and are superb swimmers. A flat, heavy tail provides propulsion in the water and balance ashore.... They are homeothermic, producing live young. The juveniles of the species cannot leave the water on their own, and they normally swim free except when feeding.... The young are parasitic, cling-ing to an adult and drawing nourishment from its blood. Although humanoid in gross appearance, the *drooroukh* have little in com-mon with Mankind....

The average local measures 1.7 meters in length, not including the tail, with hairless, slick skin which ranges from gray-green to black in color.... Although possessed of two sexes and a fairly typical reproductive cycle, the *drooroukh* have little concept of family, regarding child care as the collective responsibility of the group....

Civilization: Several thousand years ago a schism developed among the inhabitants of Polypheme. Part of the population began spending more and more time on land, except as necessary for child-rearing and mariculture.... The process led to the develop-ment of a civilization along patterns similar to Terra, with metal-working, cities, and the rudiments of scientific thought....

The second group, however, remained closely tied to the seas in a nomadic existence unchanged over a period of 50,000 years.... The nomads have enjoyed mixed relations with their land-dwelling cousins, sometimes trading with them, at other times in conflict.... Most researchers see them as locked in a cultural dead-end....

Commonwealth Contact: Prior to the Semti War Polypheme was nominally a part of the Semti Conclave, but the Semti had little interest in the planet and leased development rights to the neighboring Toeljuk Autarchy.... The Toels found conditions on Polypheme familiar and applied many of the techniques invented in their own climb to power to exploiting the new world.... Though poor in metals ashore, Polypheme offered resources in abundance at sea, where a species of small aquatic grazer, the "shelljet," was found to extract and concentrate metals in its shell. A number of large harvester ships, and bases to support them, were established by the Toeljuks on Polypheme.... The project was abandoned about the time of the Semti War due to the collapse of the Autarchy's economy in that period....

For close to a century Commonwealth contact was limited to a few scientific teams and the missionary work of the Uplift Foun-dation.... Three years ago Seafarms Interstellar put forward a pro-posal to duplicate Toel harvesting techniques, using the abandoned Toeljuk facilities as a basis for new operations....

—Excerpted from *Leclerc's Guide to the Commonwealth Volume VI:*
The Toel Frontier,
34th Edition, published 2848 AD

Chapter One

Is it how a soldier lives that matters? Isn't it how he dies?

—Colonel Joseph Conrad,
French Foreign Legion, 1835

Legionnaire Second-Class Alois Trousseau shielded his eyes against the dazzling light of the setting sun. Twilight on Polypheme was the stuff of romantic poetry, long, lingering, with brilliant hues of red and orange illuminating the low-lying cloud banks and reflecting off the vast empty stretches of the Sea of Scylla. The light caught the crescent shape of Nonhomme, Polypheme's satellite, as it loomed overhead looking close enough to reach out and touch, and reflections from the water rippled and danced everywhere.

But Trousseau paid little attention to the beauty that was Polypheme as he crossed the docking platform and knelt near the water's edge.

Displacing just under a hundred thousand metric tons, *Seafarms Cyclops* was a huge vessel. There were four of these docks spaced around her wide hull, but this was the best one for Trousseau's purposes. Designed to accommodate smaller ships with stores and equipment destined for the engineering spaces, this platform was rarely used or even visited.

And the setting sun would help hide Trousseau as he left the vessel in the raft he held bundled under one arm. By the time anyone noticed he was missing, he would be far from the confines of the huge harvester ship.

He'd planned his desertion carefully. Even the time was perfect. Not only would the sun help obscure his movements, but it was close to 0400 by standard ship-time. Polypheme's 47-hour rotation didn't mesh well with the cycles of bodies evolved for Terrestrial conditions. Most of the ship's personnel were asleep, and those on watch were likely to be slow responding.

In another few hours they would be leaving the Cape of Storms behind, and with it their last contact with solid land for a month or more. He had to act tonight if he was to escape.

Trousseau pulled the ring and listened to the hiss of the raft's inflation with a satisfied little smile. Once ashore it would be a long, hard march before he reached the native city of Ourgh. But it would be worth it to be quit of the Foreign Legion.

He knew some starport workers who would smuggle him aboard the next ship out for the hundred sols he's been hoarding for the last few weeks. Once they put in to the systerm on the outermost planet of the system he'd be able to come out of hiding. Maybe a ship would need an electronics technician. He'd put in enough time as the platoon's C^3 operator to get a job handling any commlink or computer a small ship could mount.

The raft slid slowly into the water. Trousseau lashed it to the cleat and ran through a last mental checklist.

Free! He was finally going to be free of the Legion, of the martinet NCOs, of the overbearing officers. Free of the boredom. He'd never imagined it could be so boring until he joined the garrison on Polypheme.

With a last glance around, Trousseau turned his back on the *Seafarms Cyclops*—on the Fifth Foreign Legion.

Something splashed at the forward end of the dock, and Trousseau's trained reflexes made him spin to face it before he was even consciously aware of the sound.

He found himself staring down at a bulky figure with smooth gray-green skin. It seemed to take forever for the legionnaire to register it as one of the Polypheme sophonts, a "polliwog" to use the slang of humans living on the planet. By the time he realized what it was it had already climbed free of the water to stand on the platform, its stalked eyes focused on Trousseau with an unfathomable alien expression.

It—no, *he*—was one of the planet's ocean-dwelling nomads, clad in nothing more than a loose harness that held an assortment of primitive weapons and implements. An intricate pattern of tattoos on his chest identified his tribe, but Trousseau had never taken adchip instruction on nomad symbols or tribal signs, so it was unintelligible.

The wog was large for his kind, nearly two meters long without the flat tail that balanced his slightly forward-leaning posture.

But Trousseau was only vaguely aware of the creature's size. His attention was focused, instead, on the small device clutched in one long-jointed, web-fingered hand. A slender tube mounted atop an alien pistol grip....

The alien raised the tube to point at Trousseau's chest and squeezed the trigger.

The impact of the 5 mm rocket projectile made Trousseau stagger back. His duraweave coverall—and the short range, which kept the rocket from building up to full impact velocity—had saved his life, but the legionnaire was stunned. He struggled to keep his balance, but couldn't.

Suddenly his feet weren't on the solid deck anymore. Salt stung his eyes and made him gag as he fell into the dark water. Trousseau came to the surface spluttering, gasping for air. Long fingers closed around his throat, pulling him down again.

Trousseau knew he would die.

He let himself go limp, then kicked away again as the grip relaxed. Wincing at the pain, he took another breath and let himself sink, his fingers operating the keys on his wristpiece computer. He couldn't outfight the nomads in their own element, but at least he could warn the others they were here before it was too late.

An artificial voice whispered in his ear. "Please give the password for computer access."

Damn! What was the password? Trousseau twisted away from another wog and broke the surface again. "Nightwing!" he spluttered, gasping for air. "Nightwing!"

"Access accepted. Please—"

"Security code India!" Trousseau shouted. A knife blade slashed through his coverall, and pain lanced through his back. "India! Intruders on Deck One, En—"

The knife struck again, and again.

And Legionnaire Alois Trousseau bobbed to the surface, staining the water with his blood.

* * *

Subaltern Toru Watanabe rolled out of his bunk as the ululating alarm shrieked through the bowels of the *Seafarms Cyclops*. The metal was cold under his bare feet, but the shiver that ran up his spine had nothing to do with the temperature.

Watanabe had hoped for a cruise as boring as garrison life back at the Legion's base, in the installation the humans on Polypheme called "Sandcastle." But the security alarm meant there was trouble aboard the harvester ship—serious trouble.

Still groggy, Watanabe crossed the cabin and slapped the call button on the intercom mounted above the desk. Like all the human equipment aboard *Seafarms Cyclops* the intercom had an improvised, unfinished look that stood out in contrast to the flowing lines and exotic patterns of the original vessel. The contrast reminded him vaguely of the blend of high-tech and traditional styles of art and architecture his Japanese ancestors had brought with them from Terra to his native world of Pacifica.

He forced himself to concentrate on the problem at hand as the heavy features of Sergeant Yussufu Muwanga filled the viewscreen. "Operations," the sergeant said gruffly.

"What have you got, Sergeant?"

"Computer just sounded the alarm, sir," Muwanga replied. "We're trying to find the source now. It wasn't any of our lookouts."

"A false alarm?" he asked hopefully.

Muwanga frowned. Watanabe rubbed his forehead absently. He knew the answer the man would give. Why had he let himself show his uncertainty so plainly?

"*Someone* put through an India code, sir," the sergeant said slowly. "The computer can't just come up with one on its own."

"Then get Trousseau down there and ask *him*," Watanabe snapped. "Meanwhile, order Sergeant Gessler to assemble the men in Hold Two. I'm on my way down."

"Yessir," the sergeant replied. The screen went dead.

Watanabe slumped into the chair behind the desk, feeling drained. *Why can't I keep a lid on my temper?* he asked himself bitterly. A year ago he'd never have lost control like that. Toru Watanabe had the reputation for being quiet, soft-spoken, calm in any crisis—a competent platoon commander.

Since then, though, Toru Watanabe had changed.

He dressed quickly in duraweave fatigues, boots, and a beret, his mind on the past year. First, the excitement of getting his assignment. It was rare for a top Academy student to request the Fifth Foreign Legion, but Watanabe had gone after the posting with a single-minded determination to follow in his father's footsteps and be a part of the Legion tradition. He'd made it, too, earning a platoon command.

But then came the fighting on Hanuman, the long overland retreat through hostile territory after a coup d'état had cut his company off from outside aid. And at the climax of the campaign the legionnaires had been forced to make a desperate stand against overwhelming odds, and Toru Watanabe had watched as his precious platoon was all but destroyed. Somehow he'd come through the fighting alive, but he knew he'd never be the same again.

War wasn't like the stories you saw on the holovid shows, or the textbook accounts of maneuvers and counter-maneuvers. It took courage to command men in battle; not just personal bravery, but the kind of resolve that would let an officer order his men to their deaths. Toru Watanabe wasn't sure he had that kind of courage anymore.

But if the alarm was genuine, he might soon have to find that kind of courage again.

His mind was still grappling with doubts as Watanabe left his quarters and sought out the Operations Center, a windowless cabin two decks below his quarters near the heart of Legion country commonly known as "C-cubed." *Seafarms Cyclops* was a huge ship, originally designed to carry a crew of several hundred gregarious Toeljuks on an extended cruise. Since her refit for human personnel she needed less than fifty men for a crew, and there was more than enough space for a thirty-four-man Legion platoon to have private quarters, rec facilities, drill spaces, a secure armory, and everything else they could possibly want to make a three-month tour at sea bearable.

Sergeant Muwanga looked up from a control console as Watanabe entered. "Sir, Trousseau won't answer. And he didn't assemble with the others."

Watanabe crossed the cramped room and bent over a computer terminal beside the sergeant. "Did you check his quarters?"

"Empty, sir," Muwanga said with a gesture at a viewscreen. It showed a small, spartan cubicle. There was no one visible, and the bunk was neatly made up. A locker stood open nearby, obviously empty as well.

"Goddamn ..." Watanabe said softly. He punched up a code that would allow the computer to trace the legionnaire's helmet communications gear.

"No response from beacon," the computer voice said. "Helmet has been damaged or disconnected."

Muwanga and Watanabe exchanged looks. "Desertion," the black man said. "Has to be."

Watanabe sank into a chair. "Damn stupid place to desert," he said.

The sergeant shrugged expressively. *"Cafarde,"* he replied.

Watanabe nodded. *Le cafarde*—the expression meant *cockroach*—was a disorder that had been a part of Foreign Legion lore from the very beginning. A compound of boredom, instability, and confusion, it caused men to react in bizarre ways. Some committed suicide, some deserted, some picked fights, a few just went mad—all from *cafarde*. Some superstitious legionnaires talked of it as if it really was an insect, a bug that crawled into their ears and whispered to them in the night.

Cafarde was becoming a problem on Polypheme, as boring a duty station as any legionnaire was likely to see. But Trousseau had never seemed like the sort to crack under that particular pressure.

Muwanga turned away to operate another console. He held a headpiece speaker to one ear. "Sergeant Gessler says the men are ready, sir," he said. "What are your orders?"

Watanabe stared down at the monitor, eyes locked on the empty cabin. Trousseau had been with him on Hanuman, one of the handful who survived. He'd picked the legionnaire to be his new C^3 technician personally. It was like a betrayal....

"Sir?" Muwanga insisted.

He looked up at the sergeant. "Didn't Trousseau like to go out on one of the docking platforms to get away from everyone?" he asked quietly.

Muwanga hesitated. "Yeah ... Yes, sir. I'm not sure which one."

"Check the monitor cameras on all four of them, Sergeant." Excitement was putting a sharp edge in his voice. If he was right....

Muwanga's fingers skimmed over a keypad. "Nothing ... nothing ... Hell! Portside aft platform doesn't have a camera feed. Must be out."

Watanabe leaned past him to stab at the intercom button. "Sergeant Gessler! Take the platoon to the docking platform, portside, aft. I'll meet you there!"

Sergeant Muwanga stared at him. "Not much to go on, sir...."

"*Someone* set off that alarm, Sergeant, and Trousseau's the only one not accounted for. And if he really was making a break for it, he would have knocked out the camera so you wouldn't see him." Watanabe ran from C-cubed, hoping inwardly that his guess was right.

*   *   *

Corporal Dmitri Rostov dropped to one knee and peered cautiously around the corner. The broad corridor leading to the docking platform was empty, and the door beyond was sealed tight. He hoped they weren't chasing shadows. That warning siren was sweet music, promising action, and action was just what he needed right now.

He glanced over his shoulder at his lancemates. "Vrurrth ... Slick ... Corridor's clear. Move up and flank the door."

Legionnaire John Grant—"Slick" to the rest of the lance—nodded and slid past Rostov noiselessly. Vrurrth, the hulking legionnaire from Gwyr, followed more slowly. Rostov had a grin at the contrast between the slender teenager and the big alien. The three of them had been on Hanuman together and made a tight-knit team.

The other two members of Rostov's recon lance moved closer. They were new to the unit. Legionnaire First-Class Judy Martin was a veteran who handled her laser sniper's rifle like she'd been born with it, but he still didn't know much about how she was likely to react. As for Legionnaire Jaime Auriega, he was a nube, a newcomer fresh out of training at the Legion's depot on Devereaux. As such, Rostov thought with another suppressed smile, he was the lowest form of life. He'd remain so until he proved he could cut it with the Legion.

"Cover 'em, Martin," he said. "Nube, when I move, you move. Got it?"

Auriega nodded dully. He wasn't bright, but he was willing, and that often counted for more in the Legion.

Rostov leaned around the corner again and gave Vrurrth a curt hand signal. The Gwyrran gave a ponderous nod and undogged the hatch. Like most of the fittings on the harvester ship it was of original Toeljuk design, manually operated and made to accommodate their squat bodies. Vrurrth pushed it open with a grunt, and Slick, his FEK gauss rifle held at the ready, rolled through the hatch with a smooth motion that looked like a move in an intricate ballet.

Slick came up on one knee, spraying autofire at unseen targets.

"Recon!" Rostov shouted, springing to his feet and pounding down the corridor to support the young legionnaire. Auriega's heavy footfalls echoed just behind him.

Slapping the helmet control that operated his radio, Rostov cut in the channel to Platoon Sergeant Gessler. "We got bad guys, Sarge! Better send some help!"

* * *

Watanabe heard the call from the recon lance over the commlink in the helmet he had donned in place of his uniform beret. He speeded up, ducking his head to avoid the low overhang of a Toeljuk hatch. Without a helmet he could walk through shipboard doorways without any trouble, but the extra communications and computer gear in a command helmet made it bulge up in back an extra three centimeters, just enough to be a problem.

Platoon Sergeant Karl Gessler turned to meet him. "You heard, Sub?" he asked.

Frowning, Watanabe nodded. "You could've sent more than one lance to check it out, Gessler," he said sharply.

The sergeant shook his head. "Rostov's boys were the first ones to draw their weapons. I sent them on ahead—per your orders, sir." His tone was cold. Gessler obeyed his platoon leader, but Watanabe knew there was no respect there. The sergeant had seen Watanabe struggling with minor decisions too often lately.

"Let's get some more men up there now, dammit!"

"The rest of Light Section's already on the way," Gessler said. "And I was *about* to get the rest moving...."

"Then do it!" Watanabe turned away from the sergeant, cutting the conversation off.

"All right, you sandrats! By lances! Let's mag it!" Gessler's voice sounded even colder and harsher than usual.

Watanabe followed the legionnaires, trying hard to ignore the growing conviction that he deserved every bit of the sergeant's contempt.

* * *

Rostov ducked through the outer hatch, swinging his FEK to the ready. The wind was starting to rise on the exposed platform, probably a sign of one of Polypheme's fierce storms moving into the area. He ignored the weather as he sized up the situation with experienced eyes.

Slick and Vrurrth were crouched side-by-side a meter from the hatch, spraying FEK fire across the platform into a small group of natives clustered at the forward end of the dock. Several locals already lay sprawled on the deck, their bodies shredded by the tiny gauss-propelled slivers that were the primary ammo of the Legion assault rifles.

He heard a sound behind and above him and whirled.

A large-eyed alien face leered down at him from the smooth sides of the superstructure. The polliwogs were equipped with sucker-like appendages on their arms and legs, which helped them cling to boulders and cliffs in the tidal flats that were their primary ecological niche.

This native clutched a knife in the feeding tendrils curled below its mouth. It seemed to move in slow motion, freeing one arm, taking the knife in a flat, long-digited hand, raising its arm to strike....

Rostov's finger tightened on the trigger of the FEK and the face disappeared in a mass of blood and torn flesh. The knife clattered to the deck beside his boot.

"Look out, Corporal!"

Rostov barely had time to register Auriega's voice before the big legionnaire slammed into him, shoving him to the deck. There was a bright flash and a hiss of burning propellant.

Then Auriega sagged to the deck, his own face ruined. Beyond the dead legionnaire Rostov saw another wog clinging to the super-structure. It clutched an unfamiliar-looking pistol in one hand. He fired before the alien could shift aim and shoot again.

More men burst through the door from inside the vessel, led by a pair of figures clad in armor from head to foot and carrying onager plasma rifles in their bulky ConRig harnesses. The unbearably bright flash of a plasma bolt was like an extra sun shining on the deck. A nomad gaped down at the leg the shot had severed before falling over backward into the sea.

A native surfaced nearby, opening its mouth to give an eerie, deep-throated cry that Rostov couldn't translate. Suddenly the rest of the natives were diving into the water of their own free will, escaping.

Rostov stood slowly, checking his magazine and surveying the cramped battlefield. Much as he craved action, he wasn't about to follow those things into their own element.

*　*　*

Watanabe followed Gessler through the hatch and onto the dock. A pair of legionnaires were busy pushing native bodies over the side, but the splatters of blood were still plain testimony to the savage little fight.

Corporal Rostov met them and gave a sketchy salute. "One man dead, Sub," he said, pointing to a still form under an improvised shroud on the deck nearby. "Auriega. The new man."

Watanabe noted that Rostov avoided using the legionnaire's scornful "nube." The man had proved himself, and paid the highest price for doing so. "What about Legionnaire Trousseau?" he asked quietly.

"We found some of his gear on that raft, Sub," Rostov replied. "No sign of him, though."

"Then it's almost certainly *two* dead, corporal," Watanabe said wearily. They couldn't have helped Trousseau, but if Gessler hadn't sent the recon lance in ahead of everyone else Auriega might not have been killed.

But Gessler wasn't to blame. Watanabe was the platoon leader, and responsible for every death.

"Found something else I thought you'd want to see, Sub," Rostov went on. He held out a pistol of some kind. "Some of the lokes were carrying these."

Watanabe examined the weapon. It was small, looking more like a child's toy than a real pistol, and made almost entirely of some lightweight plastic with a peculiar rubbery finish. But it was clearly an autoloading rocket pistol, more primitive than the FE-PLF he carried on his hip, but using the same principles.

Principles none of the natives of Polypheme were supposed to have mastered, not even the most civilized of the shore-dwelling cultures. Crossbows and blowguns were the limit of native technology.

Until now, it seemed.

He handed the pistol to Gessler. "Have this thing scanned and analyzed. I want to know what the owner of this thing had for breakfast!"

"Yessir."

"Corporal, did you see anything else that looked out of place, unusual?"

Rostov shook his head slowly. Another legionnaire, the kid they called Slick, looked around. "Uh ... Sub? I saw something that struck me kind of funny."

"What?"

"Well … uh, our briefings said the natives were highly aggressive when they got into a fight, and swarmed on an enemy until one side or the other was dead. But these wogs broke off the attack when things started to go sour. Looked like an officer down in the water was giving them orders, sir."

Rostov nodded. "He's right, Sub," the corporal agreed. "I didn't really think about it, but Slick—er, Grant—put his finger on it. Those bastards were fighting like they knew what they were doing."

Watanabe looked away, staring at the choppy sea.

High-tech weapons and a new style of fighting. The nomads of Polypheme's open oceans were definitely becoming more of a threat than anyone had imagined was possible.

Captain Fraser would have to know about this.

Chapter Two

A new planet is just another place for legionnaires to die.

—Colonel Maurice Lequillier,
Second Foreign Legion, 2238

Captain Colin Fraser squeezed through the throng, dodging around a pair of polliwogs arguing over the price of a bolt of plush cloth. The bazaar at Ourgh was a riot of color and sound, a scene that might have come straight out of Medieval Terra had it not been for the alien forms of the shopkeepers and passersby who filled the narrow streets. The noise they made was an assault on the ears as they haggled, individual voices blending together in an unearthly cacophony.

Here and there among the wogs there were even stranger forms as well. Some were company employees, like the majority of the humans on Polypheme, but Fraser was startled to note a party of squat Toeljuks waddling awkwardly on thick, stumpy tentacles, hampered by gravity twice what they were used to. Once the Toeljuks had been virtual masters of the planet. Now only the occasional trading ship kept up the contact between the Autarchy and Polypheme.

"Slow down, Colin!"

He turned back to see Kelly Winters struggling to push past a local who was busy unloading goods from the back of a stubborn-looking *groogh*, one of the oversized beasts of burden the land-dwelling wogs used for hauling heavy loads and plowing fields ashore. She finally got around wog and beast and joined him, out of breath.

"I thought you said you wanted a rest," she accused.

He grinned. "After two weeks behind a desk this *is* a rest, Kelly." It was hard to think of her by her new name, her Legion name, Warrant Officer Fourth-Class Ann Kelly. She had been a combat engineer with the Commonwealth Navy, stationed on Hanuman, when he was still a newly posted Lieutenant serving as Exec with a Legion company there. Then came the rebellion and the long march out of hostile territory. Fraser's CO had died, forcing him to assume command of the unit; Kelly, the only survivor from outside the Legion, had accompanied the troops. At first she had shared the scorn for legionnaires most "decent" people felt, but over time she had come to respect them.

And in that final harrowing battle, when her own Navy people had left the legionnaires standing alone against horrible odds, Kelly had fought alongside Fraser's men. Her expertise in combat engineering had contributed to the victory they had somehow wrung from seemingly certain death. But when it was over, she'd made her contempt for the Navy clear. Instead of returning to duty, Kelly had volunteered to join the Foreign Legion, and Fraser and his superior had contrived to arrange her "death" in the official records of the fighting.

Sometimes Fraser's conscience gave him a twinge of guilt over his involvement in her desertion, but his unit owed Kelly Winters too much to refuse her. Signed on as a warrant officer specializing as a sapper and pioneer, Kelly had accompanied Fraser's men when they went back into hostile territory to put down the rebellion. Now she commanded a platoon of Legion sappers attached to the garrison on Polypheme.

They spent a lot of time together. Shared experiences, common interests, a similar way of looking at things ... Fraser wasn't sure yet if it was love, but it was certainly a friendship that made life on Polypheme a little more bearable.

"Wish you my wares to see, *Ukwarr?*" a vendor asked. Fraser had chipped the principle local tongue, but there were many dialects and variations. This native seemed to be speaking one of the nomad tribal languages, but Fraser wasn't sure.

He glanced down at the blanket the native had spread on the ground, then knelt for a closer look. Being bimodal, the wogs found it perfectly comfortable to drop down on all fours whenever they had to, though most of the merchants in the bazaar had carts or tables. That confirmed Fraser's suspicion that this was a nomad. They didn't use carts—there was little call for the wheel in their oceanic lifestyle—and a nomad wouldn't be likely to be carrying a table in a pouch on his harness.

"Take a look at these, Kelly," he said, picking up one of the delicate pieces. It was a piece of bone, intricately carved with symbols and designs that seemed to bring out natural patterns in the material.

Kelly dropped to one knee beside him. "It's beautiful, Col." She took it from him and held it up, letting the reddish rays of sunset play across the ornate surface.

"*Akurg muuin ghoourak?*" Fraser asked the vendor. "Free Swimmers carving made?" He hoped he was interpreting the curious dialect correctly. The sentence structure was quite different from what he had learned for dealing with the citizens of Ourgh, and nomads could be touchy.

The native's eyestalks twitched with pleasure. "Yes ... yes, tusk from *woorroo* Free Swimmers carved. *Woorroo* hunt most difficult."

Fraser glanced at Kelly, who continued to examine the tusk. She seemed to share his fascination with the alien artist's ability to blend the natural appearance of the bone with the delicate strokes of a knife.

He smiled. There weren't many humans on or off Polypheme who could appreciate the nomads' art. Even the people who had to work regularly with the locals—scientists, and the businessmen from Seafarms Interstellar—were inclined to dismiss the nomads as worthless savages.

"On Terra about a thousand years back there were humans making carvings like that," he commented in English. "Scrimshaw, I think it was called."

"Who, primitives?" she asked.

He shook his head. "Sailors. Navy men on the old surface ships with too little to do on long sea trips." He held out his hand, and she passed the carving to him. Turning back to the vendor, he went on in the nomad dialect. "Barter for this would we."

The nomad held up a feeding tendril. "One *drooj, Ukwarr,*" he said.

That would be at least ten times its real value, Fraser thought. The nomads understood money well enough from centuries of trading with the land-dwellers, but it didn't stop them from carrying on their own traditions of barter and hard bargaining.

"*!!Ghoour,*" he replied, not quite getting the double clicking sound at the start of the word. "No. One *vroor!* is too much."

They bargained until Fraser was sure the nomad's sensibilities would be properly satisfied. It took a careful touch to keep from offending the sea-dwellers in transactions like this one. Offering too much for an item was almost as serious an insult as paying too little. He handed over four *vroor!,* small iron coins that were legal tender here in Ourgh. Then he turned back to Kelly.

"Looks like old Navy customs die hard," he said, handing her the carving. "A little scrimshaw to take your mind off the boredom."

"You saw it first, Col. Don't you want it?"

He shook his head. "It's yours. Take it, before I change my mind!"

She grinned and slipped it into her shoulder bag. Her full-dress Legion uniform looked out of place in the bazaar, but the Seafarms management had made it clear that they wanted legionnaires to show a high profile in the town. The uniform certainly did that, with a khaki jacket and slacks, a blue cummerbund, red and green epaulets, and a kepi. Kelly's headgear was white with a broad black stripe, while Fraser, a Legion officer, wore the traditional *kepi noire.* It was a needlessly gaudy uniform, but it traced its history through all of the units that had counted themselves as "Foreign Legions" all the way back to the original French Foreign Legion of pre-spaceflight Terra.

Fraser suspected that the company was probably insisting on high visibility as a way of overawing the locals with Commonwealth military prowess, despite the fact that there was no more than a platoon of legionnaires on duty in town at any one time, and their sole purpose was to act as military police to look after the legionnaires who could turn a town into a small-scale war zone while enjoying an overnight pass.

It was galling. There were exactly two combat companies, plus a few specialist troops, stationed on Polypheme, but Seafarms treated them like a full-fledged garrison. Nor was it comforting to know that the company regarded the legionnaires as their own private corporate police force.

But Seafarms Interstellar was a wholly owned subsidiary of Reynier Industries, and even a subsidiary of the company that held the monopoly over the Commonwealth's production of interstellar drives commanded a lot of clout—at least enough to get Colonial Army troops assigned as glorified security guards on this worthless backwater world.

"You're getting that look again," Kelly commented as they left the scrimshaw vendor behind. "What's wrong?"

Fraser shrugged and pointed to her bag. "I guess that thing reminded me of boredom. It's a topic I've been running into a lot lately."

"More trouble with *cafarde*?"

He nodded. "Somebody in Alpha Company hung himself last night. And we've had three attempted desertions in the past week." He shook his head. "One of them was Gates—one of the Hanuman vets."

"It's getting pretty bad, then." It was more of a statement than a question.

"Yeah. These men are combat soldiers. Sticking them in a garrison is begging for trouble." He paused to dodge an aggressive shopkeeper hawking his wares. "They say the only real cure for *cafarde* is a loaded rifle and plenty of targets. Not much chance of that here."

She pulled him into an empty alley mouth. "You can't keep blaming yourself, you know," she said.

"Yeah. Right. The damned Commission is breathing down the neck of every Colonial Army unit in the sector. And I'm the hot potato no CO wants to be stuck with!"

Fraser didn't even try to keep the bitterness out of his voice. For a while there on Hanuman, it had looked like his luck was turning....

He had been a rising star in the Commonwealth Regulars, son of the hero of New Dallas, General Lovat Fraser of Caledon. Posted to Intelligence with a lieutenant's commission and a spotless record, Fraser should have been set for life. No struggling for recognition like his father, no long career with nothing but Citizenship papers and a few distorted holovid stories to show for a lifetime's dedication, not for Colin Fraser!

That was before Fenris, though. The rebellion on Fenris had taken everyone in the Commonwealth by surprise, of course, but once it had erupted it should have been easy enough to put down. But Major Richard St. John, the officer responsible for overseeing the planetary intelligence-gathering effort, had turned out to be incompetent, and men had died. A lot of men, and Commonwealth Regulars at that.

Colin Fraser had been St. John's aide, and in the inevitable inquiry that followed the disaster he gave the evidence that sealed the man's fate. The major resigned the service ... but the story hadn't ended there.

Major Richard St. John was the nephew of Senator Warwick, and Senator Warwick was an important man on the Commonwealth's

Military Affairs Committee. Warwick had pulled a few strings and contrived to take down the man who had ruined his nephew, and Colin Fraser's promising career had evaporated overnight.

Volunteering for the Colonial Army had been the only real option open to him short of court-martial or resignation. The Colonials weren't as glamorous as the regular Terran regiments, but they offered more action, more opportunity to really *do* something for the Commonwealth. General Fraser had risen to command the Caledon Watch in the Colonial Army.

But General Fraser's patronage was no match for Senator Warwick's displeasure, and it turned out that the Fifth Foreign Legion was the only haven left open. The rising star of Intelligence had ended up as exec in an infantry company—that seemed somehow inevitable, military organizations being what they were—posted to Hanuman.

Bravo Company, his new outfit, had pulled off a miracle in the jungles of that primitive planet. After bringing his men across fifteen hundred kilometers of hostile territory and winning the battle that stopped the native insurrection cold, Fraser had suddenly seen new opportunities opening up. Promotion to captain and command of his beloved Bravos, a key role in the pacification of Hanuman, favorable notice from his superiors in the Legion ... notoriety like that could have put his career back on track.

Should have put it back on track.

The Commonwealth Senate had chosen the wrong time to start one of its periodic witch hunts for corruption in the Colonial Army. Members of the Military Affairs Committee—including Senator Warwick—were on the prowl through the frontier sectors searching for someone to nail to the cross. Suddenly, notoriety and a promising future were the last things Colin Fraser needed. As a bona fide hero, Fraser was likely to attract the Senator's attention, and no one wanted to risk being caught in the fallout if that happened.

His previous CO, Commandant Isayev, had explained it carefully to Fraser. "Don't get me wrong, son," he had said. "The Legion looks after its own. But you know how the Commission does its business— none better, I'd bet. What we need to do is get you out of sight for a while. That's better for you, and it's better for the Legion."

When Seafarms Interstellar requested Colonial troops to safeguard their harvester project on Polypheme, the Legion had responded by forming a provisional battalion. Fraser's company had been one of the first units picked for the new formation, and so far only one other outfit had been posted to Polypheme.

He realized that Kelly was still watching him with a worried frown. "I could have asked for a transfer. Or resigned. That's what I should have done in the first place."

"You wouldn't be Colin Fraser if you ran from a fight," she said. "There were a dozen times you could have taken the easy way out on Hanuman, but you didn't. This is the same thing."

He tried to smile. "Yeah, that's me. I don't know the meaning of the word surrender."

"Right," she agreed, the frown melting into an impish grin. "Too many syllables for a legionnaire to handle."

"I'd stop knocking the Legion if I were you, Warrant Officer Kelly," he said, happy to keep the conversation in a lighter tone. "Of course, everybody knows you aren't really a Legion sapper."

"I've told you before, I'll work on the beard," she protested. Like the uniforms, that was an old Legion tradition. Sappers and pioneers almost universally wore long, full beards, except for the obvious exceptions like Kelly.

"You do, and you'll have to find someone else to go to town with."

Her response was cut off by a shout from the street. Fraser turned, craning his head to see the source over the milling locals.

The shout was repeated, and Fraser spotted the source. A native—a large, menacing female with an infant clinging to her back—had just thrown a piece of *kwuur-fruit* at a Terran girl in the coveralls of a Seafarms port worker. "Where are your offworld promises now?" the native shouted.

Another local took up the call. "Fifty young carried off last night! Seventy more in the past six-day!"

Muttering spread through the crowd, and Fraser could almost *feel* their mood, like a sudden shift in the wind, turning cold and nasty.

"Kelly ..." He paused, sizing up the situation. "When you see their attention on me, circle around and get her out of sight. And use your 'piece to alert the ready platoon. We don't want to hang around."

"I'll say," she concurred. "Be careful, Col."

He edged clear of the alley as the crowd started to close in on the girl in the Seafarms coverall. Whether at sea or on land, natives responded aggressively to any perceived threat, and it was hard to distract them once they fixed on a target. According to the chip he'd studied on early Terran contact with Polypheme, entire nomad tribes had thrown themselves at a handful of Terrans with autoweapons, refusing to run or exercise the most rudimentary tactics until the entire band was slaughtered.

Sometimes it had been the Terrans who had died, though. Mob tactics were messy, but they had a way of working when the mob didn't care about casualties.

He squatted down to pick up a loose piece of tile that had fallen from a roof. Hefting it in his hand, he gauged the natives carefully before throwing it at one of the largest males on the fringe of the crowd. The wog gave a bellow that was more surprise than pain and focused his eyestalks on Fraser.

"Over there! Another one!"

"A soldier!" someone shouted. "Soldier! What about the young?"

"Why can't you stop the swimmers?"

It had been a problem simmering for a long time, far longer than Terrans had been on Polypheme. The land-dwellers had built them-selves a fine civilization ashore, but their life cycle made it necessary for their young to spend most of their time swimming. They could cling to an adult for a short time, sucking blood for nourishment, but they needed to swim. No native city was very far from the sea where juveniles could swim aimlessly, supervised—"herded" was probably a better word—by a few adults.

But the nomads, who recognized no bounds of territory or property, often raided around cities to capture juveniles who could be raised as slaves for the tribe.

The company policy of high visibility, of pushing the power of the Commonwealth military forces, was bound to collide with the slave-raiding problem sooner or later. There was no way for two companies of legionnaires to police hundreds of kilometers of tidal flats and coastal waters against slavers, even if the job was part of their mission on Polypheme. But pressure had been building ever since the Legion started arriving, and a raid the night before apparently had been enough to set the whole thing off.

"What good are your guns, Terran, if you won't use them?" a voice called out.

"Your friendship is as empty as your faces!"

The mob was focusing on him now, allowing Kelly to reach the girl. She was speaking urgently into the microphone on her wristpiece computer. It would relay her message to the main computer at the Legion barracks here in town, and help would be dispatched.

He hoped it would come in time.

Chapter Three

I'd rather face an army in the field than a mob in the streets.

—Captain Guillaume St. Andre, speaking of the Aberdeen
Massacre, Third Foreign Legion, 2398

Spear! There's trouble over on the north side of the canal!"

Legionnaire First-Class Spiro Karatsolis cut the power to the vidmagazine he was wearing and removed the holovid viewer. Corporal Selim Bashar was buckling on a rocket pistol, his face grim. "What's wrong, Bashar?" he asked.

"The call—it's from Miss Kelly. She's with the captain, and there's a riot brewing." Bashar picked a rifle from the weapon rack by the door.

"Goddamn!" Karatsolis was out of his seat in one fluid motion, his magazine forgotten. "What'll we take? Floatcar?"

Bashar shook his head. "They're warming up a veeter for us now."

Karatsolis grabbed an FEK riot rifle as he followed the corporal out of the old Toel warehouse that served as barracks for the legionnaires posted to duty in Ourgh. Outside, two legionnaires were just stepping clear of the veeter.

It was a small vehicle, barely big enough for two men and a weapons mount. It lacked the range and endurance of the floatcars and magrep APCs the Legion normally used, but the veeter had one tremendous advantage over those: It was a true aircraft, propelled by powerful tilt-rotor turbo-fans mounted on either side of the tiny fuselage. It was intended for scouting and short-range battlefield use, but the veeter was also ideal for fast movement through crowded or built-up areas.

Bashar took his place at the control console. Karatsolis mounted in front of him and ran through a quick check of the gun in the bow of the craft. It was a kinetic energy cannon modified for riot work, firing anesthetic slivers, instead of conventional needle ammunition, at relatively low muzzle velocities. It wouldn't be worth much in an ordinary fight, but it was perfect for crowd control.

"Ready, farm boy?" Bashar asked from behind him.

"Any time," Karatsolis replied. "Just make sure you steer clear of the buildings!"

The fans whined, building to a crescendo that made the veeter shudder. Bashar pulled back on the stick and the craft rose slowly, kicking up clouds of dust. Nearby more legionnaires were clearing the way for an armored magrep APC, floating slowly out of the motor pool on a magnetic cushion.

The driver, Corporal Sandoval, had his hatch open. He flashed the veeter a quick thumbs-up.

Karatsolis returned the gesture, then checked the weapon again—just to be sure.

* * *

The crowd surged down the narrow alley like a snake striking at its prey, shouting unintelligible epithets and hoarse-voiced exhortations. Colin Fraser ducked behind a garbage bin as a stone struck the masonry a few centimeters to the left of his head. He drew his FE-PLF and chambered a round. He didn't want to use the 10 mm rocket pistol unless he absolutely had to. It wasn't much use for crowd control, and a Terran killing native civilians in a nominally friendly town would only make the difficult political situation that much worse.

But the mob didn't look like it planned to give the Terrans much choice.

Kelly had her Navy-issue laser pistol out. She waved it as she urged him toward the door niche where she knelt beside the other Terran girl. The laser was even less suitable for this situation than his own sidearm.

He sprinted from cover in a crouching, zigzag run. A thrown bottle shattered against the corner of the bin behind him. Kelly squeezed off a shot, angling her fire over the heads of the crowd. The beam was invisible, but the crackle of superheated air and the tang of ozone were unmistakable. Fraser dived and rolled, coming up beside Kelly and facing the advancing mob.

"Your charge'll last longer if you use a low-intensity beam!" he said as she fired again.

She flashed him a quick grin. "Any lower and I'd be holding them off with a flashlight," she answered. "I'll cover you two."

"You go—" he began.

"Go!" she cut him off sharply. "Save the male heroics … and your ammo!" She fired into the trash bin he had been hiding behind, nodding in satisfaction as something inside caught fire. A few natives shied away from the flames, but the mob continued to press forward.

Fraser pointed down the alley. "Run!" he told the girl in the Seafarms coverall. He noticed that the nameplate said *K. VOSKOVICH*. "I'll be right behind you."

She nodded and scrambled to her feet. Fraser hesitated a second longer, reluctant to leave Kelly to face the mob alone.

But Kelly Winters knew how to take care of herself. She had led a charge into the middle of overwhelming enemy forces at the climax of the fighting on Hanuman. Fraser forced himself to follow the civilian, Voskovich. She was the one who needed protection right now.

Behind them a native screamed as Kelly fired straight into the crowd. On low-intensity a laser pulse was rarely deadly, but it could cause a serious burn. Most opponents would be quick to run from a weapon that struck invisibly, but the wogs only seemed to become more aggressive. They sensed a threat to the community, and instinct was beginning to overwhelm reason.

The narrow alley opened onto a major street. Fraser caught up with Voskovich a few meters from the intersection. He grabbed her elbow and pushed her against the nearest wall. "Wait!" he hissed.

A curious crowd was already gathering there, attracted by the shouts from further up the alley. Fraser could sense their growing agitation as they picked up something of the urgency of the other mob.

The Terrans were trapped.

*   *   *

Kelly Winters fired again and glanced over her shoulder nervously. Were the others clear of the alley yet? The charge indicator on her pistol showed that the power cell was almost exhausted. Two or three more shots was the best she could hope for.

The mob surged forward again.

She fired twice, then lunged from the shelter of the door, running. Something wet and smelly hit her square in the back, but she ignored it and kept sprinting. Angry shouts followed her.

"Terran liar!" a native yelled.

Again something hit her, in the leg this time, a heavy, jagged stone instead of a ripe fruit. Pain lanced through her calf, and Kelly stumbled. She caught herself by grabbing at the nearest wall, then pushed off to run again.

She fell, the impact against the cobblestones knocking the breath out of her for a moment. Gasping for breath, Kelly rolled over into an awkward sitting position and raised the laser pistol. But it was empty now, useless.

The natives advanced.

Then Fraser was there, standing over her, his PLF rocket pistol leveled in a marksman's brace. He fired three times with scarcely any pause between the shots. Each one found its mark, but it slowed the natives only for a few seconds.

Fraser helped her to her feet. "The alley's blocked!" he said, firing again. "More natives!"

It took Kelly long seconds to realize what he had said, and what the words meant. The mob was sure to finish off the three Terrans before they worked their bloodlust off.

It took her even longer to react to the explosion of noise that erupted from the sky.

"There! There they are, Bashar!" Karatsolis shouted over the roar of the veeter's engines. He pointed at the narrow alley off the left side of the little flyer's nose.

"I see them, Spear," Bashar acknowledged. He angled the aircraft down toward the three Terran figures, then let off a string of curses in his native Turkish. "Can't get near them while they're in that strakking side street." Small as the tilt-rotor was, it couldn't operate in the confined space between those close-set native buildings.

Karatsolis leaned forward and flipped a switch on his control panel. The public address speaker slung from the bottom of the veeter crackled. "In the open, skipper!" he said into the mike. "Get into the open so we can cover you!"

"Hang on to your lunch!" Bashar called. The veeter dipped and swerved alarmingly, and buildings flashed toward them until Karatsolis was convinced they would crash into one. He forced himself to ignore everything but his gunsights, swinging the weapon to fire into the smaller of the two native mobs hemming the Terrans in on the ground.

The stream of narcotic rounds cut a swath through the locals. A few fell immediately, but it took time for most of the natives to go down. Karatsolis kept gripping the firing stud on the gauss gun as the little aircraft pivoted again for another pass, fighting a wave of nausea from the violent maneuvering. The buildings that blocked the veeter were hampering his line of fire, but he could see the locals scattering as the strafing continued.

"Birdman, Birdman, this is Cavalry," the radio announced, using the call signs Subaltern Leonid Narmonov had assigned to the mission as they had scrambled for action.

"Cavalry, Birdman," Karatsolis replied. "Go."

"ETA your position is six minutes," Sandoval, the APC's driver, told him. "Longer, if these damned crowds get any heavier. Can you hold until we get there?"

"We have a choice?" Bashar muttered behind him.

"We'll do what we can, Cavalry," Karatsolis said. "But you'd better mag it if you don't want to miss the party."

"Roger that. Cavalry clear."

The veeter hovered for a moment, and Karatsolis pumped narco rounds at the largest clump of natives. He hit the PA switch again. "Work your way clear of the alley, skipper, so we can give you some cover!"

He saw Fraser waving an acknowledgment, and the three Terrans pressed through the path the strafing had opened up. Karatsolis fired again, keeping a worried eye on the ammo indicator. Veeters didn't carry as much of an ammunition reserve as most combat vehicles, and he was burning up rounds too fast.

Without some fire support, the captain would never hold out long enough for the APC to make it.

* * *

They broke from the alley entrance at a dead run, with Fraser in the lead and Voskovich supporting Kelly, who was favoring her injured leg.

A native lashed out with an improvised club, but Fraser shot him at close range and he reeled backward, clutching at his wounded arm. The roar of the veeter rotors overhead swelled again as the aircraft dipped low over the alley mouth, its heavy MEK gauss gun keeping up a steady stream of fire, keeping the mob at bay.

The way they were using up ammo, though, they wouldn't be able to maintain their support much longer.

Fraser pointed at the open market square, signaling for the veeter to land. It would be a tricky approach, but Bashar—that *had* to be Bashar at the controls, nobody else in the outfit handled a vehicle with the same combination of skill and stark insanity—could handle it. He kept repeating the hand signals until he was sure the crew had seen him.

The veeter settled slowly to the cobblestones, still firing. Fraser grabbed the civilian girl's arm and pulled her toward the aircraft as the forward hatch popped open.

Legionnaire Karatsolis rolled out of the gunner's seat, dropping to one knee and raising a Legion riot rifle to cover the alley mouth. Like the veeter's MEK, the riot rifle was a modification of the basic gauss rifle design which fired narco rounds. Unlike the MEK, or the standard-issue FEK battle rifle, the riot-control weapon wasn't set up for full-auto fire.

"Get aboard!" Fraser shouted at Voskovich over the noise of the rotors. "Move it!" With more hand signals he ordered Bashar to get the veeter, and his new passenger clear.

Bashar opened his hatch long enough to toss another riot rifle out. Fraser caught the weapon with one hand and helped the girl close her hatch. He rapped twice on the canopy and laid down cover fire for Karatsolis, then followed him to the shelter of an abandoned vendor's stall. The rotors revved louder.

"Kelly! Grab on to the outside and ride it out. It'll carry the extra weight!"

She shook her head. "Forget it! I'm sticking this one out on the ground!"

The veeter stirred slowly, then lifted, turning north and climbing fast.

He'd taken care of the civilian, his first duty here. Now he had to keep three legionnaires alive until help arrived.

Fraser raised the rifle and started firing.

* * *

The M-786 Sandray plowed through a native stall as Legionnaire Second-Class Enrique Sandoval gunned the motor and turned onto the wide street that led to the Square of the North Gate Bazaars. With its broad manta shape the APC was ill suited to work inside a wog city, where only a few of the main avenues were large enough to accommodate the vehicle, but it was the only way to deliver a large number of troops to a trouble spot quickly. With only a platoon to cover the entire city, the legionnaires needed the speed. And the Sandray was also large enough to hold several prisoners. The usual problem that would require a Legion response was a brawl at one of the bars or the Company-sponsored brothel on the riverfront near the port complex.

Dealing with major native riots in the heart of the bazaar district hadn't been a priority—until now.

"ETA?" Subaltern Narmonov stuck his head into the driver's cabin to ask the question. It was the fifth time he'd asked since Bashar's report that the veeter had recovered one civilian and then withdrawn, out of ammo.

"Two minutes, Sub," Sandoval replied. He slowed the APC as a cluster of natives ran into the street in front of the vehicle. "Maybe longer, if these stupid lokes don't stay out of the way."

"Make some revs, damn it!" Narmonov told him.

"Yessir." Sandoval responded, hiding a grimace of distaste. Narmonov was frantic at the thought of Captain Fraser facing the native mob.

Fraser wasn't even in command of Narmonov's company, he thought, but he sure had everyone worked up. Bashar and Karatsolis, for instance; like Sandoval, they were in the demi-battalion's Transport Section, not part of either of the two regular combat companies. They'd served with Fraser before, of course—but with Narmonov it was different.

Sandoval shrugged. Captain Fraser was the one running things here on Polypheme. Alpha Company's CO, Captain David Hawley, was the senior officer of Demi-Battalion Elaine and thus the commander of the whole Legion force in the system, but everyone knew that Hawley was incompetent. As the garrison's second-in-command, Fraser ran virtually everything while Hawley remained in his own private fog, a useless dreamchip addict, and alcoholic.

Maybe Fraser was the indispensable man on Polypheme. Sandoval doubted it. As far as he was concerned, officers hardly ever pulled their own weight. Not even in the Legion.

He gunned the engine again and grinned as wogs scattered ahead of the Sandray. All it took to keep these lokes in their place was a little force, a little willpower. Nothing else mattered.

* * *

Fraser checked his magazine and swore softly. Even without full-auto capability, the hundred rounds it carried were being consumed entirely too fast, and there were no refills available. The crowd wasn't making much headway against them, but neither were they breaking up the way a human mob would have under such steady firepower. They were still gathering, growing more enraged as the Terrans held off the attack.

He could feel the air throbbing with subsonics. Like the urge to swarm and overwhelm a threat, that was a legacy of the natives' aquatic origin, the use of low-frequency sound as a method of communication. It wasn't much use out of the water, and even in the seas they couldn't send more than the most basic of signals, but it was still disconcerting.

"How's your ammo?" he asked Karatsolis.

"No good, Captain," the Greek replied. He spat expressively as he picked out another target and fired. "Damned popguns!" His contempt for any weapon lighter than a turret-mounted plasma cannon was well known among the Hanuman veterans.

Behind them, pressed up against a wall, Kelly made a sour noise. "You think you've got problems?" She clutched Fraser's rocket pistol, empty now.

"If they rush us, sir, ma'am, keep behind me," Karatsolis said. "I'm better equipped."

"Are you talking about size or armor?" Fraser asked, trying to keep his tone light. The big legionnaire was wearing his Legion battledress without a combat helmet. He'd be slightly better protected against the mob, but still vulnerable.

Karatsolis didn't have time to answer. With a roar of powerful propulsion fans, a Sandray rounded a corner and drove into the square, gathering speed. Its stern ramp was dropping as it plowed through a stall and slid sideways, placing its armored bulk between the thickest part of the crowd and the three legionnaires.

Soldiers in battledress ran down the ramp and fanned out on either side. A subaltern waved urgently to Fraser. "Get aboard, sir! Get aboard!"

"Go!" Fraser shouted at Kelly. She started forward, limping. "Help her, Spear!"

The big Greek sprang after her, gathering her in his powerful arms and running for the APC. Fraser followed, clutching the riot gun. The thin cordon of soldiers fired into the mob with measured precision, holding them off.

As Fraser mounted the ramp, the subaltern was already shouting orders for the legionnaires. "Mount up! Mount up! Let's go!"

They remounted the Sandray smoothly, moving by the numbers without confusion or wasted effort. "Secured, Sub," their section leader told the subaltern. The officer slapped the switch that controlled the ramp and passed orders to the driver through his helmet commset. Stirring on magrep fields and fans, the Sandray lifted slowly and turned.

Rocks and bottles beat an uneven tattoo on the armored hull, but nothing in Ourgh would stop the APC. Fraser sank to a bench in the stern compartment, waving away a medic.

He realized vaguely that he was exhausted.

The subaltern sat down beside him and pulled off his helmet. He was young, fresh-faced, with the blond good looks that would have been perfect for a Colonial Army recruiting poster. But the handsome features were marred by a worried frown.

Fraser nodded to him. "Good job, Mr., ah …"

"Narmonov, sir."

"Good job, Narmonov." The man's platoon was a credit to Alpha Company. Captain Hawley's unit wasn't noted for efficiency, like their commander. It was good to see that some of them still took their soldiering seriously. "I'll be glad to get back to the city barracks."

Narmonov shook his head. "Sorry, sir, we've had orders to head back to the Sandcastle."

"Orders?"

"Yessir. From Citizen Jens."

Fraser winced. Sigrid Jens was head of the Seafarms operation on Polypheme. She had the habit of treating the legionnaires on the planet as her own personal corporate security guards. "What does she want this time?" he asked wearily, picturing another stormy meeting over the question of further thinning out the garrison to handle another of the company's schemes for a wider presence on Polypheme.

Narmonov swallowed. "There's been an attack on the *Cyclops*, sir," he said slowly. "Nomads. Watanabe reports they were carrying high-tech weapons."

Kelly, nearby, looked up from where the medic was examining her ankle. "If the nomads have high-tech weapons …"

"Then we've got trouble," Fraser said grimly.

He felt more exhausted than ever.

Chapter Four

The French, a people of etiquette, imagine that the Legion is full of criminals and barefoot savages.

—Colonel Fernand Maire,
in a letter from his deathbed,
French Foreign Legion, 1951

Officially it was known as "Cyclops Project One," but workers and legionnaires alike called the huge complex "The Sandcastle." It rose from the tidal flats a hundred and fifty kilometers southeast of Ourgh, a squat, ugly, starkly functional compound surrounded by a fifteen-meter high fusand wall. Even from a distance the base's nonhuman origins were plain.

The Toeljuks had constructed the Sandcastle as part of a chain of similar installations when they leased the world from the Semti Conclave centuries ago, and their characteristic architectural style was stamped on every building enclosed by those massive parapets. The walls, composed of a fused sand compound developed by the Toels, made the base look like an elaborate military fortress, but in fact their main job was to hold back a natural enemy, the water that coursed across the plain at high tide.

Tides on Polypheme were like nothing Colin Fraser had encountered before. They could raise the water level along the coast by as much as ten meters—more, during the fierce storms that boiled out of the equatorial latitudes during the *bhourrkh* season. In the space of an hour a stretch of open plain could be completely covered by water.

At high tide the Sandcastle became an island, and those walls were the only barrier to the lashing force of the flood tide or a raging *bhourrkh*.

The base had to be located on the tidal flats. When the waters closed in, it could become a port for the huge ore-extraction ships the Toeljuks had introduced to these seas. The corrosive content of the oceans here made frequent maintenance essential, so the Sandcastle was fitted with massive seagates which opened to flood the center of the complex and allow vessels to enter. Then the water could be pumped out, turning the compound into a dry dock where the ship could be unloaded and serviced.

At their peak, the Toeljuks had operated a fleet of thirty giant extraction ships, each one with its own home base. Since the Commonwealth had acquired Polypheme, most of the bases had fallen into ruin along with the ships. But Seafarms Interstellar had can-nibalized the old Toel fleet to put the *Seafarms Cyclops* back in service, and the Sandcastle had become a port facility once again, all part of a pilot project designed to explore the possibilities of large-scale oceanic mineral extraction.

The tide was at the flood stage now, just beginning to rush in around the walls of the base. Fraser had moved into the driver's cab beside Legionnaire Sandoval, where he had direct access to the vehicle's communications gear. Glancing at the video monitor that showed the terrain ahead, Fraser tried to gauge the time left before the water would crest. About forty-five minutes, he thought. When the waters were at their highest the nomad threat would be greatest. If the nomads really were a threat ...

Watanabe's report from the *Seafarms Cyclops* didn't leave much room for doubt. He'd spent the trip reviewing the computer file, trying to evaluate the implications of the subaltern's observations.

Any combination of high-tech weaponry and the kind of ferocity he'd seen for himself in Ourgh would be deadly. Moreover, Watanabe was suggesting that the nomads were using tactics more sophisticated than anything seen on Polypheme to date.

It all pointed to an outside influence. And odds were that the confrontation wouldn't stop with the abortive skirmish aboard the *Seafarms Cyclops*. ...

"We're here, Captain," Sandoval said quietly.

Fraser looked up to see the massive seagates swinging slowly open to admit the APC. Water swirled into the center of the compound, turning the parade ground into a sea of mud.

The gate closed behind the APC as Sandoval guided it across the complex toward the motor pool. Like the rest of the habitable part of the base, the motor pool was built into the inside of the wall, with doors that could be sealed tight when the interior was open to the sea.

A cluster of figures were waiting there, tension plain in their stances.

Sandoval guided the APC up a ramp and into the structure, then cut fans and magnetic fields to allow the Sandray to come to rest. Fraser turned in his seat to call orders to the legionnaires in the rear.

"Mr. Narmonov, keep your men ready to return to the city. I think it would be a good idea if we kept you as an escort for the company people, in view of what happened this afternoon."

"Sir!" The response was crisp, parade-ground correct.

He glanced at Kelly Winters. "Kelly, if this is going to be a full staff meeting, I'll want—I mean, Captain Hawley will probably want you there."

"I'll come with you, Captain," she replied formally. The medic had pronounced her fit, beyond a nasty bruise on her leg and a few abrasions from her fall.

He opened the hatch and clambered out of the vehicle.

"Captain," the smooth, cold voice of his Executive Officer greeted Fraser as he crossed the wide fusand floor. Lieutenant Antoine DuValier was tall, lean, and aristocratic, and Fraser still found him something of a mystery. His disdain for his surroundings was all too clear, and Fraser thought he sensed a personal dislike behind the young officer's aloof manner. He did his job efficiently enough, but Fraser was uncomfortable relying on DuValier as XO.

But because Captain Hawley needed his help running the demi-battalion, Fraser had been forced to leave Bravo Company almost entirely in DuValier's hands.

The man in Legion battledress beside DuValier was the only reason Fraser could allow the lieutenant to oversee his company at all. Gunnery Sergeant John Trent was another Hanuman veteran; an experienced NCO Fraser was willing to trust with his life. Without Trent, Fraser knew, Bravo Company would never have escaped from the jungles of Dryienjaiyeel or survived the desperate fighting in that last battle.

"Glad to see you in one piece, skipper," Trent said, genuine relief playing over his craggy features. "When the reports came in I—"

"Time for congratulations later." A small woman with short blond hair and wearing a conservative business coverall stepped forward. "Fraser, we've got problems on the *Cyclops*."

"I know, Citizen Jens," Fraser said, keeping a tight rein on his temper at her abrupt manner. Sigrid Jens was said to be the youngest Project Director in the Seafarms hierarchy, and also the most aggressive. She was, so everyone said, destined for great things at Seafarms, maybe even in the parent company, Reynier Industries.

She was also, Fraser thought, a royal pain.

"I've been looking over the report," he went on, still trying not to betray any emotion. "From the looks of things you've got a hell of a security problem, Citizen, and I think we're going to have to reevaluate the entire setup on Polypheme if we're going to handle this mess."

The woman's assistant, Edward Barnett, stepped forward belligerently. "If you people had done your job, the nomads would never be able to threaten the *Cyclops*," he said. "I recommended more troops for the ship right along, Fraser, but you and your precious Captain Hawley overruled the suggestion."

Fraser turned an angry glance his way. "Good thing, too," he said. "You wanted a whole company on board the *Cyclops*, and that would have stretched our resources way past the limit."

"Nonsense!" Barnett exploded. "You don't seem to realize how important the security of that ship is."

"Gentlemen," Jens said, holding up a manicured hand. "We need to take action, not pass out blame."

"Yes, ma'am," Barnett said quickly. He shot Fraser a sour look. "But I want to go on record as saying that we should have had more support from the Legion."

Fraser ignored him, turning to Jens. "This situation could get out of hand fast, Citizen," he said quietly. "I hope the corporation will be willing to work with us. Unless we deal with the nomads now, we could all be in serious trouble."

* * *

Warrior-Scout !!Dhruuj of the Clan of the Reef-Swimmers relaxed and let the flow of the tide carry him closer to the Built-Reef-of-the-Strangers. There was danger in swimming the tides so close to the massive stone walls, but !!Dhruuj felt no fear. He was a Warrio r-Scout, and the best in the Reef-Swimmers apart from old Soor. He had claimed the honor of this swim, since Soor was still recovering from the wounds he'd suffered in the fight with the fangmouth three ebbs ago.

He felt no fear, just as his hand would feel no fear of its own even if he was to reach out to grasp a stingfloater stranded in a tidal pool. !!Dhruuj was a Hand of the Clan now, performing his function.

The water was already more than a head deep around the Built-Reef-of-the-Strangers, enough to keep him hidden. The Strangers-Who-Gave-Gifts had warned that the Strangers-Who-Lived-Within-Walls had powerful charms that allowed them to see clearly in the dark of the open air, and others that could chart the depths even more plainly than a Warrior-Scout, but the Stranger-Who-Betrayed-Clan had sent word from within that no such underwater magic was at work here. !!Dhruuj would be safe as long as he remained in the water.

He reached out to grasp the wall as the tide carried him toward it, then used his suckers to attach himself to the uneven surface. Inching slowly upward, !!Dhruuj raised his eyestalks and snorkel out of the water cautiously, and settled in to watch.

The Clan would need whatever information he could gather before they arrived to assail the Strangers above.

* * *

"You have to admit, Captain Fraser, that two companies of legionnaires was not what we were promised for the garrison here. We understood an entire battalion was to be stationed on Polypheme."

Fraser looked at Sigrid Jens and then shrugged. "A provisional battalion, Citizen," he replied carefully. "That isn't necessarily the same thing."

"A battalion's a battalion, isn't it?" Barnett said with a sneer. "Or doesn't your Foreign Legion use the same military units as the rest of the Colonial Army?"

"A provisional battalion is formed from scratch, Citizen Jens." Fraser went on, as if Barnett hadn't spoken. "To put one together, the Legion takes whatever extra companies happen to be handy and puts them into a unified command. Two companies plus support troops isn't unusual, especially for a hurry-up job like this. More companies are scheduled to join us later, unless something else diverts them in the meantime."

"Meaning we get whatever nobody else wants, I suppose," Jens muttered darkly.

"What else could you expect with the Legion?" Barnett asked her. "Criminals and screw-ups ..."

Across the table from him, Gunnery Sergeant Trent made a low-voiced comment. "Criminals and screw-ups who might just have to save your ass from the nomads, Citizen."

Fraser broke in to keep the exchange from going any further. "If you would reconsider the plan I submitted last month for native auxiliaries, Citizen Jens, we might be able to police things the way you want without any more Legion troops."

"Native auxiliaries!" Jens laughed. "Get into orbit, Fraser! You've seen the locals. Lazy, shiftless ... what use would they be as soldiers?"

"I think you're underestimating them, Citizen. I've ... seen the townies at close range, and they'd make good enough fighters." He rubbed a bruise on his left arm as he spoke. "The nomads are even better material. They have the local knowledge we need to really make ourselves effective on Polypheme."

"You'd trust the nomads? I've seen the xenopsych reports, Fraser. They don't think anything like us. No concept of loyalty to anything higher than their own Clan ... no understanding of tactical coordination...."

"We all know how you Legion types like to set up native armies so there will be plenty of soft billets for your legionnaires to fill as officers and noncoms," Barnett said. "But the whole idea of arming and training the wogs ... that's ridiculous."

"Someone doesn't think so," Fraser commented. "Someone's equipping them with high-tech gear, and they're discovering tactical coordination fast enough, too."

They were sitting in the conference room set aside for the garrison staff, adjacent to the suite of offices and living quarters that housed Captain Hawley and his small staff. Formal discussions wouldn't begin until the captain joined them, but that hadn't kept anyone from airing his views.

Fraser studied the two civilians. They shared the common attitude most outsiders held for the Legion, but that was nothing unusual. More surprising was the contempt they directed at the natives. It was fashionable for the idle rich back on Terra to spout human-supremacist nonsense, but out on the frontiers those attitudes were usually rare.

Barnett, especially, puzzled him. The man had been doing fieldwork on Polypheme for three years. How could anyone research a culture for that long and still hold it in such low regard?

DuValier spoke up from further down the table. "Actually, Captain Fraser has already shown that nomads can be used in conjunction with our troops, at least as native scouts," he said in his flat, toneless voice. "He has been training twenty of them for several weeks now."

"On what authorization?" Jens asked sharply.

Fraser glared at his Exec before answering. "Captain Hawley and I agreed it would be a good idea to look into the possibility," he said. "Nor do I think that Seafarms can overrule the military command on this kind of point." Inwardly, he was seething. As if he didn't have enough trouble with these civilians, now his XO was complicating things.

What the hell was DuValier's problem, anyway?

The door at the far end of the room slid open with a complaining whine. Gunnery Sergeant Istvan Valko and Lieutenant Susan Gage strode briskly through the wide, squat doorway. Valko, Alpha Company's senior NCO, marked out a brisk "Ten-hut!"

The legionnaires in the room, including Fraser, stood as Captain David Hawley followed the others. As Hawley took his place at the head of the table, Fraser watched him sadly.

A phrase Father Fitzpatrick, Bravo Company's chaplain, was particularly fond of ran through Fraser's mind. "There, but for the grace of God, go I."

Hawley was old for his rank, well past fifty, and looked even older after years of hard drink and the neglect that went with dreamchip addiction. His expression was vague, his eyes empty, a sure sign that he had been in dreamland when Gage and Valko roused him for the meeting. The man spent a lot of time in the living dreams of his habit, feeding fantasies directly into the brain by way of the computer implant in his skull.

Almost thirty years ago, David Hawley had been the hero of the fighting on Aten, when marauding Ubrenfars had nearly plunged most of the frontier into war. A lieutenant in the Legion, Hawley had stopped the Ubrenfars cold with a perfectly executed ambush by the survivors of his company. Promotion and recognition followed, but somehow it had all gone wrong. Hawley was shunted from one deadend post to another, his brilliant mind wasted in minor administrative jobs and routine garrison duty. He turned to dreamland for stimulation, but the mock battles he fought in his mind proved more real to him than his waking life.

The classic pattern of dreamchip addiction … with the inevitable aftermath. Hawley lost out on promotions he might have earned, and gradually slid into obscurity.

There, but for the grace of God … Fraser was all too aware of how similar his career was to Hawley's early days.

He could end up like David Hawley, a superannuated Legion captain, grasping at memories and might-have-beens. The thought made him flinch, made his skin crawl.

"Ah … Mr. Fraser, why don't you, ah … take things in hand," Hawley said, blinking vaguely.

"Yes, sir," Fraser replied. He knew a lot of officers who treated Hawley with contempt, but he had vowed never to be one of them. Somewhere under the drink and the chip addiction, the hero of Aten remained.

He touched a stud on the table to call up Watanabe's report on the monitor screen mounted on the wall behind him. "*Seafarms Cyclops* was attacked around sunset by a strong force of nomads armed with high-tech weaponry and employing tactics that are far beyond anything previously credited to the locals on this planet." He manipulated a computer pointer to indicate specific features on an image of the captured alien weaponry. "This is a five-millimeter rocket launcher. The design is unfamiliar, but as you can see here the grip is obviously intended to accommodate hands not unlike a wog's. The whole mechanism is covered in a substance similar to duraplast. Subaltern Watanabe believes it is intended to insulate the weapon from the effects of corrosive seawater, and Warrant Officer Koenig, my Native Affairs specialist, concurs."

"Wait a moment, Fraser," Barnett said. "Are you trying to tell us that these things are manufactured locally? The wogs don't have that capability, and you know it!"

Fraser shook his head. "My people think that these are being brought in from off-planet, but they've been designed specifically for conditions on Polypheme." He paused a moment to let the implications of that sink in. "Someone is not only running guns to the natives, they're doing it as part of a consistent policy involving a long-term manufacturing commitment off-planet."

"Who?" Lieutenant Gage asked. "Any indications?"

"I'd put money on Semti renegades," Trent growled. The Semti, once the rulers of a vast interstellar sphere, had lost control to upstart Terrans after the destruction of their capital by a human battle fleet nearly a century ago. Semti administrators now worked diligently for their new overlords, but more than one plot had been uncovered in the decades since the end of the war. The fighting on Hanuman had been inspired by Semti agents, and probably the Ubrenfar campaign Hawley remembered as well.

"Could be Semti," Fraser agreed. "Or the Toeljuks. They leased the planet from the Semti, and I'm sure their leaders would like to get it back. Or we could be talking about human gunrunners, you know." He glanced at Barnett and Jens. "There's a lot of profit in instability, after all."

Barnett looked away. Jens met Fraser's stare with a level gaze of her own. "Surely it's a moot point, Captain," she said. "I would think we'd be better employed talking about security measures, not picturing plots and revolutions."

"What, ah … what do you have in mind?" Hawley asked.

It was Barnett who answered. "Obviously the first imperative is to protect the *Cyclops*," he said. "I would say our first priority should be the dispatch of at least one more platoon, preferably two more, to the ship."

"Unacceptable," Fraser snapped. "We have no idea what kind of reach the opposition has, or what their object might be. Diluting our defenses would be the worst possible thing at this point."

"What do you recommend, then, Captain?" Jens asked.

"Recall the *Cyclops* to port at once. Keep her here where we can concentrate all our forces until we know what we're facing. Shut down operations in Ourgh, too, and bring all Terran personnel out here. Right now we're spread too thin."

Barnett started to make an angry response, but Jens overrode him. "I'm sorry, Captain, but that's equally unacceptable. The corporation is on Polypheme to make money, and we can't do that crouched here in the Sandcastle. The Cyclops Project can't be jeopardized at this stage. We have to show that it can operate at a profit, or the whole concept will be abandoned. And that would be a disaster, not just for Seafarms but for this whole planet. Without something like the mineral extraction operation, the Commonwealth will pull out entirely."

Fraser leaned forward in his chair. "I think you should reconsider, Citizen," he said quietly. "If you want the Legion to provide security, you're going to have to let us do it right. Otherwise ..."

"You know as well as I do that your unit is answerable to civilian authority—my authority—as long as it is deployed on Polypheme," Jens said flatly.

"Except in cases where Commonwealth security considerations are stronger."

She smiled without humor. "I'd suggest you have some pretty powerful proof before you go invoking that clause, Captain. Unless you're planning an early retirement? I'm sure Reynier Industries can arrange it ... if you fail to show the proper spirit of cooperation."

Fraser bit back an angry reply. He glanced at Hawley again.

There, but for the grace of God ...

CHAPTER FIVE

We are nothing now but Legionnaires, and Legionnaires die better than any men in the world.

—Captain Jean Danjou, at Camerone,
French Foreign Legion, 30 April, 1863

Legionnaire First-Class Angela Garcia hated the Sandcastle. She hated the big horseshoe-shaped computer and communications desk in the base command center that was her standard duty station, and she hated Polypheme and Seafarms Interstellar and even, she was beginning to think, the Legion itself.

Le cafarde ... the symptoms were easy enough to recognize, but harder to ignore. A lot of soldiers would have given anything for this kind of duty—a quiet backwater garrison, comfortable quarters, no threat of combat—but Garcia couldn't see beyond the routine. The boredom.

Somehow she hadn't really pictured boredom as going together with her posting as chief C^3 technician under Colin Fraser. Garcia had handled the command, control, and communications position for Fraser throughout the fighting on Hanuman, and by the time the long march was over she had learned to respect him. But he was different since the company had shipped out to Polypheme—more aloof, more concerned with administrative detail than the needs of the company.

It felt like a betrayal.

She shuddered at the thought, remembering how her husband had deserted her years ago. She'd only been eighteen at the time, a poor colonial without any living relatives, no skills, no hopes, her life shattered by the way Juan had treated her. Angela Garcia had joined the Legion to find a home, people who would always stand beside her.

Now the bug was inside her head, whispering hate. She tried to put those thoughts aside.

A buzzer brought her out of her reverie. She tapped the intercom button.

"C-cubed. Garcia."

"This is the main gate," a bored-sounding voice said. "We have a Company floatcar approaching."

"So? Let them in."

"Funny, Garcia," the legionnaire replied. "They say they've got a wog bigshot on board to see Citizen Jens. You want to lay on a formal reception, or what?"

Garcia muttered a curse in Spanish. "All the brass is in conference," she told him. "Call out the officer of the watch. Better get Mr. Koenig down there as well. I'll let the captain know we've got visitors."

She cut the intercom and patched in another line, a private channel that hooked up to the earpiece receiver Sergeant Trent was wearing. "Gunny? Main gate reports a Company floatcar coming in with a native VIP on board. I'm having Reynolds and Koenig do the honors. You'd better find out if the captain wants to see the wog now, or keep him on ice for a while."

Her message delivered, Garcia turned her thoughts back to Polypheme. Trouble aboard the *Cyclops* ... the riot in town ... now a native leader coming to see the Project Director.

Legionnaire Garcia had a feeling that her boredom wasn't going to last long. The favored treatment for the cafarde was said to be a loaded rifle and plenty of targets. From where she was sitting it looked like the prescription was about to be filled.

∗   ∗   ∗

"If this project fails, the corporation will hold you personally responsible. I don't think either of you wants that."

Fraser glanced at Captain Hawley, but the older man just shrugged at Barnett's comment.

At this point in his career, Hawley had little to fear. No matter how much influence Seafarms or Reynier Industries wielded, it wouldn't make much difference one way or the other to David Hawley.

But it could be the final deathblow to Fraser's future.

He glanced down at the recessed monitor screen in the desk in front of him. Gunny Trent's memo stared back at him "COMPANY FLOATCAR WITH NATIVE COUNCIL REP HAS CLEARED MAIN GATE." That was the last complication he needed in the situation right now. The riot in Ourgh was still fresh in his mind.

"If I might suggest," Kelly was saying reasonably, "I think it would be better to concentrate on ways to *keep* the project from failing, instead of trying to hand out the blame in advance."

"Which is precisely why we have to send more troops to the *Cyclops*," Barnett shot back. "The ship was attacked, and we have to take steps to protect her."

"Not at the cost of weakening us everywhere else," Trent said. "Unless you're ready to give us the native auxiliaries we need, we just don't have the strength to waste."

Fraser cleared his throat. "I think we'd better wait. A native VIP from Ourgh is on his way up. He may have something to say that will have a bearing on all this."

Jens and Barnett reacted as he expected. "From Ourgh?" the woman said, plainly surprised. "What's he doing out here?"

"Perhaps lodging a protest over the way the Legion acted in the disturbance this morning," Barnett responded smoothly.

"Your own people sent him out in a floatcar," Fraser told Jens. "Presumably he came from your office in town."

She frowned. "Then it must be important. Damn." She seemed about to go on, but a chime from the intercom cut her off.

"Elder Houghan!! of the Governing Council of Ourgh, to see Citizen Jens," Legionnaire Garcia's voice announced.

Fraser glanced at Jens, who nodded. "Send him in," he replied, leaning back in his chair and trying to look more relaxed than he was.

Houghan!! was old for a wog, his skin dark and wrinkled, especially around the eyestalks, which looked stiff, even brittle. He was fat, and wheezed as he sank uncomfortably into an empty chair near Hawley's seat at the conference table. The Elder was dressed in brightly colored robes and carried a satchel slung over one shoulder.

There was nothing old about the native elder's voice, though. "The Council has sent me to discuss the issue of defense against the nomads," he said bluntly, the sound coming from the lower gill slits exposed by gaps in his robes just above his hips. "In the past three moon-cycles we have suffered five raids, and you Terrans have given us no aid whatsoever."

Jens held up a hand, a very human gesture. Houghan!! swiveled his eyestalks slowly to look at her. "Elder," she said carefully. "Elder, we have been over this before. Terra is here to trade, not to fight. We still feel that it would not benefit anyone if the Commonwealth took on so much responsibility ... not if you wish your government to remain sovereign."

Houghan!!'s feeding tendrils twitched in disgust. "Words!" he said. "You hide behind words! When the Toels traded here, they enforced the peace."

"And had most of their dealings with the nomads," Jens pointed out. "Your town, all the cities ashore, depended on nomad traders for everything."

"But the nomads who traded with the Toels had no need for raids. Since the Sky Lords and the Toels left, the nomads have become impossible to tame. And your people do nothing to discourage them."

"You know the size of our garrison here," Jens said quietly. "Do you really think we could patrol hundreds of kilometers of seacoast effectively? Your own troops cannot cover the waters-of-raising. How do you expect the Terran garrison to do it?"

The Elder blinked. "But ... your achievements are so far beyond ours. All know that you have instruments to see in the dark and through the waters, and artificial voices to carry over great distances. Weapons that can kill a foe you cannot even see. Your garrison could guard our shores so easily...."

Fraser spoke up for the first time since the Elder's arrival. "Our soldiers can do many things, Reverend Ancient," he said smoothly, using the most respectful mode of the local dialect. "But we cannot be in many places at once. There are too few of us to do everything we would like to do on your world, or we would surely provide the protection you desire."

The words earned him an angry look from Barnett. Seafarms Interstellar and Reynier Industries, like most corporations developing the Commonwealth's new frontier worlds, were forced to balance carefully between enough protection to ensure their own safety and the kind of full-scale Colonial Army presence that would turn Polypheme into a Terran Client, with a Resident-General appointed by the government and safeguards built in to ensure that the locals were protected from exploitation.

Inevitably Terra's corporate interests tried to hold the government at arm's length, and keeping garrisons weak was one way to keep the Colonial Office from getting too involved on planets like this one. But it was those selfsame corporations that screamed loudest when their holdings were threatened and the Commonwealth couldn't instantly field enough troops to deal with the danger.

Houghan!! regarded Fraser with interest. "You are the commander of the soldiers?" he asked.

Fraser shook his head, then remembered that to the natives the gesture connoted agreement. "No … sorry, no, Reverend Ancient. I am only the deputy here." He indicated Hawley with a gesture. "But I believe I speak for the Reverend Ancient Captain Hawley in this."

The other captain looked up. "Ah, yes … yes, Captain Fraser is my deputy here. Yes."

The native made a gesture Fraser wasn't familiar with. "Then if you cannot aid us directly, you could certainly supply us with these weapons and devices for our own soldiers to use. We would pay well, very well. In food, or labor, or whatever else you need."

Before Fraser could reply, Jens took charge of the conversation again. "That, too, is something we cannot do," she said. Unlike Fraser, she was using the mode of speech reserved for equals. "At least not until I have time to refer back to my superiors on Terra. We must see how this would influence our agreements with your Council."

"Agreements!" The Elder's feeding tendrils writhed. "There will be no agreements unless we receive aid! Or is this a part of your plot against us?"

"Plot? What are you talking about?" Jens asked sharply.

The Elder set his shoulder bag on the table ponderously and drew something out of its depths. "This was found after the nomad attack yesterday. It killed six of our soldiers before they were even aware there were nomads in our waters." Houghan!! tossed it on top of the satchel with a contemptuous flourish.

Trent picked it up carefully, and Fraser watched him turn the weapon over in his hands. It was a larger, heavier version of the rocket launcher in Watanabe's report, plainly designed for conditions on Polypheme but far beyond local technology.

More proof of outside meddling.

"Deny that this is an offworlder device," Houghan!! said with a sneer. "Deny it!"

Fraser replied. "Yes, Reverend Ancient, this must have come from offworld. But my people and I have nothing to do with it."

"This I cannot believe," the Elder said. "You Terrans have control of the trade. Even the Toels who still visit must do all of their business through your company port. These would not be here unless you wanted them here."

Jens looked worried now. "Believe me, Reverend Ancient," she said, now adopting the supplicant's mode. "Believe me, these are not here with our approval. Smugglers ... enemies ... someone is bringing these in without our knowledge."

Biting off a comment, Fraser made a quick note on his computer terminal to check security on incoming cargoes. In theory everything was carefully checked and crosschecked, but there was ample room for corruption at a port as poorly staffed as the Polypheme facility. Were these weapons coming through the terminal, or was someone conveniently failing to notice incoming ships that landed away from Ourgh and contacted the natives directly?

Another note appeared below his own: LEGION STAFF ON APPROACH MONITORS? Fraser glanced up, his eyes meeting Trent's. The sergeant had put the weapon down, and his fingers rested on the keys of his own terminal. Fraser nodded slightly, and Trent responded with a quick nod of his own. It was always gratifying to find Trent's thoughts running so close with his own.

He focused his attention on Houghan‼ again. "If your enemies are doing this," he was saying, "I cannot see why you will not protect us. Give us some proof of your good intentions, or we will follow our own currents henceforth."

"Your Council signed the agreements...." Barnett began.

"They will not be honored," the Elder broke in. "Not until we see some proof of your good intentions." He rose slowly, his massive bulk suddenly very alien, hostile. "When you are ready to deal fairly, contact the Council and—" His words were cut off by the wail of warning sirens.

* * *

Karatsolis threw down his cards in disgust as the siren sounded. The other legionnaires clustered around the improvised table looked startled, not quite grasping what the ululating warning meant. *Not surprising,* Karatsolis thought wryly. *They haven't even grasped the basics of poker yet.*

"Look alive, you apes!" he said, reaching for his rifle. "That's the perimeter security alarm!"

"Jesus!" one of the legionnaires muttered. He was a nube, part of a draft of replacements for the demi-battalion's transport section who had arrived straight from the Legion depot on Devereaux only a week ago. His name was O'Donnell. "Jesus Christ, Spear, what the hell's going on?"

"When I know I'll tell you, nube," Karatsolis snapped. "Grab a rifle and get moving!"

The legionnaire looked confused until a more savvy comrade thrust an FEK battle rifle into his hands. Karatsolis waved toward the parade ground. "Let's mag it!"

The five legionnaires followed him as he ran down the motor pool ramp and across the parade ground. Shouts and the whine of FEK fire were coming from the western side of the compound near one of the gates, and in the absence of higher direction Karatsolis led them in that direction. Off to the left he spotted Narmonov's platoon turning out. More legionnaires were racing into the compound from other parts of the perimeter wall.

"Come on!" he shouted as he reached a stairway that led up to the scene of the fighting. There was a scream up above, and a body came tumbling past him to lie in the mud. He recognized the man as Subaltern Reynolds, one of Alpha Company's platoon leaders. The body was clad in a Legion dress uniform, but much of the officer's chest had been blown away.

Feet pounded up the fusand steps behind him. Karatsolis raised his rifle, his thumb groping for the selector switch to go to full auto before he remembered that he was still carrying the riot gun from the encounter in Ourgh. He cursed, and kept cursing as he noticed that there were less than twenty rounds left in the magazine.

A native, bare-skinned but marked with the elaborate tattooing of the nomad tribes, heaved himself over the wall, brandishing a pike and shouting a hoarse battle cry. Karatsolis fired twice at close range, and the wog toppled backward. Nearby a second nomad was waving a pistol. O'Donnell let loose with a full-auto salvo. Dozens of needle-thin slivers tore through the native's torso.

Karatsolis ran to the wall and looked over the edge. "God in Heaven ..." he muttered, reeling back.

A half a hundred or more natives were climbing the smooth fu-sand wall, and more shapes were visible in the water around the base of the fortress.

O'Donnell pushed past him. "What is it, Spear?" he asked, leaning over the edge with his battle rifle at the ready.

Suddenly he jerked back, dropping the rifle. It clattered on the rampart next to Karatsolis's boot.

O'Donnell's hands clutched feebly at the native crossbow bolt that protruded from his neck. The legionnaire staggered and fell, Karatsolis dropped to one knee beside him, but it was too late for first aid, too late for anything. Legionnaire Third-Class O'Donnell was dead.

Karatsolis had never even known the kid's first name.

He grabbed O'Donnell's FEK and snatched the magazine pouch from his belt.

As he rose, the natives swarmed over the wall all around him.

Chapter Six

There is the tradition which is so strong that a man cannot be for long in the Foreign Legion without wanting, like his comrades, to do better than the soldiers of any other regiment.

—Legionnaire Adolphe Cooper,
French Foreign Legion, 1933

ights! Get some lights on out here!" Fraser was shouting, as he buckled on a plasteel chest plate over his tattered dress uniform jacket.

They were clustered on the wall above the headquarters complex. The civilians—Jens, Barnett, and the native Elder—had followed the legionnaires, despite Fraser's orders to remain in the conference room.

He didn't have time to deal with them now. There were too many other things to be done first if the defense was going to pull together.

"Why not use infrared?" Hawley asked, as Trent passed the order to light up the compound.

"Native eyes are better adapted to darkness, sir," Fraser said. "Especially the nomads, who spend so much time underwater. Twilight is an advantage for them—probably the reason they decided to attack now. Bright lighting inside the compound might dazzle them enough to give us an advantage."

Hawley nodded slowly. "Good ... very good, Captain. Use their weaknesses. Yes."

"With your permission, sir," Fraser went on, "I'd like to deploy Alpha Company and the support troops to the walls, and get Bravo Company together as a ready reserve."

The senior captain looked indecisive for a moment. "That's a pretty big reserve," he said slowly, closing his eyes for a moment. Fraser felt impatience rising within him. Why couldn't Hawley *act*? "All right, Captain. Do it. You know how to handle this."

"Thank you, sir," Fraser said. Before he turned away he could see relief spreading over Hawley's features. The other captain was plainly happy to be able to turn the responsibility over to someone else.

Floodlights started coming on all around the central well, turning the gathering gloom day-bright. More lights were coming on along the walls. Fraser saw the fighting on the far wall by the gate clearly now. Nomads, taken by surprise by the sudden glare, seemed to be wavering, but there were all too few Terran figures up there to take advantage of the moment.

"Garcia! Garcia!" Fraser swung around in search of his C^3 technician. She was just emerging from the building, still settling the field computer and communications pack on her shoulders. "Comm-link! General command channel."

Cursing his lack of a helmet with its built-in commo gear, Fraser took a handset from her. "This is Fraser. Alpha Company platoon leaders, Defense Plan Four. Perimeter deployment. Wijngaarde, Bartlow, assemble your platoons near the center of the compound."

"On the way," Subaltern Vincent Bartlow responded over the radio.

"Acknowledged," the First Platoon CO, Subaltern Henck Wijngaarde, added an instant later.

Fraser turned to the others. "Lieutenant DuValier, take Gunny Trent and join the rest of Bravo. You're in charge, but don't commit the men without my orders. Kelly, I want your sappers to take the west perimeter, you'll have to spread them pretty thin. I want Alpha Company to be able to concentrate around the gate. That's where most of them are."

"As you wish, Captain," DuValier said calmly. He managed to look like he was on his way to a social engagement instead of a battle.

"I'm counting on Bravo Company," Fraser told Trent quietly. "I know you won't let me down."

Trent gave him a sharp salute and headed for the stairs. Kelly hesitated a moment, then nodded and followed him.

Fraser turned his attention to Susan Gage. "Lieutenant, take charge at the gate." He pointed across the compound. "Clear those natives away. If they can plant explosives or get to the gatehouse controls...."

She nodded grimly. If the legionnaires lost control of the gates, the nomads could open the whole compound up to the waters lapping outside. That would give them easy access to the interior ... Gathering up Gunnery Sergeant Valko with a look, the lieutenant followed the other staffers.

He turned back to Garcia. "Pass the word to seal all the inner doors once our people are deployed. I want this place shut up tight."

The C^3 technician nodded curtly, then frowned. "I can get through to our own people," she said, shooting a look at Jens and Barnett. "It'll take longer to get the civilians to cooperate."

The Seafarms technicians stationed at the Sandcastle kept their distance from the Legion. Even their computer and communications facilities were segregated. Jens and Barnett had made it clear many times over that they wanted no interference in corporate activities by the Legion garrison.

Before Fraser could answer Jens broke in. "We'll take care of our end, Captain."

Houghan!!, the native Elder, wheezed self-importantly. "I will remain here to observe how you deal with these nomad scum," he said in the dialect of Ourgh.

Fraser hesitated, wanting to order him away, but knowing the Elder would refuse to obey. Maybe it would help if Houghan!! saw the Legion in combat with his enemies. Nodding, he responded in the supplicant's mode. "As you wish, Reverend Ancient," he said. "But I pray you will be heedful of your safety and remain away from the walls. The nomads may wish to eliminate so vital a member of the Council of Ourgh."

The Elder didn't answer, but Fraser saw his eyestalks studying the walls with an expression that might have been apprehension.

That left Fraser, Hawley, and Garcia to deal with the battle. Fighting the temptation to join in the fighting, Fraser helped Garcia take off the backpack and set up the portable command/control unit. Hawley joined them after a moment, his eyes distant. *Probably getting the computer feed direct through his implant*, Fraser thought. It irritated him that Hawley had one of the rare computer interfaces hooked directly into his brain, when the captain couldn't or wouldn't put it to practical use. Hawley used it mostly for his battle simulations.

Something like that would be damned useful for fighting a real battle, Fraser knew, but implants were expensive off Terra, and only a privileged few colonials ever had the operation.

Hawley was plugged in to the information but obviously didn't plan to do anything with it. Fraser bent over the computer's small monitor screen and watched as Garcia called up a battle map. Data from individual helmet sensors and the larger surveillance systems mounted on the base walls was interpreted on the screen to give a fairly accurate picture of the unfolding battle. Of course, the computer might not pick up all the legionnaires out there who weren't in battledress, and the count of the nomads was necessarily vague, but it was enough to give Fraser an overview of the fighting that would be invaluable in deploying his defenders.

He only hoped it would be enough.

* * *

Warrior-Scout !!Dhruuj listened to the voices of the deep, his senses extended to their fullest. Already his clan-brothers were swarming over the Built-Reef-of-the-Strangers, and the sounds of their struggles pulled at the innermost core of his consciousness. The pull of the Clan was hard to resist, but !!Dhruuj willed himself to remain still. He could serve his clan-brothers better by remaining clear of the fighting, watching, listening.

It was less tangible than the Weapons-of-Far-Death, but !!Dhruuj wondered if this new teaching, this discipline and division of duties, might not be the greatest of all Gifts. Better weapons meant power, true, power even over the city-dwellers and their perverted ways. But the knowledge that instinct could be mastered by will was something that would outlast the War-Leader-of-Clans and all his works.

The knowledge would certainly be with them long after the Strangers returned to their distant homes and left the Free Swimmers to their endless realm.

He heard the Voices echoing through the deeps, far-off, faint. !!Dhruuj strained his senses to hear the Words-That-Were-Not-Speech.

The message repeated twice. When he was sure he knew what the Voices had said, he shouted the orders through the water in ordinary speech.

It was time to launch the second stage of the attack.

* * *

A pair of bearded sappers in full Legion battledress rushed past Fraser, their FEK gauss rifles catching the harsh spotlights on gleaming barrels. Fraser watched them unfolding bipods and positioning the weapons to cover the angry sea.

"Keep a sharp eye out, lads," he told them. "Those loke bastards can climb right up the walls."

One of them, a grizzled corporal with a beard that would have done a Biblical prophet proud, flashed him a quick thumbs-up. "Dinna worry, cap'n," he said, his words thick with the familiar accent of Caledon. "Ye can count on us."

That dialect was like a taste of home. "What's your name, Corporal?" Fraser asked him.

He beamed proudly. "MacAllister, sir," he said. The sapper paused to check his magazines carefully before he went on. "I was with yer auld feether, sir, back on Geryon."

"With the auld Watch?" Fraser asked, unconsciously lapsing into the dialect himself. "Why...?" He choked back the question that would have violated one of the oldest codes in the Legion. *Never ask about a man's background. He is a legionnaire—nothing more, nothing less.*

The man grinned at him through the beard. "Long time it's been, cap'n. But you remind me of him, and that's nae mistake, sir."

Fraser turned away suddenly, overcome with emotion. What had made this Caledonian soldier seek refuge with the Legion?

"Sir," Garcia said quietly. "Sir, most of First Platoon Alpha is pinned by heavy fire near the gate. The wogs are setting up heavy stuff everywhere they've got a foothold."

"What about our own heavies?"

"Still kitting up, sir."

"Damn," he muttered. Legion heavy weapons—onager plasma guns, Fafnir rocket launchers, and semi-portable CEK gauss cannons— were too big and bulky for routine use and weren't issued for normal watchstanding duties. But it took time to prepare them, especially the onagers with their full-body armored suits that protected the gunners from the intense heat generated by the weapon. He remembered a kid in Watanabe's platoon named Grant who had suffered extensive burns in the last big battle on Hanuman after firing on enemy troops with a salvaged onager and no protection.

He could also remember a time or two on Hanuman when delays in deploying the heavies had damn near cost him a fight.

Fraser shook his head slowly. Memories of Hanuman wouldn't help him here. He had to deal with the present, not live in the past.

Like Hawley.

He glanced at the captain. Hawley had strapped on chest armor and a holster with a rocket pistol, and he looked alert enough now. But since the start of the fighting his only comment had been the question on Fraser's decision to hold back the reserves from Bravo Company. Otherwise he had seemed content to leave Fraser in command.

"Pass the word to the Armory to send out the Fafnir gunners as soon as they're ready. Lances aren't to wait until everyone is equipped—we need troops out there *now*."

"Yes, sir," Garcia responded, reaching for the channel selector. "Sir—behind you!"

He spun in time to see the sapper, MacAllister, reeling back from the rampant with a bolt embedded in his shoulder. The other legionnaire swung his FEK and fired downward.

A *whoosh* and a thunderclap silenced the FEK as an explosive-tipped rocket projectile caught the second sapper square in the chest. The man flew backward, trying to save himself, but he slipped and fell. He landed in the mud below and lay still.

A dozen bulky, inhuman shapes clambered onto the parapet, their ill-assorted weapons gleaming in the light. One of them pointed a rocket rifle at Fraser and fired.

* * *

Karatsolis sprayed autofire into a cluster of nomad soldiers and shouted encouragement to the handful of legionnaires still on the wall nearby. The defending force was shrinking fast as the enemy advantage in numbers began to be felt. The duty section at the gate was down to six unwounded men—more than half of the original force dead or seriously injured—and the handful of reinforcements Karatsolis had brought from the motor pool was simply not enough to make a difference.

He wondered how Narmonov's men were faring. They'd been pinned by heavy weapons fire for a while, and the last time Karatsolis had managed a look down into the compound the Alphas were still working their way forward to take out the position, a heavy multi-barrel Gatling gun firing rocket-assisted projectiles.

It didn't help that most of the legionnaires had been caught unready. Karatsolis, Legionnaire Sandoval, and Narmonov's men had been in battledress after the riot in Ourgh, but most of the rest of the troops inside the Sandcastle had been in light duty fatigues or even, like Reynolds, in dress uniforms. Many of the men wearing battledress didn't have their helmets.

Karatsolis wished for the armored security of a magrep APC, or at least a veeter. He found himself grinning sourly at the thought of Selim Bashar, safe back in Ourgh. Bashar was probably putting some moves on the girl they'd pulled out of the riot.

The corporal was missing one hell of a fight.

With a wild scream a native flung himself over the wall, crashing into Karatsolis before the legionnaire could react. The FEK clattered across the fusand rampart while Karatsolis gasped for breath. Brandishing a wickedly curved sword, the nomad rose over him, the eyes on the end of their stalks wild with battle.

The legionnaire lashed upward with one foot, catching the nomad on his intricately tattooed stomach. It was like kicking a solid wall, but the nomad recoiled with a hoarse, wordless cry.

Then Sandoval was there, his FEK whining as he pumped round after round into the nomad. Dark blood splashed across Karatsolis as the wog fell.

"Thanks, Sandy," Karatsolis gasped, as he groped for his rifle.

"De nada," Sandoval answered, turning his fire on another clump of nomads. "Hey, man, how long until somebody decides to help us out?"

Karatsolis grunted. It seemed like they'd been fighting for hours, but he knew the battle had started only a few minutes ago.

Three nomads were wrestling a bulky object—another of the Gatling launchers, from the looks of it—into position on the roof of the gatehouse. From there it would command most of the compound ... and put Narmonov's men in a crossfire.

He fired again, but the FEK chattered once and fell silent, the magazine empty. He checked the ammo readouts. The needle rounds were exhausted, and none of the legionnaires in the Sandcastle had been issued any rifle grenades.

Karatsolis swore and reached for a fresh magazine before he remembered that he'd already used up all the reloads O'Donnell had carried. With a final curse he flung the weapon aside. "Sandy! Come on!" he shouted, sprinting toward the nomads and their weapon.

* * *

Lieutenant Susan Gage tapped the side of her helmet as the command channel to Fraser's position went silent. Were those explosions she had heard over the commset? It was hard to separate the radio sounds from the noise of battle around her.

She was crouching behind a pile of cargomods with two squads from Third Platoon Alpha huddling under cover close by. Withering fire from the walls was keeping her troops from getting together an organized assault, and she was painfully aware of each passing second. There couldn't be more than a handful of men left around the gate. Unless they could mount an effective attack soon, the legionnaires were in danger of being drowned once the nomads flooded the compound.

Now Fraser was out of touch. *Damn!* she thought. *If he's gone, so is Captain Hawley. That makes me senior....*

If only Hawley had been able to direct that battle himself! Then the two captains wouldn't have been together, and she wouldn't be stuck holding the bag. Her past experience had been confined to administration, not combat, and Gage wasn't sure she could come up with the right answers. Not like Fraser, who seemed to know exactly what to do.

Seconds ticked by as she studied the walls, searching for a weak spot, a flaw in the nomad position she could exploit. There were other Alpha Company troops pinned down nearby, she knew. Narmonov's men were right up against the wall, but they couldn't reach a ladder or stairway without taking fire from those Gatling launchers.

They needed a break in the action, a distraction that would let her force-rush the enemy.

Reluctantly she gestured to her C^3 tech. "Patch me through to Bravo Company," she said with a tired sigh. "We need backup."

* * *

"Follow me! Come on, you strakks, you want to live forever?"

Gunnery Sergeant Trent moved to block Lieutenant DuValier. "Sir, our orders were to stay in reserve until the captain—"

"Fraser's out of touch, Sergeant. Probably dead." DuValier's expression was hard to read. Was that triumph in his eyes, or just the excitement of battle? "Lieutenant Gage needs help at the gate, and she's in charge now."

Trent felt a chill run through him. Fraser dead? After everything they'd gone through on Hanuman, could the captain really have died?

He'd lost his last CO in the massacre that triggered the fighting on that primitive world, and he had always felt secretly ashamed that he hadn't been there when it had really counted. Fraser had seemed a poor replacement for a man who had been his commanding officer and friend for nearly a decade, but as the long jungle march went on Trent had recognized the younger man's potential. By the time of the final battle, Fraser had been able to handle the company on his own, without the Gunnery Sergeant's advice and encouragement.

Trent didn't want to think he'd lost Fraser so soon.

"Sir," he said levelly. "If the captain has been attacked, we have a security threat on the western perimeter. I submit we should respond there as well."

DuValier frowned at him. "Damn it, Sergeant, I said—"

"We can't turn our back on a gap in the defense, sir!" Trent persisted.

The lieutenant hesitated for a moment, then nodded. "Very well, Sergeant. Take the two recon lances and check it out. Coordinate with Warrant Officer Kelly—she's in charge back there. Now, move!"

"Pascali!" Trent shouted. "Braxton! Your lances with me! Let's go!"

He wouldn't believe that Captain Fraser was dead. Not until he saw a body.

Meanwhile, he knew that Fraser was counting on him.

Chapter Seven

With the bayonet, mes enfants. *It's nothing but shot!*

> —Captain Arnaud-Jacques Leroy Constantine,
> French Foreign Legion, 1837

Karatsolis pulled his knife from its forearm sheath and slashed at the nomad in front of him. The native tried to parry with the cumbersome crossbow he carried, but Karatsolis reversed the direction of the attack at the last moment and thrust the weapon straight for the face. It sank to the hilt just below the left eyestalk, and the wog jerked back so hard that it tore the weapon from the legionnaire's grasp.

Behind him he could hear Sandoval's FEK whining. The sound cut off abruptly.

"Caracoles!" the Hispanic legionnaire swore. "I'm dry!"

Karatsolis snatched his knife from the dead wog's body and sprang forward, ducking to avoid a pike-thrust. He stabbed one tattooed torso, twisted to one side, then slashed again. The native was bellowing in pain or rage. A curved sword missed the legionnaire's head by centimeters.

Then Sandoval was beside him, swinging his FEK. The high-tech club took out the native with the sword, while Karatsolis finished off the pikeman with another knife thrust.

Only two more natives stood between the legionnaires and the nomads setting up the rocket launcher.

And one of them was already drawing a bead on Karatsolis with a pistol....

* * *

Corporal Mike Johnson dropped prone behind the cover of one of the massive struts that supported the complex cradle in the center of the Sandcastle. The structure was designed to hold the *Seafarms Cyclops* when she docked for maintenance or repairs, but at the moment it was the perfect place for the legionnaires of Bravo Company to take shelter as they gathered for their assault.

His duraweave battledress didn't quite keep out the ubiquitous mud. The interior of the compound was usually muddy, especially after vehicles had come in while the tides were rising. Johnson ignored the wet goo that seeped in through his boot tops and focused his attention on the job at hand.

He peered cautiously around the bulky pillar and chambered a mini-grenade in his FEK. At least the troops from the barracks had been able to get grenade clips. If the poor devils out on the perimeter had only been issued the explosive ammo, the natives might never have reached the ramparts.

"What's it look like, Corp?" Legionnaire Delandry asked.

He glanced at her. In battledress, with an FEK in her hand, Elise Delandry didn't look much like a medic, but in the Legion every soldier, no matter what specialty they were trained for, was a rifleman first and foremost. "Hell, Delandry, what does it always look like?" he asked sarcastically. "Swarms of wogs, and not enough of us!"

She grinned at him. "Good. Place was getting too damned dull."

Johnson chuckled. He and Delandry had both lived through Hanuman, and at least twice they'd come close to buying it in a hopeless fight to the death. Both times Colin Fraser had pulled off a miracle and got them out. "You'd rather get in another scrape and make the Captain rescue us again? What's the matter, Delandry, are you trying for a spot on his personal staff? You'll have to do something about his Navy bitch first!"

"Didn't you hear, Corp?" Legionnaire Abban spoke up. "They're saying the Captain's bought it! Old Do-This-n-That's in charge now."

Delandry crossed herself. *"Merde,"* she said softly. "No ... I don't believe it. Not Captain Fraser...."

"I heard it from Maxton, and he said he got it from somebody who was talking to Dubcek," Abban insisted. "The Exec's C-cubed boy should know, huh?"

The corporal opened his mouth to reply, but a crackle in his earphones cut him off.

"First Platoon Bravo, go left, Second Platoon right," DuValier's voice was saying coldly. "Make as much noise as you can. The idea's to distract the wogs so Alpha can take them down. Move! Move!"

Johnson rolled out from behind the strut and scrambled to his feet, firing a spray of needle rounds. Legionnaires shouting battle cries and hoarse-voiced obscenities followed him.

Rocket fire and a few crossbow bolts probed toward the attackers. An explosion less than a meter to the left made Johnson swerve and stagger, but Delandry steadied him and he kept running.

Nearby, Abban went to one knee and fired a three-round burst of grenades at the wall. He started forward again, but a rocket caught him square in the face.

Delandry started toward Abban as the legionnaire fell, then turned away as she saw what the round had left of the man's head. She looked sick.

Johnson kept firing until his magazine ran dry, then ejected the spent clip and slapped a fresh one into the FEK's side-mounted receiver, all without breaking stride. A crossbow bolt clattered harmlessly off his plasteel chest plate.

His foot slipped in the mud, and this time he went down. The landing was enough to knock the wind out of him. He groped for his FEK and tried to take stock of the battle.

There were a lot of other legionnaires down, many of them not moving at all, others moaning, writhing, or trying to crawl toward safety. Not that there was much of that on this killing ground. At least Alpha Company was in close to the walls where they had some cover. Out here there was nothing to hide behind.

He heaved himself to his hands and knees and found the FEK in the mud. The rugged little weapon would stand up to a lot worse treatment than that.

Johnson checked the barrel of the grenade launcher to make sure it was clear, then fired a burst of the lethal 1 cm rounds. The explosions went off in a tight cluster near the closest of the nomad heavy weapons positions.

But not close enough. Johnson saw the multi-barrel monstrosity swinging toward him, streaks of flame spouting from each aperture in turn.

The explosions approached him in an uneven line, like the footfalls of a predatory beast.

He tried to rise, lost his footing again, and fell back into the sticky mud.

Then a flash, a roar, and a searing pain lancing up his leg....

Elise Delandry's face bent over his. He saw her mouth moving, heard the sounds, but nothing seemed to connect. "Leave me ... leave ... here...." he croaked, knowing she wouldn't, knowing what a target they made, knowing....

Then blackness consumed him.

* * *

Karatsolis flinched as the grenade burst hit the wall just below the native with the rocket pistol. The nomad staggered, and Karatsolis gathered himself and sprang forward. A moment later Sandoval was with him, holding off the other enemy soldier while Karatsolis grappled with the massive wog.

The native swung a powerful arm, and the impact against his wrist made Karatsolis drop his knife. With his left hand he gripped the rocket pistol and tried to wrench it free.

The wogs had powerful arm muscles designed for swimming and climbing, which made them stronger than a man, but their hands were weaker and less versatile. Karatsolis strained, forcing the alien's fingers back. Suddenly he had the gun.

He continued the motion to bring it smashing into the wog's face just above the writhing feeding tendrils once ... twice ... and again. The nomad staggered back, dark blood welling from the ruined features. Karatsolis raised the awkward weapon and pressed the firing stud, but the range was too short. The projectile dipped as it left the barrel before the rocket cut in, but it didn't have time to build up much momentum.

Sandoval pushed past him, a knife in one hand, his clubbed FEK in the other, and finished off the stunned native. Karatsolis fired at the nearest of the three wogs manning the Gatling launcher, saw the explosive round blow a hole in his abdomen.

The other two leapt from their weapon, eyes burning, hands drawing curved swords. Paralysis gripped Karatsolis for an instant. He wasn't used to soldiers who kept coming the way these wogs did. Any human soldier would have run from a foe who had charged them the way he had. These monsters didn't just stand their ground, they attacked. And kept attacking, again and again.

One of the swords sliced deep into Sandoval's arm, and he dropped the FEK as he reeled back. Karatsolis fired twice more, then lunged sideways to avoid another fierce slash. He rolled against a wog body as he hit the ground and something long and hard prodded him. His fingers closed around one of the long pikes many of the nomads had carried. Grabbing the weapon, he thrust it upward as his attacker rushed him again.

Even in his death-throes the nomad was still trying to reach Karatsolis.

The legionnaire staggered to his feet, hardly able to believe that there were no more natives close by. He ran to the heavy Gatling launcher and studied it for a moment. Somewhere nearby he heard a groan.

"Sandy? How is it, Sandy?"

The Hispanic's voice was weak. "I'll live, I think. Hey, man, are we winning?"

Karatsolis grinned. "Could be, Sandy. Least we don't have to play with those damned popguns anymore!"

* * *

The explosive round hit the C^3 pack, and Fraser returned fire with his FEK on full auto. Half a dozen natives toppled backward off the wall under the hail of needle-thin slivers, but more kept on coming. He backpedaled, still firing, trying to reach the stairwell.

Garcia was sprawled near the shattered terminal. She stirred, rolled over, and raised her own weapon, firing from her prone position. Close by Hawley crouched beside the sapper MacAllister, his rocket pistol drawn and all trace of vagueness gone from his eyes. The captain fired twice, hitting his targets. Then he was grappling with another nomad armed with a sword.

Fraser switched to single-shot and placed a high-velocity needle round squarely through the native's forehead. He toppled, and Hawley grabbed MacAllister and started pulling him back toward Fraser and Garcia.

More natives were climbing over the wall, screaming, brandishing weapons, a seemingly unstoppable living tidal wave. Fraser kept his weapon on the single-shot setting, conserving ammo, but Garcia's FEK gave off the continuous whine of full-auto fire. She had a grim smile on her face as she sprayed the attackers with lethal slivers.

"Look out, Captain!" Fraser shouted, as a nomad swung his legs over the wall just behind Hawley. He tried to line up a shot, but the captain blocked it.

Hawley let go of MacAllister's shoulders and turned, but not quickly enough. A backhand blow knocked Hawley backward, sending him sprawling over the injured legionnaire. The nomad drew his sword.

With a hoarse shout Houghan!! leapt into the fight, moving fast for a creature of his bulk and age. The Elder had picked up a sword from one of the dead nomads, and with a deft movement he parried the killing blow aimed at Captain Hawley.

Houghan!! was no match for the nomad warrior, though. The Elder fell back under a flurry of blows, barely able to fend off the attack. Fraser squeezed off a shot, cursed, fired again. The nomad fell.

And an instant later an enemy bullet exploded in Houghan!!'s back. The Elder fell forward across the body of his opponent.

Hawley was up again, still not abandoning MacAllister. "Cover us, Garcia!" Fraser yelled, leaping to help the captain.

Between them they were able to half carry, half drag the sapper back to the door that led to the stairs. The fusand corner of the stairwell gave some cover, at least.

Fraser flipped the FEK's selector switch to full-auto. "Get him inside, sir!" he said, leaning around the corner and opening fire. He shouted over the battle rifle's whine. "Garcia! Fall back!"

The C^3 operator kept firing until her magazine ran dry, then rolled, scrambled to her feet, and sprinted for the door, running in a zigzag pattern that stayed clear of Fraser's line of fire.

Hawley had the door open and was maneuvering MacAllister's limp body inside. As nomads continued to try to mass on the rampart, Fraser kept up his automatic fire, painfully aware of how fast he was using up his only magazine. The FEK ran dry just as Garcia rounded the corner. She dropped to one knee and hastily switched magazines in her own rifle.

She paused to pull out an extra clip and pass it to Fraser. "That's my last, skipper," she said.

"Take the other side, Garcia," he replied. "Make 'em count. Captain, I recommend you get MacAllister downstairs and then go find some backup."

Hawley's voice was gruff. "I should stay and fight. I don't like running." It was a tone Fraser had never heard from the older man.

"Then think of it as gathering reinforcements for a tactical envelopment," he said. "We'll keep their attention until you get back."

Hawley's chuckle was dry and no less startling. "Hang on, then, son. I won't let you down." More softly, as if to himself, he went on. "I *won't*. Not this time."

* * *

Gage shuddered as another rapid-fire salvo of rockets poured down into the ragged Bravo Company skirmish line. The nomad heavy-weapons positions were maintaining a devastating fire against the legionnaires, and she'd already seen at least twenty men go down under that withering barrage.

But the diversion had been useless after all. When Narmonov's men tried to break from cover and attack the wall, the rockets had turned on them, breaking the attack before it had really started. A similar attempt by the troops with her had fared no better.

Every man dead or wounded out there had fallen because of her foolish orders. And soon the nomads would have control of the gates. Then it would be over.

"Massire!" she snapped to her C^3 tech. "General signal to Bravo Company. Disengage and fall back!"

"That'll leave us useless," Gunnery Sergeant Valko said. He was bleeding where shrapnel had sliced open a savage gash in his left cheek.

"Damn it, Sergeant, I can't just let them keep dying out there!"

"Ma'am—" Valko didn't finish. "What the hell?"

A rocket launcher near the gatehouse had opened fire again, but not down into the compound. Rockets streaked through the air, probing at the nomads closest to Narmonov's men. The ripple of explosions was the most beautiful sight and sound Gage had ever witnessed.

"Goddamn!" Subaltern Carnes shouted. "One of our boys is still kicking!" Other legionnaires started to cheer.

"Cancel that disengage order, Massire!" Gage shouted. "Come on, boys, let's kick those strakking wogs back into the ocean where they belong! Come on!"

She led thirty yelling legionnaires across the muddy ground.

* * *

Karatsolis swung the heavy launcher, gasping at the effort, and fired again. Rockets lanced toward another nomad position, and natives on that section of the wall dived for cover.

Beside him, Sandoval was trying to figure out how the feed mechanism worked. "You're down to ten more rounds, Spear," he said. "Damned if I can reload this sucker."

"Damn," Karatsolis swore. "I hope it was enough...." He could see Narmonov's troops swarming among the nomads who had kept them pinned down for so long. There were more legionnaires crossing the compound down below. All they needed was a little more time, a little more confusion in the enemy ranks, and the Legion could get up close and personal with the wogs. Those rocket pistols were almost useless at short ranges, and duraweave and plasteel armor would stop most of the other nomad weapons.

He fired again, aiming for another Gatling launcher that was swinging to cover the nearest group of human troops. The shots weren't very accurate, but the natives' aim went wild as well.

Sandoval grabbed his arm and pointed. "Over there, Spear!" he shouted.

Karatsolis swore again and tried to turn the launcher in the direction the wounded Hispanic legionnaire had indicated. But the bulky launcher wouldn't turn fast enough.

Three nomads were wrestling their own launcher into line to get off a shot at Karatsolis and Sandoval....

He hauled at the multi-barreled weapon desperately until Sandoval shoved him away bodily. He fell and rolled over the edge of the parapet, landing with a heavy thud on the gatehouse roof a meter below.

Fire streaked through the twilight, and a dozen rockets impacted around the launcher. Karatsolis hauled himself to his feet and started forward, then caught sight of the wreckage of the launcher and the shattered body of Legionnaire Enrique Sandoval.

* * *

Captain David Hawley was feeling really alive for the first time in years. Adrenaline pumped in his veins, and the weight of the FE-PLF in his hand brought back memories long lost in a fog of implant addiction and drink. The fight on the HQ roof had left him eager for more.

He knelt beside MacAllister and felt for the sapper's neck pulse. It was weak and thready, but the man was still alive. Satisfied, Hawley rose and turned away from the unconscious man, anxious to find re-inforcements and get back to the fighting.

Down the corridor a swinging door banged open. Sigrid Jens and a handful of men in Seafarms coveralls were there, some carrying FEKs, others improvised clubs.

"We heard there was a breakthrough up there," Jens said. "I brought as many people as I could."

Hawley gaped at her. Jens and her assistant had been a thorn in his side since the moment Demi-Battalion Elaine had arrived on Polypheme. Somehow he'd never expected the Seafarms people to lift a finger in their own defense.

Not that they'd be much use in the fighting. But the weapons they'd scavenged....

"Thank you, Citizen," he said, the words seeming inadequate to convey his feelings. "Thank you." He hesitated, trying to decide on the best course.

Decisions always came so hard these days. Young Fraser could snap out orders with barely a pause, like everything was perfectly clear from the moment he first saw it.

Once David Hawley had been able to do that. Once, but not anymore.

"Ah … look, Citizen, ah … I'll take the men with rifles back to the roof. I need you … I need you to find some legionnaires and get them to back us up. Can you do that?"

She nodded quickly. "Got it. Anything else?"

He grappled with the question a moment. "Ah … get someone to the Armory and turn out the heavy-weapons lances. Tell them … tell them…." He tried to remember the order Fraser had been about to pass when the nomads had first attacked on the roof. "Tell them lances shouldn't wait to be fully equipped before they deploy. Get the Fafnir gunners out as soon as they're ready."

"Fafnir gunners. Right." Jens gave another curt nod. "Good luck, Captain."

"Follow me, citizens!" he said, waving the PLF and urging them toward the stairs. He felt like a leader for the first time in many, many years.

* * *

Warrior-Scout !!Dhruuj croaked a complex, wordless message in his farspeaking voice, reporting the news Clan-Warlord Khroor! had ordered him to send.

The Strangers-Within were winning the fight. Their warriors were counterattacking the walls in strength, and the attack on the gates had already been turned away. The Clan would fight to the end, of course, but it was clear now that even the clever two-pronged attack had not been enough to keep the Strangers from rallying in defense of their mysterious domain.

Perhaps the War-Leader-of-Clans would have an answer, or could get one from the Strangers-Who-Gave-Gifts. !!Dhruuj felt a thrill of certainty within himself. The War-Leader-of-Clans was the mightiest warrior ever to swim free, mightier than any nomad, any city-dweller ... mightier than the Strangers-Within.

Long minutes went by as !!Dhruuj listened for the Voices to reply. Then, faintly, he heard the distant sounds.

!!Dhruuj hesitated for a long moment before interpreting the Voices for the Clan-Warlord clinging to the wall beside him. It seemed unthinkable ... unnatural....

But it was the order of the War-Leader-of-Clans, and the Reef-Swimmers had sworn to obey him as they would their own Clan-Leader.

"The attack to end," he said at last. "The swimmers to retreat. The scouts to watch and await new orders."

The Clan-Warlord grunted understanding. He seemed to sense !!Dhruuj's unease with the orders. "Wisdom there is in this," he said slowly. "Withdraw now, and we can renew the attack later to our advantage. Stay, and we destroy the Clan to no gain."

!!Dhruuj studied the Clan-Warlord with a feeling of sudden comprehension.

The battle wasn't really over. The Swimmers would return to finish it—when the time was right.

Chapter Eight

I can refuse nothing to men like you!

—Colonel Combas, Mexican Army,
to the survivors of Camerone,
French Foreign Legion, 30 April 1863

They'll be back," Fraser said flatly. "Count on it."

They were back in the conference room, now that the fighting was over, but it was far more subdued than the wrangling of their previous meeting. Even Barnett seemed a little less inclined to pick unnecessary fights. The man looked jumpy now, as if he were afraid that nomads might burst through the door any time.

He spared a glance for Captain Hawley. The older officer had lapsed back into apathy now that the immediate danger was over. The comparison between Hawley bending over the fallen legionnaire with pistol in hand and this more familiar figure slumped carelessly in his chair aroused strong emotions in Fraser, but he wasn't sure which was more powerful, pity or disgust.

Fraser closed his eyes, remembering the captain leading the armed civilians back onto the roof. They had come just in time, as Garcia and Fraser had been running out of ammo. By the time the defense was weakening again, Gunnery Sergeant Trent and two lances of recon troops had reached the building. Not long afterward, the natives had retreated.

But they'd left their mark on the Sandcastle. Medical teams were still counting the casualties and treating the injured, while the rest of the Legion checked damage to the walls and strengthened the defenses. He'd ordered Kelly to take charge of the work instead of returning to the meeting, but now he regretted not being able to bounce ideas off her. She was one of the few people in the Sandcastle he could use as a sounding board.

"The measures we are taking now should prevent a recurrence," DuValier was saying. He alone of all the officers in the room seemed unaffected by the native attack.

"Here, perhaps," Fraser said, looking at the cold, self-contained lieutenant. The contrast with Hawley's Exec, Susan Gage, was startling. She had come back from the fighting with a haunted look in her eyes, and she had contributed nothing to the discussion. "Deploying heavy-weapons lances with the troops on watch and rigging up some strong-points on the walls should keep the wogs at arm's length. But we have two other problems to address." He turned to study Sigrid Jens.

She shifted uncomfortably. "We had no idea the nomads could field that kind of a force," she said. "Obviously this puts a whole new complexion on the Project. I will issue orders for the recall of the *Cyclops*."

"You can't!" Barnett said sharply. "It'll finish the Project."

She shrugged. "Maybe. And us with it, as far as Seafarms is concerned. But the safety of the Terran personnel on Polypheme is my responsibility, Edward, and I'm not putting those people at risk. We may still be able to salvage the Project, but only after we've figured out a way to deal with the nomad threat."

"I'm glad you feel that way, Citizen," Fraser said, cutting off whatever reply Barnett had been about to come back with. "But at this point *Cyclops* is only part of the problem."

"How do you mean?" she asked, lifting one eyebrow in surprise.

"I think you should pull out of the Seafarms facilities in Ourgh as well," he said. "Everything should be centered here at the Sandcastle. The danger in the city is probably far worse than aboard the ship."

"This is ludicrous!" Barnett exploded. "We can't possibly relocate our entire operation. And there's no reason for it! The nomads won't attack Ourgh, even with rocket guns. Damn it, there's enough militia in town to handle any nomad clan without even calling up the off-duty reserves!"

Fraser leaned forward and rested his elbows on the table. "First of all, Citizen Barnett, those nomads could go through the Ourgh militia faster than a nova takes out planets. They damn near beat us, and the Legion isn't some useless loke mob. Second, don't assume the nomads are operating with the same clan structure as they used to have."

"Now, wait a moment, Captain Fraser," Jens said. "I understand your concern, but our studies have shown that the nomad clans cannot work together. They are simply incapable of accepting leadership from outside the Clan grouping, and the concepts of a committee or ruling council are completely foreign to them."

"The city-dwellers understand them well enough," Trent commented.

"Yes, Sergeant, they do," Jens said. "But land and sea-dwelling cultures on Polypheme are totally different, almost like they were separate species."

"The point is," Fraser said, "That they *aren't* completely different. The city-dwellers were an offshoot of the nomads, and they evolved new cultural standards to respond to different needs. Mr. Koenig, my Native Affairs specialist, has been studying the wogs for a long time, and his feeling is that the nomad cultures could learn to work together if they found it necessary, particularly if a charismatic warlord were to unite them against an outside threat."

"Like the city-dwellers," Gunnery Sergeant Valko said. "Or us."

"This is all pure speculation," Barnett protested. "Theory. The tribal tattoos on those natives were all the same. I don't know which Clan—"

"Reef-Swimmers," Susan Gage said softly. It was the first time she'd spoken, and the comment was offered diffidently.

"All right, the Reef-Swimmers Clan," Barnett said. "One group. No sign of some kind of coalition."

"No direct proof, yet," Fraser agreed. "But consider this. Just a few hours ago the *Seafarms Cyclops* was attacked by nomads. Watanabe's report didn't include the name of the Clan—it isn't one of the ones we've studied like the Reef-Swimmers—but the follow-up should have more information. Point is, it's a different tribe, but using the same weaponry."

Trent looked up. "And even more important, the same tactics," he added.

"Exactly," Fraser said with an approving nod. "The same tactics. Up until today no nomad Clan would break off an attack while there was still a perceived threat to other Clan members. Today two different groups, hundreds of kilometers apart, suddenly demonstrated this new idea. No way it was independently developed, Citizen … no way at all."

"So you suspect an overall leadership," Jens summed up.

"Right. One that has made contact with an off-planet source of armaments. I don't know if the tactics are a local innovation or something these helpful suppliers suggested, but I'll bet damned near any stakes you want that there's a central authority, probably a group of lokes, behind these attacks. And several native Clans working in h arness together could wipe out Ourgh without even bothering to stop for a breather afterwards."

"Not all of them carry the high-tech stuff," Barnett pointed out.

"That's about all that saved us today. They attacked before they were fully equipped. Probably the nomads are over-eager. Even if the Semti were controlling them, I doubt the nomads would be very easy to control. They've got new toys."

"So they want to use them," Jens said.

Fraser nodded. At least she was getting it. Her assistant still looked stubborn.

"How can you be sure the nomads would attack us in the city? Aside from the slaving raids, the nomads haven't tried to take on the city culture openly before. Their interests don't coincide."

"Right now nomad interests seem to involve us," Trent pointed out. "And if we've got people in Ourgh …"

"That's not the only factor," Fraser said quietly. "You all heard what Houghan!! had to say before the battle. The city-dwellers think we're dealing with both sides, and cutting them out of the weapons deals."

"But that's nonsense," Barnett protested.

"Sure. But look at it from their point of view. The emissary they sent to protest about the weapons isn't coming back. And they only have our word that he was killed by a nomad while trying to help Captain Hawley." Fraser paused; steepled his fingers, and rested his forehead on them wearily. "We lost a lot of good men today, but Houghan!!'s death really turns what should have been a victory into a major defeat. The Council in Ourgh won't trust us again, and the mood in the city is already swinging against us because we won't provide protection."

"Meaning?" Hawley asked, finally seeming to be aware of the discussion.

"Meaning, Captain, that in one stroke we've lost our last chance to recruit ourselves some sepoys to build up our troop strength, and also lost Ourgh as a safe haven. That riot I was in will look like a picnic when the lokes really start getting organized." He turned to Jens. "Once again, there just aren't enough legionnaires to cover your facilities and people in town. We have to concentrate out here, where we won't be overextended."

"You make a convincing case, Captain Fraser," Jens said with a trace of a smile. She glanced at Barnett. "Perhaps if I'd been given advice like this from the start we wouldn't be in this mess now."

"You're not going to buy this?" Barnett was out of his chair, his face flushed. "We've got to keep the port and the warehouses open!"

"That's enough, Edward," Jens said flatly. Her tone made it clear she wasn't listening to any more arguments. She turned back to Fraser. "If you'll assign an officer as liaison, we'll try to work out an evacuation plan that will meet all our needs. Military as well as corporate."

Fraser leaned back in his chair, relief draining the tension from his shoulders. He hadn't been sure anyone connected with Seafarms would listen to reason. "Thank you, Citizen Jens. Your cooperation will make this a lot easier."

He looked down the table for a moment. "Captain Hawley, if you can spare your Exec for a while I think she'd be a good choice for this."

Hawley shrugged. "If you think she can do the job, by all means, Captain."

"All right, then. Citizen, if you and Lieutenant Gage can get on this right away, we'll start the evacuation as soon as I'm sure the Sandcastle is secured. And I'll also need you to give the orders for the *Cyclops*...."

"I know you have a low opinion of us, Captain," she said with another smile. "But please don't worry. We really are on your side, and when I say we'll cooperate, I mean to follow through."

As the meeting broke up Fraser remained in the chair, frowning, his eyes focused somewhere past the far wall. For now, Seafarms would go along with what he said, but there was no guarantee that Jens would keep cooperating once the immediate threat had passed.

If this turned into a long siege, the civilians were likely to be the weak link in the chain. He wondered if their enemies, whoever they were, realized that time was as valuable to their cause as all the rocket guns on Polypheme?

If the Legion was forced entirely on the defensive they were all as good as dead.

* * *

The blackness was like a lake, deep and cold, and Mike Johnson was at the bottom of it. He struggled against unseen forces, fighting his way to the surface, back to light and warmth and air.

His eyes snapped open suddenly, relieved to see the harsh artificial glare of floodlights against the darkening sky.

He was on a stretcher, his arms and legs strapped down firmly. A large, bulky regen unit was attached to his left leg, humming faintly and making the skin tingle. He couldn't feel anything else, and when he tried to move the foot nothing happened.

Panic welled up inside. A regen unit accelerated the natural healing process, but its effectiveness in cases of major nerve damage was limited, and no one had found a way yet to regrow a lost limb.

A rich Terran who lost a leg could have a cyberlimb fitted, but a poor legionnaire on a backwater like Polypheme would be lucky to get an old-fashioned prosthetic job. Johnson knew ex-legionnaires missing arms and legs who had never received the therapy and retraining it took to use an artificial limb. They ended up as penniless beggars hanging around colonial street corners or systerm bars.

He tried to sit up, but the straps held him down. "Hey! Help me, dammit!" he shouted. "For God's sake ..."

"Calm down, my son," a soothing voice answered. It was Father Fitzpatrick, known throughout Bravo Company simply as "the Pad-re," the unit's chaplain. More than half of the legionnaires stationed on Polypheme were Catholics, and although Fitzpatrick's branch of the Church—based on Freehold, a world which had been cut off from all contact with Terra during the Shadow Centuries—did not recog-nize the primacy of the Pope in Rome, he took care of their spiritual needs quite well.

Johnson was technically a Protestant and paid little enough atten-tion to religion anyway, but the Padre's easy smile and gentle voice were reassuring nonetheless.

"Father ... my leg. I can't move my leg. Is it ... Will it be...?"

Fitzpatrick knelt beside him and examined the diagnostic readout on the front panel of the regen unit. He necessarily spent a lot of time helping the company's medical specialist, Dr. Ramirez, and he knew his way around Legion medical gear and facilities. "It's all right, my son," he said in his quiet voice. "The unit has administered a local nerve block for the pain. You can feel a tingle, can't you?"

Johnson nodded.

"Then you're fine, my son. You'll be off your feet for a while, but you'll still have both of them when you recover." A smile creased the round, open features. "I've seen soldiers who did more damage tripping over each other after a rough night on the town."

Forcing himself to relax, Johnson sighed gratefully. "Thanks, Father. I ... I was afraid...."

"No need to tell me, my son. Fear is not on any of the lists of sins I've seen."

"Have you ... have you seen Legionnaire Elise Delandry, Father? She's a medic. She was helping me after ... after I was hit."

Fitzpatrick nodded gravely. "She has been helping Dr. Ramirez with triage. I'll tell her you asked for her." He was gone before Johnson could thank him again, moving among the other wounded men who surrounded him. He tried to count the litters, but by the time he reached twenty he felt himself slipping back into oblivion.

$*\quad*\quad*$

Lieutenant Antoine Duvalier spotted the Padre kneeling by one of the wounded and crossed the open ground to join him. Fitzpatrick bowed his head in prayer, sketched the Cross, and straightened up slowly.

After a long moment the chaplain signaled to a medic. "Private Conneau is dead," he told the man. The soldier nodded, but didn't show much emotion. In the middle of all this suffering, one more death didn't cause much of a stir.

But DuValier felt the pain. Quietly, from behind the Padre, he said, "Conneau was a good man. He told me once that his parents were from Toulon before they emigrated to Devereaux."

Fitzpatrick gave a start, surprised by his silent approach. Then he recovered. "Toulon was where you were born, was it not?"

He nodded. "How bad is it?" he asked, his gesture taking in the casualties.

"Not good. A lot of men will be taking the dirt today." Many legionnaires took the soil from the graves of comrades, carrying a few grains of dirt from each planet on which they'd left brothers-in-arms. "I haven't heard a full count yet."

"This should never have happened," DuValier said harshly. He paused to rein in his emotions, further irritated that he had allowed his control to slip in the sight of the Padre. But Fitzpatrick just nodded solemnly and moved toward the next casualty in the line, leaving DuValier alone with his bitter thoughts.

For two years he'd been locked in a downward spiral, his career ruined. No one but the Legion would accept an officer with his record, so it was to the Legion he had come for his last chance to change his luck. DuValier had vowed that this time, *this* time he would not let himself give in to weakness. He would do what he had to do, no matter what stood in his way. But it wasn't easy.

And his superior, the man who commanded Bravo Company, just made the struggle that much harder. Colin Fraser....

The fighting in the compound had brought DuValier face to face with all the old memories again, and he knew the nightmares would start again tonight. The horrors of Fenris were never far below the surface in any case, but being under fire again had brought back every terrible moment.

Two years now since the rebellion on Fenris, two years since the orders to the 33rd Mobile Response Regiment to search out the suspected nest of rebels in Loki Province. They'd been issued detailed intelligence reports describing specifics on rebel strengths and probable deployments, and the Colonel had worked out the sweep in detail. It should have been routine.

But the reports were based on faulty data and sloppy interpretation, and the rebel strength had been nearly twice what they'd been led to expect. And they had far more anti-air and anti-armor capability than the 33rd planned on.

DuValier could still remember that day. He had been a freshly promoted lieutenant then, in charge of the rear guard. That was what had saved him—along with less than eighty soldiers out of a regiment of over eight hundred men. All because of the intelligence screw-up.

All because of one Colin Fraser, then also a lieutenant in the regulars but now, ironically, a hero, a captain, and Antoine DuValier's new CO.

He viewed the accounts of the court-martial in a vidmagazine, both the initial stories where Fraser put the blame on his superior, Major St. John, and the later interviews with Senator Warwick, that uncovered the plot to hurt the senator through St. John, all hinging on Fraser's testimony. Warwick's opponents had protected Fraser from the blame; men swept him under the table afterward. Why else would he be in the Legion now? If he was blameless, he'd still be in some comfortable staff job.

DuValier had suffered for two years, messed up too many assignments because of his personal problems. He had transferred to the Legion in hopes of making a fresh start, but somehow he'd been tapped to fill the vacant Exec's position in Fraser's company after the Hanuman campaign. He was sure Fraser knew nothing of his record, and so far he'd kept a tight lid on his feelings.

For a few minutes it had looked like Fraser had died, and it had been a shock to find out that he was alive after all. Thoughts of killing Fraser had crossed his mind once or twice, but he couldn't give in. He'd never accomplish his goal if he murdered a superior officer.

But if the man died in battle …

He pushed the thought away. A time or two he'd come close to sharing his doubts with Fitzpatrick, but it was something he couldn't bring himself to talk about. He was probably closer to the chaplain than he was to any other man in Bravo Company, but his past wasn't something he wanted to share … and neither was his hatred of Colin Fraser. Fitzpatrick wouldn't understand that, anyway. He'd been on Hanuman, regarded Fraser as a hero. Just like the others who'd served with the man before.

DuValier looked at the bodies littering the compound. If the Padre knew how he felt about Fraser he'd be shocked, and DuValier would lose a friend. That was one casualty he wasn't going to give up to the murderer who'd destroyed the 33rd on Fenris.

Chapter Nine

Superb men, but the scrapings of every nation, an amalgam of every state, of every profession, of every social calling who have come to join one another and many of them to hide.

—Lieutenant Arnaud-Jacques Leroy Constantine,
French Foreign Legion, 1837

eels good to be back where we belong, huh, Spear?" Corporal Selim Bashar asked, as he powered up the magrep fields aboard the M-980 Sabertooth FSV. "I mean, those veeters are okay, but I'd rather be in the *Angel* any time, wouldn't you?"

The voice in his headphones grunted a distracted response, and Bashar frowned. Spiro Karatsolis was the best friend Bashar had in the Legion, maybe the best friend he'd ever had, and he was sensitive to the Greek legionnaire's moods.

They'd met during basic training on Devereaux, two nubes surprised to find that they came from the same homeworld, New Cyprus, though everything else about them was different. Bashar had come from a city background, his father a wealthy merchant shocked by his only son's desire to join the Colonial Army. His father's resistance and a desire for adventure had driven Bashar to the Legion, where he could start fresh, beyond even his father's long reach.

But Karatsolis had come from a poor background, growing up on a farm raising the sheep that were the only Terran livestock that had adapted to New Cyprus. For the Greek kid's family, military service was a way for the boy to better himself, and the Legion the service of choice because other family members had served with the unit in times past. From background to ethnic heritage to goals and desires, the two young soldiers hadn't shared much in common, but still they'd gravitated toward one another.

Since earning the *kepi blanc*, Bashar and Karatsolis had managed to stay together, first in a regular infantry unit, then through specialist training and assignment to a Legion Transport Company. They'd soldiered together on more planets than Bashar cared to recall. On Hanuman, they'd lost the battle-scarred Sabertooth Karatsolis and christened *Angel of Death*, but they had weathered the long march. The Greek had even saved Bashar's life. That was nothing unusual, of course; they'd been pulling each other out of danger since the first day of recruit training. Danger was something Bashar and Karatsolis thrived on, though of course like any veteran legionnaire neither would admit it.

Now they had a new Sabertooth, the *Angel II*, and enough danger on the horizon to keep a whole division of bored legionnaires happy. But Karatsolis had been withdrawn ever since Bashar had returned to the Sandcastle in response to orders recalling the Transport Section to prepare a major convoy to carry out the evacuation of offworlders from Ourgh. Since the riot in town, something had happened to disturb the normally cheerful Greek.

Karatsolis had been in a battle, of course, and by all accounts he'd been as close to death as he'd ever been. Rumors were already flying around the unit that the Greek was being recommended for the Commonwealth Legion of Merit for seizing an enemy rocket launcher and turning it on the wogs at the critical moment in the battle, and Bashar believed what he'd heard. Captain Fraser would be quick to recognize any legionnaire who deserved it.

What was bothering Karatsolis, then? Bashar wasn't sure, and that realization worried him almost as much as his friend's all too obvious pain.

"Roundup Escort, Roundup Escort, this is Alpha Two," a new voice crackled in his headphones. "Status check."

"Alpha Two, Roundup Escort," Bashar replied, using the call sign selected for the FSV for Operation Roundup, the evacuation mission. "Receiving you five by five. Power at maximum charge. All diagnostics nominal."

"Confirmed, Roundup Escort." Lieutenant Gage sounded tired and worried. Bashar shrugged the thought off. The responsibility of putting together the entire mission, and the problems of making several hundred civilians cooperate once it was ready, would be enough to make anyone sound frayed. "Estimate time of departure at 1730 standard."

Bashar entered the time on his computer terminal. "On the board, Lieutenant," he replied. "You set 'em up, we'll knock 'em down."

"Standby, Escort," was Gage's flat response. The command circuit went dead. Bashar could picture her in the command APC, a variant on the ubiquitous Sandray design filled with computer and communications gear, running through a careful check of each vehicle's status before giving the orders to depart the Sandcastle. She was a competent, careful Exec.

But he couldn't help but wish that Captain Fraser or Gunny Trent was in charge. He still remembered Hanuman. Gage was a good officer, but Bashar had trouble envisioning her handling a hannie attack in the middle of the jungle.

He leaned back in the driver's seat and cut in the intercom circuit. "Hey, Spear," he said carelessly. "If we're pulling an evac maybe we'll get to carry Katrina. She was real grateful for the ride on the veeter yesterday. I mean, *real* grateful." Actually the girl from the riot, Katrina Voskovich, hadn't said more than four words from the time she got aboard, but Bashar needed something to get the banter started up.

Karatsolis didn't rise to the bait. "I got a fault on my tracking scope, Bashar," he said. "Give me another diagnostic on sensors, will you?"

Bashar sighed and punched the appropriate orders into the computer. Between the Greek and Lieutenant Gage, his own morale was starting to crack.

* * *

Floodlights held back the darkness and glinted harshly off the hulls of the vehicles parked in the center of the Sandcastle's open courtyard. Looking around at the preparations for the convoy into Ourgh, Colin Fraser felt a tug of guilt. He would have preferred to take charge of the evacuation himself. The idea of letting someone else take responsibility for such a difficult undertaking was still hard to deal with.

He almost smiled at the memory of a similar problem back on Hanuman. That time he had wanted to take command of a rear-guard party, but Gunny Trent had convinced him that his duty lay in organizing the Legion's withdrawal from a beleaguered fort. Now, just when his experience would have counted for something, he was stuck back here in the Sandcastle.

This time it had been Kelly, not Trent, who pointed out where his responsibilities were. For all intents and purposes he was in command—Captain Hawley, despite the flash of energy he had shown rescuing the old sapper during the battle, was obviously unable or unwilling to exercise his authority—and the CO had to remain in the command center and coordinate the overall operation.

There were Sandcastle defenses to put into order, recon drones to watch, contingency plans to be made, and though these could be done from the Sandray command van if necessary, they required his full attention.

But knowing that she was right didn't make it any easier to accept.

The convoy didn't inspire much confidence. When the legionnaires had been assigned to Polypheme, no one had envisioned much need for mobile operations. The transport section attached to the demi-battalion, sixteen men and ten vehicles before the nomad attack, wasn't even sufficient to lift out a full company of a hundred and ten soldiers. There was only one Sabertooth fire support vehicle, a command van, two veeters, four standard Sandray APCs, and a pair of cargo vans. Those would carry fifty passengers in reasonable comfort, or perhaps twice that number under emergency conditions.

To make up the difference between the hundred people the Legion vehicles could hold and the estimated eight hundred plus workers, technicians, dependents, and other Commonwealth civilians in Ourgh, they would need to press every Seafarms vehicle into service, right down to the starport's magrep forklifts. Jens had also promised that a bargelike contraption used in outfitting the *Cyclops* would have magrep modules fitted in time for the evacuation. It would be able to hold cargo and perhaps ninety more people, but it would have to be towed. That could be dangerous, especially if there was trouble in Ourgh.

For all of that it would still require at least two trips to get everyone out, especially since they'd have to take up some of the available passenger space with troops to guard the civilians and whatever equipment and personal effects they brought out. Edward Barnett had argued against sending legionnaires—apparently he was more afraid that they'd decide to loot the Terran Enclave than he was of native intervention—but Jens had overruled him. It looked like the woman really was ready to let the Legion take charge now.

That made him think of the *Seafarms Cyclops*. True to her word, Jens had ordered the ship's captain to head for the Sandcastle, but it was a trip that would take several days. When Fraser had spoken to Watanabe, he'd come away with the feeling that the young subaltern was relieved to be on the way back. Hopefully, the nomads wouldn't try any more attacks on the extractor ship, but Fraser knew he couldn't count on it.

Those nomads were showing enough of a grasp of tactics to know that they'd be best served by picking the Terrans apart while they were separated. The next few standard days would be the most dangerous.

Gunnery Sergeant Valko was outside the command van, nodding sagely as he reviewed a compboard with a worried-looking civilian in a Seafarms coverall. The NCO looked up at Fraser's approach and saluted smartly.

"What's the word, Gunny?" Fraser asked him, forcing an encouraging smile.

The sergeant didn't smile back. "On schedule, sir," he said slowly. Valko was a man who weighed his words and his decisions before he committed himself. "I see no major problems as long as the civilians hold their end up."

The Seafarms man flushed and looked away. Like many of the more hard-bitten legionnaires, Valko didn't bother to hide the fact that he had as much contempt for civilians as people like Barnett had for the Legion.

But friction between the military and civilian organizations could undermine the security of the Sandcastle in the days ahead.

"I'm sure everything will be ready, Gunny," he said firmly. "And if not, I'm sure that you'll be able to work things out." He nodded toward the van. "Is Lieutenant Gage aboard?"

"Yes, sir," Valko replied. He rapped on the rear door, then moved off with the civilian in tow as the ramp dropped. A young legionnaire, probably fresh out of the training center on Devereaux, blinked at Fraser in surprise. "S-sir?"

"I'd like to see the lieutenant, son," Fraser said. As the soldier disappeared into the bowels of the APC he suppressed a smile. He wasn't really that much older than the legionnaire, but lately he'd been feeling distinctly paternal. *A few more years and I'll sound just like any other gruff old officer*, he thought.

Lieutenant Gage came out of the command van's center compartment, where the C^3 gear was housed. Her face was creased into a dark frown. "You wanted to see me, Captain?" she asked.

Fraser nodded, feeling distinctly uneasy. Concern was plain on her face, in her voice, and that sort of thing could be contagious. "Just to see you off, Lieutenant," he said, trying to sound confident and at ease. "Valko tells me everything's going smoothly."

"So far, sir," she said. "But I'm still not certain how to handle things if the Council in Ourgh gets nasty. If you or Captain Hawley were along ..."

"Let Citizen Jens worry about the Council," Fraser told her. "She's been dealing with them since before we got here, and I think you can trust her judgment. You stick with handling the technical side of the evacuation. Captain Hawley and I have full confidence in you."

A flicker of anger clouded her features. Fraser wondered if he was sounding too patronizing, or if she was reacting to his reference to Hawley. No doubt she knew that Hawley hadn't expressed any such sentiment. Alpha Company's captain hardly noticed what his Exec did to keep the unit running. Fraser had never heard him utter a word of praise—or of reproof, for that matter. Hawley simply didn't care.

"Keep a close eye on your people," he went on, changing the subject. "We can't afford a lot of conflict with Seafarms, so don't let anybody decide the civilians are being uncooperative if it's really just a case of a murphy getting out of hand."

She nodded. "I'll do my best, sir."

"Good." Fraser hesitated before going on. "And if you need help, we'll do everything we can from this end."

"Thank you, sir," she responded, voice carefully neutral.

"Is Citizen Jens on board?"

"No, sir," Gage said. "She took a floatcar back to Ourgh to start putting things in motion there. Her assistant's with her, too."

He fought back a twinge of irritation. It would have been better if Jens and Barnett had stayed to coordinate the civilian side of the operation more closely with the Legion, but probably that had been too much to expect. Although Jens now seemed willing to go along with his suggestions, she was still the same decisive executive she'd been all along, and her temperament wasn't well suited to waiting when there was something she could be doing.

As he gave Gage a final salute and let her return to work, Fraser found himself thinking how much he and the Seafarms Project

Manager had in common. He still wished he could join Operation Roundup himself.

* * *

Sigrid Jens cocked her head to one side and focused on the information coming in from the floatcar's computer by way of the tiny implant in her brain. It was a curious sensation to be hurtling through the dark night, only a few centimeters above the angry water, in the small magrep vehicle, with her full attention focused entirely on statistics, progress reports on the dismantling of the corporate office in Ourgh, and dozens of other pieces of highly technical information.

The unaided human mind could never have juggled so much data even without the distraction of the floatcar's high speed motion. With the computer implant linking her to the onboard terminal and, via microwave link, to the master computer system at the corporate office building near the starport, she had complete access to everything in the files, from personnel records to specs on all Seafarms equipment. The computer could turn her thoughts into voice communications by way of any computer terminal or portable compboard or wristpiece hooked into the Seafarms network.

An implant was power, real power on a frontier world, not just the fashionable status symbol it had become on Terra. They were scarce out here—the only other one on Polypheme belonged to Captain Hawley—and they were valuable in direct proportion to that scarcity.

Thinking of Hawley made her grimace in distaste. How could a man have an implant and waste its potential on pointless games? Hawley was as bad as the addicts who sold their souls for some pornographic dreamchip. Too bad Fraser didn't have an implant: He was a man who would know how to use it.

Beside her, Barnett spoke for the first time since they'd left the Sandcastle, evidently taking her grimace as a sign that she'd finished her computer work. "I still think this is a bad move," he said.

"You've made that clear, Edward," she told him. "But I think the legionnaires made some valid points, and I have the final say."

She glanced at him. Barnett looked pale, nervous, as if he were afraid of something. What?

"We're perfectly safe in Ourgh," he insisted. "Why uproot everything and everyone, because some paranoid legionnaire wants to play at being some kind of big hero?"

She cut the mental connection with the main computer and sighed. "I'm not going to keep having this argument with you, Edward. The evacuation goes through, and so does the recall order on *Cyclops*. If you want a future with this company, you'll stop trying to second-guess me. Got it?"

Barnett subsided, suddenly meek. "Yes, ma'am." He paused. "But this mess could mean the end of the company anyway."

Silence followed. Jens contemplated her assistant with a trace of guilt. She knew his background: his parents killed in a border clash with the Ubrenfars, raised in an orphanage on New Atlanta, apprenticed to the Reynier Industries work-training program at age sixteen. Barnett had worked his way up to a position of responsibility despite a lack of formal education and all the attendant handicaps that had conspired to keep him back. His whole life centered on the drive to find security, and the company meant everything to him. Her threat must have cut deep.

She opened her mouth to apologize, but at that moment her implant signaled urgently for her attention. Although it was entirely computer-generated and quite inaudible, her brain interpreted the input as a tone as loud and clear as the whistle of the wind past the floatcar.

Jens focused her mind on the implant and mentally pronounced the code that established the computer link. At once she seemed to hear a voice, the dispassionate words of the computer system back at the Sandcastle. "Departure of Legion convoy at 1730 standard hours. Estimated time of arrival, Ourgh, 1815 standard hours."

So it had started. She acknowledged the signal but kept the computer link intact. There was still a lot of work to do if this evacuation was going to be carried out smoothly.

*   *   *

Warrior-Scout !!Dhruuj listened to the sound of rushing water and extended his eyestalks above the surface to investigate. The tide was ebbing slowly, but that had nothing to do with what he was hearing.

He remembered the Strangers-Who-Brought-Gifts telling the Warrior-Scouts about the huge mechanical pumps that drew water into the center of the Built-Reef. They created an artificial tide that could flood or empty the interior of the Built-Reef at will, allowing the Strangers to enter or leave without sending an uncontrollable rush of water through the gates as they opened.

Then the Strangers-Within were preparing to leave! Surely that was important.

He waited.

The sounds died away, and then a harsh, mechanical noise filled the water: grating, wholly unnatural, and alien. The gates rolled slowly apart.

As !!Dhruuj had expected, there was water inside the Built-Reef now. He watched expectantly for swimmers to leave, but instead saw an ungainly shape riding on—no, actually it was *above*—the waves. More followed, each large enough to hold many swimmers. Some carried devices that looked much like the far-reach weapons the Clan was using, and one mounted a pair of deadly looking rocket shapes.

Weapons. The Stranger-Warriors were leaving the Built-Reef in force, well-armed.

That might create opportunities the War-Leader-of-Clans would want to exploit.

!!Dhruuj croaked two signals; one to the other Clan scouts who waited among the rocks closer to the land, the other directed at the War-Leader-of-Clans himself.

He felt a burning pride. The Clan would be that much safer for his actions ... and the Strangers-Within far more at risk.

CHAPTER TEN

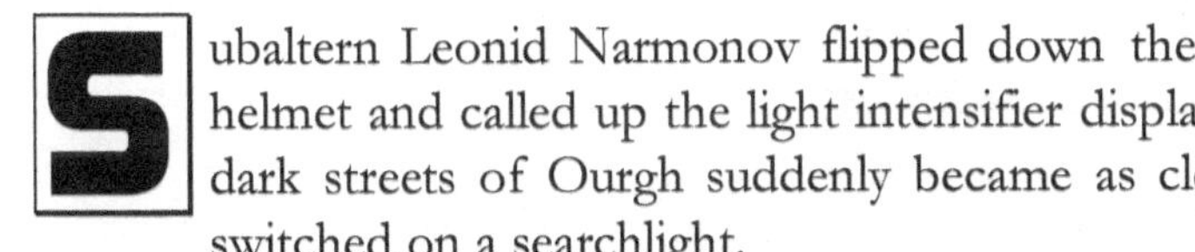

Make every shot count. Each one you kill now will be one less to fight tomorrow.

> —Commandant Jean-Michel Soubiran,
> to the guerrillas on Devereaux,
> Fourth Foreign Legion, 2729

Subaltern Leonid Narmonov flipped down the faceplate of his helmet and called up the light intensifier display. Details of the dark streets of Ourgh suddenly became as clear as if he had switched on a searchlight.

The planet's slow rotation made the nights seem endless. More than fifteen hours had passed since the nomad attack on the fort, and that had been just after sunset. It was still night, and would be for several more hours.

Nights that lasted close to a full standard day were just another petty irritation of life on Polypheme under normal circumstances, another strangeness that drove men to *le cafarde*. But this night was worse, far worse.

"Sergeant," Narmonov said, keying in his private comm channel to his platoon NCO. "I want the recon lance to check out those lights on the northeast perimeter."

"Sir!" Platoon Sergeant William Carstairs always sounded like the stereotypical noncom from an old historical holovid. Rumor in the platoon claimed he had been an actor before joining the Legion, a victim of the decline in live-action entertainment now that dreamchips and other computer-generated diversions had taken over such a large share of the market. Narmonov could believe the stories. Carstairs had a flair for the dramatic gesture. But he made an efficient platoon sergeant nonetheless.

He studied the flickering lights through the image-intensifier, but the range was too great to allow the system to resolve many details. He thought the light was coming from torches, and it looked like a large number of wogs were moving around. Hopefully his recon specialists could give him a better estimate of the threat, if any.

The evac had already run into more than enough glitches. Seafarms people had been ready enough to move out, but it had turned out that they had a lot more equipment and cargo to send to the Sandcastle than anyone originally had planned for. Two full loads of evacuees had already left Ourgh, and the third was gathering on the starport field in anticipation of the convoy's return. The extra time meant exposing legionnaires and civilians alike to the dangers posed by the natives.

And those dangers were getting stronger with each passing hour. An angry delegation of Elders had come to the port making demands. Narmonov hadn't been present during the meeting, but the rumors spreading through Alpha Company hinted that the city-dwellers were accusing the Legion of withdrawing and leaving Ourgh at the mercy of the nomads. Apparently there were questions about the fate of their earlier envoy, too.

The Project Director and her assistant had gone to meet the Council face-to-face, over the objections of Lieutenant Gage. Despite the guarantees of safe-conduct offered by the lokes, the Lieutenant had been afraid it was a trap to take valuable hostages, but by all accounts she'd been unwilling to force the issue and risk friction with the civilians.

It sounded like an unwarranted risk to Narmonov. He wondered how Captain Fraser would have handled it.

If the Elders were turning hostile, how much longer would the dwindling human population be safe? He thought about the riot that had nearly killed Fraser, and shuddered.

Behind him Narmonov heard a low-pitched whine. He turned as the Toel shuttlecraft lifted off from the landing field, the only ship in port. Apparently they'd finally given in to arm-twisting by the Seafarms people to cut their commercial mission short. That was one less problem, at least. No one would have welcomed the Toels as refugees inside the Sandcastle. The Toels were a long way from popular in Commonwealth circles.

"Sir?" Carstairs said over the comm channel. "Sir, Corporal Haddad is in position. Do you want a verbal report or a vidfeed?"

Narmonov thought for a moment before replying. "I'll take a vidfeed," he said at last. He motioned to Legionnaire Mattea, his C^3 technician. "Link to Haddad," he ordered.

Seconds passed. Then, suddenly, his view of the spaceport faded as the helmet display switched over to showing the screen relayed by Corporal Haddad's camera.

Unlike Narmonov, Haddad was using infrared imaging, and the sudden shift was disorienting. Even processed through helmet-mounted microcomputers, the IR view was distinctly different from an LI display.

Torches flared bright over the mass of wogs. They were not obviously armed, nor did they appear especially agitated. Haddad's radio picked up their shouts and chants, but not clearly enough to allow Narmonov to translate.

It looked like nothing so much as a protest march, heading from the center of town in the general direction of the starport.

For now, it was orderly enough, but a mob like that could easily turn violent.

"Corporal," Narmonov said. "Withdraw your lance to the port at once."

"Yessir," Haddad responded. The image on the faceplate display lurched abruptly, and Narmonov knew the corporal was turning to organize the five men in his unit.

Narmonov flipped up the faceplate. "Discontinue, Mattea," he ordered. Then, switching back to the command channel, he said "Sergeant Carstairs!"

"Sir!"

"Pass the word to the platoon to prepare for riot control."

"Yes, sir!"

"How's the work going along the perimeter fence?"

"Three more minutes," Carstairs replied. Narmonov had ordered some of his men to jury-rig a connection between the fence and the port's generator facilities. It wouldn't work for long, but in an emergency they could electrify the perimeter and buy some time.

But that would have to be a last resort. If there was an accident, the native reaction would be to turn actively hostile.

"Tell them to make it two minutes, Sergeant," he said. "But they're not to switch on until Lieutenant Gage or I give specific orders."

"Sir!"

Narmonov cut the transmission and turned back to Mattea. "Get me the Lieutenant," he said.

It would be a relief to let someone else start making the decisions.

* * *

"All right, Subaltern," Susan Gage said slowly. "You've done well. Keep monitoring the situation and report to me if anything changes. But do not engage the rioters unless absolutely necessary for the safety of the port or the evacuees. Understood?"

"Understood, Lieutenant," Narmonov's grave voice replied. She thought she could detect a trace of his native Russian accent. There was a joke in Alpha Company's officer's mess that Narmonov spoke better Terranglic than anyone else in the unit. He only showed traces of his Ukrainian boyhood when he was especially worried or distracted.

She thought he had every right to be worried. With the exception of Gage, Valko, and their C^3 specialist, Massire, Narmonov's platoon was the total Legion force available in Ourgh right now. And it was understrength, too, from the casualties they'd taken in fighting at the Sandcastle. If there was trouble now, twenty-six soldiers wouldn't buy the civilians much time.

"Good," she said at length. "Roundup Command, clear." She glanced across the command van at Legionnaire Massire. "ETA on the convoy?"

"Ten minutes, Lieutenant," the C^3 specialist told her. "Longer, if they have more trouble with that barge contraption." His teeth showed very white against his dark skin in the dim-lit compartment.

The barge that Seafarms had improvised had all the promised capacity, but one of the magrep generators was faulty. It had already broken down once, during the first trip out to the Sandcastle.

Damn the Seafarms people and their "extra equipment." If they'd been properly prepared, everyone would be safe back in the Sandcastle now. She'd been tempted to tell Jens to ditch the gear, but Fraser's instructions on keeping Seafarms happy had held her back. Now she was regretting the decision.

She remembered her feelings in the battle inside the Sandcastle, her horror as Bravo Company had been pinned. If there were more casualties today, it would be her fault again.

Damn Seafarms!

That reminded her of Jens and Barnett. They had opted to stay with the Elders as long as possible in hopes of convincing them to stick with the Commonwealth. It was time to get them back to the port so they could come out with the rest of the evacuation.

"Get me the Project Director," she told Massire abruptly. As he bent to work at his communications console, she swiveled her seat to face Gunnery Sergeant Valko. "What do you think of putting up a recon drone to keep an eye on that crowd, Sergeant?" she asked.

"Good idea," Valko replied, nodding. "I'll get on it." He paused. "You may want to reroute the convoy through either the east or the south gate, Lieutenant. Just to keep them clear of the lokes."

Gage gave a nod. "Yeah. That makes sense." The first two convoys had come and gone through the main gate, the one that faced north toward Ourgh. It was larger, and with most of Narmonov's security concentrated on that side it made it easier to use. Now, though, there was too much chance of trouble. "We'll use the east side for now, but keep the south gate for a bolt-hole. Massire, I'll talk with Sergeant Franz while you're trying to raise Citizen Jens."

It didn't take long to update the Transport Section commander on the situation and order the change of route. When Franz acknowledged the orders, Gage leaned back in her chair, tapping her fingers on the armrest. The two executives were taking their time about answering Massire's call.

Damn them!

* * *

The commlink shrilled again, but Jens ignored it as she listened to the Elder with the missing eyestalk.

"Unsatisfactory! Unsatisfactory! None of your answers can be proven!" His words were echoed in English by a whisper only she could hear. Although she'd chipped advanced courses in the city-dweller dialect, Jens felt safer letting the computer translate.

The Elder sat down, and Jens formed the reply she wanted to make in her mind. The implant fed her a sentence that took into account not only the literal meaning of her reply, but subtleties of emotion and mood.

"Please, Reverend Ancient !Broor!, this is not fair. We have dealt in good faith from the beginning, Reverend Elders," she said slowly. "The Reverend Ancient Houghan!! accepted our words before he died. Fighting for us, for the safety of one of our people." Actually, Houghan!! had never said that he believed the Terrans, but Fraser's account of what had happened during the nomad attack made it clear that the Elder had recognized the Terrans as friends in the end.

"We have only your word for this," another council member said. "And for the hostility of the nomads to your kind, for that matter!"

Jens felt the anger surge inside her. "Then come to the Sandcastle and see the dead, damn it!" she flared, not bothering to wait for the computer to provide suitable words.

"And walk into a trap," !Broor! said flatly. He rubbed the scar where his missing eyestalk should have been. "Nomads did this to me thirty winters ago. I'm not giving you a chance to turn me over to them now, the way you did with Houghan!!."

The commlink shrilled again, and Jens looked down at it irritation. *Damn the legionnaires!* she thought. Couldn't they carry out the evacuation without bothering her with petty details every ten minutes?

"Your pardon, Honored Elders," she said with a sigh. She picked up the commlink. "Jens. What the hell do you want this time?"

Lieutenant Gage sounded as annoyed as Jens felt. "Pack it up and get back to the port, Citizen. The last load mags out of here in less than half an hour."

"That's not convenient," Jens said. "Can't you hold it up for a while longer?"

"There are rioters assembling outside the perimeter fence," Gage replied. "The longer we stay, the more likely we get involved in an incident nobody wants. We pull out as soon as everything's loaded."

"Then I'll follow in my floatcar with Edward when I'm done here."

"Negative, Citizen," the lieutenant said sharply. "My orders say everyone comes out now." There was a pause. "Please, Citizen, don't complicate this any further."

"If I leave now, we may never get the Elders to cooperate again." She tried to keep a reasonable note in her voice. "I'm sure Captain Fraser—"

"Lieutenant!" someone's voice interrupted her, faint but distinct. "Lieutenant, we have trouble on the north perimeter. Shots fired!"

"All right, that's it," Gage said firmly. "We've got hostiles outside the port, Citizen. Get back here right away. No arguments!" The channel went dead before Jens could frame a reply.

She glanced up at Barnett, then looked at the Elders arrayed at their semicircular table facing the two Terrans. "Reverend Ancients," she said slowly, trying to find the most diplomatic way to end the meeting. "I assure you again that the nomads are as much our enemies as they are yours. But it is clear that we cannot convince you of this tonight. As you know, my people are withdrawing to the old Toel base. We believe … We believe that the presence of Terrans in Ourgh may have much to do with the nomad attacks in this area. Perhaps once you have seen that they are concentrating on us instead of you there will be a chance to reach a new agreement."

"They shouldn't be allowed to leave!" one of the council members, somewhat younger than the rest of the Elders, shouted, slamming a fist on the table. "Once the Terrans are safely out of the city they can launch the nomads against us without fear! Keep them here!"

!Broor! answered, "No, Traur!, no. Let them leave. We will not be the ones to start hostilities, Terran, but we will be ready for any tricks you may use against us." He paused. "I hope that you are telling the truth. But even if you are not helping our enemies, you have been poor friends. Any new agreement we make with you will have to re-dress the wrongs your people have done. Now go, before there is further trouble."

Jens rose slowly, grateful that the old councilman was honorable despite his obvious distrust. "I thank you, Reverend Ancient," she said. "And I hope those wrongs can indeed be redressed." She looked at Barnett. "We have to get back, Edward. Right away."

As they left the Council Chamber Sigrid Jens wondered if there would be any way to make a fresh start with the natives on Polypheme. It was plain that Seafarms had underestimated the problems of dealing with the locals—perhaps fatally.

* * *

"Switch power to the fence!" Narmonov shouted. "Now, goddamn it! Now!"

Something whooshed in the distance, capped by a small thunder-clap. "That sounded like a Fafnir, Sub," Corporal Haddad said.

"Yeah, or like one of those strakking rocket guns the wogs were using at the Sandcastle," another legionnaire added.

Narmonov keyed in his helmet commlink. "Chandbahadur! Are any of your men firing?"

Corporal Chandbahadur Rai, the little Gurkha who commanded one of the platoon's two heavy-weapons lances, answered promptly. "No, sir. We've had no orders to fire."

He knew that Chandbahadur's lance was the only unit that could have been using Fafnir missile launchers. The other heavy-weapons lance, commanded by Legionnaire First-Class Lynch, was helping to sort the Seafarms people among the convoy vehicles that had set down in the compound only a few minutes earlier.

"Maintain status," he ordered the Gurkha. Switching off the commlink, he shot a look at Carstairs. "It's not our people, Sergeant."

Carstairs had his faceplate down, so it was impossible to see his features. He was facing toward the sounds of the rockets, his whole body tense, straining. "Sir," the exactor said softly. "I've got a party of what look like nomads on the city wall, bearing three-five-four. They're firing into the crowd."

"Into the crowd!" Narmonov flipped to image-intensification and lined up on the bearing Carstairs has indicated. Several natives were clustered on top of the mud-and-stone wall. In the magnified firelight their tribal tattoos showed up plainly. As he watched, one raised a rifle and fired.

The projectile dipped before its rocket engine ignited, sending it into the civilian mob below.

"What the hell are they doing, Sub?" Haddad asked.

"Getting the townies to do their dirty work for them," Narmonov said slowly. He raised his faceplate. "If the city wogs don't know who's attacking, they're going to assume it's us...."

"God," Carstairs breathed, his role forgotten for once.

"Where's your sniper, Haddad?" Narmonov asked the recon lance commander.

Haddad grinned wolfishly. "Killer! Time to go to work!"

Legionnaire Second-Class Arnold Kelso looked more like a scholar than a legionnaire, slender, almost meek, despite his battledress and field kit. But his deadly accuracy with the Whitney-Sykes HPLR-55 laser rifle had earned him his nickname. "What's the target, Corp?" he asked, as he joined the others at Narmonov's makeshift command post.

Haddad pointed out the nomads and Kelso nodded. Unfolding a bipod on the front of the laser rifle, he set it up carefully on an upended, empty cargomod and carefully scanned the nomad position through his helmet II gear. Then he plugged a lead into the rifle sights and into his helmet, feeding an electronic image directly to his faceplate display. Narmonov dropped his own faceplate back down.

It seemed to take forever before the man finally squeezed the trigger. There was a crackle, a tang of ozone as the laser beam ionized the air, but no flash or telltale beam. But a nomad on the wall suddenly fell, with a neat centimeter-wide hole punched directly through his braincase. An instant later a second nomad went down, then a third. The remaining natives scrambled for cover.

"Carstairs! Get to the vehicle park. I want spotlights turned on that position now. Got it?"

"Sir!" The sergeant left at a flat-out run. Searchlights might dazzle the wogs up there ... and they might draw attention to the nomads, and defuse the mob before it got ugly. Shouts echoed through the night, then crashes and a harsh crackling noise. A stench of burning meat made Narmonov choke on his rising gorge.

The rioters were attacking the fence. It was too late to turn them aside now.

* * *

"Forget the rest of the equipment," Lieutenant Susan Gage said. "Get everyone else on board the convoy now."

"I'll tell them, Lieutenant," Massire replied. "But I hope the Seafarms people don't screw it up."

Gunnery Sergeant Valko cleared his throat. "Would you like me to explain it to them, ma'am?" he asked with a predatory smile.

"Do it," Gage said shortly. The sergeant left the APC hurriedly. "Massire, what's the status on Jens?"

"On their way, Lieutenant," he told her. "But with that mob in the streets, they'll have to be careful."

She rubbed an eye as she thought. "Order Bashar and Karatsolis to break through the mob with their Sabertooth. Find Jens and get her party out of town. Abandon their floatcar—we don't need it for the evac now."

"Got it, Lieutenant," Massire said, reaching for the communications panel again.

She turned to the monitor displaying the recon drone's view of the city. Viewed from above, the mob looked like some bizarre single-celled organism flowing hungrily toward the perimeter fence. So far the generators Narmonov had hooked up were still feeding power, and it was holding them back.

The southern side of the port was still clear of lokes. She hoped that the FSV could get out that way and circle around the worst of the mob. The alternative was unthinkable: letting the Legion vehicle cut through the rioters. It would be a massacre.

Gage prayed she wouldn't have to give the order that would trigger that bloodbath.

*   *   *

The south gate swung open to allow the Sabertooth to exit, and a legionnaire at the gatehouse leaned through the window to wave the vehicle through. Bashar gunned the rotors, raising a dust cloud as the FSV sped through.

They were out of the port.

The Terran enclave nestled on the south side of Ourgh, with the starport on the very edge of town. Beyond were farmlands leased by Seafarms, where local workers grew Terran foodstuffs under contract to the company. Bashar was happy to have some maneuvering room. On Hanuman, the last time he'd driven a Sabertooth in a combat situation, the dense jungles had been a major problem. Here, at least until he had to move back into the city, he could push the vehicle to the limit.

"Look sharp, Spear," he said over the intercom. "The Lieutenant said there are nomads out here, and I don't want to tangle with them if I can help it." So far, their arsenal hadn't included anything that could threaten the Sabertooth, but if they had kept something more lethal in reserve ...

"I'm watching on IR," Karatsolis replied. "And I've got a fix on the floatcar. Feeding to your terminal now."

"Thanks, man," Bashar said. That was the most the Greek had said since the start of the operation.

The trace for the floatcar lit up on a computer display map of Ourgh. Bashar nodded approvingly. The Seafarms vehicle was moving well, and it was headed for a gate in the city wall well clear of the fighting. That would make things easier.

"Targets! Targets!" Karatsolis warned sharply. "Straight ahead— range fifty meters!"

Bashar cursed as he wrenched the Sabertooth hard to the left. "Fifty meters! How the hell did you miss them?"

"They just popped out of nowhere!" Karatsolis said. "Damn it! More targets. Straight ahead at seven-five meters."

"Allah!" Bashar turned again and cut the vehicle's speed. "Go to LI and pop a flare, Spear."

The image on his external monitor changed subtly as the light-intensifier setting cut in. "Flare!" Karatsolis announced. The launcher at the rear of the FSV thumped.

A second later the flare glowed, not a harsh or particularly bright light, but a soft, steady radiance that was just enough to illuminate for the LI gear.

Bashar used a joystick to manipulate the external camera view. As he swung through a full circle around the Sabertooth, he heard a sharp intake of breath through his headphones. Karatsolis had seen the same thing he was looking at.

The farmlands were riddled with long, shallow pits, each one deep enough to conceal several wogs ... and each one a potential obstacle to a magrep vehicle.

Chapter Eleven

—Legionnaire Alan Seeger,
French Foreign Legion, 1916

Legionnaire Second Class Lin Wu-Sen raised his faceplate and nudged his lancemate in the ribs. "Hey, Reese, got a 'stick?"

"Come on, Lin." Legionnaire Third-Class George Reese sounded annoyed. "You know we're not allowed to smoke, man. We're on duty."

"Quit talking like a nube, Reese," Lin sneered. "Who's going to report me? You?"

"Convoy'll be coming out soon...."

"Yeah, so this is my last chance. Come on, kid, hand 'em over."

With seeming reluctance, Reese slung his FEK and dug in his belt pouch for a packet of narcosticks. Lin took one and put it in his mouth.

"How about a light, kid?" he mumbled around the 'stick.

Reese produced a lighter, punched the recessed button, and waited a moment for the coil to heat up. As it started to glow red he held it up to the narcostick. Lin took a few trial puffs, savoring the heady taste of the smoke. They were against regs, of course, but narcosticks were popular with soldiers on boring garrison duty. They gave a man a lift without dulling his reactions....

A bright streak cut through the night with a soft *whoosh*, and Reese flung the lighter away. But it was too late. The rocket projectile hit him squarely in the stomach and exploded. Reese staggered back, doubled over, and fell.

Lin flung himself to the ground, groping for the FE-MEK lance-support weapon he'd left leaning on the gatehouse wall. Another explosive bullet hit just behind where his head had been a moment before.

He spat out the narcostick and flipped his faceplate down, trying to assess the situation on IR. As he scanned the night, he hit the general comm channel. "First Platoon Alpha! East gate is under attack. Repeat, east gate under attack, probable nomad force!"

He thought he caught movement, and swung the MEK to cover it. He squeezed the trigger, hearing the deep-throated hum of the heavy kinetic-energy rifle as it spat needle rounds into the darkness.

Legionnaire Lin never saw the rocket that killed him.

$$* \quad * \quad *$$

"Nomad attack on the eastern perimeter, Lieutenant," the C^3 technician reported coolly. "No details. Sergeant Hooks is deploying First Platoon to check it out."

Susan Gage frowned. Subaltern Reynolds, First Platoon's CO, had been one of the first casualties in the Sandcastle fighting, and his platoon had taken the worst of Alpha Company's casualties. She hoped Hooks could handle the unexpected fighting without further support. There weren't enough legionnaires to go around.

"Tell Franz to leave by the south gate," she ordered. "And order Hooks not to get too heavily engaged. When we pull out, we're pulling *out fast.*"

As the C^3 tech turned back to his console, she swung the aerial recon drone around to the eastern side of the port to get a better look at the threat. The nomads had struck a little bit early, she thought with a grim smile. If they'd just waited a few minutes longer, they would have caught the convoy. But this way the Terrans had some warning, and the south gate was still open ... at least, so far. And it would only be a few more minutes before they had the civilians ready to move.

Massire broke her train of thought. "Sergeant Valko says everything's ready, Lieutenant. He says, uh ... he says, 'Let's mag the Topheth out of here.'"

She smiled at that. Valko was never hesitant about letting his superiors know what he thought. "Okay. General order, all units. Legionnaires to disengage and fall back. We'll keep the APCs back to pull them out. All other vehicles to move through the south gate. Once they're clear, top speed back to the Sandcastle."

She smiled again. Maybe, just maybe, she could pull off this operation after all.

*　*　*

"All units. All units. Convoy departing via south gate immediately. Legionnaires disengage and fall back on assembly point three. Roundup Two, Roundup Three, hold at assembly point to embark rear guard."

Bashar cursed as the voice crackled in his headphones. The nomads were thoroughly dug in down here, with traps and forces that would carve up the convoy with barely a pause. They couldn't withdraw this way.

He stabbed the comm button. "Roundup Leader, this is Escort. South gate exit is blocked, repeat blocked. Estimate three hundred nomad warriors with extensive fieldworks and traps in place. Do not use south exit."

Cutting the comm channel without waiting for a reply, Bashar spun the bulky Sabertooth in just over its own length and gunned the turbofans. "This is going to be bumpy, Spear," he said on the intercom. "Keep a watch for bad guys."

The fans roared, a sound that filled the cramped driver's compartment and threatened to drown out the attention signals from his control console. The light of the flare had faded, and Bashar shifted back to infrared.

"Targets ahead. Sixty-five meters." Karatsolis might have been a computer for all the emotion in his voice.

"Let 'em know we're not here to play around."

"Yeah." Barely a second passed before the Sabertooth's plasma cannon spoke. Superheated metal traced a blur across his forward monitor and hit the far edge of the wog pit. The natives still moving after the explosion were scattering. Karatsolis fired again.

The bow of the Sabertooth dipped suddenly as the leading edge of the magrep field hit the pit, but Bashar was ready for it. He increased the magrep field and stabilized the vehicle with a deft sweep of fingers over the control console. A moment later he made another adjustment as the vehicle climbed out of the other side.

It was easy enough for a driver ready for the problem. For the hodgepodge of vehicles and drivers in the convoy all trying to flee the port compound at high speed, though, it would have been a sure recipe for disaster.

For that matter, it could still be disastrous for the *Angel of Death II* if Bashar didn't stay alert. Or if Karatsolis didn't keep the wogs off-balance.

Something struck the side of the vehicle's hull and exploded, but the hull sensors reported minimal damage. Bashar fought the urge to relax and swerved to avoid another pit ahead.

He hoped his warning about the trap had come in time for the rest of the convoy.

*   *   *

Gage stared at the monitor in horror, seeing the pits, the small groups of nomads, and the trail of devastation left in the Sabertooth's wake. If it hadn't been for Bashar and Karatsolis the whole unit would have blundered into that trap, and damned few of them would have escaped it.

She'd committed one of the cardinal sins of command by not scouting out the escape route in advance.

Now what? she asked herself.

"Lieutenant?" Valko was back aboard the command van and looking at her quizzically. It took her a long moment to realize that she must have voiced her thoughts out loud.

"We have to get the hell out of here," she said. "But it looks like they've got us blocked. Any recommendations?"

Valko looked thoughtfully at the monitor. "The mess on the south side's too strakking thick to break through. I say we go for the east gate, like we originally planned."

"Even though it's under fire already?"

He stroked his thick mustache with hooded, thoughtful eyes. "It's all been too pat," he said slowly. "They stirred up the riots on the north side. Then we have an attack from the east, but I haven't seen much more than a few periodic rockets and a lot of noise. It looks to me like they're trying to herd us, Lieutenant. They want to encourage us to go out the south side."

Gage looked down at her console. "If they're really mounting an attack on the east gate, though ..."

"They wouldn't waste all that strength to the south if their main thrust was coming from another direction," he argued. "Not even if they had extra troops to burn. If they had that kind of strength they'd launch simultaneous attacks, not play coy with the trap."

"We could knock down the fence and go out an unexpected direction...."

"Some of the terrain out there is pretty rugged. Especially the west side, and that's the only place we haven't seen much activity. We'd lose that damned barge for sure." He paused. "At least that would be better than trying the southern route."

"But you're in favor of an east-side breakout."

"Yes, ma'am," he said, suddenly formal. "Perhaps on a broad front, like you suggested, instead of just pushing through the gate. Hit 'em hard enough and we'll punch right out."

She wrestled with the choices, all too aware of how bad her judgment had been so far. Valko seemed convinced, and she trusted his instincts....

"All right. That's what we'll do. But hold up the convoy until we can mount up most of our troops. We'll need them for firepower, since the Sabertooth's already busy."

"That'll throw a lot of responsibility on whoever gets picked for rear guard," he pointed out.

"I know," she admitted. "Do you think Narmonov's up to it?"

He nodded.

"Then let's get on it. And pray we don't run into anything else we didn't expect."

*　*　*

"Fall back! Fall back!" Narmonov was shouting, even though his commlink carried his words clearly to everyone in the platoon. He ducked as a crossbow bolt skimmed just over his head and scrambled toward the last line of defense.

Hold as long as you can, his orders had said. In the face of the native mob, though, those orders were easier given than carried out.

The electrified fence had held them for a while, of course, and if the withdrawal had gone according to the original instructions the platoon could have disengaged easily. But with the delays and the sudden changes in plan, the platoon had been left hanging in air as the lokes smashed through the fence. Many natives had died, but the rest were just more inflamed than ever. And this wasn't just an unarmed crowd, either. There were a fair number of city militiamen mixed in, armed with crossbow, spears, and an assortment of melee weapons. Not much against Legion technology, but sheer weight of numbers and the absolute fearlessness of the wogs made the results inevitable.

What the hell was Lieutenant Gage doing, anyway? These sudden reversals of orders were screwing up everything.

He dove over a cargomod and rolled. The last line of resistance had been improvised from the equipment and supplies abandoned when the pressure had started to mount. Now fifteen legionnaires waited, crouched behind the barricade with a wall of alien flesh closing in on them. Narmonov didn't even have any heavy weapons left. Gunnery Sergeant Valko had pulled the two heavy lances out of the fighting line to give the breakout an extra punch. But that left the remaining defenders with precious little firepower ... and their ammo stocks were starting to run low.

"Command reports the convoy's making its move on the east fence," Mattea reported. An MEK purred nearby, joined by the higher-pitched whine of an FEK.

"Where's our APC?"

"On the way. Sergeant Valko had it making a demonstration down by the south gate."

"Wonderful," someone nearby muttered.

"Legionnaires, ready to fire!" Carstairs shouted. Narmonov and Mattea joined the rest of the defenders along the barricade, leveling their weapons as the natives rushed forward. "Fire!"

The entire line opened up simultaneously, their sustained fire tearing through the first ranks of the natives. The pressure from the rear caused confusion, as more wogs became entangled in the carnage.

"Grenades!" Narmonov called, switching from needle rounds to grenades on his FEK. The four MEKs lacked the integral grenade-launchers and kept up automatic fire, but the rest of the legionnaires opened fire with the lethal little explosive rounds, raining more death and confusion into the enemy.

With a roar of fans, a Sandray APC suddenly burst out of the darkness, setting down near the end of the barricade with a flourish. The kinetic-energy cannon in the vehicle's remote turret mount chattered, keeping the mob busy while the ramp dropped in the rear of the Sandray. "Come on!" a legionnaire in the back of the APC shouted, waving urgently.

Legionnaires sprinted for the safety of the Sandray. Narmonov stayed where he was and kept firing, along with Haddad and the men of the recon lance. Nearby Kelso was firing with calm, cool deliberation, picking off one wog after another with precise laser fire.

But the wogs kept pushing forward. Any professional army Narmonov had ever heard of would have broken by now, but these disorganized rioters kept on coming.

"Hurry!" someone shouted. "Before they get to the ramp!"

"Recon lance, move!" Narmonov shouted, abandoning his position at last.

By the Sandray, Carstairs and a handful of legionnaires were laying down extra covering fire of their own, but still those wogs showed no sign of wavering. Narmonov ran, desperate to reach the APC.

"They're gonna beat us to it!" Haddad shouted.

Carstairs must have come to the same conclusion at the same time. He waved his four companions forward and they ran straight at the rioters, firing from the hip as they went.

The humans plunged straight into the first rank, still firing, but now the mob was pressing in from all sides. Narmonov saw the exactor fall, as a wog clubbed him repeatedly from behind. Nor were the others faring any better.

But the threat they posed was causing the natives to concentrate on that handful of legionnaires. Narmonov and his men reached the ramp as the mob started to lurch forward again. By then it was too late to stop the platoon from escaping. The APC was stirring on magrep fields and turning away before the ramp had even started to rise.

Narmonov collapsed on a bench, hardly realizing that they were clear.

In his mind, all he could see was Carstairs playing out that last and most dramatic scene of his career.

* * *

Corporal Chandbahadur Rai smiled with satisfaction and patted the comfortable bulk of his onager plasma gun. He was a Gurkha from

New Victoria, where a small settlement of his people kept alive the old ways and supplied troops for the Gurkha Regiment of the Commonwealth's Colonial Army. He would have still been among them, if he hadn't disgraced himself during the uprising against Terra on Tien-kuo. In the fighting he had been separated from his unit, and lost all of his weapons while eluding the enemy. Although his superiors had seen nothing wrong with his actions, Chandbahadur had not been willing to remain among his fellow Gurkhas thereafter. Instead he had joined the Fifth Foreign Legion.

There wasn't much chance of losing his weapons today. The onager was attached directly to his armor by the ConRig harness that assisted targeting and control.

Now, crouched on top of one of the two manta-shaped cargo vans towing the laden barge, Chandbahadur was ready for action.

The barge would have to go out over the relatively level ground around the east gate, where enemy activity had been reported. That was fine by Chandbahadur. There was nothing like a good fight—nothing.

He saw legionnaires from First Platoon climbing onto the nearest vehicles. They'd been holding this position since the first attack on this side of the port, but now they had to mount up fast or be left behind.

"Clear the fence," Sergeant Valko's voice said quietly in his helmet speakers.

Chandbahadur raised his onager and activated his ConRig system. The harness slaved the movements of the gun to a sighting reticle, which picked up motions of his eyes and translated them to power-assisted movement of the weapon's barrel. He sighted carefully on the nearest portion of the fence, then opened fire. The onager moved smoothly along the line of the fence, sending round after high-energy round into the posts. Up and down the line other onagers, Fafnir rockets, and grenades were doing similar damage.

Seconds later the APC lurched forward, gathering speed. It rammed into what was left of the fence and plowed over the twisted metal wreckage.

Nomad rocket guns opened fire out of the night. With each telltale flash Chandbahadur sighted a nomad gunner and returned fire. In seconds their barrage fell silent.

The convoy sped through the darkness.

* * *

The FSV swerved to avoid another obstacle, and Spiro Karatsolis clung to the trigger mount of the plasma cannon.

"That's the last of them, Spear!" Bashar's voice rang loud and cocky in his headphones. "I think we're through!"

He glanced at his sensor screen. "Confirmed," he said shortly. "Looks like everything's behind us now."

"Hey, man, what else did you expect?" the Turk shot back, his tone bantering again. "When you ride with the Bashar you don't need a gunner!"

That should have been the signal for a typical comeback, something like "That's because you run into all our targets and bash them flat." But Karatsolis didn't answer. He didn't feel up to banter anymore.

It had started with the battle at the Sandcastle. First the nube, O'Donnell, had been cut down, and then Sandoval had saved Karatsolis and died from a shot that should have killed the Greek. Why were all these men dying?

He'd lost comrades before, even a few he'd called friends. You expected that in the army, especially in the Legion. Less than a quarter of all the soldiers who signed on with the Legion lived to complete a five-year enlistment. Hanuman had killed a lot of good legionnaires, but he'd come through it all without thinking about it much.

But this time was different. Part of it was the feeling of helplessness that came with any sort of garrison duty on a hostile planet. Karatsolis was a magger, a vehicle crewman, and though on the one hand he was used to sitting inside the cramped confines of the FSV, on the other he was used to a mobile war, where you didn't just sit and wait for the next attack. When men died, at least it wasn't just more attrition with nothing to show for the deaths.

It felt like O'Donnell and Sandoval had died such useless deaths. Who would be next? Bashar? Karatsolis himself? He'd joined the Legion because he felt that a soldier could make a real difference defending the Commonwealth, and not be just another statistic in the casualty reports.

He realized that Bashar had called his name again.

"Come on, Spear, look alive up there!" the corporal was saying. "Get me a range-and-bearing on that damned float-car."

He checked the instruments and read off the figures.

"Right," Bashar said. "Heading right for us. Get that oversized narcostick lighter of yours warmed up. We'll punch through the wall up here and head 'em off before they try for one of the gates."

Karatsolis acknowledged the order gruffly and ran a quick diagnostic on the plasma cannon. As he went through the routine motions, his mind was still wrestling with the overriding question. *Why am I a legionnaire?*

* * *

Edward Barnett fingered the small handgun in its hidden pocket and tried not to betray his fear.

Everything is going wrong.... The thought seemed to echo over and over again in his mind. From the moment the nomads had launched the attack on the Sandcastle, everything had gone wrong, and it would take desperate measures to regain control of the situation.

He darted a glance at Jens, sitting beside him in the back seat of the floatcar. If she'd just stayed tough with the thrice-damned legionnaires ...

It might be too late even if he could take control now. Once they were cooped up inside the Sandcastle, would Fraser let any of the Terrans leave again?

He had to. Once the nomads started in on the Sandcastle there would be no stopping them, and Edward Barnett had no intention of being caught in the middle of that battle.

That supposed, of course, that they ever got out of this rabbit warren of a city. They had finally reached the walls of the Old Town, but getting to a gate and then making it through were starting to look like risky propositions at best. The damned legionnaires must have really stirred things up down by the port. Rioting had spread through a huge chunk of the city. Fires were burning only a few blocks away, and it was at least two kilometers to the port.

Help was supposed to be coming, but Barnett doubted the Legion could do much for them.

An explosion rocked the floatcar. A large section of the city wall erupted inward, showering the street with shattered masonry. The driver swerved to avoid rubble and skidded to a halt.

Framed in the gap opened up in the wall was a big armored vehicle, floating less than a meter off the ground on a magrep cushion. The Legion rescue party!

"Seafarms floatcar!" a PA announcer boomed. "Abandon your vehicle! We're here to take you back to the Sandcastle!"

Jens was looking as relieved as Barnett felt. She turned away from him, reaching for the door release.

Barnett pulled the rocket pistol out of his pocket. It was similar in design to the ones the nomads were using, but smaller, concealable, with a four-round magazine. An ideal holdout weapon, or so he'd been told when he'd been given the pistol and the secure comm unit hidden in his briefcase.

He waited until she had the door open and was halfway out before he shot her in the back. Then he palmed the weapon and rolled out of his side of the vehicle. "Snipers! Nomad snipers!" he shouted. "Caldwell, help the boss! Quick!"

The driver tried to scramble to where Jens had sprawled on the street. With a glance to make sure no one aboard the Legion vehicle could see him, Barnett fired twice more. Caldwell collapsed over the body, unmoving.

Barnett tucked the weapon into a hidden pocket in his left sleeve, grabbed his briefcase, and ran toward the hole in the wall, still shouting warnings of nomad snipers. The vehicle turned, dropping a ramp.

He held his breath. If there were troops there, they might examine the bodies, even collect them, and that might reveal too much. But no one came out.

He ran up the ramp in feigned panic.

*   *   *

Now Sigrid Jens was out of the way. Now he could take charge of the Project, and put right everything that had gone wrong.

Chapter Twelve

Subaltern Torn Watanabe entered the bridge of the *Seafarms Cyclops* feeling like a gladiator on his way to confront a hungry lion. The captain's summons had come before Lieutenant DuValier had finished telling him about the latest problem over the Legion's secure commlink.

He took a deep breath and tried to control his expression, as Captain Ian MacLean turned from the navigation table and frowned at him.

"Ah yes, Watanabe," the ship's captain said gruffly. "I imagine your headquarters people have already updated you on our orders, hmm?"

Watanabe nodded curtly. "I've been told. But I don't think I understand, Captain."

"Not much to understand, is there?" MacLean asked with a shrug. "Acting Project Director Barnett has ordered us to resume normal operations."

Watanabe lowered his voice so that only MacLean could hear him. "Look, Captain, I thought you agreed with the last batch of instructions—the ones from Citizen Jens. We were on our way back to the Sandcastle."

"I agree, Mr. Watanabe, with whatever orders the company sees fit to hand me. Right now those orders are to keep the *Cyclops* at sea, so that's what we're doing."

"And what about the nomads? That attack happened, and no set of orders is going to erase the fact that they're still out there."

"The nomads are your problem, Watanabe. You and your men are on board to deal with any further attacks."

"Captain Fraser isn't very happy about this, sir," Watanabe said carefully. "I fully expect him to invoke Section 34 and require Seafarms to submit itself to military authority."

Maclean laughed. "Section 34, eh? Martial law? Your precious Captain Fraser had better be damned sure of his grounds before he starts playing games with civil authority. The Commonwealth doesn't take kindly to military men overriding local government, especially when it has the kind of connections Seafarms can bring to bear at the hearing. A lot of promising careers have been wrecked on Section 34, kid."

Watanabe scowled at him. "I still think this is ill advised," he said angrily.

"And I still think this is my ship, Watanabe. And my bridge. You've got your instructions ... now get off it."

Watanabe turned and stalked out, not trusting himself to answer the man.

*　*　*

Legionnaire John Grant kept one eye on the computer's sonar display and the other on his two lancemates. Since the attack, standing orders required three men on watch in Operations at all times, but usually there wasn't enough to keep three men occupied. Normally the most junior would have been on watch while his betters amused themselves, but not this time. Slick had the job, so that Dmitri Rostov could use the opportunity to further the education of the Recon Lance's newest member in the basics of poker. The game was completely new to Legionnaire Third-Class Myaighee, who less than a year before had been a low-caste worker on Hanuman.

Myaighee stood a meter tall, with the dark olive skin, powerful arms, hairless head, and quilled neck-ruff of the species humans usually referred to as "monkeys" or "hannies." That species was hermaphroditic, without any gender distinctions; since words like "he" and "she" didn't apply, the hannie term "ky" was used to refer to members of the race. Ky wore a uniform specially tailored for the hannie frame, leaving most of the neck-ruff uncovered. Myaighee would wear a plate of plasteel armor over it in combat, but the quills were sensitive enough to make that sort of covering too uncomfortable for routine use.

The alien had helped warn the Terrans of the treachery that sparked off the rebellion on Hanuman, and ky had joined in Bravo Company's long march to safety. Ky had learned Terranglic from chip lessons on the way, and developed a real bond with the Terrans. At the final battle at the end of the march it was Myaighee who had helped Colin Fraser spring a crucial ambush that saved the survivors of the unit.

Ky had chosen to join the Legion after that rather than try to return to kys own kind, who probably would have viewed the hannie as a traitor anyway. Although ky had never been to Devereaux for formal Legion training, Myaighee had demonstrated considerable skill, and Watanabe had assigned ky to the Recon Lance to replace Legionnaire Auriega.

The hannie was showing equal skill in mastering the nuances of poker.

"How many cards?" Rostov was asking.

The alien's neck ruff twitched like a cornfield in a stiff breeze. Movements of those slender, poisonous spines were supposed to convey emotional content, but so far no one in Bravo Company fully understood the complexities of reading them. "One, Corporal," Myaighee said, in kys customary diffident tone.

"One, eh?" Rostov said, watching the movements of the neck ruff speculatively. As the hannie looked at the card, the ruff continued to move. Grant couldn't tell if it changed at all, if there were new emotions at work, and he was fairly sure Rostov couldn't either. Certainly Myaighee's face betrayed nothing.

"Dealer takes two," Rostov said, still eyeing the alien. His own emotions were plain enough. Was Myaighee excited because ky held a good hand, or because ky was trying to bluff? "What say we raise ... ten?"

Myaighee didn't even look at kys cards again. "Ten ... and twenty more, Corporal."

"Twenty more?" Rostov shook his head. "You're out for blood, aren't you?" He paused. "That's too steep for me. You take it."

Myaighee tossed kys cards down and raked in the pot without any apparent change in expression, though Slick noticed the neck ruff was no longer so agitated. Rostov reached out to pick up the cards.

"Hell, I don't believe this," he said. "A pair of deuces? This blasted monkey just bluffed me out of a week's pay with a pair of deuces."

"Serves you right, Corp," Slick said. "About time you found out what it was like to be a sucker!"

"That's enough out of you, kid," Rostov told him, laughing. "Hell, it's violating that natural order of things. Third-Classes were put in this universe for the express purpose of filling the pockets of First-Classes and Corporals, not the other way around."

"And where does that leave me?" Slick asked, looking up and grinning. "What are Second-Classes supposed to do?"

"When we know that, kid," Rostov shot back, "I'm pretty sure we'll have solved the basic mystery of life."

At that moment the computer cut the conversation short by sounding a shrill warning tone. Slick cursed as he looked down at the sonar display. "Multiple targets, Corp. Heading this way. Range about half a klick and closing."

"A school of fish, maybe?" Rostov suggested hopefully, as he joined Slick at the Operations console. The corporal cut the computer's insistent buzz.

"Only if we're talking about goddamned big fish that learned how to swim in a military academy," Slick said sourly. He pointed to the monitor. The targets were arrayed loosely, but they were certainly in formation. And the computer was reading the echoes as man-sized or larger.

"Looks like more company," Rostov said. He settled into the chair beside Slick and slapped the general alarm button, then picked up a mike. "Condition Three, condition three," he announced. "Natives spotted. Subaltern Watanabe, report to Operations."

Slick and Rostov exchanged a grim look. It looked like another attack was on the way.

* * *

As the insistent clamor of the alarm filled the corridor, Watanabe shoved past a startled crewman and into the ship's sensor center. Two more crew members looked up from their consoles.

"Intercom!" Watanabe snapped. One of the sailors pointed to the panel. "Check your sonar," he continued. "I want a display."

He stabbed the three-digit code for the Operations Center. "Watanabe here. What have you got?"

"Corporal Rostov, Sub," came the reply. "Bearing three-four-one, range four hundred meters. They're on a converging course, and the computer is scanning them as man-sized biologicals."

Watanabe watched as the crewman brought up the display on a wall-screen monitor. "I'm looking at them, Corporal. Looks like a major attack from here."

"Yes, sir," Rostov said. There was a pause. "Computer's estimating a hundred and fifty targets. There could be more, though."

"Yeah." Watanabe studied the screen. "Judging from the reports we had from the Sandcastle, these wogs might be planning some kind of ambush or surprise. Wait one, Rostov." He rubbed his forehead, trying to concentrate. "You—what's your name?"

"Brown, sir ..."

"What kind of bottom are we passing over, Brown?"

The crewman superimposed a high-resolution chart on the sonar display. Watanabe felt the familiar sensation of having pieces of a puzzle fall into place as he examined the monitor. He hit the intercom button again.

"Rostov, the charts up here in the sensor room say we're over rocky ground. Concentrate scans on the bottom. I have a feeling we may have some friends waiting for us down there."

"Yes, sir," the corporal acknowledged.

"Next, alert Gessler. It'll take me a few minutes to get aft, but I want the platoon mustered and deployed right away. Cover all four docking platforms. Recon and one heavy-weapons lances on mobile reserve." Watanabe paused. "Have Sergeant Muwanga take over for you ... and send for Forbes, too." Legionnaire Warren Forbes had taken over Trousseau's duties as the platoon's C^3 technician, though he remained part of Radescu's rifle lance.

"That will mean Radescu will only have two other men in his lance, Sub," Rostov pointed out.

Watanabe cursed under his breath. He had forgotten that Myaighee, the legionnaire he'd assigned to the Recon Lance, had transferred from Radescu's unit. "All right, Rostov, put Radescu on the entrance nearest the ready room. Understood?"

"Got it, Sub. We'll get things moving down here."

"Do it. I'll be down as soon as I take care of something up here." Watanabe cut the intercom, then punched in the Bridge combination.

"Bridge," a sailor responded.

"This is Subaltern Watanabe. I want the captain."

There was a pause before MacLean came on. "What the hell's going on, Watanabe?" he asked gruffly.

"We're tracking what we believe is an enemy formation off the port bow, less than a half kilometer away now. There is also a chance of a second force concealed somewhere nearby. I want a change of heading. We can outrun those bastards and avoid a fight."

"Run from a bunch of savages?" MacLean sounded incredulous. "Nonsense! Anyway, we still have to go this way sooner or later. The Scylla Passage is the only convenient way into the Polar Ocean, and that's where we're going. Your legionnaires will just have to deal with any of the wogs stupid enough to attack us."

Watanabe slapped the cutoff switch, unwilling to waste more time arguing. Obviously nothing was going to turn MacLean from the path his orders had set down.

As he left the sensor room, he remembered the uncertainties he'd been feeling on the day of the first nomad attack. Now his doubts about his ability were taking second place to his concern over the foolishness of the Seafarms people.

If the Terrans on Polypheme were defeated, it would be because Seafarms refused to look beyond their narrow interests or to accept the locals for the threat they were.

*　*　*

Corporal Dmitri Radescu kept his eyes on the surface of the Sea of Scylla, watching for any sign of the nomads. It was morning at last, the first planetary morning since Trousseau and Auriega had died, though thirty-six hours had passed by Terran reckoning.

He shrugged off the thought. Better to concentrate on the ocean.

Beside him Legionnaire Hoyt checked the magazine of his MEK and spat over the side of the docking platform. "Wish something would happen," he said, his growl of a voice matching his bearlike appearance.

"Yeah," Legionnaire Steiner agreed. He looked deceptively relaxed, with his FEK slung under his arm. Radescu had seen Steiner swing the battle rifle up and pick off a target at three hundred meters with barely a pause. "We missed out on the fun last time. Rostov's glory boys got all the action, as usual."

Radescu shrugged. "Luck of the draw, man. You want the truth, I wish they were out here now."

"Losing your nerve, Count?" Hoyt asked with a laugh. Radescu sprang from Transylvanian peasant stock, and though his family had been forcibly relocated to the colony world of Hecate when he was only ten, he had kept the accent of his youth. His lean build, dark hair, and pale complexion combined with that accent to make him the butt of endless Dracula jokes.

"Just wishing we had a full lance," Radescu told him. "Three men against an army isn't my idea of good odds."

"Hell, it's like Steiner said. The glory boys get all the best. They take a casualty, somebody else transfers in."

"Yeah, but look what they got," Hoyt said. "I'm glad to lose that little ale creep." He wasn't known for liking non-humans, even the ones who joined the Legion.

Radescu knew how Hoyt felt. He'd fought the monkeys on Hanuman, and he could still remember what it was like to watch a horde of the little creatures drop out of the trees in ambush or swarm over the walls of a Legion outpost.

Right now, though, even Legionnaire Myaighee would have been a comforting addition to his depleted lance.

Steiner pointed suddenly, "Hey, Count, what's…?" The words trailed off in an all-too-familiar gurgle as the legionnaire slumped to the deck. There was a crossbow bolt protruding from his throat, bare centimeters above the collar of his duraweave battledress.

Dropping prone on the deck, Radescu trained his FEK on the ocean, squinting against the dazzle of sunlight on the water. Beside him Hoyt was on one knee. The big gunner swept his MEK in an arc, firing on full automatic and keeping up a running stream of curses that nearly drowned out the hum of the weapon's gauss-generator.

Then there was an explosion and the MEK fell silent. Hoyt was down, too, with a ruined mask of blood and torn flesh for a face.

Radescu keyed in his commlink and swallowed, tasting fear. He opened fire as he mouthed an incantation his grandmother had taught him, a chant that was supposed to ward off the servants of evil.

* * *

"Attack on Docking Platform Two! Rostov, take your lance."

"On it, Sarge," Rostov acknowledged Platoon Sergeant Gessler's order. "Let's do it, Recon!"

"Recon!" the rest of the lance echoed in unison. Rostov felt a surge of pride. It was a good team.

They ran out of the ready room, with Slick on point and the hulking Gwyrran, Vrurrth, just behind. Rostov was third, backed up by Myaighee and the sniper, Judy Martin, bringing up the rear. It was a formation the lance had drilled in countless times, with the hannie taking the place of young Auriega as if ky had been with them all along.

Slick rounded the last corner, crouching low. Vrurrth stopped, flattened himself against the wall, and held up his hand to signal a stop. Rostov and the others halted as well.

"Hatch is still open," Slick's voice sounded softly in Rostov's ears. "Explosions outside … I hear an FEK."

"Someone's still alive, then," Rostov said. "Back him up, kid. Let's go!"

Slick had stopped by the hatch and was firing through it as the rest of the lance sprinted down the corridor. Through the opening Rostov could see glimpses of battle: the dead body of a big legionnaire with an MEK, a wog sprawled nearby, another nomad grappling with Corporal Radescu. More wogs were climbing out of the water.

A burst from Slick's FEK cut down the native fighting with Radescu. "Get inside, man!" Rostov shouted, joining Slick on the firing line. "Vrurrth, get ready to dog the hatch."

The Gwyrran nodded ponderously.

Rostov, Slick, and Myaighee were all firing now, covering the Romanian corporal's retreat. Radescu stopped to retrieve Hoyt's MEK, then maintained steady fire as he fell back.

They all stopped firing as Radescu dived through the hatch. Then Vrurrth slammed the hatch shut.

"Will the hatches hold them?" Martin asked. She didn't seem to be speaking to anyone in particular.

"Not against explosives," Rostov, who was trained as a demolitions specialist, said quietly. "We'd better set up a barricade and let Sarge and the Sub know what's happened."

* * *

"Both entries on the port side were attacked. Platform Two was lost; the boys on Number One drove back the wogs."

"What happened on Two?" Watanabe asked.

Sergeant Muwanga shrugged. "That was Radescu's lance. Rostov says they were short-handed to start with. Apparently two of them were taken out right away, but Corporal Radescu made it back inside after the Recon Lance started laying down some cover."

Watanabe glanced across C-cubed at Legionnaire Forbes. The man was looking sick.

No wonder. Half his lance gone in a matter of seconds, and Forbes hadn't been there to help them. A five-man lance in the Legion was closer than most civilian families.

"Any further activity from Two?"

"Rostov reported hearing some noises through the hatch, s ir. He believes they'll try to blow it and break in. Sergeant Gessler wants permission to deploy more men there."

Watanabe sat down heavily. They didn't have very many reserves left, and if there was another attack somewhere else they'd be hard-pressed to respond.

But if Rostov wasn't backed up and the natives broke through, they'd be damned close to the engineering spaces. Assuming the enemy knew something about the layout of the *Cyclops*—and that was an assumption the legionnaires had to make, even if it e rred on the side of caution—they could render the huge ship helpless if Rostov couldn't hold.

Either way the legionnaires would be in trouble.

"Sir ..." Forbes broke in suddenly, looking up from the monitor with a look of horror on his face. "Sir, I've got targets on the bottom scan ... at least two hundred. They're hiding in the rocks, but there's enough motion for the computer to pick them out of the clutter."

"Motion? What kind?"

"Ship's passing over them now, sir, and they're starting up toward us."

"Where the hell are they going to hit?" Muwanga asked, his big fist slamming the corner of the console. "Where?"

"Wherever it is," Watanabe said, "I'm not sure we can stop them. There's just too damned many of the bastards."

He turned away, staring at the wall. The only way to head off disaster was to break up the attack in a big way. Something unexpected. Something clever....

You're the one everyone says is the clever tactician, he told himself.

And an old memory surfaced slowly, a memory from his boyhood on the watery world of Pacifica, and the commercial fishing vessel his older brother had worked on the summer before Watanabe had left for the Academy.

He found himself smiling as he turned back to explain his plan.

* * *

The banging and scraping had stopped, and now the corridor off Docking Platform Two was as quiet as a graveyard.

Slick crouched behind the barricade they'd improvised out of a dozen cargomods filled with spare parts from a nearby storeroom halfway down the passageway, hardly daring to breathe. Myaighee and Rostov waited on either side, with the others poised further back, at the intersection.

"What are they waiting for?" Slick muttered.

"Probably scared of you, kid," Rostov said with mock cheerfulness. "Maybe they're waiting for you to die of old age before they rush us." His FEK never wavered, and he kept all of his attention focused on the hatch.

Slick hated the waiting. He'd never liked enclosed places or static defense; he was more at home on a recon patrol in the open or a sudden ambush where he set the pace of the fighting.

Back on Hanuman he'd nearly broken a time or two, in situations like this. He'd learned to deal with it, but he still didn't like to be pinned down this way.

The seconds dragged by interminably.

"Maybe the Old Man knew what he was doing when he decided against sending any help," Rostov commented, "Maybe the attack here was just a diver—"

And at that moment the hatch erupted inward in fire, thunder, and hurtling fragments, and alien shapes appeared through the smoke, their rocket weapons held at the ready.

Chapter Thirteen

I am asking for six hundred men of the Foreign Legion who are able, if need be, to die decently.

—General Joseph Gallieni,
French Foreign Legion, 1896

"All right, are you clear on what we're doing?" Watanabe paused in his restless pacing in front of the six legionnaires who made up his only reserve. They were the men of the platoon's two heavy-weapons units, but they had put aside their onagers and Fafnir rocket launchers in favor of FEKs. Instead of regular battledress or plasteel armor, each member of the strike force, including Watanabe, was clad in a Legion-issue hardsuit, the only type of diving gear practical for use on Polypheme.

"We're ready, sir," Sergeant Gessler answered for all of them.

"Then it's time ... Let the games begin." He forced a smile before lowering the faceplate on his diving helmet and checking the seals.

As the other legionnaires followed his example, Watanabe keyed in his commlink. "Muwanga? Communications check. Alpha, Bravo, Charlie ..."

"Read you five-by-five, sir," Muwanga replied. He and Forbes would continue coordinating the legionnaires from C-cubed. "Zeigler's ready on Platform Four."

"Good. We're moving out now. Tell him to drop the first charges in one minute ... mark! Channel clear." Watanabe cut the commlink and picked up the FEK, feeling constricted by the stiff armor of the hardsuit. The diving gear was constructed as full-coverage protection for underwater combat, though on Polypheme it had always been considered more important that the suits resisted the highly corrosive effects of the ocean. Ordinary materials didn't last long in that environment.

He followed the others down the corridor toward Docking Platform Four. This plan would put his team into serious danger, challenging the wogs in their own native environment with a considerable disadvantage in numbers.

Watanabe could only hope that the surprise he had planned would keep the nomads off balance long enough to give the legionnaires a chance to hit hard.

These natives had been showing a flair for unorthodox tactics. Now it was time to even the score.

*   *   *

Sergeant Ralph Zeigler watched the digital countdown on the inside of his faceplate and raised his arm. On either end of Docking Platform Four a member of Vane's Rifle Lance braced a foot on a canister and turned a young, worried face to look for Zeigler's signal.

Four ... three ... two ... one ...

The sergeant dropped his arm and the two riflemen kicked their tubes. They hit the water so close to simultaneously that Zeigler heard only one splash.

"Get ready, Vane," Zeigler ordered. He saw Corporal Vane tighten his grip on the remote-control box that would detonate the explosives in the two improvised depth charges.

Putting explosives into the water to take out the wogs ... the subaltern had really outdone himself this time. The canisters were the standard buffered transport containers for stocks of PX-70, the obsolete military demo charges used by the company for survey works and other scientific and engineering applications. A few minutes' work dismantling the buffers and slapping detpacks into the explosives had transformed safe shipping modules into very large, very lethal underwater bombs.

A new countdown was ticking off on his faceplate, the time left to detonation. Watanabe wanted those charges to go off fairly deep, partly to protect the *Cyclops*, partly to catch as many of the wogs still on the bottom as possible.

"And three ... and two ... and one ..."

One of the legionnaires went down as a barrage of rocket fire opened up from the forward end of the platform. A large tattooed shape heaved itself onto the deck, brandishing a heavy mace studded with wicked-looking spikes. Legionnaire Bergmann fired, killing the wog, but another was climbing out of the water to take the dead nomad's place.

"Hit it, Vane!" Zeigler shouted, bringing his own FEK into action.

The corporal hit the button.

Then Vane was down, clutching at the stump of his wrist where a rocket had exploded. The remote-control box skittered across the deck. Everything seemed to be moving in slow motion. Surely the canisters should have detonated? Had something gone wrong?

Just then twin geysers erupted aft of the ship, one close to the rear end of the platform, the other further astern. Water surged across the open deck, knocking Bergmann down and sweeping him toward the edge.

But the legionnaires had been expecting the blast, while the nomads had not. Zeigler and the other riflemen clung to nearby handholds and kept firing, clearing the rest of the natives off the platform.

No others appeared, though a number of bodies were rising to the surface, either stunned or dead.

Zeigler grabbed Bergmann and helped him to his feet. "First aid for Vane, then get him to sick bay," he ordered. "The rest of you stay on your toes. If you see a wog, shoot him ... Even the ones that look dead."

FEKs whined.

Then Sergeant Gessler, ungainly in a hardsuit, came through the hatch. Zeigler flashed him a thumbs-up.

Now it was time for the counterattack.

* * *

Slick shouted a colorful curse he'd picked up from Rostov and held the trigger of the FEK down, spraying full-auto fire into the nomads crowding through the blown hatch. An analytical part of his mind was thankful that Rostov had placed the barricade far enough back to avoid the worst effects of the blast when the hatch blew. Any closer and they would have been too stunned, too blinded by smoke, and the nomads would have overrun them.

It was lucky the natives didn't use hand grenades. They weren't very practical underwater weapons, but a single grenade would have cleared the corridor easily.

Unfortunately, these wogs were too bloody adaptable. One of them would think of using their explosives as a satchel charge soon enough.

All they could do, though, was keep on pouring fire into that hatchway, keeping the natives from shooting rockets down the corridor and praying that Subaltern Watanabe was right in assuming that this wasn't going to be the main enemy drive.

Suddenly there were no fresh targets. "Goddamn!" Rostov said. "They're not supposed to be able to disengage that way!"

Something moved in the hatch, and Legionnaire Martin shouted "Look out, Corp!" She fired, the laser beam crackling invisibly over Slick's head. A wog toppled through the hatch onto the bodies of several of his comrades, but not before something bulky bounced and slid partway down the passageway.

"Satchel charge!" Rostov called. "Get back!"

Myaighee was a blur of motion, leaping over the barricade and running toward the sack. The hannie grabbed it with both hands and threw it back with a strength anyone that didn't know kys race would never have believed possible.

A crossbow bolt struck the alien near the base of the throat, and Myaighee fell.

"Cover me, Corp," Slick said, starting over the barricade to retrieve his lancemate. He heard a staccato *thunk-thunk-thunk* from Rostov's FEK as the corporal fired a three-round burst of grenades.

Just then the satchel charge detonated, and Slick used the confusion to sprint to the fallen hannie. He stooped, picked the small body up, and ran for the barricade.

There was no enemy fire from the hatchway.

"Explosion must have cleared the platform," Radescu said from the corridor intersection. "We can take it back now."

"No way," Rostov said. "Sub said we let 'em stay put until he does his thing. That's what we do."

Slick carried Myaighee to the intersection and lowered the alien to the deck.

"Get back on the firing line, kid!" Rostov called from the barricade. "Martin, first aid!"

Slick hesitated, unwilling to leave the hannie. Martin knelt beside Myaighee, then looked up at him. "It's bad," she said. "But I'll do what I can until we can get a real medic."

* * *

Water closed around Watanabe's head, murky and somehow hostile. An alien sea, completely unlike the clear blue waters of Pacifica.

This ocean was home to the wogs, not to Mankind, and Watanabe was all too aware of being an intruder in this unfriendly realm.

He checked his gauges. The artificial gill mounted on the back of his helmet was drawing well, and his suit was maintaining integrity. Watanabe touched a stud on his forearm control band and the back-pack waterthruster hummed to life. It was no substitute for the mobility the lokes enjoyed underwater, but impellers in the pack would push him along substantially faster than he could swim.

The water was cloudy, filled with mud—and other things Watanabe preferred not to think about—churned up by the depth charges. He hit another control and his faceplate turned into a small-scale sonar display, less accurate than the computer-enhanced shipboard system, but adequate.

With luck the legionnaires would actually be able to "see" better than the opposition, at least for a while. Transponders in the hardsuit commlinks would tag friends; everything else would be a foe.

"Stick close," he ordered. "Let's go!"

He dived, keeping close to the hull of the *Cyclops*. The sonar display showed a few drifting bodies nearby, but nothing that looked like living targets.

Maybe the charges had taken all of them out....

As he reached the bottom of the vessel, though, he could see that his hope had been vain.

A knot of perhaps thirty wogs was swimming along the keel, moving toward the bow of the huge ship. They probably had been partially screened from the shock waves.

So far, the legionnaires had apparently gone unnoticed. Watanabe signaled for a halt, cut his thruster, and watched. What were they doing?

Then he saw it. And if the wogs reached their objective, *Seafarms Cyclops* and everyone aboard her would be helpless against the nomad attackers.

* * *

Ghrookwur!-Huntmaster clutched his head, still dizzy from the force of the explosions the Strangers-Above had set off in the water. The shock wave had knocked him out for a time, and now, as he recovered consciousness, his head and ears ached. He swiveled an eyestalk to examine his ear and saw that it was oozing blood.

May the offworlders find nothing but dry land and choking dust, he thought as he groped for his spear. It was floating close by, tangled with the body of Dur!ghur-Fartrader.

The Stormriders Clan had suffered many losses today, far more than War-Leader-of-Clans Choor! had said they would lose. Perhaps Choor! was wrong about the Strangers-Above. He claimed they were no match for the Clans United, that even without the Strangers-Who-Brought-Gifts the nomad tribes could drive away these foreign devils and save the seas for the Free Swimmers.

The War-Leader-of-Clans had brought the most powerful tribes of these seas together, bound by a common purpose instead of being separated by constant strife. He was wise in the ways of war, and he had the support of the Strangers-Who-Brought-Gifts. But so far this war on the Strangers-Above had brought little gain at high cost ... and that cost mostly in the lives of Stormriders. Perhaps Choor! really was above all Clan ties and rivalries ... or perhaps the Stormriders were being expended here so that some other Clan—the Wavesingers, perhaps, or the Reef-Swimmers—could gain that much more power among the Clans United.

That was disturbing. If Ghrookwur!-Huntmaster lived through the day, he would have much to say to the Clan-Leader and the Clan-Warlord.

If he lived.

He sensed movement in the water close by and swiveled his eyestalks. Strange shapes moved through the murk, grotesque parodies of the Free Swimmers. The Strangers!

His hands and feet closed tight around the spear, and he thrashed his tail, gathering speed. The Strangers had to be stopped....

* * *

Watanabe barely had time to react to the sudden movement from a target that had seemed dead moments before. He kicked his legs hard and dodged the wog's first rush, but the alien was fast as a striking snake. Before Watanabe could turn the wog was attacking again. His spear struck the subaltern's backpack.

Then Gessler was there, striking the alien from behind with the butt of his FEK. "Prisoner," Gessler grunted, hitting the still form one more time to be sure. He produced an inflatable buoy, secured it to the nomad, and triggered it. As the captive rose toward the surface the Platoon Sergeant informed Zeigler to expect the package.

Watanabe nodded in satisfaction. Captain Fraser would be pleased if they could get worthwhile information out of a prisoner or two, and so far it had been so damned hard to stop one of the bastards without killing them....

He studied his sonar scan again. "C-cubed, this is Bravo Two One. I need a computer feed."

"Bravo Two One, acknowledged," Forbes's voice responded. "What do you need?"

"Ship schematics for the lower decks," Watanabe told him.

"Roger that. Wait one." A moment later the sonar image faded out, replaced by a diagram showing the underside of the *Cyclops.*

And there, right where he'd thought it should be, was the intake for the largest of the ship's three main impeller tunnels.

Like the backpack thruster units, the *Seafarms Cyclops* relied on water sucked in through inlet ducts forward and forced out under high pressure aft for propulsion. The largest of these was located directly over the keel, with the intake located fifty meters from the bow.

It was an efficient piece of engineering, but if that master intake was damaged badly enough the ship would have to limp along at less than half its usual slow speed, easy prey for multiple attacks.

Probably the natives lurking along the bottom had planned to take out all three impeller tunnels, but after the explosions they were concentrating on the main one.

That meant they knew a hell of a lot about the layout of the ship....

Watanabe pushed the thought aside. It wasn't important now. For the moment the problem was stopping those wogs before they struck. They had perhaps three hundred more meters to swim before they reached the intake.

He cut the computer feed and signaled his men to follow.

With backpacks on full thrust, the legionnaires started after their targets.

* * *

"Here they come again!" Rostov shouted, opening fire. The legionnaires pumped round after round into the hatch, with Radescu spraying three-round grenade bursts past the barricade.

The nomads weren't pressing this attack home nearly as hard as before. It was just as Slick had said that first day, when Auriega had bought it. They seemed to have learned something about tactics. It felt as if they were mounting a diversion, pushing just hard enough to attract attention.

The subaltern had been right, then. But just now Rostov wished Watanabe had fallen for the trick, at least enough to send some backup. Myaighee was out of action, and sooner or later the attackers would score more hits.

Beside him Slick stopped firing and glanced his way. "I don't like the feel of this, Corp," he said. "Those bastards are up to something new this time."

Rostov nodded; it matched the feeling he'd been getting. "Yeah, but what do you think it is?"

"If they've got more explosives, they could try to open another hole."

"Hull's a lot stronger than the hatches are, kid," he said.

"Yeah, but if they're serious …"

Rostov switched on his commlink. "Hey, Sarge, do we have any outside cameras left by Platform two?" he asked.

"Cameras?" Muwanga responded, sounding uncertain. "Uh … yeah. What are you looking for?"

"We think the wogs are up to something out there. Maybe planning to blast themselves a new hatch. Can you see anything?"

"Wait one." There was a long pause. "Goddamn it, Rostov, they're setting charges about ten meters aft of your position, and right along the waterline. Get the hell out of there!"

"Radescu! Cover us! Come on, kid, we're making some tracks!"

As they sprinted up the passageway, crouching low to leave the Romanian a clear field of fire, a blast shook the corridor. Lights flickered overhead.

And they could hear the rush of water, mingling with the trium-phant shouts of wog soldiers, from the storage compartment aft of their defensive position.

* * *

"Negative, C-cubed, negative!" Watanabe gasped as he kept swimming. "If you weaken any of the other platforms, the wogs'll just have that many more places to try to break in. Rostov has to hold as well as he can. If they run true to form, they'll cut their losses if we stop them here."

He switched the commlink to the lance tactical frequency, shifted from sonar to direct-vision viewing, and raised his FEK. "Legionnaires!" he called, squeezing the trigger.

Water boiled as the gauss rifle hurled deadly needle rounds at the enemy. The fantastic muzzle velocity of the FEK was hampered very little by the thicker medium of underwater combat, though the range was sharply restricted. Nomads died in the storm of metallic slivers.

But some were quick enough or lucky enough to take cover behind the ship's keel. Rockets streaked toward the legionnaires like tiny torpedoes. Legionnaire Erlich let go of his FEK and clutched at a gaping hole in the torso section of his hardsuit. His scream echoed in Watanabe's headphones for what seemed like an eternity. Then he was dead.

"Sergeant," Watanabe ordered crisply. "Take two men. Drop deeper and get an angle on those wogs. We'll keep them busy."

Gessler stabbed a blunt finger at two of the legionnaires and pushed off from the bottom of the ship, striking out for the depths. One of the men following him took a rocket hit in one leg but kept right on going, a trail of blood marking his passage like the ink sprayed by a Terran squid.

Watanabe tried to concentrate on firing. His magazine ran dry, and he slapped a fresh clip into the receiver. Beside him Corporal Dmowski switched to grenades. They weren't quite as effective underwater as the needle rounds, but the pattern of bursts around the keel flushed one of the nomads. The remaining legionnaire killed him.

Then more of the nomads were breaking from the cover of the keel as Gessler's men opened up. They seemed ready to swim straight for Watanabe's position, obeying their drive to overwhelm the enemy at any cost.

Moments later they were fleeing, all the fight gone out of them.

Watanabe watched as the legionnaires picked off a few of the fugitives, wondering once again what it was that made these natives tick. Their battle plans were elaborate, but they still had trouble fighting their own reflexes in combat. Something was guiding them, that much was sure ... but what? And how?

Watanabe knew that the answers to those questions could be the solution to the whole native threat. He only hoped they could find them in time.

*　*　*

Rostov was favoring his left shoulder, bruised in the confusing minutes before the end of the battle. They had split up as they retreated, with Radescu, Martin, and Myaighee falling back to the nearest watertight door forward, while the other three cut their way through the wogs to secure the aft end of the corridor. It wouldn't have been enough — there was still a rabbit warren of compartments and passageways uncovered, and with explosives the wogs could have broken out at will, but the legionnaires had kept them tied up just long enough.

Then, just as C-cubed had said, the nomads had retreated. Apparently once their attempt on the intakes was compromised, they were unwilling to press on with the all-too-successful diversion.

The platoon was drawn up in Hold Two, the ready room, except for the ones like Myaighee who were confined to the ship's sick bay.

Or the legionnaires like Hoyt and Steiner, who wouldn't be attending muster again.

Watanabe had put on a dress uniform that looked out of place among the battledress fatigues. "You've done good work today, men," he said. "More than anyone had a right to expect. But I'm afraid the day's work isn't done yet."

There was a stir through the ranks.

"I've made a decision, one that will probably cost me my bar. I need your support to carry it out." He paused. "Seafarms has ordered Captain MacLean to continue the cruise. If he follows those orders, what we went through today is going to keep on repeating, over and over, until we make a mistake or we're just too worn down by attrition to fight the wogs off. I will not subject this command to those conditions."

This time the legionnaires were muttering audibly among them-selves. Rostov heard Martin whisper to Slick. "Why doesn't someone at the Sandcastle take charge, huh?"

Watanabe must have heard a similar comment. "I have decided to take action without reference to higher authority. Captain Fraser can't invoke Section 34 without running the risk of bringing Seafarms down on his back, and apparently that's about the only thing that would get them to change their orders. I can't convince MacLean to play it smart, either. But the best chance for everyone is to rejoin the rest of the demi-battalion at the Sandcastle, instead of letting the wogs wear us down separately."

He drew his PLF pistol. "This leaves it to us to deal with the situation. Who's with me?"

Rostov's voice joined with the rest of the platoon in roaring out his approval.

The Legion would stand together.

CHAPTER FOURTEEN

—Legionnaire Pascal Bonette,
French Foreign Legion, 1914

insist that you order this man Watanabe to return control of the *Cyclops* to Captain MacLean!"

Fraser frowned at Edward Barnett. "Citizen, I'm getting tired of these arguments," he said quietly. "Before you took charge, the question was settled. It was your reversal of policy that started this nonsense, and frankly I'm more than satisfied with what Mr. Watanabe has done."

"Then he's acting under your orders?" Barnett challenged.

Leaning back in his chair, Fraser looked around the conference room before he answered. It was a lean staff meeting, with Fraser, Du-Valier, Gage, and Kelly, plus Garcia in one corner recording the minutes.

And Barnett. Since his rescue from Ourgh, Barnett had stepped into the role of Seafarms Project Director as if he had been born to the job. In a matter of hours, he'd undone most of what Jens had agreed to do.

Fraser had blocked his hopes of returning to Ourgh, though. That had mostly been Gunny Trent's doing; it was the NCO's suggestion that Fraser agree to allow the Seafarms people to leave any time they wanted, provided they realized that there would be no Legion help on the return trip. Impounding all the vehicles inside the Sandcastle, even that ramshackle magrep barge, had driven the point home even further.

So Barnett and his people remained in the Sandcastle ... but they weren't even pretending to cooperate now, here or aboard the *Cyclops*. If it hadn't been for Watanabe's bloodless mutiny, the ship would still be on course for the open sea—or more likely, drifting helpless in the wake of fresh nomad attacks.

Kelly met his gaze with a warning look. She had a knack for reading him. He ignored the cautionary note in her eyes and answered Barnett.

"The fact is, I didn't issue any such orders," Fraser admitted. He paused. "But I wish I had, and my own report is going to indicate my full support for the subaltern's action."

That much was certainly true. He should have forced the issue long since, but instead he'd avoided confrontation with Barnett. The legalities of the situation on Polypheme were cloudy, and he'd told himself that caution was best, but the choice had nearly cost Watanabe and his platoon—and the crew of the *Cyclops*—their lives.

He'd almost allowed concern for his career to override his plain duty. Luckily Watanabe had taken the initiative.

Barnett leaned forward, scowling. "I'll make sure you and he both get what you deserve," he said, standing abruptly. "Your career's going to make your precious Captain Hawley's look impressive by comparison."

Fraser laughed. "If any of us live through the next couple of weeks, Barnett, you're welcome to whatever revenge you want." He hardened his tone. "Meanwhile, starting now, this base is under military authority. Seafarms has no further say in any decisions that get made here."

"You can't make that kind of decision!" DuValier exploded. "You're not even the ranking officer!"

"Captain Hawley will back me up, I think, Lieutenant," Fraser said mildly. "I discussed my views with him before the meeting, and he agrees that we can't keep letting Seafarms wreck everything we try to accomplish."

"That doddering old fool agrees with whoever's talking with him," Barnett said angrily. "You won't hide behind him when it comes to taking the blame for this—not like you did over Fenris!"

Captain David Hawley's voice cut through the room like a knife. "The 'doddering old fool' doesn't agree with you, Citizen. And whether you try to spread the blame or not, I'm ultimately responsible for everything that happens in this command."

Heads swiveled. Hawley's entrance had gone unnoticed, but his words brought instant attention. He was wearing issue battledress, and he seemed straighter and firmer than any of them had seen him before.

Fraser stood up. "Ten-hut!" he barked, and the other legionnaires followed suit.

"As you were," Hawley said with a vague gesture. He took his seat at the head of the table. "Arguments about who's in charge or who should be blamed aren't going to keep us alive. Citizen Barnett, I support Captain Fraser's position regarding military authority inside the Sandcastle. Inform your people, and then stay the hell out of our way."

Barnett seemed about to reply, but instead he stormed out of the room. There was a long silence.

"Thank you, Captain," Fraser said quietly. "I'm afraid that as long as there was any doubt about where the orders were coming from, he'd find more ways to obstruct us."

Hawley smiled. "I'm not good for a whole lot anymore, son," he said. "I've had too many light-years and too little practice to be much of a CO. But I'm *damned* if some puffed-up civilian is going to shove the Legion around!"

"Well, whatever the reason, it's good to have you in charge," Fraser said. He was surprised at the change in the man. It was like the spark that had started in the first battle had finally ignited a flame.

"Don't expect miracles, Captain," Hawley said, as if he were reading Fraser's mind. "As far as I'm concerned, you're in command of the defense here. Like I said, I'm not much of a CO anymore, but I'll do everything I can to keep up my end."

Fraser started to protest, but the older man held up his hand. "I said it before—arguing isn't going to help us now. If you want to take orders from me, take these. You're in tactical command, son. I know you've already got some pretty good ideas, so let's get them in place."

"Yes, sir," He swallowed and punched in a combination on the keyboard in front of him. "We've started installing heavy-weapons positions on the wall. My first idea is to build on these with several additional emplacements...."

As he started to lay out the plans he and Trent had been working on since the first attack, Colin Fraser was conscious of a glow of pride within. Hawley was no longer simply dodging his responsibilities, but he still respected Fraser's opinions. Hawley, the hero of Aten.

And Fraser realized just how much Hawley's good opinion meant to him.

* * *

Lieutenant Antoine DuValier left the conference room and started toward his own office. He was confused and uncertain, and he needed some time alone to reexamine his feelings.

What Barnett had said in there about Fraser hiding behind Hawley had hit close to home. It was easy to see the similarities between this situation and what must have happened between Fraser and Major St. John after the Fenris situation. Of course Fraser would use the excuse that the senior officer carried responsibility for the decisions....

Yet Fraser hadn't really acted like he was trying to use Hawley as a scapegoat. On the contrary, it had been Barnett who had suggested the idea—and Hawley, for that matter. But Fraser had fought his own battle until the older captain's appearance.

Had he misjudged Fraser? Or was Hawley even more of a puppet than anyone had thought, trotting out whatever help Fraser needed on command?

DuValier would have a lot to think about.

* * *

The meeting had broken up, but Fraser remained in the conference room, hunched over one of the computer monitors, studying one of the enclosures in Watanabe's report. He paused and rested his head in his hands, frustrated, tired. Every lead, every new scrap of information, seemed to complicate things.

"Don't let it get to you, Col," Kelly's soft voice made him look up.

"I didn't know you were still here," he said. "Sorry."

She smiled and sat down next to him. "I just wanted you to know you've got people on your side."

"Thanks. Between Barnett and Antoine DuValier I'm starting to think I've got more enemies inside the walls than outside. Lieutenant Gage won't say anything unless you prod her. Thank God for Haw- ley ... and for your moral support, too."

Kelly frowned. "Are you sure you can count on Captain Hawley, Col? I mean, as long as he's in command, Barnett could still get to him. He's not the most strong-willed man I've ever seen."

"That's like saying Hanuman was a trifle unpleasant," Fraser chuck- led. Then he turned serious. "The Captain's had it tough, Kelly. Too damned tough."

"It doesn't answer the question, though, does it? Barnett could force him to back down."

"What do you want me to do, Kelly? Relieve him on grounds of mental incapacity?"

"You could, you know. Ramirez would back you up."

He shook his head, angry. "I'm not going to do it! Damn it, he des-erves better than that!" Fraser looked away. When he went on he had control of his temper. "Sorry ... that came out pretty strong. But it's the way I feel. David Hawley got the short end of the stick. A good career turned sour ... the kind of thing I keep picturing for my own future. He could have retired, probably should have, years ago. But the army's all he's ever had. Hell, when he goes off to Dreamland it's usually a military fantasy, a battle story or a wargame. Well, I'm not going to be the one who takes it away from him, Kelly. He deserves a chance to keep whatever dignity he can."

She nodded slowly. "I see what you mean. So if Barnett goes over your head...?"

"I'll take it as it comes. Anyway, I don't think Barnett will play around with politics much more. I'm a hell of a lot more concerned with figuring out what the next move from our fishy friends will be."

"What were you working on there?" she asked, gesturing toward the terminal.

"Watanabe pulled a prisoner out of the fighting around the *Cyclops*, but the wog suicided."

"Damn," Kelly said softly.

"Yeah, that's pretty much what Trent and I said, though the Gunny put it a lot more eloquently and carried on for a few minutes longer. All we got out of the nomad was the slogan 'Long live the warriors of Choor!' and a couple of nasty epithets. Then he grabbed a knife from one of the guards and killed himself."

"Choor! ... A Clan chief?"

"Unlikely," Fraser answered. "Personality cults aren't very common in nomad society. Their loyalty is to the Clan. The individual is not as important as his role within the clan hierarchy."

"What have our native scouts come up with?"

"It's that kind of question that makes me wish you were my Exec instead of friend Antoine," he said with a smile. "The Gunny's down having a chat with them now. If we get a handle on just who or what Choor! is, maybe we'll have a shot at figuring out what to do about the nomads."

"How much reliance can you place on our wogs?" she asked.

He grinned. "You're starting to sound like Barnett. No offense intended." Fraser paused. "You know, I haven't been in the Legion much longer than you, but I'm finally starting to understand some of the mystique. Shared dangers, shared adventures ... hell, the shared miseries of eating rapacks ... It's the cement that binds these people together, Kelly. None of them are Citizens by birth, but they earn it by shedding blood together. You've seen it cross species lines—your little friend Myaighee, for instance—and it's just as powerful. The nomads who volunteered as auxiliaries had a lot of the same motives that drive our regulars. I think they're trustworthy, and I think they're going to do everything they can to help us. If only because they're in the same fix we are once the nomads hit us again."

"And if they don't know anything useful?"

"Then we'll just have to keep on fighting in the dark. Sooner or later something's got to give."

She looked grim. "Just hope it isn't us."

* * *

Gunnery Sergeant John Trent exchanged looks with the unit's Native Affairs specialist and shook his head. "You take this one, Hermann. I'm getting a sore throat from all this damned gargling."

"*Ja,*" agreed Warrant Officer Fourth-Class Koenig. He was a tall, gangling man who looked too young to hold a specialist's commission, but Trent knew the kid had two degrees in xenostudies and another in linguistics. Like a lot of the specialists who served as Warrant Officers in the Colonial Army, he had agreed to serve a five-year hitch with line troops, giving advice and analysis to pay off his tuition. It helped combat units to have experts on hand in areas like medicine, sciences, or engineering.

Right now Koenig was helping him question the native auxiliaries. If any of them could throw more light on the nature of the opposition....

Unfortunately, all of these nomads had been recruited out of Ourgh. They were mostly failed merchants from distant clans who had taken service with the Legion as an alternative to a long journey home and the disgrace of failure at the end of it. That meant they knew little about the local situation—or at least they were claiming ignorance.

Trent wished they had the facilities at the Sandcastle for a proper Intelligence setup. With a little patience, and access to a computer implant, an Intel officer could conduct direct, mind-to-mind examinations that were far more reliable than any of the old drug or conditioning techniques. Of course it was physically and mentally tough on both the subject and the interrogator, but the results were worth it.

Well, it wouldn't have mattered much. The only implant in the Sandcastle belonged to Captain Hawley, and Trent doubted the old man had the willpower or mental agility to handle the stress of that kind of questioning. If Captain Fraser had remained in Intelligence longer, or had been born on Terra, he might have had an implant. Fraser knew how to set up the whole procedure—he'd explained it to Trent once during the last stages of the Hanuman mop-up campaign—but the captain wasn't capable of handling it himself.

Which left verbal questioning of the nomads to try to ferret out useful information. He just hoped the auxiliaries would have something worthwhile to offer.

Trent leaned back as Koenig beckoned the next auxiliary to the chair in front of the desk they'd set up in the Alpha Company ready room. He checked the fit of the language chip behind his ear. He wasn't going to trust himself to translate; the computer could give it to him a hell of a lot faster, and that would help him concentrate on trying to sift useful information out of the session. A one-task chip was nowhere near as useful as an implant, but it was still a handy tool to have.

"Your name and clan?" Koenig asked the new nomad in his native tongue. Trent felt a twinge of jealousy as he realized that the warrant officer had no chip and hadn't even seen the need to take a refresher course before the session. The man's skill with alien languages was uncanny.

Then again, Trent thought Koenig knew next to nothing about laying an ambush or setting up a defensive perimeter.

"Oomour am I, of the clan of the Seacliffs," the native replied, the Terranglic words a soft whisper in Trent's ear.

"Where does your clan swim, Oomour-of-the-Seacliffs?" Koenig asked formally.

The native's feeding tendrils writhed. "Few of the Seacliffs swimming are," he replied. "Those that do ... scattered to the far waves."

"His clan was destroyed?" Trent asked Koenig in Terranglic.

The specialist nodded thoughtfully. "Doesn't happen much. Usually their interclan conflicts are like their fights with the city-dwellers—raids, skirmishes, that sort of thing. The Free-Swimmers don't have much concept of territorial possession or property rights, and it's a big ocean. Usually if a dispute arises, one side or the other just moves on."

Trent tugged thoughtfully at the corner of his sandy mustache. "The nomads have been doing a lot of funny things lately. Follow it up."

Koenig nodded. "How was your clan lost, Oomour?"

The native's gills vibrated, an expression of anger or great emotional stress. "By Choor! was the Clan attacked. Because join his tribe-of-tribes we would not."

"Orbit," Trent said softly. They had a lead.

*　　*　　*

"All right, let's run through what we know." Captain David Hawley leaned forward across the desk as he focused on Fraser's report. "This Choor! is a nomad leader who is trying to band together a coalition of clans—sort of a tribal empire. I thought that sort of cooperation was impossible. Something about sublimated territorial instincts, or some such."

From the corner of Hawley's office WO/4 Koenig spoke up. "Strictly speaking, you're right, sir," he said, a touch of pedantry in his tone. "The nomads have very little sense of physical territory, but a highly developed sense of the proprieties of their tribal hierarchies and allegiances. No Clan leader is likely to take orders from another Clan leader."

The warrant officer paused to consult a compboard note. "Apparently what we have here is a special exception. This Choor! seems to have been virtually orphaned when his Clan was ambushed by raiders—it had already fallen on hard times, and when bigger neighbors pounced on them they couldn't escape. A few survivors, including Choor!, but no more."

"So?" Hawley was getting impatient with the man's slow, deliberate presentation. "Where is this going?"

Fraser took over. "From what we've learned, sir, Choor! hooked up with another tribe. They do that, sometimes, but they're always regarded as outsiders. It's rare for a nomad tribe to fully adopt a stranger. Unfortunately for us, this Choor! is some kind of military genius. Literally, even discounting a lot of what our natives fed us as the beginnings of a cult-legend, this guy revolutionized the way his new friends fought. They started coordinating their actions and using real tactics—

the stuff we've seen in action—and that meant they could score big on their rivals."

Hawley suddenly understood. "Genghis Khan," he said aloud. "A goddamned Genghis Khan!"

Fraser nodded, clearly appreciating the comparison. "Yes, sir. Choor! seems to have discovered the same scheme Genghis Khan used with the Mongols. When he beats a tribe, they have the choice between joining up or getting squeezed out entirely."

"And they'll take his orders?"

"His *advice*, more like it," Fraser said. "In theory, he's still just a poor orphan boy without a tribe ... but the chiefs and warlords in the coalition all regard him as a trusted advisor. As long as he keeps on winning, they keep getting all the benefits of their new empire. Fewer disputes, less competition, a genuine chance to challenge the city-dwellers ..."

"And apparently, some big-time friends running guns and other high-tech gear in," Hawley added. "How much of this comes from Choor!, and how much from our unknown troublemakers?"

"Hard to say," Fraser said. "What we've learned comes from three nomads out of our auxiliaries, two of them refugees from tribes that ran away instead of knuckling under to the coalition, and the other one an ex-merchant repeating market-place gossip. There's no hint of any outsiders involved, but it's possible that this Choor! has been fed all of his 'innovations' from the word go." He shrugged. "If the Semti are involved, I'd say that's what happened. You know how they like to guide things from the shadows. But until we have more proof, I wouldn't make any definite judgments."

"Doesn't matter much in any case," Hawley said. "Either way, we've got a warlord running a coalition of tribes and getting technical help from the outside." He paused, thinking hard. "But it does give us an angle. Choor! has to keep winning to keep his hold over the Clans. Once they start figuring he's lost his touch, his advice means nothing and he loses his whole power base."

"Right," Fraser nodded. "They've already had a couple of failures ... which means that Choor! is further out on a limb than ever."

"So if we can just hold out...."

"Easier said than done, sir," Fraser said. "When he hits us again, he won't be fooling around. This guy is good, Captain, and you can bet he'll take stock of previous failures and apply what we've taught him."

"You've got a knack for turning good news inside out, son," Hawley said with a dry, humorless chuckle.

"There's something else to consider, sir. Risky, but worth aiming for."

"And that is?"

"Friend Choorl really is the indispensable man where the nomads are concerned. All we need is a crack at him, and we've got a shot at breaking the coalition for good."

Hawley allowed himself a frown. "How do we spot him? Is he even going to hazard himself?"

"I don't know, sir," Fraser admitted. "But at least we've got a couple of angles to work on now. That puts us a couple of moves further ahead than we were this morning."

"Yeah." Hawley looked across the office at the painting that depicted the Fourth Foreign Legion's last stand on Devereaux. "All we have to do is avoid pulling a Devereaux until we can exploit them."

CHAPTER FIFTEEN

Heroes of Camerone and model brothers, Sleep in your tombs of peace.

—From "Le Boudin," official marching song of the French Foreign Legion

By the standard calendar, today is the thirtieth of April. Today is Legionnaires' Day." Gunnery Sergeant Trent paused, surveying the upturned faces in the compound. It seemed odd to be making this address in a darkness relieved only by the glare of the floodlights, but it was 0800 by Legion timekeeping, despite the fact that the sun had gone down four hours ago and wouldn't rise again for nearly twenty more. Except for the duty section manning the walls, a few of the more serious cases on the injured list, and of course the civilians, the entire garrison was formed up in the open area below the headquarters building, turned out in full dress uniforms and white kepis. It made him feel good, like a renewal of his faith in the Legion and everything it stood for, to see those ordered ranks taking part in the annual ceremony that was at the very core of the unit's tradition.

He cleared his throat and continued. "One hundred and nineteen years ago today, in a cave in the highlands overlooking the Great Desert on Devereaux, Commandant Thomas Hunter and seventy-eight survivors from the Fourth Foreign Legion made the decision to attack the Semti garrison at Villastre. This was the culmination of the eight-month resistance to the Semti invasion, which had destroyed the rest of the Legion as a fighting force. The Semti Conclave's Ubrenfar and Gwyrran military forces on Devereaux at that time numbered in excess of sixty thousand, and the garrison at Viliastre alone was known to be nine thousand strong.

"The Legion's resistance had already bogged down the Semti offensive into Terran space, buying months of valuable time. With the legionnaires so badly outnumbered, Hunter and his men might have considered surrender, or they might have remained in hiding out of reach of enemy forces until help arrived. Instead Commandant Hunter organized a final raid on the port control facilities at Viliastre. The choice of the thirtieth of April was a deliberate one, for it marked the anniversary of the heroic stand by the First Legion on Terra at the village of Camerone. That happened nearly a thousand years ago, before the discovery of star-flight.

"Hunter and his men boarded several VTOL transports and flew in low, under the Semti sensor umbrella, while their orbital watch was below the horizon. They caught the garrison at Viliastre completely by surprise and destroyed the port control facilities and several warehouses loaded with the plunder of Devereaux. In the fighting Hunter and forty-one of his troops were killed. Lieutenant Eric Kessel took command of the thirty-six survivors as an Ubrenfar rapid-response unit deployed near the port.

"After an hour of sniping and two enemy assaults, the Legion force had been reduced to twelve men under the command of Chief-Sergeant Guy Marchand. The Semti governor and the leader of the Ubrenfars sent a demand to the legionnaires offering safe-conduct if they would surrender, but Marchand turned the envoys away. One hour later he and his men charged the Ubrenfar lines. Two men survived the fighting and were taken prisoner. The rest died in the service of the Legion."

Trent paused. "Their final gesture caused the Semti to shut down Devereaux as a supply port for another two months, and resulted in another ten thousand troops being added to their garrison against the chance that more legionnaires might have been lurking in the hills. But there were no more. Hunter and his seventy-eight were the last. By their stand, the last unit of the Fourth Foreign Legion may have saved Terra at a critical juncture of the Semti War. More important, though, they reconfirmed the lessons of Camerone and set an example for all their successors in the Legion to follow."

There was a stir among the men. Trent knew what they were thinking. On this Legionnaires' Day these men knew they could be facing the same kind of odds as the defenders of Devereaux ... or of Camerone. But Trent stuck with the traditional close to the speech. "I don't know if any of you apes will ever really get what it's all about. But maybe, just maybe, one of you might understand Devereaux someday." He paused again, then went on in a brisker, more authoritative tone. "All personnel will draw an extra ration of wine tonight to toast the heroes of Camerone and Devereaux. Due to the nature of the threat to this garrison, Captain Hawley has been forced to suspend the usual celebrations." There was a groan at that. Usually Legionnaires' Day was treated as a three-day holiday. "Duty rosters are posted in the computer files. Don't get so busy remembering the past that you forget the present. Now ... dismissed."

He turned and saluted smartly to the knot of officers standing nearby on the balcony that was serving as a reviewing stand. Captain Hawley returned the gesture with stiff formality.

Devereaux and Camerone ... When the Fifth Foreign Legion was formed in the wake of the destruction of Hunter's unit, the two names became the core of the fledgling organization's mystique. "To do a Devereaux" was to face enormous odds with no hope of success, only the intention of upholding the Legion's honor.

If they did a Devereaux here, on Polypheme, it wouldn't have the same value as that stand by Hunter's troops. The wogs wouldn't go on to threaten the whole human sphere, and stopping them at the cost of the entire unit wouldn't be hailed as one of the great military victories of history.

But the Legion would know ... and remember.

*　*　*

Leonid Narmonov leaned on the parapet and stared out into the darkness. It was approaching high tide, and that meant the danger from the nomads was reaching its peak. They could swim right to the walls, the way they'd done in the first assault.

They'd have a harder time launching a surprise attack now, though. A full platoon—six lances—was deployed along the wall at all times, with the others ready to provide backup at short notice. There were nomad auxiliaries patrolling the waters outside the Sandcastle when the tides were in, and a Sandray or Sabertooth when the waters receded. And today Lieutenant DuValier had been supervising some electronics technicians, Legion and civilian, in fitting sonar transducers around the outer perimeter. After the next low tide gave them a chance to finish, the Sandcastle would have a full set of underwater sensors that would warn of any approach.

So it's wine all around for these fine gentlemen, As I sing the refrain of these heroes again, The seventy-nine who died long ago, But live on in our memory of Devereaux!

Narmonov left the parapet to walk toward the source of the singing, a small knot of legionnaires clustered around a dim camp light. He recognized Haddad and Kelso from the Recon Lance, sitting together with a bearded sapper and a soldier whose collar tabs marked her as a Bravo Company medic. Kelso had a musynther, set now to reproduce a guitar, and played it with the same skill he showed lining up a laser shot.

Haddad looked up at his approach. "Ten-hut!" he said.

"As you were," he replied quickly.

The corporal sat down and produced a canteen. "Join us in the Legionnaires' Toast, Mr. Narmonov?" he asked.

Narmonov accepted it and drank to the heroes of Devereaux and Camerone. Then he paused, and instead of returning the canteen he held it up. "Let's drink another one to Sergeant Carstairs and the other good lads we've lost," he said quietly. "They kept the faith with the ones who made the Last March before."

The others drank with him. He saw the pride on the faces of Haddad and Kelso, both obviously pleased with the way their subaltern thought of his people. He thought it was easy to win the loyalty of these soldiers. And once earned, that loyalty would make them follow a man to Hell and back.

Something splashed in the distance, and searchlights swung to scan the water.

Narmonov handed the canteen back and hurried toward the nearest guard post. The moment of rapport was broken.

* * *

Oomour-the-Lost knew fear; the same fear that had gripped him the day the Clan of the Seacliffs had been hunted down and destroyed by the Clans United. He had been separated from the others that day, too far away to come to their aid in time, though the death agonies of his people had echoed clearly through the sea.

Then the Voice of the Clan, the repetitive signals that identified them over vast distances and provided a sense of identity even to those who foraged far from the Clan, ceased. Oomour had reached the scene of the last battle to find the attackers gone; his clanmates dead and stripped of the tribal property, the young vanished. His whole life had gone with the Clan, leaving him a husk, empty, useless.

No one had really believed that Choor! would follow through with his threat to exterminate any Clan that resisted him. But the massacre had been Choor!'s work. He'd seen bodies he knew belonged to tribes in the Clans United.

Another Clan, the Far-Wave-Hunters, had taken him in for a time. Not as a part of the Clan, of course, but they had treated him well enough and given him the chance to join their trading expeditions among the land-dwellers.

Then Choor! had come again, to demand the Far-Wave-Hunters join his Clans United. The Clan-Warlord had talked of fighting, the Clan-Chief of moving somewhere out of reach of Choor! and his allies. All the same discussions the Clan of the Seacliffs had held....

And Oomour had simply fled, too much afraid of seeing his new friends slaughtered as his old brothers had been. He'd fled to Ourgh, lived for a time as a beggar, then joined the Strangers-From-The-Skies to be a part of their "Legion."

Now he swam the long circuit outside the walls of their Built-Reef, a scout for the Legion-Clan, watching for signs that Choor! would attack.

He was afraid, and had to fight the urge to flee once again. Where could he swim, though, that Choor! and his Clans would not someday catch up?

Oomour started toward the surface, distracted by his thoughts. He never saw the looming figure waiting behind and above him, a figure who lashed out savagely with a nomad spear.

Pain lanced through Oomour's side, biting, searing.

Then there was nothing.

*　*　*

Narmonov ran to the watch post as a legionnaire pointed and shouted. "Something moving down there!"

Another soldier raised his FEK, but Narmonov knocked it aside. "Hold your fire, dammit!" he said sharply. "That might be one of our wogs down there!"

Lights knifed through the darkness, probing the waves. Dropping his faceplate and setting it on infrared vision, the subaltern scanned the area. Nothing … Nothing …

Something warmer than the water bobbed to the surface, a fuzzy bright patch on his display. Narmonov switched quickly to LI and the image shifted, becoming clearer, plainer. A native, floating face down, either unconscious or dead. He recognized the tattoos on the nomad's back. It was one of the auxiliaries … Oomour, that was the name.

Blood stained the water around the unmoving form.

"Send one of our other wogs out there," Narmonov ordered. "That's one of our scouts."

He caught a movement out of the corner of his eye and swung to face it.

Dark shapes were crawling up the wall of the Sandcastle near the HQ building.

"Sound the alarm!" he shouted, unslinging his FEK. "Get some men to the wall over there!"

*   *   *

"Fire! Pour it on, you sons of strakks!" Trent bellowed the order as he ran, still buckling on a piece of plasteel chest armor. He'd been checking over the next day's duty roster with Sergeant Valko and Legionnaire Garcia in the base's operations center when the klaxon sounded. Now Valko was rousing the off-duty troops while Trent headed for the wall.

The compound was ablaze with light, and searchlight beams were playing across the eastern side of the base as gunners searched for targets. Trent ran past a small, gaunt legionnaire wearing corporal's stripes on his gaudily painted armor. The man was stripping the cover off of an onager that had been rigged on a pintel mount overlooking the ocean. Further on, several Legion riflemen were leaning over the parapet and pumping full autofire into the restless waves below.

Subaltern Narmonov was directing troops nearest the threatened sector. The young Ukrainian looked harassed.

"Gunny!" he shouted as Trent approached. "Glad you're here. Take charge of getting the reinforcements on the line. And try to get our friendly wogs reeled in. We've got at least three out there, and one poor devil who's probably had it." He paused. "I'll be over there," he concluded, with a wave in the direction of the fighting. A few dark nomad shapes were mixed in among the legionnaires flocking to defend the wall, and more were climbing rapidly.

The wogs had chosen a good spot to launch a strike. The walls at that point projected outward at an angle that shielded the attackers from the legionnaires' fire. That allowed the natives to climb virtually unmolested.

So far the troops at the top were holding them, but as more attackers added their weight to the assault the legionnaires would be in trouble.

"Yes, sir," Trent acknowledged the subaltern's order. He doubted if Narmonov heard; the officer was already running for the thick of the fight, shouting encouragement punctuated by fierce oaths in Russian.

A lance from Alpha Company came up the stairs from the center of the compound. It was a heavy-weapons unit, and Trent directed the corporal in charge to deploy around the gatehouse in case of another assault in that sector. "Get those Fafnirs ready, but don't fire them until you get orders … or until the wogs are threatening to overrun you," he finished. "Explosions in the water will screw the wogs up, but some of our scouts are still out there."

"We're on it, Sarge," the corporal told him cheerfully. He was grinning. "Come on, you sandrats, let's bag us some polliwogs!"

"What's the situation here, Sergeant?"

Trent spun as Lieutenant DuValier and Bravo Company's two recon lances appeared, with the unit's junior C^3 technician, Legionnaire Dubcek, bringing up the rear. As usual the Exec was impeccably turned out, managing to make even battledress look elegant and stylish, though he looked tired. "Nomad assault, sir," the sergeant said formally, touching his helmet. "So far it appears confined to Sector One, but I've posted extra men by the gatehouse. I saw Subaltern Bartlow mustering some troops by the main pumping station, too."

DuValier nodded curtly. "I ordered him there. Why aren't you bombing the bastards in the water?"

"Sir our wogs are still out there," Trent responded, spreading his hands. "Mr. Narmonov says he saw one of them either killed or badly wounded, but the rest are unaccounted for."

The lieutenant scowled. "Damn stupid putting them out there," he muttered. "Score another for the boy genius." He seemed to recover himself. "All right, Sergeant. Continue here."

"And you, sir?"

"Since we can't blast them out of the water, I'm going to try something else. What we need is to get a better angle on those damned wogs as they climb. Some troops out there will do the trick." His gesture took in the water beyond the wall.

"That's suicide, sir!" Trent protested. "The wogs'll be all over you. Anyway, by the time you get on your hard-suits...."

"The hell with suits!" the Frenchman snapped. He touched a device hanging from his neck, and Trent realized for the first time that all of them were wearing oxymasks. They were usually used in riot-control situations, but they'd work for a short time underwater. "Come on, you misbegotten misfits! Let's do it!"

They pushed past Trent, heading for the parapet and fitting their masks in place. Dubcek started shedding his C^3 terminal. The computer and communications terminal wouldn't stand much exposure with those corrosive waters below. But that wouldn't stop Dubcek from following DuValier into action.

Trent's eyes followed them. Part of him wanted to stop the lieutenant, while another part wished he were following the man.

Then he turned. "Mr. Wijngaarde!" he shouted, catching sight of the First Platoon CO. "Can I have some riflemen for the walls here? We have to cover Lieutenant DuValier!"

In the back of his mind Trent felt a twinge of regret. It was too bad that Lieutenant DuValier had taken such a dislike to the captain. Fraser and DuValier had a lot in common.

Starting with bravery ...

* * *

Fraser burst into the command center, still cursing the alert that had awakened him from the first good sleep he'd enjoyed in three standard days. *Just when you let your guard down,* he told himself bitterly. *That's when trouble always starts.* He didn't like the coincidence of this attack on the evening of Legionnaires' Day. Had they just been lucky, or had Choor!'s clans learned that a Legion garrison usually declared it a holiday? Extra rations of wine and a wild night of celebrating would have made an attack easy....

Hawley, Garcia, and one of Alpha Company's C^3 technicians were already in the room. The senior captain looked up. "Looks like a commando job, Fraser," he said casually. "They picked a protected approach up the walls, and seem to be confining the attack there."

"Recon drones?" Fraser asked.

"Up and circling, Captain," Garcia told him. "Very little sign of activity. I think that supports Captain Hawley's theory."

"A good move, I'd say," Hawley said approvingly. "Looks a bit like the Imperial French op against the terrorists on Ys. The Ysan Freedom Brigade's garrison didn't have much perimeter security, of course. I'd say we've got a much better position than the YFB … and the wogs aren't anything comparable to the French, no matter how good this Choorl is."

"With all due respect, sir," Fraser said, "I'm afraid this isn't a wargame. We've got a fight on our hands."

Hawley didn't answer. He seemed entranced by the view on the monitor as the recon drone circled beyond the walls.

"What the hell…?" Fraser whispered, as he caught sight of humans in the water.

"Lieutenant DuValier, sir," Garcia broke in quickly. "He's got Pascali's and Braxton's recon lances."

"They're not even in hardsuits!" he said, sitting down beside Garcia. "What the hell are they playing at out there?"

"Sergeant Trent says they're trying to clear the attackers off the wall. He's deployed riflemen to cover them from the nomads."

Fraser looked away. It was a good plan, but damned risky. If nothing else, those men would be sick by the time they were fished out of the sea. Polypheme's oceans weren't quite lethal to unprotected humans, but even short-term exposure caused some nasty allergic reactions.

That was assuming the wogs didn't get them first.

"What reserves do we have left?" he asked.

The Alpha Company technician—Fraser vaguely remembered that his name was Jurgensen—checked a computer display. "Sergeant Reynolds, sir. First Platoon Alpha. Twenty-one effectives."

"All right. Pass the word for Reynolds and his men to suit up and relieve Lieutenant DuValier out there." Fraser leaned back in the chair and closed his eyes. He only hoped the backup wouldn't come too late.

Chapter Sixteen

—General Pierre Koenig,
during the siege of Bir Hakeir,
French Foreign Legion, 1942

The water stung DuValier's face and hands, and the FEK slung across his back felt heavier than the four kilograms claimed in the technical stats, but he ignored the discomfort as he pushed away from the Sandcastle's wall and fell into a slow, steady breaststroke. Behind him the rest of the legionnaires kept pace.

On the wall behind them DuValier could hear FEKs whining, laying down covering fire. That must have been Trent's work. The Gunnery Sergeant was a good man, except for his obvious attachment to Colin Fraser.

Or was that just further proof that Fraser wasn't as bad as he'd first thought?

DuValier thrust the question from his mind. What mattered now was getting men in position to clear those walls and keep them cleared. Fraser could wait.

Stopping and treading water, DuValier signaled for a halt. "Pascali, keep an eye out for bad guys," he said. The oxymask made it hard to talk clearly, but Corporal Pascali nodded and signaled her lance to disperse in a loose perimeter. "Braxton, your people concentrate on those wogs." He pointed at the wall, where at least twenty nomads were using their suckerlined limbs to climb toward the parapet.

Braxton kept his head and shoulders out of the water by using powerful kicks, and raised his FEK. As he fired, DuValier turned away to study their surroundings. Were any of the wogs taking an interest in them yet?

From the wall, shouts and screams attested to the deadly effect of the legionnaires' fire. They reminded DuValier of the cries he'd heard that day on Fenris.

It took all of his will to shut the sounds out of his mind.

"Sir!" That was Vaslov Dubcek, touching his arm and pointing to the left. "Over there!"

He followed the gesture and saw the bobbing figure thirty meters away. A wog, apparently unmoving.

Trent had mentioned a wounded or dead scout. DuValier started toward the figure, knowing that the C³ technician was following close behind.

He reached the body and rolled it over. Blood was oozing sluggishly from two stab wounds in the native's chest, but the gills were moving slowly and there was a pulse in the big artery on the front of the throat. DuValier wasn't familiar with wog first aid, and thought it would be wisest not to meddle with what he didn't know. He turned the wounded scout over again to get a better water flow past the gills, then started back toward the Sandcastle.

Something thrashed in the water nearby. He released his burden and turned in time to see a nomad driving a pike through Dubcek's chest. The legionnaire struggled at the end of the lance like a fish on the end of a spear, then went limp.

With a curse DuValier started to fumble for his FEK, then gave it up and drew his PLF rocket pistol instead. The wog wrenched the spear out of the dead C³ tech's body with a deep-throated shout and raised himself halfway out of the water, brandishing the weapon.

DuValier squeezed off a round and threw himself sideways. The spear missed him by inches. He surfaced again, ready to fire, but the wog was drifting now, as helpless as the injured scout.

He dived, squinting through the dark water, searching for fresh signs of pursuit. Something that he felt more than heard made him shake his head. Sounds, but at the very lowest limit of a human's range of hearing. They were nothing like wog speech, but there was some-thing ... *intelligent* about that noise. *Organized.*

He surfaced again beside the floating scout and wiped uselessly at his stinging eyes. Corporal Pascali was swimming toward him, another legionnaire close behind. "They're retreating, sir," she said. "And Captain Fraser's sent some hardsuited troops to take over."

He got a grip on the wounded native and nodded. "Get Dubcek's body," he said tiredly.

But although he was suddenly feeling exhausted from the short but intense clash, Antoine DuValier's mind was still racing, trying to piece together the whirling fragments of a half-formed idea.

*　*　*

"All right, Gunny, what's next?" Fraser asked wearily. The attack had ended less than six hours before, but routine had reasserted itself inside the Sandcastle. The administrative side of running a military unit had never appealed to him, but even in the face of the native threat the work had to go on.

"Four men for company punishment," Gunnery Sergeant Trent said stiffly. "Unfit by reason of intoxication."

Fraser glanced at the four prisoners lined up just outside the office door. They were flanked by a pair of guards from Alpha Company. Antoine DuValier, looking none the worse for his swim the night before, was with them as well, presumably as the officer filing the charges.

Softly, to Trent, Fraser asked, "What's the story, Gunny?"

"They're from Wijngaarde's platoon, skipper," Trent replied in the same quiet tones. "Apparently Legionnaire White, there, had a still set up down in the maintenance tunnels by the pumping station. They decided to celebrate Legionnaires' Day with something stronger than wine, and were passed out cold when the fun and games started last night."

Fraser frowned. There was no rule to prevent legionnaires from drinking, even on duty, but stiff penalties were imposed on men who rendered themselves unfit. Still, in their current situation, he was reluctant to put these four in cells. "Any way we can look the other way on this one, Gunny?" he asked.

The sergeant shook his head. "Lieutenant DuValier found them sleeping it off behind the docking cradle after the battle. He threatened them with cells in front of witnesses."

"Well, let's get to it, then," Fraser said, rubbing the bridge of his nose and wishing he could do something easy, like face another native raid.

The prisoners were brought in, and he went through the formalities of hearing their stories, and DuValier's. When the testimony was over he nodded gravely. "Sounds straightforward enough. One week in cells." Fraser paused. "White, your hobby has endangered the security of this command, so I'm ordering your still dismantled. You'll have an extra week in cells to think about, too."

The legionnaire glared at him. "Nothin' in regs about runnin' a still, sir."

"Ordinarily, I wouldn't care if you were brewing homemade rat poison to drink," Fraser told him bluntly. "But I need men who can see straight and put up a fight. Gunny, see to the punishment." He waved a hand in dismissal.

They started to leave. "A moment, Mr. DuValier," he said to the Exec.

"Sir?" As usual, the Frenchman managed to turn the polite formality into thinly concealed contempt.

Trent closed the door, leaving the two officers alone. "What the hell were you thinking of, Lieutenant?" Fraser asked.

"I don't understand, sir," DuValier said.

"The last thing we need is to throw those men into cells. They might not do us much good when they're drunk, but they don't do us any good when they're locked up, damn it!"

"Then why didn't you let them off?" DuValier challenged. "It's your decision."

"Because, Mr. DuValier, I am obligated to back up my officers even when they pull a damn-fool stunt. You threatened them publicly with punishment, and I had to hand out that punishment or undermine your authority."

"I'm not asking for your support, sir," DuValier said harshly.

Anger welled up inside Fraser. "I've had it with this goddamned posturing, Lieutenant! If you can't start playing on the team, at least quit pulling the other way!"

"At least I don't let my men down," DuValier shot back, flushing. "Not like you did on Fenris!"

Fraser stood up slowly, fighting for control. "What happened on Fenris, and my part in it, doesn't make a strakking bit of difference here,

Lieutenant. Do what you want to after we've got the nomads under control, but until then you can forget about Fenris. It's ancient history, and by God you'll keep it that way! Do you get me, Lieutenant?"

The Exec drew himself up stiffly. "I'll never forget Fenris, Captain," he said slowly. "Never. I lost too many friends there … and too much of myself." He paused. "Am I dismissed?"

Fraser sank back in his chair. He hadn't realized DuValier had been part of the fighting on Fenris. No wonder he'd been so hostile.

But there still wasn't room for a personal vendetta now. "I meant what I said, Lieutenant," he told DuValier quietly. "About the past … and about the present. Every man in this compound is needed if we're going to get off this planet alive." When the other man made no response, Fraser added a curt "Dismissed."

DuValier left the office. A moment later, Gunny Trent returned. "Rough, skipper?"

"Yeah," Fraser thought about Fenris. "Yeah, rough. What else do you have for me, Gunny?"

"Warrant Officer Kelly has some ideas she wants you to look over, skipper," Trent said. "She says she has a way to keep those wog bastards off the walls."

"Send her in," Fraser said, forcing a smile. "If she can do that, I'll put *her* in charge of this circus and go fishing."

* * *

DuValier slammed the door to the Headquarters building behind him and stalked across the compound, seething inside. For once he didn't care how much of his anger showed through.

Damn Fraser! The man was so smug, so superior, with his fatherly pretensions and his sham concern over the men. Fraser hadn't cared about the soldiers on Fenris!

He knew, now, that his first judgment had been right, that the captain really was to blame for everything. What had Fraser done last night during the attack? Nothing. But the man would probably grab the credit when the time came.

DuValier had planned to broach his ideas on the nomad coordination techniques this morning, but it was clearly useless to try now. He'd work out the rest of the puzzle on his own, then present Fraser with the finished product later, when the time was right.

Sergeant Mohammed Qazi, Third Platoon's senior NCO and the noncom in charge of Supply, hurried across the compound to intercept him. "Lieutenant?" he began, saluting.

"What is it, Qazi?" DuValier responded curtly.

The sergeant seemed to recoil from him. "Begging your pardon, Lieutenant, but you wanted to know when the sonar installation was complete. We've got all the transducers in place. I put Legionnaire Sinora in charge of the electronics end of things, since Dubcek bought it." Sinora was Third Platoon's C^3 specialist.

DuValier nodded. "Good job," he said. "How soon until it's online?"

"Sinora said four hours. Less, if he can get some help from the Seafarms technical people."

"You light a fire under the civilians, Qazi," DuValier ordered. "I've got another project I need to get on."

Qazi looked unhappy. "Sir ... C-cubed just called. I've got a meeting with Captain Fraser and Miss Winters—er, Miss Kelly, that is. Supply problems."

"Then tell Bartlow to take care of it!" he flared. "Just get that sonar system up and running!"

DuValier turned away, conscious of Qazi's eyes following him as he headed for the Sandcastle's hospital section.

*　*　*

"The main problem will be jury-rigging the power system. If we can nail that down, I think we'll be home-free."

Fraser nodded as Kelly finished, looking down at the terminal screen on his desk. He couldn't find anything wrong with the technical side of her scheme. If they could make this work ...

"Any opinions, Gunny?" he asked.

Trent spoke up from the other side of the office. "It won't be perfect, skipper. Magrep's been tried for antipersonnel work before, and there are always problems with it. But anything that makes it hard for those bloody wogs to get at us is a good idea."

"That's the way I see it, too," Fraser said. "Thanks, Kelly. That was good work."

She smiled. "Actually, the idea came from one of my sappers—MacAllister."

"Is he back on duty already?"

Kelly nodded. "Yesterday. He says he remembered something similar to this being used during the campaign on Thoth. A mobile column got pinned down by lokes in an open valley, and the CO dismantled the magrep generators and set them up as a perimeter defense." She glanced at Trent. "As you said, Sergeant, some of them got through. But it kept them alive until a relief column reached them."

The intercom on Fraser's desk buzzed. "Sergeant Qazi, sir." Garcia's voice came over the line.

"Send him in," Fraser said.

The dark, hawk-nosed sergeant always managed to make him feel uneasy. Qazi was the kind of NCO who regarded officers as a necessary evil at best, and didn't hesitate to let his feelings be known. Fraser waved him to a seat and started outlining Kelly's scheme. The noncom listened with a solemn expression to the plans for immobilizing the magrep vehicles in the compound and mounting their magnetic-field generators on the outer wall to hamper climbers.

"Have you worked out the spacing you'll need between modules to make this work?" he asked as Fraser finished.

Kelly answered for him. "It's on the computer," she said.

Qazi moved to a terminal and studied the specs. "Legion generators won't be enough," he said at last. "I don't have enough spares, and even ripping the guts out of all our MSVs won't give us enough."

"There's always the Seafarms vehicles," Trent commented. "And whatever spares they have in stock."

"Barnett will scream," Kelly said.

"Let him," Fraser told them. "Sergeant, get together a work party to dismount those modules. Kelly, your sappers can mount them. If you need help from anyone, Legion or civilians, they're yours. Do it."

As they left, Fraser turned back to study the schematics again. He told himself this was the kind of teamwork they needed. Not the kind of infighting DuValier was fostering.

If they could just stand together, they might pull through....

* * *

The wounded scout was awake, but obviously in pain. As DuValier leaned forward trying to catch his low, labored voice, he found time to admire the work Dr. Ramirez had done to patch the native up. The doctor had chipped a study on native medicine when they brought Oomour in, and it looked like regen therapy would have the nomad up and around in a day or two.

Considering how bad those wounds had been, that was getting close to a miracle, even given Commonwealth medical technology.

"The Voice of the Clan ..." the nomad said softly. "The Voice of the Clan you heard ... but ..."

His voice faded away and DuValier leaned forward, alarmed. "But what? Come on, Oomour, explain it to me! Come on!"

An eyestalk swiveled to fix on him. "Not ... the same. Not a Clan Voice...."

Another half hour of patient questioning left the wog exhausted. Ramirez finally administered a sedative and chased DuValier out of the ward, but not before he had the answers he'd been looking for.

He wished he had someone else he could use as a sounding board. Dubcek would have been perfect for that, but now he was dead. It left the Exec feeling very much alone among the legionnaires. They were Fraser's people, and Hawley's, not his own.

The best he could do was locate Warrant Officer Koenig. The Native Affairs specialist was going over the reports from the *Seafarms Cyclops*. He seemed happy to turn off his computer terminal and listen.

At length Koenig nodded. "You may be on to something here, Lieutenant," he said. "The sophonts do indeed have a method of broadcasting what you might call 'territorial signals.' It is a very low frequency sound, quite independent of normal speech. The actual information content it could convey would be quite small, however."

"But with considerable range, correct?" DuValier asked.

"Yes," Koenig confirmed. "Possibly several hundred kilometers. Before Mankind developed engine-propelled ships on Terra, whales could communicate across oceanic distances using much the same method. Very likely it was the disruption caused by these new sounds which contributed to the decline and extinction of the whale population."

"So the wogs send out signals that identify them by Clan."

"Yes," the specialist said again. "Members of the clan can track the main body as they forage, and other clans are warned away from waters a given clan is exploiting." He checked a computer reference. "I believe they also use these same sounds to herd the presentient juveniles."

DuValier nodded. "Now, the big question. You say the information content is low. Could these messages be made to transmit enough information to coordinate a battle? Last night I heard something that might have been one of these signals, but one of our wog scouts says that what he heard wasn't anything like a recognized Clan Voice. Just after I heard it, the natives retreated."

"The missing link in how they're coordinating their activities, then. Yes." Koenig looked thoughtful. "If they'd prearranged it ..."

"What?"

"A code. As long as they have a prearranged set of signals, they could handle a variety of evolutions with a relatively limited 'alphabet.' The British Navy in the Age of Sail could send dozens of specific orders, even before they developed a true alpha-numeric signaling system. It was rigid, but an intelligent officer could use it quite ingeniously when the need arose."

"We're dealing with a very intelligent officer in this Choorl," DuValier said. "But now that we know how he's giving his subordinates their orders...."

Koenig grinned. "We can make his life miserable."

"Exactly," DuValier said.

He wondered what Fraser's reaction would be when he discovered it was his despised Exec who had ended the native threat.

* * *

Low tide.

It left the open ground beyond the Sandcastle's dun-colored walls uncovered, a muddy plain dotted with tidal pools and the flotsam and jetsam left behind by the receding waters. From the parapet above the gatehouse, Colin Fraser surveyed the flat terrain through the image-intensifier of his battle helmet.

The handful of natives were plainly nomads, adorned only by harnesses and tattoos and carrying a variety of weapons. They walked toward the base with no sign of fear, secure under the blue-green banner that fluttered in the wind above them.

His chipped knowledge of nomad customs told Fraser that they were envoys. The Clans regarded land as neutral ground, ideal for holding parleys between rival parties—another reason for their hostility toward their land-dwelling cousins, no doubt, who claimed to own the tracts of land that had been ownerless in nomad eyes for aeons.

A red banner would have signaled an intent to negotiate a blood-feud; yellow would have summoned all comers to trade. Blue-green, the color of the oceans, was the color of a truce between warring clans.

Beside him Trent had his FEK out. "It could still be a trick, skipper," he said quietly. "Remember, they lump us with the city people, and I've heard of cases where nomads broke a parley to attack land-dwellers. They don't regard them as real people."

"Just the kind of trick friend Choor! would try, too," Fraser said. "He may figure that our leadership is as vulnerable as his."

"Not if his intel is as good as it's been so far. But anything that would upset morale would be a good move. After last night …"

"He needs a victory now," Fraser finished. "By whatever means he can get it. All right, Gunny, we'll talk to them from here."

They waited for the natives to advance to within earshot. "Clansmen!" Fraser said at last, through an amplifier mike hooked up to Legionnaire Garcia's C^3 pack. "You seek a parley? State your mission."

Nomads exchanged looks as if taken aback by having to talk from a distance. Then one of them responded.

"In the name of the Clans United," he began, proceeding through a litany of eighteen individual nomad tribes before reaching the heart of the message. "In the name of these, who are the voice of the Free Swimmers, the Terrans who have intruded into our world are called upon to surrender themselves or face death. We are many times your numbers, Terrans, and we swim free while you crouch within your stone reef. We pledge that you shall be allowed to leave our world in peace should you surrender, but should you choose to resist further the Clans United shall not rest until the last of your people has been killed."

Fraser switched off the amplifier. "They learn fast," he commented. "But I doubt that whoever's been feeding them this stuff is really serious about letting us go."

"Yeah," Trent agreed. "This isn't quite the same thing as taking in a recalcitrant tribe and turning it into part of the organization."

He nodded to Garcia and spoke into the mike again. "No surrender," he said shortly. "You'll have to come in here and dig us out."

He turned away from the parapet. There would be no turning back from here.

Chapter Seventeen

Getting bounced from the Legion? They don't bounce people from Hell.

—attributed to an unknown legionnaire of the French Foreign
Legion

The nomad scout was better after more regen therapy, and DuValier found him sitting up and looking alert, even restless. Aside from the steridressings on his chest and side, Oomour looked almost fully recovered.

"You I thank for bringing me back?" the scout asked DuValier as the lieutenant entered the ward.

He nodded, then remembered that among the natives it was a side-to-side movement that indicated assent. "I found you," he told Oomour. "It was luck, mostly."

"Then to you my life I owe," the nomad said. "To you a debt I would repay."

DuValier shrugged. "We don't abandon our own," he told the wog, wondering if the native would understand.

"Yes … yes, your Clan is mine now." Oomour seemed more grateful at being accepted as part of the Legion than at having his life saved.

"Well, your Clan is going to need you, Oomour," DuValier said. "When Dr. Ramirez discharges you tomorrow, see me. I want you to help me with a little project I have in mind."

"Project?"

He smiled. "Yeah. I'm going to make a Voice for the Legion Clan that'll give Choor!'s bastards a headache."

A footfall behind him made DuValier turn. Edward Barnett was standing just inside the door. "Lieutenant, I need to see you," the civilian said. He shot a look of distaste at Oomour. "When you're done here."

DuValier finished with the native quickly and joined Barnett. The civilian wouldn't speak until they were out of the medical center and out in the open. When he finally did talk, it was in hushed, conspiratorial tones.

"Lieutenant, you've struck me as the only voice of reason in this entire unit," Barnett began. "Between that incompetent Hawley and your boss Fraser, they've flouted everything Seafarms has tried to do on this planet, damn it, and neither of them seems to realize the damage they've done."

DuValier studied the civilian with distaste. He knew how Barnett felt about the Legion. He wouldn't be here, talking to a Legion officer, without some ulterior motive. "It isn't for me to criticize my superiors," he said guardedly. *Not to the likes of you*, he added to himself.

"You heard about the nomad peace offer yesterday, didn't you?"

"Yeah. A sham."

"So your Captain Fraser claims. But what if it isn't? The nomads may be giving us a way out. With negotiation, Seafarms might even find a way to deal with this warlord, Choor! or whatever his name is. But Fraser won't even think of exploring a peaceful settlement, and of course Hawley backs him up."

"The nomads, by themselves, could be offering terms, Citizen. But whoever's backing them, human or ale, knows enough about the Commonwealth to know Terra won't back down that easily. I can't see them letting the wogs arrange a peace that's liable to break down in a few months anyway. They'll want a solid victory, something to prove this place is too expensive to try and civilize."

"You seem to forget, Lieutenant, that Seafarms is the government here. As things are going now we'll probably drop the Cyclops Project and cut our losses. We can give these people exactly what they want, if that's what it takes, without any more loss of life. We can get out of this without any more battles, man. But Fraser seems determined to sit tight and take the whole planet on if he has to. And all that's going to do is get a lot of good people killed. Like he did on Fenris. You know about that, don't you?"

DuValier nodded tightly. "I ... know." He thought about what Barnett had said. It seemed reasonable enough. What did they have to lose by negotiations?

Nothing but pride. Rumor had it that Fraser was likely to be investtigated by the Warwick Commission, and giving in to the locals would be damning enough to get him into hot water even Warwick's well-connected enemies couldn't rescue the captain from. He might just take the whole unit down, if the alternative was watching his career be ruined. Like Hawley's.

"I can encourage them to take another look at negotiations, Citizen," he said carefully. "But beyond that ..."

"Beyond that, there's something else to be concerned about," Barnett broke in. "Fraser and his girlfriend have cooked up some scheme to mount magrep generators on the walls. To pull it off, he wants to rip them out of Seafarms vehicles!"

"Planning a trip, Citizen?"

Barnett snorted. "Look, quite aside from the fact that these are company assets that I don't want to see destroyed, we don't know that we won't be needing those vehicles again. What if we do strike a deal with Choor!? Hell, what if the natives pound us so bad here that we have to run for it? We could be needing those vehicles, damn it, but Fraser plans on stripping all of them down."

DuValier studied him again. It was clear that Barnett had his own reasons for preserving those vehicles intact. Was it worth it to help him?

They didn't really need the generators. As soon as he finished his work with Oomour they'd have a weapon that would be just as effective, maybe more so. And if Barnett was right about negotiating their way out....

A friend at Seafarms was a friend inside Reynier Industries, and that wasn't a bad thing for a legionnaire to have. If getting Fraser to back down on the magrep generator idea would cement an alliance with Barnett, it might be worth his while to get involved.

"Just what do you want me to do?" he asked slowly.

"Why, I thought that was obvious," Barnett said. "Relieve Hawley and Fraser of their commands, and take charge of the garrison yourself."

*　*　*

"Tide'll be coming in soon," Fraser said, glancing at the display of his wristpiece computer to confirm the tide table data. "Is that going to interfere with your work?"

Beside him Kelly was crouched by the parapet, checking a power lead. "Not unless the nomads attack again when the water's high," she said. "I'm more concerned about getting the magrep generators out of Seafarms."

"Trouble?"

"They said they'd take care of it, but I think Barnett told them to pull a go-slow. MacAllister said that their people were evasive this morning when he asked them when they'd have some generators for us."

"I'm getting damn tired of hearing about trouble with Seafarms," Fraser said. "If I get any more of this nonsense I'll throw Barnett into cells. And any of his little helpers who want to back him up."

"Careful, Col," she said quietly, hooking her circuit-tester to another lead. "Every time you back that bastard into a corner you run the risk of having him bring you up on charges. You know Warwick's just waiting for an excuse like that."

"Yeah. But if it's a choice between my career and our chances of getting out of here alive …"

"Let's try to pull off both," Kelly said with a grin. "Come on, Col. If you get kicked out of the Legion now, where will that leave me? I didn't sign on for the glamour, you know."

He wondered if she was serious. Sometimes she seemed to want nothing more than friendship, but there were other times....

Fraser wasn't about to complicate either of their lives further by pursuing that line of thought. Instead he tried to match her light tone. "Don't worry. No one's figured out a way to drop someone from the Legion yet. There's nothing lower on the social scale to drop *to*. And I could always sign on as an enlisted man if they don't want me as an officer."

She laughed. "I'd love to see Sergeant Trent cuffing you on the ear and calling you 'nube.'"

"So would he." Fraser paused. "Seriously, though, I'd better go see what Seafarms is doing. If we can get those generators in place, I think we'll even be able to hold a major assault. And with *Cyclops* due back here in another couple of days, that'll finally put time on our side."

Seafarms had taken over a disused part of the base. With more than eight hundred civilians from Ourgh now installed inside the Sandcastle, living quarters were cramped and the workshops and offices were ne-cessarily squeezed for space, but that hadn't stopped Barnett from insisting on maintaining services that duplicated some of what the Legion was responsible for, like the motor pool.

If only Sigrid Jens had lived....

He cut across the center of the Sandcastle on his way to the Seafarms motor pool. A block of legionnaires from Alpha Company was drilling on open ground below the Ops center, supervised by Gunny Valko and Subaltern Narmonov. Some Bravos from Bartlow's platoon were working with Kelly's sappers, using the makeshift magrep barge to haul the first of the generators cannibalized from Legion vehicles toward the wall near the gatehouse. There was also a gang of Seafarms people, some armed, but most of them not, checking over the struts of the cradle that would support *Seafarms Cyclops* when Watanabe brought her in. Corporal Bashar was piloting a veeter and operating a winch to lift the heavy generators into place on the wall. The corporal gave Fraser something between a wave and a salute as he hovered over the barge.

He was glad to see the work going on. It was a big improvement over the way things had been before the crisis, when *cafarde* had been threatening to ruin them all. But it was a damned high price to pay to relieve a little boredom.

Fraser stopped as he saw Barnett crossing the compound from the direction of the Seafarms section. Several armed civilians were with him, almost a bodyguard. Lieutenant DuValier and some legionnaires from Wijngaarde's platoon were with them.

"Is there some kind of trouble here, Lieutenant?" he asked as the party approached. Had Barnett caused some kind of trouble?

Something wasn't right....

"Captain Fraser," DuValier said formally. "I regret to inform you that I am relieving you of your command of Bravo Company under Article Two-oh-seven of Colonial Army Regulations. I hope it will not be necessary to place you under arrest."

"What the hell are you talking about, Lieutenant?" Fraser asked, stunned by the flat, emotionless statement. DuValier didn't sound triumphant, or defiant, or even concerned. Just cold and aloof, as always. "Two-oh-seven is relief by reason of incapacity...."

"And in my judgment, sir, your recent decisions have been proof of mental incapacity," DuValier shot back. "Perhaps the strain of having to assume so many of Captain Hawley's duties in addition to your own ..."

"It'll never stick, man!" Fraser insisted. "A junior officer can't relieve a superior when someone senior to both is available. You have to go through channels...."

"Face it, Fraser," Barnett said harshly. "Hawley is even more obviously incompetent than you are. As a matter of fact, it's your coddling of the old fool that's going to be the basis of Mr. DuValier's case when it comes up."

Fraser looked from one to the other, incredulous. Behind them, their men were a study in contrasts, the civilians grinning, the legionnaires more subdued. But they seemed ready to obey DuValier. The Legion expected obedience to authority, and in a case like this they'd obey DuValier as long as he kept quoting regulations.

If any of them had been Hanuman vets ... But they were all from First Platoon, Wijngaarde's. They were almost all new men, legionnaires he didn't know very well. DuValier was right in one respect. He'd been so busy trying to help Hawley do his job that he'd neglected Bravo Company. He didn't even know these men by name.

"This is a mutiny, Mr. DuValier," he said, trying to buy time. What could he do? "You won't succeed."

"That's enough," Barnett said. He gestured to one of his Seafarms bodyguards. "Disarm him. We'll take care of Hawley next."

He thought of fighting, but rejected it. All he'd do by fighting was give DuValier and Barnett an excuse to kill him. They would be happiest if he did ... Fraser, alive, was dangerous to their cause, at least until they were in full control. But they'd have to obey the legalities if they wanted to keep the support of the legionnaires.

He raised his hands slowly and allowed the civilian to unbuckle his gun belt. For now, he'd have to play along. There were people in the Sandcastle who knew him, from Hawley and Kelly and Sergeant Trent down to soldiers like Bashar or Garcia. Barnett and DuValier would find it hard to win over or arrest all of them....

* * *

Bashar cut back on the power and held the veeter in place as the work party below wrestled with the harness on the fourth of the mag-rep generators. It was one of the units out of the *Angel II*, and the thought made him wince. He hoped they'd be able to put the old girl back together again after the siege was over.

He glanced around the compound to take his mind off the *Angel*. Captain Fraser was talking to a cluster of civilians and legionnaires. He thought the captain had come a long way since Hanuman. From first to last he'd taken charge here at the Sandcastle, and so far they'd stopped the wogs cold.

Fraser raised his hands, and a civilian was advancing to take his gun. What...?

"Allah!" he said aloud. "MacAllister, look over there. Four o'clock."

Legionnaire MacAllister from the sapper platoon was riding in the veeter's front seat today, helping him with the placement of the generators. The old veteran's head swiveled, and Bashar heard a string of low-voiced oaths in his headphones. "What the hell are those de'ils doing?"

"I don't know," Bashar said. "But I don't like it."

He tapped his radio mike thoughtfully. This looked like a mutiny. Who could he call? Who could he trust?

Karatsolis was back at the motor pool. Like all Transport specialists the Greek was cross-trained as a general mechanic, and he'd been drafted into the party that was dismounting generators from the other vehicles. He felt the same way about Captain Fraser as Bashar did.

Bashar changed radio channels. "Repbay, repbay, this is Veeter One."

"Repbay," the bored voice of Sergeant Franz replied. "What's the problem, Bashar? The little bitch acting up on you?"

"Naw ..." He paused, thinking fast. "Look, Sarge, can you put Spear on for me? I forgot my strakking wristpiece, and I can't remember what I did with it. Spear'll know where I had it last."

"And you can't wait until you're off-duty?" Franz complained.

"Ah, hell, Sarge, give me some boost here. My dad gave me that 'piece." That was a lie, but Franz didn't know it. "And you know those thieving civilians'd just love to rip one of us off."

There was a long pause. Then Karatsolis came on the line. "What've you got, Bashar?" he asked. His voice was flat, brooding.

"I've got a Veitch problem up here," he said, using the personal code that went back to their days in training on Devereaux. Veitch had been the worst of the NCOs in their recruit unit, a sadist and a bully who liked to uncover secrets his men wanted left hidden. Ever since those days, the name had been their way of hinting that private information was coming.

There was another pause before Karatsolis answered. "I'm on headphones. What's going on?"

Bashar explained the situation. "It looks like Lieutenant DuValier and that strakk Barnett," he finished up. "We've got to do something, Spear."

"I'll get Gunny," Karatsolis replied, considerably more animated than before. "He'll know what to do."

MacAllister was listening to the exchange. "Pass the word to Warrant Kelly, too," he suggested. "I dinna think she will stand for this."

Bashar grinned. "You're right about that. I'll keep an eye on them, Spear. Let me know what's going down."

Karatsolis didn't even bother to sign off.

*　*　*

The civilian guards closed in around Fraser at Barnett's command, and the little procession headed for the Ops center. As they passed the ship cradle the Seafarms executive rounded up the workers there and added them to his force. Fraser estimated forty of them, perhaps three-quarters with outdated FEKs—the Mark-24 model that lacked the grenade launcher and had been obsolete when Hunter led his men into battle on Devereaux—plus ten legionnaires and DuValier. Substantial odds ... especially as long as the Legion loyalists they met weren't prepared for an encounter.

Perhaps he should have put up a fight after all. At least it might have attracted some attention, given Hawley a chance to muster a defense.

As if reading his thoughts, the nearest guard dug his FEK/24 into Fraser's back. "Don't give us any trouble," he hissed. "I don't want to have to kill you, Captain, but I've got my orders."

Fraser nodded, his fists clenching in frustration. He darted glances left and right, trying to size up the situation. There had to be something he could turn to his own advantage in all this.

Narmonov's men were still drilling, apparently oblivious to the mutineers. Or were they in it? No ... neither Narmonov nor Gunny Valko was likely to be involved, and if the mutiny was that well organized the subaltern and the NCO would have been neutralized by now.

He noticed that Bashar's veeter wasn't hovering anymore, and it looked like the generator work party had thinned out. Unless they were just out of sight, blocked from Fraser's angle by the ship cradle and the barge. Wishful thinking ...

"Halt!" The voice that boomed out of the portable amplifier was Trent's. Like the men around him Fraser searched desperately to spot the sergeant, then saw him on the balcony overlooking the compound. Garcia was beside him, along with a pair of soldiers in full armor carrying onagers. Behind them Fraser thought he could see Hawley giving orders to his own C^3 tech. "You people are covered," Trent continued. "Halt, or be fired on!"

There was a moment's hesitation among the mutineers before DuValier pushed his way forward. "Sergeant Trent! I order you to stand down at once!"

Trent drew a pistol. "Release Captain Fraser and disperse," he said, ignoring DuValier.

"Come on, Sergeant," Barnett sneered. He gestured to his men, who had spread out into a loose semicircle. "One volley and you people are dead."

The sergeant shook his head. "Not all of us, Citizen," he corrected.

Loud in the tense silence, dozens of *snick-snicks* were clearly audible. Fraser turned his head. Legionnaires, some of them sappers, were leveling FEKs from behind the shelter of the cradle. And from the other side Narmonov's platoon was moving toward the mutineers with weapons held at the ready.

A third group was trotting from the direction of the motor pool, the big figure of Spiro Karatsolis out in front of them.

"Give it up, Barnett," Trent continued, still ignoring DuValier entirely. "I'd rather save our ammo for the wogs, but if you force us to we'll wipe your little revolution out. I mean it."

"Damn it, Sergeant," the lieutenant said, sounding desperate. "Seafarms can negotiate with the wogs! Fraser and Hawley just want a heroic stand. They don't care what happens to us!"

Fraser shoved past two of the civilian guards into the open. He didn't have an amplifier, but he raised his voice enough so that everyone would hear him.

"Listen to me! It's true the wogs are making an offer to let us surrender, but we rejected it because we know they will not honor any agreement that leaves us alive! You've seen how they fight, how they think. They don't let threats to their tribes survive. If these nomads can't absorb an enemy, they crush him. There aren't any other alternatives!"

He paused. "Maybe you don't believe that. It's true enough, but that doesn't mean you'll buy it. Well, buy this." Fraser's gesture encompassed the mutineers. "These men think they'll get off this planet safely if they put Captain Hawley and myself out of the way and negotiate. Maybe they will, too. But anyone who supports this mutiny had better be ready to spend the rest of his life a long way outside the Commonwealth. The Colonial Army doesn't like mutineers, you know."

There were a few laughs among the loyalists. A stir went through the civilians.

"Think about what mutiny means," Fraser went on. He had every man's attention now. "After the garrison on Talbot's Rock mutinied, the Commonwealth went on tracking them down for ten years. Now normally you could hide out by joining the Foreign Legion. We take care of our own.... But of course since the mutiny was in the Legion, I guess that would be hard to manage, wouldn't it?"

More laughs. Barnett raised his voice, trying to break the spell. "Nonsense! This isn't a mutiny. You're all working for Seafarms! If there's a mutiny here, it started when my orders were ignored. No one will be prosecuted for helping Lieutenant DuValier's legal relief of two incompetent officers."

"Does anyone want to take that risk?" Fraser asked loudly. "Any legionnaire who mutinies has bought a hot shot for sure. And you civilians are looking at treason charges. All it would take is one man going to HQ and claiming this was an armed uprising."

Kelly appeared on the balcony beside Trent and took the amplifier. "How many of you are going to feel safe after all this?" she chimed in. "Look at the guy beside you. Can you trust him not to turn you in? Can you trust him not to slip a knife between your ribs to keep *you* from turning *him* in? That's the kind of life you can expect if there's a mutiny here!"

"Lay down your weapons now," Fraser ordered. "For God's sake, this thing is almost over! We can hold off those wogs, just as long as we're all fighting on the same side. Every man has a part to play in this, and I need every one of you to make it work. That's how we can beat them, by standing together. By each of us doing what he knows how to do. But if you don't believe what I'm telling you ..." He paused. "Then fire the first shot now and get it over with. Or else get back to work and save the shooting for the wogs!"

There was silence. Then, slowly, the ten legionnaires put down their FEKs. The civilians were a little slower, but, ringed in by armed soldiers, they had no other option.

Fraser let out a sigh. "Karatsolis! Mr. DuValier is relieved of duty immediately. Escort him and Citizen Barnett to cells. The rest of these ... protesters ... may go back to their normal duties."

He turned away, unwilling to let them see his face.

* * *

And Edward Barnett slipped one hand into the secret pocket in his left sleeve, drawing out the tiny rocket pistol he'd used to kill Sigrid Jens. At least he'd have Fraser....

Chapter Eighteen

> —Lt. Colonel Paul Rollet,
> French Foreign Legion, 1917

Karatsolis started forward, his FEK trained on DuValier. The lieutenant would be the more dangerous of the two prisoners, with his Legion training. Now that Barnett's thugs were disarmed, the civilians wouldn't be much of a problem....

"Look out!" Kelly screamed from the balcony. "He's got a gun!"

He caught Barnett's movement out of the corner of his eye and whirled, feeling that everything, himself included, was moving in slow motion. The tiny pistol was coming up in line with Fraser's back....

Karatsolis fired almost by instinct even as someone—was that Trent?—shouted "Don't kill him!" The FEK was set for a three-round burst, but even the short whine of the gauss fields seemed to stretch on forever.

The civilian spun away from the blast, dropping the pistol and clutching at his arm. The high-velocity rounds had torn through flesh, probably shattered the bone, and blood was spurting from the wound. Barnett stared at the arm for a long moment, then collapsed.

"Medic! Medic!" someone shouted. A legionnaire was beside the injured man already, applying emergency first aid. A moment later Legionnaire Delandry pushed through the crowd and joined him.

"Someone get the Doc," Delandry snapped, producing her medkit. "Hurry!"

Karatsolis lowered the FEK. He realized that one of his men already had DuValier covered. Everything had happened so fast that it had hardly registered on him.

Then Fraser was beside him. "Good shooting, Spear," the captain said. "Thanks. If it hadn't been for you …"

He nodded automatically. "Yes, sir. I'll … take charge of the lieutenant for you."

Slinging his FEK, Karatsolis joined the soldiers flanking DuValier. After the tense confrontation with the mutineers, the sudden action had drained him completely.

It took all his willpower to keep from stumbling as he led the detail toward the Legion's cellblock.

*　*　*

"Skipper? I think you'd better see this."

Fraser looked up from his desk at Trent. "What is it, Gunny?" he asked. It was hard even yet to keep his voice level, although more than an hour had passed since the abortive mutiny.

Trent laid a small weapon and another unidentifiable object in front of him. "The pistol's the one our friend Barnett tried to use on you," the sergeant told him. "Narmonov picked it up while they were policing all the other weapons."

Picking up the small pistol, Fraser turned it over in his hands. It had a familiar look to it.…

"Good God!" he said suddenly, as he recognized the workmanship. "This is the same technology as the nomad rocket guns!"

"Right down the line," Trent agreed. "Koenig looked it over and said the same. Barnett got this from the nomads … or from whoever's been supplying them."

Fraser leaned back in his chair, still looking at the pistol. "This isn't an infantry weapon," he said. "It was designed for concealability." He remembered the questions that had crossed his mind during the first meeting in the conference room. "You think Barnett was a spy?"

The sergeant nodded. "I had his quarters and office searched," he said. Trent prodded the other device. "Pascali turned this thing up. Transmitter."

"Pretty lightweight job," Fraser commented. "Not much range...."

"More than you'd think. Koenig says it's a Toel job, and they've got some pretty sophisticated electronics."

"And a technology designed for underwater use, like these guns!" Fraser finished the thought, angry that he hadn't made the connection sooner. "Not to mention a lot of experience dealing with the natives here, to know the best weapons designs to manufacture!"

"That's the way we figure it," Trent said. "The Toels have the biggest stake in all this. If Seafarms fails on Polypheme, the Toels might just pry it loose from the Commonwealth and set up their old operation all over again."

"Pry it loose? Hell, Gunny, if Seafarms backed off of this dump, the politicians would be glad to unload it on the Toels. Especially with a massacred garrison and a lot of nasty hostiles complicating things. The Elders in Ourgh would disown Terra if we were wiped out, and any-body trying to come back here later would have to start from scratch. It all fits."

"Gives us something to go on, at least," Trent said. "I wonder how much Barnett knows about the whole operation...."

"Maybe we can find out," Fraser said. "Have you checked with Ramirez lately on his condition?"

"He'll be all right," the sergeant said with a look of distaste. "A week or so in regen and he'll be ready for a hot shot."

"Good. Tell Garcia to turn over her duties to the other C^3s. I've got some special work for her. We'll get some answers out of Barnett. You can count on it."

"You figure DuValier was in on the whole thing?"

"I don't think so, Gunny," Fraser said slowly. "He had a personal grudge against me, but I think he really thought he was doing the right thing. There were too many ways DuValier could have sab-otaged us. He didn't.... Not until Barnett conned him with this negotiation nonsense."

"I guess you're right. Looks like Barnett was just doing his best to keep Seafarms off-balance while the bad guys did their thing."

"Yeah," Fraser said. He laughed as a thought struck him. "God, he worked so hard to keep us from bringing the civilians in here. He must have had it figured that his friends would stay clear of Ourgh and concentrate on us! No wonder he didn't like the idea of a move!"

Trent nodded gravely. "And when his boss overruled him ..."

"She died, and he started screwing around, keeping his people from cooperating with us. He's probably been passing intel to them ever since he moved in. But I'll bet the surrender bit was his own idea, to get the hell out of here before the nomads hit us."

"If they know our timetable …"

"Then they know we'll have the magrep generators up about the same time *Cyclops* gets back, fifty hours at the outside!" Fraser pounded the desk with a clenched fist. "They'll attack before then, damn it! We'll have to step up everything."

"With Barnett gone, the Seafarms bunch'll cooperate a little better," Trent said. "I'll get their tech people out on the perimeter to help with the generators."

"Good. And while you're at it, find out how many have had some kind of military training and start issuing weapons. And let's have every legionnaire ready. We'll need all the troops we can get."

Trent raised an eyebrow and stroked nervously at the corner of his mustache. "Is that a good idea? We've already had one mutiny…."

"Gunny, the next time Choor! hits us it's going to be with every nomad in his whole army. If the perimeter isn't secure by then, there's no way we can hold them off without some more troops. No way at all. We *have* to trust those people. Either that, or surrender now and let Choor! and his Toel friends win without a fight."

"God help us all," the sergeant said. He headed for the door.

Fraser looked at Barnett's pistol and radio on the desk. "Amen to that," he said softly.

*　*　*

Sparks crackled, and acrid smoke coiled from the makeshift power hookup on the magrep generator. Kelly shouted "Cut it off!" into her throat mike. She started to curse as she knelt by the housing to recheck the leads, then realized the mike was picking that up as well.

As the power cut off, she thought she could hear someone chuckling over the commlink. Kelly ignored it and reconnected the lines. Not for the first time—or the last, she suspected—she found herself wishing that the assortment of magnetic-field generators they were using wasn't quite so assorted. The equipment represented at least twenty different makes and models, some of them fifty years old or more. Some of the Legion vehicles had mounted four different units in the same chassis, many of them obsolete by any sane standards.

Kelly was beginning to believe that the mechanics who kept Legion APCs running were either geniuses or madmen, but she wasn't yet prepared to choose which.

This was a Stellectric Products Mark XVIII, probably off of the FSV Bashar and Karatsolis were so proud of. She'd hooked it up as if it were a Mark XXX, like the last one. No wonder it hadn't been working right!

"Try it again," she said aloud. Power hummed, and the improvised check light came on to indicate that the generator was up and running.

That made exactly half of the generators in place and running now. Fraser wouldn't be happy at the slow pace of the work. Ever since he'd begun to suspect that Barnett had been feeding information to the enemy, Fraser had been determined that the defenses had to be finished as soon as possible—preferably about a week ago. But it was a time-consuming job to install and hook up the magrep modules. At least they were ahead of the schedule Kelly had expected to manage.

As she gathered up her tools and moved down the line to the next unit, Kelly hoped again that they'd be fast enough.

A pair of civilian technicians was working on this one already, but Kelly wasn't planning on taking their work on faith. The mutiny was still too fresh in her mind to let her trust anyone from Seafarms, even though Fraser seemed prepared to do so.

She'd protested when he had briefed her on the situation. "You can't just ignore it, Col," she had said. "Letting everyone go back to work except Barnett and DuValier ... You're asking for more trouble with them, you know."

"I can't lock up eight hundred civilians just because they might sympathize with Barnett," he'd replied wearily. "Or all the legionnaires who might've known and trusted DuValier more than me."

"I'm not saying you should, Col," she had shot back, angry. "But the ones who were with those two bastards in the mutiny ..."

"Not even them," he'd said, looking away. "Those kids from Wijn-gaarde's platoon were just following DuValier's orders. I expect that's true of the Seafarms people as well. Once I can question Barnett I'll know for sure, but until then my main job is to get these boys and girls together. It's got to be a team effort from here on out, Kelly. Because if Seafarms really did decide to take us out and surrender, there's no way we'd stop them. We've less than two hundred legionnaires in this base now. That's the real tip-off that Barnett was improvising all this. If he'd been in a position to expect all of his people to support an uprising, he could have taken over easily, with or without DuValier."

"Yeah … maybe. But—"

"No more arguments, Kelly. Please. Just get those generators up. And pray."

He'd looked so tired, so dispirited … less confident than she'd ever seen him before, even in those rocky first days of the march on Hanuman.

That had been almost eighteen hours ago. Susan Gage and the two gunnery sergeants had been taking charge of the preparations in the fortress since that time, while Fraser, Hawley, and Angela Garcia concentrated on another project in the medical section, working with Dr. Ramirez on something no one was talking about.

Whatever it was, she hoped it would work.

*　*　*

"It's as ready as it's ever going to be, sir."

At Garcia's words Fraser looked up from the computer terminal. "Any problems?" he asked.

"You mean aside from the fact that I've never worked on a setup like this before, don't have all the right gear, and don't really believe in it anyway?" Garcia shrugged and grinned. "Not a one."

He wished he felt like joking about it. Garcia had summed up all the problems with his scheme in a nutshell, but it was their only hope of getting the information they needed.

Fraser looked past her at the two examining tables that had been set up side-by-side in the extra operating theater of the Sandcastle's medical center. The setup looked primitive compared to what he'd seen in service with regular Intelligence units, but it was the best they could improvise under the circumstances.

Most military personnel and Intel operatives were routinely conditioned against chemical methods of persuasion; that was standard procedure. In light of the dangers of modern corporate espionage, a lot of senior executives got similar workovers. Odds were that Barnett wouldn't be broken that way. If Seafarms hadn't seen to it, the Toels— if they were indeed his employers—would surely have done so.

Physical and psychological interrogation techniques would have worked eventually, but they took a long time, and time was something the Terrans didn't have right now.

That left Fraser's idea, unlikely as it was. They'd have to improvise the direct mind-to-mind questioning process that was SOP in Army Intelligence. Both theoretical and practical information were easy to come by in the files of the demi-battalion's master computer, but translating them into working interrogation equipment had taken hours of labor and all of Garcia's ingenuity. And there was still no guarantee they could make it work.

Looking through the glassed-in wall at the triage room where Ramirez was finishing a medical examination of Captain David Hawley, Fraser couldn't help but be pessimistic. Everything, literally, rode on the old man's slender shoulders this time.

At first he'd hoped that they could come up with a usable substitute for the computer implant usually used for this sort of interrogation. Externally worn adhesive chips—adchips—could do many of the same things as computer implants, and certainly the subject in one of these questioning sessions didn't need an implant. But as he'd studied the computer files, Fraser had realized that this was one place where short-cuts weren't going to work.

The interrogator and the computer had to work together on an almost instinctive level when interrogating a subject. Fraser might have been able to do it if they'd rigged up an adchip and given him several months to practice with the computer, but once again there just wasn't time. Only someone who had long experience with brain-computer interfacing could handle the nuances of mind-to-mind interrogation.

That meant there was only one candidate for the job in the Sandcastle, Captain David Hawley.

But it took a strong mind to handle the pressures of literally ripping information out of another man's memories—strong, and agile as well. Could Hawley break Edward Barnett? Or had he been retreating from reality, avoiding responsibility, for too long to be able to get the job done?

He cut the terminal, rose, and crossed to the door. Sticking his head into the triage room, he asked, "What's the verdict, Doctor?"

Ramirez glanced down at his compboard. "Physically, I see no prob-lems," he said slowly. "Captain Hawley is in good condition. But this is certainly ... unfamiliar work. Lacking formal training or experience in interrogation proceedings, I would say ten-minute sessions, at least until we see how the captain will hold up under the strain."

Hawley finished putting on his uniform blouse and favored Ramirez with an angry look. "Don't talk around the problem, Ramirez," he said harshly. "You don't think the old man can cut it, do you? Afraid I'll end up letting Barnett dominate me, instead of the other way around. Right?"

Before Ramirez could answer, Fraser intervened. "Sir, you know better than I do how much damage you can do to your mind through misuse of an implant. It takes a strong will to maintain control during an interrogation. And the doctor is right to be concerned. None of us want to see you burn out your mind fighting Barnett."

Hawley looked like he was about to flare, then nodded and sat down on the examining table. "And you're right to be concerned that I'm not up to it," he admitted. "My record's not exactly something to inspire confidence, is it?"

"Sir, your record's got nothing—"

"Don't interrupt me, Captain!" he barked. Then he smiled. "I was trained to command, son. Once. And I think I can safely say that I have more experience with this implant than most regular interrogators. If I can find my way back to reality from Dreamland as often as I do, surely I can do it this time." He paused, still smiling. "Anyway, if you're looking for a man with a strong will, what else would you call an officer who won't give it up even after twenty years of being told that a quiet resignation would be the best thing for everyone, hmm?"

Fraser forced a smile in return. "I'd call him stubborn, sir. Or perhaps 'pigheaded' would be a better term."

"There you have it. I'll have this bastard Barnett for lunch. I've been wanting a crack at him ever since the first time I heard a snide remark about how I wasn't fit to be a security guard at the Seafarms warehouse, much less the CO of the garrison. I was getting comments like that even before you got here, Fraser, and I'm getting damned sick of them!"

"You'll have your chance, sir," Fraser said. He nodded to Garcia. "Have an escort fetch Citizen Barnett from his cell. It's time he started helping us as much as he's helped the wogs."

* * *

Karatsolis leaned against the rampart, staring down at the restless waters of high tide. There was no more work for him in the repbay, now that all the magrep units had been dismounted. He had another twenty minutes of free time left before he was due to relieve Sergeant Franz, who was now operating the unit's second veeter on the south wall.

He couldn't get his mind off the mutiny. When Bashar had first called him, he had still been dwelling on O'Donnell and Sandoval, on the whole question of his place in the Legion. And he'd been no nearer to resolving it.

Then the mad rush, warning Kelly and Trent, then organizing the Transport Section at Trent's orders to help close the trap on the mutineers. Even Franz had taken his orders. Trent had made it clear that he wanted none but Hanuman veterans in charge of the operation, and to Topheth with rank.

When Fraser had started talking, his first reaction had been one of frustration. Why try to reason with the bastards?

But what he'd said about every man playing a part had hit home. And Barnett's assassination attempt....

He'd saved Fraser's life. Twice, maybe, since he'd helped organize the resistance to the mutiny. And if they held off the wogs and got off of Polypheme, it would be because Colin Fraser was alive to do it. Karatsolis had no doubt of that. None of the other officers inside the Sandcastle had Fraser's flair for tactics, or the ability to inspire the legionnaires the way he could.

One man like Fraser could really make a difference. And so, it seemed, could Karatsolis, when he guarded Fraser's back or did his part in combat.

A siren pulled him forcefully out of his reverie. "Attention! Attention!" the PA blared. It sounded like Gunny Trent himself making the announcement. "Sonar has detected large groups of targets approaching the base! All personnel to defense posts!"

Karatsolis ran for the nearest stairway. For the first time in days, he was eager to come to grips with the enemy.

To do his part.

CHAPTER NINETEEN

Death before surrender!

> —Lt. Clement Maudet, at Camerone,
> French Foreign Legion, 30 April 1863

avid Hawley jerked upright on the examination table, his link to Barnett suddenly cut off. Sweat soaked his shirt and matted his hair, and he couldn't remember the last time he'd felt so totally exhausted.

No ... he *could* remember. The last time had been on Aten, years ago, the day he'd led his men into the last terrible battle against the Ubrenfars. His clash of wills with Barnett was as close as he had ever come to the strain of that fight. Memories he'd buried for years were rushing to the surface now, memories like the ones that had driven him to seek refuge in Dreamland in the first place.

But at the same time there was something exhilarating about fighting and winning. He'd forgotten that feeling, too, even though he'd lost himself in chip wargames hoping to recapture it without having to face the darker side of the struggle. Now he realized it was that darker side that made the feeling so intense.

The flood of thought and emotion was over in an instant, and Hawley opened his eyes. Fraser and Ramirez were on either side of his table, both wearing worried expressions.

"The ... the computer terminated the session," he said haltingly. It was hard to talk out loud, after relying on the machine-induced telepathy of the interrogation.

Fraser nodded. "We're on alert, sir," he said. "Large numbers of nomads on the way in. The doctor and I need to get to our posts. Garcia, too."

"Right. Just let me get my bearings...." He tried to get up, but the room was swimming around him.

"No, sir," Fraser said. "Doctor Ramirez has a sedative for you. You need some rest, sir."

He started to protest, but Fraser held up a hand. "Captain, even trained interrogators take some crash time after a session. SOP." He paused. "We haven't seen all the transcripts yet. How'd it go?"

Hawley winced at the memory. "He's a stubborn bastard, Fraser. I didn't get much. But he *was* working for the Toeljuks and the nomads. Seems he was selling out for money. Security. He comes from a pretty bad background.... Wasn't getting very far with Seafarms, for all his strutting."

"And they call us mercenaries," Garcia muttered darkly from the corner by the computer equipment.

"I was on the track of their headquarters when the computer cut the link," Hawley went on. "He knows where they're set up—the Toels and Choor! too. But I'll need another session or two to get it."

"You'll have it," Fraser promised. "But right now you need to rest ... and we have a fight to get to." He nodded to Ramirez, who advanced with a hypo.

As the doctor applied the spray injector to his arm, Hawley felt the fatigue washing over him. "Wish I ... could be out there with you ... son...." he heard himself saying.

He was surprised when he realized that this time he really meant it.

* * *

"Grenades!" Narmonov shouted.

All along the parapet the legionnaires of his platoon switched from conventional ammo to mini-grenades, firing single rounds into the water below the east wall of the Sandcastle. The individual explosions weren't much, but they'd keep the wogs off-balance.

He still couldn't believe the size of the nomad army. Every estimate they'd been able to make so far showed there were at least ten thousand warriors out there. The ordinary clan numbered less than a few hundred. Choor! must have sent every able-bodied swimmer in his confederation against the fort.

With the magrep generators still not fully installed, it would take a lot of killing to stop this attack.

"Sir!" That was Sergeant Zold, acting as platoon NCO in place of Carstairs. "Permission to fire Fafnirs? Or would you rather use the charges?"

He glanced at the stack of explosive canisters piled nearby, then shook his head. "Save the explosives for when we know they're at the walls," he said. "Make it Fafnirs. One round each. Just to keep them guessing."

Zold gave him a gap-toothed grin. "Yes, sir!" He turned away, shouting orders despite having his helmet radio on. "Weapons Lances! Fafnirs ready! Timed detonation, thirty seconds. Launch!"

Nearby, one of the Fafnir gunners quickly programmed the instructions into the computer targeting system. The Fafnir was supposed to be a selectively targeted anti-vehicle missile, equally useful against ground or air targets, which were matched by silhouette in the missile's on-board brain. But it could also be programmed for area effect with a timed detonation, as Zold had ordered.

The legionnaire lifted the launch tube to his shoulder and squeezed the trigger. With a brilliant flare of burning propellant, the missile leapt into the air, then arced downward and lanced into the water. Elsewhere along the wall other missiles followed.

Seconds passed. Then a ripple of underwater explosions followed.

Each missile, by itself, could kill a Sabertooth or a Sandray. Going off underwater like that, they'd disrupt the nomad attack.

Too bad the stock of Fafnirs in the Sandcastle was so low. No one had anticipated much call for anti-armor missiles, on a planet where the crossbow was still considered an advanced weapon system, and there were no more than five missiles per gunner on hand. Those would have to be hoarded.

At least some of their weapons weren't hampered by ammo concerns.

"Sergeant!" he called. "Fafnirs to cease fire. Order the onagers to engage at will."

"Onagers front! Onagers fire!" Zold sounded a lot like Carstairs, barking those orders with the same crisp precision. Maybe the actor hadn't been playing a part after all. It seemed like the job shaped the men, not the other way around.

Now the fully armored onager gunners were taking position on the parapet. Narmonov saw one, armor emblazoned with colorful emblems, checking the balance on his ConRig harness and running through a quick series of tests. That would be the Gurkha, Chandbahadur Rai. He remembered warning the corporal to repaint the armor in standard camouflage a few weeks back, before the crisis had blown up. When he'd told Gunny Trent he thought the man was getting a dose of the *cafarde*, the sergeant had just laughed and said, "With a Gurkha you can't tell. They're crazy all the time."

Chandbahadur chambered a round and fired. The plasma bolt was like a controlled bolt of lightning stabbing into the sea, raising a cloud of hissing steam as the superheated metal hit the surface of the water. The onager—officially the *fusil d'onage*, or "storm rifle"—deserved its name ... and its fierce reputation.

Narmonov fired another grenade at the seething water. This was the strangest battle he'd ever fought in, with opponents who didn't show themselves and who hadn't, at least so far, started shooting back. There was no way to tell how much damage the legionnaires were doing, except by inference from the reports passed on from time to time from the civilian sonar operators in C-cubed.

Sooner or later the nomads would strike back. As he pulled the trigger yet again, Narmonov couldn't help but wonder whether the legionnaires were having any real effect on the enemy ... and whether it would make any difference to their battle plans.

*   *   *

Fraser entered C-cubed at a run, Garcia following close behind. "Status!" he snapped as the door closed behind her.

A civilian technician looked up from a computer monitor. "Sonar shows five major groups out there now, Captain Fraser," he said. "So far they just keep feinting in and out, like they're testing our defenses. The fire from the walls seems to be discouraging them."

Fraser bent over the display. "I wish this thing was designed for computer imaging," he said. The sonar systems used aboard most ships and submersibles in the Commonwealth included programs allowing a computer to interpret signals as actual images, but the improvised detectors they'd installed around the perimeter were more like the primitive devices of Terra's pre-spaceflight era. All they registered was the presence and approximate size of objects underwater, without showing any real detail.

And detection wasn't completely accurate. Targets near the sea bottom or close in to the wall probably would be obscured by clutter.

If Barnett had been feeding the nomads information, they would surely know about the sonar. And Barnett could have told them about its limitations....

So why were they limiting themselves to these highly visible demonstrations?

Beside him, Garcia stiffened. "Sir ..." She hesitated, then went on, "Sir, I helped calibrate the system, with some of our wog scouts as sample targets. Some of those ... don't look right."

"Decoys!" Fraser crossed to the communications desk and grabbed a microphone. "General call! General call! Natives are using decoys as sonar targets. Watch out for infiltration attempts! Repeat, watch for infiltration by nomad forces!"

* * *

Warrior-Scout !!Dhruuj looked up as another shock wave washed over him. So far the Strangers were focusing their fire close to the surface of the water, and their explosives were having little effect on the band of elite warriors who crept along the sea floor. Some of the big explosions had been dangerous, but they had come this far without casualties. A few more minutes and their job would be finished.

War-Leader-of-Clans Choor! had anticipated the Strangers once again. Their underwater sight was imperfect, limited in its ability to distinguish one object from another and nearly blind to anything that kept close to the bottom. So the Stranger-Who-Betrayed had reported, and the War-Leader-of-Clans had been quick to see how those weaknesses could be exploited.

What would the Strangers-Within think if they knew that most of what they were seeing now were not Swimmers at all but *woojoork*, the Swimmer-sized beasts of burden the Clans used to carry heavy loads on long treks? And would they realize that many of the Swimmers interspersed among the animals did not belong to the Clans at all, but were actually prisoners from Ourgh taken in a big raid two Tides ago?

Only a few warriors of the Clans were actually among the many targets they would be seeing now, a handful who were responsible for keeping the captives and animals threatening the Built-Reef.

And while the Strangers allowed prisoners and beasts to distract them, the Clans would strike!

The Built-Reef loomed ahead, the walls made of the sand-that-was-harder-than-sand an impenetrable barrier. The first Clan assault had aimed for the gates, the second had relied upon Swimmers going over the walls. This time they had more accurate information, transmitted by the Stranger-Who-Betrayed before the Clans had arrived in force. !!Dhruuj followed Warrior-Superior Ghoodoor along the wall of the Reef until they found the gaping hole, the *intake pipe* that the Betrayer had described. It was wide enough for two Swimmers to pass through abreast, and the barriers within were said to be much weaker than the walls themselves.

Ghoodoor signaled !!Dhruuj to summon the others, and the Warrior-Scout swam out of the hole and waved to the rest of the party. The Swimmers approached slowly, three of them heavily burdened by the explosives they carried slung in a net between them.

!!Dhruuj clung to the wall and began speaking in the Voice-Without-Words, informing the Clans of their progress. When Ghoo-door finished placing the explosives, the party would withdraw to safety and set them off. Then, as water rushed into the center of the Built-Reef, the Clans would launch their attack.

Victory floated within a tendril's grasp....

* * *

"The Sandcastle's calling, Sub."

Toru Watanabe looked toward the comm station on the other side of the ship's bridge. Dmitri Rostov had the position this watch, and his lancemate, Legionnaire Martin, was keeping an eye on the civilian pilot at the helm. Since the day he'd ordered the platoon to seize the *Seafarms Cyclops* and turn back for home, the key Bridge and Engineering posts had either been staffed or watched by legionnaires. For the most part, even the most stubborn civilians, Captain MacLean included, had accepted the situation long ago.

He crossed to Rostov's console and held a headphone to one ear. Rostov keyed in his mike at Watanabe's nod. "Sandcastle, *Cyclops*. Watanabe here."

"*Cyclops*, be advised of sitrep update," Angela Garcia's voice came back. "Hostile forces around base may include decoys, repeat, decoys. Intentions of hostile command not known. Captain Fraser advises you be ready for possible attack."

"Acknowledged, Sandcastle," Watanabe answered. He gestured to Rostov, who hit the general alarm and began passing the warning to the rest of the ship's company over the PA system. "Revised ETA is now one hour, thirteen minutes."

There was a long pause at the other end. Then Fraser came on the line, sounding worried. "Toru, you could be sailing right into a major battle here," he said. "We still don't know which way the wogs are going to jump. If you want to hold off until things are settled here, it's your discretion. You know how vulnerable that monster of yours will be coming in."

Watanabe didn't need to think the decision through. "Sounds like you're going to need a hand there, Captain," he said. "We're coming in. I'll see if I can't shave some time off that ETA, too, so we don't miss the party."

Fraser sounded relieved. "Thanks. These bastards are playing for keeps, and I'll feel a hell of a lot better with the Second backing us up. Sandcastle clear."

He set down the headphones and turned away from the comm station. "Impellers to full thrust," he ordered.

"Sir!" The civilian helmsman turned in his seat to deliver his protest. "We're already pumping at the maximum safe level...."

"I said full thrust, damn it! Even if you tear the guts out of her! Do it!"

The helmsman looked ready to argue, until he caught sight of Legionnaire Martin as she stepped toward him, her laser rifle a vivid reminder of just how far the platoon was willing to go to see that the civilians carried out Watanabe's orders.

The man swallowed twice, turned back to his console, and advanced the throttle to the maximum thrust setting.

Watanabe could feel the vibrations as the impellers churned, driving the Seafarms Cyclops toward her goal.

* * *

The wall shuddered under Narmonov's feet, throwing him off-balance. He grabbed at the parapet to steady himself, dropping his FEK with a metallic clatter. *"Bojemoi!"* he exclaimed in Russian. "What the Topheth was that!"

"Explosion," Zold said curtly. "Must've been pretty deep ... Christ! Look at that!" He was pointing behind Narmonov, into the interior of the compound.

Narmonov followed the gesture and felt his mouth go dry.

Water was pouring through a gap below the gatehouse, an un-stoppable torrent rushing into the compound.

"The intakes!" Narmonov shouted. "They've blown the main intakes!"

Zold waved his FEK over his head. "Chandbahadur! Haddad! Sinclair! Your lances with me!" The sergeant looked at Narmonov. "I'll try to set up an overwatch on that entrance, sir. Slow them down when they start coming through."

He nodded. "Do it. I'll stay here." He paused. "Good luck, Sergeant."

They'd all need luck before this was over.

* * *

"Breach in the wall, sir. Main intake pipe, below the gatehouse."

Fraser swore under his breath. They should have been expecting that, as soon as they'd realized the wogs were using decoys. A few commandos infiltrated along the bottom ... Explosives like the ones Watanabe had reported the nomads carrying in the attack on the *Cyclops*....

"We'll need more troops out there, Garcia," he said. "What's the state of our reserves?"

"We can draw off troops from the perimeter if those really are decoys out there," she said. "Subaltern Narmonov's already deployed half his platoon to the gatehouse area on his own initiative."

Fraser looked away. Choor! had already proven himself a shrewd tactician. The nomad—and his Toeljuk backers—would probably know that the defenders' first reaction would be to weaken the outer wall in response to the threat of an attack into the center of the Sandcastle.

Which meant that there would be other native soldiers waiting to take advantage of that weakening....

"Anything else?" he asked.

"Just the armed civilians," Garcia told him. "About a hundred, with a mixed bag of weapons. Sergeant Trent's been keeping them back."

"We'll need them now," he said. "Pass the orders." He paused, rubbing his forehead. "I wish I knew how much we can rely on them...."

"Just because Barnett was a traitor doesn't mean we all are, Captain," a technician spoke up from the other side of C-cubed. Fraser looked up. With a shock he recognized her. It was Katrina Voskovich, the technician he and Kelly had saved from the rioting in Ourgh the day of the first nomad attack. "We'll fight. All of us, if that's what you need. And if you have weapons for us."

One of the other technicians nodded, and another said, "That's right. Tell him, Kat."

"All right. Garcia, get together any civilian who wants to volunteer and break out more weapons from the Armory. I'll need ... three volunteers to stay here with me."

"Yes, sir," Garcia said, a smile that could have been anticipation lighting up her face.

"You're in charge until I find an NCO or an officer to take over. Move!"

The technicians were talking among themselves in low, urgent tones. Finally Voskovich and four others joined Garcia, leaving Fraser his team.

As they started out the door, Voskovich turned back and caught Fraser's eye. "Don't worry, Captain. We may not be legionnaires, but we'll show the wogs a thing or two!"

* * *

"Fafnirs! One round each!" Narmonov shouted the order, all too well aware that they might need the missiles later. But if there were natives closing in on the hole under the gatehouse, they had to be discouraged from getting any closer. "Forty-five-second fuse delay!"

The two remaining Fafnirs in his section of the wall opened fire. The others were with Zold. There had already been some firing from that direction, probably against the commandos who had blown the intake. How many men had the wogs infiltrated while the Legion sniped at decoys?

"Some bodies there, sir!" someone called, pointing.

He let his FEK hang on its sling from his shoulder and flipped down his faceplate, hitting the image-intensifier setting. The distant objects suddenly filled his vision, bobbing in the waves.

One of them wasn't even vaguely humanoid. He recognized it as the beast of burden Terrans had dubbed "sea camel." Next to the animal another body, a wog this time, was lying facedown, staining the sea with blood. *So we got one of the bastards, at least,* Narmonov thought.

But something wasn't quite right....

No tattoos, that was it. The wog wasn't tattooed, and all the nomads wore Clan tattoos.

"Damn them," he muttered. The wogs were using prisoners as well as animals for decoys. Probably a city-dweller from Ourgh or another nearby city.

A dark, suckerlined arm snaked over the parapet, grabbing at Narmonov. He stumbled backward, surprised. They'd reached the walls!

He snapped his visor up just in time to see the nomad clamber over the top, swinging one of their strange crossbows into line. Narmonov fumbled for his rifle, bringing it up as the crossbow fired. His finger twitched reflexively on the trigger, and a full-auto burst nearly tore the alien in half.

Then pain was lancing through his left shoulder. He looked down; saw the bolt, the red stain on his battledress. Even the duraweave cloth hadn't been able to stop the weapon at such close range.

More nomads were appearing on the ramparts, climbing out of the angry sea below. They'd counted on the intake explosion to weaken the wall and further confuse the defenders ... and they'd got just what they counted on.

He ignored the pain spreading through his arm and upper chest as he crossed to the pile of explosive ten-kilogram canisters, then cursed as he remembered that one of Haddad's men had the detonator box for this batch. The Recon Lance was with Zold. He should have realized it....

"Look out, Sub!" a legionnaire shouted.

He spun around in time to see another nomad looming close behind him, wielding a curved sword and shouting some unintelligible battle cry. Narmonov tried to block the wog's swing with his FEK, but the deflected blow still cut deep into his injured arm. The native wrenched the blade free and raised it for another strike, then fell as a legionnaire pumped a dozen needle rounds into his back.

Dizzy, Narmonov staggered back against the parapet, trying to fight off the fog of pain and shock closing in around him.

They *had* to blunt this attack, now....

Gathering his strength, he grabbed one of the canisters and jerked open the detpack wired to one end. Manually he set the timer, dropped it over the wall, then reached for another of the improvised depth charges.

A rocket-assisted bullet struck the wall half a meter away. He flinched but finished the setting on the second timer, throwing the bomb over the wall.

As he staggered under the weight of the third bomb, another bullet slammed into his back. The duraweave fatigues kept it from penetrating, but the impact rammed him against the parapet. He clung to the canister, fumbling with the timer.

A wog slashed at him with a bulky weapon like an out-sized battleax as he finished making the setting. Narmonov rolled onto the top of the wall, kept rolling ... until he was falling toward the hungry waves, the canister still clutched close to his chest.

He blacked out as he hit the water, and never felt the three explosions that killed him.

Chapter Twenty

*Charge your rifles. You will fire on command, then we will charge with the
bayonet. You will follow me.*

—Lieutenant Clement Maudet
at the battle of Camerone,
French Foreign Legion, 30 April 1863

"Come on! This way!"

Karatsolis was knee-deep in swirling water as he ran across
the open ground below the vehicle repbay. The orders for the
Transport Section to assemble to defend that stretch of the wall
had made him cut across the center of the base. Now, as the water rose,
he was regretting the impulse that had taken him to the far wall before
the attack.

Near the gatehouse he saw a pair of legionnaires wading through the
raging water, firing at a group of wogs who had come through the hole
they'd blasted. Three of the nomads fell, but the rest surged forward and
brought them down with a hail of spear thrusts and sword cuts.

"Come on, Spear!" Bashar called again. The corporal was standing
near the top of the ramp into the repbay, urging him on with frantic
waves. "They're going to button up in a minute!" The heavy doors were
already grinding shut.

Karatsolis dodged around the last APC lined up at the foot of the
wide ramp. As each of the Legion vehicles had been stripped of its

magrep generators, they had been towed out of the repbay and lined up in the open by a lumbering wrecker on treads to clear more space inside the motor pool. They stood in an orderly block, looking ready for a parade.

The *Angel II* was parked among them, her plasma cannon's barrel pointing at Karatsolis like an accusing finger. They hadn't finished putting in the generators, but none of the vehicles was mobile now. The Legion could really use some of them now....

He stopped dead in his tracks, staring up at the FSV. The magrep modules were gone, and she couldn't move ... but her power units were intact, and so was her weaponry. The Sabertooth might not be able to move, but she'd make a damned good pillbox. And after the water rose she'd be able to discourage wogs from swimming through the center of the Sandcastle.

"Bashar!" he shouted, pointing at the *Angel II*. "We can still fight her! Give me a hand!"

Bashar didn't seem to understand right away, but as Karatsolis scrambled up on the chassis and opened the turret hatch the Turk ran down the ramp to join him. "You're nuts, farmboy!" he shouted.

"Not as nuts as the wog who tries to play games with our little bitch!" he yelled back happily.

The water was almost up to the level of Bashar's hatch by the time the Turk climbed in and started the power-up process. Up in the turret, Karatsolis ran through the weapon and sensor diagnostics, glad to have the chance of fighting out this battle doing what he did best.

* * *

"What the hell is that?" one of the technicians muttered.

Fraser crossed the Ops center and bent over the man's shoulder to study his board. He was monitoring the gate-side sensor readouts, sonar, radar, and motion detectors. "What've you got?"

The tech pointed to the radar screen. "This sucker just lit up. A big, surface-skimming target, like a magrep. Must've been hiding behind Haven Point, up here, or we would have spotted the bastard earlier. Closing fast, too ... Must be a hell of a mover."

"Can the computer ID it?" Fraser asked.

The civilian looked blank for a moment, then punched in the code that called up the base's warbook files. Another computer monitor began running through comparison signal profiles faster than the human eye could follow, until it stopped at a probable match.

Fraser read the specs and let out a low whistle. "Good God. I didn't think the Toels would go this far helping them...."

*   *   *

Legionnaire Angela Garcia knelt behind the parapet, her FEK braced on the fusand as she covered the rapidly flooding interior of the compound. Around her, Seafarms workers were dropping into similar positions.

"Down there!" Katrina Voskovich shouted, pointing. Garcia followed the gesture and saw a group of wogs slogging through the torrent.

"Fire!" she called, her finger tightening on the trigger. The gauss rifle whined and chattered. Then the noise swelled as the civilians joined in. The nomads thrashed and struggled, then flopped backward and floated with the rushing sea.

Adrenaline sang through her veins, making Garcia feel really alive for the first time since Hanuman. This was why she'd joined the Legion, to be a part of something larger than herself, to stand against the odds and fight back against a hostile universe....

There was an explosion by the gates, and the inrush of water redoubled. Garcia saw wogs and Terrans alike being overpowered by the force of the water, but it wouldn't take long for the nomads to recover. For the humans, though, the torrent spelled death.

As the flow slacked off and the water levels inside and outside of the walls equalized, there were more explosions around the gate. The massive doors buckled and a large, menacing shape pushed through the wreckage.

It had the lean and deadly look of a shark, larger than a Sabertooth or a Sandray but riding, like them, on a magnetic cushion and propelled by powerful turbofans. Garcia had seen pictures of the Toeljuk assault vehicles known in Commonwealth parlance as "Gorgons," but this was the first time she'd seen one up close.

Wogs clung to the sides of the vehicle, brandishing weapons and shouting battle cries. They slid into the water as she watched, joining many more of their kindred who were already swimming through the shattered gates.

And a low bubble turret, mounting a pulse laser cannon, swung slowly to cover the gatehouse wall, where the fiercest fighting was still going on.

* * *

"Fall back! Fall back!" Gunnery Sergeant Trent shouted the orders, but he knew he was too late to save some of the defenders holding around the gatehouse.

He'd joined Bartlow's platoon to support the wavering Alpha Company troops, who were still demoralized by the loss of Subaltern Narmonov and the sudden two-front battle they'd been pressed into by the nomads. Subaltern Bartlow himself had been wounded in the first few moments of the fight, and Trent was in command now.

But it didn't look like he'd be in command of anything much, now that the Toel Gorgon had entered the fight.

"Weapons Lances!" he yelled. "Concentrate fire on that strakking thing! Burn every Fafnir you've got left if you have to!" Trent grabbed a retreating Alpha Company corporal. "Get your men under control, damn it! We've got to set up a fallback position and hold these wogs!"

The man nodded dumbly and pushed past Trent, but he was calling orders as he ran and looked like he was functioning again. Trent looked around wildly; saw the sappers moving a dismounted magrep generator into place across the parapet twenty meters behind them, using one of the small maglifts Seafarms normally used for bulk cargo handling. Kelly was there, too, waving for him to fall back to her position.

He cut in his commlink. "Task Force Gatehouse! Fall back on the sappers! Now!"

Then the Gorgon's laser cannon opened fire.

* * *

Garcia grabbed the handset of her C^3 pack, which was open on the rooftop beside her. "Ops! Ops! The gates are gone, and the Toels have brought in a Gorgon-class MAV. Come in, Ops!"

Fraser's voice came back, sounding worried but controlled. "Acknowledged, Garcia," he said curtly. "Bastards had it out of sight until a couple of minutes ago. What's your situation?"

Garcia looked back into the compound in time to see the laser cut loose with a string of rapid pulses that battered the fusand gatehouse, raising clouds of dust and debris with each strike. She saw a legionnaire caught in the beam, his head and torso vanishing in a flare of raw energy.

Then she saw the dark shapes in the water, swarming around the gatehouse wall and into the compound.

"We've got several hundred wogs in the compound now, Captain," she said, shivering. "That's *minimum*—there could be ten times that many too deep underwater for us to see from up here. The gatehouse is under fire from the Gorgon now, and Sergeant Trent is falling back. And I don't think there are any reserves left...."

"Let me worry about that, Garcia," Fraser shot back. "Hold as long as you can. I'll find some more men for you ... somewhere. Count on it."

As the comm channel went dead Garcia raised her FEK again and opened fire, knowing that she could rely on Colin Fraser to keep his word.

* * *

Fraser dropped the handset and turned to the technicians in the Ops center. "We can't do much more in here. Get out to the Armory and grab weapons, then report to Legionnaire Garcia."

One of the techs, an older man with a snow-white mustache, looked uncertain, "What about you, Captain?" he asked.

"I'm going to find some more reinforcements," he answered curtly. "Get moving. We need everyone we can get out there."

He followed them out the door, but turned left instead of right at the first branch in the corridor. Within minutes he'd descended two levels and crossed to the cellblock section.

The four legionnaires he'd ordered confined for drunkenness were in one large holding cell together. Fraser unlocked the door and swung it open hurriedly. "Sentence suspended," he said, forcing a smile. "Lay up to the Armory and draw some weapons, boys. We've got a situation outside."

White, the one who'd operated the still, let out a whoop. "Come on! Let's get us some wogs!" They rushed past him.

"Captain!"

Fraser turned at the sound of DuValier's voice. The lieutenant was in a separate cell three doors down.

"Captain ... let me fight too. Please."

Fraser shook his head slowly. "After the stunt you pulled? I couldn't trust you out there, Lieutenant. Forget it." He turned away.

"Wait ... please, wait!" There was a note of desperation in that voice, usually so cool and controlled. "Captain, you need me out there."

"What I need is a couple of squadrons of Airsharks and an armored regiment," Fraser said harshly. "Not—"

"Listen to me, for Christ's sake! Before ... before the mutiny I was working on an idea to screw up the nomad command and control set-up. We can block the signals they've been using to pass orders. Believe me, Captain!"

Fraser hesitated. "I didn't see anything about this...."

"Was I going to tell you about it? You know how I felt ... before...." DuValier trailed off. "Damn it, Captain, ask Koenig about it. We talked about the options the other day. I was planning on telling you once I had the whole thing ready to go. Hell, I thought it would make the magrep modules unnecessary."

"You really think you can foul up their communications?"

"I'm sure of it. Just let me get to the med center, Captain. Put a guard on me if you have to...."

"I don't have the men to spare to guard you, dammit!" he said. Reluctantly he crossed to the cell and unlocked the door. "Your friend Barnett was a traitor. I hope I'm not making a mistake believing in you, Lieutenant."

"You aren't," DuValier told him. There was no trace of hatred in the man's eyes now, only a burning determination. "You aren't...."

*　*　*

"Firing!" Karatsolis called, hitting the stud on the console in front of him. The round chambered automatically, with a metallic clang that made his ears ring. An instant later the plasma cannon opened up with a screech of superheating ammo. The turret grew noticeably hotter, worse than usual because of the water boiling around the barrel and in the path of the searing plasma bolt.

Down in the driver's compartment Bashar was monitoring the commlink. "Spear! They've got an assault vehicle up there. Gorgon-class ... one of those old Toel MAVs."

"Yeah, I know it," Karatsolis confirmed. "Remember? We ran into one of their export jobs on Embla."

"Sounds like it's got them running in circles up there," Bashar commented. "Two Fafnir gunners killed trying to nail the sucker, everybody else too busy with wogs. Can we get it?"

"Coords?"

Bashar reeled off a string of numbers. "Over by the gatehouse," he elaborated.

"This muck we're shooting through is screwing up the plasma gun pretty bad," Karatsolis said, thinking hard. "It's great for frying wogs, but I don't think it'll do much to the Gargon...." He swung in his seat, flipping a row of switches on one side. "I've got the Grendels on line. Feeding target ID ... firing!" He slammed the red launch switch.

One of the Sabertooth's Grendel missiles slid off the launch rail behind the turret, slashing through the water like a predator in search of prey. Karatsolis fired the second missile.

Seconds passed....

* * *

As the first missile cleared the water, Gunnery Sergeant Trent dropped flat behind the improvised barrier of magrep generators, shouting "Get down! Get down!"

Around him legionnaires and civilians threw themselves to the fusand rooftop. The first missile struck the massive Gorgon assault vehicle squarely in the bow and exploded in a multicolored fireball. Showers of debris rained down on the compound.

The stern of the vehicle remained suspended on its own magrep fields for a moment, before the second Grendel finished the job. One of the sappers—the old man, MacAllister—raised a ragged cheer.

Then the rest of the legionnaires were taking up the call, and even a few of the Seafarms people.

Trent rolled, fired his FEK at a nomad climbing over the parapet, and got to his feet. "Pascali!" he called. "Your lance to the inner wall! The Captain says Garcia needs some support in there!"

The battle went on.

* * *

Antoine DuValier burst into the medical center, pushing aside a burly medic in bloodstained battledress. Dr. Ramirez whirled, a look of shock on his face. "Stop him! He's broken out of cells! Somebody cover Captain Hawley!"

DuValier stopped, holding out both hands. "Captain Fraser let me out, Doctor," he said quickly. "I need to see that wog scout ... Oomour. Please!"

The doctor was joined by a pair of medics, with distinctly unmedical FEKs held at the ready. None of them looked ready to believe him....

He didn't blame them a bit. It was miracle enough that Fraser had trusted him, but in the confusion the word hadn't gone out yet. And who would trust a man who mutinied against the Legion? That was the only unforgivable sin in a unit well known as a haven for the worst humanity had to offer.

He caught sight of Father Fitzpatrick behind the others. "Padre! My word of honor ... Before God, I'm telling the truth. Believe me!"

Fitzpatrick was frowning. He didn't want to accept DuValier's word any more than the others. But they'd been friends from the day DuValier had joined Bravo Company, and the lieutenant had always played it straight with the chaplain.

Finally, he nodded. "Let him go, Doctor," the priest said quietly. With reluctance plain on their faces the others accepted the Padre's word. Not DuValier's, but the Padre's.

The shame of the Legion's hatred burned deep, but DuValier swallowed and pushed on.

Oomour was bending over a human casualty. Evidently the more lightly wounded patients were helping the doctor tend the seriously injured from the battle. "Lieutenant!" the native said, sounding pleased. "False Voice make we now?"

"Yes ... yes, now. It's urgent." He urged the scout toward the door. "We have to move fast, Oomour!"

Together they ran for the broad stairs that led down to the lowest level. DuValier had laid out a hardsuit there, together with weapons, a hand-held amplifier for Oomour, and additional communications gear for himself. He was explaining his plan as he suited up with the clumsy help of the nomad.

Finally, his suit sealed and his FEK in one hand, DuValier checked the airtight inner door and then opened the outer one, the one that led to the compound. He had to cling to a stanchion as the water poured in.

They swam out side-by-side, the nomad clutching the amplifier in a dexterous foot and cradling his weapon in his arms, while DuValier held the FEK at the ready.

He gestured to the amplifier, and Oomour shifted it to his feeding tendrils. DuValier switched on the recorder function of his communications package. A few minutes of the nomad's live performance could be turned into a permanent jamming technique ... if it worked.

Even amplified the Voice was at the very threshold of audibility, but judging from the way Oomour himself was cringing the sound must have been loud and clear to a native's ears.

DuValier swam past the alien and let himself sink slowly to the bottom. He waited, ready to protect Oomour, hoping he wouldn't have to.

Hoping he had a chance to redeem himself.

* * *

!!Dhruuj stopped dead in the water, baffled by the cacophony of sounds that suddenly filled the sea. Beside him Warrior-Superior Ghoodoor stopped as well. "What is that, Scout?" he asked.

"I ... do not know, Warrior-Superior," !!Dhruuj admitted. "It is like the Voices ... but different. Not the Voices of the War-Leader-of-Clans ... not the Voice of any Clan I have heard."

Ghoodoor's feeding tendrils writhed in uncertainty. "Could it be some weapon the Strangers are using?"

The Warrior-Superior's concern was understandable, !!Dhruuj thought. The destruction of the Gift-That-Rode-Above-the Waves had unsettled them all. But it was not the way of the Swimmers to allow a setback to keep them from victory.

But these new Voices were something different....

"Weapon or not," !!Dhruuj said at last. "I think we should withdraw."

"Retreat! We do not retreat! Not without the word of Choor!."

!!Dhruuj turned to face the Warrior-Superior. "How will we know what orders we are sent? How will Choor! hear our reports, to judge the next turning of the battle? Without the Voices, the Clans cannot work as one anymore! We become a mob again, and Choor! has said that a mob cannot defeat the Strangers-Above!"

Ghoodoor hesitated, plainly torn between instinct and obedience to the War-Leader-of-Clans. "If we withdraw, the battle is lost...."

"No! If we withdraw, we can see how far these new Voices reach, ask for advice from the War-Leader-of-Clans, mount a fresh assault when we are prepared!" !!Dhruuj knew his voice was edged with the unaccustomed fear he felt. Without the Voices he was no longer a Hand of the Clan. He was cut off, like the only survivor of a dead tribe. He knew Ghoodoor was feeling it, too.

"Others might not be retreating. We cannot contact them."

"That is why we must retreat!" !!Dhruuj insisted.

The Warrior-Superior took a long time before he finally shook his head in assent. "Withdraw! Withdraw!" he shouted in the Voice-of-Speech. "Spread out in a skirmish line and urge others to withdraw as you meet them!"

They started back toward the hole in the Reef. !!Dhruuj fought the impulse to turn back and keep fighting, knowing that the Strangers would still be there when the Clans returned. This attack had hurt the Strangers, and they would not survive another such battle.

Chapter Twenty-one

You have given the Legion too limited an objective. It has assigned itself others.

—Lieutenant Colonel Paul Rollet,
French Foreign Legion, August, 1917

DuValier emerged, dripping, up a ladder along the inside of the compound wall, with Oomour following close behind. The nomad had recorded almost ten minutes of random noises before DuValier had decided they had enough to work with.

He looked around as he climbed. There was still heavy fighting raging near the gatehouse, with legionnaires crouching behind barricades across the wall holding against fierce fire from nomads who had won a foothold. On the far side of the compound, near the motor pool building, there was more activity. That would be Lieutenant Gage with the bulk of Alpha Company, rallying against an assault which had hit soon after he'd gone underwater.

The center of the compound was growing quiet now. A mixed band of civilians and legionnaires were spread out along the rooftops of the Ops center and adjacent structures. They were still firing at random targets visible in the waters below, but on the whole it looked like Oomour's "Voice" had been enough to prompt a withdrawal.

At the top of the ladder DuValier stripped off the hardsuit and then crouched over the electronics module. He pulled out the chip that he had used to make the recording and tucked it into a belt pouch. Then he looked at Oomour. "You know what a remote speaker is?"

The nomad shook his head. "Yes. Used them I have, in training."

"All right, then. I want you to report to Lieutenant Gage. Tell her to have her C^3 technician drop a remote speaker over the wall where she is fighting." He pointed across the compound. "She's over there. If you can't find her, find out who's in command and pass on the same order." He paused. They couldn't afford another round of arguments over whether or not DuValier could be trusted. "Tell them you have Captain Fraser's authority on it. Understand?"

Oomour repeated the instructions back in his heavily accented dialect.

"Good," DuValier said. "Get moving."

As the alien hurried off, DuValier turned toward the nearer battle zone. He had to find a C^3 backpack to broadcast the message, and a remote of his own. Once they placed the speakers in the water, he could start broadcasting the jamming message. The relay units wouldn't last long in Polypheme's corrosive water, but if it bought them a respite now they could find a more permanent solution later. Hopefully that would turn the tide on the perimeter, as it evidently had inside the compound.

Hopefully....

*   *   *

"It's slacking off, Captain. Most of them are pulling back."

Fraser slapped a fresh magazine into his FEK before he responded to Garcia. "In here, maybe. They're still fighting on the outer wall."

The C^3 tech took a moment to fire a long burst at half-seen shapes moving in the water below. "What the hell's making them run?"

"Gunny says DuValier just reported in. This could be because of his jamming trick. I hope so." Fraser peered into the middle of the compound, searching for targets, but none was visible. Trent's last call had reported the situation as stabilizing now that the Gorgon had been destroyed, but the casualties by the gatehouse had been heavy. Maybe DuValier's bag of tricks would work, but Fraser didn't plan to lean too heavily on the lieutenant's scheme. He finally lowered his FEK and looked back at the C^3 tech. "Garcia, I want you to stay here with half your people. I'll take the rest to help Gunny with the perimeter."

She nodded. "Take Hodges and the other legionnaires in your group, Captain," she suggested. "I don't think we'll have much more fighting here."

It took several long minutes to sort the civilians between the two groups. Fraser heard more explosions near the gatehouse—grenades, from the sound of them—and silently cursed each wasted second. They had the wogs on the run … but it was still possible for the nomads to stage a comeback.

He had to win this fight before a new one started.

*　*　*

"Here goes, Sergeant," DuValier announced, pitching the speaker over the wall. "That'll keep the bastards from talking!"

The chip he'd made of Oomour was already broadcasting over a commlink from Legionnaire Tomlinson's C^3 pack. Tomlinson wasn't alive anymore to operate it. He'd started on the Last March saving Subaltern Bartlow from a wog spear after the latter had been wounded, so DuValier himself had the bulky computer/communications unit slung across his back. With relays in place both inside the compound and at each corner of the perimeter, the wogs would be hard-pressed to communicate anywhere within a hundred meters of the walls, maybe further.

A rocket bullet hit the wall a few meters away and exploded, reminding him that many nomads hadn't chosen to run. At least their attacks were no longer coherent. With a little bit of luck, the legionnaires would have them cleared off the walls within another hour or so.

He crouched behind a temporary barricade of magrep modules the sappers had thrown up across the rampart, and checked the magazine on his FEK. Trent and the other men on the line were maintaining a steady fire, and so far Trent had been the only one even to acknowledge his presence.

DuValier squeezed off a round, shifted his aim, fired again. What the rest of the legionnaires felt no longer mattered as much as what he thought of himself.

Yells behind him made him glance over his shoulder. Fraser was running at the head of a disorganized mass of civilians carrying an assortment of weapons, mostly Legion FEKs. Those reinforcements would clean the nomads up even faster than he'd first estimated.…

* * *

Fraser saw DuValier, wearing a C^3 pack awkwardly and holding an FEK. The lieutenant half rose from his crouching posture behind Trent's improvised barrier, shouting something Fraser couldn't pick out from the noise of the battle.

Suddenly the FEK came up into a firing position, and the blood turned cold in Fraser's veins. He'd *trusted* DuValier....

He felt the hot breath of the burst, as needle rounds sliced past him. Then he heard the deep-throated wailing behind him, and spun around in time to see a trio of wogs reeling backward against the parapet. One of the Seafarms men was gaping at the natives, paralyzed.

DuValier was beside him a moment later. "Sorry about the near-miss, Captain," he said, leaning over the wall to pump some more rounds into the water below. "I didn't think your bunch of overnight heroes were going to take care of the bastards."

Firing a burst of grenades into the water where DuValier was aiming, Fraser let out a shuddering breath. "I'm the one who should be apologizing," he said quietly. "For doubting your word."

* * *

Somehow the Voice managed to convey anger and contempt, even though it was a simple arrangement of clicks and grunts that weren't supposed to hold any emotional content. !!Dhruuj strained to hear, trying to sort out the real Voice from the faint echoes of the false Voices around the Built-Reef-of-the-Strangers. A distant throbbing sound made it even harder to hear—probably another of the Strangers' weird weapons or devices off by the Reef.

Finally, he turned in the water to face Clan-Leader Nuujuur!, the youngest of the clan leaders in the assembled army and hence the most revered for his fast rise to ascendancy. He was the Hand of Choor! here, responsible for translating the War-Leader-of-Clans' instructions into action.

"The War-Leader says we can still win, even without the lost Gift. He says that now is the time to allow the fighting madness to possess our troops, to let them attack and keep attacking until victory is ours. If we launch all of the remaining swimmers in the attack at once, he says our victory is assured."

"He's said that before," someone grumbled.

Nuujuur! silenced the offender with a glare. "If Choor! says to fight, we will fight," he said, but no one missed his pessimistic tone. The War-Leader-of-Clans had promised victory time and time again, but still the Strangers resisted.

"The Floating-Reef!" another scout called. "The Floating-Reef comes!"

The knot of officers started to scatter, and !!Dhruuj swam after Nuujuur! in case the Clan-Leader had any further messages to send. The throbbing of the water jets that drove the huge Floatin g-Reef, the thing the Strangers-Above called *Cyclops*," was suddenly loud as the massive structure drove toward them.

It had arrived sooner than anyone had expected ... sooner than the Swimmers who had been assigned to watch it had predicted after many tides of seeing it travel. A hidden reserve of speed ...

The bulk blocked the sunlight filtering through the waters, like one of the periodic passings of the moon across the face of the sun. Nuu - juur! was diving, striking for the bottom as if he were being pursue d by a hunting *woorroo*.

Something splashed into the water overhead and drifted lazily down. Suddenly !!Dhruuj remembered the reports of the explosives the Strangers had used to defend the Floating-Reef from an earlier attack, and he knew why Nuujuur! sough t refuge in deep water. Another cylinder splashed, and another, and yet another....

Long before the first explosion lashed through the water, !!Dhruuj knew neither he nor Nuujuur! would escape the blast. He doubted if any of the leaders would.

It would be a sad Tide for the Clans United when their leaders floated to the surface and led no more. !!Dhruuj wondered if their successors would be able to organize the final attack....

*   *   *

Legionnaires cheered as the great bulk of the *Seafarms Cyclops* slid through the shattered gates and into the compound. Figures on the four boarding platforms waved in response. Some of them were capering like the overexcited monkeys Fraser remembered from Hanuman.

The jubilation was infectious. He felt like shouting or capering himself, now that Watanabe had brought the big harvester ship back.

The subaltern had pushed her to the limit to get to the Sandcastle early, and on his way in had ordered that improvised depth charges be dropped every time his sonars reported contact with large groups of targets.

In combination with the defense the rest of the Legion had mounted inside the base, that would surely break up the wogs for a while. They'd bought yet another breathing space: time to regroup, reorganize ... and count the dead.

High up in the small windows of the ship's bridge, Fraser saw Watanabe's slender, stiff figure. He waved, but the subaltern didn't respond.

The butcher's bill for the battle would be horrendous. He knew that much already. He also knew there was no way they'd be able to pay that price again, even with the full cooperation of the civilians and the arrival of Watanabe's men.

And much as he wanted to think that Choor!'s alliance had been broken by this defeat, there was no way to count on it. They had to expect the nomads to strike again, once they'd recovered from today's fighting. With their resources, they'd recover a hell of a lot faster than the Legion—especially if the Toels had more surprises like that Gorgon waiting in the wings.

As the *Cyclops* maneuvered slowly toward its cradle, Fraser turned away and stared out over the wall across the open sea.

Simple survival was no longer enough. The Legion had to seize the initiative now, before the enemy returned.

One way or another, the next battle would decide this campaign.

*　*　*

He was floating in a formless mist, stark, unrelieved by any detail or variation, different from any of the countless environments David Hawley had experienced in his past voyages into Dreamland. But he was not alone. He shared the mist with another soul, Edward Barnett's, and from somewhere in the distant corners of his mind the computer implant whispered to him.

"Response Shows Resistance/Blockage At Probability 86.5%."

Hawley thought of emptiness, of loneliness, and the computer translated his thoughts, magnified them, redirected them back at the link between Hawley and Barnett. The machine had identified this as one of Barnett's weaknesses, this fear of the void. It was part of the general psych profile, and it had already broken down many of the man's barriers. But Hawley was sharing in these induced feelings and dreams, and they were taking a toll on his spirit as well.

"Again, Barnett." He wasn't speaking, but he visualized the thoughts as words, "heard" them through the mist. "Again. The location of the Toeljuk base. Give me the location, and you won't be alone anymore. Give me the location...."

It was an effective approach. Barnett was fighting him, of course, but Hawley was the only other entity in this private universe, the only link the traitor had to humanity. The poor colonial orphan inside Barnett needed that contact the way David Hawley needed his implant, needed the escape....

He thrust the stray thought aside with an effort of will and repeated the question, holding out a lifeline to Barnett.

And after what seemed like an eternity, Edward Barnett began to answer.

*　*　*

The conference room held more people than it had at the last meeting, but even so Fraser was very conscious of the ones who were missing. Neither Jens nor Barnett was there this time, of course. Since Captain MacLean, the senior man in the Seafarms hierarchy now, had been confined to cells on Watanabe's recommendation, as too thoroughly committed to Barnett's policies to be trusted, it was Katrina Voskovich who represented the civilian viewpoint—not so much because of seniority as because she seemed genuinely ready to support the legionnaires and was respected by her own people at the same time.

DuValier was missing, too. He'd insisted on returning to his cell after the battle, even when Fraser offered to release him. "What I did today I did for the unit, Captain," he had said, stiff and formal. "My opinions on ... other matters ... haven't changed, and I didn't help you so I could earn some good-conduct prize." And Gunnery Sergeant Valko was dead, killed in the fighting around the motor pool in the tense moments before the destruction of the Toel Gorgon.

On the other hand, the remaining subalterns were present for this conference: Watanabe, looking remarkably fresh, despite the fact that he'd snatched only two hours' sleep since the *Cyclops* had berthed; Henck Wijngaarde, still managing to look embarrassed over the fact that the handful of Legion mutineers had all been from his unit; and Carnes, the only platoon leader from Alpha Company still alive. The demi-battalion's warrant officers were also present: Father Fitzpatrick, Dr. Ramirez, and Koenig, plus their opposite numbers from Hawley's outfit and, of course, Kelly.

That left the people clustered around him near the head of the table. Hawley, still looking pale and strained after his time in the interrogation centers. Gunnery Sergeant Trent, who sported a large bruise on one cheek and a bandage on his left hand. And Susan Gage, who'd fought a stubborn battle by the motor pool but seemed as withdrawn and diffident as ever.

These were the men and women who would have to decide the fate of the Terrans on Polypheme. Tired people who'd been pushed to the limit ... but were still determined.

"With the magrep generators and Lieutenant DuValier's tapes in place, we can sit here and laugh at the wogs," Subaltern Wijngaarde was saying. "We've won. I don't see what the problem is."

"The problem, Mr. Wijngaarde, is what it's always been," Kelly told him. "The nomads are smart. Especially this Choorl. We can't guarantee that our defenses are a hundred percent leak-proof."

"Especially with the Toels around," Trent added. "Last time it was a Gorgon, and odds are they only had the one or they'd have hit us with more during the assault. But they probably have a ship or some sort, and they have better weaponry than they've been giving to the wogs. The magreps won't hold against high-tech, and the wogs will come in expecting the jamming."

"What can they do about it?" Warrant Officer Simms, the Alpha Company chaplain, blinked owlishly at Trent.

"Lots of things, Chaplain," Trent said. "Me, I'd put together some simple attack plan ahead of time and ditch the fancy coordination. Win by strength of numbers and sheer wog guts. Or if they've figured out how we're doing it, they could send in commandos to shut our broadcasts down."

"The point is, we're still vulnerable," Kelly said. Trent and Watanabe both nodded at that. "Captain Fraser's right when he says we have to take the war to them for a change."

"How sure are we of their base?" Koenig asked. He looked apologetic, but determined. "That jury-rigged questioning setup...."

"We're sure," Fraser said flatly. "It's another old Toel base like this one, about a hundred klicks down the coast. It was supposed to be abandoned, but when we ran through the Seafarms database it was pretty clear that Barnett had dummied up the survey reports to keep anyone from paying much attention to the place. Captain Hawley pried it out of the little strakk, and the computer puts a ninety-seven-plus probability on the accuracy."

There were a few skeptical looks around the table at the mention of Hawley's name. Ramirez cleared his throat. "I agree. Barnett wasn't holding anything back by the time Captain Hawley got through with him."

Fraser hid a smile. At least the doctor was convinced of Hawley's soundness now.

"What it comes down to, the way I see it, is whether or not we have the strength to mount an attack on the base." Heads turned as Lieutenant Gage spoke in a soft but clear voice. "We're talking about a compound just like this one, possibly defended by Toels and certainly full of wogs. If our chances of surviving another attack here are slim, what are the odds of winning there?"

"We're in bad shape," Fraser admitted. "We're going to have to break down one platoon out of each company to bring the other platoons up to something like fighting strength, and better than one-third casualties is not what I'd call sitting pretty. But Barnett's info suggests the Toels don't have much—probably no more than thirty or forty 'advisers,' and some of them would have gone up with the Gorgon. If we hit them hard, try for the element of surprise, we'll take them."

"But that sounds like you're abandoning the Sandcastle!" Gage exclaimed. "You don't seriously mean to use all the legionnaires on the attack?"

"All but the ones too badly wounded to serve as assault troops. Doc says we've got sixteen recovered enough to man the walls."

"Sixteen!" Carnes paled. "That's not enough to stand watch on the gatehouse!"

"Plus the civilians," Fraser said. "We'll take a few with us to operate the *Cyclops*, but the rest will be left here." He saw Voskovich opening her mouth to protest, and raised his hand. "I know your people are willing to do more, Katrina, but they aren't trained for a set-piece battle. Or a commando action. Or for combat in hardsuits, for that matter. Your people will have to flesh out our resources on this end."

"You're putting all the civilians at risk this way, sir," Chaplain Simms said quietly. "You've said yourself that another attack will overpower our defenses here, even with the legionnaires available. Isn't our first duty to protect these people? That's the way our orders read, isn't it?"

Hawley stirred. Even though he looked exhausted, haggard, there was a fire in his eyes. "This is the only way we can carry out these orders, Chaplain. Captain Fraser's right about this. It's the only move we've got left in this game."

* * *

DuValier looked up, surprised, as the cell door opened and Fraser entered the cramped, spartan room. "Is something wrong?" he asked, rolling out of his cot.

"Not exactly," Fraser said enigmatically. He motioned for DuValier to sit again. "We've decided on an assault on the nomad HQ. Barnett gave it to us."

"I heard," DuValier said. One of the guards who'd brought his dinner had shared the news. "You're taking the *Cyclops*?"

"Right. And every legionnaire who can fight. Fifty civilians as ship's crew, both veeters. It's all or nothing this time, Lieutenant."

He kept his response noncommittal. "Tough decision."

Fraser nodded vaguely. Suddenly he looked hard at his former exec. "We're damned short of officers, Antoine," he said. "Three subalterns, a lieutenant, one senior NCO. Captain Hawley, who might not be up to the long haul. It's bad enough we lost so many legionnaires, but its officers we really need."

"You want me to come? After what happened?" DuValier laughed harshly. "Remind me to tell you sometime what I had to go through yesterday trying to get anybody to trust me. The kind of battle you're going into doesn't have room for hesitation like that!"

"I know. But I *do* need to leave someone in command here while we're gone. Bartlow's arm is coming off; he won't be much use. The senior NCO from the limited-duty bunch is a corporal, Johnson. And I can't spare any of the other officers to take charge of the Sandcastle. But you could."

"You'd trust me with the base? With the civilians?"

"I did yesterday," Fraser said with a shrug. "You did damned good work coming up with that voices thing, even if you did screw around on procedures and not tell anyone. And you've got the touch, Antoine. The wogs won't catch you napping."

DuValier looked away. "You're not going to stick me with some watchdog to keep me honest?"

"You'll be in charge. You're the best man for the job."

He hesitated for a long moment, then nodded. "All right. I'll take it." He laughed again. "And God help us all."

CHAPTER TWENTY-TWO

The Legion's in Magenta; the job is in the bag.

—General Patrice de MacMahon,
French Foreign Legion, 1859

Sorry you came, Kelly?" Fraser asked, joining Kelly Winters by the large observation window at the bow of the *Seafarms Cyclops*. The huge ship was laboring through rough seas on a course south and east from the Sandcastle, with three more hours to go until they were in position to strike at the enemy base. He'd ordered the legionnaires to rest while they could, but hadn't been able to relax himself. It looked as if Kelly was having the same problem.

She shook her head slowly but kept on staring at the water. A nasty storm was brewing out there, one of the powerful *bhourrkhs* spawned in the heat of the tropics that would spin north or south, with winds that could make a Terran hurricane look like a summer breeze. Another reason to finish this fight fast. Tides would be higher than usual for the next few days, and as long as the storms raged the wogs would have a huge advantage in any assault they mounted on the base.

If the legionnaires didn't finish this fight today, they probably wouldn't have another chance.

"I was just … thinking about this planet," she said. "The Toels kept the peace here for centuries, even though we always talk about how brutal they are. We let Seafarms take over here, and they drove the nomads to war in a couple of years."

"Seafarms had help," he said. "From the Toels, especially. They wanted the planet back, and they knew what buttons to push to make the nomads join them." He paused. "But you're right. I think sometimes that Mankind wasn't mature enough to take on a responsibility like the Commonwealth. The government needs commercial support to make it worthwhile to be out here at all, and the corporations are so busy with their profit margins they don't stop and think about the damage they're doing. So then the military gets called out to put things right, and there are times when the only way to do that is to smash the hostiles flat...."

Kelly sighed. "When you put it like that, it sounds like you're one of those back-to-Terra people, ready to chuck it all and let the universe look after itself."

"Not really," he said. "You can't stuff the djinni back into the bottle. Terra has responsibilities we can't just ignore. We didn't know what we were getting into when we knocked down the Semti Conclave, but someone had to step in when they collapsed, and it looks like we were the ones who got picked for it. For every primitive native like Choor! and his people, there are ten who are benefiting from Commonwealth rule, one way or another. We'd create even more hardship by pulling out."

"So we just muddle through, then? That's not much of an answer."

"It's all I've got, anyway," he admitted. "We took oaths to uphold the Commonwealth and help spread civilization among the stars, Kelly. We can't stop idiots from screwing things up, and you know there'll always be idiots—politicians or bureaucrats or misguided business executives. All we can do is put things right when they do screw up, and try to leave the situation a little less volatile than it was when we found it."

"Do you think we can, here?"

"If we pull this off ... maybe. Seafarms went wrong by assuming they could simply ignore the locals except where they were useful. They won't have that option again."

"But if we break Choor!'s confederation ..."

He shook his head. "That's another djinni that won't fit back into the bottle. The nomads have found out that they can work together. It's only a matter of time before they realize it doesn't take Choor! to make cooperation work. And once the natives have a stable confederation this gaggle of independent city-states won't be viable anymore, either.

Ideas spread fast here, thanks to the way the nomads move around. Mark my words, Kelly, whether Choor! wins or loses, Polypheme won't be the same again. Any offworld dealing with the locals will have to involve a global policy, not just focus on one favored city and ignore everybody else."

"I hope Seafarms sees it the way you do."

"I left a tape with DuValier before we left, told him to pass it on or make sure it's somewhere an expeditionary force will uncover it if things go sour for us. My recommendations are in there, and I'm pretty sure the Legion will persuade the Colonial Administration to go along with them. Polypheme's going to have to be a full Commonwealth protectorate after this. Even if Seafarms doesn't want it, we can't afford to let the Toels win and move back in. We're too close to some pretty important systems here to let the Toels build this into an advanced base."

"Well ... I'd rather you delivered your recommendations in person, Col."

"Me too," he said with a faint smile. "I'm just covering all the possibilities, that's all."

"Can we really win this fight?" She turned from the window and looked him in the eye. "And don't give me the morale-building speeches you give to the others. I want it straight."

"Straight? I don't know. We don't have very many troops to pull this off with, and you know the state of our officer corps. There's a hell of a lot riding on unknowns."

"Finally having doubts about Hawley?" she asked. "He *seems* better...."

He shrugged. "Him among others." The battle plan they'd drawn up required the bulk of the legionnaires to distract the nomads in a general engagement, while a smaller, more elite force attacked the enemy base. Fraser was taking charge of the latter unit, backed up by Kelly and her sappers and by Gunnery Sergeant Trent. But it left the main battle to Hawley, Gage, and the three surviving subalterns. It was a lot of responsibility to push onto David Hawley, no matter how dramatically he had changed. And Gage didn't inspire much more confidence. "Mostly, though," he continued, "I'm having doubts about me."

She looked at him with a questioning expression.

He didn't elaborate. But the doubts had been growing since the first time the natives had attacked. He'd underestimated them in the first battle, and after that he'd allowed first Jens and then Barnett to paralyze the defense of the Sandcastle with their interference. That near-mutiny should never have been allowed to happen, either....

Now they were on the verge of being committed to a battle he wasn't sure the Legion could win. Was this how it had started for Hawley? The miracle on Hanuman had set Fraser up as a hero, but a debacle on Polypheme was looking more and more likely. If he lived through this, would he follow David Hawley's path, retreating from reality and trying to recapture the glory of that first lucky victory? Or maybe he'd be more like DuValier, searching for someone else to blame for his misfortunes and twisting his whole life out of shape as a result.

Kelly laid a hand on his shoulder. "Try not to lose that battle before we even leave the *Cyclops*, Col," she said softly. "You're the one who held things together this far. And without you in there doing your best, there's no way we'll win. Don't forget, you're supposed to be part of the Legion, so try following in the footsteps of all those Legion heroes. Go in swinging, do your best, don't give up. These people have a right to that, you know. They need you." She paused. "And I do, too. I don't want to lose you."

The observation bay was quiet except for the distant throbbing of the impellers. Fraser took her hand, and the two of them looked out at the endless ocean together.

*　*　*

David Hawley stood on the docking platform, feeling uncomfortable in the stiff hardsuit. The sun was low on the eastern horizon, just below a building mass of storm clouds. The colors of the sunrise were a spectacular mix of reds and pinks reflected from the dark and angry canopy. A bit of ancient doggerel from pre-spaceflight Terra ran through his mind. *Red sky in morning, sailor take warning....*

Next to him Legionnaire Second-Class Jurgensen cocked his head to one side as he listened to a report over his C^3 network. "That's the last of them, sir," he said. "Subaltern Watanabe's platoon is in the water."

"Then I guess it's time," Hawley said slowly, feeling reluctant to commit himself. He'd thought he could do this, but now he wasn't so sure. A lifetime of dodging responsibility was a hard habit to break....

Fraser crossed the platform from the hatch, saluting smartly. "Good luck, Captain," he said formally.

"And to you," Hawley responded automatically. He started to lower his faceplate, men stopped and fixed his second-in-command with a hard stare. "Look, Fraser ... Colin ... thanks. Anyone else probably would have eased me out of the unit a long time ago, and I wouldn't have fought very hard. But you ... you gave me what I needed. An example to remind me of what being a Legion officer is all about." He stuck out his hand. "It's been an honor to serve with you, Colin—and my personal privilege."

Fraser took his hand with a firm grip. "The honor and the privilege are both mine, sir," he said. "But thank you for the sentiment."

The reluctance was gone now. He closed his helmet and ran a quick diagnostic on the suit. Although Hawley still felt no real confidence in his ability to command the main body of the attack, he knew he'd at least go down trying. If only because he could do no less for Colin Fraser, the only officer he'd met in many long years who'd ever seen anything of value in the washed-out veteran of Aten.

With Jurgensen close behind, Hawley crossed to the edge of the platform and jumped into the water. Now it was too late to turn back. Right or wrong, he was in command.

The water was fairly clear, and with the vision-enhancement setting on his faceplate Hawley could see everything within fifty meters plainly. Beyond that they'd have to rely on sonar.

Below him, the bulk of the demi-battalion was drawn up loosely, divided by platoons. Fraser had five recon lances—the sixth, from Narmonov's shattered formation, had been broken up to provide replacements for the others—plus two heavy-weapon lances and all the surviving sappers. By breaking up Narmonov's and Bartlow's outfits and drafting most of the legionnaires from the transport section, Hawley's platoons were all close to full-strength, except for those missing lances. That gave him a total force of just under a standard paper-strength company. Not much to occupy the attention of whatever nomad forces were covering the enemy headquarters, especially when this fight would be taking place in an environment where the wogs would have all the advantages.

"Sergeant Franz!" he said sharply on the NCO channel of the commlink. "Switch to sonar, and keep me informed of what's out there."

"Clear for now, sir," the sergeant replied. He was probably unhappy at losing what amounted to autonomous command of the transport troops, but he was the best replacement they could find for Gunny Valko.

No one knew how many wogs were here. It was possible that the entire army had withdrawn from the Sandcastle once the Cyclops left, though Fraser had been fairly sure that Choor! would leave at least some of his forces to try another attack on the Legion base while it was shorthanded. But they could expect to be outnumbered, regardless, and in the water FEKs would be hampered a lot more than the rocket guns the nomads used. The legionnaires needed an equalizer....

He found himself comparing the situation to simulations he had played over the years. Ambush and good use of terrain were the best equalizers in combat, but it was damned hard to mount an ambush in what amounted to an offensive role.

Unless the side that was on the offensive was able to stand on the defense tactically.

"Trebbia, 218 BC," he muttered. "Or F'Rujukh's counterattack on Ganymede."

"Sir?" Jurgensen sounded uncertain. Hawley hadn't realized he'd spoken out loud.

"Never mind," he said.

At Trebbia Hannibal's Carthaginians, exhausted and weak from the crossing of the Alps, had drawn the Roman legions into a fight by using light cavalry to goad them into a rash attack across an icy river. The Romans had never expected Hannibal to conceal a large force behind some low hills. The resulting rout had destroyed Rome's best hope of stopping the Second Punic War before it could really get started.

And Ganymede. Marshal F'Rujukh had lost two pitched battles to Alliance forces on Jupiter's moon, but that didn't stop him from laying a beautiful trap around Frenchport. Concealing the bulk of his forces in a series of caves, he'd used a brigade of the Third Foreign Legion as bait to encourage an Alliance landing, caught them from behind, and annihilated them, thereby capturing sufficient transport to mount his brilliant counteroffensive, which prolonged the fighting on Ganymede by at least six months.

Or there was Second Manassas from the American Civil War, or ...

He stopped himself. There were dozens of precedents, and he'd fought most of those battles himself, in simulation. A weak enough force retreating from the wogs should encourage a general pursuit, while another unit lying in ambush could exploit the confusion that was sure to follow. That was the key.

He started toward the bottom on full thruster. For the first time, he was beginning to feel that he could actually be an asset to this fight after all....

* * *

"Sonar reports a large force of nomads leaving their compound. Stand by."

Selim Bashar glanced over the controls of the veeter, impatient for the order to begin the attack. Karatsolis looked anxious too, as he rechecked his weaponry.

They had to wait, though. Until the nomads were fully committed to responding to Captain Hawley, an assault on their fortress would be useless.

Minutes passed. Bashar turned in his seat, glancing first at the other veeter flying parallel to them, and then down and back at the barge hooked to the two flyers by tough flexsteel cables.

The barge had been reequipped with its magrep generators before the *Cyclops* had sailed from the Sandcastle. With the magrep fields operating, it rode uneasily just above the ocean surface. And when the time came the two veeters could tow it into action at a fairly high speed—faster, certainly, than *Cyclops* could have covered the distance to the old Toel complex. And even if they ran into trouble the ship would be intact to pull out the legionnaires when the battle was over, win or lose.

Two veeters, a makeshift barge, and sixty-seven legionnaires weren't much for an attack on the enemy headquarters. Bashar hoped they would be enough, Allah willing.

"CO Alpha reports the enemy has engaged the main body," the civilian communications tech aboard the *Cyclops* relayed.

"CO Strikeforce to all Strikers," Fraser's voice came on the line. "Commence attack!"

Bashar waited until Legionnaire Shapiro, piloting the second veeter, had signified his readiness. Then he hit the countdown button on the autopilot. Seconds later, the throttle began to advance automatically in the preprogrammed pattern that would keep the two veeters pulling evenly on their towlines. They gathered speed, slowly at first, then more quickly.

The enemy base came into view ahead, swelling as the veeters hurtled toward it. The complex was similar to the Sandcastle in overall layout and appearance, but this one hadn't been modified to accommodate Terrans. The gates on this one had never been repaired, and water filled the center of the compound. There were other differences, mostly of detail.

The large beehive shape that rose from the middle of the complex, gleaming in the morning sunlight, was the most noticeable difference of all. It had all the characteristics of a Toeljuk spacecraft, probably one of their smaller models. Fifty or sixty crew, perhaps, given the gregarious nature of the Toels. Less, with the ones that Karatsolis had taken out aboard that Gorgon.

The veeters pressed on, closer … closer.…

*　*　*

"Gunners! Stand by!" Fraser shouted.

The barge was pitching in the rough water, and he wondered for the hundredth time if his plan had any hope of success. The heavy weapons needed a stable platform if they were going to succeed in this first crucial phase of the attack plan. If they couldn't do it, they'd have to circle and attack by way of the opening where the main gates should have been. That area would be heavily defended.…

They had to try. "Gunners, fire!"

Two Fafnirs leapt into the sky almost as one, and the harsh glare of four onagers outshone the sun. The onagers kept on firing, laying down four steady streams of superheated plasma at preselected points along the wall, while the Fafnir gunners reloaded their launchers with the last two missiles in their stockpile.

Kelly had mapped the stress points carefully back at the Sandcastle, and computer simulations had given them good odds of opening a breach of the required size with the arsenal they'd selected.

Maybe he should have assigned more heavy weapons to the strike force … but Hawley would need them, too, to help equalize the odds in *his* battle. These would have to do the trick.

He dropped his faceplate and switched to image-enhancement, as the first two Fafnirs struck the wall and exploded. Those hits, at least, had been right on target. And the onagers were taking a toll as well. Fraser held his breath, willing the attack to work.…

The second wave of Fafnirs hit, and part of the wall seemed to buckle, sagging under the impact. "Pour it on!" Fraser shouted to the onager gunners. More fusand exploded under the onslaught, while the bombardment superheated the entire target area. The fusand was glowing, running, melting.

And the wall loomed closer as the veeters pulled the barge on.

* * *

"Now!" Bashar shouted, hitting the release on the tow cable and jerking his joystick hard over and up. The wall flashed under the veeter, a few surprised-looking nomads gaping up at them from the rooftops. Karatsolis swung his MEK into line and opened fire as the veeter passed, and many of the natives were left staring at the sky with unseeing eyes.

Behind them there was a flash and the roar of an explosion. As he brought the veeter around in a tight turn, Bashar felt his breath catch in his throat. Shapiro hadn't made it.

Maybe he hadn't been able to release his towline in time, or maybe he'd been a fraction of a second too slow in climbing as he approached the wall. The veeter had almost cleared the rampart, but not quite. Now pieces of the shattered flyer littered the wall and the adjacent rooftops, and the hole Fraser's men had cut gaped a little wider near the top than it had before.

There wasn't time to mourn the two men from the other veeter, though. With a muttered appeal to Allah, Bashar swung around again and passed low over the compound, giving Karatsolis a chance to sow death and confusion in their path.

* * *

Drifting free, the barge continued to rush toward the wall under the momentum of the high-speed approach. Fraser studied the breach with a critical eye.

One of the veeters scraped the wall and lost control. He recoiled as the blast lit up the cloud-darkened sky and showered them with debris. Two more men dead. When would it end...?

"Steady, boys!" Trent called out, as if unaffected by the explosion. "The old scow's a little too wide! Brace yourselves!"

Fraser grabbed a rail moments before the barge hit. As Trent had said, the gap wasn't quite wide enough for the barge to pass through, but that wasn't important. The jagged hole extended just below the waterline, and beyond, the enemy compound spread before them. "Let's move!" he shouted.

"Go! Go! Go!" Trent was yelling as legionnaires ran forward, closing the helmets of their hardsuits and springing over the rails, across the remains of the wall, and into the fort. Kelly was marshaling her sappers further aft.

"All right!" Fraser called. "Plan Tango! Kelly, you've got the Toel ship. Gunny, with me! Let's take 'em!"

He closed his hardsuit and followed the others.

The die was cast.

*　*　*

"Strikeforce is going in, Lieutenant."

Susan Gage barely noticed Massire's report, as she drew a bead on a wog and fired. The attacking force was larger than she'd expected, and it moved with a speed and discipline that were incredible to watch. It would take a miracle to keep her diversionary force out of reach until the captain sprang his trap.

A miracle she would have to pull off.

She had both of Alpha Company's platoons, less all the heavy weapons. Thirty-nine legionnaires all told, against hundreds of nomads....

Did Hawley really expect her to keep them together, keep them retreating without starting a rout? Over and over, the battle in the Sandcastle where she'd let Bravo Company get pinned down under withering fire kept replaying itself. If she made a single mistake now, her own outfit would be the one to suffer.

But another phrase also echoed in her mind, Hawley's last words as he gathered the ambush force and withdrew to the boulder-strewn terrain he'd chosen to hide them in. "Of course you can do it, Lieutenant," he'd said after she'd expressed her concerns aloud. "There's no one else I would entrust my Alphas to."

She'd always thought that Hawley was indifferent to his Exec. Now she knew he had confidence in her, and for the first time in a long time she realized that Hawley's confidence was all the respect she needed.

"Dalton! Hsien! Tighten it up!" she ordered, checking her sonar display again. "Keep it moving ... keep it moving."

Susan Gage was going to bring off the miracle—or die trying.

Chapter Twenty-three

Were you satisfied with my men?

—last words of Commandant Faurax,
killed at Dogba, Dahomey,
French Foreign Legion, 1892

Keep down! Wogs coming through!" the sapper called over his radio, and Kelly flattened herself behind the cover of a half-ruined fusand stairway, one that led up to the roof of the structure they used as the motor pool back at the Sandcastle. Moving and fighting underwater was awkward. She had thought her Navy training in zero-G operations would help, but so far she'd found it heavy going just to keep up with the rest of the sapper platoon. She was glad of the chance to rest while they waited for the band of nomads to swim past, heading for the fighting on the far side of the compound.

They had worked their way around the wall after leaving the breach, trying to avoid contact for as long as possible. Fraser and Trent were supposed to keep the defenders occupied while the sappers took care of the Toel ship. If that vessel got airborne it could cause a lot of damage, and now that the aliens had revealed themselves once they had no further reason for staying hidden. The Toeljuk Autarchy had never been slow to use whatever methods were necessary to achieve their goals. If anything, it was a surprise that they hadn't already used the ship for an attack on the Sandcastle. But the Toels probably preferred not to risk their ticket home, against the same Grendels that had knocked out their assault vehicle.

The last report from Fraser suggested he was doing his part of the job. Garcia had passed the word that the recon lances were under heavy attack from nomads, and Katrina Voskovich aboard the *Cyclops* had relayed a sonar report that suggested the wogs engaged with Hawley had dispatched most of their reserves to support the base.

That would make Hawley's situation a little less desperate, but it also meant that at least part of Fraser's battle plan was already un-raveling. He'd counted on Hawley's main body to keep most of the enemy distracted.

At least they'd bought some time this way. But if the battle here lasted more than fifteen or twenty minutes the nomads would be getting reinforcements, and that would spell disaster.

Everything was balanced on a knife edge....

Something hissed through the water from above them, striking Legionnaire Gordon squarely in his backpack thruster unit. The proj-ectile exploded, and in the same moment the thruster controls shorted out. Gordon's body convulsed a few times.

Then Kelly was too busy to notice the casualty, as more shots plowed toward her unit like so many tiny torpedoes. She rolled in the water and fired a long burst from her FEK. As she cut in her thruster and raced for cover, she saw their attackers. Not the sleek, elongated figures of the wogs, these were squat, with a dozen thick tentacles and many more smaller ones, wearing uniforms with many of the same characteristics as her own battledress and carrying strangely-shaped weapons no human hand could have made or used.

The Toels had discovered them. And there was no way any of her sappers was going to run the gauntlet and reach the spaceship as long as the fighting went on....

* * *

"Onagers forward!" Fraser called. "Stand clear!"

Four legionnaires took up positions in front of his ragged skirmish line. Unlike the rest of the legionnaires, they didn't have hardsuits. Their regular combat armor was sealed against all environments, in-cluding the incredible heat generated by their plasma weapons. Hardsuits were less effective, and it was wise to give the onager gunners a wide berth.

The Alpha Company corporal in the garishly decorated armor called out the order to fire, and the onagers flared bright in the water. They kept up a steady barrage, and after a few seconds there were no more nomads to threaten their position.

That wouldn't last long. This was the fourth wave of native soldiers that had been entirely wiped out. Choor! evidently wasn't worrying much about controlling his soldiers' fighting instincts when it came to the defense of his headquarters. And even with a sizable number facing Hawley's force outside the compound, there were plenty of wogs to expend.

"Casualties!" he snapped.

Garcia repeated the order, waited as she received replies from each lance, then responded. "Three killed. Valdez, Martin, and Llewellyn. And Vrurrth took some shrapnel in that last rocket attack, but Corporal Rostov says it's superficial."

That brought the total dead since the start of the assault to seven. "Tighten up the sonar watch," he ordered. "We've got to spot them before they launch another attack." It was getting to be a pattern. The wogs would get in the first shot by sneaking up on the legionnaires, and men would die. Then the Legion weaponry would shatter the enemy assault. He couldn't afford to keep on fighting a war of attrition, though. Not when the nomads had a seemingly endless supply of replacements, and more on the way from outside.

"Sir, Warrant Officer Kelly reports the Sapper Platoon has come under attack by Toels approximately seventy meters from the grounded ship. They are pinned down and requesting reinforcements."

Kelly....

Fraser fought the urge to snap out orders to split up his force and launch a relief mission. That would just give the nomads a better chance of defeating them all in detail. "Tell her to hang on as long as possible, Garcia," he said. "We've got problems of our own."

Even as he spoke, his sonar display showed movement to the left and down near the bottom. Another attack getting organized? Probably.

"We'll get her help as soon as we can," he finished. He shifted to the private channel that linked him to Trent. "Gunny. We're getting targets bearing two-five-seven, down."

"I see them, skipper," Trent replied.

"Let's make them uncomfortable. Take Rostov and Pascali. Call for backup if you need to." It took all his control to keep his impatience and anxiety from showing. He didn't like the thought of what would happen if Kelly was captured by those Toels. They were one of the few races that preferred slave labor to automation....

Too many enemies, too few legionnaires to carry out his ambitious attack plan. Everybody else had been right. Now they were paying the price for his mistakes.

*   *   *

Hawley watched the sonar display, fascinated by the unfolding battle. It was so much like one of his simulations, this movement of tiny dots across his faceplate display. The legionnaires in Gage's force were falling back steadily, managing to stay just out of reach of the pursuing nomads. Just a few more minutes ...

He welcomed the feeling that it was all just another elaborate simulation. When he thought of the battle in terms of a real conflict, with real casualties and an outcome that depended entirely on his own decisions, panic would scream within him.

Reality took him back to that day on Aten, to the fears of failure and the sickening realization of loss each time a man died. Far better to think of them all as units in a game, unfeeling, imaginary.

Perhaps if he could have done that, things would have gone differently all along. A few better breaks here and there and he'd be a brigadier now, ready to retire after a long and honorable career. Instead of being a failure whose single moment of glory had been lost in a lifetime of uselessness....

No! He couldn't keep mourning a lost past. It was time to live in the present. His men needed him now.

Now ...

It was time to act. "Jurgensen! Start broadcasting the wog voice recording!" He switched to the general transmission channel. "Come on, boys, let's show those wogs what the Legion's made of!"

"Legion!" half a hundred voices replied. Then someone else shouted "Hawley! Hawley!" and the others took it up. He had forgotten the thrill of it, the feeling of *belonging* that was part of being an officer of the Legion.

The legionnaires broke from cover, opening fire at the rear ranks of the nomads chasing Gage. The trap was sprung....

"Now!" Gage shouted. "Turn and give 'em hell, Alphas!"

The two depleted platoons responded flawlessly, pivoting in the water and unleashing a murderous FEK barrage against the closest wog troops. Following so close upon Hawley's ambush, this counterattack destroyed the last of their cohesion. A moment ago the natives had been a disciplined fighting force. Now they were a mob, trapped in a deadly crossfire, unable to react quickly enough as the initiative suddenly shifted to the Legion.

But the confusion didn't diminish the individual bravery of the wogs. They still fought fearlessly, and they still outnumbered the legionnaires by a wide margin. If they got a chance to reorganize, they'd still be dangerous.

She gestured to Massire. "Make sure that wog noise is playing loud and clear," she ordered. They had to make sure that Choor! didn't start coordinating this battle again. There wouldn't be much chance of that, as long as the wogs were getting a double dose of DuValier's recording from each of the two Terran forces.

Massire gave a thumbs-up, but a moment later a native rocket bullet tore a hole through his chest. He was dead before Gage could reach him....

"Tsiolkov!" she called to the nearest legionnaire. "Take the C^3 unit." She paused to fire a long FEK burst before shouting again. "Hit them! Hit them hard!"

* * *

"Hit the bastards again!" Corporal Mike Johnson shouted. "No, not like that, you stupid son of a strakk!"

He grabbed an FEK out of a civilian's hands and snapped the selector switch from full-auto to the three-round burst fire setting. "Don't just pump out a whole strakking clip, for Chrissakes! We want some ammo for the next attack, too!"

A couple of the Seafarms people laughed, sounding relieved. If the legionnaire could talk about the next fight, maybe they really could come through this....

The assault had been going on for close to half an hour now. Unlike the previous attacks against the Sandcastle, this one hadn't involved any finesse or maneuvering on the part of the wogs. They'd just come boiling out of the sea from all directions at once, trying to overwhelm the defenses.

Luckily, the magrep generators had slowed them down, so that even the armed civilians could hold the walls. The worst weak spots were the shattered gates and a short section of the wall near the Seafarms office block, where one of the magrep modules had been removed to outfit the barge Fraser's men were using for their attack on the enemy base.

Lieutenant DuValier had the gate area. It was up to Johnson to take charge at this other danger zone. But it wouldn't pay to ignore the rest of the perimeter, either. If any of the generators failed, or if the nomads forced their way through despite them, the civilians wouldn't be much of a match for the wogs.

He thrust the battle rifle back into the man's hands and pointed at the crowded waters below. "Now let 'em know you mean business!"

Limping on his injured leg, stiff and tingling inside the regen cast still strapped there, Johnson moved back. It was hard to let the civilians do the fighting while he just looked on, but Lieutenant DuValier had told him that the best thing the legionnaires in the Sandcastle could do was stay back and direct the defense. An officer couldn't allow himself to be drawn so deeply into the fighting that he didn't pay attention to what was happening all across the battlefield. And for all intents and purposes Johnson was an officer now. With two other wounded legionnaires, he was in command of what amounted to two full platoons.

It was a responsibility he gladly would have traded for his old lance command, but he wasn't going to let Captain Fraser down. Or Du-Valier, who despite the abortive mutiny had been a powerhouse, org-anizing the defense since Hawley and Fraser had left aboard the *Cyclops*.

"Corporal! Corporal!" That was Legionnaire Myaighee, the injured alien from Watanabe's platoon who was operating Johnson's C^3 unit. "Trouble by the gatehouse, Corporal. A major attack this time. Wogs have penetrated the gates and are attacking the lieutenant's position from three sides now!"

"Pass the word to Wu," Johnson ordered. "Tell him to round up … five civilians from each unit and get over to the gatehouse right away. Grab five of our people to go, too!"

The hannie saluted and hurried off. Johnson scanned the sea again. If they could just keep holding until Captain Fraser smashed the enemy base.…

* * *

DuValier crouched behind the rampart and slapped his last magazine into his FEK. He'd run out of grenades long since, and it wouldn't be long before he was out of needle rounds as well.

In which case, he told himself, he'd throw shards of fusand at any wog who tried to climb onto the gatehouse roof. If this was going to be another disaster like Fenris, he wasn't planning on surviving the massacre. This time he'd go out fighting, and he'd take as many wogs with him as he could manage. Antoine DuValier wanted an honor guard to escort him to Hell.

He leaned over the rampart and fired down, heedless of the questing rocket bullets and crossbow bolts that responded to his fire. There were only eleven Seafarms men left on the walls around him out of the fifty he'd started with, and four of them were wounded. The technician with his C^3 pack had tumbled off the roof a few minutes earlier, so he didn't have any way of raising the rest of the defenders now. Corporal Johnson would have to keep up the fight as best he could....

He kept on firing until the clip ran dry, then threw the FEK at a nomad climbing slowly up the inner wall. Another rifle lay nearby where someone had dropped it. DuValier scrambled for it, checked the magazine, and brought it up to fire a burst into a wog climbing over the parapet. The nomad screeched and fell over backward, hitting the water below with a loud splash.

Panting, DuValier crouched for a long moment. If the Sandcastle fell, at least he'd die with a weapon in his hands. Captain Fraser had given him that much.

If he had worked with Fraser all along, instead of letting his hate blind him to the man's nature, perhaps none of them would be in this corner now. Or maybe this would have been the outcome no matter what.

All that really mattered anymore was the battle. DuValier raised the battle rifle again and thrust himself back into the fray.

$*$ $*$ $*$

"Here they come again!" someone shouted. Hawley braced the FEK in his hands and strained to see through the murky water. The battle had churned up mud and blood that made it hard to spot anything more than a few meters away. That was giving the wogs an advantage, despite the Legion sonars. In this confused battle it was impossible to follow all the enemy targets successfully, and when a nomad erupted from a liquid fog at close range he had all the benefits of speed and familiarity with the environment. Most of the Legion casualties in this fight were coming from sword cuts and spear thrusts, not the high-tech weaponry supplied by the Toels.

There was an irony somewhere in there, but Hawley wasn't laughing.

Nearby, Subaltern Watanabe and a corporal named Radescu raised their weapons and fired almost simultaneously as a trio of wogs broke into view. Radescu screamed as a heavy-bladed sword drove downward through his shoulder and deep into his torso, but the nomads thrashed and bled under the subaltern's withering fire. More inhuman shapes appeared, and Hawley added his FEK's voice to the battle.

The nomads were broken as a fighting force, but they were still attacking anywhere they could. It looked as though this time they were going to keep on fighting until there were no wogs left at all. A lot more legionnaires would die as well.

The butcher's bill was going to hurt later, but for now Hawley had a battle to fight. He didn't even need the fiction of a game anymore. All that mattered was keeping these wogs tied up until Colin Fraser could win the fight inside the compound. And that was just what Hawley would do, no matter what the cost might be.

"Sir!" That was Jurgensen, sticking close beside him despite the double encumbrance of the thruster unit and his C^3 pack. "*Cyclops* reports that bunch of wogs heading back for the base has broken up. Some of them are heading for us again. Sounds like they're completely disorganized."

"Acknowledge the report," he said, his mind wrestling with the new information. It sounded like Choor!'s war machine was breaking down. Those nomads would want to rally around their own clans as the fighting became general. The wog commander would know that the defense of the base was most important, but in the long run his coalition was still weaker than the individual clan loyalties within it.

That would help Fraser. But the last thing he needed out here was more nomads....

"Captain! Look out!" Watanabe yelled the warning too late. A nomad spear seemed to come from nowhere, thrusting into the pit of his stomach. The pain was like nothing he'd ever felt before.

He tried to shoot at the wog, as the nomad yanked the spear clear and thrust again, but he'd dropped his FEK. The pain redoubled, and Hawley bent double, clutching his injured stomach and sobbing.

The wog shuddered and thrashed as a hail of needle rounds ripped through him. A moment later Watanabe was there, fumbling at his first aid kit. "Medic! Medic!" he yelled.

"Save ... save it," Hawley gasped out. "Nothing ... a medic ... can do for ... me. Not now...."

"Take it easy, sir," Watanabe was saying, as he moved closer to examine the wound. Even through his faceplate his grave expression was clear enough. The subaltern knew the wound was a mortal one.

"More ... nomads ... on the way ..." Hawley forced the words out, trying to ignore the burning pain in his gut. "Must ... unify.... Join Gage ... Hit them all together... No defeat in detail...." It was all clear in his mind, but he didn't know if he was making sense to Watanabe. Marshal Vigny had allowed an Alliance relief force to smash into his troops while they were still dispersed after the first part of the Battle of Dijon, and the afternoon battle had ended with the rout of the French and the final collapse of the Imperial resistance in Metropolitan France at the end of the Grand Crusade.

The battle was clear in his mind, as clear as this fight against the wogs. But he couldn't find the words to explain it....

Gage and Watanabe could handle the fight. They'd beat the wogs cold. With these legionnaires, they could do anything.

He rallied enough to go on. "Tell ... tell the men ... I'm proud of them all...."

And blackness descended on him for the last time.

Chapter Twenty-four

They're not men, they're wild beasts.

—a German major, speaking of the French Foreign Legion,
1916

Katrina Voskovich held the receiver to her ear and listened to the chatter from inside the enemy base. Around her, the other civilians on the bridge of the *Seafarms Cyclops* watched her, waiting. She'd never expected to be a leader, but it seemed as if the role had been forced on her anyway.

"The sappers are still pinned," she said. "And it sounds like the captain's troops are running into heavy resistance." She looked across at Warrant Officer Koenig, the only legionnaire on the bridge. "Sounds like they're in trouble."

Koenig shifted uncomfortably. Aside from him, only Father Fitzpatrick and Dr. Ramirez remained on board the ship. "What about Captain Hawley's men? Can we get any of them free to support the strike force?"

"I don't think so," Voskovich told him. "The fighting down there is still pretty confused, and that new bunch is moving in."

The warrant officer let out a ragged breath. "Then there's no way of helping Fraser's people. They'll have to handle it on their own...."

"We're available," Voskovich said flatly. "I say we go for it."

"Captain Fraser's orders—"

"Damn the orders!" she flared. "Look, he wanted the *Cyclops* safe so there was a way out if things went sour. Well, they're going sour, but none of those legionnaires will make it unless they get support fast. We may not be much, but we can turn up the heat on the wogs."

A spasm of indecision crossed Koenig's face. She pressed on. "What do the rest of you say? We've disobeyed the military people before, right? Let's make it count for something, for a change!"

The bridge crew's reaction was mixed. The ones who'd been in the fighting at the Sandcastle were cheering, but the regular ship's personnel looked sullen. Their only experience of the Legion had been Subaltern Watanabe's takeover....

Koenig looked around, then gave a curt nod. "Do it," he said shortly.

"You heard the man," Voskovich said loudly. "Get this monstrosity under way. And get everyone who has a weapon and isn't needed to operate the ship down to the boarding platforms. We'll show the legionnaires they aren't the only ones crazy enough to take on these wogs!"

$$* \quad * \quad *$$

Fraser swam past a knot of dead nomads, to join Gunnery Sergeant Trent beside one of the twisted struts that had been part of a harvester ship cradle near the center of the enemy compound. Steady fighting had pushed them deeper and deeper into the base, but they still had a long way to go to reach Kelly's position beyond the bulk of the Toel ship.

Fourteen dead and eight wounded, so far. More than half of his force were casualties now, and still the nomads kept on fighting. The wog coalition was larger than anyone had predicted, and there were still plenty of hostiles left inside their fortress. Enemy troops were closing in behind them now, and the next attack would probably come from all sides.

He was certain now that this final gesture against Choor!'s headquarters had failed. They hadn't seen anything yet that looked like it might be the native warlord's bodyguard or staff, just scores of nomad soldiers rallying to the defense. He had a good idea now of where Choor! was: The defenders were strongest in the direction of the gatehouse complex, and Fraser suspected that the lower levels there were probably flooded and occupied by the enemy leadership. But the gatehouse was even farther away than Kelly's beleaguered sappers. It didn't look like he was going to reach either target now.

Explosions erupted behind the legionnaires, a long way off but loud in his external audio pickups. They were coming from the direction of the breach, and they sounded like the depth charges the legionnaires had improvised. "What the hell…?" he said aloud.

He kicked off from the bottom and broke the surface, ignoring the risk of being spotted. Looking across the compound, Fraser spotted the breach.

The huge shape of the *Cyclops* loomed behind the hole, and civilians were streaming off one of the boarding platforms onto the abandoned barge. He thought he saw Koenig … Voskovich … even the burly shape of the guard who had threatened him during Barnett's mutiny. None of them had hardsuits, but they were firing into the water and shoving explosive canisters through the gap to confuse the nomads.

Fraser dived again. They'd disobeyed his orders to stay clear of the fighting, but he was glad of the disobedience. With this new threat the nomads would have to regroup, and in the meantime he just might be able to turn the battle around….

"Gunny!" he shouted. "Take two lances toward the breach. *Cyclops* is there, and we can catch some wogs in a crossfire if we hurry. Then go support Kelly."

"What about the rest of the men?" Trent asked. "You're not splitting us up?"

"Yes, we are. We'll smash through the nomads over there and hit the gatehouse! That should make Choor! rethink his battle plan!" He switched frequencies. "Onagers, form up in front and prepare to advance. Let's get this thing over with!"

He slapped a fresh magazine into the receiver of his FEK. This new plan still risked a defeat in detail, but the appearance of the *Cyclops* had opened up a window he couldn't afford to ignore.

Even if they failed, the nomads would know they'd been in a fight.

*　*　*

"Lieutenant!" Watanabe felt relief wash over him as he caught sight of Susan Gage in the middle of a cluster of legionnaires, advancing out of the swirling murk ahead. Since Hawley's death he'd been trying to hold his force together and close ranks with the other unit. Now, at last, he could pass the responsibility back to a superior.

Gage and her C^3 technician swam over to him. "Where's the captain?" she asked.

"Dead, Lieutenant," Watanabe told her. "You're in charge now."

"Damn," she said softly. "Just when he had a chance ..."

"He died the way he would have wanted to," he said. "Let's concentrate on saving the living."

"Right," she nodded, visibly taking control of herself. "We've broken the back on the main body. Wish we had a better idea of what's going on with Captain Fraser. That's where the real action is." She paused. "Do you have a status on those reinforcements?"

"Lost them in the clutter a few minutes ago," he said. With the bodies so thick throughout the battlefield, the sonar units were having a lot of trouble distinguishing the live targets that were still out there. "They'll be here soon...."

She brought up her FEK suddenly and fired past him, yelling "They're here now!" Watanabe rolled over and added his own weapon to hers. A cluster of nomads with mixed weaponry swam right into the kill zone and died.

Then there were more, swarming out of the murk. He maintained fire until his magazine ran dry, then drew his PLF rocket pistol.

Gage ran out of ammo at almost the same moment and fumbled for a fresh magazine. As she did, a wog raised a rocket gun and fired. Watanabe tried to shove her out of the way, but it was too late. Susan Gage was dead, too. That made him the senior surviving officer — maybe the only one. Wijngaarde had died in the early stages of the ambush, and he hadn't seen Carnes yet....

"Close up, legionnaires!" he called on the comm circuit. "Throw the bastards back!"

He heard Sergeant Gessler shouting orders and encouragement, heard the grudging respect in the man's voice as he called, "Come on, you sandrats! The Sub needs us!"

*   *   *

Kelly flinched as another of her sappers died. The Toels had the whole position ringed in now, and there was precious little cover that wasn't exposed to one of the alien soldiers. Even the arrival of the *Cyclops*, reported by Trent over her commlink, hadn't slowed the Toels down. It looked like they were letting their allies go down, while they concentrated on protecting their ship.

Beyond their defensive positions she could see Toeljuk workers loading cargo through the open bay doors near the base of the vessel. If only she could get some explosives up there....

A Toel laser probed toward her. She could feel the water temperature going up each time the pulse passed overhead. Kelly clung more tightly to the fusand wall and returned fire, but the laser was shielded behind a plasteel barrier.

Without reinforcements from Fraser, there was no way the sappers were breaking out of this crossfire. And Fraser, she knew, was busy elsewhere. There was still no sign of Trent's two lances, either.

Suddenly the Toel laser position ceased firing as the gunner let go of his weapon and drifted toward the surface, no longer moving. Another Toel nearby did the same a moment later. Through her headphones she heard a whoop of triumph.

"Rydell to the rescue!"

"Knock it off and find a target." Trent's gruff voice overrode the exuberance of the laser gunner from Braxton's recon lance. "Miss Kelly? Are you still here?"

"Alive and kicking, Sergeant," she answered, firing again. More Toels were dying, as the two fresh lances took them from behind. Trent had circled around so that his attack had come from the direction of the ship, and the Toels had never even noticed. "How the hell did you sneak up on them like that?"

"Climbed out and used the walls. Bashar and Spear have things pretty clear topside now, and the bad guys aren't paying much attention up there anymore."

She grinned inside her hardsuit helmet. For a change the Terrans had made terrain work in their favor.

"Let's move!" she shouted to her sappers. Kicking off from the bottom and cutting in her thruster, Kelly raced toward Trent and his men. A few random shots followed from other Toel positions, but at least for now the enemy was too busy to effectively cover the legionnaires.

Sappers followed, led by old MacAllister. The veteran trailed a large satchel of PX-90 behind him. "Dinna worry, lassie!" he called, as he caught up to her. "We'll blast yon bastards!"

Mbote, another of Braxton's men, passed her and dropped toward the bottom, blazing away steadily with his FEK. "We'll cover you," he said. "But make it fast!"

Trent was already swimming ahead, with Pascali's lance spread out in a loose skirmish line on either side, cutting a swath through the unarmed Toel workers around the cargo door. Kelly and MacAllister were close behind, with a handful of other sappers in tow.

There was a savage gun battle at the door itself, with a pair of Toels armed with heavy laser rifles holding the recon lance. Finally Trent and Corporal Pascali rolled through, firing a volley of mini-grenades. In the confusion, the rest of the lance was able to break in and kill the two aliens. The cargo bay was clear—for the moment.

"Go! Go!" Trent called. Kelly and MacAllister split the explosives between them and started working their way around opposite sides of the cargo bay, slapping liberal quantities of the PX-90 in place. The other sappers followed behind, setting detpacks and programming them to Kelly's shouted orders. The recon troopers kept a wary eye on the two doors, ready for any Toel reinforcements.

Kelly planted her last charge and waited impatiently for the others to finish. "Let's mag out!" she said. The Terrans swam clear of the cargo bay, back into the battle outside. Braxton's lance was giving way slowly before a determined Toel attack. Now the legionnaires hit their thruster and angled away from the ship.

Pausing to draw out a remote control unit, Kelly hit the detonator. An instant later explosions erupted from the interior of the ship. The Toeljuks pursuing them broke off the fight and headed for the vessel.

"No way they'll be leaving now," Kelly said confidently. They'd planted the charges to breach the hull in several places, and it would be hours before they could patch the ship well enough to make her spaceworthy.

They'd done their job. Now if Fraser could carry off his ...

*　*　*

Inside the Reef-of-the-Gift-Bearers, Choor! listened to the reports from his subordinates with mounting concern. All contact lost with the force sent outside the walls to face the Strangers there, no word on the progress against their fortress. And every force they'd mustered against the raiding party had been thrown back or destroyed.

How could these Terran-Strangers fight so well? The Gift-Bearers had said that Terrans were a weak race, indecisive, whose warriors ran from a losing battle and whose merchants would sell one another as slaves when they scented profit in the current. An easy victory, they had said, which would deliver Ourgh and eventually the rest of the land-dwellers into the tendrils of the Clans United with less effort then it took to subdue a hostile Clan.

But this had been anything but an easy victory. Even if they finished off these Terrans, the Clans United might never recover. Too many warriors lost, too much of Choor!'s prestige used up in useless assaults and stratagems the leaders of the Strangers had anticipated all too thoroughly. Even the Betrayer had proven useless to the Clans.

This "Legion" of Terran warriors was more tenacious in battle than any Clan, fighting, *winning* against impossible odds and never knowing when to give up. They were more like a blood-hungry *woorroo* following the scent of its prey. Animals …

But dangerous animals. Animals who had broken his dream of the Clans United.

"If you wish, you can still win free with the remaining guards," one Clan-Leader was saying.

"No!" Choor! rejected the suggestion as automatically as the most instinct-enslaved Warrior-Inferior. "No … Muster the last guards. Break these animals for me. Break them!"

* * *

The wogs erupted out of the gatehouse so suddenly that Fraser hardly had time to react. For a few minutes he'd thought the battle was over. But there were still nomads rallying to the defense after all.

Just one more battle … Surely this would be the last.

A native with a pike twice his own length charged straight at Fraser, but the huge Gwyrran named Vrurrth thrust past and grappled with the wog. The pike drifted away as Vrurrth wrenched it from the smaller alien's hands. Then the wog was thrashing, as those powerful fingers dug into the nomad's gills. A moment later the native stopped moving, and the Gwyrran pushed the limp body away with a contemptuous flourish. It floated toward the surface in slow motion, blood oozing from the gill slits.

Fraser opened fire just as another nomad, this one wielding a sword, slashed at Legionnaire Grant. The boy flashed him a quick thumbs-up as he directed a steady stream of autofire at the gatehouse door. Corporals Rostov and Haddad were close by, also firing until it seemed that the water was growing black with needle rounds.

The Gurkha corporal commanding one of the weapons lances touched Fraser on the shoulder and pointed at the gatehouse wall a few meters from the door. Fraser gave him a quick nod, then he backed away fast as the onager came into play again. The other onagers joined in an instant later, and in seconds they had opened another breach in the inner wall. Fraser gathered up a handful of legionnaires and swam for the hole. The heat of the water near the gap was almost into lerable, but he squeezed through into the building, his men close behind.

And stopped at the sight of the lone figure waiting inside.

The nomad wore an ornate dagger at this side and cradled a rocket gun in his arms. His bearing made his identity plain, though he was nothing like what Fraser had imagined.

Choor!, the nomad warlord, was a young wog, probably younger than any of the leaders he had "advised." He was distinctly over-weight, too, and looked more like one of the scholarly class from Ourgh than he did like a being who had single-handedly brought such terror to Polypheme.

Fraser hesitated. Suddenly it didn't seem right to kill this mild-looking wog.

But Choor! plainly didn't share that sentiment. He raised his rifle and fired.

A legionnaire shoved Fraser out of the way and took the round in his own arm. A moment later it was over, with half a dozen Legion soldiers pumping round after round into the nomad leader.

* * *

Gunnery Sergeant Trent climbed wearily onto the boarding platform of the *Cyclops*, opening his hardsuit helmet and taking a deep, satisfying breath of air. He could hardly believe it was over.

The civilian leader, Voskovich, hurried across the deck. "Did you hear the news?" she was asking, her eyes shining.

He shook his head wearily.

"The wogs attacked the Sandcastle again, but we held them. Corporal Johnson called a few minutes ago to report that they were running. Someone must have sent word to them about Choor!...."

"Johnson? Was DuValier...?"

She shook her head. "He was wounded in the fighting, and Johnson's in charge, but the medical people say the Lieutenant will be all right."

If Fraser wanted to press charges over the mutiny, DuValier would be wishing the wogs had killed him. Death by lethal injection wasn't a pleasant way to go....

"Everyone else aboard?" he asked, changing the subject. Another death was something he didn't want to think about just now. Not after all the killing Trent had seen today.

She nodded. "Captain Fraser brought the Toel prisoners aboard a few minutes ago. And Mr. Watanabe and the survivors of the main body are already down in Legion country." She smiled. "There was one named White who was talking about booze."

"They deserve it," Trent said. "Hell, *I* deserve it! You want to join us?" Voskovich had played no small part in getting the fight inside the base back on track.

She nodded hesitantly. "Yes … yes, I'd like that, Sergeant."

"Then give the orders to get us going, and come on down. I'm not going to stop celebrating until we sight home."

EPILOGUE

It is thanks to you, gentlemen, that we are here at all. If I ever have the honor to command another expedition, I shall ask for at least a battalion of the Foreign Legion.

—General Charles Duchesne, commander, Madagascar
expedition,
French Foreign Legion, 1895

Colin Fraser leaned on the rampart and looked out at the Navy lighter grounded outside the Sandcastle, his feelings a mixture of relief, pride … and not a little sadness. With the arrival of Commandant Miloradovich and his battalion, Demi-Battalion Elaine would be leaving Polypheme. But they would be leaving behind many comrades and many memories. That was a part of being a legionnaire.

The Commandant had escorted a new contingent of Seafarms executives, who were already busy trying to put the Cyclops Project back together. The carrier ship that had brought the legionnaires to the Polypheme system had also carried a contingent of government people, who would soon be putting together everything necessary to turn Polypheme into a full-fledged Commonwealth protectorate.

They'd have little trouble getting the natives to cooperate. The Elders in Ourgh had been more than just eager to resume their close ties with the Terrans in the wake of the battle at the enemy head-

quarters, and several of Choor!'s erstwhile confederates had approached Fraser asking for assistance in recovering now that the fighting
was over. Choor!, they said, had been responsible for the conflict. Without him, and without the warriors lost in those desperate attacks, the
individual tribes were almost helpless.

Down on the mud flats, he saw a guard detail escorting a gaggle of
Toel prisoners aboard the ship. Sergeant Michael Johnson was in
command. Getting him that extra stripe for the way he'd held together
the garrison after DuValier was wounded had been one of the small
rewards that almost made the other side of the coin, the butcher's bill,
tolerable. The Toels would be returned to their own people, but not
before the Autarchy heard just how dim a view the Commonwealth
took of interference in the affairs of worlds within the Terran sphere of
influence. The Toeljuk Autarchy wasn't prepared for a full-scale war.
Fraser was sure those Toels would be labeled "outlaws" by an
embarrassed Autarch, regardless of what the real facts of the plot might
have been.

"Captain?" The familiar voice sounded a little less cool and
controlled than it usually did. Lieutenant Antoine DuValier had
recovered from his physical wounds. Whether he had healed the scars
in his mind was another question.

Fraser turned and examined him. The uniform was spotless as ever,
and it was hard to tell the stiffness of his wounds from his usual
straight-backed stance. "What is it, Mr. DuValier?"

"I ... thought you might not have heard. Senator Warwick's cut his
tour short and headed back to Terra."

He nodded. "The Commandant told me." Miloradovich had also
told him, in strictest confidence, the reason for Warwick's abrupt can-
cellation of his witch-hunt on the Frontiers. Evidently Reynier
Industries had been applying quite a bit of pressure on the commission
to recognize a certain Captain Colin Fraser for his heroism in defending
Commonwealth interests on Polypheme. Warwick wouldn't be a party
to a medal for the captain, but he was in no position to block it. One of
the other members of the Commission would be left to deal with an
embarrassing situation.

The medal didn't matter that much, but it was good to know that
Warwick wouldn't be hovering over his shoulder, at least for a while.
He only hoped that Reynier Industries wouldn't lose sight of the other
heroes of Polypheme. Like David Hawley.

DuValier seemed unwilling to go on, but finally spoke again. "Sir … Captain … I was wondering if you'd heard anything about … what happens now?"

"Alpha Company's being dissolved," he told him. "Most of them will wind up as Bravos. The Commandant says we're being posted back to Devereaux for a few months. After that …" He shrugged. "Who knows?"

They'd be taking some other recruits with them as well, including the nomad scout, Oomour, and Katrina Voskovich, who had resigned from Seafarms to look for adventure in the Legion.

DuValier looked away. "I … was hoping.…" He trailed off. "You've done so much just by dropping the mutiny charges.…"

"You earned that," Fraser said harshly. "Several times over."

"I was hoping you'd reconsider keeping me on as Exec," DuValier blurted out. "I was wrong about you. And I'd be honored to keep on serving with you."

Fraser shook his head firmly. "I'm sorry, Lieutenant. That's out of the question. I need to know that my Executive Officer is someone I can rely on, no matter what. Someone who knows my mind better than I know it myself. Even though you've … changed a lot, I still could never give you the kind of loyalty you deserve. That's a two-way street that can't be put right by a few kind words and a little soul-searching."

DuValier looked unhappy. "I'm … sorry, sir. I hope you can find someone else who'll meet your standards."

"I already have, Lieutenant. The Commandant has already let me know that my recommendation for promoting Toru Watanabe's been approved. He'll be my new Exec."

"He's a good man," DuValier said, turning away.

Fraser followed the French lieutenant with his eyes. *So are you, my friend,* he thought. With a fresh start in a new outfit, without this hatred gnawing away at his guts, Antoine DuValier would find his feet again. He had the makings of a first-rate Legion officer. Someone Fraser would be proud to serve with again someday.

Someone even David Hawley would approve of.

BOOK THREE:
COHORT OF THE DAMNED

PROLOGUE

**eau Soleil:** Distance from Sol 94 light years ... Spectral class G2V; radius 1.0 Sol; mass 1.0 Sol; luminosity 1.01 Sol. Stellar Effective Temperature 5800° K ... Seven planets, in-cluding one habitable world, Beau Soleil III, designated Devereaux ...

Ill Devereaux: Orbital radius 0.96 AUs; eccentricity .0068; period 0.94 solar years (343.6 std. days) ... No natural satellites ...

Planetary mass 0.9 Terra; density 0.95 Terra (5.225 g/cc); surface gravity 0.93 G. Radius 6265.2 kilometers; circumference 39,365.49 kilometers ... Total surface area 493,263,949.23 square kilo-meters ...

Hydrographic percentage 64 percent ... Mean atmospheric pres-sure 0.85 arm; composition oxygen/nitrogen. Oxygen content 23 percent ...

Planetary axial tilt 21 degrees 39 feet 17.6 inches. Rotation per-iod 28 hours, 18 minutes, 14.2 seconds ...

Planetography: Devereaux is a familiar Terra-type world, offer-ing few surprises.... There are three major continents as well as a significant chain of islands which together roughly equal the smallest continent in land surface area....

Temperatures and climatic zones are within Terrestrial norms, though overall conditions tend to be slightly warmer and more arid than in equivalent Terran zones. The most noteworthy terrain fea-tures are the *Archipel d'Aurore*, the massive island chain extending through the tropical band of the planet's eastern hemisphere, and the Great Desert which dominates much of Devereaux's largest continent....

Although a diversity of native life forms is found on Devereaux, there is no native sapient life … of some interest to planetary ecologists is the impact of three successive waves of colonization over a five-thousand-year period on the planetary biosphere … the na-tive biochemistry is basically compatible with Terran life forms, and transplanted Terran species have flourished.…

People: *Population* 378,000,000; *Urbanization*: 45 percent … *Ethnic Groups*: Gwyrran 96 percent, Human (primarily French) 3 percent, Other 1 percent … *Languages*: Terranglic, French, Gwyrr-an dialects … *Religions*: Universal Church of Gwyrr 93 percent, Catholic 5 percent, Other 2 percent … *Capital*: Villastre; *Major Cities*: Villastre (18,206,963), lie de Havre (12,658,419), Premier d'Atterissage (10,743,072) … *Port Facilities*: Haut Port geosynch orbital spaceport, 5 planetary spaceports …

Government: *Type*: Commonwealth Trust … *Head of Govern-ment*: Governor Guillaume Gerard … *Local Divisions*: 5 … *Def-ense Budget as Percentage of GDP*: 2.2 percent … *Military Manpower*: 6 percent …

Economy: *Resources and Industries*: Natural Agricultural Products, Ores, Radioactives, Petrochemicals, Processed Agro-products, Alloys, Agro Byproducts, Light Manufacturing, High-Tech Systems … *Exports*: Processed Agricultural Products, Agro Byproducts, Light Manufactured Goods … *Imports*: Gems and Crystals, Heavy Manufactured Goods, Electronics … *Arable Land*: 15 percent (26,636,251 sq. kms.) … *Labor Force*: Agricultural 38 percent, Industrial 29 percent, Service 25 percent, *Resource Extraction*: 8 percent …

Finance: *Currency*: Commonwealth Sol … *Gross Domestic Product*: 737,100,000,000 sols … *Per Capita Income*: 1500 Sols …

History: Originally settled by Gwyrran colonists under the auspices of the Semti Conclave approximately 5,000 years ago, the planet now known as Devereaux formed an important center for trade, exploration, and military operations for the Conclave for many centuries. A series of devastating plagues and famines drastically reduced the Gwyrran colony during the period from roughly 1800-2200 AD and left no more than 15 percent of the predisaster population alive.… The survivors, known today as Wynsarrysa (from the Gwyrran phrase best translated as "The Lost"), suffered technological and sociological devolution, slipping back to a largely preindustrial level.... These changes were apparently viewed favorably by the Semti, who made no effort to relieve conditions during or after the plagues began....

Around the middle of the 24th century humans arrived on Devereaux following the discovery of the planet by the survey ship *CARTIER*. The initial survey mistook the Gwyrran population for a native sophont race, and permission to colonize was granted by the Imperial Minister for Colonial Affairs in 2364.... As a prime colony world Devereaux was settled primarily by French and Western European stock, both from Terra proper and from the established colony worlds of Ys and Concorde.... Roughly two million human settlers arrived before the disintegration of the French Empire heralded the beginning of the Shadow Centuries and the loss of Terran interstellar travel.

It was during this period that the Semti Conclave renewed contact with Devereaux, establishing a new Gwyrran colony on the planet. The humans, cut off from Terra and not fully self-sufficient, welcomed Semti hegemony and became willing subjects of the Conclave....

Devereaux was one of several flashpoint worlds along the Conclave frontier which helped trigger the Semti War. With the emergence of a Terran Commonwealth presence in the sector, human settlers on Devereaux appealed to their own species for assistance against what was perceived as the intolerable excesses of the Semti/Gwyrran government ... Commonwealth forces intervened and established the Fourth Foreign Legion headquarters on Devereaux to furnish protection for human colonists against the Gwyrran locals and the possibility of Semti intervention. During the Semti War, this Legion garrison was destroyed during the Semti occupation of the planet, but bought valuable time for the Commonwealth by delaying the progress of the enemy attack through a determined resistance effort....

Since the Semti War Devereaux has been a Trust, ruled by a local-born human Governor and sending Observers to the Commonwealth Assembly. A growing cadre of humans with Citizen status form the solid core of the urban population, supported by Gwyrrans of the last Semti colonization effort who have retained a high-tech, industrial orientation. Most of the Wynsarrysa prefer rural lives and serve as labor on farms and plantations. Some remain hostile to the human presence and roam the wilderness areas in war bands, making their livelihood through raiding settlements or operating overland caravan routes between remote settlements.

The planet is most notable for its continued connection with the Commonwealth's Fifth Foreign Legion. The Legion's primary headquarters and training facilities are located on the planet, and Legion garrisons continue to provide protection for the population against disaffected elements—primarily Wynsarrysa, who continue to pose a threat to the security of the colony.

—Excerpted from *Leclerc's Guide to the Commonwealth Volume V: The Cis-Conclave Frontier*, 34th Edition, published 2848 AD

Chapter One

We are the wounded from every war, the world's damned ones.

> —from "Adieu vielle Europe," Marching Song,
> French Foreign Legion

A laser bolt struck the wall bare centimeters from *Leutnant* Wolfgang Alaric Hauser von Semenanjung Burat, burning into the tough duraplast. The scorching heat of the pulse, the acrid tang of burning plastic, the hoarse shouts of his men sent adrenaline surging through his veins, and his grip on his CAR-22 laser pistol tightened as Hauser shot desperate glances left and right, seeking a way out.

He had never imagined combat would be so terrifying, never, in fact, envisioned that he might find himself in a battle at all. A commission in Laut Besar's Sky Guards was the accepted career for a young Uro aristocrat, but no one thought that they might actually face combat. It was unthinkable....

But now the unthinkable had become all too real.

"This way, *Tuan!*" *Sersan Peloten* Radiah Suartana shouted. The Indomay NCO held an enemy rocket launcher in his hands, the Ubrenfar weapon large and awkward even for Suartana's massive frame. He braced himself against the wall and raised the cumbersome weapon, unleashing an explosive-tipped projectile in the direction of the advancing Ubrenfar assault troops, completely at ease in the low gravity despite the launcher's powerful recoil. "Over here!"

Another laser bolt sizzled past his head. Hauser rolled sideways, squeezing the trigger of his laser pistol for a blind shot. Then he pushed off in a powerful leap toward the *sersan*'s position near a bend in the corridor. Telok, the inner moon of Laut Besar, was little more than an oversized planetoid, its low gravity almost unnoticeable.

He was grateful for hours of practice in the port's low-G gymnasium. It was almost second nature to turn in the air and land beside the *sersan*, absorbing the inertia of his jump with no more effort than if he'd been playing a game of air hockey with his friends from the BOQ block. They used a handrail to pull themselves around the corner and through a pair of massive armored doors, clear of the Ubrenfar field of fire.

Hauser scanned the inside of the chamber. It was one of the warehouses servicing Docking Bay Five, long and wide with a high ceiling hung with handling machinery and a catwalk running around the entire room three meters off the floor. In the port's weak gravity, terms like "ceiling" and "floor" had little meaning, but the warehouse floor could be magnetized to hold cargo modules in place and allow workers with steelloy boots to operate without the distracting effects of low-G. The power was off at the moment, but restraining nets held the scattered cargomods in place. They would provide cover, at least, if his men had to fight the Ubrenfars here.

The warehouse was also a junction for a number of different corridors, including one that led to the airlock doors of the docking bay. Inside, the frigate *Surapat* was still taking on refugees from the rest of the Telok port complex. She was the last ship in port, the last hope of escape. The other docking bays had already been overrun by the Ubrenfar assault troops who had infiltrated Telok aboard an unarmed freighter, boiling out of the hold and overwhelming every group of defenders they had encountered.

Sensors had picked up the main Ubrenfar battle fleet soon after the fighting began. Within four hours that fleet would arrive, cutting off all hope of escape for anyone who managed to survive the initial onslaught.

Hauser's wristpiece buzzed insistently. He touched a stud and watched as the small terminal screen glowed, swirled with color, and then resolved into the grim features of Major Erich Neubeck von Lembah Terang.

"Leutnant," the major said crisply. "Your status?"

"We have been forced back to Warehouse 5-C, *Herr Major*," he said. "Contact with the enemy temporarily broken. I have twenty men, from miscellaneous units. Mostly light weapons, one captured rocket launcher. Not enough to make a stand."

Neubeck frowned. "You're going to have to try, *Leutnant*," he said. "I need you to hold that position for at least fifteen minutes more, longer if possible. It's critical."

"Herr Major...." Hauser stopped, swallowed, looked around the warehouse again. "The men here aren't a coherent unit ... some of them aren't even soldiers! We have no combat armor. Ammo is running low, and morale is poor at best. I don't know how long these men can hold against a determined attack. Can you send some reinforcements?"

The major pursed his lips. "I'll see what I can do, Hauser. But that position has to be held. Do your best."

"Yes, sir," Hauser responded. "But without some steady troops here I don't know how good our best will be."

The screen had already gone dead.

Hauser glanced across at Suartana. The *sersan* seemed to read his thoughts. "We can hold the scalies for a while, *Tuan*," he said. "But not forever."

"You heard the man, *Sersan*. We defend the warehouse."

He jumped back to the center of the chamber in a single low-G bound as Suartana shouted orders. He hoped Neubeck would be as good as his word. These Indomay defenders wouldn't be able to stand up to a major attack for long, not discouraged and disorganized as they were now. If this position was as critical as Major von Lembah Terang maintained, it would have to be secured by better men than these....

* * *

"We'll be ready to lift in twelve minutes, *Herr Major*. I'll hold the count as long as possible, but I've got nearly three hundred men to think of."

Major Erich Neubeck von Lembah Terang let out a ragged sigh and nodded. "I understand, *Herr Kapitan*. The refugees have to come first." He glanced around Telok's Master Fire Direction Center, with its banks of control consoles and computer terminals. It was crowded with Sky Guards working feverishly to complete the job Neubeck had set them. They might be able to finish in time....

On the monitor screen dominating one wall of the FDC, the image of the captain of the frigate *Surapat* looked relieved. He was a Uro aristocrat, of course—officers of all the military services on Laut Besar were Uros—but he came from a minor family from one of the poorest districts on the western side of the continent of Malaya Besar. The prospect of arguing with a member of the powerful, well-connected Neubeck family would have been daunting at best. "I will keep you appraised, *Herr Major*," he said.

Before the captain could cut the connection, Neubeck interrupted. "A moment, *Kapitan*. Have you been identifying your passengers?"

"The list isn't complete," the captain told him. "But we're doing our best with it."

"Is Walther Neubeck von Lembah Terang aboard? An *oberleutnant* in the Fourth Sky Guards?"

There was a pause. "Yes … yes, he's on the list, *Herr Major*."

Neubeck tried not to betray his relief at the captain's words. "Very good. Neubeck clear." He shut off the commlink and leaned back in his chair.

At least his brother would win clear of this hell. That was some consolation.

Oberleutnant Wilhelm Stoph appeared beside him. "Third Squad just reported in, sir," he said. "Corridor twelve is sealed off now. Do you want the squad to join the demo work?"

Neubeck frowned at his subordinate, weighing his options. He had promised to find more men for *Leutnant* Hauser. The warehouse the *leutnant*'s ad hoc force had fallen back to controlled the only remaining route into the Fire Direction Center … and the only line of retreat Neubeck's men could use to reach the *Surapat*. Hauser had sounded unsure of himself, uncertain if his men could keep that route secure.

On the other hand, the most urgent task at this point was to make sure that the Fire Direction Center couldn't be used to turn Telok's two linnax railguns against the owners. Refugee ships were lifting clear of Laut Besar as quickly as they could load up. If the railguns fell into Ubrenfar hands those ships would never escape … and there was the further danger that the guns might be turned against targets on the planetary surface. With defeat looming near, Neubeck had to take those railguns off line at all costs, and the more men he set on the demolition job the quicker they would finish.

Hauser would have to make do with what he had. Neubeck nodded curtly to Stoph. "Do it," he said. He undid the safety harness that held him close to the control chair and stood up carefully in the low gravity, then dropped the faceplate on his vacuum armor and checked the seals. "Let's get this over with and get the hell out of here."

*　*　*

Sersan Radiah Suartana pushed back his uniform cap to wipe the sweat from his forehead, then stared down at his hand. The gesture was an uncomfortable reminder of how ill-equipped the Sky Guards were. The soldiers were still clad in their Class One uniforms, designed for smart, parade-ground looks rather than combat use, while the three civilians who had attached themselves to the unit were wearing technicians' coveralls. At the very least Suartana wished they had been wearing duraweave battle-dress, with combat helmets and plates of chest and back armor. Or, better yet, fully armored vacuum gear ...

But the fighting on Telok had erupted without warning, and none of the soldiers on duty in the military spaceport complex had been ready for it. They'd lost a lot of men already today to wounds even ordinary combat fatigues would have prevented. Now the men of *Leutnant* Hauser's ad hoc unit were sure to lose more. Against Ubrenfar commandos in full armor the humans were seriously overmatched.

The *sersan* darted a glance at Hauser. The Uro officer was gripping a cargo net with one hand, while the other clung tight to his laser pistol. He had a grim, determined look on his face and seemed completely oblivious to the rest of the men, Indomays all, crouching behind the improvised cargomod barricades or perched high on the catwalk watching the entry, waiting for the Ubrenfars to come.

Suartana frowned. Hauser had paid little attention to the defensive preparations. He seemed totally withdrawn into himself, a man already defeated. The men could sense his mood, too. They knew he had no faith in them, and now they had precious little faith left in themselves either.

He had known Hauser since the young aristocrat was a baby. The family was one of the best known on Java Baru, Laut Besar's smaller continent, and it had been his honor to serve three generations of the clan. Hauser's grandfather had been a member of the Chamber of Delegates; his father and uncle had both staked out promising political careers. Now young Wolfgang Hauser had struck out on his own, the first of his prominent line to join the military. The *Leutnant's* sharp, fox-faced features reminded Suartana of Karl Hauser, Wolfgang's father. He would have been proud of his son. Too bad that hunting accident had carried him away.

Too bad in more ways than one. Since Karl Hauser's death his older brother, the *Graff* von Semenanjung Burat, had tightened his grasp on the family holdings. A firm proponent of Laut Besar's Aristo-Conservative Party, Rupert Hauser had resisted every move toward political reform the government had undertaken. Despite his faction's resistance, the Indomays were starting to make progress toward equality, but it was slow going. Suartana had watched the *Graff's* nephew grow up believing in the superiority of Uros over Indomays. That was something the boy's father wouldn't have been proud of, he thought. The young officer's stubborn arrogance seemed stronger than ever now that he had earned his Sky Guards commission. And with that exalted feeling of Uro superiority came an equal tendency to denigrate the Indomay class.

And when Hauser, a Uro, was almost paralyzed with fear, he couldn't believe his inferiors capable of anything....

* * *

"I hear them," one of the *koprals*—Suartana thought his name was Lubis—said in Terranglic. "They're coming. Get ready, men." He looked nervous, but determined.

The man had every right to be nervous. *"Selamat, saudara."* Suartana said in Indomay. "Good fortune, brother." The Uros used mostly German when speaking among themselves, while the lower classes preferred the traditional tongue from the early days of the colony. Everyone spoke Terranglic, though, and it was largely replacing Indomay as the primary language of Laut Besar. Sometimes Suartana regretted that, but most of the books and technical chips that the Indomays needed to better themselves were in Terranglic.

The *kopral's* grip on his weapon tightened. *"Kembali,"* he said. "I return it."

He looked at Hauser. "The men are ready, *Titan,*" he said. *As ready as they'll ever be*, he added to himself.

Then the doors erupted in a storm of fire and smoke.

* * *

Half-seen figures loomed through the swirling smoke around the doors, hulking dinosaur shapes encased in full vacuum armor. Hauser fired his pistol, and an instant later the rest of the defenders joined in with a ragged volley of fire from their ill-assorted collection of weapons. Laser beams and the needle-thin rounds from FE-FEK/24 combat rifles chopped through the billowing cloud, but only one of the massive, two-meter tall Ubrenfars fell. Their armor protected them from most of the damage the human defenders could mete out.

The Ubrenfars fanned out, moving fast in the low gravity despite their bulk and their clumsy, forward-leaning postures. They were highly trained assault troops, specialists in space combat situations. More than a match for the Indomay defenders, most of whom had never heard a shot fired in anger before today.

He forced the thought from his mind. The men in his command weren't the best, but they were still *men*. They should be more than a match for mere ales, no matter how well trained or well equipped. He'd grown up believing in the natural order of things, the inherent superiority of Uro over Indomay, human over alien. All he had to do was rally his men to put up a solid defense. The Ubrenfars would surely give way....

"Pour it on!" he shouted. "Fire!"

The defenders kept up a steady stream of fire, and another of the Ubrenfars went down with the faceplate of its vacc helmet smashed, the face beyond a bloody pulp. Someone gave a hoarse cheer in Indomay. *"Ure!"*

Then one of the Ubrenfars raised a rocket launcher, a twin to the massive weapon Suartana had scavenged earlier. A rocket streaked from the tube, trailing flame, tearing into a stack of cargomods near the center of the warehouse. The warhead tore through the improvised barricade, and a gout of fire and whirling debris erupted from the other side. The three men using the cargomods for cover spun away, hurled bodily across the chamber by the force of the explosion in the weak gravity field. Hauser saw the body of the senior *kopral* hit the far wall and bounce. The man's face had been burned away. One of the other soldiers was dead, too. The third was gaping at the stump of his forearm, eyes wide with shock. Then a laser shot bored straight through his chest, and the eyes glazed over. The man hadn't screamed, had hardly seemed to understand what was happening to him.

Swallowing sour bile, Hauser tried hard to stay in control.

"Got one!" a rifleman on the catwalk above Hauser's position shouted. He was waving his FEK in triumph. "Got one of the scaly bastards!"

Then a whole barrage of laser fire from the assault troops probed the human positions. Four rapid pulses of raw energy sliced into the soldier on the catwalk, nearly cutting his torso in half. Unlike the other men, he had time to scream.

Wolfgang Hauser knew he'd hear those screams for the rest of his life.

Something *whooshed* from the doorway. The rocket struck the wall near Hauser's position and exploded in a fury of light and sound. Smoke billowed and fragments careened off the walls like bullets. Pain stabbed through Hauser's leg, and he looked down to see blood oozing from a gash in his thigh. Someone was moaning nearby.

He scrambled for fresh cover, with *Sersan* Suartana close behind him. As the smoke cleared, Hauser could see the shattered bodies of four more of his men sprawled nearby. The rest of the defenders were wavering, their fire slacking off as they hunkered down behind the cargomods.

Eight dead in seconds, out of a scant twenty. And they'd taken only three of the enemy with them....

Hauser grabbed Suartana's massive shoulder. "We can't hold them! We've got to pull back! If we can seal the corridor behind us ... get to the frigate...!"

"What about our orders, *Tuan?*" Suartana asked. "Major Neubeck said—"

"Damn what Neubeck said!" Hauser exploded. The major had promised him more men, then let him down....

He fought down the waves of fear and anger, trying to regain at least a semblance of composure. Suartana was right. He couldn't just abandon this position without checking in with Neubeck first. But if the major didn't send help right away the defenders in the warehouse would be overwhelmed, and Hauser's first responsibility had to be to the men in his outnumbered unit.

Hunkering down behind the cover of stacked cargomods, Hauser activated the communications function of his wristpiece computer. As the screen began to glow he raised his arm to speak into the sound pickup.

A laser bolt sizzled through the air less than a meter to his left, and he flinched from the crackling, the stench of ozone in the air. With or without support from Neubeck, he wasn't sure how much longer he could face the Ubrenfar attack.

* * *

"Just hang on for a few more minutes, Hauser," Erich Neubeck said, frowning at the wall screen. "We're almost finished up here."

The young *leutnant* hesitated, and opened his mouth to speak. An explosion went off nearby, and the picture on Neubeck's screen jumped wildly as Hauser moved, the vision pickup following the motion of his arms. Against a backdrop of whining FEK fire and crackling flames, someone was screaming.

Hauser's voice cracked as he shouted orders. "*Kopral!* Have somebody see to that man!" There was a short pause. "Damn it, Suartana, too many of the scalies are leaking through! Can't you *do* something?"

The edge in that voice worried Neubeck more than anything else. The kid was cracking under the pressure....

"Major, my men can't hold this position without immediate reinforcement," Hauser went on, speaking into his wristpiece again. "Where are the men you said you were sending me?"

"I need them here," Neubeck shot back. "For God's sake, man, we're all shorthanded! You've got to try to tough it out with the men you've got!"

More combat sounds filtered through the commlink. "What I've got is a handful of men who can't hold any longer," Hauser said tightly. "We can't do it! We just can't!"

"Hauser, I'm ordering you to—"

But the *leutnant* wasn't listening. "Pull back!" he shouted. "Pull back now, Suartana! Regroup at the corridor head!"

The channel went dead without warning.

If those men in the warehouse fell back now, Neubeck's troops in the Fire Direction Center would be cut off. They'd have to act fast if they wanted to retrieve the situation.

"Stoph!" he shouted. "Tell one section to open up a retreat route through the warehouse! If you can get there in time to keep that bastard Hauser from falling back we might still get out of this!"

The *oberleutnant* saluted and hurried off, shouting orders and checking the charge level on his laser pistol as he trotted toward the door. Other men joined him, trading demo packs for rifles.

When the airtight door slid open, Neubeck thought he could hear the distant echoes of combat drifting up the corridor from the warehouse.

Sending Stoph and his men would slow the demolitions work, and any delay now could be fatal. But they had to try to win through the Ubrenfar lines.

Deep down, though, Neubeck knew it was probably too late to try....

Chapter Two

Hope no longer existed. Still, no one thought of surrender.

—Corporal Louis Maine,
Report on the Battle of Camerone,
French Foreign Legion, 1863

P ull back!" Hauser shouted. "Pull back now, Suartana! Regroup at the corridor head!" He cut power to the wristpiece comm.-link function. "Now, damn it!"

Neubeck had promised men to stiffen his meager defense force, but he had been lying all along. There never had been any rein-forcements. The major had no right to expect Hauser to sacrifice his entire command to carry out impossible orders....

And he wasn't about to listen to any more screaming casualties on Neubeck's behalf.

Suartana hesitated a moment, staring deep into Hauser's eyes. Then the big *sersan* gave a single curt nod. "Ujo! Yahia!" he called. "Maintain fire but keep your heads down! The rest of you fall back!"

It didn't take much encouragement to get the troops moving toward the door at the far end of the chamber. The two soldiers the *sersan* had singled out kept firing, covering the retreat. The others were leaping for the safety of the corridor that led to the docking bay. The Ubrenfars picked off several men as they broke cover.

Hauser checked the charge of his laser pistol and rolled to the edge of the debris they'd taken shelter behind, ignoring the throbbing pain in his leg. He clenched his teeth, determined not to give in to fear, to hold here until all his men were safe. Leveling the CAR-22, he squeezed off a shot.

Suartana pulled him back. The *sersan* crouched beside him, clutching the captured rocket launcher. "Get clear, *Tuan!*" he said. "I'll hold the bastards ... for as long as I can." He fired as if to emphasize the words, and an explosion erupted in the doorway, smashing into the mass of Ubrenfars still pouring into the warehouse.

Hauser hesitated, unwilling to abandon the Indomay, but knowing there was little enough he could do to help him, either. Finally, he nodded tightly. "I'm ... I'm sorry, Suartana...."

"Go, *Tuan!* Go!"

Ignoring his wounded leg, Hauser pushed off, leaping toward the rear doors. Suartana's rocket attack had forced the Ubrenfars to keep their heads down, and the trio of shots fired in his direction all went wide.

As he used his good leg to absorb the shock of the jump against the wall beside the door, *Serdadu* Yahia joined him, his FEK trailing behind him as he leapt with the receiver empty. The soldier slapped the pressure plate to open the doors just as an Ubrenfar rapid-pulse laser punched a half dozen neat holes through his lower torso. Hauser shoved the body away in horror and dived through the doors. A hundred meters further on, the five surviving men from his shattered command were clustered around the airlock that led into the docking bay.

He looked back into the warehouse. Despite Suartana's rocket fire, more Ubrenfars were pouring into the chamber now that the volume of defensive fire had slackened. Some of the assault troops were already breaking off to bound toward the corridor that led off toward the Fire Direction Center. That would be their principal objective, of course. Control of the linnax railguns would ensure control of any ship traffic trying to move to or from orbit....

And Neubeck's men were up there, cut off now. Hauser swallowed, realizing for the first time the wider implications of what he had done by ordering the retreat. More than just his own little command had been riding on what happened here, but he had focused entirely on his own men instead of seeing the wider picture. But it was too late now. He didn't have enough men to counterattack successfully even if he could have found it in himself to give the orders for what was sure to be a suicide attack.

Hauser swiveled his head in response to another explosion. Suar-tana was maintaining his lonely defense, but now the *sersan* had only two more rockets. After that, there would be nothing left to hold back the enemy tide....

* * *

"That's the last of them, *Tuan*. All charges in place and ready to detonate."

Erich Neubeck accepted the detonator from the Indomay *sersan* and verified the program entered into its chip memory. One coded sequence to arm the mechanism, then a single touch of the activator stud would be enough to trigger all the charges in a set sequence.

He nodded, satisfied, and clipped the device to the belt of his vacuum suit. At least they had carried out their mission. There wouldn't be much left of the Fire Direction Center once the explosives were set off. It wasn't only the controls that had been mined. Soldiers in vacuum suits had also used the access shaft that led from the FDC alongside the number one railgun and out to the surface of Telok to plant charges that would disable the linnax system itself. Even if the Ubrenfars managed to jury-rig a new control system, at least this gun would be unusable ... more if the other sabotage teams had carried out their jobs.

The difficult job was finally done. All that remained now was to find a way out....

A muffled explosion rumbled in the corridor outside the airtight door. Neubeck leapt across the room, shouting to the other soldiers to join him. Stoph and his men hadn't been out there for very long, and it sounded like they'd run into resistance already.

Damn Hauser for letting the invaders through!

He hit the control button and the door slid open, letting in a tumult of combat sounds. A laser beam crackled past the door, and somewhere down the corridor there were hoarse shouts and an inhuman cry that must have been a wounded Ubrenfar.

Neubeck hesitated before plunging out into the corridor, and in that moment he heard Stoph's voice calling out. "Retreat! Retreat back to Fire Control! We can't do anything else here!"

The major gestured to a pair of Indomays armed with RG-12 grenade launchers. The men dived through the door to take up pos-itions on either side of the corridor. One of them fired a rocket-propelled projectile, aiming high, and it leapt from the barrel with a *whoosh* of burning propellants.

Soldiers hurried up the corridor, taking full advantage of the light gravity to cover the distance quickly. One stopped at the door and turned to fire his FEK back down the passage, but it only chattered uselessly on an empty magazine. The Indomay cursed luridly and ejected the clip as he rolled into the Fire Direction Center. Then he threw the weapon violently against the far wall as he realized he was out of ammunition.

A trio of men landed together, awkwardly, two Indomays with slung rifles supporting Stoph between them. The *oberleutnant* was bleeding from half a dozen wounds, and one arm dangled uselessly. Pale and wild-eyed, Stoph stumbled through the door. Neubeck caught him and guided him to one of the control chairs.

"It's ... no good, sir," the Uro gasped. "They were already in the corridor. Too many ... too well armored. I couldn't break through ... couldn't ..."

"Easy, Stoph," Neubeck said quietly. "You did everything you could."

The *oberleutnant* coughed. "Trapped up here ... no way to get back to the docking bay now...."

"*Tuan!*" an Indomay shouted. "That's the last of them! What do we do now?"

"Lay down a heavy barrage of grenades and then get those two inside. Seal the doors. That's all we can do, for now."

An Indomay *kopral* in Sky Guard full-dress uniform pointed to the entrance to the maintenance shaft beside the wall screen on the other side of the room. "Some of you could still get away, *Tuan*," the soldier said. "The ones in suits. Out the access shaft to the surface, then across to the docking bay. It's only about two hundred meters...."

Neubeck bit his lip. He had ten men, including himself, who could use that escape route, twenty-five more who could not. It galled him to even think about abandoning them to their fate, but the alternative was to stand in place and die a useless death.

At least he could send the rest of the troops with vacc suits out. A few might survive this deathtrap that way....

Stoph grabbed his arm. "Take the ones you can, sir," he said, coughing again. "I can stay in charge here ... until the scalies come." He looked significantly at the detonator hanging from Neubeck's belt.

Neubeck hesitated. It didn't make sense to throw his own life away with the rest, but honor was important to a Uro, particularly a Uro Sky Guard officer. He didn't want to be seen to abandon his proper place, to run away from death. That could dishonor the proud name of the Neubecks von Lembah Terang.

"Please, sir," Stoph insisted. "Please … let me do this.…"

Reluctantly, Neubeck nodded. This time the honor belonged to Wilhelm Stoph.

*　*　*

"Throw me a rifle!" Hauser shouted. It was too late to do anything about the Ubrenfars heading for the Fire Direction Center, but he was damned if he would abandon Suartana to his fate.

A green light flashed above the airlock doors as the mechanism cycled, and the massive doors rumbled open. One of the Indomays looked from the airlock to Hauser and back again. Then he grabbed an FEK from one of the others and bounded back up the corridor, leaving the other four men to pass through the heavy doors.

The soldier thrust his extra rifle into Hauser's hands and crouched beside him at the doorway. Turning to look over his shoulder, Hauser shouted instructions. "Get to the *Surapat!*" he ordered. "Warn them the Ubrenfars could break through any time!"

One of the Indomays acknowledged the order with a wave of his rifle. The doors ground together, shutting with a clang that had the ring of grim finality.

"Suartana!" Hauser shouted, turning back to search the chamber for the massive figure of the *sersan*. "Here, man! Get back here now!"

The big man gave no outward sign of having heard the call. He lifted the rocket launcher to his shoulder again, bracing his body against a cargomod. The rocket streaked straight into the smoke and debris from his earlier shots. Then he turned and jumped, covering the dis-tance in one easy bound. Hauser and the Indomay *serdadu* beside him laid down a heavy covering fire, but despite that the other soldier in the rearguard, Ujo, went down as he sprinted for the safety of the corridor.

As the *sersan* scrambled through the doors, Hauser hit the pressure plate above his shoulder to close them. They'd hold no longer against Ubrenfar weapons than the ones that had led into the warehouse, but at least the defenders would have a few moments of comparative safety.

If they could wreck the airlock controls on this side, the Ubrenfars would be stalled until they could bring up something heavier than rockets. Those doors were proof against almost any portable weapon....

Hauser pointed to a small sphere dangling from the belt of the Indomay trooper. "You've got a grenade," he said. "I want it rigged on the control panel there. Before we cycle through. We'll pull the pin before we go and let it wreck the panel before the scalies try to follow us."

"Yes, *Tuan*," the soldier acknowledged crisply. He crossed to the panel, unhooking the grenade. Despite the horror of the fight, the man still had some spirit left.

Knowing how close to the edge he was himself, Hauser wondered how much more the Indomay could take. He watched the man return to the airlock and begin to rig the makeshift demolition charge. He and Suartana fell back slowly, keeping their eyes and weapons trained on the warehouse doors.

Behind them, Hauser heard the doors grinding open. At almost the same instant the warehouse doors burst open in a roar of smoke and searing flame.

"Pull the pin! Let's go!" Hauser snapped.

The soldier at the panel started to respond, but his reply turned into a throaty gurgle as a laser beam slashed out of the smoke cloud and caught him in the back of the neck. He sagged slowly to the floor.

Suartana fired his last rocket with an Indomay curse, then flung the launcher aside. Diving past the dead *serdadu*, Hauser grasped the pin on the grenade and yanked it out. He was grinning as he turned back for the airlock door....

And a searing heat scorched his side. He smelled burning flesh and realized it was his own. Hauser gasped, staggered, feeling dizzy with pain and a sudden, overwhelming fatigue.

Huge hands closed over his shoulders, pulling him through the airlock door. The door seemed to take forever to slide shut. As it slowly cut off his view up the corridor, Hauser saw Suartana's last rocket detonate just as a pair of Ubrenfars trotted out of the smoke.

Before he passed out, Hauser heard their inhuman cries, but they were drowned out by the memory of his own men screaming as they died.

His last thought, before blackness claimed him, was the hope that he would never have to wake up and face that memory again.

* * *

Oberleutnant Wilhelm Stoph shifted in the control chair and winced at the searing pain that lanced through his chest and arm. The makeshift Sky Guard unit hadn't included any medics, and the only first aid kit anyone had carried was near the end of the corridor now, overrun together with its dead owner by the Ubrenfar assault. He couldn't find relief in painkillers ... but Stoph knew he wouldn't have to fight the pain much longer.

The access hatch to the maintenance shaft was open, and the troops wearing pressure suits were starting through. The major hung back until the last, his face hard to see inside the plashield helmet, but his body language making his reluctance to abandon the other defenders plain. Stoph held up the detonator with his good hand, and the helmet inclined in an exaggerated nod. Then Neubeck straightened to attention and snapped off a salute before turning to follow the others through. A pair of unsuited Indomays sealed the hatch behind him.

Outside the other door, something clanged loudly against the wall, and every eye inside the Fire Direction Center focused on the entrance.

"Get set, men," Stoph said quietly. He gestured to one of them. "You ... give me a hand."

The soldier helped him across the room to a better position, shielded from the door by a bank of sensor monitors.

"Thanks," he told the Indomay. As the soldier started to move away, he gripped the man's sleeve. "No," he said. "Stay here. If I'm hit, make sure you set off the charges."

The man nodded and unslung his rifle, checking the magazine. Neubeck had urged the defenders to draw the Ubrenfars into a fight at the end, so that there might be a concentration of them in the FDC when the explosives went off. It was only a gesture at this point, but all they had left now was gestures. Dignity. Honor. Stoph would take as many of the enemy with him now that his time had come.

He checked the detonator again, then entered the code sequence to arm it into the keypad. A red light glowed above the activator stud.

They waited.

He didn't know if seconds were passing, or minutes ... or even hours. It seemed like an eternity of tension and pain and fear.

More clanging sounds echoed through the door. Stoph summoned his strength to speak. "They're going to blow the door," he said, his voice a dry croak that somehow still sounded loud in the still room. "Get set ..."

The door burst inward in a shower of arcing debris. Thick smoke obscured everything, but he could hear the heavy-booted feet of the attackers as they poured into the room.

"Fire! Fire! Pour it on!" His shouted order trailed off into a spasmodic cough, but the Indomays obeyed. FEKs whined, their gauss fields hurtling high-velocity slivers of metal into the smoke on full auto fire. The alien cries he had heard out in the corridor before broke out again, louder this time, a cacophony of wailing and hooting that might have been pain or anger or sheer blood lust.

But the attackers wore combat armor, and the heavy firing produced comparatively few casualties. Saurian shapes broke from the swirling smoke, their combat lasers pulsing as they sought out targets. A panel nearby exploded from a direct hit, and the men behind it were down. Another Indomay rolled out from behind a stanchion near the door, firing as he scrambled for better cover, but an Ubrenfar cut him in half with rapid-pulse shots from its laser rifle.

A massive shape vaulted over the panel Stoph was crouching behind. The Indomay who had helped him twisted to one side and tried to fire, but the attacker was too fast. The man's head disappeared in a red haze as the Ubrenfar found its mark.

Stoph stared up at the alien for what seemed an endless moment. The Ubrenfar shifted its aim to cover him.

With a last smile of triumph, Stoph jabbed the detonator stud....

And his world disappeared in fire and smoke and thunder.

*　*　*

"Keep together, men," Neubeck said into the microphone of his suit commlink. "It's not much further."

Behind him the nine suited figures moved slowly, awkward in the narrow confines of the access shaft. It was necessary for the soldiers to make use of handholds spaced along the wall to pull themselves toward the surface. The temptation to leap against the weak gravity was offset by an awareness of how easy it would be to tear a suit or break a faceplate on an unexpected projection. Galling as their slow pace was, it was the safest course. Since passing through a safety hatch near the bottom of the tube they had been in a vacuum, where any mistake could be instantly fatal.

He reached the top of the shaft. Looping one arm over a handhold, Neubeck worked the hatch controls to open it up. Blue-green light reflected from Laut Besar blazed bright overhead as Neubeck scrambled out of the tube and bent over to help the next man up.

Somewhere behind them, there was a distant rumble.

"Move it! Move it! Get clear!" he shouted over the commlink. The soldiers hastened to obey as the rippling explosions at the far end of the shaft spread and intensified.

All but one of them made it out before the shock wave erupted from down below. Fragments of the airlock hatch hurtled like bullets straight up the shaft, and one of them tore a two-centimeter hole through the unlucky man's stomach. The body twitched for a moment, then fell back, drifting very slowly down the deep access shaft.

Another man lost, along with everyone in the FDC. Neubeck swallowed sour bile and bit back a curse. "Come on, men. The docking bay is that way ... just beyond those rocks over that way. Let's move out."

As they started forward in ground-eating bounds, Neubeck thought again of *Leutnant* Hauser. If the man hadn't run from the warehouse fighting, they might have saved most of Neubeck's unlucky command instead of this pitiful handful of survivors.

He hoped the Ubrenfars hadn't killed Hauser during the *Leutnant's* retreat. Neubeck wanted to confront the man himself someday ... so that Hauser would know in full measure the price of his cowardice.

Chapter Three

—Legionnaire Frederic Martyn,
French Foreign Legion, 1889

The carriership loomed large in the observation lounge viewport, a vast, spindly web of metal that blotted out half the sky. Only a handful of the separate docking modules held ships, and most of them were battered and battle-scarred from running fights with the Ubrenfar Navy. It was a miracle any of them had eluded the invasion fleet.

Wolfgang Hauser was one of the dozens of refugees crowded into the lounge to watch as the passenger liner eased closer to the Commonwealth carriership *Solomon*. Just over a week had passed since *Surapat* had blasted clear of the Telok port complex. Hauser had spent most of that time in the frigate's sick bay, sharing limited regen facilities with the scores of other wounded aboard. The doctors had told the dramatic story of how Suartana had brought him through the airlock and aboard ship with only minutes to spare before she sealed up for launch, but Hauser hadn't felt much like thanking the Indomay. The painful memory of the desperate fighting in the warehouse on Telok still burned within.

Perhaps it would have been better if Suartana had left him for the Ubrenfars, he told himself bitterly as the slow, stately dance of the docking continued outside. Thanks to his mistakes, a lot of good men had died back there. He had no business being alive....

He thrust the thought from his mind and tried to concentrate on the activity on the screen. Hauser had never traveled beyond Telok's orbit, and this was his first encounter with one of the huge carrierships that were the heart and soul of all interstellar travel. Under other circumstances he would have been totally absorbed by the excitement, but today he found it hard to feel anything but regrets.

It seemed wrong to be here, fleeing Laut Besar's star system and the invaders who had occupied his homeworld. But he'd been given little choice in the matter.

Surapat had fled from Telok to Danton, the cold, dreary planet-sized moon of Barras, the huge superjovian world occupying the outermost orbit of the star system. Perpetually locked with one face toward its brown dwarf primary, Danton was a world of fire and ice, heated by the faint radiation of Barras on one side, but bitterly cold across the face away from the giant planet. Still, Danton was considered marginally habitable, and the Terran Commonwealth had leased the world from the government of Laut Besar as the site for a scientific research station and the system terminal, *Systerm Liberty*, from which visiting carrierships were serviced.

The commonwealth science station on Danton had transformed in a matter of days into a huge refugee camp crammed with fugitives from the fall of Laut Besar, while a handful of surviving Besaran ships and military units, including the frigate, remained on active duty ... but only under the protective umbrella of Commonwealth forces. Even the Ubrenfars would hesitate to stir up a direct confrontation with the Terrans. Decades of minor clashes and border disputes had made both sides wary.

But how long the Commonwealth would continue to extend protection was still unknown. Once the nearest regional Governor got involved, anything could happen. If he decided that protecting Laut Besar's refugees wasn't worth the risk of war with the Ubrenfars, Danton wouldn't survive as a safe haven any longer....

The world was fast becoming an armed camp, and as quickly as ships could gather in the refugees they were being shipped out by way of Systerm Liberty to the waiting *SOLOMON*. The carriership had dropped out of irrational space during the first week of the crisis, a lucky coincidence for the fugitives from the Ubrenfar invasion. Laut

Besar wasn't on any regularly scheduled carriership routes and frequently went months without receiving a visit from one of the huge FTL transports. *SOLOMON* had made the short side trip from the nearby Commonwealth world of Robespierre, and the commander of the military contingent attached to the carriership, Brigadier Nachman Shalev, had taken stock of the situation quickly and deployed his troops to Danton on his own initiative. Three regiments of Commonwealth colonial troops seemed little enough to challenge the Ubrenfar invasion force, even with the help of the reorganizing Besaran units which had escaped the fall of their homeworld. But as long as higher authority within the Commonwealth didn't overrule Shalev, those units on Danton would at least make the Ubrenfar commanders pause before escalating their incursion into a full-scale confrontation with Humanity.

Hauser had still been carried on the sick list when *Surapat* dropped him off with the rest of the refugees at the systerm, and the authorities had ordered him transferred to the liner *Freiheit Stern* rather than allowing him to stay with the military units assembling on Danton. He hadn't been given any other options, but that didn't help salve his conscience much. He was abandoning Laut Besar, just as the military and the core of the government had left the planet to the tender mercies of the Ubrenfars.

The most disturbing part of it all was the sense of relief he had felt at the news. Hauser had never thought of himself as anything but a patriot ... until now.

On the wall-sized viewscreen a carriership docking cradle dominated the scene now as the liner maneuvered closer. Long seconds later, there was an almost imperceptible jar as the ship made contact. The liner's hull echoed with the clangs of boarding tubes and support conduits hooking up, turning the ship into an integral part of the vast carriership complex.

The wall screen went blank for a moment. Then it displayed the nebula-and-starship logo of the Commonwealth Merchant Service. A pleasant, well-modulated voice, a shade too even to be human, began to speak. "I am *SOLOMON*. Welcome aboard. Your cabin terminals are now integrated into my database, and you may feel free to question me at need. Passengers are invited to leave the ship to visit other docking modules, but please allow one hour for final docking checks before you debark." There was a short pause while the carriership's enormous artificial intelligence attended to some other duty … or more likely a whole host of duties. Hauser had heard about the sentient computers that piloted the huge interstellar transports, but he had never expected to meet one of them. Only an intelligent computer could handle the myriad computations necessary to maintain a Reynier-Kessler irrational field.

Carrierships by themselves were impressive enough, massing millions of metric tons of interstellar drives, AI computer networks, and support systems. But the carrier-ship proper was really only a framework in which a host of smaller vessels took passage from star to star. This trip *SOLOMON*, which was referred to by the masculine pronoun "he" instead of the more traditional "she" of classic naval usage, would be running light. He would be carrying no more than twenty assorted liners, freighters, and transports, all of them filled with refugees from Laut Besar. Most of the ships he had brought into the system—warships and military transports, for the most part—were staying behind in support of the deployment on Danton. A strictly commercial operator would have been screaming over the waste, but like all carrierships *SOLOMON* was a part of the Terran Commonwealth's Naval Reserve Fleet, subject to activation at need. The *SOLOMON* computer, technically classed as an intelligent being, was now carried as a warrant officer in the Commonwealth Navy for the duration of the ship's service.

The voice of the computer resumed smoothly. "We will shortly be departing from Danton orbital space. As we have been assigned two yard tugs, the maneuver will be made under constant acceleration, and we will reach the Reynier Limit in just under six hours. Throughout that time, escort will be maintained by the Commonwealth Navy. Please do not be concerned for your security or safety during the departure operation."

Hauser let out a low whistle at that. Carrierships were designed for deep space operations, with low power thrusters for minor course corrections but no large-scale normal-space drives. Operating between systerms at the fringes of inhabited star systems, there was rarely a need for anything beyond a slow but steady progress in a minimum-fuel solar orbit to carry the carriership and its docked craft beyond the Reynier Gravity Limit that inhibited use of the interstellar drive. *SOLOMON* was being treated differently now though, assigned a pair of tugs to maintain constant boost and greatly reduce the transit time between Systerm Liberty and the transition to irrational space.

Plainly, Brigadier Shalev wasn't planning on wasting any more time than absolutely necessary. The faster *SOLOMON* left Danton behind, the quicker he would reach neighboring Robespierre for another ship-ment of Commonwealth troops and ships.

"Screens will be reactivated when the departure maneuver com-mences," the computer went on. "Thank you for your attention."

The voice went silent and the logo faded from the screen. There was a long silence in the crowded passenger lounge as the refugees considered *SOLOMON*'s words. Hauser looked around one last time and then pushed his way through the door and into the corridor outside.

The disturbing feelings associated with leaving Laut Besar were getting to him again more than ever. He needed solitude, the privacy of the suite he shared with *Sersan* Suartana, to consider those feelings more closely.

Wolfgang Alaric Hauser von Semenanjung Burat felt like a coward. That was something he would have to come to terms with somehow if he ever expected to hold his head up among his peers again.

* * *

"The departure of this latest contingent of troops and ships under-scores the importance of Laut Besar to the Commonwealth," the r-eporter on the trideoscreen was saying. She was an attractive woman with a strange, lilting accent and blond hair cut in a style Hauser thought too mannish, but that was in line with her very presence anchoring a news broadcast. On Laut Besar Uro women lived pam-pered, sheltered lives, and rarely worked at any of the male-oriented aristo careers. Indomay women were a different matter, of course.

Hauser wasn't sure he approved of a society that allowed Uro women to be thrust into the public eye.

But he was no longer on Laut Besar, and standards here were different. Since *SOLOMON* had arrived at the systerm on the fringes of the Soleil Fraternity star system, *Freiheit Stern* had been on her own again, shaping her course for Robespierre along with the rest of the ships which had taken passage on the carriership. The trideo broadcasts from Robespierre gave the new arrivals a chance to get a glimpse of their destination before they had to face the problems of direct interaction with a strange culture.

It was ironic that the normal-space trip from the outermost world of the system to Robespierre would take longer than the three-day Reynier-Kessler irrational drive voyage from *Soleil Liberté.*

The reporter on the trideo was still talking. "Among the units included in the most recent draft of reinforcements for Operation Cordon is an ad hoc battalion of the famous—some would perhaps say notorious—Fifth Foreign Legion. The battalion includes three light infantry companies, including the unit commanded by Captain Colin Fraser which served in the high-profile Legion operations on Hanuman and Polypheme over the last two years." On the screen, the reporter was replaced by a scene of smartly dressed soldiers in khaki dress uniforms with blue cummerbunds and red epaulets marching at a slow pace down a crowded city street.

The reporter continued her voice-over commentary. "This will actually mark the second time the Fifth Foreign Legion has been called upon to intervene in Besaran affairs. The first occurred sixty-two years ago, when the Besaran aristocracy called upon the Commonwealth to help put down a massive insurrection by the lower class which threatened to oust the established government in favor of a popular democratic movement. Many people both then and now have criticized the government for taking this stand in favor of a ruling class which has been characterized as greedy, self-serving, and repressive, but the Commonwealth's commercial interest in the onnesium supplies on Laut Besar has always outweighed any anti-aristocratic or prodemocracy sentiments."

"Trideo off," Hauser said with a snort. The three-dimensional image faded as the monitor switched off, leaving Hauser to stare at the blank imaging tank with a lingering feeling of disgust.

It was obvious that the media on Robespierre knew next to nothing about Laut Besar, even though the planets were the closest of neighbors as interstellar communities went. The distorted view of Besaran society these people held made it sound as if the Ubrenfars were actually justified somehow in their decision to launch the unprovoked invasion of Hauser's homeworld.

In a way, he supposed, that attitude was inevitable, no matter how wrong it might have been. Laut Besar had been settled under the provisions of the French Empire's notorious Clearance Edicts, drawing involuntary colonists from Terra's Southeast Asia region and putting them down on the new world with a minimum of outside support. Those Clearance Edicts had ended up sparking the collapse of the

Empire, galvanizing resistance to Paris instead of siphoning off the malcontents as the Imperial government had intended, and within half a century of being settled, Laut Besar had been virtually abandoned. The war that had brought down the Empire led into the era known later as the Shadow Centuries, when interstellar contact among Terra's colonies had all but broken down. Like so many of the planets settled through involuntary colonization, Laut Besar had fared poorly during that time. The colony had all but failed by the time the next wave of Terrestrial exploration rediscovered the planet, and the Indomays who had survived had lost most of their technology and civilization in the process.

They didn't really understand the situation here on Robespierre even today. It had been a prime colony, not a dumping ground for Terra's excess population, and though they had lost interstellar travel and were forced to fall back entirely on local resources, the French-descended inhabitants of Robespierre had never really fallen on hard times like their neighbors on Laut Besar. If they had seen what the first Uros had found among the Indomays, they might have comprehended the forces that had led to the development of modern Besaran society.

The Terran Commonwealth had ultimately emerged from the Shadow Centuries to reclaim Terra's sphere of influence, and the first survey mission to revisit Laut Besar had found the Indomays on the verge of complete collapse. But they had found something else of critical importance, a discovery that had put Laut Besar on the star charts in a way no one could have predicted. When the Imperial surveys had first mapped the planet they had noted the presence of large quantities of onnesium, a rare element which existed in an island of stability beyond the short-lived radioactives on the periodic table. At the time it had merely been a curiosity, the apparent result of a mammoth asteroidal strike which had crippled the planetary ecology and reshaped the face of the world in an earlier age.

But in the interim between the first and second surveys, onnesium had become important, vitally important, and the deposits on Laut Besar boosted the planet into interstellar prominence. Onnesium had become the principal element used in plating the field coils of Reynier-Kessler interstellar drives. Interstellar travel was possible without onnesium, using the technology of pre-Commonwealth times, but those early drives had been primitive and inefficient compared to the new models that made use of onnesium plating. Since it was still comparatively scarce, any large deposits merited exploitation and development. Laut Besar's plight had aroused sympathy but little action … until the critical commercial value of a viable settlement there had emerged. Then, suddenly, everyone was interested in assisting the Indomay "lost colony."

Specialists in mining and industry had come to the planet from the Commonwealth courtesy of Lebensraum Bergbau und Ingenieurwesen Korporation, a resource exploitation company. They reintroduced advanced technology to Laut Besar and helped the Indomays recover from the long years of isolation and decline, and in the process managed to gain long-term control over the major onnesium deposits and, just as importantly, the new factory complexes and other industries they were bringing to the world. The Indomays had lacked the knowledge and the assets to do any of this for themselves, but they'd been more than happy to share in the prosperity the Uros were bringing. That had laid the groundwork for the development of the Besaran class system, especially after the corporation relocated its main offices to Laut Besar and began to encourage large-scale Uro immigration. The Uros, few in numbers but in possession of the sophisticated skills needed to make Laut Besar rich, had slowly transformed into an aristocracy ruling over the more numerous but less advanced Indomays who had preceded them.

Then came the Semti War, when Mankind faced its most formidable opponents in a full-scale interstellar conflict. It was at the height of the war that the Uros on Laut Besar decided to sever their political connection with the Commonwealth, not out of disloyalty but rather in the hope of gaining a better deal with a Terran government already notorious for colonial exploitation on the most unfair terms. With the need for onnesium more urgent than ever because of the war, the Terrans had been willing to recognize the Besaran Declaration of Sovereignty, providing the supply pipelines stayed open. After the war the Uros had skillfully played the Commonwealth against the other emergent interstellar power of the postwar era, the Ubrenfars, who had quietly occupied a habitable world in the third system of the trio of stars that contained Laut Besar and Robespierre several decades before. Each interstellar government was eager to support a neutral and fully independent Laut Besar if the alternative was losing access to the onnesium. But the Commonwealth had always regarded the Besarans with suspicion and no little disdain for their secession, and the growth of the aristocratic society on the neutral world had only added fuel to the fire among Commonwealth citizens who regarded democracy as the only reasonable form of government.

Hauser, like most Besaran aristos, had no real quarrel with the principles of democracy ... but conditions on Laut Besar hadn't been right for a completely open government by all the people. The Indomays were slowly learning the intricacies of modern civilization, and some day they'd be ready for full participation. But not yet. Not for many years to come.

Now, though, everything had changed. One or more of the semi-independent Ubrenfar warclans had evidently decided to risk Commonwealth intervention in order to win total control of Laut Besaran onnesium. The Commonwealth was sure to rally behind the legitimate Besaran government. They had sent assistance in the past, and they were doing so now. But after a hundred years of talking about the inequities of "greedy, self-serving aristocrats" who "exploited their Indomay compatriots," the Commonwealth news media might be slow to break old stereotypes and recognize that the Besarans were their allies, the victims rather than the villains of this particular drama.

Thinking about Commonwealth misconceptions, Hauser found his own personal doubts had vanished. He loved his planet, his culture, his people ... and these things deserved to be defended, whether it was against the slurs of outsiders on Robespierre or the guns of Ubrenfar invaders.

Wolfgang Hauser would go home again someday, go home to fight. No other course made sense.

Chapter Four

A sense of honor is a wonderful thing for an officer or a civilian, but I'd rather see a legionnaire with a sense of self-preservation any day.

—Colonel Alexandre Villiers,
Third Foreign Legion, 2397

The walls surrounding the Besaran consul-general's huge country estate were made of stone, built with modern technology in a style that predated human spaceflight. They looked out of place here on Robespierre, a full Member World of the Terran Commonwealth with all the high-tech trappings of modern life that political status implied.

Those walls served no real purpose beyond their impressive, anachronistic appearance. For true security there would be a whole host of detectors and sophisticated intruder deterrent systems scattered around the perimeter. But the high stone walls and brooding iron-wrought gate gave the compound an atmosphere of aristocratic splendor that made the estate a small slice of far-off Laut Besar. The homeworld was three light-years away, but looking at this compound, Wolfgang Alaric Hauser von Semenanjung Burat couldn't help but feel a little bit homesick. The place looked like the Hauser family's seat on Java Baru and was a bitter reminder that he wasn't likely to see that home again any time soon.

With a high-pitched whine of revving turbofans, the hired floatcar set down a few meters from the gate. Hauser touched the small ident disk adhering to the base of his neck and pressed it against the scan-plate of the computer terminal mounted in front of him. The vehicle's on-board computer processed the transaction, shifting twenty-two sols from the Commonwealth account of the von Semenanjung Burat family to Transport Capitale and recording the time, date, place, and nature of the business in its own files and in the tiny chip inside the ident disk itself.

The scanplate flashed green, and the computer's synthesized voice said, "Thank you, sir." The passenger doors swung upward with a sigh, and Hauser and Suartana stepped out of the automated vehicle. When its sensors detected that they were clear, the computer closed the doors and the floatcar lifted on its magnetic suspension cushion, hovering a meter and a half above the ground. The turbofans kicked in, raising a cloud of dust as the car sped back in the direction of Cite Capitale.

Hauser watched it all with an expression of mild distaste. Like any civilized world Laut Besar made extensive use of computer technology in all avenues of life, but there was something faintly obscene about the preponderance of totally automated systems on Robespierre. Here virtually every job was conducted by computer-control equipment, with little room for human involvement.

The high-tech base left the populace little useful work to perform, a whole planet of idlers. Cheap fusion power and the nearly inexhaustible resources of an interstellar society had left their mark on society as a whole, and the inhabitants of the rich worlds of the Commonwealth able to take full advantage of these high-tech blessings had no need to work in order to survive, though some still found activity more bearable than enforced idleness. Some found jobs in the areas that still required human intervention, like government service or supervisory and executive positions in business. Others turned their attention to creative pursuits. But for many there was no incentive to do anything productive with their lives. The population of a full Member World received universal Commonwealth Citizenship and thus were eligible for the basic living wage of the ever-present Citizen's dole. It was a microcosm of conditions on decadent Terra, and the whole idea made Hauser cringe.

At least on Laut Besar wealth and technology had not completely ruined society. Onnesium deposits had made the planet wealthy even beyond Commonwealth member worlds like Robespierre, and the Uro aristocrats who controlled the extraction and sale of the mineral were very rich individuals indeed. But they were still expected to work, by the force of custom and family honor if not for economic incentives, and work they did, managing family estates and business concerns, filling government posts, serving as officers in the Sky Guards, the Navy, or the Planetary Defense Force.

And the Indomays, whom the Uros had rescued from certain economic and social collapse by the introduction of high-tech industry and onnesium mining a hundred years back, they were expected to work as well. The Uros had avoided the pitfalls of the welfare state so evident on worlds like Robespierre. Wasn't it wiser to let the lower classes earn their living as workers, farmers, drivers, or whatever instead of subjecting them to the demoralizing, debilitating influence of the monthly dole?

Laut Besar enjoyed access to the same level of technology as the Commonwealth worlds, but by restricting the uses of that technology the planet had been able to preserve a social structure closer to that of the various Commonwealth Colonies, where the number of true Citizens was small and most men still had to work if they wanted to survive and prosper. That gave Laut Besaran society a vigor that was lacking on worlds such as Robespierre, and it was the preservation of their unique culture that had led the Uro ruling class to resist many Commonwealth attempts, some quite strongly made, to bring Laut Besar into the mainstream of Terra's interstellar empire.

Despite the problems—the ongoing balancing act between guaranteeing the Indomays their basic human rights without creating total chaos by giving them more political or economic power than they were prepared to handle, for instance—the Besaran system had worked just fine. Until now.

Now that the Ubrenfars were entrenched on Laut Besar, it was going to take Commonwealth assistance to free the planet. Even if liberation was achieved it was possible that the Besaran debt to the Commonwealth would be too large to permit the leadership to ignore a new request for Laut Besar to join. One way or another, the homeworld would never be the same again....

Hauser shook off his gloomy thoughts and turned toward the gate. During the past week, as *Freiheit Stern* had made the crossing from the systerm to Robespierre, Hauser had spent a lot of time considering his options. He had shied away from committing himself to the cause of Liberation at first. It would have been easy enough to resign his commission and sit out his exile in luxury. The von Semenanjung Burat mining and shipping interests had amassed a sizable account balance here on Robespierre, unaffected by the Ubrenfar occupation of the homeworld. Plenty of other Uros had already opted for that course of action, and Hauser's meager skills surely wouldn't be missed even if there really was a counterattack against the invaders.

But much as he feared the prospect of facing combat again, and especially the thought of leading others into danger, Hauser was more afraid of giving in to that fear. Unless he tried again, he would always have to live with his failure on Telok and the recurrent dreams where he heard dying men screaming in agony. At least by returning to duty he would have the chance to redeem that failure, to prove himself. In the end, that argument had carried the day.

His Sky Guard staff post was gone, of course, and in the confused state of things among the refugees there was no clear-cut organization, no solid chain of command to report to any longer. Lacking any better options, Hauser had decided to seek out the Free Laut Besaran Regiment forming among the refugees here on Robespierre. All the media reports had featured the unit's call for volunteers to serve under *Oberst* von Padang Tengah, the hero of the campaign against the Indomay rebellion on Java Baru a decade ago. The newscasts had indicated that there were still plenty of openings for junior officers.

The *oberst* had arranged to quarter and train his recruits here, on the extensive country estate reserved for the use of the Besaran consul-general and chief commercial representative. So Hauser had left his luxurious hotel suite in the capital, with *Sersan* Suartana in tow, to see if he could arrange a posting. He only hoped there were as many vacancies as the reports indicated.

Unfortunately, the Hausers, prominent as they were in homeworld politics, had few connections in the military establishment, and that could be a handicap. Both the Sky Guard and the PDF establishments relied heavily on patronage for the placement of qualified officers. Hauser had obtained his staff position through a *feldmarshall* who had owed his uncle a favor, but there were precious few other connections available for him to call on now. It was different for a well-connected military family like the Neubecks von Lembah Terang, who could get preferment anywhere they applied.

Hauser felt a momentary burst of anger that he couldn't use his links to his mother's family. *Oberst* von Padang Tengah was a distant connection of the Wrangel family, and should have been a useful ally.

But the scandal of Hilda Wrangel-Hauser's mental breakdown and bizarre suicide had opened a huge gulf between the two families. There had even been a pair of duels in the wake of the incident, and now neither clan would even acknowledge the existence of the other in public. There would be no help from that quarter ... in fact, the *oberst* might actually block his application if he was close enough to the main branch of the Wrangels to care about the old feud.

He would just have to hope that the manpower shortages were real, that he could win a slot in the regiment even without a patron to speak on his behalf.

The gate was closed and locked, but he spotted the adjacent inter-com system and buzzed for attention. A moment later the speaker squawked an interrogative.

"Applicant for the FLB regiment," Hauser responded. "Uro. Active commission in the Sky Guard as *leutnant.*"

There was a short pause. Then the gate swung slowly open and the speaker came on again. "Please wait in the gatehouse. Transportation has been dispatched." He couldn't tell if the voice belonged to a person or to another computer.

Minutes passed before a civilian model floatcar, hastily repainted in a camouflage scheme and bearing the Free Laut Besaran *binatanganas-head* crest on each door, appeared and settled to the ground outside the gatehouse. This vehicle wasn't automated, at least. An Indomay bearing *kopral's* stripes was driving, and a *serdadu* rode alongside him. Both saluted smartly as Hauser climbed into the car. Suartana sat with him, maintaining a respectful silence.

The estate proved to be even larger than Hauser had first envisioned, a sprawling compound given over mostly to rolling hills and unspoiled woodland. Purchased from the government of Robespierre soon after the inception of the lucrative onnesium trade, the land was classified as a foreign embassy and thus technically Laut Besaran soil. It included a small shuttle port with control, repair, and warehouse facilities, all highly automated in Robespierran fashion, plus the Inner Sanctum, where the Residence, business officers, and servants' and workers' quarters were located.

The block of apartments that had formerly housed the serving staff had been turned over to the regimental headquarters staff for the duration of their stay on Robespierre, while the landscape was dotted with makeshift housing. Not all of the latter was military, though. There were large numbers of Indomay refugees living on the estate now. Unlike the Uros, most of the Indomays lacked the wherewithal to support themselves, except for those like Suartana directly attached to a Uro's personal "tail." There was no work for refugees here, and as non-Citizens they couldn't even qualify for the Commonwealth's dole. Government relief measures were still being debated. In the meantime, the consul-general had invited the refugees to stay on the estate grounds, and was purchasing food and other supplies for them out of government discretionary funds.

Still, the precarious position of the refugees made it certain that there would be no shortage of recruits for the regiment's enlisted ranks. Their pay, at least, would be guaranteed for the foreseeable future.

The floatcar grounded outside the Residence, and the *kopral* pointed toward a doorway flanked by a pair of smartly dressed sentries. "Officers' recruitment is through there, *Tuan*," the noncom said. "First door on the left after you leave Reception. Go straight through if there's no one at the front desk."

"Terima kasih," Hauser replied. "Thank you." The two Indomays looked surprised and more than a little pleased at his use of their own phrase. It was a courtesy his father had always insisted on, though one rarely seen among Uros today. But Karl Hauser had been a progressive politician whose chief platform had been the advancement of Uro rights. Wolfgang Alaric Hauser had never paid much attention to the politics of the Indomay rights question, but he had always tried to live up to his father's insistence that the Indomay people, lower class or not, deserved to be treated with dignity.

The reception room was empty of either visitors or staff, so Hauser took the NCO's advice and led the way down the corridor to the indicated doorway. It was standing open, and inside he could see the makeshift office furnishings that had replaced some Residence staff members' quarters. A Uro wearing a naval *leutnant's* uniform and a regen cast on one leg sat in front of a desk. Behind it three more officers, all Sky Guards, were ranged in a row, questioning the man.

It took Hauser several seconds to realize that he knew two of the men.

The younger man, wearing an *oberleutnant's* insignia, had been a classmate of his at the Academy, never a close friend but at least an old acquaintance ... Walther Neubeck von Lembah Terang. And next to him was his brother, Major Erich Neubeck. Hauser had seen his frowning features last on a commlink screen during the fight on Telok.

He hadn't given any real thought to what might have happened to the major after things went sour back there....

Just then Erich Neubeck looked up and caught sight of Hauser. Anger twisted his handsome features into a dark frown. "Hauser!" He managed to turn the bald name into a venomous snarl. "What are *you* doing here?"

Hauser stepped back, taken by surprise by the hatred and contempt in the major's tones. "I—this is a mistake. I didn't mean to disturb you gentlemen." He strove to keep his voice even, to maintain the polite forms even in the face of the older man's obvious fury. The aristocracy of Laut Besar placed a premium on keeping up a public mask of civility even under the most stressful conditions.

Major Neubeck stood, a flowing, catlike movement. "Not so fast, *Leutnant* Hauser," he said firmly. "I asked you a question. Why are you here?"

"Maybe he wanted to apply for a position in the regiment," Neubeck's brother interjected. Unlike his brother, he sounded more amused than angry, but there was a razor-sharp edge hidden under his light tone. "That would be a real laugh, wouldn't it, Erich?"

The major's blue eyes were cold. "Not funny to me, little brother," he said. "There's no place in this outfit for a man who would disobey orders and desert his post."

The words stung, but Hauser fought down his rising anger. Both of the Neubecks were being openly scornful, without making any pretense of civility. That kind of treatment implied that Hauser wasn't a real gentleman, that he wasn't within the bounds of polite society. Hauser had always had trouble keeping control of his emotions. His temper had always been short, his sense of honor touchy at best, but this time he was determined to stay calm. He couldn't let the Neubeck brothers goad him into an outburst he'd regret later.

"We retreated because we couldn't hold that position against the scalies," he said, trying to sound reasonable. "Because *you* didn't send the reinforcements you promised. That wasn't a matter of disobedience or desertion. We simply couldn't hold the position without proper support, and your men weren't there to help."

"The men I sent ran into Ubrenfars in the passage *your men* were supposed to be securing," Neubeck shot back. "Thanks to you, all but a handful of my people were killed."

"You made it out," Hauser said. Everything the major accused him of was a distortion of the truth ... but it struck just close enough to home to hurt. "I was one of the last men out of the warehouse. How is it *you* escaped if so many of your men were killed?"

Neubeck looked as if he'd been struck. "You … you dare to suggest …" He took a step toward Hauser. "I won't take that kind of talk from a damned coward like you, Hauser!"

All of Hauser's anger and frustration came to the surface at once. He had tried, really tried, to keep from losing his temper, but this was more than he could take. There was no way he could stand there and let Neubeck call him a coward, not in front of other Uros. His honor had been insulted publicly, and there was only one way a Uro gentleman could react to that.

"Coward is it?" Hauser grated. "Coward? Take that back, Neubeck, or by God I'll …"

"You'll what?" the major taunted. "There's nothing a gutless softsnake like you can do to me, von Lembah Terang. Nothing!"

"I said retract it, Neubeck … unless you'd rather meet me with steel."

The major laughed coldly. "A duel? A puppy like you would challenge me to a duel? Did you hear that, brother?"

The younger Neubeck followed his brother's lead. "Maybe he's never seen you fence, Erich," he said, grinning. "He wouldn't last five minutes in a fight with you."

"Last?" Major Neubeck laughed again. "He doesn't have the guts to *show up* for a duel. He'll run again, just like he did on Telok."

"You think so, Neubeck?" Hauser said quietly. "You really think so? You'll see differently soon enough." He turned away, pushing past Suartana and striding down the hall briskly with the Neubecks' laughter echoing in his ears.

Erich Neubeck was a well-known duelist back on the homeworld, and Hauser knew he didn't have much hope of winning a fight. But this was a question of courage and honor, not of skill, and he was determined to prove to the two brothers that he was no coward.

At the same time, perhaps he could prove his courage to himself as well.

Chapter Five

The old legionnaires were made of quite different stuff and were in it for reasons ranging from manslaughter to unrequited love.

—Legionnaire David King,
French Foreign Legion, 1914

Hauser returned the Indomay sentry's crisp salute and strode through the high-arched double doors into the courtyard. Suartana stayed close behind him, rigid, precise, his attitude never deviating from perfect correctness toward his Uro superior yet somehow managing to convey a faint hint of disapproval at the same time. Their booted feet clattered on the cobblestones as they crossed the open space within the walled garden.

There were already five figures waiting by the fountain in the center of the courtyard. The two Neubeck brothers and the major's Indomay attendant barely acknowledged Hauser's arrival with narrow-eyed glances. Another Uro, wearing a Besaran naval officer's uniform with the insignia of the medical corps, was plainly the doctor required by the formalities. The fifth, also a Uro but clad in exquisitely tailored civilian clothes, was Freidrich Doenitz von Pulau Irian, Laut Besar's consul-general and chief commercial representative on Robespierre and owner of the estate. He was the neutral party here, the man responsible for overseeing the final arrangements for the duel.

"Ah, *Freiherr* von Semenanjung Burat," Doenitz said cordially, stepping forward with his hand extended. "I wish we could have met under more ... congenial circumstances. I knew your father quite well before his unfortunate accident."

Hauser took the proffered hand. "He spoke well of you, *Freiherr*," he replied. "My uncle, as well."

The consul-general gestured toward the Neubecks. "A sad business, this," he said softly. "At a time like this, with the Homeworld overrun, shouldn't you save your anger for the Ubrenfars? We need all our young officers if we are to regain our homes."

Shrugging, Hauser half turned from the diplomat. "This is a matter of honor, *Freiherr*. Surely you don't expect me to disgrace my family's name?"

Doenitz shook his head sadly. "There are many kinds of disgrace, young man," he said in the same low voice. "I only hope you can choose between them." He walked back toward the others, leaving Hauser to his own thoughts.

Custom had dictated every move in the intricate dance of the dueling code. Hauser had made the challenge in anger, but the outburst had been in front of other Uros, witnesses of power and substance. With no graceful way out, the only face-saving choice was to follow through with the affair. Suartana had delivered the formal challenge to Neubeck's Indomay retainer, who in turn had presented the major's acceptance. Time, place, weapons, all had been arranged with scrupulous regard for tradition.

Now it was out of the question to even consider backing down. Neubeck had been a champion fencer at the Sky Guard Academy, so his choice of sabers had been no real surprise. His reputation made it all the harder for Hauser to stop the duel. That would look too much like the very cowardice Neubeck had accused him of, and Hauser would never be able to mix with his peers again if the label of "coward" clung to him any longer.

Duels were rarely pursued to the death. He would fight Neubeck to prove his courage, and even though he would probably lose, his honor would remain intact.

"Gentlemen," Doenitz called suddenly. "It is time."

Hauser stalked toward the fountain slowly, acutely aware of everything around him. Suartana loomed over his left shoulder, tense, a coiled spring as tightly bound by tradition as Hauser himself. The Indomay had tried to talk him out of the fight. Now, caught between his promise to the family to protect Hauser from harm and the strict rules of the duel, Suartana had the look of a rembot caught in a program loop, unable to choose one course of action over another.

"I will ask you both one more time," the diplomat said in even, measured tones. "Won't you settle this matter without shedding blood?"

Woodenly, Hauser stepped forward. His voice sounded like it belonged to someone else, some actor playing a trideo role. "He has already called me a coward. Why should I give him further reason to make the claim?"

"If you'd stood on Telok we wouldn't have to be here, Hauser," the major said harshly. He spat eloquently, a contemptuous gesture that had no place in polite society. "But you won't stand up to my blade now any more than you did to the Ubrenfars then. You don't have the guts for it. So let's get this charade over with now."

Doenitz looked grim. "Very well, *gentlemen.*" He made the word sound like an obscenity. "Weapons will be sabers. Select them, if you please."

At Hauser's gesture Suartana moved forward, and Neubeck's Indomay joined him. That, too, was custom. If the Uro principals showed too much interest in the weapons selection it would be an implied criticism of the neutral arbiter's impartiality. While Doenitz was clearly no dedicated duelist himself, that would be an affront to honor even he wouldn't have been able to overlook.

Suartana returned with the saber. It was heavier than Hauser had expected, with a wide, slightly curved blade honed to a razor-sharp edge. Long before the age of spaceflight, weapons like this one had played major roles in Terran battles, but now they were anachronisms. Officers carried swords as part of their dress uniforms, but by and large they were strictly for show.

But on some worlds, including Laut Besar, dueling was an accepted social custom, a challenge of courage, manhood. There were few tests of personal bravery better than facing an opponent armed with cold steel.

Hauser tested the balance of the blade, made a few quick practice cuts, and gave a satisfied nod. It was Besaran manufacture, a genuine Kohl saber from the famous swordmakers of Djakarta Baru. A fine weapon, elegant and deadly.

"If you please, gentlemen," Doenitz said. "This engagement shall be to first blood—"

"What?" Major Neubeck's voice was an angry whip-crack in the still morning air. "I specified a fight to *angenehm aufgeben*. Is this more of your damned dodging, Hauser?"

He opened his mouth to make an angry denial, but Doenitz answered first. "Will your honor not be satisfied by drawing blood, Major? I really do feel that ..."

"*Angenehm aufgeben,*" Neubeck said, cutting him off.

Doenitz looked at Hauser.

"*Angenehm aufgeben,*" he echoed flatly. Much as he appreciated the old diplomat's gesture on his behalf, Hauser couldn't help but feel angry at the interference. Now it looked as if he had been trying to save himself by altering the agreed-upon conditions of the fight.

The terms of the fight to *angenehm aufgeben*—"acceptable surrender"—required the duel to go on until both parties agreed to end it. A ruthless duelist could press the battle to the death, though that was a fairly rare result. But it did give Neubeck the chance to thoroughly humiliate his opponent, perhaps wound him seriously, before accepting a surrender, rather than simply going through the form of a quick engagement to first blood that would satisfy most questions of honor.

Hauser knew he wasn't a match for Neubeck in a prolonged duel. But he was willing to accept the humiliation of an unbalanced fight if it would prove once and for all that he wasn't a coward who would run from personal danger.

"The fight is to *angenehm aufgeben,*" Doenitz conceded. "It will continue until one party yields and the other accepts the surrender. Gentlemen, take your places ... *anfangen!*"

As the diplomat stepped back, Hauser dropped into the proper fencing stance. He had fought saber back at the Academy, well enough to be on the first-string fencing team in his last year. But he was nowhere near Neubeck's skill level.

And there was a vast difference between Academy matches, with blunt-edged weapons and heavy protective padding and electronic scoring, when compared with the reality of facing an armed man in actual, lethal combat.

Neubeck's blade flicked back and forth in tiny, neat strokes, beating against Hauser's saber, probing, testing reactions. The major's fencing style was a reflection of the man himself. Controlled and precise, he refused to commit himself to an attack until he had taken the measure of his opponent.

Such a careful style was kilometers away from the crowd-pleasing swashbuckling antics so dear to the hearts of the spectators in Academy tournaments, but in the long run it was exactly the kind of fighting that won the match.

Or the kill.

Hauser beat his opponent's blade aside and lunged suddenly, trying to take control of the tempo of the duel. If he allowed Major Neubeck to stick to the slow, deliberate pace he was building, the major's greater experience and talent would be sure to carry the day. But if he was thrown off his preferred speed, particularly now while both of them were still fresh, then anything might happen. Hauser needed every advantage he could get. Neubeck was seven years older, but the younger man couldn't count on any advantage in stamina. The major was trim and fit....

And agile. Neubeck danced back from the attack, dodging Hauser's hasty stroke easily. An unpleasant smile showed just what he thought of his younger opponent's tactics.

Suddenly the major exploded into action himself, and Hauser recoiled under a flurry of quick cuts and thrusts which took all of his ability to hold off. There was no room here for parry and riposte, nothing but hasty blocks and retreats that left the initiative squarely with Neubeck.

The man's final slash was a fraction too fast for him to deflect, and Hauser stifled a cry as steel bit deep into his right arm just above the elbow.

Neubeck stepped back, still on guard, still sneering. "Too much for you, Hauser?" he asked, voice dripping sarcasm. "If you throw away your sword and run, I probably wouldn't bother to chase you. Running away should come easily enough to you." He wasn't even breathing hard.

But Hauser didn't have the wind to talk and fight. He just shook his head and tried to ignore the warm, wet, sticky trickle of blood running down his sword arm.

The major renewed his attack abruptly, leading with the *beat-beat-beat* of a double disengage that turned into a whistling cut aimed at Hauser's neck. Again he managed to block the attack, but this time Neubeck didn't break off once the block was made. He bore down against Hauser's blade with his full weight until they stood *corps a corps*, glaring at each other over crossed steel.

They held the pose for what seemed like an eternity before Hauser twisted suddenly to the left. Neubeck recovered his stance with the speed of a cat, but not before Hauser managed to score a hit of his own, a shallow cut across his opponent's thigh. It wasn't much, especially when set against Hauser's bleeding arm, but it was a hit.

Knowing that the man wasn't invulnerable after all was as important to Hauser at that point as the wound itself.

Neubeck backed away, keeping his guard up and regarding Hauser with a new look that might have been grudging respect. They touched blades again tentatively, the initial flurry of aggression now replaced by caution.

Now Hauser led off with a foot-stomping attack, but the distraction didn't break Neubeck's concentration for so much as an instant. He parried Hauser's thrust easily, almost casually, and riposted in a smooth, flowing motion. Giving ground, Hauser blocked three quick slashes, then parried a fourth and counterattacked. But it was useless, and in seconds he was falling back again, thoroughly outmatched. He skipped back out of reach as Neubeck stepped into a classic lunging attack, a move more common to foil or epee fencing than saber, but still effective. The major grimaced as he took his weight on the injured right leg, and he was slower than usual recovering to the guard position.

Not that it was much of an advantage, especially now that Hauser's arm was starting to give him just as much trouble. Each block and parry made it throb, and he was having trouble controlling the blade as the hilt grew slippery with his blood.

On Neubeck's next attack the saber went flying from his grasp when he tried to parry. The cut landed on his right forearm this time, not deep but painful. Hauser threw himself sideways, hitting the ground in a roll that brought him up on one knee beside his sword. He scooped it up in his left hand, and shifted immediately into a block against a fierce slash aimed at his head. As Neubeck dropped back, he rose awkwardly and dropped into the guard position, still using the left hand.

The major was smiling again, no doubt thinking that his opponent would be handicapped fighting with his off hand. Few people knew that Hauser was ambidextrous. He had rarely fought left-handed at the Academy, but he had practiced often enough in the *Ortwaffen* on the Hauser estate under the harsh eye of Otto Roehiyat, the half-breed *anteilzucht* fencing instructor, who, like Suartana, had served three generations of the Hauser family.

Now he finally had an advantage of sorts. Fighting a left-handed fencer was almost always unsettling for fighters used to right-handed opponents. Neubeck's experience might actually work against him for a change.

No ... he actually had *three* advantages. The major's overconfidence, and his injured leg, would both be valuable allies if Hauser could only make them work for him. For the first time he began to believe that he might have a real chance to win this duel.

But his right arm was still throbbing painfully. Advantages or not, he couldn't keep this up indefinitely.

Neubeck renewed the fighting without warning, catching Hauser by surprise. He fell back before the major's assault, almost tripping as he stepped off the cobblestone pavement into a flower bed. As he parried a whole string of fast strikes, Hauser cursed inwardly. Apparently the only one who was suffering from overconfidence right now was Wolfgang Hauser.

He rallied and counterattacked, less graceful than the major but fierce enough to make the man recoil. Back on firm footing, he decided not to press the offensive. At this juncture he needed to bide his time and stay in control. Conservative fencing was the need here, not a rash gesture that could throw away his hard-won advantages. Roehiyat had told him repeatedly that his two most dangerous shortcomings as a fencer were his impatience and his short temper, and he could still remember how he had lost the championship bout during his last year at the Academy by letting blind rage take over where reason and caution should have held sway. It was almost as if he were reliving those times again instead of facing Neubeck. Hauser told himself that this time around he wouldn't make the same mistake....

Their contact again broken off, the two duelists faced each other for a long moment. The older man was sweating and short of breath now, but he still seemed to be holding up better to the exertion than Hauser. Neubeck was regarding him with a narrow-eyed look of concentration, calculation, assessment. Perhaps he was actually feeling some concern for the first time in the fighting. At the very least he had learned to treat Hauser with some caution.

Hauser lunged forward once more, driving, slashing, forcing the tempo, trying to make Neubeck use his wounded leg as much as possible. The major did give ground at first, but suddenly changed tactics to meet a savage cut with a solid stop-thrust. Again their sabers locked, standing close enough together for Hauser to feel his opponent's hot breath on his cheek.

Neubeck shifted his weight suddenly, twisting his blade to bear down hard on Hauser's sword. He tried to counter the unexpected maneuver ... and his saber flew free from his grasp like a live thing. It spun in the air as if in slow motion, catching the morning sunlight. The sword clattered on the cobblestones five meters away, too far this time for Hauser to dive for it.

Hauser looked down at the point of the major's saber, bare centimeters from his throat.

"Do you yield?" Neubeck asked coldly.

"Yield," he agreed, almost choking on the single word.

The blade remained poised for long seconds, as if Neubeck were debating whether or not to renew the attack on his disarmed opponent. Then the major lowered the sword with a careless shrug and turned away. "Surrender accepted," he said gruffly. He stalked back toward his brother, handing the sword to his Indomay attendant without another word. It was as if he had dismissed the duel from his mind already.

Hauser picked up his saber, grinding his teeth in frustration and anger. For all the advantages, all of his self-deluding hopes, he had still lost the fight to Neubeck. And now the man wasn't even following through with the accepted forms that would be accorded to any gentleman after the conclusion of an affair of honor.

Freidrich Doenitz was glaring at the Neubecks, obviously just as concerned that proper customs should prevail. He stepped forward, darting a glance at Hauser before returning his attention to the major and his brother, then clearing his throat noisily. "Ah ... *Freiherr* von Lembah Terang ... you will surely acknowledge now that *Freiherr* von Semenanjung Burat is no coward...?"

There was a long moment of utter stillness in the courtyard. Then Neubeck looked up at Hauser and Doenitz and laughed, a cruel, callous sound. "I suppose the puppy's not a coward," he responded, laughing again. "Too stupid to be a coward. He's soft in the head ... just like his mother."

Coming on top of the pent-up anger and frustration from the duel, the words and the cold laughter were more than Hauser could take. Something inside him snapped. "Damn you, Neubeck!" he shouted, pushing past Doenitz to get at the man. "You'll pay for that!"

Hot fury consumed him, made him lash out at his enemy in an outburst of hatred. Half blinded by a red haze of raw emotion, he was hardly aware of the weapon in his hand, hardly aware of anything except the overpowering need to strike out.

The jarring impact of his saber sinking deep into flesh sobered him instantly.

Too late.

Neubeck staggered back, almost jerking the sword out of Hauser's hands before the blade came free. The major sagged to the ground with blood pouring freely from the ugly gash in his neck. The saber had sliced deep through the neck and throat, almost to the bone, and Neubeck's head, half severed, hung at an impossible angle.

There was a moment of stunned silence, broken by the navy doctor. The man dropped to one knee beside Neubeck's stricken form, raising his left arm to speak urgently into his wristpiece computer terminal. "Ambulance to the Doenitz estate. Now!"

Hauser could do nothing but stare at the tableau. His sword slipped from nerveless fingers and clattered on the stonework again unheeded. Then Doenitz and Suartana were there, urging him toward the Residence. Unresisting, he let them lead him.

At the door he paused as Neubeck's brother spoke for the first time. "This isn't over, Hauser," the *oberleutnant* said harshly. "You'll pay! You hear me, you dirty murderer? You'll pay!"

Chapter Six

A good legionnaire is a man who needs to find something in the Legion. If he has a past he wants to forget and needs a lifeline to cling to, and providing he is in good physical condition, he will have the right motivation to succeed with us.

—Colonel R. Forcin,
French Foreign Legion, 1984

The study in the consul-general's Residence was decorated in dark paneling, a quiet, somber room that suited Hauser's bitter mood. He sat in a straight-backed chair at the richly inlaid *kajudjati* desk Doenitz had brought to Robespierre from Laut Besar, holding his head in both hands and staring unseeing into the glossy, polished hardwood desktop.

He could sense Suartana hovering nearby, but ignored the Indomay. The *sersan* had tried to attend to his injured arm, but Hauser had waved him away. Neither had spoken for a long time now, and the silence of the study had been broken only by the brief flurry of noise in the courtyard as the ambulance had arrived to pick up Erich Neubeck.

Long minutes passed before Doenitz came in. Hauser looked up at him hopefully, but the consul-general shook his head. "It's no good, Wolf," he said slowly. "It took too long. There's no hope of reviving him now."

The words knocked down the last hope Hauser had been holding on to. Medical technology on a world as sophisticated as Robespierre could work miracles, and even a mortal wound like Neubeck's might have been treated at a high-tech hospital facility. But without a regen capsule on hand to keep the body on life support until the ambulance arrived there had never been much hope of that. Now there was no hope at all. Erich Neubeck was dead.

"What about ... his brother?" Hauser asked, turning away from Doenitz.

"He left with the body. But he's more determined to even the score than he was when you left. They were ... a close family."

Hauser nodded. "What'll he do? A challenge? Or is there some legal action he can bring instead?"

"Neubeck provoked the whole thing," Doenitz replied. "A Uro court would find in your favor, since the man so obviously flouted the conventions. You satisfied the demands of honor and yet he continued to insult you."

"Unfortunately, this isn't Laut Besar and there are no Uro courts available," Hauser pointed out grimly. "I've seen how they feel about the Besaran aristocracy around here."

"The offense took place on Besaran soil," the consul-general pointed out. "Robespierre has no jurisdiction ... but there's no organized homeworld civil authority that Neubeck could turn to. He might argue that it's a matter for a military court. That would mean the *Oberst* von Padang Tengah."

"Who is married, if I remember correctly, to a Neubeck," Hauser finished the thought glumly.

"It's more likely he'll issue a challenge of his own," Doenitz went on. "And he's nowhere near as good with a saber as his brother. You could probably beat him."

Suartana cleared his throat. "You might beat him, *Tuan*, but you know that wouldn't be the end of it."

"Yeah." Hauser slumped in the chair. "There must be a dozen Neubeck connections in the regimental mess alone ... including the *oberst*."

"Nor would von Padang Tengah be too happy if you kept fighting his officers. You know the Neubecks will turn this into an outright blood feud. All duels to the death ... not just an agreed capitulation. So either you die in a duel, or you keep killing off officers until the *oberst* decides that military court is in order."

"Always assuming that *Freiherr* Neubeck sticks to the proprieties," Suartana added hesitantly. Indomays were usually careful to avoid questioning Uro honor, but the *sersan*'s words were blunt even if his tone was not. "If he's really out for revenge he might just round up a few of his men and ambush you somewhere."

"He's an honorable man," Hauser said, but he made the admonishment more from habit than conviction. "But the alternatives don't sound too good...." He trailed off. Inwardly he was cursing the hot temper that had made him strike Erich Neubeck down. It was a betrayal of everything he believed in. Hauser had cut off more than a man's life in that courtyard. Honor, reputation, both his and the Hauser family's, had died on the cobblestones alongside the major.

"I warned you," Doenitz said. "You were worried about the disgrace of cowardice, but what you've ended up with is ... worse. Infinitely worse."

Hauser turned in the chair and met the old man's eyes. "What do you suggest, *Freiherr* Doenitz?" he asked softly. "What would you do in my situation?"

The consul-general's dark eyes were sad. "There's nothing left for you here, Wolfgang. Home, family ... those are gone already. If you stay and fight for your name, you only condemn yourself to death, and I hate to see anyone throw away a life to no good purpose."

"What's the alternative?" Hauser asked.

"Leave Robespierre. Turn your back on all this ... and find something to do with your life. That's my advice."

"Just ... abandon my honor? My family's good name? I don't know if I could do that." The idea went against everything that Wolfgang Hauser had been brought up to believe.

"Your other choice is to stay and die. It's that simple. It doesn't matter if you die fighting some pointless duel, or if you're condemned by a court martial, or if a gang of hired thugs attacks you in a dark alley some night. In the end, you'll die unless you leave ... and leave quickly."

"The von Lembah Terang money gives the Neubecks a long reach, *Tuan* Doenitz," Suartana commented. "How safe would it be to stay in the Commonwealth?"

Doenitz looked thoughtful. "That's a good point, Suartana. A very good point." He was quiet for a long moment. "There's one option you might consider, Wolfgang," he went on at length. "But it's a drastic one."

"It sounds like anything I do will be a drastic measure," Hauser said. "What is it?"

The diplomat didn't answer right away. When he did, his voice was soft. "There is a place where people can run from their problems, where they can take on a whole new identity if they wish. It's a Commonwealth military unit, but it accepts anyone who can measure up to its standards. They're tough, but you have what it takes, I think … if you want to try."

"The Fifth Foreign Legion," Hauser said slowly.

It was one of the best-known military formations in the Terran sphere, a unit which carried on a romantic tradition that stretched back through centuries of human endeavor. The Fifth Foreign Legion had been called an elite fighting force and a haven for the worst social outcasts in the Commonwealth, and such was the power of the myth surrounding it that no one could really say which description was more apt.

But the Legion was certainly known as a safe haven, where recruits could vanish into the anonymity of a military life. Legion recruiters didn't care if a man was wanted for a long list of crimes, as long as he had the potential to be a good soldier. And they were supposed to protect their own, no matter what.

Wolfgang Alaric Hauser von Semenanjung Burat would never have considered joining the Legion … but the man who had killed Erich Neubeck and forever stained his name and honor would fit in perfectly among the other flotsam of human space. The thought that he might somehow expiate his dishonor among such men was seductive.

"Do you really think they'll take me?" Hauser asked.

"Well, it takes more than a strong back to be a soldier," Doenitz said. "But you've already had military training at the Academy. If anything, your background as an officer puts you ahead of most of the recruits they take in. You could get tapped as an NCO if they think you're leadership material."

Hauser shrugged. "After Telok I'm not sure what kind of leader I'd make," he said somberly. "But that doesn't really matter, I guess." He paused, frowning at Doenitz for a long moment. "You sound sure of yourself, *Freiherr*. Have you dealt with the Legion before?"

Doenitz shook his head. "Not me, no. But I had a brother once, Wolfgang … he joined the Legion a long time ago, after a quarrel with our father. He … never came back. But the last holo I had from him was full of stories about Legion life. He said it was a harder life than he'd ever imagined, but also the most rewarding." The diplomat looked away for a long moment, then turned his sad eyes back on Hauser. "I was proud of him, Wolfgang. People said he turned his back on our way of life, but I was proud of him. Do you understand?"

Hauser nodded slowly. "I think I do, *Freiherr*. I hope you can be as proud of me ... even after what I did today."

For the first time since the end of the duel he felt as if he had a future. He would join the Fifth Foreign Legion, and he would prove himself the only way he still could, now that his old life was closed to him. And maybe he could make this one old man proud.

*   *   *

"Name?"

"Wolfgang Hauser von Semenanjung Burat."

"God, what a mouthful," the NCO at the computer terminal commented wryly. His stripes identified him as a *sersan*, but Hauser had already learned that rank titles were different in the Legion from the ones he was used to at home. "You expect us to call you that, kid?"

"Wolfgang Hauser will do, sir," Hauser said quietly. He spoke slowly, carefully. It had been a long time since he'd used Terranglic, and he hadn't taken a chip course to brush up on the language for years.

"Not 'sir,'" the man told him. "Sergeant. You reserve 'sir' for officers, politicians, journalists, and other scum." He entered Hauser's name. "Are you a Commonwealth citizen?"

"No. I'm from Laut Besar."

"Ah ... one of the refugees." The sergeant looked at him. "Look, son, far be it from me to turn away a recruit. Lord knows we can always use fresh meat. But if you're enlisting with the idea of fighting the Ubrenfars, stick with the Besaran army they're putting together out in the country. There's no guarantee the Commonwealth'll even get involved, and even less that you'd get a posting to your systern after Basic. Any good card player knows not to play against the odds, see?"

Hauser shrugged. "I wasn't counting on anything, Sergeant. And I have my reasons for preferring your Legion...."

The sergeant gave him a knowing look. "Like that, huh?" He grinned. "Well, whatever it is you've done, the Legion'll look after you. We'll protect your identity ... you don't have to tell anyone anything more about your past than you want to, once you're in. But we'll need a complete history before we can process you."

"Whatever you want, Sergeant," Hauser said. Despite the commitment he'd made to himself at the consul-general's Residence, part of him still felt empty, as if he was just going through the motions.

Consul-General Doenitz had handled all of the arrangements once Hauser had made up his mind to enlist. The diplomat had placed a call to the Legion's Robespierre recruiting office, arranging for a floatcar to pick Hauser up at the estate. It had arrived a little more than an hour later, giving Hauser time to make arrangements to have his meager personal effects picked up from his hotel in the capital. Nothing he had left there had any particular value or usefulness, and anyway Doenitz had said the Legion wouldn't let him take much of a personal kit, but he needed to wrap up the loose ends in his life. It was almost a symbolic gesture, closing out his past life to clear the way for his Legion career.

But there was one loose end he hadn't known how to wrap up. Radiah Suartana had insisted on accompanying Hauser into the Legion, and despite all of Hauser's protests and orders the Indomay had bluntly refused to be put off. Even after it was pointed out that the Legion might not let them stay together the big *sersan* had remained set in his intentions. He had been told to watch over Hauser by the family he had served for years, and he would not give up that charge under any circumstances.

In a way Suartana's stubbornness was comforting. A part of Hauser recoiled from the idea of this complete break with his past, and the unswerving loyalty of the Indomay, despite everything that had happened, was something Hauser could draw strength from as he faced the most difficult moment in his life.

The Legion floatcar had been piloted by a tough-looking, scar-faced man wearing the insignia of a *kopral*, but he was a Uro—of Old Terran European stock, at least—and he told Hauser and Suartana to address him as "corporal." He was plainly a long-service veteran, with close-cropped hair beginning to go gray. Each of his five hash marks indicated completion of a five-year hitch in the Legion, and in response to a question from Doenitz he indicated that his sixth term was nearly over. Most legionnaires on recruiting duty were approaching their retirements, and this man was no exception.

For all his long military experience, the corporal was good at dealing with civilians. He was polite to Doenitz, brisk and businesslike toward Hauser and Suartana. They had surrendered their ident disks to the noncom, then followed him to the floatcar for the hour's trip to the

Commonwealth military installation on the fringes of Robespierre's principal spaceport.

The Legion occupied its own compound within the larger complex, a building surrounded by a high chain-link fence topped by barbed wire. Over the single gate was the inscription *Legio Patria Nostra*—"The Legion is our country"—one of the many unofficial mottoes of the Fifth Foreign Legion. The two would-be recruits were escorted to a waiting room outside an office on the first floor, where the corporal left them to take their ident disks inside. Hauser spent the time examining his surroundings.

It was a spare, Spartan room with few furnishings, white walls contrasting with tile floors colored red. Holopics and paintings depicting legionnaires in a variety of situations and environments hung on the walls. Looking at scenes of combat on far-off worlds had brought back the remembered horror of the fighting on Telok, and Hauser had nearly elected to back out at the last minute. Yet there was something compelling about those images, too, something that touched him on a deep level of his soul where romance and adventure reigned supreme. They made Hauser feel as if he were poised on the brink of something large and mysterious which he simply had to explore, no matter what the consequences might be.

He hadn't been given much time to debate the question, though. The corporal had emerged from the inner office, pointed at Hauser, and jerked his head toward the door. The NCO had knocked sharply as Hauser approached, and a voice inside had growled "Enter!"

So now he was inside, seated on a hard chair looking across a broad, cluttered desk at the sharpest and most alert man Hauser had ever encountered. Like the corporal, the recruiting sergeant was an aging veteran with short, grizzled hair and an air of tough competence. His sleeves were rolled up to reveal well-muscled arms covered by intricate tattoos, and his chest was decorated with three rows of colored campaign ribbons and the space-helmeted death's head insignia of the Legion's elite assault troops.

"You'd be surprised how many people try to join up thinking they can get a billet without any kind of background check," the sergeant went on amiably. "We'll take damn near anyone who meets our require-ments, but even the Legion has some standards!" He laughed as if he'd made a brilliant *bon mot*, then checked his compboard and asked another question. "Date of birth? In standard reckoning, please, no local calendars."

Hauser had to use his wristpiece to translate Besaran dates to the Terran Commonwealth's system. The questioning continued from there as the sergeant led him through the list of questions. He answered each one as truthfully as possible, and the sergeant seemed satisfied even after Hauser recounted the story of the duel and Neubeck's death. After half an hour he leaned back in his chair. "All right, Hauser. The crime, or whatever you'd call it on Laut Besar, occurred out of the Commonwealth's jurisdiction, and anyway it probably wouldn't change anything if you'd murdered a man in the middle of the capital. What matters to us is your qualifications … and your aptitude. You'll be given scholastic, physical, and psych tests, and you'll have time to record your personal history in more detail. I'd also suggest you chip Terranglic. You're pretty good, but you'll be expected to understand and obey orders promptly, so you'd best be comfortable with it."

Hauser raised an eyebrow. "Does that mean I'm in, ah, Sergeant? A legionnaire?"

"Hell, no!" the sergeant said with another laugh. "You are now a Probationary Engaged Volunteer. That means you're under military discipline, but we haven't made up our minds about keeping you. Pass your evaluations and you can drop the 'probationary' … but you won't be a legionnaire unless you get through Basic Training first."

"I see.…"

"Don't worry, Hauser. You can back out as long as you're still under Probationary status. A lot of guys pull out as soon as they sober up and realize what five years in the Legion really mean."

"I won't back out, Sergeant," he said flatly.

The recruiter smiled. "Think it over, Hauser. It's a damned dirty job, you know. We're not one of the glamour regiments, y'know. The Legion's been getting the short end since before Mankind had spaceflight. If you don't die in some worthless skirmish on a frontier world helping some politician or corporation carry out some half-assed policy, then you'll probably get a dose of the bug and go nuts … maybe you'll try to desert, and get caught and sent to the penal battalions. Or maybe you'll pull it off and end up stuck on some dead-end frontier world without a way off planet."

"You make it sound like you don't want me," Hauser said.

The sergeant gave a shrug. "Throw your life away any way you want, kid. Just keep in mind that the Legion isn't about glory, or romance, or adventure, or any of that crap you might come across in a vidmag. When you join the Fifth Foreign Legion, kid, you're giving us everything ... body, mind, and soul. The Legion looks after its own, and we'll expect you to be there for your buddies the way they'll be there for you. And if you survive your hitch, you'll get citizenship, a stake on some new colony planet ... and the knowledge that you were part of something special. The Legion's tough, Hauser ... but if you're the right man for the job you'll find out there's no going back. Think about whether you want to make the commitment ... and *why*." He turned away. "That's all, Hauser. You'll spend the night in the barracks room here, then we'll shuttle you and our other recruits up to the transport *Bir Hakeim* tomorrow morning. Recruits take Basic on Devereaux, at the main Legion depot, so unless you flunk out on your tests en route that's where you'll end up in about ten weeks. After that ... well, that's up to you and your drill sergeant." The sergeant gave him a lopsided smile. "And may God have mercy on your soul. Now wait outside again until I've finished with the other applicant. Then someone will show you to your quarters. Dismissed."

Hauser left the recruiter's office with an unexpected jumble of impressions and ideas whirling through his mind.

The Legion sounded far more complicated than it had seemed when he'd first decided to join.

CHAPTER SEVEN

There will be formed a Legion composed of Foreigners. This Legion will take the name of Foreign Legion.

—Article 1 of the Royal Ordinance establishing the French Foreign Legion, 10 March 1831

A different corporal had the task of escorting Hauser and Suartana from the sergeant's office to a barracks room on the second floor. The door slid smoothly open as the non-com approached, and from inside came a swirl of narcostick smoke and chatter in half a dozen different languages. There were perhaps thirty people in the room, some sitting around a small square table playing cards, the rest lying in three-tiered bunk beds. All of them stood as the corporal entered the room.

He jabbed a finger at the closest man. "You," he said flatly. "Show these men their beds and let them know what's expected of them."

The man gave a broad, pleasant smile. "Aye, Corporal," he answered. He spoke Terranglic with a lilting accent Hauser couldn't place. It was nothing like the French-influenced tongue he'd heard in use here on Robespierre. "Dinna worry. I'll see to the laddies."

Apparently satisfied with this, the corporal left without another word, leaving Hauser and Suartana standing just inside the door, taking in their temporary home in silence.

They were still wearing the formal Besaran day clothes they'd worn for the duel, and were the only ones in the room in civilian garb. The others wore plain gray ship-suits, the simple coveralls that were standard for spaceship crews. Lightweight and comfortable, they would convert easily to pressure suits with the addition of gloves, boots, and a bubble helmet. No doubt they'd been issued so the recruits would be ready for the shuttle flight the sergeant had mentioned.

For the moment, though, they made Hauser feel uncomfortable. He knew he stood out from the crowd, and that was never a good thing even among social equals. With such a diverse mix of backgrounds represented among the people in the barracks, he would have preferred more anonymity.

"So, fresh meat for the Legion machine, eh?" the man appointed to look after them was still smiling. He was slightly built, with reddish brown hair and fine-sculpted features. The hand he extended to Hauser was soft and delicate, almost feminine. "The name is MacDuff. Robert Bruce MacDuff, Younger of Glenhaven. If you're a civilized man, ye'll ken that to be on Caledon."

Hauser answered his smile as he took the hand. "Then I'm afraid I'll have to own to being a barbarian," he said. "I've never heard of Caledon, much less of Glenhaven. My name's Hauser. This is Suartana."

MacDuff flashed his easy smile at the Indomay, but something in Suartana's stolid stance and expression kept him from offering his hand in that direction. Instead, he turned and pointed. "We've still got a few free bunks left. The accommodations are not precisely up to the standards recommended by Harker Travel Guides, but they're tolerable. A mite drab, but ye'll see worse, no doubt, if you stay in the Legion."

They followed him down the double line of bunks. MacDuff paused once to tap impatiently on the end of one of them. "Here, Carlssen, why don't you see if you can round up kits for our two new gentlemen of fortune, eh? They'll probably be ready in a minute or two."

The blond man in the bunk shrugged and nodded amiably. "Sure, Mac," he said, rolling out of the bunk.

MacDuff grinned at Carlssen's retreating back. "Poor laddie made the mistake of drawing tae an inside straight last night. He's working off his debt in a few wee favors." He looked at Hauser. "And do you play cards at all, lad?"

Hauser shook his head. "Sorry, not me. I decided a long time ago that you can't call it gambling if you always lose."

The Caledonian laughed. "A man who kens his ain limits. I like that." He pointed. "One of those bunks will do for you and your quiet friend."

He started in the direction MacDuff had indicated, then stopped at the sight of a short nonhuman figure lying on the lowest bunk in the tier. He turned toward MacDuff and gestured toward some empty bunks on the opposite side of the aisle. "How about those, instead?"

MacDuff studied him for a long moment with a poker face, then shrugged. "Suit yourself, laddie."

Hauser nodded to Suartana, who sat on the bottom bunk without speaking. Checking the mattress on the middle bed, Hauser tried to ignore the feeling that the little alien on the other side was watching his every move.

Nonhumans made him nervous. The few aliens who lived on Laut Besar permanently knew their place in society, but since arriving on Robespierre Hauser had been thrown together with all too many who seemed to regard themselves as the equals of the humans they traveled among. It was an aspect of Commonwealth culture Hauser had never really been aware of. Back home the natural order of things was clear. Uros might be far above Indomays on the social scale, but any human, even the poorest Indomay peasant, came ahead of the things.

He thought of the Ubrenfars and shuddered. Mankind had made a sorry mistake leaving their worlds alone after the fall of the Semti Conclave. The attack on Laut Besar only proved how wrong it was to allow alien races free access to space....

Did the Legion really accept aliens as regular soldiers? Or would they be assigned to segregated units once the selection process was completed? He hoped that would be the case. Soldiers had to know they could rely on each other, and he could never bring himself to trust a nonhuman.

Just then the recruit named Carlssen appeared, carrying two com-pact bundles. He passed one to Suartana, offered the other to Hauser, then headed back to his bunk without a word. He was tall and pale, with hair so blond it was nearly white, and younger than Hauser had thought when he saw him the first time. Shy, too, from the looks of it, completely unlike the brash Caledonian, MacDuff.

He had wondered if he would fit in among the "typical" prospective legionnaires, but now Hauser was beginning to wonder if there was any one type who *was* typical. So far he'd seen an alien, a shy teenager, and an enigmatic gambler with the composure of an aristocrat. In that mix, maybe he and Suartana with their military backgrounds were the closest to how he'd always pictured legionnaires.

Hauser laid out the shoulder bag on his bunk and opened it up. It was small but well stocked, with two of the gray shipsuits and a single set of hostile environment accessories to go with them, plus work boots, undergarments, and a personal kit that included grooming supplies and a small first aid pouch. He opened the bottle of antibeard lotion and wrinkled his nose. It was a cheap brand, the kind of thing Indomays might have bought at one of the teeming floating markets of Kota Delta back home. He replaced the cap hastily and checked the bag again, coming up with a small, cubical chip library.

The touchpad on the end accessed the index chip. Holding it to the side of his head just behind the left ear, Hauser closed his eyes and "saw" a catalog listing each of the tiny computerized books in the library. There were courses in Terranglic, Legion history, military pro‑tocol and procedures, and a variety of basic academic subjects. A careful thought brought up another, similar mental vision, this one a recommended study program. He knew there would be other infor‑mation in the index program as well, such as a simple orientation covering various ships so that he could find his way around the tran‑sport they were embarking aboard in the morning. For now, he wasn't interested in exploring the chips further, so he cleared his mind and lowered the box.

One of the listed chips, though, was important to him. This was his ident disk, which hadn't been returned to him before. He removed the disk carefully from its slot in the box and frowned. It wasn't the one he'd worn before. This one didn't bear the familiar Hauser family crest.

Unlike the adchips in the library, the ident disk was meant to be ac‑cessed through a computer terminal. He spoke a soft‑voiced command to his wristpiece, then watched the data scroll across the small screen. This disk identified him only by a serial number, and the credit balance recorded there was only five hundred sols, the enlistment bounty award‑ed to all new Commonwealth recruits. He frowned for a moment, then shrugged. He'd heard they made new recruits break with their pasts completely when they joined the Legion. If he ever needed access to his own credit balance or personal history again, he could get a new ident disk through Doenitz. Hauser touched the adhesive disk to its accus‑tomed place on his neck, then started to strip off his civilian clothes.

MacDuff was still lounging against stacked bunks nearby. He cleared his throat and jerked his head toward the back of the barracks room. "If you want tae preserve your modesty, lad, you may want to change somewhere else."

Following the gesture, Hauser finally noticed the woman lying in one of the bunks, staring straight up at the mattress above her. She was dressed in the same garb as the other recruits and seemed oblivious to the rest of the room.

Hauser hadn't thought that the military career was open to women in the Commonwealth. No woman on Laut Besar—at least no Uro woman—would dream of joining any of the services. Thinking of the newscaster he'd seen on the trip in, he realized he probably should have made the connection. Women on these worlds didn't lead the same sheltered lives they did back on Laut Besar.

He shrugged again. "Doesn't look like she's taking much of an interest," he said, trying to sound nonchalant. He went ahead changing, though he turned away and stepped behind the bunks for some added privacy. There were a lot of things he was going to have to get used to, it seemed, before he'd be able to fit in to this new life.

As he closed up the coverall, he looked up at MacDuff. "Look, thanks for all the help. I'm going to need all the help I can get steering around all the cultural differences around here."

The Caledonian nodded. "Dinna fash yourself, lad. It's a big Commonwealth. Room for all kinds."

"Yeah." Hauser thought of the alien and the woman. That was already more "kinds" than he'd expected. "So what kind are you, Robert Bruce MacDuff? You look and sound like a gentleman, not a soldier. So how do you come to be in the Legion?"

"I'm not the only one who looks more like an aristocrat than a soldier," MacDuff replied. "But—"

"Excuse me," a quiet, diffident voice interrupted him. The alien had stood up and come up beside MacDuff. Short, bald, wearing a coverall that had been cut down to size and tailored to expose the ruff of quills at the alien's neck, the humanoid figure was almost a parody of humanity. "It is generally considered to be very poor manners in the Legion to ask about another's past. Such information may be volun-teered, but should never be a subject for questioning."

"This is a private conversation, ale," Hauser said harshly. "And among *humans* it's considered bad manners to interrupt someone who is talking or push yourself into the company of your betters."

The alien's quills moved as if they were being stirred by a summer breeze, but the expression on its face was unreadable. MacDuff took a step back, as if startled or shocked. "Look, Myaighee, don't worry about it," he told the little alien. "I don't care who knows my story. But thanks for the reminder."

Myaighee continued to study Hauser's face for several long seconds. Then it turned away and walked back to its bunk.

"Take some well-meant advice, lad," MacDuff added quietly to Hauser. "Ye'll nae get sae far around here with that kind of attitude. Whatever it may be like where you're from, here there is equality between species."

Hauser bit back an angry retort and nodded. "Yeah ... okay," he said. "Sorry if I gave offense, MacDuff. Like I said, I'm new in these parts."

The Caledonian let out a careful breath, then grinned. "Aye, and anyway we strayed from a subject of much greater importance. Namely myself! You were asking how I come to be in such princely surroundings."

He nodded and gave an encouraging grin.

"Truth is, lad, my auld feether owns half the land in Glenhaven, and I was aince destined for a career as a banker. But cards and dice have always been my weakness, and while I'm more than a match for any honest gambler ye care tae set against me, even I canna beat the house when the games are rigged. After I ran through two trust funds and all the money I'd saved from my ... other sources of income, the auld man cut me off cold. Said I had to reform before I could be trusted with high finance again." MacDuff paused. "I had been considering the military life already, but with some more decent outfit like the Caledonian Watch. Unfortunately, one of the gents who claimed I still owed him money sent some laddies with more muscles than brains to collect the debt. I'm afraid we had a wee tulzie, and one of the braw lads happened tae end up on the wrong end of my needier. Rather than stay around tae argue the differences between self-defense and manslaughter with the compols, I felt a tour in the Foreign Legion might be just the sort of change of pace I was looking for. For my health, you'll understand."

Hauser studied the Caledonian. His expression hadn't changed, but there was a faint twinkle in his hazel eyes that suggested the man wasn't completely serious.

He didn't know if the story was true or not, but there was something about MacDuff that made him instantly likable, and Hauser decided he wanted the man for a friend.

Nonetheless, he resolved never to underestimate the slight, in-offensive-looking Caledonian. For along with that humorous twinkle, Hauser had seen something else in those eyes. Something dangerous.

Bright and cheery, the shuttle terminal was a place of gleaming duraplast and cheap, gaudy furnishings. It was a civilian area temporarily appropriated for military use, and the thirty-four recruits in their matching shipsuits looked out of place in a lounge that should have been thronged with colorfully garbed tourists.

But all the regular military terminals were tied up with last-minute, feverish preparations to load troops and supplies outbound for a rendezvous with *SOLOMON* and the voyage to *Soleil Liberté*, and the draft of recruits setting out for Devereaux weren't high enough on the priority list to warrant interfering with the logistical nightmare of supporting Brigadier Shalev's expeditionary force. So instead they had been brought here to wait for a shuttle that would carry them to the *Bir Hakeim*, a transport lighter scheduled for an overhaul at Lebensraum's orbital shipyards. Since the transport was heading in something approximating the right direction, it would carry the recruits from Robespierre until they met up with another ship bound for Devereaux.

Hauser leaned back in one of the molded chairs and studied the other recruits. Actually, only a few of them came from Robespierre. Aside from Suartana, there were two Indomays from Laut Besar. Hauser knew the type, poor, desperate men, probably on the run after breaking faith with a Uro employer or landholder. Most were like MacDuff, though, drifters from a score of worlds who had signed up for the Legion for one reason or another and who had been moved from one world to another following the vagaries of available shipping.

There was one group of recruits, though, who held themselves aloof from the others. MacDuff had told him that they had all been sent to the recruiting office from a regular Legion outfit, where they had already been serving as legionnaires for some time. Apparently the Legion did a lot of local recruiting, but regulations required th at they all pass through the official training course on Devereaux at some point before they could proceed with their military careers. Both the woman he had seen in the barracks—her name was Katrina Voskovich, but beyond that and the bare fact of her Legion experience Hauser hadn't learned much about her—and the alien Myaighee numbered in this group.

He saw the two talking together in the far corner of the lounge, Voskovich nodding vigorously at something the short humanoid was telling her. Hauser wondered how they had come to join the Fifth Foreign Legion in the first place.

"Out of my way, aristo," a deep, gravelly voice growled. Hauser looked up, startled, taking in the sight of an oversized recruit he'd heard referred to as Crater, presumably from his scarred, pockmarked face … or perhaps from what he did to other people's faces, judging from his bullying tone. "I want to sit here, and you're in the way."

Before Hauser could react, Suartana was there, looming behind Crater and reaching out to touch the man's beefy shoulder. Crater jerked away and spun to face the Indomay, but stepped back as he looked into Suartana's grim face. "Don't make trouble," Suartana said quietly. "It wouldn't be smart. Got it?"

"What's going on here?" a new voice broke in. A legionnaire in camouflaged fatigues and sergeant's stripes had appeared behind the two glowering giants at the entrance to the shuttle boarding tube.

Suartana smiled gently at him. "Nothing at all, Sergeant," the Indomay said. "I'm afraid I was clumsy and bumped into my friend here. He was startled."

"Yeah," Crater said, with a sidelong look at Suartana. "Startled."

The sergeant studied them for a long moment, then nodded. As he moved off, MacDuff's slender form settled into the chair beside Hauser. "Pretty good setup ye've got there, laddie. I never thought to bring my ain bodyguard into the Legion with me." He was grinning, silently daring Hauser to deny it. But Hauser was still watching the sergeant, who had still been within earshot as the Caledonian spoke. The noncom's eyes narrowed as he looked at Hauser, and he jotted a note down on his compboard.

"All right, you nubes, listen up!" the sergeant shouted. "I'm Sergeant D'Angelo, and I'm in charge of your little tour group while you're enjoying the good life on the old Beer Hatch. Shuttle's ready for boarding. Line up, single file, and get aboard. Let's mag it!"

Hauser, MacDuff, and Suartana were near the end of the line. As they filed through the extendible boarding tube into the passenger compartment of the shuttle, another Legion NCO, a corporal this time, directed them into acceleration chairs. Gesturing with a stun baton that hummed faintly, the noncom placed Hauser into the seat next to the woman.

When the last of the recruits was strapped in, Sergeant D'Angelo sealed up the lock and faced them. He was another old veteran, like the legionnaires at the recruiting station, but he was easily the fittest man aboard. "For the benefit of you newcomers, I'm supposed to start exposing you to the Legion. Maybe one in five of you will actually make it in, but from here on we're going to pretend you've all got a shot." He glanced at his wristpiece. "In just under six minutes we'll be boosting for orbit. The transport lighter *Bir Hakeim* will be taking us on the next leg of our trip to Devereaux."

He paused before continuing. "The transports used by the Legion are operated by the CSN, but they are procured using Legion funds and are devoted exclusively to Legion missions, because the Legion is considered a part of the Colonial Army instead of being counted among the Regulars. Every other Colonial Army formation is supported by its own planetary navy, but even though the Legion calls Devereaux home it isn't officially associated with any individual planetary government. So even though you're headed for a navy ship, it's really part of the Legion, as much a part of the service as any of our units. That may not mean much to you now, but those of you who make it through Basic will understand some day. Legionnaires have no home except the Legion ... and ships like the *Bir Hakeim* are part of that home. After you've been shot up in a tough op on some godforsaken planet somewhere you might appreciate it."

D'Angelo's eyes roved over the recruits slowly. "Legion transports are named for the places legionnaires have shed blood for the Contract. *Bir Hakeim* was a battle fought on Old Terra long before they had spaceships. Like a lot of Legion battles, it was an uneven match between a small force from the French Foreign Legion—the original outfit we trace our descent from—and the forces of a nation-state called Nazi Germany commanded by a general named Rommel. The computer library aboard the ship has a full account of the battle. While you're aboard, chip it. That's not a suggestion ... that's an order."

There was a murmur from some of the recruits, quickly stilled at the corporal's shout of "Silence!"

"Before boosting to a rendezvous with any Legion transport, it is customary to remember the heroes who helped give that vessel its name. MacDuff ... the names inscribed under the colors in the ship's auditorium, please."

MacDuff's voice piped up from near the rear of the compartment. "Koenig, Pierre. Amilakvari, Dmitri. Messmer ..."

The whole ritual struck Hauser as foolish, and the sound of the Caledonian faithfully reciting names of people long dead whose memories remained alive only in the traditions of these outcasts from the Legion made him smile. Then he chuckled. These legionnaires seemed to set more store in the past than the present. Would they be expected to ride animals into battle next?

Sudden pain lanced through his arm and shoulder as the corporal lashed out with the stun baton he'd used to direct traffic earlier. The man glared down at him. "Quiet, nube," he growled.

"Messmer, Pierre," MacDuff resumed after faltering for a moment. "Travers, Susan. And the other officers and men of the Thirteenth DBLE, First Free French Brigade."

"We will remember them," D'Angelo said quietly, his eyes resting thoughtfully on Hauser. He turned away a moment later and started strapping himself into an empty seat.

Hauser was still rubbing his throbbing shoulder as the shuttle lifted. He had learned an important lesson about the Fifth Foreign Legion already....

They took their traditions and customs seriously here. And he would have to learn to do the same, if he intended to get along in this strange new life he'd chosen.

CHAPTER EIGHT

You're like in a cage. There's people from all over the world there. There's a lot of fights because there's no discipline. All you're doing is waiting. Waiting to get that red band that says you're clear. I think that if you can get through Aubange you can get through a lot.

—an anonymous legionnaire,
French Foreign Legion, 1984

Bir Hakeim had been designed to transport a full company of legionnaires plus support troops and all the equipment needed to conduct independent operations on a remote planet. Carrying less than forty recruits plus a handful of NCOs heading back to the depot on Devereaux for one last assignment before they retired from the Legion, the transport had barely a quarter of the available troop berths filled. The accommodations should have seemed luxurious, but the recruits weren't given a chance to enjoy that luxury.

The noncoms seemed determined to make sure that there were no idle hands among their charges. Recruit labor was put to work in a variety of menial tasks, everything from chipping old paint to cleaning latrines to donning pressure suits and working on structural repairs that would have been done when the ship reached the shipyard anyway. There was little consistency to the schedule, and Hauser doubted that it was intended to do anything more than occupy idle hands.

Hauser, Suartana, and seven other brand-new recruits who had joined up on Robespierre were spared these work details during the first leg of the journey, but this didn't mean they had any leisure time. They were kept busy with a seemingly endless battery of tests supervised by the transport's Navy doctor. After they rendezvoused with the carrier-ship *ARISTOTLE* and shifted to Reynier-Kessler drive for the inter-stellar voyage out from *Soleil Egalité*, much of the testing was taken over by the computer itself.

The tests ran the gamut from physicals to academic quizzes to psychological profiles. Hauser had never realized just how carefully new recruits for the Legion were screened. Given their reputation for taking any outcast, they seemed surprisingly concerned with picking and choosing their new soldiers.

The criteria used to select suitable recruits was hard to follow. The NCOs seemed impressed by Hauser's past military training and aca-demic preparation, for instance, but they acted just as interested in a tough little Robespierran peasant named Lauriston whose only evident qualification was superb physical fitness and a calm, phlegmatic manner that no amount of testing could shake. On the other hand, the big recruit named Crater, whom Hauser had picked as a stereotypical legionnaire, was bounced by the time *ARISTOTLE* reached Mecca Gideed, the first stop on the long voyage to Devereaux. Rumor had it that Crater was pronounced too psychologically unstable to make acceptable Legion material. Apparently even the Legion drew the line at taking in people who enjoyed violence too much.

One of the Indomays left the transport at the same time, down-checked due to medical problems, but a draft of new recruits joined up, and the process went on as *ARISTOTLE* set a course for another colony world, Bonaparte.

Hauser had completed all the required testing sessions, but a final verdict on his acceptability still hadn't been handed down. Recruits who had been passed for Basic received a red shoulder band to wear with their shipsuits, but even after the stopover at Bonaparte Hauser still hadn't received that final stamp of approval, and he was growing concerned. They hadn't failed him yet … but neither had they taken him in. When Suartana earned his red band and started full-time duty with the rest of the recruits on work details, Hauser couldn't help but feel ashamed. Additional tests were scheduled. Some were obviously intended to verify his academic and military knowledge, and these didn't worry him. But he recognized others as new psych exams, and those were disturbing. Hauser had never considered himself a candidate for a down-check based on instability.…

Yet when *Bir Hakeim* separated from *ARISTOTLE* at Bonaparte's systerm to pick up another carriership heading for Lebensraum, Hauser received orders to transfer along with the rest of the recruits to a new, larger transport, the *Kolwezi*, which was joining up with *ARISTOTLE* to complete the trip to Devereaux. *Kolwezi* carried another, larger contingent of recruits, a few of whom were reportedly from Terra itself. There were also more noncoms, but despite the additional supervision less time could be devoted to individuals. When the carriership left the star system behind, Hauser still didn't have his red armband, but he was assigned to many of the same work details as the others while the NCOs and *ARISTOTLE* reviewed his case further. It gave him time to get to know the others in his bunkroom a little better.

At first most of the recruits were strangers, but as time went on Hauser got to know many of them as individuals. Some, like MacDuff, were friendly from the start. MacDuff's background was enough like his own for the two of them to hit it off right from the start, th ough the young Caledonian's outgoing personality stood out in startling contrast to Hauser's own reserve. Addicted to games of chance of every variety, and a natural master of scams and cons, MacDuff didn't act like any aristocrat Hauser had ever seen, but there was something about the man's inborn assurance and easy leadership that made it plain he'd been accustomed to money and power from birth.

Not everyone was as approachable to Hauser, and he found it took a special effort on his own part to win any sort of acceptance among them. Some found his manner too reserved for their taste, and for some reason they found his unwillingness to make friends with the alien Myaighee as grounds for resentment.

Hauser didn't exactly dislike the alien, but he did find its presence disturbing. As the one recruit who had more than a year's worth of actual Legion experience, Myaighee was in a strange position that left Hauser feeling uncertain and confused. How much weight was he supposed to give to that experience? He wasn't sure how nonhumans were supposed to be treated in Commonwealth society.

Plainly they were regarded with more respect than would have been the case back on Laut Besar. It particularly bothered him when the alien tried to impose its own values on him, such as in their first encounter in the barracks on Robespierre. He saw others having similar problems relating to the ale from time to time, but somehow no one else seemed to elicit the same reactions he did.

After the recruits had transferred to *Kolwezi*, for instance, Myaighee had a run-in with one of the NCOs who had been in charge of the recruit contingent already on board the new transport. The little non-human had corrected Chief-Sergeant Colby when the noncom referred to Myaighee as "he." The proper word, so the alien insisted, was "ky," a gender-neutral term used on its homeworld of Hanuman. Myaighee's species was hermaphroditic, and concepts of "male" and "female" didn't apply. Colby had hardly listened to the explanation, and went right on calling Myaighee "he." So did almost everyone else, except a few of the recruits who had been with the ale from the very start.

Chief among these was the woman, Katrina Voskovich. Short, dark-haired, and quite a bit different from the Uro women Hauser was used to in both looks and attitude, Voskovich was a fierce partisan of Myaighee's and hence kept her distance from Hauser. He learned a little bit about her through MacDuff, who seemed to be able to find out anything about anyone. She had been an electronics technician employed by a large corporation with interests on Polypheme, a backwater world where a Legion company had fought a desperate campaign against hostile natives. When it was over, the company's hold on the planet had all but collapsed even though the legionnaires had won the war. Voskovich had actually been involved in some of the fighting together with other volunteers from the ranks of the corporate employees, and had chosen to enlist in the Legion rather than remain in her old job. Unlike Myaighee, she didn't have all that much experience, but she shared the alien's high opinion of their unit, Captain Colin Fraser's Bravo Company.

Few of the others really stood out. Young Carlssen and the tough little peasant Lauriston were both friendly with MacDuff, and seemed to like Hauser well enough. Suartana, of course, remained a rock he could always rely on, though as time went on he saw less and less of the Indomay, apparently on the orders of the chief-sergeant. According to one rumor that went around the bunkroom, Suartana was a big reason for the delay in passing Hauser's application to the Legion. He was regarded as a symbol of Hauser's aristocratic background, and apparently the aristocracy was viewed with some distrust by the legionnaires. They seemed to feel that Hauser was too soft to make a good soldier, though his other qualifications were excellent.

At least he still had a chance of earning a place in the Legion. He resolved to work harder and hope for the best.

*　　*　　*

Legionnaire Third Class Myaighee sat cross-legged on a mat in the center of the gymnasium and tried to picture home. Following the advice of Corporal Rostov, kys lance leader from bravo Company, Myaighee had saved up a large stock of synthol and offered it to the Navy CPO in charge of Environmental Systems maintenance aboard the transport in exchange for permission to use the variable-climate training compartment when it wasn't needed for other purposes. As Rostov had suggested, the exchange had been welcomed enthuse-iastically. The clicontrol system allowed the user to set the chamber to virtually any combination of atmosphere, pressure, temperature, and humidity, but nothing could bring back the sights or sounds of nighttime in the jungle or the hubbub of a village market.

The world humans called Hanuman was far away, and Myaighee had not been home in over a year. Ky missed the jungles, the friends and family left behind, and knew ky was not likely to see any of them again.

Feelings like these had stayed comfortably far away when ky was serving in Colin Fraser's Legion company. During the desperate fight on Polypheme ky had never felt lonely. There were friends enough within the ranks of the Legion, friends like Corporal Rostov and Legionnaire Grant and the female-human Kelly, who had been a Navy officer before becoming a Legion combat engineer. Kelly had been kys first friend, the one human who had taken an interest in Myaighee during the horrible days of the company's retreat from Dryienjaiyeel. Ky—no, "she" was the word for a female-human—had helped Myai-ghee see that giving up home did not necessarily mean giving up life itself.

After Polypheme the company had been ordered to Devereaux, and Myaighee had accepted the assignment to recruit training with the thought that kys friends would be close at hand. But en route the crisis on Laut Besar had erupted, and the company had been diverted on reaching Robespierre. But the draft of recruits had been sent on to finish their training.

Now Myaighee's friends were in the thick of another crisis, and Myaighee wished ky could face it with them.

A few other recent recruits had been shipped out with Myaighee, but none with kys seniority. Katrina Voskovich, a civilian technician who had helped the legionnaires on Polypheme, seemed friendly enough, but Myaighee barely knew that female-human. There were complete strangers among the recruits who were more like friends than that one.

So many strangers ... such a strange place....

Loneliness could do strange things. There had been the alien from Polypheme, Oomour, a native scout from a primitive nomadic culture. Oomour's entire clan had been wiped out, and the scout had adopted the Legion as his new home. But the cramped confines of a transport lighter had been too much for a being accustomed to ranging the seas of his native world unhindered, and Oomour had committed suicide long before the legionnaires reached Robespierre. Corporal Rostov had given Myaighee a piece of the rope Oomour had used to bind his gill slits closed, claiming it would bring good luck. Myaighee still had it, but couldn't see how it could be lucky to carry the ill-omened object.

All the cursed thing did was remind Myaighee of how much ky had in common with Oomour. Both aliens from backward cultures in a place shaped and dominated by humans. Both far from home, struggling to adjust to new ways....

Most humans didn't even try to recognize Myaighee as an individual. Insisting on treating ky as a male-human instead of a hermaphrodite of the *kyendyp*, for instance, that was something kys old lancemates would never have done. Despite Myaighee's best efforts to educate the other recruits, ky was almost always referred to by male-human pronouns.

And humans like Volunteer Hauser seemed to actively despise Myaighee. Ky had known human scorn before, back on Hanuman before becoming a legionnaire, but ky had always assumed it was because they were so advanced and the *kyendyp* so obviously backward. Here there was no such standard for comparison. If anything, Myaighee should have commanded respect because ky had been part of Bravo Company. Unlike the other recruits, Myaighee already held the rank of Legionnaire Third Class, already had a right to wear the coveted white kepi. But all these things didn't change the sense of scorn ky felt when some humans were near.

It made Myaighee wonder if ky had been right to leave the jungles of home behind in pursuit of an intangible *something* ky had sensed in the Fifth Foreign Legion.

The door to the gymnasium slid open with a sigh and a sudden blast of cool, dry air. Myaighee looked up, saw the slender, fair-complexioned figure of Hauser in the doorway.

"Allmachtiger Gott!" The recruit's words were in a language Myaighee didn't know, but ky recognized a human's cursing when ky heard it. "What's with the sauna?"

Myaighee felt kys neck ruff rippling in confusion, but knew few humans could understand the emotional content. "I do not understand some of your words," ky said mildly.

"Why is it so goddamned hot in here?" Hauser said, a look of exasperation crossing his alien features.

"Ah, the heat." Myaighee mimicked a human shrug. "These settings make the air much like my homeland on Hanuman."

Hauser mopped his forehead with his sleeve. "Then God save me from getting posted there," he said.

"If you wish to use the room, I will leave. I was almost finished in any case."

"Finished? You were sitting on the floor staring at the walls. What was that, some weird ritual the ales do back on your planet?"

Myaighee stood slowly. "I try to spend my free time remembering my home," ky said slowly. "It has been a long time since I saw it last. Remembering helps … relax me.

The human shrugged. "Hell, what you do when Chief-Sergeant Colby isn't looking over our shoulder is your business," he said. "But I can't figure why you'd leave your own kind and try to mix with humans in the first place."

Kys ruff bristled. "Are you, then, among your own people? You do not fit in as you would like to, true?"

The shot seemed to hit home, and Hauser fell silent. Myaighee crossed to the clicontrol panel and cut the settings back to their Terran-standard norms. Then ky turned to Hauser, who was still staring at Myaighee. "If you wish, perhaps you would like to learn the relaxation technique I was using when you came in." Ky paused. "Actually, it is a 'weird ritual' native to a planet called Pacifica, and I learned it from the human who was my company's Exec."

Myaighee pushed past the tall, lanky human into the cool air of the corridor outside. Ky didn't feel any less lonely, but at least there was satisfaction in knowing that the humans kys people had once thought of as demons or gods were, in fact, not that much different from ky after all.

* * *

"Fall in! Fall in, you straks! Move it! Move it!"

Wolfgang Hauser unstrapped the seat harness and shoved his way into the ragged double line of recruits forming up in the center aisle of the shuttle passenger compartment. A trio of corporals in Legion battledress moved through the motley group, shouting orders and curses and laying about freely with their stun batons as they tried to enforce order. From time to time they used their fists instead. Hauser obeyed the bellowed commands and tried to keep from drawing attention to himself. Three months in transit had taught him the value of remaining unobtrusive. Gradually order emerged from chaos as recruits shouldered bags or grabbed suitcases and found their places in line.

The shuttle grounded with a sharp lurch that nearly bowled over the recruits and set the noncoms to lashing out all over again. Over fifty would-be soldiers in a cramped, ancient landing craft took a lot of controlling, but these legionnaires knew how to do the job.

Colby, the burly chief sergeant in charge of the passenger compartment, ran a cold eye over the recruits and then slapped the switch beside the stern loading ramp. With a groan of long-used machinery the doors swung open and the ramp dropped slowly to the ground, letting in a blast of hot, dry air that made Hauser's skin prickle. The fierce glare from outside was brighter, more intense than the familiar orange glow of *Soleil Liberté* or the muted artificial lighting of the ships that had been his home for nearly three months now, and he had to blink back tears as the corporals prodded the line into motion down the ramp and out onto the planet surface.

Chief-Sergeant Colby stopped at the foot of the ramp, facing a gate in the duracrete berm that surrounded the shuttle pad. A guard dressed in full Legion parade uniform—white kepi, khaki trousers and jacket with archaic red-and-green epaulets, green tie and blue cummerbund— took two brisk steps forward, his rifle coming to port arms. Behind the man, flanking the gate, two flags fluttered in the hot wind, one the stars-and-globe of the Terran Commonwealth, the other a tricolor emblazoned with the V emblem of the Fifth Foreign Legion. Colby saluted each flag crisply. "Recruit detail to enter the post," he rasped.

The guard gave a sharp rifle salute in return. "Detail may enter. Major Hunter welcomes you."

"Devereaux shall not fall again," the chief sergeant responded. The grim, almost fanatic note in their voices fascinated and repelled at the same time. Like the old-fashioned legionnaire's uniform, the ritual was part of the tradition of the Fifth Foreign Legion. Hauser had studied some of the background en route, but the reality made him shiver despite the desert heat.

The gate slid open as the guard stepped aside to let the recruits pass through. Fort Hunter was the main training depot for the Fifth Foreign Legion, standing near the town of Villastre near the edge of the Great Desert on Devereaux. Near the present military base, over a hundred years ago, Commandant Thomas Hunter of the Fourth Foreign Legion had led a ragtag band of legionnaires in a desperate raid against terrible odds as part of a prolonged resistance to alien invaders. The legionnaires had perished almost to a man, but their sacrifice had helped buy valuable time for the Commonwealth in their bitter war against the Semti Conclave. When the Fifth Foreign Legion was established out of the ashes of the Fourth, Hunter and the fighting on Devereaux had formed a key part in the deliberately cultivated mystique of the new organization.

Hauser could still remember the stun-lashing he'd received after scoffing at Legion tradition that first time in the shuttle leaving Robespierre, but even that beating hadn't completely driven home the genuine seriousness with which the legionnaires regarded their unit and its history.

As the recruits shuffled slowly through the gate, he realized that he still had a lot to learn. The long voyage to Devereaux was over. Now the training would begin.

He was still a little bit surprised at having made it all the way to Devereaux. His red armband had finally been awarded a few days out from Bonaparte, after a final round of evaluations supervised by Chief-Sergeant Colby, who had come all the way out from Terra on *Kolwezi*. A few words from Suartana had helped Hauser pass those last tests. Once he'd realized how much he was hurting his own cause, he had made a conscious effort to tone down his stiff-necked pride. Colby had inadvertently helped him get a grip on himself by insisting that Hauser demonstrate his proficiency with the saber in a practice fight in one of the training compartments. The match—against Colby himself, a tough bulldog of a man—had reminded Hauser vividly of the duel with Neubeck and the way his short temper and touchy sense of honor had forced him to seek refuge in the Legion.

The fight had helped another way, too. Apparently Commonwealth standards of swordsmanship were a lot lower than Laut Besar's, because Hauser actually managed to impress the NCO with his prowess with a blade. Few people on *Kolwezi* had succeeded in impressing Colby at anything.

Fifty-five recruits had boarded the shuttle in orbit over Devereaux, the candidates deemed acceptable after the selection procedure. Suartana was the only other Besaran left. The other two Indomays hadn't made it, the one because of his medical problem and the other for some unknown failing only the Legion understood.

Somehow, Hauser had made it through the tests, though he'd come close to failing more than once. Chief-Sergeant Colby had been brutally direct in summing up his future with the Legion. "You've got the education and the intellect to be an officer," he'd said harshly. "But you'll have to shake off that goddamned snob routine and learn how to take orders if you're gonna make it as a marchman. I'm passing you ... but instructors at Fort Hunter might not be so charitable. Just watch yourself!"

Something in the sergeant's words had given Hauser pause. The Fifth Foreign Legion was widely regarded with scorn by more spit-and-polish units both inside the Commonwealth and beyond its borders. Despite the hard-fighting reputation of the unit, the Legion was known as a refuge for the misfits, the malcontents, and the no-hopers who couldn't make it anywhere else. But Colby's tones had held nothing but haughty pride and superiority, as if Hauser was in danger of not measuring up to the Legion.

Since that interview, winning the acceptance of men like Colby had suddenly become very important to Wolfgang Hauser.

CHAPTER NINE

The curious thing was that the regiment, which formed a compact unit because of an esprit de corps which bordered on fanaticism, was composed of the most diverse elements.

—Legionnaire Charles-Jules Zede,
Souvenirs of My Life,
French Foreign Legion

It took half an hour for Hauser and the others to reach the actual grounds of Fort Hunter's Recruit Training Center, a huge, semi-independent compound surrounded by its own security fence and linked to the main fort by a maglev tube network. Nothing in the orientation sessions had prepared Hauser for the full scope of the Legion facilities, and in answer to another recruit's comments on the subject Colby had just laughed and pointed out that there were several other Legion bases scattered around Devereaux just as large if not quite so important. Devereaux was the Legion's headquarters and administration center, the planet every legionnaire called home regardless of where duty might take the individual unit. A large percentage of the civilian population on Devereaux directly supported Legion activities, from the food processing workers who produced their rations to the factory technicians who turned out munitions and other supplies to the prostitutes, male and female, who worked the off-base brothels. And there were no small number of former legionnaires on the planet as well, veterans who had chosen to invest their stake in this adopted home planet rather than seeking a post-Legion life on some other developing world.

Colby formed the recruits up into a double line outside the tube station and led them at a trot across the RTC compound toward the cluster of large buildings near the center of the complex. Hauser was surprised to note that the structures at the very hub of this fort-within-a-fort were not barracks or administration buildings, but rather an imposing museum which faced a monument across a reflecting pool. The familiar slogan *Legio Patria Nostra*, in two-meter tall letters, frowned down from above the entrance to the museum. Without breaking stride, Colby informed the jogging recruits that the museum was devoted to the history of the Legion and its four predecessors, while the other structure was reputed to be an exact replica of the original *Monument aux Morts*— the Monument to the Dead, a raised globe guarded by four stern-faced soldiers of the old French Foreign Legion. In the days before Mankind had left Mother Terra, such a monument had stood, first in the old Legion's headquarters in the colony of Algiers, later in a camp in southern France. The original had been destroyed in the fighting that ended the Second French Empire, defended to the last by the Third Foreign Legion. This replica, though, carried the tradition down across the centuries. It wasn't an exact duplicate, though. At the four corners of this monument were modern additions, further statues depicting soldiers of each of the four Legions that had followed the original.

Finally, Colby signaled a halt outside of a long, low building near the edge of the central sprawl. The sign outside the door proclaimed that they had arrived at Hut 4, Processing.

"All right, you slugs!" Colby shouted. "You're ready for the final stage of processing, starting now. First order of business is to file inside that building in an orderly fashion. When you get inside, stow your luggage in the bins by the door. Make sure they've been tagged with your assigned serial numbers. If you don't have 'em tagged, you won't get 'em back!"

The sergeant paused, glaring fiercely. "Next item. Once you've stowed your luggage, peel down to your underwear. Keep your clothes with you until you're told otherwise. You may want to make sure any personal effects you want saved get stowed in your bags. That includes wristpieces, pictures or holocubes, and other mementos. Keep your ident disks on you until someone says different. When you've done all that, your troubles are over. All you have to do after that is wait. Listen for the last two digits of your serial number to be called. Keep the noise down so everyone can hear their numbers called. Think you straks can handle all that?"

A ragged chorus of voices answered him. Colby exchanged a weary glance with one of the corporals and then shrugged. "Right, then get moving! Now!"

Hauser was one of the last ones inside, and he found that even the straightforward instructions Colby had issued had produced chaos among the recruits. Voices were raised in noisy complaints or questions, and several recruits had simply found a corner and sat down to wait, fully dressed and with luggage close at hand. Others were wrestling with bags too large for the bins.

Here and there Hauser caught sight of a few who had managed to get everything right, but even a few of these were generating their share of disorder. A pretty blond woman unzipping her shipsuit was the object of comments from a small male audience led by a dark, good-looking kid who looked even younger than Swede Carlssen ... certainly too young to be a legionnaire recruit. "*Sì! Sì!* Spogliarello!" he said with a whistle. Then, in Terranglic with a thick accent Hauser couldn't identify, he continued. "Take it off!"

"Quiet!" A new voice bellowed, cutting through the hubbub with the quality of a spacecraft launching with booster assistance. "I said QUIET!"

The room fell silent as a squat, stocky man with a bullet head emphasized by his short haircut strode from the inner door. Though physically almost the opposite of the massive Chief-Sergeant Colby, the newcomer had the same air of self-assured competence Hauser would have recognized even if the man's uniform had not been marked with a sergeant's stripes.

"That's better," the man said in a voice only slightly less penetrating. "I am Gunnery Sergeant Ortega, and I'm in charge, heaven help me, of your recruit training. I do not like noise, and I do not like disorder. Right now, that means I do not like you. Let's see if you can improve my opinion of you straks before I get you out on a parade ground somewhere. Now go about your business in an orderly manner. If you have a question or need assistance, raise your hand and wait for me to help you. I'll get to everyone in time, so be patient and we'll make this as painless as possible." He turned his glittering stare on the dark-haired youngster who had been voicing his approval of the blonde and raised his stun baton under the youth's chin. It wasn't switched on, but the sergeant's thumb was less than a centimeter from the power button. "As for you, lover-boy …" he said in a low, dangerous voice. "What's your name?"

"Antonelli, *signore* … sir," the kid replied. Despite the menace of the baton his voice was cocky.

"You address me as 'sergeant' when you talk, boy," Ortega said, his voice a whipcrack. "Now listen to me, Antonelli. The whores in town'll be glad enough at all the things you can do—if you really can, that is. Save the enthusiasm for them and leave her the hell alone. Got it?" He didn't wait for an answer.

Hauser's bag was small, all he needed for the small kit he'd collected en route. He double-checked the label to see that the serial number was clear, opened it up long enough to transfer his wristpiece computer and a few odds and ends from his pockets inside, then sealed it and tossed the bag into a bin. He stripped off his clothes quickly and cast around in search of a place to sit.

He looked for MacDuff, but the Caledonian was surrounded by a mob of other recruits already, including the hannie Myaighee. Hauser didn't care to mix with the ale again. He had tried to soften his resentment of the non-human after hearing Suartana's advice on trying to adopt more Commonwealth-oriented attitudes, but that didn't mean he liked the bald-headed little monkey any better. So far it had stayed away from him, and he didn't intend for things to change now.

Instead, he finally found a cold metal chair next to another recruit, a big, raw-boned man with auburn hair and a collection of scars on his chest. A tattoo on one arm showed a crest of some kind, together with the words "Third Assault Marines" and the slogan "Death Strikes From Orbit." Hauser hoped his own appearance wouldn't stand out too much among the rough characters in the waiting room. Most of the skin displayed carried scars or tattoos of some kind, though there were others who looked more like Hauser than the big man next to him.

There was little conversation under the watchful eye of the sergeant. Periodically, someone would call out a number from the inner door, and another recruit would leave. Then it was Hauser's turn.

"Number forty-eight! Forty-eight!" There was a pause. "Serial number 50-987-5648!"

Hauser suddenly realized the call was for him and stood up with a jerk.

"Waiting for a goddamned engraved invitation?" Sergeant Ortega asked him harshly. The NCO lashed out with a stun baton, and Hauser's forearm tingled and burned as the blow landed. "Mag it, strak!"

As he crossed the waiting room, Hauser knew he was taking the last steps in his journey. He found himself hoping, too late, that his decision really had been the right one.

At the door, he was called upon to surrender his ident disk. Then the processing began, a seemingly interminable job that lasted more than four hours and left Hauser weary, discouraged, and less sure of himself than ever.

Despite weeks of preparation in transit, it seemed as if Hauser was starting from scratch. There was a fresh physical examination, with another long look at the lingering traces of his wounding and regen treat-ment. A psych team questioned him yet again, concentrating on his familiarity with chip training procedures. Then came a haircut, a sonic shower, vaccinations against various bacteriological and viral threats, and the injection of a five-year birth control agent. Legionnaires contracted for a term of five years and gave up all right to formally sanctioned marriages or any chance of children. In the Fifth Foreign Legion, personal ties were always frowned upon.

Through it all, the officers, noncoms, and civilians remained completely impersonal. The recruits had numbers and were never referred to by name. Hauser had never felt so completely removed from his aristocratic background. It rankled to be referred to by an ident number instead of a name, but somehow he held his tongue and avoided further trouble.

He had thought he'd be drawing a Legion uniform, but instead ended up in secondhand coveralls and boots a size too large. The explanation offered by a bored noncom at the supply counter was that uniforms and kits would not be issued until training actually began, perhaps as much as another two weeks off. *ARISTOTLE* had brought only about half of the recruits who would comprise Hauser's training company. More would arrive to fill out the unit when the carriership *PETRONIUS* arrived in-system. Meanwhile he and the other recruits would wear these secondhand clothes. It was another Legion tradition. The new recruit made a clean break with his past. A fresh start. Though they would be allowed some personal effects, there was something symbolic in having the new arrivals start out this way, wearing used clothing as anonymous as the identification numbers and nearly as impersonal.

The process ended in a small office in the administration building, a large structure which faced the Monument aux Morts and the museum along the broad extent of the road the legionnaires referred to as "The Sacred Way." Room 2312 was windowless, with the wall behind the desk dominated by the Legion colors. A woman with captain's bars gestured to the lone chair beside the desk as Hauser was shown in.

She consulted her wristpiece. "Number 50-987-5648. Hauser von Semenanjung Burat, Wolfgang Alaric."

"Yes, Captain," he responded. It was a relief to hear his name used at last.

"Good, good. Needless to say, you've been accepted for a five-year enlistment in the Foreign Legion. You are aware that you may take this enlistment under a pseudonym, a *nomme de guerre*, as the French used to call it?"

He nodded slowly. That, of course, explained the pointed avoidance of using names throughout the processing. From the time their ident disks had been taken, the recruits had been in a sort of limbo. Anyone who wanted to could take new names upon entering the Legion, to make the break with the past complete.

"It is not required that you change your name," the captain went on. "In some cases it is essential, such as when we accept a recruit with a criminal record. The change of identity, which includes issuance of complete records—birth certificate, passports, everything—the change is designed to protect the Legion and the legionnaire alike. If you were wanted for murder on Caledon and we got a query regarding Wolfgang Hauser, we could honestly say there was no such person, and produce complete records to prove it. That's been a basic building block of the Legion for hundreds of years."

She looked at him with a smile. "That doesn't apply to you, though. However, a lot of legionnaires choose to change their names just for the tradition, the romance, the sense of adventure … and frankly we encourage the change because it helps cement the new beginning you're making with us. Have you given any thought to a *nomme de guerre*?"

Hauser shrugged. "Not really, Captain," he said slowly. "I suppose a change might be a good idea. Even if I'm not considered a criminal, there's a few Besarans who might not be too pleased to know that I'm here."

She nodded. "The possibility had occurred to us, based on the background information you gave the testers aboard *Kolwezi*. Mind you, the Legion looks after its own, no matter what your name might be. But you could save yourself, and us, a lot of trouble. What name shall we enter you under, then? Or would you prefer we give you some random identity selected by computer?"

He looked away. The Hausers had always been known as the "Wolves of the West," after their holdings on Java Baru's Western Peninsula. His given name, Wolfgang, echoed the old nickname....

And his father, Karl Hauser, had always called him "Little Wolf."

"Legion tradition or not, I don't like the idea of completely breaking with my past. My father's memory, at least." He spoke more to himself than to the captain. "I'd like the name Karl Wolf, Captain."

She touched some keys on her wristpiece. "Karl Wolf. Very good. The name is now entered on your ident disk and in our files. You are now Engaged Volunteer Karl Wolf. Welcome to the Fifth Foreign Legion."

*   *   *

The man who now called himself Karl Wolf leaned back in his bunk and stared at the tattered mattress slung above him. He barely noticed the noise made by the other recruits crowded into the transients' barracks. For the moment he was too wrapped up in the gloomy knowledge that they faced yet another delay before the training would begin. It seemed that boredom was more likely to claim his life than any enemy on the field of battle.

After finishing in Room 2312 he'd been ordered to the barracks building. The assignment was temporary, until the new training company was fully assembled and settled into standard quarters. Twenty men shared this dormitory, mostly others from Wolf's batch of new arrivals. There were a handful, though, who had been in residence for over a month already, some of the holdovers from the last training company which had formed at Fort Hunter. Wolf hoped he wouldn't end up like them, forced to wait for yet another batch of new recruits to be assembled.

His bag had arrived ahead of him. There had been a few moments of worry over that, but the seals had been untouched and the contents all accounted for.

"This my bunk up here?" a gentle, lilting voice broke into Wolf's private world. He turned his head to see the big redhead from the processing hut looking down at him, holding what looked like a military-issue kitbag in his beefy hands. The voice reminded him of MacDuff, and was completely at odds with the man's powerful build and hard eyes, and Wolf wasn't sure which to go by. He'd heard of bullies in situations like this forcing weaker men out of choice spots ... like lower bunks.

Wolf raised himself on his elbows. "I figured we were supposed to sleep wherever they tossed our stuff, but I haven't seen any sign that we're actually assigned anywhere," he told the big man in his most reasonable voice.

The redhead nodded. "That's what I thought. They did the same thing at ..." He trailed off. "At another military base I heard about once."

The tattoo with the Assault Marine crest was hidden by the man's coverall sleeve, but Wolf's eyes strayed to the forearm anyway. When he met the recruit's level gaze again he saw a tiny smile. "That's my story and I'm sticking with it," the redhead said in a quiet voice. "Look, boyo, I mass about twice what you do, and this bunk looks like it was part of the base they had here back when this fellow Hunter was stationed here. Would you rather sleep in the upper or run the risk of having me fall through and smother you in your sleep? Doesn't matter to me."

Wolf grinned back. "Put that way, I'm inclined to be generous," he said, sticking out his hand as he swung his feet to the floor. "The name's ... uh, Wolf. Karl Wolf." He had almost forgotten his *nomme de guerre*.

"Tom Callo—Tom Kern," the other responded, taking his hand in a powerful grip. "The names take some getting used to, don't they?"

Nodding, Wolf relinquished the bunk. He was surprised to find himself warming to this man even though he was obviously nothing at all like the people he'd been friendly with back home. There was something about Kern that made him almost instantly likable despite his fearsome appearance.

Kern didn't sit down immediately. Instead he turned to the drab gray locker beside the bunks and started emptying his kitbag, staying well clear of Wolf's meager possessions. That done, he dropped the bag into the bottom of the locker and stripped off his coverall, hanging it neatly. In fact, all his motions were precise and careful, further con-firmation that he had plenty of experience living out of a military kit or a barracks locker.

A recruit stirred on the upper bunk next to them. It was Antonelli, the dark-haired kid who had been making trouble in the waiting room. "Hey, Red," he said easily, a trace of accent overlaying his Terranglic. He pointed to the tattoo. "You a *veterano*, man? Why would an Assault Marine end up in a jerk-ass outfit like the Foreign Legion, huh?"

Kern shot him an angry look, but didn't answer the boy.

"Hey, come on, Red," Antonelli persisted. "We're supposed to be *compagni* ... comrades in arms, now!"

"Quiet, there!" The kid's bantering tones were cut off by the harsh voice of Gunnery Sergeant Ortega. The NCO had come up behind the youngster as he was talking. Now he was peering up at the kid with an expression of supreme distaste. "Everybody, on their feet! At attention!" His stun baton lashed out to prod the kid, who scrambled out of his bunk hastily. The other recruits were falling into line beside their bunks, shaken out of their complaisance by the sergeant's penetrating shout.

"All right, stand easy," the sergeant growled. He surveyed the bunk-room with a withering look. "You lot will be spending two to three weeks in these transient quarters until the rest of your training company arrives. Until then, technically, you aren't even part of the Legion, because your contracts don't start until the company is formed."

He looked straight at Wolf. "That means you still have a few days to back out if you want to. A five-year commitment to the Legion might sound exciting or adventurous back home, but I'm here to tell you it's nothing of the sort. It's not like some holovid or dreamchip scenario where the stalwart heroes fight it out on some sanitary field of honor, then go back to swap yarns over a bottle somewhere. Legion life is month after month of duty so boring it'll drive you crazy, followed by a few days or hours when you're too busy trying to save your ass to realize that you're really in one of those exciting battles you heard about back when you were a civilian. Think about it.... Five years of whatever duty we think suits your qualifications. That's what's waiting for you even if you manage to make it through Basic."

Antonelli spoke up. "Uh, Sergeant, what happens if we wash out of the training?" He managed to look brash and nervous at the same time.

Ortega glared at him. "There are just four ways out of the Legion once the contract is in force. You can wash out of Basic, or resign if you decide you can't take it. Pass Basic and your options get slimmer. Then you can complete five years' service and get your H-and-F stamp on your discharge papers, or you can take the Last March or get yourself wounded bad enough to pull a medical out, or you can desert. I wouldn't recommend deserting. We don't like deserters, and you won't like what we do to you if we catch you trying."

There was a stir in the barracks room, but no more questions. "In short, just remember one little rule and you'll get along fine. Stay out of trouble. As long as you obey orders and don't go screwing up we'll all be one happy family." Ortega looked around the room. "Just because you're not official doesn't mean you get a vacation. You'll work until *PETRONIUS* brings the rest of the company in. That starts tomorrow. Lights out is at 2300 hours tonight, with reveille at 0430. Keep in mind that you've got a 27-hour rotation period here, and set chronometers accordingly." He paused again. "Dismissed."

Wolf followed the sergeant's stocky form with wary eyes. The non-com made him nervous. Ortega seemed to look straight at him every time he spoke of people not measuring up. It reminded him of Colby, of the recruiting sergeant back on Robespierre. It was as if they all expected him to fail. Was he really too soft to be a part of the Fifth Foreign Legion?

A sign on the wall caught Wolf's eye: YOU LEGIONNAIRES ARE SOLDIERS IN ORDER TO DIE, AND I AM SENDING YOU WHERE YOU CAN DIE. The sign attributed the words to a General Negrier of the old French Foreign Legion. The quote had been uttered over a thousand years ago, and it was still part and parcel of the unit's tradition.

That said more about the Legion than anything Ortega or any other legionnaire had put into words.

Chapter Ten

It takes an iron hand to bend such diverse elements into the same mold.

—Comte Pierre de Castellanne,
French Foreign Legion, 1845

ll right, you straks, ten-HUT!"

The recruits had been milling around the parade grounds on their own for the better part of an hour, and the sudden shout caught most of them by surprise. Wolf found a spot in the second row as they formed up into three lines in an approximation of military attention. One hundred twenty men, women, and non-humans stood sweating in Devereaux's afternoon sunlight, assembled for their first official muster as Training Company Odintsev. They still looked more like a motley assortment of convicts than a military unit, with their secondhand coveralls and sloppy, unmilitary bearing, but from this moment the process of turning them into legionnaires would begin.

The arrival of the transport *Sevastopol* had ended three long weeks of boredom. It hadn't come a moment too soon as far as Wolf was concerned. Ortega had decided he was best suited for latrine duty, and five days of scrubbing out the facilities with a toothbrush and a pile of rags was enough to make almost any other duty sound attractive.

The shuttle from *Sevastopol* had touched down shortly before noon, and while the new batch of recruits was going through the processing routine, Wolf and the others had been drawing their Legion kits and getting ready for the changeover from boredom to Basic. Almost everything he'd need for the next five years was stowed in the bulky kitbag beside him—shoes, boots, five grades of uniform from duraweave battledress up to the khaki shirt and trousers of full dress, a canteen and mess kit, and other accoutrements, including the white kepi that was the Legion's unique badge of office. None of them would be allowed to don the sacred headgear until they had convinced their instructors that they really were Legion material.

Those instructors were standing in a cluster behind the stocky figure of Gunnery Sergeant Ortega. Unlike the recruits, they wore comfortable gear for Devereaux's mid-afternoon heat, shorts and T-shirts in khaki and green with the Legion motto *Legio Patria Nostra* emblazoned in bright scarlet letters across their chests. The casual rig revealed that Ortega had a tattoo on his forearm even gaudier than Kern's, a skull and crossbones with the motto "Living by chance, soldiering by choice, killing for fun" running under the picture.

A pair of stiff figures emerged from the administration building behind the noncoms and crossed the street at a leisurely pace. They wore crisp khaki uniforms and black kepis, and the one in the lead had *hauptmann*'s—no, captain's—bars. Behind him was a woman wearing a lieutenant's insignia. Gunnery Sergeant Ortega saluted, and the captain returned the gesture casually.

"I am Captain Dmitri Odintsev," he said, raising his voice to make himself heard over the whining turbofans of a passing MSV cargo carrier. "Today you will begin your Basic Training as members of Training Company Odintsev. I expect good things from the recruits under my command. My units have won the Training Company Commendation three terms running, and I intend to make it a fourth time with your help. You will find the work here hard, and not all of you will finish the process. That is only to be expected. Even the ones who wash out of Legion training should hold their heads up high, because as long as you give us your best you will know that you've been part of something special, something ordinary soldiers will never under-stand. Regardless of what some people claim, the Fifth Foreign Legion is a good outfit ... the *best* outfit ... and for those of you who do measure up I can promise that you'll find a home for life."

Odintsev paused. "As Company Commander, most of my duties are strictly administrative, and the same goes for Lieutenant Du-Chateau, my Exec." His gesture took in the woman beside him. "Most of your training will be directly supervised by Gunnery Sergeant Ortega and the rest of the Training Company's noncommissioned officers. In addition, some of you may be assigned instructor duties in areas where you have demonstrated particular proficiency. However, even though the lieutenant and I won't be directly involved in day-to-day training, we're still available if you need us. The Legion looks after its own, and even though you aren't full legionnaires yet rest assured that I take care of my recruits ... for good or for ill.

"Most of the academic work you do in Basic will consist of chip education coupled with practical applications classes," the captain continued. "Part of your screening included tests on your tolerance for chip learning, so none of you need to be concerned by any stories you might have heard about some people being unable to handle chip learning. You should, though, keep in mind that training through direct mind-computer links may be faster and easier than any other form of education, but will still vary in quality according to your individual aptitudes and desire to learn. Don't expect to retain everything perfectly just because you review a chip on a subject. You may have to repeat a chip several times before you fully understand the material."

He paused again before continuing. "The purpose of applications classes is to put some of what you learn from adchips into actual practice. You will find that you'll retain information much better when you do it, as opposed to merely studying it. Your progress will be monitored, and where necessary you may be assigned extra course loads or the assistance of a tutor to help you. Do not be discouraged by any problems you may have. I've known old legionnaires from Neusachsen and Beaumont who never learned Terranglic well enough to shed their native accents, even after years in the Legion and plenty of chip instruction. They muddle through. So will most of you."

The captain moved on to other topics, touching a number of subjects briefly. "Now as far as the overall training program goes," he said at last, "I'll lay out what you can look forward to in the months ahead. For the next three weeks you will undergo your initial indoctrination here at Fort Hunter. This will consist of physical conditioning, courses in military discipline and etiquette, Legion background, singing, first aid, basic weapons familiarization, and so on. At the end of that period you will have two more weeks at Hunter in intensive training with Legion equipment, including weapons, some vehicles, and your combat helmet and battledress capabilities.

"Following this will be a series of two-week courses designed to familiarize you with various environments and to give you actual field experience. Fort Kessel in the Nordemont mountain range, Fort Marchand in the jungles of the Archipel d'Aurore, Fort Souriban in the deep desert, and the orbital station of Fort Gsell will each serve in turn as your home base during the appropriate stages of training. As Christmas falls within this period, many of you will also be participating in extracurricular activities related to the holiday, and training will be interrupted for a week around Christmas so that the entire training battalion can celebrate together here at Hunter. The final two weeks of your basic training will consist of a series of tests to determine your fitness to graduate the course and receive the white kepi of the legionnaire."

He studied the recruits for a long moment. "That's all I have to say for now ... except for one more thing. Welcome to the Fifth Foreign Legion." He smiled, then turned toward Ortega. "All right, Gunnery Sergeant, they're all yours." They exchanged salutes again, and the two officers headed back for the admin building.

Ortega waited until they were inside before raising his voice again. "Let's get a few things straight right now," he shouted. "Captain Odintsev is listed as Training Company Commander, but you'll find that you'll see a hell of a lot more of me than you will of the officers. When you address me you will salute and call me 'Sergeant.' Do you understand?"

There were sprinkled replies, a ragged and discordant chorus. Wolf didn't join in. Behind Ortega the other noncoms were fanning out to move through the ragged formation, dressing the lines and frowning at the recruits.

"Do you understand?" Ortega repeated, sounding menacing.

More soldiers answered, but it was still a dispirited response. Wolf chuckled ... until the numbing shock of a stun baton across his shoulders made him gasp. Other recruits were getting similar treatment up and down the line from the corporals moving among the ranks.

"We'll keep this up until you get it right," Ortega announced loudly. "You will salute and say 'Sergeant' when addressing me. The proper answer to any question asked of you is 'Yes, Sergeant' or 'No, Sergeant,' DO YOU UNDERSTAND?"

This time Wolf joined in the chorus, all too aware of the hovering noncom near him. "YES, SERGEANT!"

Ortega nodded, a quick, curt gesture. "You straks ... no, that's an insult to every damned strak that ever jumped into the Mistfloor Gorge.

You lot aren't straks ... and you certainly aren't men, so you must be the lowest form of life. Nubes. Newbies. Recruits. You nubes are the best of a bad lot, the sorry-assed few the processors couldn't get rid of any other way. So now you'll spend fifteen weeks finishing your basic training here and elsewhere ... unless you screw up first, and I'm sure most of you will! While you're here you'll learn how to be a legionnaire, but odds are none of you will ever be fit to breathe the same air as a real legionnaire. By the time it's over every last one of you'll be wishing you had just signed up for Hell, 'cause pitchforks and eternal flames would be comfortable compared to what you'll be doing!"

He paused, looking them over slowly, contemptuously. "For the rest of the day you'll be settling in to your permanent quarters. The company will be divided into four platoons of thirty recruits each, and each platoon will be assigned to one barracks building. Those of you who've been with us for a while will be glad to hear you'll be getting more locker space and semiprivate cubicles. After we've divvied you up by platoons, sections, and lances, you'll spend the afternoon getting squared away. Evening mess is at 1800 hours. After that you'll have two hours of free time, with retreat and lights out at 2100. Reveille is at 0300 hours."

Ortega checked the tiny screen of his wristpiece computer. "In addition to myself, twelve NCOs are responsible for the bulk of your training, though you'll also be given specialized lectures by other officers and noncoms as necessary. You will obey these men at all times. If you have a problem, you go through the chain of command. That means you see the corporal in charge of your section first, and if he thinks it's worthwhile you see the sergeant in charge of your platoon. Heaven help you if they think it has to be brought to me ... or if you bother me with some damned complaint without seeing them first!" Ortega gave a savage little smile and made a gesture to the NCOs nearest him. "All right. Tell 'em off by lances and sections and get 'em moving. This isn't some strakking picnic!" He turned on his heel and stalked off.

One of the noncoms took Ortega's place. "First Platoon!" he bellowed. A corporal took over with a shout of "First Section. Alpha Lance!" He recited five names, including Suartana's, then added, "Form up over here. Now!"

The process seemed to go on interminably. There were a few mutter-ings in the ranks until the corporal who had hit Wolf lashed out a few times with his stun baton. Then the other recruits were quiet.

First Platoon was filled out, and the sergeant in charge was leading them away at a trot. After a few minutes more Wolf saw the corporal with the well-used stun baton stepping clear of the ranks.

"Second Platoon, Second Section, Delta Lance! When I call your names fall in behind me. Antonelli, Mario! Kern, Thomas! Myaighee! Scott, Lisa! Wolf, Karl!" He paused before starting in on Echo Lance.

As the corporal continued assembling his section, Wolf studied the recruits beside him. He knew Myaighee, of course, along with Kern and Antonelli from his transient barracks room. The redhead was friendly and good-natured; the young Italian's brash manner made him unpopular, but for all that there was something about the kid that would have been engaging if he hadn't been trying so hard to play the role of the cocky tough guy.

The last member of the group was the same blond girl Antonelli had been admiring in the processing hut that day. She was tall and slender, and moved with a catlike grace. Her short hair and worn coverall couldn't hide the fact that she had once been used to power or money. Like MacDuff, she looked like an aristo. He wondered what her background was, what had led her to join the Legion.

The corporal finished calling names, and a tall, rugged sergeant with a face scarred beyond the ability of reconstructive surgery to repair bellowed for Second Platoon to follow him. They struck out at a brisk trot, following First Platoon through a gate into a fenced-off compound containing several buildings and a large central parade ground. They stopped outside a building labeled Barracks 18, where the two sections separated and were called to order by their respective corporals.

"All right, you miserable nubes, stand easy and listen up!" the NCO told them. "I am Corporal Stefan Vanyek, and until you put on the kepi or wash out of training the second section of this platoon is under my authority. For the next fifteen weeks you'll be answerable to God, two sergeants, and me ... but not necessarily in that order! When I say jump, you'd better ask how high. Screw up and I'll be all over you like scales on an Ubrenfar. Got it?"

"Yes, Corporal!" the section members answered in unison.

"Good! Now ... each of you has four lancemates. Think of your lance as your family. You'll train together, march together, eat together, sleep together, and God willing fight together for as long as you're here. Got it?"

"Yes, Corporal!"

Beside him, Antonelli smirked at Wolf and jerked his head at the blond woman. "Sleep together, huh," he whispered. "Hey, man, maybe this ain't gonna be so bad!"

Vanyek whirled and stalked toward them. "Who said that?" he demanded, looking at Wolf. No one answered.

"All right, nubes. Delta Lance, take a lap around the parade ground. Mag it!"

They fell out of ranks and started running. Antonelli set a brisk pace, and pulled out ahead almost at once with the girl following close behind. Wolf noticed Kern and the hannie holding back, choosing a steady ground-eating trot over Antonelli's faster gait. Though he wasn't sure about the alien's reasons—perhaps those short legs just couldn't manage anything better—Wolf decided Kern probably knew what he was doing and fell into step beside the big man. Although they weren't pushing themselves particularly hard, they were soon drenched in sweat, and the dry, hot air seared Wolf's throat before he had rounded the last corner of the field.

The run completed, they fell back into the line and Vanyek resumed his harangue.

"Next time one of you nubes mouths off in ranks you'll get a real punishment, not just a warning." He paused. "As I was saying, the lance is everything. Your best friends, your family. One of you screws up, the whole lance screws up. Keep it in mind."

A shuttle roared overhead, drowning out the sounds of Fort Hunter. Vanyek waited until it was gone, then continued. "One recruit from each lance will be appointed as lance leader. The lance leader is responsible for discipline and all actions of the lance. You will obey your lance leader's orders except as overridden by higher authority."

He looked at Wolf's lance with an expression of distaste that Wolf was coming to recognize as the standard look of the NCO instructors at Fort Hunter. As Vanyek called up information on his 'piece, Wolf suppressed a smile. Kern's military background and aptitude would make him the obvious choice for lance leader, and that would suit Wolf well enough. Or perhaps his own education and Academy training would count for something, as Doenitz had suggested back on Robespierre. Although he had disclaimed any desire for a leadership role, he wouldn't shirk the responsibility if it was offered....

"Delta Lance," Vanyek mused. "Hmm ... you, the ale. Your file says you've already had Legion combat experience?"

The alien nodded, a completely human gesture. "Yes, Corporal. With Captain Fraser's company on Hanuman and Polypheme—"

"Did I ask for a service history, nube?" The corporal cut the alien off short. His gaze swept over the rest of the lance. "When the Legion recruits locally, during a campaign, there isn't always time for the regular training process. Myaighee here is an example. He has served in two campaigns already. Since you have combat experience, Myaighee, you'll be the designated lance leader for Delta Lance. Understood?"

"Yes, Corporal," the alien replied.

"But—" Wolf burst out. He stopped himself.

"What is it, nube?" Vanyek asked sharply.

"Uh … nothing, Corporal. Nothing …"

Vanyek gave him a long, speculative look. "I've seen your file, Wolf. It says you think you're better than most people. Is that so, nube?"

"No, Corporal," Wolf responded crisply.

"Ah … well, then that means you think the psych tester lied about you. Right?"

"No, Corporal," he repeated.

Vanyek snorted and gave Wolf a brief touch of the stun baton on low power, making the muscles in his arm jerk spasmodically "Get something straight, nube. And the rest of you trash. If you've got any hang-ups about an ale as lance leader, you'd better swallow them double quick! We don't worry about how many arms you have or whether you hatched from an egg or whatever. Anyway, all nubes are the lowest form of life, so trifling differences aren't gonna bother you. You got it, nubes?"

"Yes, Corporal," they all responded.

Vanyek shoved his stun baton under Wolf's chin. "What about you, nube? You got any problems taking orders from a hannie?"

"No, Corporal. None." Wolf swallowed, uncomfortably aware of how the man's words were hitting home. He'd heard about Myaighee's Legion experience back on the *Kolwezi*, but he'd assumed a nonhuman would never have a shot as a leader at any level.

"You think you could lead this lance better'n Myaighee, nube?" Vanyek persisted.

"No, Corporal!" he replied quickly … perhaps too quickly. Vanyek regarded him for a long minute before finally nodding. "Myaighee, Delta Lance." He moved down the line. "Now, Echo Lance … hmmm …"

Wolf's attention wandered as the corporal moved to the next group of recruits. It seemed the Legion wasn't making any allowances for the differences between people, between whole cultures, even though it drew manpower from across the Terran sphere and beyond. He had expected to find differences, of course. His ancestors had emigrated to Laut Besar largely to get away from some of the stricter aspects of the Commonwealth, and in just over a hundred years the two cultures had diverged. Now he was expected to adapt, and with people like Vanyek pushing him it just made the job all the more difficult.

He glanced at Myaighee. Did the hannie find it hard to understand human ways? Of course the alien had already been exposed to the Legion before coming here. Alone of the recruits in Training Company Odintsev, Myaighee wore the insignia of a Third Class Legionnaire. He—Wolf refused to use the alien word *ky*—was already a veteran, and would probably go back to his old unit no matter what.

That was as galling as the hannie's sudden promotion to lance leader.

Wolf felt his jaw tighten. He'd adapt to these Legion ways, all right ... if only to see how Vanyek and Ortega reacted. If that meant treating an alien as an equal, even a superior, so be it.

A few moments later, Vanyek was finished with the lance leader assignments, and the section followed him into the barracks building. It was designed to hold an entire platoon of thirty men, with quarters on the ground floor and a basement gymnasium and exercise area underneath reached by a flight of stairs and an airlock arrangement. The exercise room, Vanyek explained, could be set for a variety of different environmental conditions, much like the training compartments in the transports.

The quarters block was divided lengthwise, with one section occupying each side of the main floor. Each lance shared a room with five semiprivate cubicles and a common room. At one end, near the only outside door, the Section NCO had an office and private room. The other end contained another office/quarters suite, slightly larger, for use by the platoon NCO, Sergeant Konrad, plus a large communal latrine and shower room that was shared by the entire platoon.

Delta Lance had the quarters adjacent to the shower. Initially, Wolf was inclined to grumble about the arrangement, especially when several First Section recruits started using the showers and he realized how much noise they could make. But Kern only smiled and pointed out that he'd be a lot happier with the arrangements when everyone in the building was eager for a shower and Delta Lance would have the advantage in getting there first.

The quarters themselves were comfortable enough, far superior to the transient's bunkroom. Each cubicle had a cot, a small writing desk and computer terminal, and an individual locker, with a lightweight folding door that could give at least the illusion of privacy. The common area at the center of the room was as Spartan as the cubicles, with no more furnishings than a table and some chairs.

Compared to his private room at the Sky Guard Academy it was appalling, but judging from other aspects of Legion life, Wolf felt lucky to have such good quarters.

As he unpacked his kitbag, the memory of Vanyek's words kept coming back. They were determined that he would fail, that he couldn't handle life in the Legion. And maybe they were right.

CHAPTER ELEVEN

The Legion is a moral paradise but a physical hell.

> —attributed to an unknown colonel of the French Foreign
> Legion

All I'm saying is that some of these guys are pretty damned free with their stun batons, that's all," Wolf said.

The recruits had finished their evening meal and were back in barracks, enjoying their last night of comparative freedom. Everything they'd heard since arriving on Devereaux suggested that Basic was going to be tough, but at least they had one more evening of calm before the storm.

Wolf was sitting at the table in the common area with Kern and Lisa Scott. Myaighee had closed himself off in his cubicle with an adchip on leadership principles, while Antonelli was perched on his bunk watching the others and absently shuffling a deck of cards.

The conversation had started after Sergeant Konrad had finished up his inspection. He hadn't found any faults with Delta Lance, but there had been some excitement a few minutes later after he handed out extra duty to everyone in Echo Lance as punishment for one recruit's sloppy locker. When the sergeant left, Volunteer Lauriston had taken it on himself to chastise the offender, a small recruit with features like an Indomay, named Kochu Burundai. The resulting fight had been quickly broken up by Konrad and Corporal Vanyek, but not without some heavy-handed use of stun batons.

Hauser had seen a lot of that sort of thing, both here at Fort Hunter and back aboard the two transports, and it still grated. On Laut Besar even Indomays didn't get that sort of treatment, yet in the "enlightened" Commonwealth no one could make a move without worrying about being subjected to a stun-lashing.

Tom Kern didn't seem particularly shocked, though. "It's rough, I'll give you that. But they've got their reasons. You'll find the military always has a pretty good motive for whatever it does, even if it doesn't look that way to an outsider."

Volunteer Scott laughed. "I can't buy that one, Kern," she said, raising an eyebrow at the big ex-Marine. "You can't tell me that anybody in his right mind would have put together this lance."

"She's got you there, Tom," Wolf chimed in. "Look what they decided would make a compatible unit. We're not exactly a typical bunch, are we?"

Kern shrugged. "I've seen stranger."

"Sure. A deserter from the Marines—"

"I never told you that!" Kern shot back, sounding more amused than annoyed. During the time they'd spent together in the transients' barracks waiting for the company to form, Wolf had picked up plenty of clues about the backgrounds of some of the other recruits, including Kern and Antonelli.

"Okay, okay, a Marine veteran, then," he amended. "Then there's a street kid who was sentenced to the Legion against his will." He darted a glance at Antonelli, who flashed a cocky grin. "An ale that doesn't know what sex it is. I'm the token aristocrat with the shady past, I guess ... and of course there's our mystery guest here."

Lisa Scott looked away, blushing faintly. She was close-lipped about her past, and so far no one had breached Legion tradition to interrogate her. That didn't stop her new lancemates from speculating, though.

"Not exactly the ideal outfit," he concluded. "How in hell did anybody come up with a team like us? Somebody program the master computer to pull practical jokes?"

"They're supposed to match psych profiles," Kern said. "And yes, scoff if you will, the pair of you, but they really do know what they want. You've had military experience, haven't you, Wolf?" At his nod, Kern went on. "Well, so have Myaighee and I. I'd guess you haven't, Scott ... and I know Antonelli there hasn't. They try to pair up novices with people who've had some kind of training. And mixing social background is supposed to get us used to interacting without thinking about status and all that shit."

"They sure don't take background into account in the training, do they?" Wolf commented. "Hell, that guy they nailed for a messy locker never even saw running water until he went on board *Kolwezi*...!"

"Yeah, I know," Kern replied. "I heard that Burundai was a herder on Ulan-Tala before he signed up. They reverted to a nomad culture during the Shadow Centuries, but they weren't as lucky as your bunch. They never had anything worthwhile to attract new settlers to yank them back into a modern frame of mind. That's the whole problem with the Legion. Regular outfits have the glamour and get the best recruits, while the Colonials are mostly drawn from common backgrounds. But in the Legion they're getting recruits in from everywhere, from Terra to Ulan-Tala and anything in between. That's the reason for the tough physical discipline."

"Come again?" Lisa Scott asked.

Kern spread his hands and looked at the tabletop, but his mind seemed light-years away. "The theory is that the instructors can give lectures until Sol goes nova, but some of them might never understand what we're telling them. Would you really want to explain to that herdsman why civilized people use a latrine instead of a convenient bush? Multiply that by a hundred and twenty, because every last recruit comes from a different background and culture with different ideas of what conduct to call proper. It's a hell of a lot easier to get people to accept a single standard of behavior by showing them a good, selfish reason for it—keeping their precious skins intact—than it would be to individually overcome each recruit's lifetime of social training."

"And here I thought Vanyek just liked to make people twitch," Wolf said dryly. "How'd you pick up so much on what makes these people tick, Kern?"

The big redhead looked away for a long moment. "I was a DI in the third ... for a while." He paused. "I'd rather not think about that now, though."

As the conversation died away, Antonelli rolled out of his bunk and approached the table, still practicing a one-handed shuffle that would have made Robert MacDuff envious. "Hey, let's knock off the heavy philosophy and have some fun," he said. "Come on, it's our first night, and it's free time. What d'ya say we play some cards, huh?"

"No thanks," Wolf replied automatically. He stood up. "I think I'll emulate our great leader and chip something until they call lights out."

"I just thought maybe you'd like to sit in on a game or something, you know?" Antonelli put the cards on the table and tapped the deck.

"Thanks anyway." He still wasn't sure what he thought of Antonelli. The kid tried hard to make others like him, but he had a knack for saying the wrong things. Like his comment on the parade ground, or the way he'd acted the day they'd processed in.

"Just trying to be sociable." Antonelli turned away. "How 'bout you, Red?"

"Not for me, mate," Kern said, affably enough.

Antonelli sat down at the table. "Man, what a bunch of killjoys they stuck me with," he complained. "Come on, just a coupla hands, okay?"

Kern shook his head slowly. "Maybe after we get our first pay slip, all right? I used up my whole advance before we even got off the transport, and gambling's no good without stakes."

From his cubicle, Wolf watched Antonelli shrug and look across at Lisa Scott. "You'll play, won't you, honey?" Antonelli said loudly. "I'll bet we can think of some stakes worth playing for, huh?"

She didn't answer. Instead, she crossed to her locker, took out a towel, then headed for the door. A few moments later the sound of running water confirmed her destination.

Antonelli leered again. "Hey, maybe she's got the right idea. Maybe I'll just clean up, too...." He got up and followed her.

Wolf rolled out of his cot. "Maybe we'd better help out Scott...."

"Better wait and see if the lady needs any help, boyo," Kern advised. "Could be old Mario's in for a surprise or two from that one."

Before he could respond there was a shout from the shower room, then a string of curses in hoarse tones barely recognizable as Antonelli's. Wolf raced for the door with Kern close behind. Myaighee joined them as they ran down the hall to the showers.

Antonelli was backed against the wall next to the door clutching his left arm. Blood seeped through his fingers and dripped to the tile floor. "She cut me! The bitch cut me!"

Lisa Scott took a step toward the bleeding man. She made no effort to cover her nude body, and the knife in her hand, held at the ready, never wavered. "I'll cut you worse if you come near me again," she said in a soft, dangerous voice. "And in some place a lot more painful than your arm. Depend on it."

"What's going on in here? Get out of the way!" Corporal Vanyek's strident tones broke through a babble of voices from the corridor, where members of the other lances were gathering in response to the commotion. "Out of my way, I said!"

The corporal brushed past Wolf and took in the scene with a single glance. "All right, back to your quarters. Now! Mag it!" He halted Wolf and the other members of Delta Lance. "Not you straks."

He turned away, toward Lisa, then suddenly whirled around and slammed a fist into Antonelli's stomach. The recruit doubled over, gasping, and Vanyek hit him again, this time in the face.

"You stupid bastard," Vanyek said, almost in a monotone. "You strak-faced piece of ghoul shit." For emphasis he struck again, then signaled for Wolf and Kern to pull the injured man to his feet. "The Legion wasn't set up so you could party with female legionnaires, Antonelli. You got that?"

Antonelli nodded weakly, and Vanyek hit him again. "I don't think you're hearing me, nube! I don't know how it is in whatever sewer you grew up in, but in the Legion there's no distinctions drawn between men and women. None! That means there'll be female soldiers in your units, here and out in the field. But they weren't put there as playthings for the likes of you." He raised his fist as if to strike again, then seemed to think better of it. The recruit was barely conscious as it was. "Now get this, nube, and get it good. You can screw whoever or whatever you like, whenever you like, on your own time. We've got whorehouses to take care of the troops outside the fort. If some legionnaire is crazy enough to want you, that's fine, too, but you better make sure we're talking consenting partners here. You get me, nube?"

He nodded, gasped out, "Yes, Corporal!"

Vanyek smiled coldly. "Good ... because you try a stunt like this again, and I'll personally make sure that whatever the woman leaves intact gets carved up anyway."

"Yes, Corporal," Antonelli repeated weakly.

The corporal turned his angry eyes on Lisa. "You, nube. You made it clear that you didn't want anything to do with him before you pulled the knife."

She met his eyes without flinching. "Yes, Corporal. Several times today, and again when he came in here."

He frowned at her. "And you brought that thing in here with you. You always take a knife into the showers, nube?"

Flushing she gave a grim nod. "Yes, Corporal," she repeated. "I do. Since I was seventeen. I have a right to defend myself."

Vanyek was suddenly a blur of motion, his hand snaking out to chop at the wrist of her knife hand as he stepped past her guard. The knife clattered on the wet tile floor as the corporal gave the naked girl a backhanded slap that sent her reeling. "Get this straight, nube," he roared. "You don't have any rights while you're here! None! And you certainly don't have the right to go carving up members of your own unit! How did you get that knife into the barracks in the first place?"

She rubbed the red spot on her face where he had hit her. "It was in my bag. There's a hidden compartment...."

"So you just smuggled yourself a weapon onto the base," he finished. He spat for emphasis.

"No one said anything about forbidding weapons, Corporal," she said quietly. "And I never intended to do anything but protect myself...."

"Shut up!" he bellowed, raising his hand as if to strike her again. Then he dropped it and went on in lower tones. "We'll go to your quarters and have a look through the rest of your things, just to make sure you haven't brought in any other little surprises."

Vanyek bent down and retrieved the fallen knife. "This weapon is confiscated, and if I catch you with another one I just might decide to use it myself." He tucked it into the top of his boot. "I could have you and Antonelli both on your way out of here, but I'm going to recommend leniency. This time, that is. The Legion doesn't like to waste recruits in barracks knifings. And there are good reasons why we don't like our recruits running around with weapons unless we give them to you. Get the picture?"

She nodded tightly, but didn't answer. Vanyek ignored the silence and went on. "I'm putting you down for twenty hours extra duty in an unarmed combat class, starting tomorrow. Use what you learn to discourage any other rutting straks you run across, and save the cutlery for the enemy."

Swallowing, she found her voice at last. "Yes, Corporal."

Vanyek fixed Myaighee with a harsh look. "I don't want any more trouble out of either of these two again, you hear me? Next time your whole lance draws punishment."

"Yes, Corporal," the hannie said, the quills of his neck ruff twitching. Wolf had heard that those spines moved in response to strong emotion.

"Antonelli, you get two hours a night extra duty starting tonight, and until I decide otherwise. You can draw a toothbrush and clean the shithouse after you wrap up your arm. Let's get going!"

Vanyek slammed the door open and led the way back to their barracks room, with Myaighee following. Kern and Wolf got on either side of Antonelli, supporting his stumbling figure. As they left the shower room, Wolf saw Lisa Scott rub her jaw once before turning to pick up her clothes. She trailed behind them, drying herself with a towel, and stood aside as Vanyek went through her locker.

Finally satisfied that she wasn't hiding any other weapons, Vanyek favored them with a last savage glare. "All right. That's enough excitement for one night. Patch up that strak's arm and send him to my office. The rest of you ... lights out in ten minutes!"

Myaighee had already broken open a medical kit hanging on the wall near the door, and with Kern's help the alien started bandaging Antonelli's wound. Wolf looked at them for a moment, then headed for his own cubicle. Next door, Lisa Scott started to close the screen, caught his eye, and shrugged.

"Not much point in modesty anymore, is there?" she said with a sardonic smile. But she closed the screen anyway without waiting for Wolf to reply.

He stretched out on his cot, then picked up the adchip he had been about to study before the trouble began. He frowned at it for a moment, then put it down. After everything that had happened, he doubted he could get into a chip lecture before the call for lights out sounded. Reluctantly, he leaned back, listening to Antonelli cursing while Kern and Myaighee applied the bandage.

Wolf wondered, again, what he had gotten himself into by joining the Fifth Foreign Legion.

*   *   *

It was quiet in the barracks building now, half an hour after the PA order for lights out. Engaged Volunteer Mario Antonelli wiped the sweat from his forehead with his sleeve and winced as the motion set his arm to throbbing again. It was all so damned unfair ...!

Having the bitch pull a knife on him had been bad enough, but then Corporal Vanyek had beaten him until he could hardly move. Now the noncom expected him to spend two hours on his hands and knees cleaning toilets. Vanyek had left little doubt that another beating, worse than before, would follow if the work wasn't done to the corporal's satisfaction.

"This shit is crazy," he muttered aloud. "*Pazzo*. Goddamned judge ..."

Antonelli had never intended to join the military, much less a hard-luck outfit like the Fifth Foreign Legion. But here he was, against his will, with no hope now of escaping.

He had been born in Rome, on Terra, and at the age of fifteen he'd become a full Citizen with all the rights and privileges that went with that simple title. A hundred and fifty nations on Terra and a score or so major world governments extended Commonwealth Citizenship to their entire populace automatically. In theory it meant the right to vote in Commonwealth elections, and the Citizen was supposed to have precedence over Colonials and other non-Citizens in all things, from the chance to own Colonial land to the best seats on shuttles or floatbuses.

In practice, though, most Citizens on Terra didn't give a damn about any of it. The one thing the vast majority of the beeswarm billions of the Mother World's overcrowded cities cared about was the Citizen's dole. With cheap fusion power, artificially intelligent computers, synthetic foods, and the wealth of an interstellar empire to draw on, nobody on Terra had to hold down a job to survive. The dole took care of basic needs. If a Citizen wanted more, there were opportunities he could take advantage of, all the way up to emigration to some frontier world where Citizenship carried real power.

But like so many of his kind, Antonelli had been perfectly willing to accept state-sponsored housing and the minimum dole rather than exerting himself to find some kind of use or meaning to his existence. Instead he'd drifted casually into a life of petty crime and dissipation, mostly out of boredom and because it was the only way to rebel against a cold, impersonal society. He'd run with I Paladini Blanci, the White Knights, a gang of like-minded youths, none of them really violent or dangerous characters, but they acted tough and expected him to do the same.

Then he'd stolen a floatcar and gone on a joyride among the rez-plexes outside of Rome on a dare from some of the Knights ... and the compols arrested him and the judge sentenced him to a term in the service. And not just any service—the Fifth Foreign Legion. His Citizenship was suspended, and only by completing a five-year term of enlistment would he get it back again. Otherwise he'd be sent to one of the Colonial Army penal battalions, and when his term was up there would be no more dole, no more state housing ... nothing.

He hadn't really thought much about being a Citizen until the judge had taken the title away.

But for a time the idea had seemed exciting, like anything but punishment. A chance to get off Terra, get away from endless mobs of people, find adventure on distant planets ... he'd leapt at the chance. The Legion had a murky reputation back home as a haven for all the cast-off scum of a hundred worlds, but at the same time there was a romance about the lonely life of the soldiers who guarded distant frontiers that had made him dream of coming home covered in glory.

He had even told his parents that he had volunteered. His mother had cried, but old Sergeant-Major Enrico Antonelli had beamed with pride. The old man was getting on in years, and the artificial heart they'd put in him after the fighting on Horizon was giving him trouble these days, but when he thought the son of his old age was finally going to follow in his footsteps there had been no doubt of his feelings. Antonelli had shipped off Terra feeling good for the first time in a long, long time.

Now he was in the Legion, and the glory had vanished like a mirage in the desert. Why couldn't he fit in here? He'd tried to put up the same tough image that had won him respect with the Knights, but he'd been rebuffed at every turn. The corporals and sergeants were worse than compols, and then the girl ...

In the crowd he ran with back home, any girl would have understood him. He had been showing his appreciation for a good-looking woman; that was all. Sure, if she'd been interested they could have had some fun, but he hadn't planned to force her or anything. Antonelli didn't need to use force to get a girl. It had all been in fun, the kind of macho horseplay all the Paladini Blanci went in for. He'd intended it to break the ice with the legionnaires, nothing else.

Until the bitch had pulled the knife and slashed his arm. Now he was branded a rapist, and the noncoms would come down twice as hard as before. And he was off on the wrong foot with his lance, with the whole outfit in fact. He would have to work twice as hard to be accepted now.

Antonelli bit his lip and leaned forward to start scrubbing again, favoring the bruises where Vanyek had hit him in the stomach. He couldn't afford to fail with the Legion, not if he wanted to win his Citizenship back. Not if he wanted to see that same look in his father's eye the next time he went home.

He *had* to make it work.

Chapter Twelve

You have to be tough with recruits. We get very hard men coming into the Legion, and hard men expect hard treatment. That's why they join the Legion.

—A drill instructor French Foreign Legion, 1984

Reveille! Reveille! Come on, you nubes, up! Up!"

The numbing shock of a stun baton between his shoulder blades made Wolf scramble out of his cot, groggy and barely able to remember where he was. The attention was entirely impersonal, though. Corporal Vanyek was already moving on to prod Volunteer Scott into wakefulness. Across the common room Wolf saw Antonelli, face and torso mottled with the bruises of the beating in the shower room, leaning against his locker door and fumbling with his clothes.

"Come on, people, what are you waiting for?" Vanyek demanded. "Let's get with it! Assembly on the parade ground in five minutes. Wear your sweats, 'cause that's what you're gonna be doing out there! Mag it! Mag it!"

Wolf groped in his locker for his clothes and dressed, still trying to clear his head. By the time he was done, Kern and Myaighee were helping Antonelli, and the whole lance poured out of the building at the same time. They formed up alongside the rest of the platoon, shivering in the cold predawn wind that blew off the Great Desert. The other platoons of the training company poured out of adjacent buildings.

Sergeant Horst Konrad blew a whistle and trotted into view, looking too fresh, too alert. "What a sorry bunch of nubes!" he shouted.

"When reveille sounds you people had better mag it out here on FTL, or I'll know the reason why! Now all of you drop and give me fifty!"

He pushed them through a grueling series of calisthenic exercises, with frequent repetitions when anyone failed to perform to his satisfaction. Wolf kept expecting to see Vanyek or one of the other noncoms wielding their ubiquitous stun batons among the sweating, straining recruits, but they were nowhere to be seen.

Finally, it ended and they were back in line, standing stiffly at attention. "All right, you nubes!" Konrad said brusquely. "Chow line forms in ten minutes. Change to fatigues before you eat, and police the barracks! Go!"

Wolf and the rest of the lance trotted back into the barracks, only to find their room a complete shambles. While they had been exercising, someone had dumped the contents of their lockers on the floor and overturned all the cots. Wolf discovered that his uniforms had been thoroughly soaked in the scented antibeard lotion he'd purchased at the base exchange a few days before. Judging from the noise coming from elsewhere in the building, the other lances had found similar scenes waiting for them as well.

"Cristo!" Antonelli moaned, righting his cot and sitting on it with an air of hopelessness. "Why the hell did they do this? As if we don't have enough grief already!"

"What's the matter, nube?" Vanyek's mocking voice came from the doorway. "You want your mother to come and clean up for you?" The corporal's cold blue eyes fixed on Wolf, and he gave an exaggerated sniff. "Fancy perfume. Too good for the common soldiers, I'd say, but just right for a fancy aristo. Smells expensive. Was it expensive, Aristo?" He didn't wait for an answer. "There's no servants in the Legion to keep you fine aristocrats from getting your hands dirty. You'd better get this mess cleaned up and get changed in a hurry if you want to have any breakfast!" He spat eloquently and moved on, leaving the recruits staring at the mess in dismay.

Myaighee broke the spell. "Kern, you and Antonelli get the cots in order." The alien's nose wrinkled. "Wolf, see if you can find a set of fatigues that isn't too wet. Scott and I will start folding clothes and putting the lockers in order, yes?"

Wolf had to suppress the urge to tell the hannie to mind its own business. Myaighee was his lance leader, and if Vanyek or Konrad found out he'd disobeyed the alien's orders there might be trouble.

And, after all, Myaighee had told him to do exactly what he would have done anyway....

It took nearly twenty minutes to restore order from the chaos and lay out each locker in the exact order prescribed by the Legion. By the time they reached the mess hall, they had only ten minutes left to go through the chow line and get a few bites to eat. The strong smell of antibeard lotion made several other recruits make comments about his taste in perfume, but Wolf wasn't the only one in the company who'd been given the treatment. Volunteer Kochu Burundai, the nomad from Ulan-Tala, had found all of his uniforms lying in a pool of water in the showers. He promptly received the nickname "Soak" and was the butt of at least as many jokes as Wolf.

Then Konrad was blowing his whistle again and shouting orders. Wolf gulped down a bitter cup of Ysan tea and joined the race for the parade ground.

Once outside, the sergeant set them to running, leading them at a brisk pace across the camp and out into the rugged desert beyond. Konrad and the other noncoms didn't seem to find it a strain, but the recruits, already tired and hungry, were hard-pressed to keep up. Corporals with stun batons helped the laggards find a second wind, though. Somehow Wolf forced himself to keep going, though it took every ounce of willpower. He saw Vanyek darting looks in his direction from time to time, but he was determined not to give the corporal the satisfaction of seeing him fail.

Antonelli wasn't so fortunate. After what Wolf estimated was five kilometers the recruit stumbled and fell, and Vanyek's stun baton couldn't get him moving again. The unit kept going. As other stragglers fell by the wayside, a medical van on screeching turbofans skimmed by, stopping to gather in the casualties.

Eventually, the torment was over, and they were back on the parade ground gasping and panting. Wolf's uniform, still smelling faintly of antibeard now thoroughly mixed with sweat, was making him itch, and the long run had almost done him in. But he had made it, seen it through, and that was what was important. Konrad dismissed them with curt orders to shower, change into fresh fatigues, and assemble in ten minutes.

When Wolf stumbled back onto the parade ground, Vanyek gave him a quick cuff and a jolt from his stun baton for being the last man back from the showers. Antonelli and the other stragglers were back in ranks now, looking dejected. Wolf thought he could detect a few fresh bruises on the battered youngster's face.

He wasn't sure what to expect next after the hard pace of the morning workout. Incredibly, what followed was two hours of singing practice under Konrad's stern tutelage.

"You nubes will learn the songs of the Legion," the sergeant told them harshly. "You will practice until you can sing any song, any time, to my satisfaction!"

He started with the words to "Devereaux Lament," a slow, sad ballad of the Fourth Foreign Legion and Hunter's last battle against the Ubrenfar and Semti forces more than a hundred years back. Shouting the words a line at a time, making the recruits repeat them back over and over, Konrad looked like some mad choirmaster with his crisp fatigues and close-cropped head. Wolf almost laughed, until he saw Lisa Scott chuckle and then gasp as Vanyek used his stun baton on her.

It seemed absurd, but one of the lectures he'd chipped aboard *Kolwezi* had discussed the importance of singing in Legion training. Songs helped transmit the spirit and mystique of the Legion, and singing bound the recruits together on a basic, very human level. Like so many other aspects of the training program, it was one of the old, solid traditions that went back almost to the beginnings of Legion history.

Once he got past the seeming silliness of it all, Wolf had to admit he enjoyed the interlude.

Unfortunately, after two hours it was time to parade for lunch, which meant falling in to ranks again, going through another round of calisthenics, and then trotting off after Konrad, singing "Devereaux Lament," to the mess hall. They had more time for this meal, but there was still precious little chance for relaxation before the training started up again.

$$* \quad * \quad *$$

That first day set the pace for the next three weeks of Basic. Mornings were spent in physical training, exercising, marching, running, singing. After the noon mess call, the platoon usually shifted to academics in the lecture halls of the admin building, where the recruits went over material from individual training chips and had a chance to do practical, hands-on work that reinforced the chip courses. The period following the evening meal was supposed to be set aside to give them time to study chips or relax, though Wolf soon discovered that this "free time" was frequently taken up by extra duty imposed at the whim of Vanyek, Konrad, or Sergeant Baram, Konrad's deputy.

This standard pattern was by no means a constant, though. Some days the morning march turned into an all-day excursion, and during the second week the whole company covered fifty long desert kilo-meters on foot, then made camp overnight and returned the next day. It was hard work, far harder than anything Wolf had experienced in the Sky Guard Academy, and as the days passed, he found himself wondering more and more if the noncoms who had doubted his ability to measure up might have known what they were talking about after all.

Still, he kept on trying. During that first overnight march, he man-aged to stick with the column all day, though there were others who fell behind. Two days later, Wolf was pleasantly surprised to find himself selected to give instruction to the rest of the platoon in saber fighting, and for at least an hour a day he could feel that even Vanyek and Kon-rad had to respect him a little bit.

Throughout these early weeks, the drills and lectures were only a part of the overall training process, though if it hadn't been for Kern's observations Wolf might never have noticed the deeper significance of the work. The Legion program started with the assumption that every recruit was completely inexperienced not just in military matters but even in many of the accepted norms of education and proper social behavior. At first it seemed a waste of time and effort, but as time went on Wolf could see how the recruits absorbed the lessons that made the Legion a common denominator for all of them. Rich in tradition, the Fifth Foreign Legion was almost a culture apart, as far removed from Antonelli's origins on the streets of Rome as it was from Wolf's aristo-cratic Besaran heritage. Though Wolf remained cynical about the whole process, he watched men like Burundai latch on to their new "culture" eagerly, and understood how the Legion could breed the fanaticism he had seen in some of the noncoms' eyes.

On a purely military level, it was probably right to approach the training in such a stolid, step-by-painful-step way. Out of his training company of one hundred and twenty recruits, forty-eight admitted to prior military service, but there was a wide gap between Wolf's Sky Guard background and the experience of Engaged Volunteer Hosni Mayzar, a twenty-year veteran of the Commonwealth's crack Centauri Rangers who was leader of Second Platoon's Echo Lance. And the ones with no military background at all had to learn even the simplest of things from the ground up. Those with some soldiering experience were expected to help the others along, whether they were giving formal instruction like Wolf's saber training, or just passing along advice and useful tips as Kern seemed to do for his lancemates almost daily. The "veterans" didn't get a break from the training routine just because they already understood something, though. They were expected to relearn the military trade the Legion way.

Like so much in the Legion, it made sense when viewed dispassionately, but it was damned hard to deal with the Legion's ruthless but often painfully slow approach to turning the recruits into soldiers.

As the end of the first phase of the training program drew near, the recruits in Wolf's lance were beginning to draw together into a solid, close-knit unit. Wolf grudgingly gave much of the credit to Myaighee, the hannie. He—no one in Fort Hunter bothered with the alien term "ky"—didn't seem likely as lance leader, but somehow Myaighee did the job without losing the soft-spoken, diffident manner that was the little being's most noticeable characteristic. Although he came from a background entirely unlike anything the human members of the lance could comprehend, Myaighee seemed to understand the Legion and its ways better than any of them. Perhaps that came with experience. Myaighee had started out as a servant employed by Terrans on Hanuman, his home planet, but during a rising by his people against the human population, he had thrown his lot in with the offworlders and ended up joining a column of legionnaires marching across hostile jungles to the safety of the main Terran enclave. In the course of the campaign the alien had helped the legionnaires on more than one occasion, and when it was all over he had chosen to stay with the unit rather than return to the home he had left behind. Another campaign on Hanuman, and one on the watery world of Polypheme, had followed.

Wolf still had trouble accepting Myaighee as a superior, or even as an equal ... but surely once they were in the field the natural order of things would assert itself and the nonhuman members of the legion would find the proper place. After all, according to the background chips less than ten percent of the Fifth Foreign Legion was made up of nonhumans.

Mario Antonelli was still the odd man out in the lance, but the young man's brash, cocksure attitude had softened under Legion discipline. Antonelli's background typified everything the Uro aristocracy of Laut Besar objected to in the Commonwealth. Convicted of some minor offense—no one in the lance knew what he'd done, and the Legion tradition of asking no questions about a man's past kept it that way—Antonelli had been sentenced to serve a hitch in the Legion, one of a handful in the training company who hadn't volunteered.

Strangely, it was Myaighee who got along best with the moody youngster. The alien claimed that one of his lancemates from his old outfit had come from a similar sort of background, and encouraged him to devote his free time to wood carving and other hobbies with surprisingly good results. In training he tried hard and seemed determined to succeed, but he frequently ran afoul of Vanyek and Konrad through carelessness. Wolf found it hard to show much sympathy to a man from such a completely foreign social strata, and Lisa Scott continued to treat Antonelli with disdain. Nor did the Italian seem particularly interested in overcoming their low opinions. Everything he did seemed focused on the bare effort to hang on no matter what the Legion threw at him.

On the other hand, everyone found Tom Kern easy to talk to but hard to know. The big redhead was a quiet man. He never spoke of his past or his reasons for joining the Legion. He spent most of his free time alone. He knew a great deal about the training process and occasionally let slip comments about his past as a drill instructor. Most of the recruits figured him for a deserter who had sought out the anonymity of the Legion to ply the only trade he knew.

Whether the speculation was true or not, Kern was the ideal lancemate. Though he rarely sought out the companionship of others, he was always willing to put aside his own problems and share an hour in spinning a yarn or playing cards, and on the parade ground his consistently cheerful, solid competence was valuable to the entire lance. Academics gave him more than his fair share of problems, but Wolf had started as his tutor early on and they were making good progress. And though Kern in his way was as far removed in background and social standing as Antonelli, Wolf regarded him as something more than just another member of the unit. He was no substitute for the faithful Suartana, whose posting to First Platoon kept him well out of Wolf's orbit, but he was as close as Wolf expected to find in the Legion.

The fifth member of the lance was altogether more of a puzzle. Lisa Scott's background was even more mysterious than Kern's. No one had an inkling of why she had joined the Foreign Legion or where she had come from, but Wolf thought he recognized in her the quality of another aristo. She was not from Laut Besar, of course, but she plainly came from a good bloodline and had enjoyed the same kind of wealth and good education he'd received. But she was a startling contrast to the pampered, protected daughters of the Uro aristocracy he'd known on Laut Besar. Self-assured, independent, and as tough as any of the men in the training company, she should have seemed as alien as Myaighee in Wolf's eyes, but somehow the qualities he would have found repugnant in a woman of his homeworld seemed ideal for Lisa Scott.

He might have sought a closer relationship with her, but the memory of that unwavering knife and her cold blue eyes in the confrontation with Antonelli made Wolf cautious. She remained completely aloof from all the recruits, male, female, and alien alike, a loner who did her job but seemed unable or unwilling to lower her barriers and let anyone else get close.

He could sympathize with the feeling. The more he saw of these people who had chosen the Legion life the more Wolf wondered at his own choice. Sometimes he felt like more of an alien than Myaighee. It was a feeling he wasn't sure he liked … but the alternative, becoming a part of all this, scared him even more.

*　*　*

"All right, next up! Antonelli! Let's go! Let's go! We could spend your whole strakking enlistment waiting for you to get moving! Go!"

Wolf suppressed a smile as Antonelli stumbled on his way to the weapons rack at the front of the Barracks 18 exercise room. For all of his tough talk, the youngster couldn't manage to keep his cool in the face of one of Sergeant Konrad's badgering tirades. The sergeant came from Lebensraum, where most of the Besaran Uros had originated, and his uncompromising drive for perfection never failed to remind Wolf of his own grandfather. Konrad was no aristocrat, but he would have been right at home supervising an onnesium mine or running an industrial complex on Laut Besar … at least, on Laut Besar before the Ubrenfars came.

Antonelli selected a saber and stepped onto the strip facing Wolf. Saluting the Italian with his blade, Wolf dropped into the guard position.

"I want you to try the disengage I showed you earlier," he said. "Remember that the idea behind the disengage attack is to mislead your enemy, to make him parry a false blow and leave himself open to your real strike. Do you understand?"

The youngster nodded a little uncertainly and dropped into guard stance without a blade salute. Wolf frowned, then dismissed the slip. Antonelli had enough trouble with the practical end of saber fighting without further confusing him by insisting on precise adherence to the proper forms. Later Wolf would have to go over the etiquette of dueling.

For just an instant Wolf looked over his blade at Neubeck, not Antonelli, and knew a moment's revulsion. The feel of the sword in his hand kept bringing back bitter memories of that day on Robespierre. He fought back the feeling and nodded. "Begin."

Antonelli beat his blade once, a brief tap lacking authority. His second beat, on the same side of the blade, was a little firmer, and Wolf nodded in encouragement. The younger recruit screwed up his face in concentration and struck Wolf's blade a third time, then twisted his wrist to the left to make the disengage attack. Wolf parried the blow and stepped back, lowering his saber.

"All right," he said with another nod. "Now that one wasn't too bad, but you need to work on your technique. You've been chipping too many swashbucklers, kid, and you've got a tendency to make your attacks a little too wild. Keep your attacks precise and controlled. That's the way to win the point."

The younger recruit nodded, but Wolf wasn't sure how much he actually understood. Before he had a chance to go on, though, he was interrupted by Sergeant Konrad. "Right! Platoon ... muster on the parade ground for calisthenics! Move! Move! Move!"

The order caught Wolf by surprise. He had thought they'd have another half hour or so of fencing. But Konrad was nothing if not unpredictable, and he shrugged and headed for the weapons rack to put his saber away.

Konrad intercepted him as the rest of the recruits filed out of the exercise room at a trot. "You, nube," he said, his voice harsh. "You are a good fencer."

The sergeant rarely paid a compliment without balancing it with something scathing, and Wolf halted in mid-motion at the words. "Thank you, sergeant," he said tentatively.

"A good fencer ... but the Legion doesn't want good fencers." Konrad picked up a saber and hefted it in his hand. "We are not training recruits to fight saber in the Commonwealth Games, nube. Or to fight in duels between aristos, either. Do you know why we train our legionnaires to fight with blades, nube?"

"Uh ... I *thought* I did, Sergeant," Wolf replied. "It speeds the reflexes, sharpens perception ..."

"Nein! Nein!" Once again Wolf was reminded of his grandfather as Konrad lapsed into the German of Wolfgang Hauser's youth. "We fight with swords because some day we may have to use them in battle, nube! Many times our garrisons are on primitive planets where the sword is a major weapon. The Wynsarrysa outlaws right here on Devereaux use blades, for instance, when they can't take anything better from settlers. So we learn enough that a legionnaire can fight with whatever weapons come to hand. *That* is why we learn saber ... and knife fighting, and hand-to-hand combat, and all the rest. Do you understand that?"

"Yes, Sergeant," Wolf replied slowly. He still wasn't sure why Konrad had decided to point all this out to him, but he was learning from experience to be careful in dealing with the man.

"When you train my men," Konrad went on, "I want you to stop worrying so much about proper forms and good technique. I want my legionnaires to know how to defend themselves with a blade, not how to score points in a match. Understand me?"

"Yes, Sergeant," Wolf repeated.

"Good. Keep one thing in mind, nube, and we'll get along just fine. In the Legion, we fight to win. Not for any other reason. We fight to win."

Konrad turned away abruptly. "Now move it, nube, or I'll have you on report!"

Chapter Thirteen

There are many, too many, who join the Legion with no sort of qualification for a soldier's life, and these men do no good to themselves or to France by enlisting.

—A Legion recruiting officer,
French Foreign Legion, 1889

Look sharp! Look sharp! It could come at us from anywhere!"

Wolf hunkered lower behind the protective bulk of a rock outcropping and blanked his mind to access the interface chip that controlled his combat helmet. The tiny computer could translate thought into orders that could govern a variety of helmet functions, from communications to vision settings to tactical data displays, though it was far less complex than a conventional adchip or computer implant. An ordinary soldier not only didn't need full-scale computer access, but in fact would be handicapped by having too much information available at times when survival depended on combat instincts rather than sophisticated data retrieval. But the combat helmet was a versatile tool he was finally beginning to master.

He called up a sensor map on the inside of the helmet's faceplate. Superimposed on the computer-generated topographic chart, five green triangles showed how he and his four lancemates were spread out over the barren ground in a loose skirmish line. He took careful note of their positions to avoid any chance of mistaking one of them for the hostiles who would be trying to penetrate the defensive zone sometime in the next few minutes.

"Look sharp, people," Kern repeated, voice gruff. Despite his experience, he sounded as much on edge as any of them.

Wolf switched off the map and raised his faceplate to get an eyeball view of his surroundings. The Legion combat helmet was an amazingly versatile piece of equipment, fitted with a computer-coordinated sensor system that could generate a wide range of different displays, including maps, optical sighting, passive and active infrared, light-intensification, and electronic magnification and image enhancement, but none of them was a completely satisfactory replacement for the human eye and brain. He still trusted his own senses best.

Motion to his left attracted Wolf's attention, but it was Lisa Scott running a zigzag course to reach a gully that would give her a better view of the battlefield. The lance was fitted out as a heavy weapons unit, and she was acting as a spotter.

He shifted the bulky tube of the Fafnir missile launcher in his hands. It was a versatile weapon that packed a powerful punch, its programmable targeting system equally effective at seeking out and destroying any specific target type, ground or air. But he didn't care much for the job of Fafnir gunner. The notion of having only five warheads and a pistol to fall back on when his ammo was used up made him appreciate the standard-issue FE-FEK battle rifle with its hundred-round magazine of Mylar-coated plastic needles and the 1 cm autogrenade launcher. *That* was a weapon that could keep a soldier in a firefight....

But for now he had the Fafnir, and the tacdata briefing had reported the likely opposition would be small, fast-moving Ubrenfar attack pods which wouldn't be vulnerable to ordinary small arms fire. That put most of the burden on Wolf and Antonelli, who was carrying the unit's onager plasma gun.

"Motion! Motion bearing three-two-three degrees!" Kern called out.

"Gunner ready!" Myaighee chimed in.

Wolf swung to face the indicated stretch of terrain. It was dominated by a series of low, undulating ridges that could mask the approach of an enemy.

The on-board fire-and-forget tracking system on the Fafnir could be programmed to discriminate an Ubrenfar attack pod—or almost any other type of vehicle, aircraft, or installation the Legion expected to come up against—and attack it at long range, unhampered by considerations of intervening terrain or line-of-sight. Wolf opened his mouth to request a "weapons free" order from Myaighee, then bit back the question. Over and over again during weapons training he'd been given stun-lashings by Vanyek and other instructors for trying to tell the lance leader how to do his job. That was a mistake he wouldn't dare to make again.

Anyway, it might not *be* an attack pod. Without visual confirmation he might just be throwing away a missile to no purpose. Better to play it safe....

At that moment, as if to taunt him over his decision, the attack pod darted into view from behind the cover of the ridge at lightning speed. The flattened sphere paused, suspended on magrep fields as its turret sensors swiveled in search of a target. Wolf gritted his teeth and fought the urge to open fire with his Fafnir. Doctrine required him to give the onager gunner first crack at a target. The Fafnir's limited ammo supply could be a drawback in a firefight. But the *fusil d'onage* Antonelli was carrying, on the other hand, was good for twenty high-powered shots and could be recharged from any fusion power source. When the target was in plain line of sight, the onager had priority.

But the onager wasn't firing, and the attack pod was starting to move once again.

"Fire, damn it!" The angry voice was loud in Wolf's ear. "Fire the goddamned onager! Fire *something*, for Tophet's sake!"

The Ubrenfar vehicle was gathering speed, closing on his position. Wolf's fingers danced over the Fafnir's programming keys, feeding in the target type information the fire-and-forget missile needed to lock on and attack.

Suddenly a bolt of raw energy surged across the open field as Antonelli opened fire at last. A clump of scrub a good fifty meters to the left of the target vanished in the searing fury of the onager bolt. The attack pod shot off at an angle on powerful fusion airjets, disappearing behind another low ridgeline. Wolf squeezed the trigger on the Fafnir, watching the missile streak skyward and then arc down.

There was a flash before the warhead was even below the masking terrain. A moment later the attack pod was in sight again, its weapons trained precisely on Wolf's foxhole.

Then the image flickered and faded out as the holographic projector creating the illusion cut out.

"You're dead, Stinky!" Vanyek shouted from behind him. "No more perfume for you, ever, and all thanks to Lover-boy!"

"Ah, shit, man," Antonelli said, clambering out of his own foxhole and pulling off the heavy-duty combat helmet that covered his face. "If he'd started shooting before the machine broke cover that *bastardo* never would've come close."

Wolf didn't respond. For three days now Vanyek's section had been training with support weapons, with each lance in turn acting the part of a heavy weapons unit on the firing range. The standard doctrine for engagements like this one had been drummed into them over and over, but Antonelli seemed unable or unwilling to comprehend the role each weapon was supposed to play in combat.

"Get your sorry asses down here," Vanyek snapped. "Now!"

Wolf checked the Fafnir's safety and trotted back from the firing line to the trench where Vanyek and the other recruits waited. It took longer for Antonelli to cross the distance, hampered as he was by the bulky onager and the full body armor required to protect him from the weapon's deadly, scorching backblast. As the Italian appeared at the lip of the trench and started to climb down, Vanyek swore and darted toward him.

"Christ Almighty!" the corporal said. His hand reached up to yank the power cord connecting the weapon to Antonelli's ConRig harness assembly. A red light on top of the onager went out. "You strakking idiot, you didn't safe your weapon! You could've fried everybody, damn it!"

Antonelli blanched and stammered his response. "I-I'm s-s-sorry …"

"Sorry doesn't cut it, you stupid bastard!" Vanyek shouted, thrusting his face a few centimeters from the Italian's. "Never, ever leave the firing line without safing your weapon, for God's sake! Now get out of that armor. You're done for the day."

As Kern and Scott moved forward to help Antonelli start to un-strap his armor, Vanyek turned away to address the section as a whole. "All right! Critique! What did these two straks do wrong out there? Myaighee!"

The hannie shot an apologetic glance at Antonelli before he replied. "Volunteer Antonelli should, by doctrine, have engaged the target as soon as it was in plain sight. The Fafnir must be preserved as a weapon of last recourse, except as specified otherwise by higher authority."

"True enough," Vanyek said. "Mayzar?"

The leader of Echo lance answered briskly. "When he did fire the onager, Antonelli overcompensated on the aim. The onager is more responsive than it looks, because the ConRig slaves the tracking system to the operator's eye movements." He sounded like he was reciting from the instruction chip. "As a result, his shot was too wide to do any good, and there was no opportunity for a second attempt."

Vanyek gave him a curt nod. Mayzar had spent more than his share of time trying to get the hang of the tricky ConRig system. Although he was one of the most experienced soldiers in the recruit company, his time with the Centauri Rangers had stressed other skills than heavy weaponry, and he was sadly out of practice. It was no wonder he could quote the chip instructions verbatim. He'd gone over them often enough.

"Who else noticed mistakes?"

None of the other recruits answered. After a long pause, the corporal turned to face Wolf. "All right, here's a few. Wolf waited to program his target type until he had visual verification of the pod even though he knew that was what we were going to be up against...."

"But—" Wolf bit off the rest of his protest too late. He grunted as Vanyek slapped his arm with the stun baton.

"It takes no longer to reprogram a Fafnir than it does to program from scratch," Vanyek went on as if nothing had happened. "If your intel briefings say you're up against a specific weapons system you should be ready to handle it. Just make sure you're also ready to handle surprises quickly as they arise. Preprogramming the Fafnir might have given you the edge to hit the bastard while he was still scurrying for cover."

He let the point sink in for a moment before jabbing his baton at Kern. "And you, nube. Where were you in all this?"

The redhead looked glum. "I should have laid down sustained fire as soon as the pod came into view, Corporal," he said. The big ex-Marine looked down at the MEK he still cradled in his hands. It was a larger, heavier version of the FEK with a bigger magazine and larger-caliber ammo, useful for antipersonnel and general suppression fire.

"That's right," Vanyek said with a sarcastic edge to his voice. "Your fire might have caused the bad guys to hesitate even if you couldn't penetrate their armor. The mix of weapons in your lance is designed to be mutually supporting, and you weren't pulling your share. Why not?"

Kern looked embarrassed. "I guess I knew that the simulation wouldn't be diverted that way, Corporal," he admitted slowly. "So I didn't want to waste the ammo."

Vanyek looked at him with an expression that mingled disappointment and distaste for a long moment. "We'll give you some time to think about that doing a few laps around the range in place of lunch," he said at last. He raised his voice. "I expect you all to treat every exercise exactly like the real thing. You understand me?"

The corporal glared at the recruits. "Next point. Myaighee, you're the lance leader. Why weren't you taking charge?"

The hannie looked back at Vanyek, neck ruff stiffening. "I understood this to be an exercise for the gunners, Corporal," he said slowly.

"The lance is a unit, damn it!" Vanyek shot back. "You should know that by now! In the field it would have been your job to encourage your gunners ... and to give the order releasing the Fafnir sooner. You said it yourself: higher authority is supposed to decide when to override doctrine. Your job! Nobody fired until I said something, and they don't issue instructors in your battlefield supplies!"

There were some chuckles from the rest of the section. Wolf started to smile, not so much at the corporal's joke as at the satisfaction of seeing Myaighee taken down a peg or two. Because of the hannie's past Legion experience the little alien had always come across as a cut above the rest of the recruits. And although Wolf had come to admire his skill in handling the disparate characters in the lance, he still found it hard to accept a nonhuman as a superior. Now that the hannie had made a mistake, maybe attitudes would be changing....

"And you can wipe that grin off your face, Stinky," Vanyek said sharply, jerking Wolf out of his reverie with a quick brush of his stun baton. "Just because you didn't have orders is no reason to sit still and do nothing!"

He replied without thinking. "But doctrine ..."

Vanyek jabbed him in the stomach with the stun baton, and he doubled over in pain as the muscles of his stomach and diaphragm went into spasm. "Doctrine is no excuse for stupidity, nube," the corporal told him. He stepped back, raising his voice for the benefit of the others. "When are you straks gonna get it through your heads that this is combat training? Kill or be killed, that's the name of the game. Out on the battlefield you have to think for yourself. If you stick to one set of rules and freeze up when you can't find some tenet of doctrine to cover your ass you're gonna end up dead ... maybe take a bunch of your buddies out with you, too. So you use doctrine, but you use your own initiative, too. If you see that something's not going the way it's supposed to—and that pretty much describes any battle you'll ever be in—then you have to adapt. Act. Don't just sit still and wait to get killed."

Lisa Scott raised a diffident hand. "Corporal?"

"What is it, Scott?" Vanyek's voice was almost gentle, now. She was the only one of the five who hadn't drawn his ire.

"If we're supposed to think for ourselves, why drum the by-the-book doctrine into us?"

The corporal gave a thin-lipped smile. "Because the rest of the army, not having the benefit of seeing screwups like you, still believes in a perfect world," he said quietly. "It's true that under textbook conditions it would be best to take out an attack pod with an onager and save the Fafnirs for better targets. And we'd rather see you try it that way because Fafnir warheads are expensive and we don't want to waste them ... nor do we want to use up all our shots the first time the bad guys show up, and end up with nothing but rocks to throw at them later on. So we teach you to give the onagers a chance at the easy targets first."

Vanyek's voice became harder. "But at the same time you've got to learn to really put yourself into a fight. It won't be a practice exercise when you're out in the field. Mistakes will kill people. So you've got to learn to judge when to play it by the book, and when to throw the book aside and make it up as you go along."

Wolf was still feeling the effects of the stun baton, but the corporal's words struck a familiar chord. He remembered the battle in the corridors on Telok, the moment when he'd panicked. Maybe if he had shown more initiative then, instead of giving in to appearances, things might have gone differently. Not just the battle, but everything that had followed. The quarrel with Neubeck ... the duel ... his flight from Robespierre....

The pain of that battle was still like a raw nerve, but he forced himself to think about it. His lack of sound judgment in that fight had convinced him. He would never be a leader of men.

Now he was beginning to realize that it could keep him from being a soldier as well....

*   *   *

Mario Antonelli listened to the corporal's systematic critique of the lance with a sinking feeling of failure and despair. *Nothing* he did ever

seemed to come out right. Somehow he'd avoided washing out of training so far, but he was making no more than a barely passing mark. Sooner or later he wouldn't even manage that, and then it would all be over.

Why couldn't he deal with the training better? Why couldn't he fit
in here?

All the talk about the legionnaires being a family, helping out each
other, that had been a big lie. No one had offered *him* any help. If you
weren't a perfect little rembot who snapped to on command, you were
beat up, and nobody lifted a finger to save you. They all said they cared.
"The Legion takes care of its own" was how they kept putting it, but it
wasn't so. He was an outcast, would always remain an outcast among
these people who always demanded more than he was able to give.

Sometimes he thought it would be better to just give up, leave the
Legion and serve out his sentence with a penal battalion. At least then
he wouldn't have to face the constant pressure, the continual bullying
from the instructors and the unspoken amusement of his lancemates.

But if he didn't make it with the Legion, he'd lose that look of
pride he'd finally kindled in his father's eyes. The old man probably
wouldn't survive the shock if he found out his son had been con-
signed to a penal battalion.

The sharp pain of a stun baton across his shoulder blades made him
jump. "You want to get with the program, nube?" Vanyek bellowed
into his face. "Or am I boring you?"

"N-no, Corporal!" he said, snapping to attention.

The NCO struck him again, but the shock setting was lower and
just made his shoulder and neck tingle. "What you did out there was
bad enough," he growled. "But ignoring the range safety regs is a
screw-up you don't make twice in *my* unit. You get me, nube?"

"Y-yes, Corporal." The reply was anything but crisp.

Vanyek hefted the baton in one hand as if contemplating the best
place to apply it, then lowered the wand and turned away from the
Italian.

"All right, that's enough for this morning," Vanyek said at last.
"We'll try another drill this afternoon. Get your gear, fall out, and head
for the mess hall."

The recruits looked surprised. By rights he should have kept them
on the firing line for at least another quarter hour, and after what had
happened none of them would have been shocked if he'd kept them
longer....

As Antonelli started to bend over to round up his equipment Vanyek stopped him with the baton, its power turned all the way off this time. "Not you, Antonelli. You stay here. We still have some things to talk about." He turned away again. "And you, Kern, you start your laps. I'll let you know when to stop!"

The redhead nodded and moved off at a trot, leaving the others to round up his MEK and combat helmet. When everyone was gone Vanyek spoke again, his tone quiet and almost sympathetic.

"Listen to me, Antonelli," he said slowly. "And listen good. I know the training is tough, and I also know that you've been trying as hard as anyone. But you're still making mistakes—stupid mistakes—that you should have stopped making the first week of training. Normally I'd work you over for a while with this." He hefted the stun baton for emphasis. "You'd have a few aches and pains to remind you to do better, and we'd move on. But I've done that enough to know that it isn't gonna help this time. The question is, what *will* get you motivated?"

Antonelli didn't answer, didn't know how to answer.

The corporal looked at him for a long time in silence, then shook his head. "I just don't know. I really expected you to snap in and start showing some skill, kid. Your kind usually do well in the Legion. But it's clear you're heading straight for an unsatisfactory mark on your training record. That means you struggle on for days or weeks longer, with noncoms using you for a punching bag and poking these glorified joy buzzers at you until you do something really dumb and get sent to the penal battalions ... or you might not do anything spectacular and still wind up doing hard labor because your performance just isn't up to specs. Maybe you ought to just drop it now and save yourself the grief."

"No!" Antonelli said, pulling back. "No! I can cut it ... I *have* to!"

"It's not that big a deal, kid. Penal battalions are no picnic, but it's not really as tough as the Legion in some ways. You won't get your Citizenship back, but ..."

Antonelli shook his head violently. "Let me keep trying, man! Please!" He hesitated. "*I miel genitore* ... my parents, my whole family ... they don't know I was sentenced. They think I volunteered. And they were proud of me...."

"That won't help you much if you pull an unsat rating, kid," he said gently.

"It will kill *mio babbo*, my father, if I don't make it," Antonelli went on as if he hadn't heard. "It'll kill him. I've gotta keep trying...."

"I can't force you to put in for the penal battalions, kid," Vanyek said reluctantly. "If you won't go voluntarily, you'll have to earn yourself a trip there. Which is what you'll do if you don't buckle down and show some improvement pretty damned quick. What'll your parents think if you keep screwing up the way you did today, huh, kid?"

The recruit didn't answer.

"All right," Vanyek told him. "You've had your warning. Just remember that you're about a centimeter shy of an unsat already, so you'd better get your act together. You'll pull two hours a night extra duty on the indoor weapons range for the rest of this training phase. By the time you're through I expect you to take that onager and use it to light a narcostick a klick away without hitting the guy who's smoking it. Think you can handle that, nube?"

"Y-yes, Corporal," Antonelli responded, pulling himself to attention. There was a long pause. "And ... *grazie*. Thanks."

"Don't thank me, nube," Vanyek told him. "Not until you pass. Now ... what shall we have you do to learn about range safety? Maybe what you need is some exercise with your buddy Red, hmm?"

Antonelli followed his gesture and saw Kern rounding the far end of the practice range. He suppressed a groan and started to run, but inwardly he was elated. He had a second chance ... and he would work twice as hard this time to make it work.

Chapter Fourteen

As for myself, my tongue was down at least to my feet, but I kept going, knowing what awaited stragglers.

> —Legionnaire Eugene Amiable,
> Mexican Campaign,
> French Foreign Legion, 1863-1867

Engaged Volunteer Wolf. Four weeks' service. Delta Lance, Second Platoon, Training Company Odintsev. At your orders, Sergeant!"

As he went through the ritual recitation of name and unit, Wolf drew himself up to rigid attention beside the door to his cubicle. In thirty-four days the recruits had become accustomed to the routine. Twice each day, just before breakfast and before evening lights out, the NCOs held an inspection of the recruit quarters. A noncom in a bad mood could find plenty of things wrong during inspection. Even if the lockers and bunks were flawless, like as not Corporal Vanyek would tip a recruit's belongings on the floor and then punish the luckless trainee and the rest of the lance as well. One night Vanyek had rescheduled evening roll call four times before finally letting them turn in at 2600 hours.

This morning, though, Gunnery Sergeant Ortega was conducting the inspection in person. Wolf hoped the senior NCO would be satisfied with what he saw.

Ortega prodded the contents of Wolf's locker with his stun baton and gave a reluctant nod. "Better, nube. Better," he said grudgingly. He started to turn away, then looked back at Wolf. "But I can still smell your perfume. Ten push-ups, nube."

Ten push-ups, after the calisthenics program the Legion had put him through, was little enough. Wolf dropped to the floor....

And Corporal Vanyek stepped nimbly onto his back. "Begin, nube," he ordered harshly.

Wolf strained to lift the extra weight. Somehow, he got through the exercise as Ortega moved to the next cubicle. He was surprised when Vanyek held out a hand to help him up.

It was somehow typical of the training regimen, he thought as he snapped back to attention. Just when it seemed as if the instructors had finally gone too far, pushing a recruit beyond the limits of endurance, some little gesture like this one put everything back into perspective.

The company had spent a full two weeks at drills like the one with the simulated Ubrenfar pod, learning how to handle all sorts of special Legion-issue equipment. By the time it was all done with, Wolf knew how to handle a Fafnir or an onager, an MEK or a laser sniper's rifle, all in addition to the basic FEK. The recruits had learned all the useful functions of their combat helmets and had discovered the effectiveness of the climate-controlled, chameleonweave battledress fatigues in constant practice maneuvers. They had even been exposed to some of the more exotic gear in the Legion arsenal, like the Galahad anti-personnel mine and the complex C^3 communications backpacks. The program finished up with exposure to the APCs and AFVs that made up the Legion's mechanized arm. Some of what they learned was intended only as an introduction, since many of the more advanced systems were properly the realm of Legion specialists who had completed their first five-year hitch and gone on to advanced training, but the recruits learned enough to get by with virtually anything they might encounter in the field. Between chip instruction and practical experience, the recruits developed their skills quickly, though their progress was far from uniform. Wolf found his efforts drawing grudging approval from Vanyek and the other NCOs by the time it was over, but it was Kern, and more surprisingly Lisa Scott, who earned most of the praise in the lance. Kern was a natural with virtually all heavy weapons, especially the onager, while the blond woman showed a genuine flair for handling magrep armored vehicles.

Antonelli, on the other hand, continued to struggle. Although Kern, at Corporal Vanyek's direct order, devoted an hour of free time each night to extra tutoring, the Italian's performance was still barely up to the minimum he needed to stay in Basic. That put him under even more pressure than the rest of the recruits. Wolf could wash out of the training, even choose to resign voluntarily, and would be no worse off than when he'd started. But if Antonelli failed, he would end up sweating out his five years in a penal battalion with no hope of seeing his Citizenship restored. Even after his sentence was finished he'd still be paying the penalty for his petty crime, cut off from the easy life of the dole and without any worthwhile skills to help him make a fresh start.

His case drew sympathy from the other recruits, and even some of the instructors seemed concerned for him, but all the goodwill in the world couldn't make up for the simple fact that Antonelli wasn't cut out for the soldier's life. Five weeks of training had already seen twenty recruits dropped from the company, and it was clear to everyone that Antonelli wasn't far from joining them.

More and more, Wolf was beginning to feel a certain kinship for the youngster. Though he was doing far better than Antonelli in training, deep down Wolf was still an outsider. The rituals that bound the Legion together didn't reach him the way they did many of the others, and he was still conscious of the gulf that separated him culturally, socially, and intellectually from the rank and file around him. Sometimes the only thing that kept him going was pride. He was still determined to prove the doubters wrong and see the thing through, despite everything. But the knowledge that he didn't face the dilemma that hovered over Antonelli tempted him sometimes.

Now they were finished with weapons and equipment orientation. Tomorrow the recruits would move on to a new phase of their training. For the past five weeks Basic had concentrated on teaching the essentials of soldiering, and as Captain Odintsev had pointed out during one of his infrequent appearances at morning assembly a few days earlier, the recruits were now at a point that would have qualified them for active service in any of the armies of Terra before the days of starflight. But they were only a third of the way through the Legion's course, and what remained was a far more difficult curriculum than what had gone before.

He was roused from his reverie by Gunnery Sergeant Ortega. "You straks might be worth keeping after all," he growled. "At least until we get some real legionnaires in here. Right, then, listen up! Tomorrow you begin the next phase of training, the first of a series of two-week tours for intensive specialized training in multienviron operations. Your first assignment is to the Archipel d'Aurore for practice in jungle and amphibious warfare ops and advanced recon."

The soldier of the Commonwealth was expected to serve on a variety of different worlds, each as complex and diverse as Laut Besar or Old Terra. There was no way to prepare the recruits for every possibility, but according to the training chips this phase of Basic was designed to get them accustomed to as many different environments and situations as possible. As Kern had put it in a late-night bull session, the purpose of the multiple-environ portion of the program wasn't so much to prepare them to serve in the specific conditions they would be exposed to, but rather to make the would-be soldiers aware of the range and diversity of their possible duty stations ... and to drive home the simple but often overlooked fact that every new environment possessed its own unique properties, its own tactical realities. And its own individual dangers.

"For the rest of the day you'll be getting ready to move out," Ortega continued with the faint smile the recruits had come to associate with trouble on the horizon. "But I don't want any of you to get the idea that you'll be short of work to do. Corporal...?"

Vanyek consulted his compboard. "Delta Lance ... you'll be getting a workout down at the shuttle bay, loading platoon equipment onto the transport."

"In addition, you will be responsible for packing up your own kits and policing the barracks here," Ortega went on smoothly. "And each of you will be expected to draw the background chip on Fort Marchand to get acquainted with your new duty station before you leave the base tomorrow morning. Any questions?"

There were none. Ortega smiled again and checked his wristpiece. "Ah, yes. I almost forgot. Antonelli!"

"Yes, Sergeant!"

"Starting tonight, you will spend one hour of each free period working on a special project."

"Yes, Sergeant!" Antonelli was learning that it was best to stick to the safe response, though he still forgot and talked back sometimes in the heat of drills or practice sessions. Wolf wondered, though, how the young Italian would handle yet another extra assignment. He was already spending most of his free time trying to keep up with his studies, and it was a rare week that didn't see him pulling nighttime punishment details as well.

The sergeant smiled coldly. "Good attitude, nube," he commented. Shifting his glance to take in the others, he went on. "Christmas comes in just under five weeks. One of our regular ways of observing the holiday is to hold competitions in the construction of cribs, Nativity scenes. Since you've shown special aptitude working with your hands, Antonelli, I thought you'd be a good candidate for your platoon's team. Volunteer Mayzar is in charge of the proceedings. Report to him in the repbay tonight. The work will continue when you get settled into your new duty station, and up until the Christmas training break. Understood?"

"Yes, Sergeant!" Antonelli's expression didn't reveal if he was happy or unhappy with this added duty. Nor did anyone seem to find it odd that Volunteer Hosni Mayzar, a native of Mecca Gideed where over ninety percent of the population was made up of Moslem extremists, was in charge of preparing a Christian Nativity scene. Just as everyone attended Sunday services with a Catholic chaplain, so the entire unit was expected to follow the Legion line when it came to holidays and observances.

"If any of the rest of you can carry a tune, Corporal Vanyek will be in charge of the holiday music program," Ortega went on. "You're expected to teach the other singers at least one carol from your native culture ... if, of course, your culture observes Christmas." His eye rested on Myaighee, and it looked like he was trying to hide the ghost of a smile. Maybe even fanatics like Ortega realized the irony of some of their actions, at that.

"All right, that's enough small talk. Fall in on the parade ground for the march to the mess hall. Mag it!"

Wolf thought he heard Kern humming some old Irish carol as they headed out the door.

Perhaps, he thought with a twinge of uncertainty, perhaps the Legion knew more than he did about involving recruits in the life of the unit.

* * *

The preparations that day took as much time and effort as a long training session, but eventually the work was done and Wolf and the others could tumble into their bunks for some much-needed rest.

Reveille came an hour early the next morning, and all four platoons of the training company traveled by maglev tube to the shuttle port.

At Sergeant Konrad's order Second Platoon filed aboard the TH-19 Pegasus hypersonic transport at Docking Bay Eight. Wolf already knew the sleek craft's lines all too well from the loading duty the previous day. The Pegasus was an old shuttle design, no longer used much in frontline duty except by the Legion. It could reach any point on a Terrestrial-type planet in less than an hour, and performed ground-to-orbit service as well, but the design definitely emphasized rugged efficiency over comfort. Wolf stowed his field pack under the bench seat between Kern and Lisa Scott, then strapped in, but it was a long time before the shuttle received clearance to take off.

He spent the time reviewing the background on their new base, knowing they'd probably be quizzed by some of the NCOs before the trip was over. The Archipel d'Aurore was a scattering of large islands to the east of the primary continent which stretched in a loose arc right across the planet's broad equatorial zone. Instead of the dry barrens around Fort Hunter, the recruits would now be coping with the tropical heat and humidity of a region popularly referred to by older legionnaires as the Devil's Cauldron.

Although most of the islands were covered by dense jungle, they were far from uninhabited. The Archipel d'Aurore was the source of one of Devereaux's most important exports, the sap of the *arbebaril*, and plantations raising the stubby, multitrunked trees dotted the island chain. The Legion outpost where Second Platoon would receive its jungle warfare training had been founded on the largest of the islands— actually more of a small continent—to protect the plantations. Its role in the training process was only secondary. For the first time the recruits would be facing actual field conditions.

That might mean a certain amount of danger. Although the region around Fort Hunter was thoroughly settled, civilized, the same couldn't be said of the eastern island chain. Like most of the back-water areas of the planet, the Archipel d'Aurore was home to large numbers of Wynsarrysa, and many of them were hostile to the human colonists on Devereaux.

The Wynsarrysa were the original inhabitants of the world, not native to the planet but descendants of a Gwyrran colony planted there nearly a thousand years before the first visit by Terrans. The Gwyrrans had been a key client race in the old Semti Conclave, which had exercised rigorous control over its subjects in everything from interstellar movement to technology to social organization until they were finally overcome by vigorous, unpredictable humans.

Devereaux had been a major point of contention in the Semti War. The Gwyrrans—massive, ponderous, slow-thinking, but with a reputation as warriors that nearly matched the Ubrenfars—had proven unable to make their settlement flourish, and the colonists had lapsed into a state of barbarism which the calculating Semti had found entirely to their liking. When Terran explorers had first arrived, they found the locals to be few in number and too primitive to be a significant factor in planetary development, and promptly planted a human colony on the primary continent.

The new Devereaux colony had suffered during the war. The Semti, with their Gwyrran combat auxiliaries, reoccupied the planet and set out to put an end to human resistance. The struggle had seen the end of the Fourth Foreign Legion, which had been assigned to protect the world. Commandant Hunter's band of guerrillas were the last to resist, but in the end they'd fallen almost to a man ... but they had won the Commonwealth valuable time to organize a counterthrust that ultimately destroyed the artificial world that had formed the heart and soul of the Conclave.

The Wynsarrysa had flourished again for the brief months of the Semti occupation, only to be disarmed and dispossessed by the new waves of human colonists who arrived after the fighting was over. Most had been absorbed into society, but there were a stubborn few who refused to bow to the new masters. They continued an uneven guerrilla struggle, raiding settlements and living a marginal, outlaw existence. And the Fifth Foreign Legion remained on Devereaux to keep them in check, guarding the inhabited regions of the planet from outposts like Fort Marchand.

That meant that the recruits would be training in an area that could erupt into violence at any time. The dense jungles of the archipelago region were especially favorable to the rebels, who could use the cover to dodge orbital and aerial drone reconnaissance efforts. That meant that even though the Wynsarrysa were no match for legionnaires in a stand-up fight, anyone who strayed too far from the fort or straggled during a march would be fair game for guerrillas. The orientation chip had made that point abundantly clear.

As he'd expected, the assistant platoon leader, Sergeant Baram, spent most of the time they were in the air barking out names and questions about Fort Marchand, the Archipel d'Aurore, and the conditions they could expect to encounter in the region. The trip took less than half an hour, but it seemed three times as long in the face of Baram's relentless interrogation. Fortunately, the one question that came Wolf's way, regarding Chief-Sergeant Guy Marchand's role in the last stand on Devereaux, was one he could answer. Antonelli was less fortunate, and earned himself another five hours of extra duty for failing to remember the percentage of the planetary export revenue attributable to *arbebaril* sap.

At last they grounded and the questioning ended. As Wolf and his lancemates filed down from the shuttle, he was struck first by the heat, so different from the arid climate around Fort Hunter. It had been hot there at the edge of the Great Desert, but this heat lay over everything like a heavy, soaking blanket. His first deep breath of outside air made him sputter and cough.

The other thing he noticed was Fort Marchand itself.

It was a compact base surrounded by a perimeter fence dotted by prefab watchtowers and presumably ringed by sensors and, perhaps, mines. The shuttle had grounded in the northwest corner of the compound, inside the fence, which helped drive home the danger of the region. Usually shuttle bays were kept at a discreet distance from inhabited areas in case of an engine failure, but that wasn't the case here.

Looking around, Wolf couldn't help but draw the comparisons with Fort Hunter. This was no ceremonial headquarters and training center. There was a functional feel to the camp ... and to the grim-faced legionnaires who stood watch over the perimeter.

Fort Marchand was part of the real world.

"All right, you nubes!" Corporal Vanyek barked. "Enough gawking! Mag it! Mag it!"

They trotted across the parade ground, full kits hitched high on their backs, urged on by the noncoms. The block of transient barracks that served as the compound's training center was cramped, and their new quarters made the facilities back at Fort Hunter look positively luxurious by comparison. But there wasn't much time for grumbling. Less than fifteen minutes was allowed for stowing gear before the platoon was assembled in front of the building to sweat at attention while Konrad addressed them in ponderous, heavy-accented tones.

"Welcome to the Legion!" he began. "Up until now you nubes have lived the good life and thought it was hell. Now we'll show you how legionnaires really live every day of their lives. You'll soon think back to the easy days at Fort Hunter and feel wistful for the good life, I assure you." He waved his stun baton, a gesture that took in the entire compound. "Fort Marchand is a real Legion post manned by real legionnaires, and you nubes will do well to stay out from underfoot except as your duties require. Remember that these men have jobs to do, and in the field the smallest disruption can cost lives.

"There have been reports of Wynsarrysa activity in this area in the last several weeks," Konrad continued harshly, his gaze wandering over the ranks freely now. "It is probably nothing significant, and it will not interrupt the training schedule ... but you must all be constantly aware of the fact that out here things are not the same as they were in Fort Hunter. Out here you must behave as if you were really in the field, where a mistake can be deadly not just to you but to all of your comrades." The sergeant's eyes seemed to be resting on Wolf. "Do not let your guard down. Not even for a moment. Because the legionnaire who lowers his guard is a dead man."

Chapter Fifteen

oin the Legion, they say. Adventure. Excitement. Why the hell did I ever listen to that shit?"

Wolf smiled as the other legionnaire, a massive, shaven-headed black from Uhuru, spat expansively without missing a beat in his grumbling commentary. Volunteer Otema Banda had raised discontent to an art form, but somehow never seemed to run afoul of the NCO instructors.

"Ah, but just think what you would've missed by not signing up, laddie." That was Robert Bruce MacDuff, Banda's lancemate. "Why, who would have believed you could stuff ten healthy soldiers into such a small space and expect them not merely to survive, but in fact to fight like demons when they emerge? Mind you, it's my theory that anyone would go out and defy death in battle knowing that the alternative is climbing back into one of these floating coffins!"

Laughter filled the compartment. Ten recruits from two of Second Platoon's lances were crowded into the back of the M-786 Sandray armored personnel carrier, and although it was supposed to carry twelve plus a crew of two in "ordinary field use," the vehicle was by no means spacious. Even though the platoon was getting used to the routine of recon exercises after more than a week at Fort Marchand, no one claimed to find the confining ride in a Sandray comfortable.

Today's mission was a typical one-vehicle, two-lance patrol. Wolf and the rest of Myaighee's Deltas were equipped as a heavy weapons lance again, with Antonelli carrying the onager and Wolf the Fafnir launcher just as they had before. They were accompanied by Charlie Lance, from the platoon's first section, and for a change Corporal Vanyek wasn't supervising the exercise. This time they were under the orders of the assistant platoon leader, Sergeant Baram. Vanyek was conducting a separate exercise with Echo and Foxtrot lances somewhere else in the far-flung Archipel d'Aurore, and Wolf for one was glad to be out from under his stern eye for a change.

It was the first time in weeks that Wolf had been thrown together with Robert Bruce MacDuff, and that was another welcome break in the routine. Though they were members of the same platoon, they rarely saw one another. Most of the time exercises were performed by individual lances, or sometimes by sections, and it was only since the start of the second phase that they had started to work in two-lance groups like this one. By the end of their stay at Fort Marchand they were supposed to be into full-platoon operations, which would be considerably more complex.

For the moment, though, the chance to renew the acquaintance with MacDuff was enough of a boost to Wolf's morale to let him put aside concerns for the future. The young Caledonian, irreverent and carefree as ever, seemed to have adapted well to the training program.

The Sandray lurched, throwing Wolf sideways against Lisa Scott. He straightened up quickly, but not before she elbowed him just under the chest plate. It was just typical recruit horseplay, nothing serious, but it was a hard enough jab to make him grunt. That brought a laugh from some of the other recruits.

"Goddamned student drivers," he said, bracing himself with one hand on a strap beside his head. The contingent acting as the platoon's transport unit was drawn from veteran legionnaires who were going through advanced training as vehicle crews, and some of them still hadn't learned how to control their responsive charges. The APC rode on magnetic suspension fields, moving under the thrust of powerful turbofans, but sudden shifts in direction were just as violent for the passengers as anything an old-fashioned groundcar would have caused. Wolf noticed that Antonelli, the full body armor that went with his onager complete except for helmet, gauntlets, and power pack, was looking distinctly pale at the uneven motion. He'd earned himself a hundred push-ups two days earlier after throwing up during one exer-cise, and Wolf hoped the younger recruit wasn't going to be sick again today.

At least the exercise wasn't likely to offer any surprises. These prac-tice recon runs went down pretty much the same way each time. The Sandray carried two lances out to some remote island, the troops practiced quick deployment under simulated combat conditions, and then proceeded to conduct reconnaissance and attack exercises in a variety of different terrain conditions. The tacdata briefing chip for today's mission had indicated they'd be focusing on movement through marshes and thick secondary jungle, and that didn't sound like it would offer any unusual complications. Wolf was beginning to get an old hand's tolerance for the repeated exercises.

The Sandray skewed sideways at high speed, an even more violent motion than before, and recruits around the rear compartment cursed and held on.

"Listen up, back there," Sergeant Menachem Baram's voice crack-led in Wolf's headphones. He was in the cab up front, with the driver, occupying the seat that would normally have been reserved for a gunner for the Sandray's kinetic energy cannon. "We're diverting to check out a possible trouble spot. When you get the order to dismount, do it fast and clean. This won't just be another exercise. So don't screw it up!"

The channel went dead, and for a moment everything in the troop compartment was quiet. Then Banda spat again. "Yeah. Right. I guess they think we'll jump through hoops for them if they peddle this 'not just another exercise' shit. Bastards just don't give up."

"I'm not so sure," Kern said softly from his seat beside Wolf's. He had flipped his helmet's faceplate down. "Take a look at the feed from the forward cameras."

Wolf fumbled for a moment getting his own faceplate down and patched into the Sandray's video system. Suddenly he was gazing across a broad expanse of ocean at a humpbacked island swelling noticeably as the APC sped toward it. Most of the visible land was covered by a dark tangle of jungle. Numbers scrolled along the bottom of the view, readouts of the vehicle's speed, course, and precise location, but he paid only minimal attention to any of them.

It was the black smear of smoke coiling above the island that held Wolf's attention. He let out a low whistle. "I don't like the looks of that," he said somberly.

"Me, neither," Lisa Scott said, her voice muffled by her own helmet. "From the grid coordinates, that would have to be the Ile de Mouton, wouldn't it?"

Wolf checked the numbers unreeling across the lower left-hand corner of the display and tried to match them in his mind to the area map they'd been studying for the past week, but he wasn't sure enough to verify her conclusion. She was better at map work than he was, and he suspected that her excellent memory was the product of a computer implant in her brain. Frustrated, he cut the feed and raised the faceplate.

"Ye've got that right, lass," MacDuff said a moment later. He flipped his own faceplate up. "Right there on the map ... not very large, but there's a plantation marked on the northeast side. It just calls the place Savary's here."

"It could just be a fire," Katrina Voskovich, another member of Char-lie Lance, spoke up. Like Myaighee, she had come to training from Colin Fraser's Legion company, but she didn't carry herself like a veteran. Her tone was more hopeful than convinced. "The briefings said that *arbebaril* sap is flammable...."

"Yeah ... but the fire could've been set, too." Kern snapped his faceplate up again. So did Scott. "By rebels. We'd better figure on hostiles in the neighborhood. If it turns out it was caused by a careless foreman with a narcostick, then we get a pleasant surprise. But it's better to be ready for the worst."

"Like the man said, it isn't just an exercise this time," Engaged Volunteer Yen Chen, acting lance leader of Charlie Lance, said. He was a small Oriental whose talent in hand-to-hand fighting was a legend in Second Platoon, and Wolf had heard him described as completely unflappable. But he sounded tense and preternaturally alert now.

No one else spoke as the APC continued on its way. Each of the recruits checked over weapons and field kits, actions they'd performed hundreds of times under the cold eyes of their instructors but which seemed somehow different, more urgent, now that the drills had become terrifyingly real.

Even Antonelli seemed to have his mind completely on the job for a change. Kern and Myaighee were helping him into the last of his onager armor, finishing up by settling the heavy helmet over his swarthy features. Unlike the standard combat helmets, the rest of them wore, Antonelli's didn't have a movable faceplate. It covered his whole head and fastened to the collar of his chest armor, providing a sealed environment that was proof against any atmosphere as well as the incredible heat generated by the plasma rifle he carried. With the addition of air tanks to replace the filter intakes at the rear of the helmet Antonelli could have worn the same garb in vacuum.

The Italian checked the power connections on the onager and powered it up just long enough to confirm it was fully charged, then safed the weapon and sat down again on the bench. The extra practice he'd been putting in, Wolf thought, was paying off now.

Wolf checked his Fafnir just as carefully, but not without a wistful glance at the FEKs most of the other recruits were carrying. The Wynsarrysa guerrillas didn't have access to the kind of heavy equipment the missile launcher was designed to counter, and it was likely he'd have little to do in the event of a fire fight. The thought reminded him to check his FE-PLF rocket pistol, the backup weapon he would use in case of a close-in threat. The laser sniper's rifle MacDuff was carrying would have suited him far better.

"Approaching target," Baram reported from the driver's cab. "We've got fires and heavy smoke around the OZ, so go to Echo Charlie Three and set your vision circuits to Image Enhance."

"Echo Charlie Three, Image Enhance." Myaighee, as the ranking recruit lance leader, repeated the orders back. Environmental Condition Three called for lowered faceplates and the attachment of a breathing filter across the lower portion of the combat helmet, while image enhancement would use computer processing to improve the quality of helmet-mounted video cameras using normal light and magnification settings.

Wolf unhooked the filter attachment from his web gear and snapped it into place, taking a few deep breaths to make sure it was working properly. Then he dropped the faceplate into place, turned on the cameras, and switched to the image enhancement mode. The image flickered, but in the well-lit compartment there was nothing for the computer to interpret and the view didn't change noticeably. All around him the others were going through the same drill. They were ready.

Or at least as ready as they could be....

The whine of the turbofans rose in pitch as the Sandray slid crabwise around some obstacle. Then the vehicle halted suddenly and grounded with an abrupt jar. "By lances, deploy!" Baram shouted over the comm circuit. "Standard dispersal and perimeter! Mag Out!"

The rear door was dropping as he spoke, and Voskovich and one of her lancemates, whose name was Owens, were already on their feet and moving before the ramp reached the ground. FEKs at the ready, they scrambled out and took up crouching positions on either side of the Sandray. Yeh Chen and Banda followed moments later, to take their places as the first two fanned out further. MacDuff, his laser sniper's rifle cradled in his hands, was next out.

Then it was time for the Deltas to go. "Delta Lance, move out," Myaighee ordered calmly.

Antonelli, with the heaviest firepower, followed MacDuff, moving more slowly than the other recruits but secure in the knowledge that there were few weapons on Devereaux outside of Legion arsenals that could have penetrated his combat armor. He was followed by Myaighee and Scott. Kern, carrying the bulky MEK, and Wolf with his Fafnir, dismounted last.

He dropped to one knee beside Scott at the base of the ramp and scanned the terrain cautiously. The computer chip in his helmet needed a few seconds to fully interpret the smoke-obscured surroundings, but it slowly began to fill in the details as he looked. The effect was like having a haze slowly lifted under the morning sun.

It was a scene from hell.

The plantation consisted of a broad clearing holding five prefab colonial buildings surrounded by orderly rows of multitrunked barrel trees. At a guess, Wolf estimated it would have housed twenty or thirty people, and given the Commonwealth's tendency to use rembots for manual labor instead of lower-class workers that would have been about right for a midsized Devereaux plantation.

Not one of the buildings was intact now. The two-story manor building directly in front of Wolf and Scott was burning fiercely, and most of the doors and windows had been shattered. He thought he could identify the pockmark cratering on the wall around the main door as the scars from a wild barrage of 1 cm grenades fired from an FEK on the full-auto setting. Off to the left the blackest roil of smoke came from a windowless building that looked like a storehouse, where there were probably tanks of sap still smoldering.

But the real horror had nothing to do with the buildings. Eight bodies lay between the recruits and the manor house, and the sight of them made Wolf turn his head away for a moment before he could force himself to study them objectively.

From the look of it none of them had been killed there. They had been dragged from other parts of the compound, stripped, and laid out with arms and legs spread-eagled. Even from a range of twenty meters Wolf could see that the bodies had been mutilated as well.

Bile rose in his throat.

"Report!" Baram's voice was sharp, jerking Wolf back to reality. The savages who had done all this might still be somewhere near. He focused his attention on a thorough scan of the surrounding jungle as Yeh Chen's recruits made their observations in the order they had debarked.

"Charlie Two," Owens said. "No sign of life. Just burning buildings and … bodies."

"Charlie Five." That was Katrina Voskovich. She sounded sick. "That's all I see. Nothing moving. Nothing alive."

The others had the same negative reports. Even MacDuff's usually jaunty manner was distinctly subdued, and Antonelli didn't speak at all when his turn came.

Myaighee, on the other hand, was matter-of-fact, stepping smoothly into the awkward silence left by Antonelli. "Delta Leader. I see nothing in motion. Two groups of casualties, one north of the Sandray, one southwest. Eight bodies in each. All buildings showing smoke, but fires seem to have died out. My estimate is that it has been several h ours since this area was attacked."

The rest of the Deltas added nothing significant. Antonelli, when he finally managed to make his report, was barely able to speak, and Lisa Scott broke off halfway through, gagging. Wolf was last. "Delta Four," he said harshly. "I concur. Whoever was here is gone now."

"An observation based, no doubt, on your vast experience," Baram said sarcastically. He appeared in the rear door, in full kit with an FEK held at the ready. "Reassuring as Volunteer Wolf's opinions may be, I want this area searched. Thoroughly. Charlie Lance will carry out the recon in pairs, while Delta maintains overwatch from here. MacDuff, you're with me. Myaighee, you take your orders from Legionnaire Yancey. Understood?"

There was a chorus of acknowledgements. As Baram and the five recruits from Charlie Lance split up and moved cautiously away from the APC, Legionnaire Second Class Yancey spoke up. "Wolf, Scott, take a closer look at the casualties," the Sandray driver ordered. "Helmet cameras on relay. I'll record from here. The rest of you maintain watch. Mag it!"

Wolf handed his Fafnir to Kern and drew his rocket pistol. While Scott stood watch with her FEK, he moved cautiously to the first line of bodies and dropped to one knee beside one of them.

"Booby traps," the blonde said curtly.

He nodded, remembering a lecture Gunnery Sergeant Ortega had given early in Basic regarding the ways an unwary soldier could be maimed or killed by carelessness in the field. He studied the body carefully, trying to block out the grisly reality and concentrate on the task as if it was just another Legion exercise. But it wasn't easy.

The body was a man's, eyes still wide open and staring at the smoke-filled sky. He had probably been killed by surprise, judging from the way his throat had been slit. The other wounds had apparently been inflicted later—the ears and nose had been cut off, and a deep gash in the shape of an inverted V had been cut in the stomach and chest, with the point over the breastbone. A glance left and right showed that all of the victims had that same incision no matter what other wounds showed.

"I've seen that work before," Legionnaire Yancey commented over the commlink. "It was rebels, all right. The damned savages like to leave us ... messages like that."

"I see no signs of booby traps," Wolf said, trying to keep his voice even.

"You probably won't," Yancey replied. "Not when the bodies are laid out like that. But be careful anyway, nube. There's always a first time."

All of the bodies in both of the groups were much the same as the first one, but repetition didn't make the examinations any easier. Twelve men and four women had been treated the same way. Sergeant Baram reported finding three more bodies barricaded in one of the burnt-out buildings. From the signs, Baram said, the fires had been set during the fighting, and the humans had preferred to burn to death rather than fall into the hands of their assailants.

Baram and the recruits from Charlie Lance confirmed that the plantation was deserted. Returning to the APC, the sergeant spent ten long minutes in the driver's cab, putting in a call to higher authority at Fort Marchand. When he finally emerged, looking grim, he called them all together.

"This is a bad business," he began. "The bastards that did this might be a few hundred meters away, or they might have magged out entirely. There's no way to be sure without searching this whole damned island, and two lances of nubes ain't my idea of a proper search party."

"So what are we gonna do, Sarge?" Yancey asked.

"First thing is to bury those poor devils we found, and smother the fires that are still smoldering. With one lance keeping watch while the other works that's going to use up most of the daylight we've got left." He frowned. "Unfortunately they've had some other problems with rebels around Marchand today, and they won't be able to spare any more troops to check out this area until tomorrow. We've got orders to remain in place here until a regular patrol can relieve us."

"What the hell is there to guard, for Christ's sake?" Banda burst out.

The sergeant didn't react the way Wolf expected. Instead of a reprimand or a quick stroke of his stun baton, he simply shrugged. "There's gear in the processing shed that's worth a lot of credits. Robotics. The rebels even left a couple of floatcars in the repbay. Ordinary marauders would leave that stuff if they were in a hurry, but they could just be waiting for a chance to bring a boat in and haul off everything that isn't nailed down. Anyway, even if there wasn't anything they wanted, they could still move in after we left and prepare a nasty reception for the next bunch that comes in. I've seen them do that a time or two ... let an area be pronounced clear and then set up an ambush."

"So we stick it out until tomorrow," Yancey said.

"That's the size of it. After we finish the burials we'll deploy remote sensors out in the jungle in a perimeter line to protect the clearing here. If they do try to pay us a visit, they'll run into a hell of a lot of firepower." He glared at the recruits. "Think you nubes can handle it all?"

Myaighee replied before anyone else could respond. "It doesn't sound like we are in that much danger, Sergeant," he said softly. "It isn't that much different from an overnight route march."

"Yeah ... except for the fact that there are real hostiles out there somewhere," MacDuff added from the far edge of the semicircle of recruits. "But aside from that little detail, it's just a bleeding picnic."

There were a few laughs at that, but it was nervous, uneasy laughter.

Wolf, thinking about those mutilated bodies, didn't join in.

Chapter Sixteen

ario Antonelli felt a trickle of sweat running down his back and shifted uncomfortably. The sun had been down for hours now, but the cloying jungle heat still smothered the plantation clearing like a wet, heavy blanket.

His battledress fatigues were supposed to have built-in climate controls to compensate for extremes of heat and cold, but he'd been having trouble with the settings ever since the platoon had landed at Fort Marchand. One more thing, he thought bitterly, that he just couldn't manage to do right. At least Sergeant Baram had allowed him to stand his watch with a borrowed FEK and wearing his fatigues. The onager with its heavy armored protective gear would have been doubly uncomfortable tonight.

He fumbled with the studs on his wristpiece computer to try to correct the settings, but he couldn't see what he was doing. With his helmet faceplate set to receive sensor readings from the perimeter he was working blind. Suddenly angry, he cursed and cut off the external feed, then raised his faceplate and blinked a few times before he realized that the darkness around him was as thick and impenetrable as the jungle that lay only a few meters away. Konrad had assigned him to sentry duty, monitoring the perimeter sensor net, and after staring at the readout for what seemed like hours on end Antonelli had forgotten how black the nights in the Archipel d'Aurore could get.

Switching on a tiny light mounted on the side of his helmet, Anton-elli studied the 'piece. It was hooked directly into the uniform's climate-control system, and with a few quick touches he changed the settings that governed the environmental maintenance coils woven into the fabric of the battledress. He felt cooler almost at once.

Antonelli cut the light, but left his faceplate up for the moment. There was something almost comforting about the dark. The envel-oping blackness hid the sight of the burnt-out plantation, though it couldn't blot out the memory of the grisly tableaux of mutilated bodies arranged in their neat rows in the clearing. That was a scene that would remain burned into his brain for a long time to come.

He'd been assigned to the burial detail in the afternoon, and almost inevitably the horror of the bodies, the heat and humidity made even worse by his onager armor and the swaying motion he'd endured for over an hour in the Sandray before they reached the plantation, and cumulative fatigue from too many nights without enough sleep had all come together to hit him at once. Right in the middle of the work Ant-onelli had been overcome by wave after wave of nausea. He had torn his helmet off and tossed it aside as he doubled over to throw up. Afterward Baram had worked him twice as hard, and of course he'd been singled out to take the first watch after the rest of the party had turned in for the night.

He wasn't sure how much more he could take. The extra training Vanyek had handed him, solo practice and tutoring from Kern, had helped him squeak through Weapons Training and was keeping him even with the rest of the lance now that they were at Fort Marchand, but it was grueling. On top of that he had the Christmas craftwork Ortega had assigned, an hour or more each night, and it was a rare week that didn't see him pulling some kind of evening punishment duty as well.

Antonelli wasn't sure how much longer he could keep up with the physical pace the Legion was demanding of him. Sometimes he thought that was exactly why the instructors kept throwing more evening duty at him. After all, Vanyek had tried his best to convince him to accept failure as inevitable and resign ... maybe they had decided to push him to the breaking point and force him out since he refused to accept the trip to the penal battalions gracefully.

He shook his head wearily. He didn't really think it was any kind of deliberate plot. It was just that sometimes everything seemed stacked against him.

And he was just so damned tired all the time....

He leaned his head back against the trunk of the *arbebaril* behind him and closed his eyes. Just for a moment, to help him clear his head before he went back to staring at the sensor readouts....

Just for a moment....

* * *

Movement close by brought Lisa Scott instantly awake. That was something she had lived with for five years, the hair-trigger sensitivity that made her react to the slightest hint of a disturbance anywhere around her. She sat up, eyes wide open, her hand instinctively wrapping around the hilt of the Legion-issue knife under her sleeping bag. It wasn't as good as the one that had been confiscated the first night of training, but it was good enough.

She relaxed as she saw Wolf crouching a few meters away, his back to her as he rolled up his sleeping bag. "Time for your watch already?" she asked softly, sliding the knife back into its accustomed place.

He glanced toward her. His face was hard to read in the soft illumination of one of the portable camp lights Baram had set up a few meters away, but she thought she could make out the mixture of bemusement and wariness that she'd come to expect from the aristo. He knew her foibles by now, and he went out of his way to keep his distance. That was fine by Lisa Scott. She knew in her mind that none of her lancemates, not even Antonelli, would do anything to hurt her now ... but five years hadn't erased all the scars, and she didn't entirely trust herself if she was pushed too far or backed into a corner. Not even with someone like Wolf.

"Yeah," he replied quietly. "You'd think the Sarge could've split the watch schedule between us and Charlie Lance ... but I guess that'd make too much sense."

"'Ours not to reason why....'" she quoted.

"'Ours but to do *and* die, '" he finished. "Just do me a favor and make sure Sleeping Beauty over there relieves me on time, okay?" He pointed toward Kern, who had spread his sleeping bag a few meters away from the rest of the lance. They were camped about halfway between the APC and the ruined plantation house, while Charlie Lance had set up much closer to the vehicle. Baram had insisted in spreading the recruits out, just in case. Scott found herself hoping that the precaution would prove foolish in the morning light.

"I'm perfectly capable of waking myself up," Kern's voice cut in before she had a chance to reply. "Especially when other people make all this noise. So move out before I decide to test my night shooting skills."

Wolf chuckled and straightened up.

"Need a rifle?" she asked him. Since he was saddled with the rocket launcher, Wolf didn't have an FEK of his own.

He shook his head. "Antonelli'll turn his over to me. Thanks, anyway." Stiff-backed, he donned his combat helmet and started off. Outside the circle of light, he was quickly swallowed up by the darkness.

She stretched out on the ground again, but didn't close her eyes right away. The horrors of the afternoon were still too close, ready to spring unbidden from the dark recesses of memory. There had been clustered bodies the other time, too, five years ago, and one bad memory fed on the other.

Scott shut the thought out of her mind, just as she had during the burial earlier. She took a deep breath, going through the meditation tech-nique she had originally learned to clear her mind in order to access the computer implant in her brain. Since the day the terrorists had kidnapped her from her father's estate she had found that the same formula could help her banish the nightmares ... at least for a while.

Slowly she let herself slip into the darkness.

And suddenly she was fully awake once more as the commlink receivers in every helmet in the camp shrilled an alarm simultaneously. The standby communications setting was designed to attract attention to an emergency alert message from a distance when the helmets weren't being worn, and now they were doing just that as Wolf's voice, edged with an urgency that bordered on panic, boomed from the speakers.

"Alert! Alert! Movement outside the camp!"

* * *

"Antonelli! For God's sake, man, answer me!" Wolf resisted the urge to call out, either aloud or over the comm channel, and kept his voice to a hoarse stage whisper instead. He didn't want to get the younger recruit in trouble with Sergeant Baram by calling unnecessary attention to him ... but the Italian's silence was exasperating. Where *was* he?

The image of the civilian with the slit throat rose unbidden in his mind, but Wolf thrust it away. "Antonelli!"

He had his combat helmet set for light intensification, and the faint starlight was enough to make the clearing look as if it was lit by flood-lights on his faceplate. Wolf paused and took a careful look around, getting more concerned now. The Italian had been ordered to pay special attention to the southern perimeter, where the barrel trees were thickest and approached the plantation buildings most closely. Al-though he could have monitored the sensor net from almost anywhere, Antonelli had taken the orders literally and headed for that end of the compound at the start of his watch. The clearing, as defined by the five plantation buildings, formed a U shape with the open end facing south and the APC resting near the mouth, less than fifty meters from the tree line.

If Antonelli had done the sensible thing and set up his watch near the Sandray it would have saved a lot of trouble. As it was, Wolf couldn't very well relieve the kid unless he could find him first. And so far there was no sign of the Italian....

No, *there* he was. Wolf could see his legs past the squat trunk of an *arbebaril* at the very edge of the trees. The recruit was sitting with his back to the clearing. Still, he should have heard Wolf.

He cursed silently and unbuckled the strap on his pistol holster. It was his only weapon, since he would ordinarily have taken over the FEK Antonelli had borrowed. Wolf covered the distance to the tree quickly and dropped to one knee beside the Italian. He was sprawled against the trunk, head back, faceplate up. There was no sign of any injuries, and his breathing was deep and regular....

Antonelli was asleep.

Wolf prodded him. "Goddamn it, kid, wake up!" he whispered urgently.

The Italian straightened up, looking wild. "What? What is it?"

"What a *stupid* stunt to pull!" Wolf told him, still whispering. "If the Sarge had caught you ..."

Antonelli flinched. "I didn't mean to, man. I ... I only closed my eyes for a moment. I swear!"

"Yeah ... well, now you can turn in for real. I'm supposed to be your relief. So get back to the camp and get some rest."

The younger recruit kept his eyes fixed on Wolf's face and didn't move. "Are you … are you going to report me?"

"Well … you only closed your eyes for a moment," Wolf told him with a half-smile. He knew he ought to do just that, but he wasn't willing to be the one who finally got poor Antonelli busted. The kid looked scared enough never to fall asleep on watch again. "No, I won't report you. Word of honor on that. But you know I could get a fast trip to Tophet myself for covering your ass. Keep it in mind, kid."

The Italian nodded and stood slowly.

"Okay, I relieve you. Let's see the perimeter.…" He switched from LI to sensor feed, and his faceplate lit up with a dozen blinking red dots. The unexpected sight made him forget his Terranglic. *Mein Gott!*

Each one of those red lights was a sensor reporting movement by man-sized bodies pushing through the jungle. There might be a dozen moving targets out there … or perhaps many more.

Wolf hit his commlink button. "Alert! Alert! Movement outside the camp!" He didn't even have time to repeat the warning before the whine of kinetic energy rifles erupted from the brush. He grabbed Antonelli by the web gear and pulled him down on the ground beside him. "Keep your head down, kid!" he said harshly, switching his faceplate back to LI vision again before groping for his pistol. "And let 'em have it!"

A grenade went off behind them, near the heart of the camp, and half a dozen bulky figures burst out of the jungle howling and waving a weird assortment of weapons as they ran. Wolf drew a bead and squeezed off a round, but the shot was wide. "Lay down some autofire, Antonelli! Nail the bastards!"

Antonelli clutched his FEK, but made no move to use it. He lay where Wolf had pushed him, eyes wide, his mouth opening and closing but making no coherent sounds.

Wolf fired the pistol again, then rolled sideways as one of the rebels took aim with an antiquated-looking rifle. The crack and whistle of the shot was nothing like the sound of a kinetic energy rifle, but it made Wolf duck anyway. He'd heard of old-fashioned projectile weapons, and even though his battledress was reportedly adequate protection against typical longarms of that sort he had no desire to test those reports.

The bullet missed him by a safe margin, but the massive alien shouted and pointed, and more of its comrades turned to join the fight.

Now they knew exactly where the two recruits were, and with Antonelli paralyzed it would be an uneven match.…

* * *

Lisa Scott crawled on her belly up to the protective bulk of a log, braced her FEK across the top, and got off a long full-auto burst. It was just blind, random fire, but it elicited an unearthly scream that made her skin crawl. She fired again.

The camp was a scene of chaos. The attack had started hard on the heels of the first warning, and before anyone could react explosions and shouts were already filling the clearing. The first grenade had gone off close to the APC, where a couple of the Charlie Lance recruits, Owens and Banda, had bedded down. Peering over the top of the log, she could see one body sprawled there on the ground. It was too small to be Banda, so it was probably Volunteer Owens. Dead?

No ... she could see the figure moving feebly. Beyond were the hulking shapes of Wynsarrysa rebels fanning out across the clearing, large, slow moving, but relentless as so many juggernauts. One was heading straight for Owens, holding a massive sword and baring his teeth in a savage snarl.

She remembered the mutilated bodies and opened fire again, raking the ponderous form with a stream of needle projectiles that tore into the rebel's torso. With a screech like the one she'd heard before the alien toppled.

"Legionnaires! Hold 'em, legionnaires!" That was Yancey, the Sandray driver, waving a pistol as he ran toward the APC, heedless of the swarming hostiles.

Scott opened fire to cover him. If Yancey could make it to his armored vehicle, its kinetic energy cannon would make short work of the attackers.

But at that moment the driver's back exploded in a haze of blood. At least one of the savages had a captured FEK and knew how to use the 1 cm grenades to good effect. She swallowed sour bile and squeezed the trigger again, feeling sick but refusing to give in to the nausea.

Where were the rest of the recruits? She couldn't see Antonelli or Wolf, but she noticed Kern crouching at the corner of the nearest building, the warehouse, off to the left. Myaighee had given his weapon to Antonelli when the latter had gone on watch, but the diminutive hannie was scrambling up a ladder on the outer wall of the warehouse, apparently oblivious to the shots the attackers were taking at him. She wasn't sure what he intended, but the roof would at least give him a good vantage point to act as a spotter for grenade fire.

As for Charlie Lance, she wasn't as clear. Owens was down, of course, but there was no sign of Volunteer Banda or the others. The fight had erupted so fast that she'd lost track of almost everyone.

"Come on! Hold them, damn it! Hold them!" Sergeant Baram's voice was familiar, at least, something to latch on to in the chaos. A moment later he appeared as if out of nowhere and dropped to o ne knee beside her. "Keep up the fire, Scott," he growled, spraying needle rounds at the closest clump of rebels as he spoke. "Yeh Chen! Banda! Report!"

There was a pause. Then the commlink crackled. "Yeh Chen's down, Sergeant," Banda said. "His arm's off at the elbow. I've got the bleeding stopped...."

"Leave him! Get in the game, Banda! We need to get to that goddamned Sandray!"

"Y-yeah ... yes, Sergeant! On my way!"

"Scott, MacDuff, maintain covering fire. Everyone else rushes the APC on my order!"

There was a chorus of acknowledgements. A moment later Baram was on his feet and crossing the clearing at a dead run, zigzagging, while Scott covered him with a sustained FEK burst. "Legionnaires!" Baram shouted. "Legionnaires, form on me! Nail the bastards!"

Out of the corner of her eye she saw Kern grappling with a Wyn-sarrysa rebel who had sprung on him before he could get clear of the warehouse. Myaighee gave a blood-curdling, ululating screech and leapt from his perch to help the redhead.

Then her attention was wrenched away from that melee as Baram took a hit and stumbled. The black recruit, Banda, ran past him straight into a hail of needle rounds. He flopped backwards and lay still, and there was a long moment of stunned silence.

*   *   *

One of the rebels had an old-model FEK, and Karl Wolf scrambled over the uneven ground as needle rounds whispered just over his head. Reaching Antonelli, he pried the rifle out of the Italian recruit's trem-bling hands and flicked the selector switch to full automatic. Clamp ing his finger down on the trigger and aiming up from his prone position, he raked the four charging rebels with a steady stream of fire until all went down. Then he cautiously peered around the sheltering bulk of the *arbebaril.*

Light-intensification made the darkness look bright as a cloudy winter day, and it was easy enough to spot the rebels spreading out along the edge of the clearing between the two recruits and the APC. A few of them had fallen under fire from the camp, but there were still more of the hulking alien shapes moving than the entire two-lance Legion outfit ... and there was no way of knowing, from here, how many of the legionnaires had been killed in the first rush.

His commlink didn't enlighten him much. There was a confused babble of orders and shouted warnings, but it didn't sound like Baram had established any kind of control over the firefight.

Or maybe Baram was dead already.

He decided against trying to break into the channel to ask for instructtions. Even if there was anyone left to give them, it sounded as if everyone in the camp already had enough to worry about. Instead, Wolf shut off his commlink altogether and studied the scene spread out on the inside of his helmet visor.

Three of the raiders were crouched near the corner of the nearest building, the processing plant, and several more were visible clustered around the APC. The vehicle was the key to the whole situation, of course. That heavy turret gun would turn the tide in no time. No doubt there were others in the camp with the same idea, but the clearing would be an open killing ground, hard to cross without coming under concentrated fire from the rebels.

But the rebels weren't paying any attention to their flank or rear now, and that gave Wolf the edge.

He looked back at Antonelli. The young Italian was still on the ground, plainly terrified. His hands clenched tight around the FEK in frustration, but Wolf knew it was no use trying to goad the younger recruit into action. He'd have to behave as if Antonelli was out of the action entirely.

Wolf started to turn away, then had another thought. He belly-crawled to the cluster of rebels he'd killed before, grabbed the old FEK/24 one of them had dropped, and checked the magazine. It was still half-full. Switching the selector switch to three-round autobursts, Wolf crawled back to Antonelli and thrust the antiquated weapon into his hands. The Italian stared at it uncomprehendingly.

"Use it to defend yourself, kid," Wolf hissed. "Just stay put here."

Somehow, Antonelli managed to nod acknowledgement. Wolf left him and went back to the *arbebaril*. Raising his borrowed FEK/27 carefully, he switched to the single-shot setting and took careful aim on the nearest of the three rebels by the corner of the processing building. He squeezed the trigger and saw his target collapse in a heap without attracting any attention from either of its partners.

With a quick movement he shifted his aim and fired again. This time, though, his aim was off and the rebel felt the breeze of the high-velocity needle whispering bare centimeters past what should have been its ears, if these ales had sported anything identifiable as external ears. The raider grabbed its friend by the arm, pulling it to one side and gesticulating wildly. The image would have been funny if the situation hadn't been so grim.

Wolf cursed. If he didn't move fast, those two would have the whole rebel force on top of him....

CHAPTER SEVENTEEN

Dying is what the Legion is all about.

—Legionnaire William Brooks,
French Foreign Legion, 1978

Legionnaire Third Class Myaighee felt the battle lust overwhelming kys senses. A quick thrust of kys combat knife had killed one massive Wynsarrysa rebel, and Kern had brought down a second one with a quick burst of FEK fire, but more were pouring into the plantation clearing from the jungle behind the warehouse. The surroundings and the situation took ky back to the long retreat by Bravo Company through the jungles of Hanuman, when kys own people had been the enemy.

Ky didn't have a battle rifle, but one of the rebels had dropped a heavy autopistol of Gwyrran design, more like a submachinegun for Myaighee. Ky snatched it up and studied the awkward weapon. It wasn't far removed technologically from the weaponry ky had used in the militia back home, several long ages ago. The hannie crouched over the unmoving body and checked the creature's belt, coming up with a pair of extra clips.

"Look out!" Kern shouted, cutting loose with another burst of fire. Myaighee rolled sideways just as a pair of rebels opened fire. If not for the redheaded male-human's warning, the shots would have hit ky in the head.

Myaighee raised the pistol in a clumsy two-handed grip and return-ed fire. One of the bulky aliens threw up his arms and fell, screeching like an injured *zymlat*. Others kept coming, though. Ky could feel the surge of excitement in kys veins, the stirring of the neck ruff that signaled fury. Ky gibbered a challenge and blazed away into the dark.

"Myaighee!" Sergeant Baram's voice was weak, wavering, and Myaighee barely noticed it as a distraction in kys ear. "Myaighee ... take charge! Get ... to the Sandray...."

The hannie shouted again, fired again, and lunged forward to meet the oncoming foes. The sergeant's words meant nothing now next to the fight ky already was waging.

* * *

Lisa Scott ducked behind the barricade and bit her lip as another fusillade split the air overhead. The relief she'd felt on hearing Sergeant Baram, realizing he wasn't dead after all, had given way to doubt. Myaighee hadn't responded to Baram's order, and she wasn't sure what she should do. Should she try to help Baram, or get to the vehicle? Or stick to her position and hope she could keep the hostiles from getting any closer to the wavering human position?

As if reading her mind, Volunteer MacDuff spoke up on the comm channel. "Stay where you are, lass, and keep giving those bastards hell. Voskovich and I will make a try for the APC."

"Right," she said through clenched teeth. Her FEK chattered, its magazine exhausted. She switched to grenades and got off a quick three-round burst at the nearest group of rebels, then ejected her empty clip, fished a fresh magazine of caseless needle ammo from her pouch, and slapped it into the receiver. "Make your move, MacDuff!"

MacDuff and Voskovich advanced carefully, leapfrogging forward in the classic fire-and-movement pattern they'd been taught during weapons training. Moving from cover to cover, with one laying down suppression fire as the other ran, they worked their way up the right side of the clearing opposite the warehouse. The repbay with its three large, slightly recessed vehicle-sized doorways dominated that side of the compound and gave the two some shelter.

MacDuff had discarded his laser rifle for an FEK, probably Yeh Chen's, and he used it to deadly effect as they advanced. All it would take now was one rush from the corner of the repbay and the Caledonian would be at the APC. Scott switched back to grenades and laid down a heavy pattern. MacDuff gave her a cocky thumbs-up and burst from cover, running at top speed. He moved with the sure grace of a cat, and in seconds he was at the driver's hatch of the APC, stabbing at the door controls.

A giant shape loomed out of the shadows. Before she could shout a warning Scott saw a blade flashing down, once, twice, a third time. With a gurgling cry MacDuff collapsed.

Half blinded by tears of rage and frustration, Lisa Scott was on her feet, sweeping her FEK back and forth as she ran. The alien who had struck down MacDuff fell over the body of his victim, but there were more of them out there. A rational part of her mind, detached and strangely calm, knew she would never make it to the Sandray....

She kept running.

* * *

Wolf switched to full-auto and sprayed the enemy position. As he fired, he surged to his feet and ran toward the two aliens. The needle rounds shredded through flesh and bone, and by the time Wolf had reached the corner neither of the aliens was moving. In fact, there wasn't much that was recognizable as a once-living creature left.

But the FEK was chattering on an empty clip now, and Wolf didn't have any fresh ammo, just a clip of minigrenades. Those would cause casualties, all right, but they would also draw too much attention to him ... and could put other legionnaires at risk if he overshot his target. He gave another curse, softly, through clenched teeth, at his thought-lessness. He should have taken Antonelli's extra magazine before leaving the Italian alone back there. Now it was too late. He was committed. Wolf slung the battle rifle over his shoulder and drew his pistol once more.

Without firepower there was no way he was going to make it to the APC from this position. There were half a dozen rebels right around the vehicle and several more further back, at the edge of the jungle, who would spot him if he made a move. What he needed was a diversion....

He thought of the smoldering fires they'd put out during the daylight hours. The *arbebaril* sap was flammable, and in his mind's eye Wolf could picture the maze of pipes that carried the sap from the processing building to the next building down the line, the main ware-house. The pieces of the puzzle were starting to fit together.

Wolf sprinted toward the back of the building, hugging the wall and keeping low. It didn't take long to swing around the back. He dropped to one knee at the back corner, scanning the space between the two structures carefully. Two rebels were visible beyond the complex of pipes and conduits, both of them intent on the center of the clearing. More cautious than before, Wolf crept forward until he was among the pipes. He found a keyboard for a maintenance check-valve and bit back another curse. An old-fashioned manual valve would have been easier to deal with. He considered backing off and using a grenade, but there was no guarantee of success ... and he'd only have the one chance. Discarding that notion, he pulled the interface wire from the side of his wristpiece computer, plugged into the keypad, and whispered orders to the 'piece. The self-programming chip inside quickly established the parameters of his command and began the code-breaking sequence to activate the keypad.

Precious seconds ticked by. One of the rebels near the APC fell, but more ran forward. Wolf had a glimpse of a dark-clad human figure running across his field of view, but saw nothing more of the human defenders. When there was no further change in the firefight in the clearing he couldn't help wondering who had made that desperate charge ... and what had happened. It could have been Kern, or Mac-Duff then ... even Lisa Scott, probably cut down by the rebels close to the APC. The thought made Wolf want to cry out and charge into the fighting, but he forced himself to stay put and wait for the computer to do its work.

At last a green light lit up on the keypad, and Wolf hit the control to open the valve. Thick, dark liquid oozed from the check pipe, like congealing blood. Wolf disconnected the interface and sprinted back the way he had come, leaving a pool of the viscous sludge spreading slowly under the pipes.

From the back corner he'd paused at before, Wolf waited and watched until he was sure enough sap was on the ground to give him the diversion he needed. He returned his pistol to his holster and un-slung the FEK once again, checking the magazine out of habit even though he knew all too well what the indicators read. Then he carefully aimed the rifle and fired three 1 cm grenades into the middle of the pool. Wolf was running by the time the first explosion went off, racing for the spot where he had killed the three ales. As he ran, the blasts went off in quick succession. Hoarse shouts from the clearing attested to the attention he had drawn, and a cloud of thick, choking smoke, black against the black night, roiled and twisted from the burning inferno he had created. He only hoped the surprise would last....

*   *   *

Something tore the air close enough to Lisa Scott's faceplate to make her flinch. Her Legion training took over, made her drop and roll away from the danger. Even as she came up to one knee she was searching for the source of the fusillade. She recognized the bulky shape near the rear of the Sandray as an enemy and had her weapon up and firing almost without thinking about it. Part of her was smiling inwardly. Brutal and often senseless though it often seemed, her Legion education was certainly proving effective tonight.

The alien was literally flung back against the hull of the APC by the power of her full-auto blast. She surged to her feet and started forward again, vaguely aware of Katrina Voskovich shouting support and laying down suppressive fire from off to her right.

She dodged around Baram's prone form, encouraged when she saw the sergeant moving, trying to claw his way forward to the shelter of a pile of debris left over from the original sack of the plantation. For a moment she was tempted to go to his assistance, but that would have been a wasted effort at this point. Unless someone got to that Sandray and brought its heavier weaponry into play, the entire cadet patrol was liable to be swamped by superior numbers, and there weren't enough legionnaires left on their feet now for her to take herself out of the fight just to help Baram.

The whole decision passed through her mind in an instant, and she barely broke her stride as she continued her zigzag course toward the squat APC. Ahead, a pair of rebels appeared at the door of the process-ing building, opening fire with antiquated hunting rifles. A bullet hit her squarely in the chest, splattering ineffectively on her breastplate armor. The force made her stagger, but she kept on running.

At that moment a fireball erupted from between the buildings to her right, with a flash so intense that it overloaded her LI gear. Panic gripped her for a moment. *I'm blind* she thought, stumbling over some obstacle and sprawling to the ground. She clawed at her helmet, then realized she was seeing again. The LI circuits were coming back on line, none the worse for wear.

She blinked a couple of times, then saw the two aliens gaping at the smoke and flame, her presence apparently forgotten. Groping for her discarded rifle, Lisa raised herself to her knees and cut loose with a spray of automatic fire.

The two rebels fell under the autofire, but she used up the rest of her magazine bringing them down. Grimly she ejected the spent clip and started to snap her last one into place in the FEK's receiver.

Another Wynsarrysa loomed up just in front of her, seemingly coming from nowhere. The sudden menace made her fumble with the magazine. Lisa Scott had grown up in an environment that didn't encourage foul language, but she yelled a lurid curse she had learned among the legionnaires when the clip spun out of her hand and into the mud.

The rebel's teeth were gleaming in the firelight as he raised his own FEK to finish the human off....

Nothing happened.

The Wynsarrysa gaped uncomprehendingly for a long moment before he realized that his own magazine was empty. Then he surged forward, two meters of fang and muscle and fury, clubbing the rifle and drawing back to deliver a single skull-crushing blow. Lisa stumbled backward, trying to bring her weapon up to block the savage attack, but she knew her strength was no match for the nonhuman's.

The familiar *whoosh* of a rocket bullet split the night, clear despite the noise of battle and fire that filled the plantation clearing. The alien's chest erupted in a fine spray of blood and flesh. He stood transfixed for long seconds before finally toppling in a heap beside her.

And Karl Wolf was there, the PLF rocket pistol in one hand, his rifle clutched by the barrel in the other.

* * *

Myaighee's scavenged pistol was empty now, out of ammunition, and ky threw it at the face of the closest rebel. The fight had carried the hannie, with Thomas Kern close behind, past the warehouse and almost to the jungle, rushing forward from cover to cover each time there was a brief let-up in the attack. The battle lust was starting to give way to fatigue now, and for the first time Myaighee became aware of Kern's voice shouting in his earphones.

"Damn it, Myaighee! What are you doing? Sarge said for you to take charge and get to the Sandray...!"

Ky gaped at Kern's tall, stocky form, not quite comprehending.

Then pain lanced through kys shoulder as a rebel's heavy sword slashed down, seemingly from out of nowhere. Kys battledress absorbed the worst of the shock, but Myaighee still felt the pain like fire in kys arm and upper chest.

Kern shot the Wynsarrysa rebel, and stood over the hannie....

Then the night lit up with a string of explosions, and the rebels stopped in their tracks to stare at the fireball rising over the processing building on the other side of the compound. Kern grabbed Myaighee by kys webgear and sprinted back for the safety of the warehouse.

Myaighee passed out from shock and fatigue before they reached the building.

* * *

"Come on! While we've got an opening!" Wolf shouted and turned, sprinting for the Sandray, knowing Lisa Scott would follow him.

He hopped over one body, dodged another, and reached the corner of the vehicle. Four more aliens broke from the cover of the trees, heading his way, and he squeezed off two shots in quick succession before they ducked behind a half-ruined shed. In the next instant Lisa Scott was kneeling by his side, her FEK at the ready. She fired a three-round burst of minigrenades that finished the destruction of the shed. At least one of the aliens fell, sprawled under a collapsed wall. She switched to needle rounds and laid down a murderous stream of fire across the clearing, sweeping back and forth along the tree line to suppress the enemies still lurking there.

Wolf turned the corner with the pistol held high, but there were no living rebels there. Several dead bodies littered the ground nearby, including at least one shape that had to be human, not Wynsarrysa. He forced himself to ignore the casualties and rushed up the length of the Sandray. The driver's hatch was closed, electronically sealed, but the tiny transponder in his helmet would identify him to the onboard computer as a friend and release the locks when he hit the pressure pad beside the door.

Another ale popped out from behind the cover of the Sandray's blunt nose, and Wolf fired from point-blank range. The rocket bullet didn't have time to build up enough velocity to do much damage, and the rebel shrugged off the stinging hit in its shoulder and raised a massive, curved sword of native make.

But Lisa was right behind him, and her shots did more than just sting. The alien flopped on its back with its chest and throat shredded by the hail of needle rounds the woman had fired over Wolf's shoulder.

"I'm out of ammo," she said, throwing the FEK away. "Needles and grenades both."

He didn't answer. His fist rapped the door release, and with a hiss of escaping air the hatch swung up. He clambered in, then turned to help her climb up after him.

"Fire up the fans," he said. "I'll take the gun."

She nodded agreement and settled into the driver's seat as he scrambled to the other side of the cab and took the gunnery chair. The turret on top of the Sandray with its kinetic energy cannon was remotely operated in the APC, and in a pinch the driver could handle both jobs. But two were better, especially in a situation like this one.

The hatch sighed shut, and Wolf discarded his helmet, thankful to be rid of the clumsy thing. Soft red lights illuminated the compartment, and the monitor screens along the front of the cab lit up as Lisa ran her fingers over a bank of control switches. She had taken her helmet off as well, and even in the faint battle lights her face was pale and drawn, smudged with dirt and a large bruise on one cheek.

He checked the power supply for the turret and smiled. Now they had the edge they needed....

Lisa Scott revved the fans, and the Sandray stirred ponderously from the ground on interlocking maglev fields. Wolf moved the joystick in front of him, lining up the glowing green crosshairs on his monitor with a clump of *arbebaril* trees where a trio of rebels had disappeared a moment earlier.

"Firing!" he shouted as he hit the trigger stud.

Lisa wasn't sufficiently familiar with the vehicle to completely compensate for the shot despite his warning, and the Sandray slid back and to one side, but the shell tore into the target. Wolf fired again, then a third time, as his lancemate steered the APC toward the jungle at a deliberate, menacing speed.

He wasn't sure how much longer they kept at it, but eventually it was over. The rebels were in full retreat, and Lisa Scott turned the Sandray back toward the plantation. The battle was won.

Now came the job of counting the cost of that bitter victory....

* * *

Morning found the legionnaires back in the protective confines of the Sandray, speeding back across the open sea toward distant Fort Marchand. They had spent the remainder of the night huddled close to the APC, with one cadet constantly on watch in the vehicle's cab and two more walking the perimeter. Only six survivors had come out of the fighting more or less able to carry on, half the original contingent, and the new watch schedule had stretched their resources thin. Not that any of them thought much of sleep in the wake of the battle.

Soon after dawn they'd finally been relieved by a larger patrol in a trio of maglev vehicles, not cadets this time but crack veterans stationed at Fort Marchand for just this sort of work, responding to rebel attacks and tracking their enemies to their lairs in the wild. They were part of a larger force that was spreading across the district in search of the Wynsarrysa rebels who had survived the night's encounter.

Weary from their long night, the cadets had gratefully turned over the responsibility for the plantation to the new arrivals. Now they were safe aboard the Sandray, with a driver/gunner team assigned by the lieutenant in command of the patrol and a medic from his platoon to look after the wounded. In another hour, maybe less, they would be back at Fort Marchand, and the ordeal would be over.

Mario Antonelli wanted to believe that, but he knew that his problems were far from done.

He sat huddled in one corner of the rear compartment, hardly aware of his surroundings. It was a good place to be alone. The medic and his two seriously injured charges were the only other occupants, with the rest of the cadets in the middle chamber. Antonelli wanted to be alone right now. He couldn't face the others ... not yet.

He couldn't remember much of what had happened in the night, beyond a feeling of paralyzing terror that had gripped him from the moment he and Wolf had first spotted the enemy, but he knew he hadn't taken part in any of the fighting that followed. Antonelli wasn't even entirely sure how he'd come back to the camp after it was all over, though he had a vague memory of Karl Wolf pushing him bodily out of the jungle with a look of utter contempt on his haughty, aristocratic features.

The cadet knew he merited that contempt several times over. He had fallen asleep on watch and allowed the rebels to get close to the camp ... and when the battle started, he had been completely unable to force himself to do anything useful. From first to last, he had let everyone down, and as a result four men were dead and two more seriously injured. Sergeant Baram and Volunteer Yeh Chen would recover after a stint in the fort's hospital. The same couldn't be said for Corporal Yancey or the three volunteers from Charlie Lance, Banda, Owens, and MacDuff. They would be coming back in another Sandray, wrapped in body bags, making their final trip home.

"No," he muttered aloud. "It's not my fault. It's not."

"What was that, Cadet?" the medic, a corporal named Alvarez, looked up from the litter that held Sergeant Baram.

"Uh ... nothing, Corporal," Antonelli said hastily. "Sorry."

It *wasn't* his fault, though, he told himself vehemently. Not entirely. Ordering a bunch of half-trained cadets to stand watch over the ruined plantation ... expecting Antonelli to stay awake after the kind of grueling pace they'd been forcing on him for so many weeks ... not posting other guards or a watch in the Sandray....

No, it wasn't all his fault. He had to believe it. The alternative, to accept responsibility for everything that had happened, was simply unthinkable.

Chapter Eighteen

A lot of youngsters feel that by joining the Legion they become men—but you don't become a man overnight.

—Corporal-chief James Campbell,
French Foreign Legion, 1984

"Ten-HUT!"

Wolf drew himself to attention as the door to the tiny classroom opened to admit Commandant Akiyama and his aide. The officer had been appointed to investigate the battle in the Archipel d'Aurore, and Wolf had already had several interviews with him over the course of the past two weeks. But this was the first time all of the survivors of the fighting at Savary's plantation had been assembled together to meet with the commandant. Rumor had it that today's session would be the last.

Even the battle hadn't been enough to halt the juggernaut of Legion training. The survivors of the battle at Savary's had been granted a day off to rest after their ordeal, but after that it was back to the regular grind. The investigation into the night's events proceeded, but it wasn't allowed to interfere with the ongoing classes at Fort Marchand. In due course the jungle warfare/reconnaissance course was wrapped up, and Training Company Odintsev moved on to the desert warfare training center at Fort Souriban, located deep in the Great Desert that covered half of Devereaux's primary continent. Akiyama's inquiry went on after they settled in to the new post, with hearings squeezed in to free periods or arranged to fit in with the platoon's training schedule.

Wolf hadn't been surprised to see this further proof of the Legion's single-minded determination. Nothing about the Fifth Foreign Legion surprised him anymore.

"At ease," Akiyama said.

"Take your seats so we can get this thing started," Sergeant Baram growled. He waited as the recruits found places near the front of the classroom, then limped slowly to find a seat off to one side. His kneecap had been shattered in the battle, but after two days in Fort Marchand's hospital he had been returned to limited duty, his leg encased in a regen cast that supported the limb while regeneration stimulators encouraged the regrowth of bone and tissue. Wolf couldn't tell if the irritated expression on the sergeant's face arose from the continuing pain in his leg, or from the prospect of the hearing itself.

At least Baram was back on full duty. Volunteer Yeh Chen had lost an arm in the battle, and that was something the ordinary regeneration process couldn't cope with. He was slated for a medical discharge as soon as the investigation was closed out. The recruit hadn't said much about it, but Wolf knew he must feel cheated. The Legion hadn't even offered to fit him for an artificial limb. His enlistment would be marked as satisfactorily completed and given the customary H&F stamp, which would grant the wounded man the full privileges of Commonwealth Citizenship, but that was all. No accumulated bonus for years of service, and no help to a man who had sacrificed so much to the cause of the Legion. Just a Citizen's dole for the rest of his life ... and the knowledge that he had been all but abandoned.

Commandant Akiyama and his aide sat at a desk at the front of the room. The investigating officer had a compboard, which he consulted at length before finally beginning to speak. "This inquiry has been convened to consider the events of the past 23 November, standard calendar," he said, matter-of-factly. "The fighting at Savary's in the Archipel d'Aurore, to be specific. It is based principally on the reports each of you has filed, in combination with findings made by other Legion troops on the scene after your patrol was relieved." He looked up from the compboard in front of him to study the recruits. "For the benefit of you trainees, we call an inquiry of this kind any time a Legion unit loses personnel in combat. It is not to be considered a military court ... although it would be within my power to recommend a full court martial if I felt that events warranted one. As it happens, this matter has proven fairly straightforward, and all questions of punishment can be handled through ordinary administrative disciplinary channels."

Akiyama looked down at the compboard again. "Sergeant Menachem Baram...?"

"Sir!" the sergeant responded crisply. He rose awkwardly and stood at attention.

"Sergeant, I find that you showed poor judgment in your precautions against a possible night attack by the Wynsarrysa at Savary's. You should have been aware of the fact that the rebels frequently double back on targets they have previously attacked for the express purpose of ambushing our forces. Our records show that you chipped the appropriate intel bulletins prior to being authorized to lead recruit patrols in the field. Do you deny this?"

"No, sir," Baram said flatly.

"Are there any mitigating circumstances you feel should be taken into account in connection with this finding?"

"No, sir," the sergeant repeated. "I should have posted more guards and kept someone in the APC. I badly underestimated the threat from the rebels, and accept full responsibility for the mistake."

"Very well." Akiyama made a note on the computer's screen. "Sergeant, you are sentenced to a reduction in grade and relief as a recruit instructor. You will be transferred to a line unit as soon as you are certified for a return to unrestricted duty and a vacancy becomes available. Is that clear?"

"Yes, sir," Baram said.

"Legionnaire Myaighee!"

The hannie stood and saluted smartly, none the worse for wear despite his injuries in the battle. A short set of regen treatments had been sufficient to deal with the wounds. "Sir!" Although Myaighee looked efficient enough, Wolf thought he could detect a note of concern in the alien's voice. The quills of the hannie's neck ruff were twitching.

"Myaighee, we expected good things from you as a recruit lance leader. After the death of Corporal Yancey, you were the most experienced legionnaire under Sergeant Baram's command and had the responsibility of taking command of the entire unit when your superior was incapacitated. The evidence we have gathered shows that you did not, and your own report indicates that you failed to live up to your responsibilities. Do you dispute these findings?"

"No, sir," the hannie replied. "I ... allowed myself to become too involved in hand-to-hand fighting and was not fully aware of what was happening on the rest of the battlefield."

Akiyama nodded and jotted down another note. "The fact that you were engaged in combat at the time is certainly a mitigating circumstance. But you have demonstrated that you are ill-suited to a leadership position, and I will be recommending that you be relieved from your current position as Recruit Lance Leader."

"Yes, sir." The hannie didn't betray any more emotion in his voice, but the neck ruff remained in constant motion. Myaighee sat down again, and Akiyama consulted his notes once more.

"Now ... Volunteer Mario Antonelli."

The Italian stood up slowly. "S-sir," he stammered.

"The reports filed by Sergeant Baram and Volunteer Wolf made it clear that you must bear much of the responsibility for the loss of life in the battle. The attack began as you were in the process of turning over your watch to Volunteer Wolf, but the proximity and number of the attackers suggests that they were able to get into position largely as a result of inattention on your part. Moreover, it is evident that you took no noticeable part in the actual fighting."

Antonelli was pale. "I ... I ..."

"Go ahead, Volunteer. What did you wish to say?"

He shook his head. "N-nothing, sir."

The captain regarded him for a long moment before continuing. "Your record has been rather spotty throughout training, Volunteer. Any form of poor performance or misconduct is certainly enough to justify terminating your service with the Legion ... which could cause you to revert to the penal battalions for the duration of your enlistment, that being your only other option under the terms of your original court sentence. But I am recommending a further investigation of this case, specifically to discover if you might be guilty of gross negligence. If the deaths of your comrades are directly attributable to some failure on your part ... sleeping on guard, for instance, or being unfit for duty as a result of intoxicant use ... then you can expect to be sentenced to the penal battalions for an additional period of time to be determined by a court martial board."

The Italian recruit looked stricken. He turned a mournful glance on Wolf, then stood straighter and met Akiyama's piercing stare. "I understand, Commandant," he said softly.

Wolf looked away from the tableau. He had been honest in his report regarding Antonelli's failure to join in the fighting, but had said nothing about finding him asleep. That had been a hard decision to make. His first impulse had been to bury the young Italian. It had been Antonelli's fault … and Robert Bruce MacDuff and the other casualties had paid the price for his lapse. But he had given his word of honor not to say anything about finding the kid asleep … and when the time came he hadn't been able to go back on that word. But now Antonelli would probably think he had been betrayed.

"Pending further investigation, you are relieved of all duties and placed on administrative restriction. That means you will drop out of your lance. Transient quarters will be provided. You have the run of the fort, but you will not leave without my express permission or orders from a higher authority. And you will make yourself available for de-tailed questioning until I am satisfied that I have reached the truth in this matter. Should I find sufficient evidence of negligence, I will order court martial proceedings. Is that clear to you, Mr. Antonelli?"

"Yes, sir," Antonelli said again. He sat down, his shoulders slump-ing in defeat. He was no longer Volunteer Antonelli … and because the courts had taken away his citizenship and wouldn't restore it unless he completed honorable service, he wasn't even Citizen Antonelli anymore. Wolf had never given the matter much thought before, but now he could see how much the honorific might mean to someone like the Italian.

"Now … last on the list. Volunteer Karl Wolf."

Wolf stood reluctantly, wondering why Akiyama was singling him out. Would he be held jointly responsible, with Antonelli, for failing to spot the rebels before the attack? Or had Antonelli lied about Wolf's part in the fighting in an effort to save his own skin?

"Volunteer Wolf, the attack began at a time when you were officially on guard duty, but it is the opinion of this investigation that you could not have issued a warning any earlier than you actually did. Therefore, you are exonerated of any responsibility for the attack itself."

"Thank you, sir," Wolf said, relieved.

"All reports agree that it was your initiative and steady performance which was largely responsible for the retreat of the enemy force. The Legion demands obedience, but we also encourage initiative. You have been recommended for an Award of Valor, Second Class, and a copy of that recommendation has been placed in your permanent service file. If a Review Board finds in your favor, you will receive the decoration and a twenty-point boost in your recruit standings, which in your case, I believe, would place you near the top of your class."

Wolf didn't respond. He had been treated like a hero ever since the battle, but he still didn't feel much like a hero. He had done what he'd been trained to do, no more. And luck more than courage had carried him through the battle.

The real heroes were the ones who had died. Like Robert Bruce MacDuff, killed trying to reach the Sandray at the height of the fighting. MacDuff, who had been his first friend among the cadets.

"Additionally, Volunteer Wolf," Akiyama continued. "I am recommending that you be awarded the Lance Leader position which Legionnaire Third Class Myaighee previously held. Although Volunteer Kern's combat proficiency scores are higher than yours, your academic standings put you at the head of your lance ... and I believe your performance at Savary's indicates that you have leadership potential we would be well advised to tap. Your platoon leader will have the final say, of course." The officer gave him a thin smile. "But it is very rare for a noncommissioned drill instructor to ignore the recommendations of an Investigating Officer."

"Y-yes ... sir. Thank you." Wolf could hardly choke the words out. He had always hoped, secretly, that Myaighee would be relieved of the lance leader's position, but he had never thought they would give it to him instead. It should have been Kern....

"Very good. This inquiry is adjourned. Carry out your orders."

Kern slapped Wolf on the back, grinning, and Lisa Scott pumped his hand, but he hardly heard their words of congratulation. His eyes were on Antonelli as the young Italian walked out of the room, no longer cocky or confident.

He had been angry at the kid for surviving when MacDuff died in the battle. His friend's bravery had stood out in sharp contrast to Antonelli's paralysis, and it just hadn't seemed right that the hero should die while the coward lived on. But this was no fair trade. Antonelli had tried hard and just couldn't measure up ... but did he deserve an even longer stay than he was already guaranteed with the Colonial Army's infamous penal battalions?

Wolf was the only one who had seen Antonelli asleep that night. His word could condemn the Italian youth to an extra term of hard labor ... at the cost of Karl Wolf's honor.

He shook his head slowly. Punishing Antonelli further wouldn't bring MacDuff or the others back. The best thing he could do, now, was to let Antonelli know that Akiyama had no evidence of negligence to go on, and wouldn't get any from Karl Wolf. It wouldn't save the kid's Legion career—that was gone, one way or another—and it wouldn't even save him from the penal battalions, since whatever original crime he had committed back on Terra had warranted the choice between the Legion or prison service. But at least Wolf's forbearance would leave him with a shred of dignity.

That was little enough, but it was all Wolf could give him.

* * *

The Great Desert was bleak, a seemingly unending expanse of rock and sand where Beau Soleil, the system's primary, beat down without mercy. Legionnaire Third Class Myaighee didn't mind the heat—the temperatures in the jungles of Hanuman soared higher even on a cool day. But ky wasn't accustomed to the parched atmosphere, the dryness so completely unlike anything ky had seen before. The fatigues ky wore, specially tailored for the hannie's small frame, contained climate control settings that adjusted to almost any extremes of temperature, but they weren't designed to deal with different levels of humidity. Myaighee felt the effects of the desert much more than kys comrades, and needed to drink frequently to replenish precious body fluids.

The whole platoon was on the march, another exercise in desert warfare operations contrived by Platoon Sergeant Konrad less than an hour after the end of the hearing back at Fort Souriban. When they had mustered on the parade ground outside the block of classrooms where Akiyama had passed judgment on them, Konrad had already known the results. He had curtly informed Mario Antonelli that all his effects had been moved to transients' quarters during the hearing, and he had sent the young male-human away without a further word or thought. Katrina Voskovich, the only survivor of Charlie Lance able to return to duty, had been reassigned to Delta Lance in Antonelli's place.

And Karl Wolf had been confirmed as the new lance leader. Myaighee wasn't sure how to take that part of the hearing. Ky had never been happy at being a leader. On Hanuman, kys caste had been everything, and ky had always been a servant. In the Legion ky had found a measure of respect, but as junior member of a lance. The leadership role hadn't come naturally, and ky was relieved not to have to face the responsibility.

But to have Wolf in charge …

The male-human from Laut Besar hadn't displayed his contempt for Myaighee openly for a long time, but ky knew it was still lurking under the man's polished veneer. It rankled ky to have the male-human promoted in Myaighee's place … as if in confirmation of the man's arrogant claims of superiority.

If only ky had been able to stay in control during the battle at Savary's. In previous fights ky had seen some desperate moments, and the battle madness had helped ky survive. But this time had been different. Ky had paid the price for ignoring the rest of the battle.

It was a price ky was determined never to pay again.

*　*　*

Lisa Scott was grateful for the climate-control features of her uniform coverall. The heat of the Great Desert seemed to suck up every vestige of moisture, but the cooling coils woven into the fabric made it almost comfortable … which meant she could focus on a dozen other hardships instead. Her aching feet, for instance, sore after the long route march through the rocky desert. Or the outcome of the hearing, the end of Antonelli's long struggle to make good.

She had no high regard for Antonelli, but Scott couldn't help feeling disturbed by the whole thing. It was all so impersonal, not at all the way she had pictured the life of ordinary soldiers. There was the gigantic military bureaucracy at the top, of course, cold, heartless … all the things she associated with her father and his cronies. But she had imag-ined more sentiment, more of a feeling of fellowship, among the or-dinary fighting men and women.

At least the inquiry was over. Now maybe they could put the past behind them. She hadn't known any of the dead recruits very well, but she knew MacDuff had been a good friend of Karl Wolf's. He had been distracted and withdrawn ever since the battle, and his mood had in-fected her of late. Today, though, Wolf had seemed more concerned with Antonelli's fate, and she didn't know what to make of that. There had been little love lost between the street kid and the aristocrat….

Wolf still looked glum, plodding through the desert sands just ahead of her with his eyes fixed on some unknown point beyond the horizon.

She'd expected him to be more pleased at his promotion—after all, he'd never been very happy at taking orders from Myaighee, Legion toleration lectures or no—and at the possibility of a medal. The recruit had certainly earned it, that night at Savary's. But he seemed equally oblivious to both ... and indeed to the whole world around him.

The slightest of motions made her look down at Wolf's feet. She shouted a warning and lunged forward to push him out of the way....

And felt a searing fire coil around her left ankle.

*　*　*

Wolf stumbled, barely keeping his balance after the unexpected shove from behind. A curse sprang to his lips, but died as he turned to see Lisa Scott falling heavily to the ground. She screamed once, a sound of sheer agony, as the muscles of her leg spasmed uncontrollably and she thrashed on the ground like a woman possessed.

He rushed to her side and started to kneel, one hand reaching for the first aid kit on his web gear. But Kern loomed up beside him and grabbed his shoulder roughly, pushing him back.

"Hold on, boyo," the redhead ordered, his voice harsh. "Sandray ..."

The Devereaux sandray, which had lent its name to the Legion's primary APC, resembled nothing so much as a Terran manta ray adapted to the environment of the Great Desert. A burrowing predator, it hid under a thin layer of sand with only the tip of its long, flexible tail showing. The appendage contained a breathing tube, a motion-sensitive organ that detected the approach of prey, and a poison stinger. Any of the large animals that lived along the fringes of the Great Desert were prey for the sandray.

They didn't hunt Man by choice, but anyone foolish enough to wander the desert without precautions was likely to make a meal for one of them.

Kern rolled the stricken recruit clear of the sandray's hole with the butt of his FEK, and Myaighee, his own weapon unslung, fired a long, full-auto burst into the ground. The hannie only stopped when dark red blood soaked through the sand layer.

They didn't have much time. Sandray poison spread fast, causing the muscles to convulse and then go rigid. Already she was curling into a tight fetal position, arms wrapped around her stomach, still twitching horribly. Wolf knew that the sandray venom would stop her breathing and her heart within a minute unless she was given prompt first aid....

Then Corporal Vanyek pushed past Wolf, his own first aid kit ready in his hand. "Take it easy, Scott," he said. "This is the antivenom patch." He was already positioning the adhesive pad over her carotid artery as he spoke. Then he produced a knife to cut away the leg of her coverall to put another patch over the wound itself.

The convulsions seemed to ease somewhat, but she was still curled up, her breathing shallow and ragged. She didn't seem aware of any of them.

Vanyek, though, appeared satisfied. "Wolf, Kern, monitor her vitals. I'll call for medevac. The rest of you straks keep your eyes open! This ain't some goddamned walk in the park!"

Wolf bent over her, shaken. It had all happened so quickly, but one fact stood out. She must have seen the questing tail as it moved to strike him, and in pushing him out of the way had taken the attack in his place.

She had saved his life.

"Thanks ... no thanks are enough," he said quietly, not sure if she could even hear him. He produced his own medical kit and found a sedative patch to position on her wrist. "This'll relax you. Put you to sleep, maybe. You hang in there, Scott. Do you hear me? Hang in there...."

Chapter Nineteen

It is to the mystery of his origins that the legionnaire owes much of his character.

—Legionnaire Georges Manue,
French Foreign Legion, 1929

ail call! Form up for mail call! Aiken!"

"Here, Sergeant!"

"Ambrose!"

"Here!"

Wolf skirted the edge of the small cluster of recruits, cocking his head to listen as the names were called. Mail call was far from the minds of most of them. More than half of them, after all, had joined the Legion to break their ties with the past entirely, and even those who had signed on with the knowledge of friends or family were unlikely to start getting messages for some time to come. With interstellar communications limited to the speed of the fastest carriership, eight weeks was scant time for anyone on a distant homeworld to have learned that a recruit had actually been accepted, much less dispatch a holetter or message chip.

But on this particular day a lighter had arrived from the carriership *METTERNICH*, fresh in from the frontier around Robespierre. Fort Hunter had forwarded the mail to Fort Souriban promptly. That was one thing about the Legion. They were always good about getting mail from home into the proper hands. Mail call had sounded just as the evening free period began.

"Antonelli!"

"Here," came the listless reply. Wolf started to angle across the parade ground to intercept him. He hadn't been able to talk to the Italian since the hearing had adjourned the day before, and it was still important to him that he let Antonelli know that Akiyama's comments hadn't been based on anything Wolf had reported. But by the time he reached the spot where he had last seen the failed recruit, close by Sergeant Konrad and his mail sack, Antonelli was nowhere to be seen. Wolf lingered for the rest of the mail call, just in case something might have arrived from Freidrich Doenitz von Pulau Irian, the consul-general who had befriended him on Robespierre.

As it happened, there was nothing for him, but when Sergeant Konrad noticed him waiting the NCO shoved a small package at him. "Something for one of your lancemates, nube," he growled. "Take care of it."

The address chip on the front responded to his touch with a voice that echoed deep in his mind. "Recruit L. Scott, Fifth Foreign Legion Training Center, Fort Hunter, Devereaux." Almost immediately it grew hot under his finger, and Wolf shifted his grasp on the packet at once. He'd heard of privacy chips before, but hadn't encountered one before. Only the intended recipient could order the chip to open the package. Anyone else who tried to tamper with it would get a nasty burn.

Its presence confirmed Wolf's opinion of Lisa Scott. Only someone very rich or very important was likely to seal correspondence with a privacy chip.

She was still in the fort's tiny hospital, after the sandray attack the previous day. Luckily Vanyek's first aid had come fast enough, and the fort's medical warrant officer had been able to set her up on a full detox program as soon as the medical APC had brought her in from the field. Wolf was glad of an excuse to stop by and see her. Exercises had kept the recruits occupied almost constantly since the accident, and he still hadn't been able to stop in and thank her properly for what she had done. The thought of taking a dose of sandray venom made his skin crawl....

The ward was small, and Lisa Scott was the only patient. She looked up as he came in, smiling.

"Package for you," Wolf announced, holding it out. "Maybe it'll take your mind off the hospital food for a few minutes." He grinned.

Her welcoming smile turned into a black frown. "Package. But who … how…?"

She took it from him, held her fingers over the address chip for a moment. "No! God damn it all, no!" Lisa threw the package at the wall with savage fury. "I should have known he'd find me here!"

Wolf took a step toward her, then checked the movement and the question he had been about to ask. The Legion's no-questions-about-the-past policy was something none of the recruits was likely to violate anymore. Gunnery Sergeant Ortega had already made it clear that no one would enjoy going against that particular quaint tradition.

But she looked so miserable, lying there staring at the offending packet where it had landed beside the door. He struggled to find the right thing to say, then crossed over to the offending object, retrieved it, and raised one eyebrow. "This obviously doesn't belong here," he said lightly. "What should I do with it? Dump it in the fusion hopper? Or plant it out on the grenade range?"

That drew a reluctant smile. "Too easy," she said, her voice husky with suppressed emotion. "I'd want something more creative." She hesitated. "I guess I'd better take it until we come up with something." Another quick smile crossed her face, but her eyes were still bleak.

As she composed herself Wolf laid the packet on the table beside her bed. "At the risk of violating all sorts of Gunny Ogre's rules, is there anything I can do?" he asked quietly. "I've got a sympathetic ear, if you want one. And Lord knows I owe you."

She sat down with a sigh. "I don't know," she said slowly. There was a long pause. "Hell, if the message is what I think it is I won't be keeping secrets long here anyway. Dear Daddy will see to that."

"Daddy?"

She nodded slowly. "Next to the rest of you guys I don't have a very exciting past to run from. I mean, Antonelli's got … had … his criminal record, and Myaighee turned his back on his own kind to stay with the legionnaires, and whatever Big Red's hiding must be a really big deal. And you … the messtalk has it that you're on the run from the war on Laut Besar." She plunged on without waiting for a response. "I'm just a rich kid who got sick of being a prisoner in my own house. So I cut loose and joined the Legion, figuring I'd be safe even from Daddy's long arm. But he found me anyway."

"If what we were told is the truth," he said slowly, "I don't think his finding out is going to make any difference. They claim the Legion looks after its own, no matter what."

"Yeah, and I believe in the Milky Way Magician and all ninety-nine of the Ubrenfar hero-gods, too," she said bitterly. "My father's one man who can get his way, Legion or no Legion." She hesitated. "Senator Herbert T. Abercrombie sits on the Military Affairs Committee, after all. If he says he wants his daughter discharged, the Legion's not going to buck him on it."

He let out a long, low whistle. "Abercrombie…?" Even on Laut Besar, where Commonwealth politics weren't of much interest, Abercrombie's name had been well known. The terrorist attack two years back that had killed the Senator's wife and left his only daughter wounded.…

His only daughter …

"You're Alyssa Abercrombie?" he went on, hardly believing it. "The one who—"

She nodded wearily. "Yes, the teenaged heroine who avenged her mother by killing a terrorist and making a daring escape from a hotel window." She recited it in a singsong voice. "God, you'd think the media would have got sick of it before the story made the interstellar circuit. They never bothered to cover the trial where the rest of the gang got off on some legal shortcut the compols took arresting them."

"That kind of attention … it must have been pretty tough."

"Yeah, and the Semti War was a mild disagreement between reason-able beings," she shot back. "First I was the famous heroine. And by the time the story finally started dying down Daddy was convinced I'd be a bigger target than ever, and that's when it really got bad."

"So you decided to strike out on your own."

"You sound like you really understand it," she said, a note of sur-prise in her voice. "Anyone I ever talked with before thought I was crazy for wanting a life of my own." She looked across at the unopened package on the table beside her. "Money and clout never seemed very important. I mean, it was nice to have, but I would have given it all up if it could have brought my mother back. And living for what everybody else wants … it's … I don't know. I can't really explain it right …"

He thought of his own life. His father was long dead, but his uncle had expected young Wolf Hauser to be a good aristocrat. Those expec-tations had taken him to the Sky Guard Academy … to the fighting on Telok and the duel on Robespierre. "I hear you, Lisa. Alyssa, I mean.…"

"It's Lisa here," she told him. "And … thanks. It's nice to know there's one person who doesn't think I'm just an ungrateful, spoiled little rich girl."

He gave a sour laugh. "Hell, you turned your back on it all to go after what you wanted. My family had money and political connections, too, and I spent my whole life doing exactly what I was told to do just because that's the price an aristo's supposed to pay. Noblesse oblige, and all that garbage."

"So what changed? How'd you end up here?" She raised an eyebrow. "If you don't mind my asking ... at the risk of violating all sorts of Gunny Ogre's rules."

"The Ubrenfars took away my planet," he said bitterly. "And some of my own kind took away my honor. I decided that was one price I couldn't pay."

*　　*　　*

It was a letter, an old-fashioned scribed letter that had been dictated to a computer and printed on paper. His parents had never been able to afford a holorecorder.

Antonelli crumpled the paper in his hands, but the action couldn't erase the words that had burned into his mind. *What else can happen?* he asked himself bitterly. *Haven't enough things gone wrong already?*

He had been struggling to keep up with the other recruits, and had even started making some progress ... right up until the battle at Savary's. That had ruined everything. The commandant's announcement that he would be headed for the penal battalions hadn't been much of a surprise. Antonelli had been prepared for that inevitable consequence of failure for a long time. But the possibility that he might be punished for his part in the battle was something else entirely. He'd never expected that. Never thought Wolf, for all his arrogance and superiority, would betray him.

And now his father was dead, and his mother was sick. Uncle Giuseppe's letter made it clear where the blame lay. Salvatore and Nunzio and some of the others from the old gang had started shooting their mouths off, and his father had overheard them, learned about the court sentence. It had been too much for the old man's heart to learn that his son had dishonored the family, had lied about everything. All that pride gone in one moment, and nothing to take its place but death....

Tears stung Antonelli's eyes, and he sat down heavily in the single chair in his Spartan transients' quarters, still clutching the letter in one fist. His parents' pride had been all that had held him on course. Without it, what did he have left?

The penal battalions would claim him now. After all his efforts, all his struggles. They'd all been useless....

Antonelli chucked the paper away. There was really only one option open to him now, and he had to take it quickly, before he lost the will to go through with it....

* * *

Wolf paused outside the hospital door and checked his wristpiece. The miniature computer was tied in to the fort's much larger database, and it was easy to query the personnel files for a room assignment. After a few seconds the screen displayed the information he'd asked for, and Wolf gave an approving nod and set off across the compound.

It was high time he saw Antonelli. He'd put off the confrontation too long. Somehow the whole incident, from the battle at Savary's right through the hearing and even Lisa Scott's accident, had all made Wolf doubt his place in the Legion more than ever. MacDuff had died, and Scott had come close to it herself, and either one of them was better Legion material than he was from start to finish. And Mario Antonelli, though he wasn't much of a soldier, had tried with all his will to make it and still failed. Wolf hadn't put in one-tenth the effort to fit in. What right did he have to succeed where the kid had failed?

And what guarantee was there that Wolf *would* succeed, in the long run? Myaighee, who had the advantage of past Legion experience, hadn't kept his lance leader's star. Even if he kept his nose clean and did everything the Legion demanded, a rebel bullet could still strike him down the next time he had to fight....

He had always understood the dangers of a soldier's life. The possibility of death was something he'd accepted long ago, even before the Ubrenfars attacked Laut Besar. But he had come to terms with the problem by thinking of it in the traditional aristo fashion. He was an aristocrat, and it was his duty to fight, and if need be die, for his world. His honor and his family name demanded no less.

But what was he putting his life on the line for in the Legion? His name wasn't even his own. These weren't his own people, by any stretch of the imagination. Their customs and beliefs were like nothing he had been raised to revere ... with these notions of species equality and all the rest of it. The Fifth Foreign Legion was nothing but a mercenary unit in thin disguise, fighting for money or personal glory or the sheer love of violence. Wolf found it hard to think of putting his life on the line for any of those things.

His mood was thoroughly black by the time he reached the transients' block. This Foreign Legion adventure had been a mistake, pure and simple. Wolf ... *Hauser* knew that now. He should have taken his chances with Neubeck's family.

But he still had a duty to perform here and now. Wolf stood for a long moment outside the door of Antonelli's room, gathering his thoughts, trying to put aside his own problems and focus on the Italian instead. Perhaps he could tap Doenitz on Robespierre for a loan to help Antonelli out once his sentence was finished...?

There was no answer when he pressed the intercom buzzer.

Wolf shrugged. Maybe Antonelli had heard about Volunteer Cromwell's secret still and was out drowning his sorrows. He would just have to keep trying.

As he passed the single tiny window next to the door, an odd flicker of motion caught his eye. Wolf looked into the room, curious.

The limp body of Mario Antonelli was swinging back and forth from a rope dangling from a light fixture on the ceiling. He was clearly dead.

* * *

Antonelli's funeral was quiet and subdued, with only a handful of the recruit's comrades and instructors in attendance. Wolf stood rigidly at attention between Kern and Volunteer Mayzar, convinced that Konrad and the other NCOs were keeping close watch on him.

It was a Catholic service, like the majority of religious observances in the Legion. When Mankind reached out for the stars it had been a largely European effort, with Catholic France in the vanguard of interstellar expansion, and when France became an empire and dominated Terra and the colonies the religion had taken firm root on dozens of worlds. Perhaps as many as three-quarters of the people who called the Legion home followed some version of the faith.

But on Laut Besar it had been different. The Indomay community followed Moslem, Hindu, or Buddhist beliefs on the whole, with a sprinkling of Catholic and Christian Protestant adherents, while the Uro upper classes who had any religion at all were almost entirely Protestants who had brought their faith with them from the German-settled colony world of Lebensraum.

Wolf himself had grown up in a largely agnostic atmosphere, and tended to scoff at religious pomp and ceremony. But today, standing in the hot afternoon sun, there was something comforting about Father Chavigny's solemn words.

The chaplain finished by making the sign of the Cross, and Ortega nodded to Vanyek. The corporal stepped forward, and Wolf, Kern, and Mayzar followed. They lifted the plain wood coffin and lowered it carefully into the ground. As the four men stepped back, Chavigny sketched the Cross again before turning away.

A work detail with shovels moved in to cover the coffin with earth, and the funeral was over.

There would be no eulogy, no headstone, nothing but a shallow, unmarked grave for Mario Antonelli. He hadn't even died a legionnaire. Just a suicide who had found his disgrace impossible to bear.

Wolf lingered, looking down at the grave as the others left. He tried to analyze his feelings and found that he could not. Antonelli hadn't been much of a lancemate, but he had deserved better than this. It was typical of the Legion to ignore him in death after hounding him to the breaking point in life.

Something stirred behind Wolf, and when he looked he found Myaighee there beside him. The hannie hadn't been told off as one of the pallbearers because of his small size, but as one of Antonelli's few real friends the little alien had come to the service, Wolf found himself wondering what Myaighee thought of the human religious service, then realized that he had probably seen it many times before while serving in Fraser's Bravo Company.

The alien knelt beside the grave and rambled with something at his throat. It was a small vial which hung from a chain, hidden by the neck ruff. Myaighee opened the vial and carefully added a few grains of sand from the earth the workers had used to fill in the grave to a layer of dirt inside the container. Then he sealed it up and returned the vial to its place.

"A custom from your planet?" Wolf asked the hannie.

"No," Myaighee said quietly. "A custom of the Legion. When a comrade falls, dirt from the grave is collected in one of these containers. I carry a reminder of all the friends I have lost, and of the worlds they fought for, wherever I go."

Wolf sniffed disdainfully. "Another Legion tradition. Wonderful."

"I have learned that there is great comfort in tradition, Wolf. It might help you, if you would only let it." The alien didn't wait for a reply. Myaighee turned away, leaving Wolf alone beside the grave.

He stood there for a long time, lost in thought. When he finally walked away, he saw Vanyek coming back into the quiet cemetery. Wolf stopped and watched the corporal from a distance and was surprised to see the man kneel and take a small sample of dirt from the grave.

CHAPTER TWENTY

You're given a hard time and you can't relax. If you can't take it, you shouldn't have joined in the first place. I've changed a lot since I joined the Legion.

—an anonymous legionnaire,
French Foreign Legion, 1984

The sign over the bar door read The White Kepi, and the entrance was flanked by a pair of mannequins clad in Legion dress uniforms. It was a popular watering hole for legionnaires from Fort Hunter, located a block from the maglev terminal in the seedier side of Villastre known as Fortown. The owner, Jacques Souham, was an ex-Legion NCO who had chosen to invest his retirement money and Citizen's stipend to build a business on Devereaux, rather than migrating to some more popular world. That was how the Commonwealth did business. Citizens had power and prestige on frontier worlds like this one, and over the years their numbers grew until they could bring the planet painlessly into Terra's star-spanning empire.

Karl Wolf clutched the package in his hand a little more tightly and went inside. The bar was dimly lit and crowded, and though there were plenty of legionnaires within there were a fair number of civilians as well. He even noticed a table of Gwyrran-descended Wynsarrysa natives in one corner. Not all of the ales on Devereaux were rebels.

The smell of narcosticks and cheap synthol made him choke, and Wolf regretted agreeing to use the bar as a meeting place. He hadn't particularly wanted to come into Villastre in the first place, even though this was the first pass the recruits had been granted since the start of training. Since the training battalion had gathered back at Fort Hunter for the holiday break in their schedule, Wolf's idea of recreation had been to seek out some precious moments of privacy so he could think ... and try to map out his future.

But Lisa Scott had wanted to do some Christmas shopping in town, and she had talked him into coming with her. They had split up at the maglev station, setting The White Kepi as their rendezvous point, and Wolf had dutifully battled the crowds in the city's commercial district in search of token gifts to give to the rest of his lance. He wasn't very satisfied with his purchases, but thought it was probably just his bad mood influencing his judgment.

He spotted her, sitting alone at a table near the Gwyrrans in the corner. She waved, and with a curt nod he pushed his way through the crowd to join her. When he reached the table he saw that she had turned to examine a display of knives on the wall above her. Her inter-est in them brought back a flash of memory, the sight of her that first night in the platoon shower room, her knife at the ready to hold off young Antonelli.

A lot had happened since then, he thought bitterly as he put his package on the table and sat down opposite her. More than he cared to think about, today.

"Glad to see the decor's to your taste," he said, trying to keep his tone cheerful and light. In the ten days since Antonelli's suicide he had been fighting hard to avoid letting his ill humor show, but it took an effort. Wolf had never been much interested in small talk, and it was harder than ever to keep from sitting and brooding when the people around him were enjoying themselves.

She smiled at him. "You bet. This guy Souham's got a great collection. So how did you make out? Find what you were looking for?"

A waitress in a tight-fitting, low-cut parody of Legion fatigues appeared to take their drink orders. He checked the chrono function of his wristpiece. Another maglev car would be leaving for the base in thir-ty minutes. Enough time for a beer, perhaps....

He ordered, then looked back across the table at Scott. This excur-sion had been her idea. Was she ready to head back yet?

"Find what you were looking for?" she asked again, seemingly ignoring his byplay with the 'piece.

"Some," he said shortly. "But I still agree with what my father told me when I was a kid. If we had been meant to mingle with crowds of shoppers, God never would have invented computer shopping networks."

She laughed. "That would take all the fun out of it," she told him. "Anyway, you can't haggle over the price with a computer."

"I wouldn't have imagined you as the haggling type," he said absently. "Not much need to haggle when you've got money...." The words were already out by the time he realized what he had said. Since that day in the hospital at Fort Souriban he had been careful not to mention anything about her background.

But Lisa didn't seem put off by his comment. "Where else do you want to try?" she asked. "We've got time."

He sighed. "Look, I think I'd rather head back to the tube station and catch the next car to Hunter. I've had about all the holiday shoping I can take."

"If that's what you want," she said with a shrug. "But if you still have stuff you need to pick up ..."

"Hell, I don't even know what to buy," he told her. "I mean, you and Kern are easy enough, but what the devil am I supposed to buy for an alien who never even heard of Christmas until he joined the Legion? What *do* you buy a hannie, anyway?"

She looked at him with a stern expression. "You really don't like Myaighee much, do you?"

Wolf shrugged. "I don't dislike him," he said defensively. "It's just that nonhumans aren't real common back home, and I don't know how to deal with them."

"Try treating them the way you would anybody else. As long as you keep thinking of every nonhuman you meet as something different, you'll always treat them as inferiors. Myaighee's a better person than a lot of humans I've met, and he doesn't deserve this human superiority act of yours."

"Hey, I went along with him as lance leader. I took his orders when he bothered to give any."

"Sure, but everyone could see that you resented it, Wolf. How would you like it now if one of us started acting that way toward you?"

He looked away. "Doesn't matter much now," he said slowly.

"What are you talking about?"

"I don't think I'm going to Kessel next week," he said slowly. The thought had been nagging him for days, and he said the words with a feeling of making a decision at last. "I don't think I can make the grade in the Legion, Lisa. Maybe it's time I just admitted it and left the soldiering to the people who are qualified for it."

"Nonsense!" Now she looked angry. "You've got the highest score in the lance, and I heard Konrad telling Vanyek the other day that you're still in the top ten in the whole company. You can't just give up!"

"We're only partway through," he pointed out. "There's plenty of time for me to screw up yet ... especially now that they gave me the lance. Look what happened to Antonelli. He was finally starting to show some progress. Then he screws up once and ..." He trailed off, picturing the body swinging back and forth in the tiny barracks room back at Fort Souriban.

"Antonelli was a whole different case," she said. "Nobody knows the whole story. He did, but he'll never tell it now. He muddled through as long as he could, but you know how close he was to a downcheck the whole time. When they finally cut him, he couldn't take it. Pure and simple. So don't sit there and use Antonelli as an excuse. He didn't have what it takes. You do."

"Do I?" he asked. "Really? The only thing I had in common with the kid was not fitting in around here. I just can't buy into all the mystique. The traditions they try to foist off on everybody to turn us into obedient little drones. 'Honor and Fidelity' and 'the Legion takes care of its own' and all that drivel. They didn't take very good care of Antonelli when the chips were down ... or even Yeh Chin, who couldn't help getting hit before the real fighting started."

He looked down at the table. "I didn't see anybody rallying around to help Antonelli when he got in trouble. Not the rest of our class, and certainly not the regular legionnaires. Do you know that when a lance came to take down the body and investigate his quarters they took the rope he'd used and cut it up to sell as *souvenirs?* Another of their damned traditions...."

"I know," she said. "It's supposed to be a good luck charm, or something. The superstition goes back to the very beginning of the Legion, back on Terra."

"My point is, they weren't worried about *him.* Just like most of the other recruits didn't even bother to come to the funeral." He thought about Myaighee and Vanyek taking dirt from the grave, but dismissed it. Just another superstition ... it had nothing to do with their feelings about Antonelli himself. "So where do they get off preaching about camaraderie and dying for the Legion and all that garbage? You've got to believe if you expect to get anywhere in this outfit, and I just don't believe."

"Oh, come off it," Lisa said harshly. "You don't believe the advertising hype, and right away you think that makes you doomed to failure? That's ridiculous." She reached across the table and took both his hands in her own, fixing his eyes with her ice blue stare. "Yeah, the mystique can be pretty damned silly sometimes. But it isn't just empty words. If that was true, Banda would have left Yeh Chin to bleed to death when the fight started at Savary's. And your friend MacDuff wouldn't have rushed the Sandray trying to save the rest of us. Do you think he believed all the crap they've been feeding us about Camerone and Hunter and all the rest? I doubt it. But he thought enough of his duty ... and of the rest of us ... to put his life on the line when we were in trouble. As I recall, you were doing the same thing. But where was Antonelli? Crouching out in the woods somewhere, wasn't he? You never said so, but I saw the way you were looking at him later on. He was afraid, wasn't he? Don't compare yourself to him, Wolf. And don't try to make him a martyr. He killed himself, because he couldn't take the pressure."

"Yeah. Maybe." He nodded reluctantly. The scorn in her voice hammered at his newfound resolve, but deep down he wasn't convinced. And he was sure that Antonelli had taken his life largely because he believed Wolf had betrayed his trust, and that was a stain on Wolf's honor that couldn't just be dismissed as unimportant.

The waitress returned with their drinks before he could say anything more. He took a cautious sip of his beer and set it down with an expression as sour as the beverage tasted. Most of the crops grown on Devereaux picked up a tart flavor from the local soil. But all legionnaires professed to enjoy Devereaux products, and even though he had enough money in his ident disk to buy offworld imports he had decided long since that it was best to blend in as much as possible.

He was starting to think that protective coloration wasn't worth the assault on his taste buds. Beer had never been his favorite drink before signing up anyway, and this local brand ...

Not that it mattered much anyway. If he went ahead and resigned, he wouldn't have to keep up the pretense much longer, and even though Lisa Scott had made some good points she hadn't really said anything to make him change his mind.

Lisa gave a sudden, mirthless laugh. "Wouldn't you know it," she said with a bitter smile. "You want out, but I'm the one who has a father pulling strings. And I'd give damn near anything to stay...."

He couldn't find any way to answer that.

The silence went on, and deep in thought, Lisa Scott drank her beer without noticing its tart flavor.

She had joined the Legion with the firm intention of keeping others at arm's length. That was another legacy of the kidnapping, and its aftermath, the reluctance to allow anyone to get close again. Long ago she had started dividing the universe up into three distinct groups—the masses of people who had nothing to do with her or hers, the ones who wanted something from her, and the few who were genuinely worth caring about. The latter category, she had found, were in danger of dying or being sent away. Alyssa Abercrombie had vowed that she wouldn't hurt—or be hurt by—anyone else again.

But Karl Wolf had gotten past her defenses somehow. She still wasn't sure how to define her feelings about him. There was some physical attraction there, but she thought of him more as a friend than as a potential romantic interest. Growing up as the Senator's only child, she could only imagine what a brother might have been like, and perhaps that was how she regarded Wolf. An older brother, someone who understood her, someone she could look up to....

But it was hard to reconcile the Wolf she was seeing today with the man who had turned the tide at Savary's. If he went through with this idea of resigning, it would be a terrible waste. Not that it could really matter to her. As she had expected, the package from her father had been one of his holocube lectures, ending with the promise that she would be out of the Legion just as soon as the paperwork was over and done with. Another week or two, at most. She wouldn't even get the chance to put on the white kepi.

It was ironic that Wolf wanted out even though he had everything going for him, while she wanted to stay in but couldn't escape her father's long arm. People adapted to the Foreign Legion at different rates, she decided, thinking back to a discussion in the lance's barracks at Fort Marchand a few nights before the battle at Savary's.

They had been comparing their views of the training process. Kern had talked about the main obstacle that every trainee had to overcome sooner or later, called "the Hump" by some, "the Wall" by others. Every military recruit, whether he served in the Legion or the Centauri

Rangers or the Commonwealth Space Navy, found it hard to make the transition from civilian to soldier. In the Legion the pressure was particularly hard because the conditions were much harder than in ordinary services. The first goal of any Basic Training, according to Kern, was to break down the individuality of recruits so that they could learn to subordinate themselves to the army as a whole. In a state as diverse as the Commonwealth, and particularly in the polyglot Foreign Legion, harsh treatment was one way to encourage would-be soldiers to let go of that individuality. Not only were tongue-lashings and the occasional beating effective methods of getting a point across, but the recruits also tended to be drawn together by a common resentment toward their instructors. It was a tough process, and the only options open were to adapt or to fail. That was the real essence of the Hump.

Most Legion recruits just opted out, earned their down-check and gave up all hope of a successful five-year hitch with a Citizen's benefits at the end of it all. But for some, the Hump was too much, especially when there were pressures from other directions that made failure as impossible to face as the training the recruit couldn't handle. When that happened, anything was possible. It was like *cafarde*, the classic Legion disease, starting with a little voice whispering the gospel of hopelessness and ending with madness, suicide, desertion ... depending on the individual recruit, almost anything could happen.

It had happened to Antonelli, though he hadn't actually broken until after the Legion had ordered his discharge. But she had never expected to see it happen to Karl Wolf. And it worried her ... in more ways than one. Why was she suddenly so concerned over how Wolf lived his life?

But whether she liked it or not she did care. But she didn't know how to reach him. Plainly he needed to cling to that sense of individuality the Legion was just as determined to squash. She could understand that much, at least. An aristocrat, accustomed to command, would find it hard to surrender the freedom that was an essential part of his makeup. It was easy enough for her to make it past the Hump, because compared with life with Senator Abercrombie the Legion for her was a genuine taste of freedom.

If only she could help make Wolf see that he could become a part of the Legion without giving up everything of himself....

"Well, fancy that," a voice said at her elbow. "A couple of genuine junior white-caps in for a look at the big city!"

She looked up. A trio of teenagers in motley civilian dress were looming over their table. The speaker was short and slender, and his cocky manner reminded her instantly of Mario Antonelli in the early days of training. His two friends were larger and seemed ready to take their lead from him.

"Hell, I guess we're lookin' at the future of our fair planet," one of them rumbled. "The next generation of protection from the lokes and the ales, huh?"

Neither recruit answered. Lisa took another drink and studied the display of knives on the wall.

"Hey, junior white-caps," the leader persisted. "Maybe you can tell us why your Legion won't let us change things around here. We're ready here for Membership ... but it's you white-caps who won't let us have it. Isn't that right? Explain it to me, why don't you?"

She looked him over slowly, coldly. "I'm not up on local politics," she said in a quiet, reasonable voice. "We're just marchmen signed up for a hitch."

The political situation on Devereaux was a complicated powder keg with twists and turns she was only vaguely aware of. The planet's human population had once been ruled by the Semti Conclave, but the Terran Commonwealth had liberated the world and made it a Trust. In the usual course of things, a slowly expanding Citizen base would eventu-ally have been able to form a government able to apply for full Mem-bership, with votes in the Grand Senate and a voice in the admin-istration of the Commonwealth as a whole. But conditions weren't that straightforward. There was the ongoing problem of the Wynsarrysa rebels, for one thing. And there was also the problem of the Fifth For-eign Legion.

Devereaux was the official home of the Legion. It had been built on the ruins of the Fourth Foreign Legion that had died defending the world in the Semti Wars, and for over a hundred years it had been home to the current outfit. But unlike other units of Terra's Colonial Army, the Legion was not permitted to be directly tied to any one Member of the Commonwealth. Individual worlds fielded military forces that served in the Colonial Army—the Black Watch from Cal-edon, for instance—but by statute the Legion was drawn from all parts of the Commonwealth and even from worlds outside the Terran sphere. If Devereaux became a Memberworld, the Legion's connections would have to be severed, and that was something most legionnaires found unthinkable.

There are inevitably rumors that the Legion had blocked every attempt to gain Devereaux a better place in the Commonwealth, even accusations that the Legion was secretly fostering the Wynsarrysa risings in order to make itself seem indispensable for the planet's defense. And there was a vocal body of human colonists who were calling for the expulsion of the Legion....

"C'mon," the agitator insisted, getting louder. "You come here to our planet to perpetuate your Legion rule ... but you don't want to own up to it, do you? Afraid people will learn the truth about you? We're sick of having the scum of the galaxy calling this their home. So why don't you leave and find some place that wants you?"

A few of the other civilians applauded. The other legionnaires, though, had gone silent. The atmosphere was suddenly tense.

Wolf stood, a smooth, fluid motion. "Why don't you go peddle your politics to someone who cares, Citizen?" he said, soft-voiced.

"Citizen!" The agitator hooted. "You think me and mine have a chance to be Citizens? Hah! The only way we get to be 'Citizens' is if we go out and take what should be ours! Like this!"

His fist lashed out at Wolf, but the aristo parried the blow easily. Then one of the toughs grabbed him from behind, and the other reached for Lisa Scott....

She ducked and pushed back her chair, bringing her foot up in a roundhouse kick in the same motion. Her boot caught him in the kneecap, and he fell heavily. Wolf elbowed his attacker in the stomach and pulled free. They were back to back now, facing the two remaining rabble-rousers. A few other civilians were starting to move toward the fight, as if to join in....

Until the legionnaires scattered around the bar surged forward.

There was a long moment of deadly silence. Then a loud humming broke the quiet. A scarred man wearing an apron over old Legion fatigues with the name "Souham" prominent on the right breast stepped onto the floor, a stun baton in each hand. From the pitch of the hum they were both set on full power. "Break it up, you scum," the man growled. "Take your politics out of here and leave my comrades-in-arms alone!"

For emphasis he lashed out at the leader of the toughs. The young man screamed and backed away, clutching at the livid welt on his bare arm.

As suddenly as it had started, the fight was over. Civilians and legionnaires alike drifted back to their tables and started drinking and talking again. But a couple of noncoms stopped to clap Wolf on the back, and Souham ordered another round for the two recruits, on the house. He shook Wolf's hand before retreating behind the bar again.

Sitting down opposite Wolf again, Lisa Scott smiled. "Looks like you've got to take back a few of the things you were saying before, Wolf," she said.

He raised an eyebrow. "Such as?"

"Well, if you don't call that rallying around a fellow legionnaire, I don't know what would qualify."

Wolf looked thoughtful as he took another swig of beer.

Chapter Twenty-One

I started out a soldier of this Foreign Legion, and now that we are reunited once more I know that nothing can defeat us.

> —Marshal F'Rujukh's Order of the Day,
> Battle of Frenchport, Ganymede,
> Third Foreign Legion, 2419

A holiday air filled the familiar confines of the mess hall. According to the intricate conversion of the standard Terran calendar and clock to local Devereaux time, Christmas Eve had started at 0934, and had run for over twenty hours now. Legion tradition guided the celebration of the holiday as it did so many other things, and according to that tradition four training companies and the entire staff of Fort Hunter had gathered in the mess hall at 2630 hours local—about 1700 hours GMT, Christmas Eve, according to Terrestrial timekeeping—to start an ongoing round of eating, drinking, and partying punctuated from time to time by more serious or ceremonial moments. This was the Christmas vigil, and everyone not on duty was expected to attend.

Wolf sat in a dim corner of the hall, feeling out of place amid the merrymakers. At the far end of the huge room a space had been cleared. At "midnight" an improvised altar would be moved into place so that Father Chavigny could hold mass. For now, though, the area was a stage where groups of recruits were putting on skits or singing Christmas carols to entertain the audience. Right now six recruits and Corporal Vanyek were singing a haunting holiday song that had origin-ated with the noncom's Slavic ancestors. Another group was huddled to one side hastily improvising the skit they were supposed to do next.

He took a long swig of punch and set the empty cup on the table beside him. Ever since the excursion with Lisa Scott he hadn't been able to put his feelings in order. Part of him still wanted to make it through Legion training, to prove that he really did have what it took ... but he was growing more aware each day of his inadequacies as a soldier. A very basic part of him resisted the entire process of giving up his individuality. He wasn't sure he'd ever be a cog in the Legion machine.

On the maglev tube car heading back from Villastre he'd asked Lisa for advice. Somehow she seemed able to deal with the situation even though her background, like his, had been one of privilege and ease.

"It's all a matter of giving them what they want," she said with a shrug. "I got used to that from years of pleasing my father. It isn't an all-or-nothing proposition, Karl. You can bury your individuality far enough to please the powers that be without losing sight of who you are entirely."

Watching the other recruits mingling amid the Christmas festiviti es, he wondered again if he'd ever be able to strike that balance.

"You're quiet tonight," her voice broke in on his sour thoughts. He looked up to see her standing behind his chair, sipping a glass of wine and watching him through thoughtful eyes.

"Yeah. Still a lot on my mind."

Lisa smiled. "The least you could do is let down for Christmas! What's it take to put a smile on that face, anyway?" She didn't wait for an answer. "Did you see the cribs? They're really incredible!"

Each company had entered one Nativity crib in competition, and the four entries were lined up along one wall. Wolf had been drafted into the work party Sergeant Ortega had put together to set them up. "Yeah," he said slowly. "Er, they're not ... not exactly in the holiday spirit, some of them."

She flashed another smile. "I'll say. Especially ours."

Training Company Odintsev had submitted a crib that showed three bearded legionnaires abseiling from a hovering transport lighter into the midst of a typical Nativity scene. Volunteer Hosni Mayzar, who'd been in charge of the project, had entitled the composition "The Hostage Rescue of the Magi." No one was entirely sure if the Moslem recruit was having his own little joke at the expense of his Christian comrades....

But it was eye-catching, intricately detailed, and Vanyek thought it stood a good chance of winning Father Chavigny's First Prize award despite—or perhaps because of—the unusual blend of theology and small unit tactics.

The thought made Wolf smile despite himself. Mayzar, at least, had kept part of his own individuality intact. And Antonelli had played a big part in the design and execution of the crib before his untimely end. Maybe Lisa had been right after all.

"Did you see the one Schiller's bunch did?" he began, trying to keep up this end of the conversation. "It's—"

He was interrupted by a disturbance at the double doors ten meters away, where a cluster of officers and noncoms had suddenly stopped comparing notes on the training program so they could greet a new arrival. Wolf had to strain to see through the throng.

The object of all the attention was an unprepossessing sight, a frail, white-haired woman in a life-support chair. Her legs and lower torso were completely enclosed by the chair's mechanism, but she wore a Legion uniform jacket. The rank device was like a sergeant-major's, but with an extra rocker and a black star added, and a long strip of chevrons denoting her time in service. Wolf wasn't familiar with any such insignia, but plainly the legionnaires around her, even the officers, were treating the old woman with considerable deference and respect.

She had a right to respect, Wolf thought, just on the basis of age. Regen therapy could extend life by a fair number of years, and bionic and geriatric medicine could do even more. But sooner or later—say after a hundred and twenty-five or so—the human body just couldn't keep repairing itself no matter how much artificial assistance the high-tech doctors could bring to bear. At that point, full-support wheelchairs or beds were the only way to keep the aging body alive. More often than not the mind went first, though.

But this woman's eyes were sharp, almost supernaturally alert and bright. And, frail though she looked in that chair, it was plain that she wasn't ready to give up the fight for life just yet.

"Who the hell is she?" Wolf asked aloud. Beside him, Lisa shrugged.

"Keep your voice down, nube," another voice countered in a hoarse stage whisper. It was Sergeant Konrad, leaning against the wall nearby. He moved forward and took a seat beside Wolf. The platoon NCO had plainly been drinking and looked as unsteady as he sounded. "Show some respect. That's Aunt Mandy."

"Aunt?" Wolf asked, raising an eyebrow. "Whose aunt?"

Konrad looked disgusted. "That's what we call her in the Legion. That's Amanda Hunter, for God's sake."

"Hunter.... You mean, as in *Fort* Hunter?" Lisa asked, echoing Wolf's thought.

The sergeant nodded curtly. "Of course. Commandant Thomas Hunter's wife. She was hiding out up in the hills of the Nordemont range when her husband died in the attack on Villastre."

"That was a hundred and twenty years ago...." Wolf said softly. "That means she must be ... what? A hundred and fifty?"

"One hundred fifty-three last month," Konrad said with an air of pride. "She's the last surviving member of the Hunter family. And the only living link to the Fourth Legion. When they ordered the Fifth established, she was given the honorary rank of chief-sergeant-major. When she finally dies it will really be the end of an era."

"But what's she doing here?" Wolf pressed. "A woman with her name could have her pick of the high society balls on Devereaux. Age and a historical name are always a sure route to invitations."

"She's here, nube, because this is where she wants to be," Konrad hissed. "Every year since the Fifth Legion was formed she's attended one of the Legion Christmas vigils at Fort Hunter. This year she chose the Training Battalion. You should count yourself lucky, nube. Aunt Mandy might not be around too many years longer." The tough sergeant looked like he was about to break down and cry at the thought.

Gunnery Sergeant Ortega got behind her chair and helped guide the old lady toward the front of the mess hall. Vanyek and the other carolers had finished, and the recruits preparing for the next skit looked relieved at the interruption.

Long minutes went by as the officers and NCOs arranged themselves around the life-support chair. Then an officer, resplendent in dress uniform and heavy braid, stepped forward and nodded to the legionnaire at the sound systems panel. The technician adjusted the directional sound pickup, and the officer cleared his throat.

"Good evening and Merry Christmas," he said. His voice was clear throughout the mess hall, but didn't sound distorted or amplified. "Many of you don't know me by sight, but you've cursed my name often enough. I'm Commandant Stathopoulos, commander of the Training Battalion here at Fort Hunter. Tonight we have been honored by a visit from a very special lady we fondly call Aunt Mandy. Every year she picks out one unit at the base to share Christmas with. This year it's our turn, and as usual Aunt Mandy has picked out some presents for all of you here. When you hear your name called, come up to the front and take your gift."

A sergeant took over, bawling out a name at a volume louder than any technical augmentation would have allowed. Wolf tuned out the proceedings and muttered an excuse to get away from Sergeant Konrad. The NCO was fearsome on the parade ground. Half-drunk and maudlin he represented an entirely different set of problems.

Lisa Scott followed him to the door. "You're not leaving, are you?" she asked. "You'll be in trouble if they call you up and find out you wandered off."

He shrugged and sat on the floor beside the open doorway. A cool breeze was coming off the desert, and it felt good after the heat of the crowded mess hall. "More of their precious tradition," he said gruffly. "They trundle this woman in here and get her to hand out little trinkets to make the recruits think somebody really cares." He shook his head sadly. "They fall for it, too."

Lisa slipped her hand inside her uniform jacket and drew out a flat package. "Well, here's one trinket that comes from somebody who does care," she said. "Go ahead ... open it."

The plain wrapping paper covered a plastic case. Inside rested a silver medallion. He drew it out and squinted at it in the poor light.

On one side the medallion bore the tricolor-and-V of the Fifth Foreign Legion. On the other ...

"How in the name of God did you find this?" he demanded. The reverse side bore the stylized coat of arms of the Hauser family. "I never even told you my name...!"

"No," she admitted. "But you had that crest stamped *on* the inside of your wristpiece. I ... er ... exercised my reconnaissance skills one night when you were showering, and a craft house in Villastre did the rest."

"It's ... great." Words weren't adequate.

"When you look at it, think of it as the balance you've been looking for, Karl." She smiled. "I just hope you don't opt out now. Not after I had them put the Legion emblem on it."

He swallowed. "I'll have to keep that in mind. Thanks, Lisa." He smiled at her. "Alyssa. I don't feel right thanking someone who doesn't really exist, you know."

Wolf spotted a silver chain coiled in the box and went through the motions of attaching the medallion to it. With Lisa's help he settled it in place around his neck and tucked it under his uniform shirt.

"I bought you a present, too, but I'm afraid I can't give it to you for a few weeks," he told her.

"What is it?"

He grinned. "A knife, to replace the one our beloved corporal took that first night."

"A knife. Now there's a fine present to give at Christmas!"

"Well, if you don't want it … I mean, it's just a Novykiev Spring Knife, no big deal."

"A Novykiev …" Her eyes were wide with surprise. "How did you lay your hands on one of those?"

The lineal descendent of a weapon first used on Terra before star-flight was born, the spring knife combined a fine hand-to-hand edged weapon with a powerful spring mechanism that could propel the blade thirty meters or more with deadly accuracy. The best were made on the colony world of Novykiev, where they had enjoyed considerable vogue as a hunting weapon for a time. Since the Riots of 2839 and the imposition of martial law, though, Novykiev Spring Knives had become scarce as hens' teeth.

"Found an old legionnaire who'd picked up a couple as souvenirs back in thirty-nine," Wolf said with a smile. "He decided he could afford to part with one."

He didn't mention the fact that it had taken most of the credit in his ident disk to buy the weapon from old Corporal Souham in town. He had gone back to the bar the day after the fight specifically to get the weapon for her. The cost hadn't seemed important even though he had nothing left now but his meager Legion salary … and if he ended up resigning he wouldn't even have that.

But he owed this woman his life … and more. The knife was perfect for Lisa Scott.

"I—I don't know what to say," Lisa told him. "You shouldn't have gone to that kind of trouble.…"

He touched his jacket where the medallion lay. "I thought it was the best way I could pay you back after you helped me start to sort things out the other day. Among other things. And whether you stay in the Legion or your father pulls you out, you'll need the extra edge. A very sharp one."

Lisa made a face at the pun. Before she could reply. Kern's gentle voice interrupted her. "They're going through the gifts up front by units," he said quietly. "Our platoon is up next, and it might be a good idea if we were ready for it. If it wouldn't be interruptin' anything important here, that is." Wolf looked up to see the big redhead favoring them with a suggestive leer.

There was a line of recruits moving past the officers and NCOs by Aunt Mandy's life-support chair. Lisa and Wolf joined the line.

They moved forward slowly, but eventually they approached the old woman. Wolf couldn't hear what was said to Myaighee or Kern, but as Lisa's turn came he heard Gunnery Sergeant Ortega say her name and saw Amanda Hunter nod. She looked up at Lisa and held her eyes for a long moment before speaking.

"Captain Odintsev tells me there has been a request for a certain Lisa Scott to be released from her provisional contract immediately," she said in a dry but surprisingly firm voice. "From what I hear there is quite a lot of pressure being applied from a very high level indeed."

He could see Lisa's shoulders slump in defeat. The old woman gave a dry chuckle, and it was all he could do to keep from stepping forward and shouting at her. Why had she ruined Lisa's Christmas this way?

Then he caught a glint of gold in her hand as she held something out to Lisa. "My gift to you is a choice, my dear. The ident disk you're wearing is about to be updated with new orders requiring your discharge. This one, on the other hand ..." She chuckled again. "The Lisa Scott this one describes has a different serial number, a whole different background. We don't often change a legionnaire's identity again so soon after starting Basic, but if you don't want to leave the Legion ... Well, by the time anyone found out and started searching for you again, you'll have the white kepi, and no one can make you leave then, my dear. No one."

For the second time that night Wolf saw Lisa speechless. She took the gleaming ident disk and finally managed to stammer out an awkward thanks.

Then it was his turn.

"Volunteer Karl Wolf," Ortega said. At Amanda Hunter's gesture he backed away out of earshot.

When the old woman looked up at him, Wolf could see her eyes glittering with something that might have been amusement ... or understanding. She nodded slowly. "I've seen your file," she said. "Your real one, not Karl Wolf's recruit file. I like to know a little something about the people I give gifts to, you see, and I'm old enough and respected enough to get my way."

She held out a flattened box, an adchip module. "You've come to the Foreign Legion from a culture that's quite different from your own, Wolfgang Alaric Hauser von Semenanjung Burat," she went on. "Not as different as some alien ones, admittedly, but still ..." She seemed to pause to gather her thoughts. "It may seem like you're facing pressures no one else has ever had to meet. When my husband was alive ... but that's a different story. The fact is, the path you're on now has been well trodden over the centuries, young man. You might benefit from seeing how one of the ones who went before walked that path. A merry Christmas to you ... Karl Wolf."

He smiled and nodded and mumbled something he hoped was app-ropriate and moved on, surprised at what she knew about him and hardly aware of the gift in his hand. The old lady had put a lot of thought and effort into these gifts, more than he would have believed reasonable. Earlier he had sneered about the Legion snaring foolish recruits with worthless trinkets. Now he knew better.

Wolf found a chair and touched the chip module to the side of his head, just behind and below his left ear. The chip clung there after he released it from the module. He closed his eyes and triggered it with a thought.

For a moment he was far from Devereaux, on an empty, airless plain below a cluster of half-ruined domes. Without being told he knew this was Ganymede, a colony known as Frenchport, and the end of the French interstellar empire was drawing near.

A figure was visible in the scene, only vaguely humanoid with four arms and a low, domed sense-organ cluster instead of a head. Even clad in an old-fashioned vacuum suit the alien seemed to exude an air of authority and competence.

"In 2419 AD the only nonhuman ever to hold the rank of Marshal of France faced his last and greatest challenge," a voice only Wolf could hear said deep in his mind. "Marshal F'Rujukh, outnumbered, out-gunned, without hope of retreat or relief, led a mixed army of Imperial forces into combat in a campaign that would cost him his life. But in the process he earned a place few can match in the annals of military history."

There was a fanfare of music. "F'Rujukh ended his life a Marshal of

Imperial France, but his beginnings were by no means so auspicious. Forced to flee his homeworld of Qwar'khwe when the planet fell under the sway of a military dictatorship, F'Rujukh entered the Third Foreign Legion as a common soldier. Years later he lived up to an ancient Legion saying: 'The only way for us foreigners to repay our debt to France is to die for her.'

"Though not of Terra, he shed his blood for Mankind's sake."

Wolf terminated the biochip and returned from Dreamland bemused. A few weeks before he would never have thought that he could be interested in the career of an alien, no matter how distinguished his place in history.

Now he was looking forward to studying that career in the hopes that it might help him shape his own.

Chapter Twenty-Two

To be a good soldier, one has to leave his personality at the barracks gate, become wax which receives all impressions, put his tongue in his pocket, hide the resentment in his eyes ... and despite all that display everywhere a finesse and a superior intelligence.

—Legionnaire Charles des Eccores,
French Foreign Legion, 1873

The Christmas holiday was over, and the training had moved into a new phase which Gunnery Sergeant Ortega had promised would be at a more intense level than ever before. Where the specialty work before the break had focused primarily on honing specific skills, the new round of instruction was supposed to bring everything the recruits had assimilated before together into a single, unified approach to soldiering.

The recruits had been given passes into town for Christmas afternoon, and the following day was one of light duty. At morning assembly on the parade ground a new set of reorganizations had been announced, abolishing the training company's fourth platoon entirely and absorbing the lances from that outfit to fill in vacancies in the other lances. It still left Wolf's platoon, the Second, under-strength, with only four lances instead of six. Charlie Lance had ceased to exist as a result of the casualties taken at Savary's, and Foxtrot Lance was now broken up to fill in other vacancies in the TO&E. Any further losses, they were told, wouldn't result in further changes in the company's organization.

Wolf's lance was unchanged by the reshuffling of other units, to his relief. The problems of trying to lead a lance were daunting enough when he knew most of his troops from their weeks of shared training. Katrina Voskovich was already an unknown quantity, and he was happy there would be no others to deal with.

Somewhere between the Christmas Eve vigil and that first post holiday assembly the idea of Wolf's resigning had faded away. He wasn't sure what had turned the tide. Aunt Mandy's presents, both to him and to Lisa Scott, had made him reexamine his image of the Legion ... but the medallion his lancemate had given him was like a talisman. It seemed to symbolize what was possible, and he was unwilling to put it aside. Unwilling, also, to let her down after she had shown confidence in his ability to continue.

He wasn't sure if he had actually found his way over the infamous Hump during the holiday, but at least Wolf had found a new resolve to keep on trying, whatever might happen.

Now they were on the move again, heading for a new base of operations near Fort Kessel in the rugged Nordemont region a few hundred kilometers north of Villastre and Fort Hunter. Unlike their previous training assignments, this time around they would be spending the whole two-week period in the wilderness, conducting full-company exercises in competition with some of their opposite numbers from one of the other training companies. They might go the entire time without ever seeing Fort Kessel, sleeping in field habitats or under the open sky.

As with the previous changes of base, they were ferried into the mountains aboard a Pegasus transport carrying all the troops and equipment assigned to the platoon. This time they weren't to have any vehicles, which meant they would have to hump their gear over rough terrain on their backs. Still, Wolf told himself, it was probably better to handle this part of the training in the Nordemont than, say, in the Archipel d'Aurore. Long marches with full field packs in those dense jungles, and with the threat of Wynsarrysa rebels lurking behind every tree ... he was definitely glad they had done their vehicle patrol exercises at Fort Marchand. First Platoon had drawn field exercises there, and he didn't envy Suartana and the others in that outfit.

The Nordemont mountains were a startling change from the other regions where the Legion carried out training exercises. They were well to the north of the subtropical zone around Villastre, and latitude combined with altitude to make the area considerably cooler than the more heavily settled areas of Devereaux. The climate was still largely arid, and the mountains, though far from barren, were clad in a sparse scrubby growth. Down in the valleys there were lush forests, but so far these had gone largely unexploited by the human colonists. Large bands of Wynsarrysa were reputed to roam those valleys, some hostile, some merely hoping to be left alone. Few were ever seen along the higher slopes.

Their transport's landing site commanded a particularly spectacular view, and even hard-bitten noncoms like Konrad and Vanyek were drawn to the edge of the plateau where the platoon had been instructed to set up camp to look down into the deep, narrow confines of Mistfloor Gorge. The Blanc River, the largest on the continent, had carved a deep canyon through this part of the mountains. Dropping over a magnificent waterfall, the river vanished below a perpetual cloud of mist at the valley floor.

According to Wolf's chipped briefing, the Mistfloor Gorge was also the termination of the annual migration route of the nasty little animal native to Devereaux known as the strak. Combining the worst features of several Terrestrial species, including the rat, the lemming, and the cockroach, straks traveled in huge bands from their breeding grounds in the northern wastelands, dying by the thousands here at the Mistfloor Gorge every year. It was little wonder that their name had passed into the Legion lexicon as a sort of all-purpose swearword that could refer to appearance, uncleanliness, stupidity, sexual obsession, or any of a number of other bad qualities commonly attributed to the disgusting little creatures.

And the gorge held a special significance for the Legion, as so many things did. Somewhere on the far side of the canyon a network of caves had been used by the Fourth Legion as a base during the guerrilla campaign against the Semti, and later as a refuge by Amanda Hunter and other family members after the legionnaires had doubled back into the inhabited regions along the edge of the Great Desert.

Looking down into the tumult of white froth deep in the canyon, Wolf thought he could understand why the Legion would esteem this place. It was the sort of landmark around which legends were bound to be built.

"What's the matter, you straks?" Vanyek's voice broke into his reverie. "Want to follow your kin and take a jump? Well, go ahead ... or else get back to work!"

The spell was broken. Wolf turned away from the vista and concerned himself with the practical problems of helping Kern and Myaighee set up Delta Lance's field habitat.

*   *   *

Six days of arduous marching and mock fights that were difficult to distinguish from the real thing had confirmed the promise of harder work in this new phase of training. They never remained in the same camp for more than a few scant hours, rising well before the local dawn each day to pack up their gear and set out through the wilderness for a new position. These forced marches made Wolf long for the routine twenty-kilometer hikes of days gone by, and they were usually punctuated by skirmishes with Training Company Hamilton either en route or at the end of the day's journey.

They fought their battles using modified FEKs and support weapons fitted with low-powered training lasers that registered hits by interacting with the microcircuitry in their fatigues. A hit would cause the chameleon cloth to turn a lurid red, making it quite clear when a recruit had become a casualty. By the fifth day Wolf was becoming quite used to being seen in red ... and to the inevitable dressing-down Vanyek or Konrad would give him and the other simulated casualties for allowing themselves to become targets in the first place.

Tonight, though, the lecture he was receiving was of a different kind.

"If your lance had been in its proper position, nube, the ambush would have gone perfectly." Vanyek jabbed him in the chest with two fingers, but Wolf stayed at attention. "As it was, your little band of nightslugs was twenty minutes late showing up, and you came in from the northeast instead of the east. That gave the enemy just the kind of opening they needed."

The exercise had been an elaborate battle of maneuver, with the four lances of Konrad's platoon each taking a different route through the hill country to converge on a command post in a centrally located valley. Delta Lance had set out at the same time as the other units, but Katrina Voskovich, who had been rotated to duty as the lance's pointman for the day, had managed to take the wrong path halfway through the march. By the time anyone had realized it, they'd been committed to the new route, which led to a point near their target but took them over much rougher terrain.

Wolf fought down the impulse to respond to Vanyek, and the co-rporal jabbed him again, harder this time. "If it hadn't been for Mayzar, those reinforcements coming in from the east would've cut up our assault faster than you could say 'dishonorable discharge.' In a *real* fight, nube, you can bet we'd be licking our wounds now, all because you decided to take the scenic route instead of following orders!"

Again he held back. His instant reaction was to defend himself from Vanyek's charges. He wouldn't have picked Voskovich for the point position in the first place, but she had been foisted on him by Vanyek's own rotation schedule. Kern wouldn't have made a mistake like that ... even Myaighee would have done better. Although Voskovich, like the hannie, had seen action with Fraser's famous Bravo Company, she had been a civilian electronics technician who had been forced by cir-cumstances to fight alongside the Legion, and her experience had been minimal. She still didn't have very good combat instincts despite her training, and though she had been brave enough at Savary's her con-tribution there hadn't proved very helpful overall.

And the whole mess had been her doing from first to last. That, to Wolf, made the corporal's tirade doubly bad. Wolf had done his best to redeem the situation....

But he held his silence. The Legion's creed held that the unit was supposed to look after its own, and Delta Lance was Wolfs outfit. The leader had to take responsibility for what all of his charges did ... and there was no point in complicating the situation by trying to make Voskovich share the blame.

Vanyek's eyes bored into his own for a long moment. Finally, the corporal stepped back. "All right, nube," he said. "Your lance pulls the mule duty for the rest of the week. And you ... I want you on guard tonight. All night. You get me?"

"Yes, Corporal," Wolf responded.

"All right. Free time for two hours. Fall out!"

Fuming inwardly, Wolf headed across the platoon's campsite until he found Kern and Myaighee putting the finishing touches on their field habitat, or fab as it was commonly called, the portable, inflatable hut that could hold a five-member lance with minimal discomfort. Lisa Scott handed him a rapack and a mug of thick Devereaux coffee fresh off the fire, and Wolf sat down on a log to eat and sip and think.

He had learned, these last few months, that legionnaires looked out for one another, and that a leader should always accept responsibility for the actions of the soldiers in his command. But he had learned something else from the Legion as well. No mistake ever went unpunished. Sooner or later, any error had to be redeemed by proper action. In the case of Katrina Voskovich, the punishment for her inattention at point would be shared with the whole lance when they had to undertake mule duty, carrying all the excess baggage of their section on future forced marches. Each lance was responsible for personal and lance gear, but there were always extras that had to be carried—medical supplies, demolitions gear, spare ammo for the heavy weapons, and so on. When there were no vehicles on hand, some legionnaires had to be told off to carry this additional baggage, and it was a common form of punishment to assign the duty to individuals or lances who were under a cloud.

So Voskovich would not face any specific penalty to encourage her to think twice the next time she tried to read an electronic map at a crucial fork in the road. Not unless Wolf himself handed down that punishment....

He had seen lance leaders in the company teach an errant recruit a lesson by tying them inside a sack and getting the rest of the outfit to kick and punch the helpless target. That kind of brutality repelled him, but it was all too common in the Legion's ranks.

Wolf looked up from his steaming mug to see Vanyek watching him from the far side of the camp. Something in the corporal's expression told him that Vanyek was expecting him to take some sort of further action. If he didn't, he was all but inviting trouble. The corporal could give Wolf low marks if he didn't handle the situation right ... or he might step in and start handing out fresh punishments that were a lot less pleasant than mule duty.

Voskovich couldn't be allowed to escape punishment completely, so it was up to Wolf to handle it in such a way that it didn't go further than Delta Lance.

On Laut Besar, Uro women were cherished and protected. That had been part of what made Lisa Scott interesting, her independence and ability to look after herself. But it was hard for Wolf to even consider meting out punishment to a woman like Voskovich ... harder than he would ever have imagined. Despite all the Legion training, there was still a lot of the Uro aristocrat in him. But something had to be done, and as he finished his drink and his evening rations he thought he had a way to handle the problem.

"Listen up, people," he said, hardening his resolve. "We've got some time to ourselves here. I think we could put it to good use brushing up on unarmed combat techniques."

"Unarmed combat?" Kern said, an eyebrow raised in curiosity. "Any particular reason, boyo?"

"Yeah," he said. He motioned Kern closer and then gave him a quick jab to the ribs. "Yeah. Because I say so, that's why. Any problem?"

The blow hadn't been a hard one, and the big redhead could have come back and flattened him. But the punch and cuff were the accepted signals in Legion ranks that a superior intended an order to be c arried out, and Kern just grinned and nodded. "Unarmed combat it is," he said cheerfully.

He led them away from camp to a clearing screened from view by a line of trees and set them to work. Each recruit in turn took on Katrina Voskovich in one-on-one combat. The attackers could rest while a comrade took her on, but Voskovich herself had to keep on fighting. By the time it was all over, two grueling hours without rest had taken a toll on Voskovich and left her with a set of bruises to remember it by. Nonetheless, the violence had been controlled throughout.

Wolf felt smug as he led them back to their fab afterward. Perhaps he was finally getting the hang of leadership after all.

* * *

And Stefan Vanyek, watching the proceedings from the cover of the trees, nodded approval as Delta Lance left the field. For a time, Volunteer Wolf hadn't been considered good Legion material. He was too independent, too conscious of his own privileges, to be a legionnaire, no matter how well he performed academically.

But Vanyek had always believed there was a capable legionnaire somewhere inside the pampered aristocrat, and now he knew he had been right.

Wolf would make it after all.

* * *

After the end of the Nordemont training, the company was reassigned to Fort Gsell, the Legion's orbital facility positioned in a synchronous orbit over Fort Hunter, for the final phase of their instruction. The other companies in their training battalion shared this duty, uniting the entire recruit force for the first time since the beginning of the process three months earlier. Things would have seemed crowded, but Fort Gsell was a large station, and in zero-G, space utilization was far more efficient than anything possible on the ground, so the quarters and training areas allocated to the platoon were actually roomy.

The focus of the training in the orbital station was on zero-gravity and zero-pressure combat, learning to convert ordinary battledress fatigues into space suits. Wolf was in his element now, for the Sky Guard training he had received back on Laut Besar had included extensive training in these areas, and he had practical experience as well.

In fact, the training was an unpleasant echo of the last fight for Telok. He woke up several nights running from a nightmare replay of the battle, thrashing against the tether cord that held him in place while he slept in zero gravity. A medical warrant officer prescribed a sleeping patch which helped some. So did a long talk, off duty, with Lisa Scott. It helped to tell her about the fight on Telok, and afterward the dreams weren't quite so vivid or terrifying.

The most notable event of their stay was the arrival of fresh news from the Republic Trisystem. The Ubrenfar leadership had rejected a Commonwealth demand for the evacuation of Laut Besar, and the CSNS *Genghis Khan* had been attacked by a small squadron of Ubrenfar patrol ships inside the orbit of Danton. The Warlord-class cruiser had driven her assailants off, destroying two and forcing a third to surrender. According to unconfirmed reports leaking from the Commonwealth news media, the attacking Ubrenfar ships had belonged to a different warclan from that which had staged the original occupation, suggesting that the confrontation was now widening on both sides of the frontier.

The batch of letters and messages accompanying the news had included a brief holo from Consul-General Doenitz. Wolf had holoed him a few times during training, but this was the first message back. The old diplomat congratulated him on his progress in the Legion, and mentioned in passing that the Free Besaran units Neubeck had been mustering were now on Danton, preparing for the expected push to reclaim Laut Besar from the invaders. Viewing the holetter, Wolf felt a twinge of regret. He had been questioning his reasons for serving with the Legion, when there were reasons aplenty for him to be part of that army confronting the Ubrenfars. His mistakes dealing with the Neubecks had barred him from taking part in the only military career that would have been truly worth his support....

He didn't send a reply right away. The holo had raised new questions in his mind, and Wolf wasn't sure how to deal with them. It was pretty much accepted that he would pass Legion training with flying colors, and on one hand the thought of overcoming all the obstacles he had faced along the way was encouraging. But the knowledge of past failures diminished the achievement in his mind.

The zero-G portion of the training proved relatively easy overall, though the company suffered four men killed in the company from suit accidents over the course of the first week. Then they moved into more complex operations, practicing high-altitude atmospheric insertions in Legion transport lighters. The drills taught the recruits the basics of High-Altitude/High-Opening parawing operations, so that the legionnaires could jump from a ship high in the atmosphere and have a fair chance of reaching the ground in one piece. There were three more deaths in that stage, and Lisa Scott came out of the training with a regen cast on one leg but an unyielding determination to pass the final test that would determine which of the recruits had the honor to don the white kepi at last.

Wolf knew that test would be a tough one ... but he also knew that he could pass it. He could be—*would* be—a legionnaire.

Chapter Twenty-three

I figure it's like this: being a civilian is easy; being a legionnaire is easy; but the difficulty is the change.

—an anonymous legionnaire,
French Foreign Legion, 1984

ive minutes! Five minutes to drop coordinates!"

The interior lights of the assault shuttle switched to red, and recruits began checking each other's gear one last time. They had done this plenty of times during the last week at Fort Gsell, but Wolf could feel the difference in the air, in the purposeful movements of his comrades ... and most of all in himself. This assault jump was unlike any they had practiced before. This time he and his lance-mates would be on their own from start to finish.

Sixty-eight recruits had finished the orbital operations course at Gsell with high enough marks to move into the last phase of their training—the two-week cross-country endurance test which was the final challenge for every legionnaire. They were to be dropped high above the Nordemont wilderness, descending by parawing. Each lance was supposed to come down, assemble, and then make their way overland with minimal equipment, ending up at Fort Hunter. The lances that made it through would pass the training. Those which didn't ... some might be picked up by Search and Rescue craft later. But the drill instructors had made it clear that no recruit class ever underwent the final test without suffering casualties.

The fact that he was aboard the shuttle today was proof th at Wolf really did have what it took to be a legionnaire. In fact, he was number six in the training company, a respectable score indeed. But even the best of them could still wash out in this course.

"Three minutes! Delta Lance, on the line!" Gunnery Sergeant Ortega was serving as Jump Master today, checking to make sure each recruit was fully prepared when he leapt from the hatch. After that, the sergeant's responsibility ended. Tomorrow, in fact, he would be working against them, leading a small force of legionnaires and instructors into the wilderness in search of the recruits. Ortega's troops were one extra hazard to be overcome. Anyone captured by the patrols would get an automatic downcheck.

The five recruits made their way to the rear of the fast-flying shuttle, weighed down by their field packs and the bulky parawings strapped to their backs. Wolf looked them over one last time. He knew that Ortega was doing the same, but this was too important to leave to anyone else. The arrangement of personnel and equipment for the drop might be absolutely crucial to their survival.

Kern would jump first. The big redhead was the strongest member of the lance, and he was weighed down by more than his fair share of the equipment. Myaighee was too small to carry a full load, so Kern had to hump the hannie's share of the communal load. The little ale would be following Kern down, ready to assist him on the ground. Voskovich, and then Lisa Scott, would go next, with Wolf jumping last. He hoped he could coordinate the descent so they wouldn't become too badly separated on the way down....

They looked ready. Wolf gave a tight nod and turned to face Ortega. "Delta Lance, ready, Sergeant," he reported crisply.

The Hispanic noncom pointed to the hatch. "Coming up on one minute," he growled. "Get ready."

Ortega moved down the line, starting with Wolf, checking parawing packs and other fittings. He tapped Wolf on the top of his combat helmet before moving on to Scott.

Finally, he reached the head of the little line, finished inspecting Kern, and slapped the switch beside the hatch. It swung open, and air whipped around them like a small hurricane. Wolf was glad for the safety line that held them together until the moment came to jump.

"Ten seconds!" Ortega called, reading off the numbers displayed over the hatch. "Five ... four ... three ... two ... one Go! Go! Go!"

One after another the recruits jumped. As Wolf reached the head of the line his eyes met Ortega's, and the sergeant gave him a brief smile. Wolf dropped his faceplate down and stepped through the hatchway.

The wind tore at him like an animal, and for a moment he was back in the freefall conditions he'd become so familiar with from all the practice at Fort Gsell. Wolf closed his eyes, and the image of the fight in the warehouse on Telok flooded into his mind unbidden. The same thing had happened every time he'd practiced, a few seconds of near panic, disorienting, almost paralyzing, until he could force himself past the memory.

When he finally opened his eyes he could see two parawings open far below and off to the left. Kern and Myaighee, probably ... Wolf adjusted the image intensifier setting of his faceplate and nodded. The redhead and the alien had their wings extended to ride the air currents all the way down. A flashing sequence on his helmet's HUD display counted down the seconds before his own parawing would unfold.

The number hit zero, but nothing happened....

Malfunction! Wolf fought back another tide of panic and groped for the manual release. His fingers found the control at his belt and tightened around the trigger grip. An instant later he felt the straps around his chest and shoulders dig into his flesh as the wing opened up and checked his plummeting descent. His sigh of relief was almost audible over the rushing of the air past his helmet.

The parawing was a lineal descendent of the old-style parachutes of ancient Terra. Constructed of extremely lightweight materials, it could be stored in a small backpack, but unfolded into a small glider which gave the rider excellent maneuverability in the air. The wings were independently managed by a small computer which could alter their configuration to get the best possible lift and control in any situation. The descent could be left entirely to the computer's discretion, or modified as necessary by simple commands entered through the belt control box.

Wolf called up a descent profile on his combat helmet's faceplate. The miniature computer's projection said he was right on target for the preselected LZ, so he let go of the belt control and let the parawing do its work unattended. Instead he concentrated on making sure the rest of the lance was also going in according to plan.

He had checked each of his lancemates in turn when he lost sight of Kern's parawing. Even though he'd been expecting it, Wolf went through a moment's fear before he reminded himself it was all part of the program. The parawings were made of the same sort of chameleon cloth that was woven into Legion battledress. The helmet chip, tied into sensors in the fatigues, picked up surrounding light waves, analyzed them, and altered the reflective value of the fabric to duplicate the background shades as closely as possible. From above, the parawing tended to blend in with the greens, browns, and grays of the planet's surface below, while an observer on the ground would have trouble telling the wing apart from clouds and blue sky. A quick change of his faceplate setting called up flashing symbols that identified the location of each member of Delta Lance, and he was able to relax again. Everyone was on target....

Long minutes later, with the ground perceptibly closer, Wolf switched from computer to manual control of his parawing, using the airflow to bank in a long slow circle over the LZ. From this vantage point he could scout out their surroundings and make sure Ortega hadn't arranged any special surprises to complicate the landing exercise. Finally, he keyed in his commlink.

"Delta One to all Deltas. Lima Zulu is clear. Repeat, Lima Zulu is clear."

"Delta Three, acknowledging," Kern responded. "Commencing final approach ... now."

Each recruit glided in to the narrow clearing Wolf and Kern had selected as the landing zone during their pretest planning. Although the instructors knew the general area, even Ortega himself didn't know the exact spot where the lance was landing, a clearing along the banks of a stream that fed into the Blanc River just above the Mistfloor Gorge. They had covered this ground thoroughly during the Nordemont training exercises. There was a route down from the plateau into the lower land below the gorge, and their plan called for a stealthy overland move to another tributary of the Blanc to the south. There they could build a small raft that could take them downriver quickly and in comparative comfort. By moving only at night, and concealing themselves along the bank in daytime, Kern had figured they could make it to Fort Hunter in a week. That would give them an ample cushion in case they encountered unexpected difficulties along the way.

Wolf came down last, a little clumsy despite all the practice they had put in. He overshot the clearing and ended up touching down in shallow water, much to the amusement of Kern and Lisa Scott.

But in this test style didn't count. They had made the drop success-fully, and that was what was important. Now all they had to do was elude the hunters and reach their destination....

Myaighee moved through the brush silent and unseen, like one of the phantoms of kys homeworld's rich tradition of myth and legend. Twenty-eight hours had passed since the lance had touched down, and they were still working their way through the rugged hills toward the mouth of the Mistfloor Gorge. The terrain was supposed to be familiar from the training exercises they had gone through prior to the tour at Fort Gsell, but familiarity didn't help that much. It was still a confused tangle of trails and tracks. Ky remembered the time Katrina Voskovich had misdirected them, and was doubly wary as a result. Wolf had assigned the hannie point duty, and ky was determined to come through for the lance. The memory of Savary's, and the shame of being replaced by the male-human aristo, were both burning reminders that ky needed to do the best possible job on this test, no matter what.

And today's reconnaissance was absolutely vital to their march. This section of the Nordemont range was well guarded by the Legion against the possibility of a Wynsarrysa incursion. Several hostile tribes lived to the north of the so-called Hunter Line of fortifications and outposts, and the Legion's main function was to keep those potential foes from penetrating this perimeter and threatening the settled lands to the south, especially the city of Villastre. Checkpoint Tatiana, a permanent outpost manned by a reinforced section of Legion infantry, was perfect-ly placed to interdict the route the recruits wanted to take down to the Blanc River, and it was vital that they work their way past the position without being noticed. Right now Myaighee's job was to determine just how tough a job they faced, and ky was determined to do the job quick-ly and well.

It wouldn't be easy, though. Ky had already spotted several areas covered by a mixture of remote motion sensors and clusters of Galahad antipersonnel mines. The latter, fortunately, were on stand-by mode. In a combat situation the Galahad could be set up for any of a number of trigger systems, including a recognition-friend-or-foe setting which would set the weapon off the first time anything of roughly human size moved into the lethal radius without a working combat helmet broad-casting an acceptable identification code. But that was impractical for permanent defenses, and Myaighee had determined that these mines were all controlled from the checkpoint itself by remote detonators.

The sensors were another problem. But Myaighee's size made ky the ideal scout in this situation. Like the Galahad recognition system, the sensors were set to pick up certain types of body heat, sound, or moving objects of a roughly human-sized mass. Ky was small enough to move in among the sensors. Those which threatened the unit's safe progress could be temporarily disrupted with the right equipment from Myaighee's small field pack.

Ky could hear the sound of running water nearby. That would be the Sinueux River. Checkpoint Tatiana should lie on the far bank beyond the bulk of the low, humpbacked hill ahead....

Myaighee sniffed the air. Something was wrong ... a smell that didn't belong....

The smell of fire. Of scorched wood and charred vegetation. Of burnt flesh.

Ky flipped up the visor of kys combat helmet for a better look. The late afternoon sun was dipping low beyond the hills to the west, but there was plenty of light to see by. And the coil of smoke rising from the direction of the checkpoint confirmed Myaighee's first fears.

It took five more minutes to reach the bank of the river beyond the projecting ridgeline. Crouching in dense brush, Myaighee studied the far bank with a sinking feeling gnawing at kys stomach.

A long time later, ky departed as cautiously as ky had approached, heading back along the path in search of the others. They had to be told.

The exercise had just turned deadly.

*   *   *

Checkpoint Tatiana was still smoldering.

The five recruits had reached the outpost well after dark, but their LI gear made the nightmarish scene all too visible as they crossed the narrow footbridge and passed through a gap in the surrounding duracrete berm. Wolf couldn't help but remember Savary's as he surveyed the damage here. There had been no ritual mutilations here, but the attackers had sacked the place even more thoroughly than the Wynsar-rysa had at the plantation. And there were plenty of bodies in evidence.

The post wasn't large, just a low berm enclosing a few buildings, a landing area large enough for a Pegasus transport craft, and a reinforced command bunker near the center of the installation. Four of the buildings were little more than permanent fabs, one for each lance normally stationed there. A fifth structure had served as a storehouse and armory, but there wasn't much left there now. The attackers had ransacked the place first, then burned everything they didn't want or couldn't carry off.

The attackers had been Wynsarrysa tribesmen, apparently, if the scattering of Gwyrran bodies around the perimeter was any indication. The defenders hadn't taken very many foes with them, which Kern claimed probably meant a surprise assault. There were mysteries which needed to be cleared up, such as how the attackers had penetrated the sensor and mine nets in the first place. There were also three bodies which didn't belong at all ... humans in civilian garb, all apparently cut down by FEK fire just outside the command bunker. Who they were and what they were doing in the outpost, were questions Wolf had to put off answering, though. They had other work to do.

It was plain the perimeter line had been breached. A body of rebels that got past Checkpoint Tatiana was well placed either to strike toward the inhabited zone between the mountains and the Great Desert, or to turn northeast and overpower Fort Gsell from the rear. And the garrison at Kessel had been reduced to provide Ortega's roving patrols for the training exercise.

The Legion had to be warned. But how?

"The command bunker's a wreck," Katrina Voskovich reported as Wolf finished his examination of the three unknown humans. "An explosion went off inside. Knocked out the commlink, the whole C-cubed set-up ... the remote detonators for the minefields, too."

"So there's no transmitter," he said quietly.

"Nothing. And you can bet we'd have heard them on the air if they'd been able to get off a message before the place was hit. They're in the dark back at Kessel."

"How about our helmet commlinks?" Wolf asked.

It was Kern who shook his head. "In these hills? Forget it. No way we can reach Kessel. Maybe—*maybe* we could get lucky and raise a patrol or some of the other recruits, but I doubt it. The drop zones were scattered pretty wide, and it would be one chance in a hundred."

"So what's the answer?" Wolf asked, looking from Voskovich to Kern and back again. He felt helpless, boxed in by events he couldn't control. The recruits had to do something ... but it looked like all his options were closed off.

Voskovich rubbed her chin. "There's one thing we could try...."

"Shoot. I'll take anything."

"I might be able to rig up something makeshift. Hook a helmet commlink into the outpost antenna, maybe get the kind of range we need. I don't guarantee anything...."

"Do it," Wolf said. "I want it yesterday."

"You'll have it in six hours ... if you get it at all. Can I use Myaighee to help me?"

"Myaighee? Is he the right one for high-tech work? I thought his race was pretty backward."

She looked disgusted. "He's been in the Legion for two years, Wolf. He probably knows more about field maintenance on a commlink than you do."

"Sorry I asked," he said curtly.

She looked like she was ready to say more, but just then Lisa Scott appeared, breathless from a run across the compound. "You'd better come, Wolf," she said. "I found a survivor."

*   *   *

"Take it easy, Corporal," Lisa Scott said. "You've lost a lot of blood."

That was an understatement if ever she'd made one. By rights the man should be dead, but somehow the corporal had lived through the battle and hours of unattended misery. He had been hit by FEK slivers that had pierced his battledress fatigues and cut up his left side, and a pair of deep slash wounds across his chest looked like the products of an attack by one of the heavy Wynsarrysa scimitar-type swords. She had seen plenty of suffering these last few years ... her mother, the terrorists she had shot, the casualties at Savary's. But seeing the corporal now was worse than anything she'd been forced to look at before.

"Drink this," Wolf added. "It's a stim pill in water."

"Wolf," she said softly. "In his condition ... a stim pill ..."

"I know," he said harshly. "But we need him at himself to answer some questions."

The corporal took a long drink, then dropped the cup. "The kid's right," he said, his voice labored. "I'm for the Last March anyway ... got to do something worthwhile before God starts calling the muster." He tried to sit up, but Wolf pushed him back gently.

"Lie easy, Corporal," he said. "Just tell us what happened here."

"Civilians ... said they needed help. First aid. We spotted them on sensors downriver and sent a patrol ... found one of them shot. They said ... hunting accident. So we brought 'em back."

"How many?" Wolf urged.

"Six. Guess we ... didn't pay enough attention to the ones who weren't hurt. One of 'em ... tossed a grenade into the bunker. Whole damn thing went up...."

"Why? Why would humans want to knock out the defenses?"

"Separatists ..."

Scott remembered the three young thugs in the bar in Villastre. It was hard to picture them involved in something like this.

"Separatists," the corporal repeated, gasping for breath. "Some kind of deal with the rebels, I guess. They took out the defenses ... next thing we knew, those screaming devils were all over the wall. Too damned many to fight ..."

"They've moved on into the lowlands, haven't they?" Wolf asked.

The corporal shook his head. "I heard ... I heard them talking. They'll hit Kessel. The armory there ... enough to give them some real firepower. Unless they're stopped." He closed his eyes.

Wolf straightened up slowly. "Make him as comfortable as you can, Lisa," he said. "Find out anything else you can. If he's right about an alliance between the Wynsarrysa and the separatists, getting through to Fort Kessel's more important than ever."

She nodded grimly and bent over the injured man, too worried now to notice the horror of his wounds.

Chapter Twenty-Four

Like your ancients, you will serve with all the force of your soul, and if necessary up to the supreme sacrifice. This LEGION is your FATHERLAND ...

—Momento du Legionnaire,
Recruiting Pamphlet,
French Foreign Legion, 1938

Delta One, this is Kessel Command. Wait one." The voice was thin against the static, and Wolf had to strain to hear it. The commlink Voskovich had cobbled together from damaged gear and her helmet system left a lot to be desired. It hissed and crackled like frying bacon, and the signal was apt to fade without warning or reason, but it worked. Fort Kessel had answered his desperate calls at last.

He only hoped it wasn't too late.

Wolf drummed his fingers on the lowest girder of the antenna assembly in growing exasperation. *We don't have time for this waiting!* he thought bitterly. Voskovich had finished in just under five hours instead of the six she'd promised, but in that time the rebels would have covered a lot of ground. He had already repeated his story three times, to three different people on the other end of the commlink, and it was starting to seem like he would never convince them of the danger in time.

"Delta One, this is Ogre," Gunnery Sergeant Ortega's voice suddenly crackled over the commlink. Despite his anxieties, or maybe even because of them, Wolf had to fight back the urge to laugh at the drill instructor's use of his training company nickname as a call sign. "Wolf, if this is some kind of stunt …"

"Everything in the report is accurate, Sergeant," he said, irritated. "Corporal Gallagher passed most of it on to us … before he died. An hour ago."

There was a short silence. "Gallagher … we were on Gwyn together." The gunnery sergeant, usually so gruff, sounded genuinely disturbed. But the moment passed. "We've confirmed parts of your report, Delta One. We diverted a Pegasus when your call came in, and we've spotted your rebels. Commandant Czernak has already started coordinating an operational plan to deal with them."

Wolf breathed out a relieved sigh. "Thank God. I wasn't sure if we'd be able to get through in time."

"Don't bring God into it just yet, Delta One," the sergeant told him. "Not until you hear what's in store for you next. The commandant's plan requires a unit to block the rebel retreat route up the Sinueux, and you're the only ones in position. It won't be easy, Wolf, but we need you.…"

He listened in growing horror as Ortega began spelling out the plan.

*   *   *

"Fight? That's a laugh. Every rebel in this district is out there, Wolf. How are we supposed to fight them all?"

Wolf studied Katrina Voskovich for a long moment, then shrugged. "They've left it to us," he said. "If we can't do anything, we're to head up into the hills and try to avoid contact. But if that happens, the rebels will just escape. If we could do something to slow them down, maybe the people who died here won't have died completely in vain."

He wasn't convinced himself, so there wasn't much reason to expect as much from the other four recruits gathered around the base of the antenna array. Ortega and Commandant Czernak had outlined a plan to counter the rebel attack, but it sounded like nothing short of suicide for Delta Lance.

Czernak was calling in all the patrols and as many recruits as they could assemble to bolster the strength at Fort Kessel, while a fast-moving rapid response force would drive north from Fort Hunter to catch the rebels in a pincer. It was a classic military operation, lacking only one thing to make it foolproof.

The missing ingredient was a way to slam the back door on them. Right now Delta Lance was the only group in a position to even try. Ortega had promised to send more men into Checkpoint Tatiana as soon as possible, but it still might take hours. Those men were needed everywhere, and prying enough legionnaires and equipment loose in time to do any good was easier to promise than to deliver.

And Wolf knew as well as Ortega did that it was poor policy to reinforce a forlorn hope when other forces needed the manpower more....

It reminded Wolf all too vividly of Erich Neubeck's orders on Telok. Wolf was supposed to hold the enemy as long as possible, with a vague promise of help to sustain him. In the fight with the Ubrenfars he had tried to hold, but superior numbers had quickly overcome his ramshackle outfit. The reinforcements had never arrived, and good men had died before he had the chance to extricate the handful of survivors from disaster.

His initial reaction to Czernak's plan had been a mixture of horror and disbelief. He couldn't face a replay of Telok. And he couldn't try to lead his lance to certain death. These people were his comrades ... his friends. Their deaths would hurt even worse than the ones he'd caused on Telok that day.

But he had listened to Ortega without comment, and gravely promised to see if there was any action Delta Lance could take to block the retreat route, at least for a few hours. On the surface it sounded impossible, but the situation Wolfgang Alaric Hauser would have found impossible, Karl Wolf, soldier of the Fifth Foreign Legion, was willing to examine. He couldn't do less.

For too long Wolf had been on the run. He had failed at Telok and run. That had led him to the duel with Neubeck, and he had run again, his honor further stained. He had nearly run from the Legion when the going got tough, but Lisa Scott and the woman called Aunt Mandy had convinced him to stick it out.

He had discovered something these past weeks with the Legion. Honor, reputation, even life itself weren't worth anything unless they were backed up by a genuine commitment. It could be to family or to country or to some cause, but without commitment there was nothing else.

It had taken him a long time to find what a legionnaire was commit-ed to, but Wolf thought he understood it now. *Legio Patria Nostra* ... the Legion is our Fatherland. They had sounded like empty words before, but he knew better now. A legionnaire was committed to the most important cause, the greatest of fatherlands ... the Legion itself.

Wolfgang Hauser had failed to uphold his honor, his family, his reputation, and his planet, and that failure had led him from aristo-cracy to this last asylum of misfortune. But Karl Wolf wasn't going to fail again.

"I'm not much on suicide missions, boyo," Kern said, managing to sound cheerful. "Just because we're on Devereaux 'tis no good reason to *do* a Devereaux like our esteemed predecessor, Commandant Hunter. At least not for an empty gesture. Do they really think five people can make a difference against a few hundred?"

"If the minefields could still be switched to active, the rebels wouldn't have much chance of getting away," Lisa Scott ob served. "But with the command bunker smashed ..."

He looked across at Voskovich. "You were able to rig the comm-link. What about the mines?"

She looked thoughtful. "It might be done. But anything we rig will be vulnerable. I can't keep them from shutting everything down if they get to the controls we rig here."

"That means defending the place," Kern said slowly. "It still leaves us with the original problem. Five against hundreds ..."

"Corporal Gallagher told me there was a hidden ammo stock under one of the huts that the rebels didn't get," Scott said. "The sergeant in charge didn't like keeping all his eggs in one basket. That gives us something better than our exercise load to play with."

"Thank God for small favors," Kern said with a grin. The recruits were carrying FEKs, but the only ammo they had been issued consisted of riot control munitions, smoke grenades, and anesthetic needle rounds. With some real ammunition they had a chance.

"We'll have the edge on them in firepower," Wolf said. "Except for what they looted here, they probably aren't all that well equipped, and they won't be all that familiar with what they have picked up."

"Don't make the mistake of underestimating them," Myaighee warned. "Some of them have been fighting for a long time."

"And a club can kill you just as dead as a grenade if you don't watch out," Kern added. "But I'll agree with you on this much, boyo. We can make the bastards know we're here."

"It's damned slim," Wolf said. "If you want to opt out, now's the time. I know you can't run a military unit like a democracy, but I'm not going to decide for the rest of you. Anyone who wants to run for the hills has my blessing. And Gunny Ogre's, too, if that makes any difference. He said to make sure you know this is strictly for volunteers."

"Well," Katrina Voskovich said. "You aren't going to get those mines back on line unless I stay. So I guess I'd better get to work. What about you, Myaighee?"

The hannie's neck ruff twitched. "I let everyone down before, at Savary's. I will not do so again."

"Good enough," the woman said. "What say we tackle the job together, then? With your permission, oh great lance leader ..."

"Ah...." Wolf hesitated. It was hard to bring himself to actually speak the words he needed to say now. "Myaighee, you're still a Legionnaire Third Class, not just a recruit like the rest of us. You've had more experience in real combat situations. I think ... I think you should take back command of Delta Lance for the duration."

Myaighee crossed his arms, the hannie gesture of denial. "No. No, I was not suited to leadership. I am content to take your orders, Wolf." He paused. "But thank you. This was ... a gesture I will not forget."

Wolf looked away, uncomfortably aware of the new respect, not just in Myaighee's eyes but in Voskovich and Kern's as well. The hannie and the electronics expert stood up and turned toward the command bunker, already starting to talk over ideas.

"What about you, Tom?" Wolf asked.

The big redhead didn't answer right away. When he finally spoke, his look was focused far away, and he might have been talking to himself. "I joined the Legion because there was nothing for me in civilian life," he said softly. "I ruined a good career with the Marines. Killed a recruit by accident, then skipped out instead of taking my term in the penal battalions. But I didn't fit in anywhere, Wolf. The only life I was any good at was the Service. So I decided I'd finish out in the Legion. I intend to die fighting, and whether it's today or ten years down the line ... well, it doesn't really matter that much. I've got no reason to run."

He stood up. "I'll walk the perimeter, make sure everything's in order." Then he was gone.

Wolf looked across at Scott. She cut him off before he could say anything. "Let me ask the question," she said. "What are *you* planning? Once upon a time you didn't think Legion traditions meant anything. It must be strange for you, thinking about the oldest tradition of all."

"I'll fight," he said. "Not because of any Legion tradition about lost causes, though. Because we really can make a difference here. And we might be able to give some meaning to the sacrifice the garrison already made. I won't believe Gallagher held on all that time, gave us that information, to no purpose at all."

"Noblesse oblige?" she asked with a faint smile.

He shook his head. "The Legion takes care of its own."

*　　*　　*

Karl Wolf peered over the top of the low berm and studied the valley below Checkpoint Tatiana with growing dismay. The longer he waited and watched, the more his doubts gnawed away within. How could five Legion recruits even consider stirring up a hornet's nest of over two hundred armed rebels? The odds against them were more than just numeric. These Wynsarrysa were tough, fanatic outlaws, well used to fighting as a way of life. Like the Ubrenfars who had overwhelmed his troops on Telok....

He tried to ignore the memory and concentrate on the problem at hand, but it was hard to separate past and present.

Dawn would be breaking over the mountains soon. They had spent a long night getting ready, but now the time for waiting was almost at an end. Somehow Katrina Voskovich had managed to rig up a control for the Galahads, using a mine recovered from the field by Myaighee, components from her wristpiece computer, and odds and ends scavenged from damaged equipment in the bunker. The mines were no longer on standby. From here on out, anything the size of a man that moved through a minefield would set off the devices.

In fact, they had already seen them working. The rebels had started drifting back up the river valley soon after planetary midnight. Evidently the assault had run into the first Commonwealth resistance, and this unexpected loss of surprise had been enough to persuade some of the fainthearted to turn in search of a retreat route. A small party had run straight into a minefield. None of them had survived.

But the next group had spotted the casualties and guessed the truth. Wolf had tried to confuse them by having the recruits launch some of their stock of smoke grenades into the woods on the other side of the refugees. Some, apparently convinced the Legion was close at hand, tried to break through the mines, with the same results as their late friends. The rest withdrew back down the valley in haste.

That had been an hour back. Since then the rebels had been gathering in the valley, gradually marshaling themselves for a concerted effort. Someone down there, perhaps one of the human separatists, had realized that the key to escape lay in retaking the outpost and shutting down those mines. Otherwise the Wynsarrysa wouldn't win free before the main body of legionnaires caught up with them. The Galahads had been carefully positioned over many years by legionnaires thoroughly familiar with their business, and the antipersonnel mines were designed to flip an explosive charge into the air each time the device was triggered. With multiple warheads, Galahads could be lethal again and again before they finally ran dry, and that made them doubly effective at barring escape through any of the narrow valleys that opened up around Tatiana.

So the only way out for the rebels lay through the heart of the out-post. And five would-be legionnaires stood ready to defend the position.

Movement caught his eye. The LI setting on his faceplate showed the rebel force clearly even in the predawn darkness. He zoomed in on the enemy and studied them for a moment.

"They're coming!" he shouted, bracing his FEK on the wall of the berm. The wall would have been a substantial barrier if the power cells in the central bunker hadn't been thoroughly wrecked by the explosion there. Topped with electrified wires, the berm could have held up an assault for a long time if the defenders had been able to tap into a generator, but they'd have to do without that defense now.

Kern dropped to one knee at the other end of the east wall, his own weapon held at the ready. This time they had full combat loads, grenades and needle rounds. The other three recruits were posted behind Wolf and Kern, defending a slit trench the redhead had dug overnight. It made the ideal fallback position, halfway between wall and bunker. Wolf expected the three of them to be quite a surprise for the rebels to meet once they overcame the wall itself.

They waited. Slowly, the enemy advance gathered strength, surging up the valley. Wolf estimated there were forty or fifty of them, waving an assortment of weapons and shouting hoarse cries exhorting one another to glory.

The two recruits opened up.

With no restrictions on their fields of fire, they used their 1 cm minigrenades first. Explosion after explosion burst amid the enemy force, and even those that did little damage contributed to the morale loss of the Wynsarrysa vanguard. After less than a minute of sustained fire the rebels wavered, crumbled.

And the waiting began again.

*   *   *

Lisa Scott and Legionnaire Myaighee were on the firing line when the second serious attack developed. Kern and Wolf had run through nearly half of their meager stock of live minigrenades, so the fresh magazines had been moved forward. Kneeling at the berm with the enemy main body in the crosshairs of her faceplate target display, Scott wondered what Senator Abercrombie would think if he knew what his daughter was doing. For years he had treated her like a possession, not a person. Now she felt free for the first time....

Perhaps it would also be the last.

The rangefinder showed they were coming close enough to be hit hard, and Scott began firing. Across the compound, at his post overlooking the riverbank, Myaighee lid the same.

It was just as Wolf had described it, more like a dreamchip game than a real battle. She fired, and kept firing as long as there were targets in her sights. As before, the rebels broke long before they were a threat to the berm, and there was little return fire.

Maybe, she told herself, the odds weren't as overwhelming as they had seemed after all....

"Fafnir! Fafnir to the front! Hurry!" Myaighee's shout was almost gibberish, but somehow the words penetrated her brain and Lisa Scott cut back the magnification on her image intensifiers to get a panoramic view of the battlefield.

That was when she saw them. A pair of flattened turtle shapes, hovering a few scant centimeters off the ground with the morning sun glinting off gleaming armor. She blanked her mind to access her computer implant, and almost instantly her mind was filled with the information she had asked for. They were Sandrat APCs, the predecessors of the Legion's Sandrays. Many had found their way into civilian use after being phased out of the Legion ... and it seemed that these two, at least, were still doing duty with an army after all these years.

Two armored magrep vehicles, even if they didn't mount any heavy firepower, would be proof against the firepower available to the recruit defenders. Except, of course, for the Fafnir. The missile launcher was an easy match for any APC.

But the hidden military stores at Checkpoint Tatiana had contained only one missile for the launcher, and there were two enemy vehicles out there.

* * *

"Go! Go!" Wolf shouted the order and practically lifted Katrina Voskovich out of the trench. The dark-haired, stocky woman sprinted for the berm, clutching the Fafnir tight in her hands.

He had considered taking the weapon himself. Through most of the training he had been assigned as the Fafnir gunner for heavy weapons drills, and he'd slowly developed an affinity for it. But Voskovich had scored better marks with the launcher ... and a gunner rarely had the luxury to oversee a whole battle the way an ordinary rifleman could. That was why the typical lance in the Fifth Foreign Legion didn't burden the lance leader with any specialty work, though of course there were frequent exceptions.

She ran for the berm, and Wolf cursed under his breath. He hadn't expected vehicles. Most of the Wynsarrysa were primmies, living from hand to mouth, unable to survive except on what they scavenged. Who would have thought they could have kept the APCs in working order?

Wolf vowed not to underestimate his opponents again. If he lived to profit from the lesson....

Voskovich reached the wall and steadied the Fafnir. An instant later, the APC was on top of them, turbofans whining as it picked up speed. At that moment something flashed from the top of the vehicle. For a moment Wolf thought they were using a weapon mounted in a small remote turret, but then he realized it was a Gwyrran with a heavy rocket launcher lying on top of the vehicle.

The rocket streaked toward the wall. Toward Voskovich.

The explosion tore a hole in the berm twice the width of the vehicle, sending chunks of duracrete spinning in all directions. Wolf saw Voskovich fall, the unfired Fafnir rolling from her arms as she clutched at her stomach.

He was out of the trench in an instant, racing toward the discarded launcher. Wolf barely had time to throw himself sideways and scoop it up as the armored monster drifted almost casually, arrogantly, through the gap. The rocket gunner was sitting up now. So was another rebel, this one with a heavy machine pistol.

The second one was raising his massive weapon slowly, training it on Karl Wolf....

Chapter Twenty-Five

Are you worthy to be a legionnaire?

—Sergeant Georges Manue,
French Foreign Legion, 1941

The Sandrat was less than ten meters from Wolf, floating on its magnetic cushion with the turbofans cut back to a dead idle. With the vehicle dominating this side of the compound, the rebels could advance unhindered, supported by their comrades on top of the APC and their weaponry. Wolf knew, though he couldn't see directly, that the second Sandrat was closing fast.

Time seemed to move in slow motion, and every thought, every action, had a crystal clarity about it unlike anything Wolf had ever experienced before. He could see the muzzle of the machine pistol coming into line with him, and could feel the soft stirring of the air kicked out by the slow-burning fans. Behind him he could hear someone shouting his name....

Then, like the breaking of a dam, time returned to normal. Something struck him in the back just as the machine pistol spat, and a slug tore through the battledress fatigues just above his elbow. If it had not been for the shove Lisa Scott had given him, the bullet would have taken him square in the chest. As it was, fire burned in his arm, and it was all Wolf could do to keep from dropping the Fafnir.

Lisa hit the ground and rolled, coming up with her FEK whining on full-auto. The rebels on top of the APC both rolled back and off the vehicle under the intense impact of the high-velocity needle rounds.

He struggled to his feet and fumbled with the rocket launcher, cursing his throbbing arm. At point-blank range the computer targeting system was as useless as it was unnecessary, and Wolf had to override the settings and aim and fire strictly by sight. The Fafnir roared from its tube and streaked to the APC, striking it squarely above the driver's hatch. The missile penetrated before it exploded, and the clang of debris ricocheting around the interior was audible where Wolf stood.

Slowly, painfully, the vehicle settled to the ground as the magrep fields collapsed. The fans continued their slow, rhythmic beating, but the APC was too heavy for the fans to lift.

Wolf staggered, caught himself before he fell, and tossed the empty launcher aside. Kern sprinted past and knelt by the wall, FEK blazing away at full automatic. The missile shot had knocked out one target, but there was still a battle out there.

Wolf kneeled beside the bloodstained form of Katrina Voskovich. Lisa appeared beside him, but he angrily waved her back to the wall. "I'll take care of her," he said. "Pour on the fire! Go!"

The injured woman stirred at the sound of his voice. Ignoring the pain in his arm, Wolf half carried, half dragged her back to the slit trench. At least she would be out of the line of fire there. Dropping into the bottom of the trench beside her, he opened his first aid kit and put painkiller patches on her carotid artery and over the worst wound, a deep gash in her upper leg dangerously close to her femoral artery. Then he dug into the kit again for the roll of sterilite cloth. Working quickly, he wound it around and around the leg, finally cutting it off with his combat knife. As the woman's body heat interacted with the bandage, it would tighten to conform to the shape of her leg, hopefully stanching the flow of blood.

He waited for a long moment, looking down at her. They had never been close, not since the day he had first met her back in the Legion bunkroom on Robespierre. But she was part of his lance, and it had been his decision to let her have the Fafnir that had led to this. His decision …

Then he shook off the mood. Wolf returned the knife to its sheath in the top of his boot and clambered awkwardly out of the trench. The rest of the lance was still in the fight. His duty was to them now.

* * *

The second Sandrat closed more slowly than the first, but the lower speed allowed a trio of rebels on the hull to maintain a steady fire as the APC approached. Needle rounds chewed at the berm just to the left of Myaighee's position, and ky flinched once as tiny shards of duracrete rattled off kys faceplate.

Myaighee could feel the battle lust stirring once again just as it had back at Savary's. Ky had started out a servant, not a warrior, but each time ky had gone into battle ky had lost control that much more easily. The lance couldn't afford having one of their number out of control but Myaighee wasn't sure ky knew how to keep from becoming lost in sheer savage fury.

Maybe the male-human Wolf was right after all. Perhaps the *kyendyp* race really was closer to its animal roots, its barbaric heritage. Ky had seen humans go berserk at the height of a fight, but somehow they seemed to channel it better. For all of kys progress these last two years, ky still hadn't adapted to this strange world of gods and demons and forces beyond the comprehension of kys own kind.

Like Oomour ...

Out in the valley the rebels were shouting epithets and curses as they ran, waving their weapons overhead. The protective fire from the Sandrat was making the defenders keep their heads down more often than they could shoot and the mass of the enemy force was pressing forward unchecked. This time they might carry the wall. When that happened, the battle would be over.

Ky fired again, trying to pick off the passengers on the hull of the APC, but the shot didn't have any apparent effect. Myaighee swore, a human curse of the kind favored by Corporal Rostov back in Bravo Company. Nearby Kern was trying to lay down a sustained blanket of fire, but the big male-human was drawing unwelcome attention from the enemy. Myaighee lifted kys weapon again.

The second Sandrat put on a burst of speed, leaping straight for the gap the first one had opened up. It slammed into the grounded hull of the first APC and hovered for long seconds, as if the driver had been stunned by the collision.

Then Myaighee realized the real reason it had stopped. The rear door was dropping, and ky could see hulking shapes pushing toward the ramp....

Ky hardly thought, letting instinct take over entirely Swarming over a pile of rubble, ky leapt for the top of the APC, a motion kys tree-climbing ancestors would have been proud to witness. Myaighee jabbed the muzzle of kys gun into the opening hatchway and squeezed the autogrenade launcher's trigger tight. Round after round pumped into the rear of the vehicle, and the whole APC seemed to shudder as explosions ripped through it.

But at least half of the passengers had already dived out the back as they realized what the hannie was doing. One of them, an oversized Wynsarrysa with a string of human ears around his neck and a huge scimitar in one hand, swept his blade in an upward cut. The massive sword caught Myaighee in the stomach, and the force of the blow knocked ky off the vehicle.

Legionnaire Third Class Myaighee lay still on a mound of debris, staring at the open sky. Kys last thought before death claimed ky for its own was the knowledge that ky need worry no more about civilization or savagery, whether ky was bound for the Afterlife among the Blessed Sky Gods kys own people believed in, or the Heaven the chaplains preached about in the human Legion.

The long struggle was over.

*　*　*

"Fall back! Fall back!" Wolf shouted the order as Myaighee went down. The unexpected enemy APCs had wrecked his careful planning, drawing the recruits out of their prepared position at just the moment when the full shock of the rebel attack was sweeping toward them. Instead of a withering fire from the trench, the rebels would encounter nothing but disjointed, individual resistance.

The little hannie's leap to the top of the Sandrat, and his grenade attack on the vulnerable interior, had been the acts of a real hero, but he—ky—had died nonetheless. So it would be with all of them. They could fight on with all the courage they could muster, but in the end Wolf's faulty plan would bring them all down.

"Fall back!" he shouted again.

Kern had clubbed his FEK and was wading through a crowd of Gwyrrans. More were swarming over the berm, too. Wolf lost sight of Lisa Scott entirely....

The high-pitched whine of another battle rifle took Wolf by surprise. He fired again, heard the loading mechanism shatter as his magazine ran dry. As he discarded the FEK, Wolf realized that the new firing was coming from the slit trench.

From Katrina Voskovich. Seriously wounded, she had still dragged herself upright. Now she was leaning against the lip of the trench, clutching her battle rifle like a talisman to ward off the pain and the terror and pouring autofire into the enemy ranks. As the rebels recoiled, Wolf ran for the trench. Kern followed, and after a moment Lisa Scott appeared, bleeding freely from a gash in her forehead but wielding a long, slightly curved sword like an outsized dueling saber and waving a Gwyrran pistol in the other hand.

"We've got to get back to the bunker," Wolf panted. "We can block the door ... try to hold the bastards a little while longer...."

"Somebody has to stay and lay down cover," Kern said. "So you three mag it out of here."

Voskovich shook her head. The effort seemed to cost her most of her remaining strength. "I can't run anyway. And I'd slow you down if you tried to carry me. I'm the one to stay." As if for emphasis, she turned away from them and started firing again, cool, calculating. But Wolf could see the sweat on her forehead, the lines of pain around her eyes and mouth. It was a miracle she was still standing at all.

But she was right.

"Do what you can," he said softly. "What you have to." Wolf pushed Lisa out the rear of the trench. "Mag it! Go! Go!"

Bullets plucked at his uniform as he ran for the command bunker, but the only one that hit was almost spent. Beside him, Kern wasn't as lucky. A bullet slammed into the redhead's back. The big man stumbled and fell. Wolf threw himself down beside Kern, checking his back. There was no blood, no sign of penetration. The duraweave had saved his life.

"I can make it!" Kern snapped, rising unsteadily and plunging on. Wolf was right on his heels.

They had just reached the bunker when the firing slackened by the trench. Voskovich was out of the action. Dead? Or just exhausted at last, overwhelmed by shock and blood loss and the painkillers in her veins, lying in a heap at the bottom of the trench? It didn't matter much now.

They closed the door and barred it, but there wasn't much they could do now to defend themselves. The bunker hadn't been designed to defend against a sustained attack ... and they were down to their knives, a captured pistol and a bloodstained saber for weapons. The Wynsarrysa still outnumbered them despite the heavy casualties they had suffered in the attacks.

Now it was just a matter of time....

Something thumped against the door, once, twice, and again.

"They won't use explosives," Kern said. "The bastards don't know what our set-up is in here. Probably figure wrecking our new controls will keep the mines active."

"Will it?" Wolf asked.

The big man gave a curt nod. "The way they're set now they'll go off no matter who goes through there. No recognition function." His eyes met Wolf's. "I know what you're thinking, but we can't wreck them ourselves. Our own people will be driving into those mines soon."

"They don't know that," Scott pointed out. "Maybe we can cut some kind of deal...."

Kern shook his head this time. "They won't keep it. No honor. We'd be better off going out still fighting. If we're captured ... it wouldn't be pretty."

The blonde shuddered. Outside, the thumping continued, louder now. The door bucked and strained under the blows.

Wolf took the sword from her. "Then let's do it."

The door splintered. Wolf shouted a Germanic oath and leapt forward, blade slashing fiercely. The attackers gave ground, and he was suddenly outside again. The large Gwyrran who had killed Myaighee loomed in front of him, his scimitar a menacing gleam in the morning sunlight.

The other rebels were jeering and shouting, but none made a move against Wolf. The swordsman stepped closer, turning a casual-seeming move into a sudden blurring attack. Wolf's blade flashed up to meet the sweeping cut. In the same motion Wolf pressed forward. Surprised, the Gwyrran gave ground, defending himself from Wolf's sudden follow-up lunge. His left-handed attack seemed to have his opponent off-balance.

In Wolf's mind he saw the duel with Neubeck again. He pushed the image away, launched a slashing attack that drew blood from the Gwyrran's right shoulder. But the wound didn't seem to bother the other at all. He counterattacked, a vicious, savage attack that pushed Wolf back step by step toward the door to the bunker. The Wynsarrysa was bigger, stronger, with a better weapon. He had all the advantages.

Just like Erich Neubeck....

Then the alien slashed again and wrenched the saber from Wolf's grasp. It spun, end over end, catching the sunlight. The crowd was silent for the first time.

"The loss is disgrace," the Gwyrran rumbled in broken Terranglic. "In defeat ... death." He gestured arrogantly to a pair of rebels close by. "The human is taken. Bind him. The sport comes later."

Wolf flinched as the Gwyrrans closed in, then staggered and dropp- ed to his knees. In a single lightning-motion, he drew his combat knife and threw it. It sank into the Gwyrran's back, just below the neck, and the rebel collapsed in a heap. There was a long, stunned moment when nobody moved.

Suddenly shots rang out as Lisa Scott came out of the door with the machine pistol blazing. The silence ended in shouts and screams, chaos. It was only a temporary respite, but Wolf smiled faintly anyway.

It had been like living through the fight with Neubeck all over ag- ain, but this time Wolf felt no guilt over lost honor. This time he hadn't given in to hatred or instinct. He had done as he had been taught, and he thought his Legion teachers would approve.

The legionnaire fought to win, not merely to score points or prove superiority. And even if he died in the next instant, Wolf knew now that he had truly become a legionnaire....

*   *   *

"Bank left! Over there!" Gunnery Sergeant Ortega tapped the pilot of the Pegasus on the arm and pointed, and the corporal nodded and followed his order.

The transport shuttle stooped low over Checkpoint Tatiana. The cluster of rebels around the command bunker had already started to break up, and the sudden appearance of the Legion craft, twin Gatling guns hammering into the crowd without mercy, was enough to keep them on the run. Two more shuttles swept over the humpbacked hill on the far side of the river, their own guns raking the enemy, to finish the job.

As they passed over Tatiana, Ortega saw the three ragged figures by the door. Delta Lance had done everything they had been asked to do, and more. Soon the main body of Czernak's legionnaires would come up and round up the rebels who had fled.

A notable victory … won by a lance of recruits.

Ortega smiled. That was a story that would be told to future recruit classes … perhaps for as long as Mankind fielded a legion of foreigners.

*   *   *

They buried Myaighee at Checkpoint Tatiana, alongside the legionnaires who had died in the first surprise attack. He was the only one of the lance dead, though Katrina Voskovich's fate still was far from sure despite the high-tech miracles of Commonwealth medicine. Wolf, Kern, and Lisa Scott had all been wounded in the fighting, but they were in attendance alongside the veteran legionnaires of Czernak's strike column and an assortment of their fellow recruits who had been pulled in from the field when the exercise had turned real. The regen cast on his arm was an inconvenience, but Wolf steeled himself to keep from trying to scratch at the healing flesh encased in the cylinder.

Father Chavigny, as the Training Company's chaplain, had been flown out to conduct the ceremony. He read the burial service in slow, measured tones, and Wolf found himself making all the appropriate responses right along with the others.

As Father Chavigny finished the service and put away his prayer book, Wolf couldn't help but think of the funeral they had held for Antonelli. These honored dead were heroes of the Legion, and treated as such. He knew the difference now.

It was old Legion tradition for the lancemates of a dead legionnaire to divide up his personal effects among themselves. Kern had taken a length of rope Myaighee had claimed was used by another alien legionnaire to commit suicide, but Wolf had been interested in only one item the hannie had left behind.

As the service broke up he produced Myaighee's tiny vial from under his shirt and took it off its thin chain. Wolf kneeled by the open graves, and put a tiny quantity of soft earth inside. He straightened up and drew out the medallion Lisa had given him. It had helped him find the balance in his life at a time when he had needed it, but in the past days he had learned that the true source of that balance was within.

He weighed the medallion in his hand for a moment, then tossed it into Myaighee's grave. It was the last honor he could pay to a better soldier, a better legionnaire, than he would ever be.

EPILOGUE

The training affects people in different ways. Yes, there were times when it was rough, but I survived.

—A legionnaire of the 13th DBLE,
French Foreign Legion, 1984

Dusk was gathering over Fort Hunter.

It was an evening just like any other, but for Karl Wolf and fifty other recruits from Training Company Odintsev it was anything but ordinary. The shrunken company stood in ranks on the parade ground with an air of anticipation and excitement, wait-ing for the officers and noncoms to settle into place on the reviewing stand in front of them with ill-disguised impatience.

Tonight was the ceremony of the *kepi blanc*. After this, the training would end. They would be legionnaires.

Gunnery Sergeant Ortega made a curt gesture, and a line of Legion security troops ignited their hand-held torches in unison. The flickering light of the flames highlighted fifty-one drawn but happy faces.

Standing at attention in full dress uniform with his white kepi held behind his back, Wolf thought back over the weeks of training and wondered how he had made it through. The battles had tested them to the limit ... but the calculated training of the Legion's noncoms had prepared them well for those fights by pushing them beyond their limits.

Now the survivors of that difficult process of molding and tempering were about to be accepted into the ranks of the Fifth Foreign Legion.

From his position in the first line, between Kern and Scott, Karl Wolf couldn't see many of the other recruits, but he knew them like brothers and sisters now. Hosni Mayzar, the fiendish Arabic lance leader ... Soak Burundai, who had overcome his poor start to stand here tonight ... Lauriston, MacDuff's friend ... Radiah Suartana, whose path had rarely crossed Wolf's during training, but who remained as faithful now as when they had signed up together.

And Katrina Voskovich. She was out of danger but facing a long recovery period. Alone of the training company she had already received her orders back to Colin Fraser's Bravo Company, still stationed in the Trisystem facing the Ubrenfar invaders. The long trip back would be time enough for her to heal from the physical wounds. Other scars might run deeper, Wolf thought. But if anyone could overcome those, it was Katrina Voskovich.

Wolf jerked his attention back to the ceremony. There was a galaxy of important people in attendance, including Aunt Mandy and Corporal Souham, the barkeeper who was also president of the Legion Veterans Association. Captain Odintsev and Commandant Stathopoulos, commander of the Training Battalion, had already given their speeches, laying emphasis on the fine work and bright prospects of the recruits now that basic training was over. But the third officer to speak held Wolf's complete attention.

"For over a thousand years the white kepi has been the symbol of the legionnaire," Colonel Jason Carr, the commanding officer of Fort Hunter, said in solemn, measured tones. "Through the centuries the units which have taken the name and symbolism of the Foreign Legion have carried the kepi in victory and in defeat, fighting for the good causes and the bad. We legionnaires are a strange breed, true not so much to the colors that fly above us as we are to ourselves and our traditions. There are those who call us mercenaries, others who call us scum ... but we shall always know that we are first and foremost *legionnaires*, bearers of the sacred white kepi. And it is for the honor of our comrades, of our Legion, and of our sacred kepi that we make the pledge of honor and fidelity. The day may come when you must emulate the heroes of Camerone or Devereaux or a thousand other desperate battles." He glanced toward Delta Lance, and Wolf drew himself up a little straighter. "In fact, some of you already have. If and when that day comes, I know each of you will remember your pledge and redeem it with the heroism that is the essence of the legionnaire."

He nodded sharply, and his C^3 technician touched a key on the reviewing stand's soundboard. The slow, stately notes of *"Le Boudin"* the ancient marching song of the Legion, filled the air.

The music had been passed down over hundreds of years almost unchanged, but the words went back only a century or so to the formation of the Fifth Foreign Legion. Wolf was surprised to find himself joining in with the rest of the recruits as enthusiasm and a stirring feeling of belonging welled up inside him.

Under strange skies so unfamiliar, By the light of a distant sun, Stands the sentinel, the warrior, Of the Fifth Foreign Legion.

To die with honor is our wish, For the Glory of past Legions; We shall all know how to perish, Following old traditions.

One world's unnumbered blood was shed, For Honor and Fidelity, Heroes of war, our hallowed deed. We know you shall judge us worthy.

As the final words of the song rang out, Captain Odintsev gestured to Gunnery Sergeant Ortega, whose swarthy face managed to look stern and proud under the flickering torch light. Ortega nodded, and with the last trumpet flourish all fifty-one men and women in the recruit company donned their kepis as one.

It was done.

There were more speeches, but the magical moment was over. They held the rank of Legionnaire Third Class now, and their five-year contracts had gone into effect the moment the ancient kepis had touched their heads.

Wolf listened to the speeches with a sense of unreality. It was hard, now, to think of life outside of Fort Hunter. The recruits would be moving on, to advanced training or to assignments in the field. There was even word that drafts of reinforcements would soon be on the way to the Republic Trisystem as the confrontation over Laut Besar continued to escalate.

And Karl Wolf had made a decision. He would be there. He had been forced to abandon his home, and then the cause itself. And even though he had found a new place here among these legionnaires, he knew he would never be truly free of his past until he laid his ghosts to rest.

After the ceremony, he and Lisa Scott walked across the grounds, past the *Monument aux Morts* and toward the tube station. It was quiet now, the perfect night for a walk and a chance to talk about the future. He valued Lisa's advice over all others, and he thought she would approve of his choice.

As they talked, the gates to the tube station swung open and a trio of noncoms led a ragged line of mismatched civilians through. They looked young, for the most part, baffled, awed, scared....

Fresh recruits ... for Fort Hunter to turn into legionnaires.

GLOSSARY

 **dchip:** Short for "adhesive chip," any of the button-sized minicomputers designed to hook directly into the human nervous system for total sensory interaction. A cheap alternative to computer implants.

Airshark: Ground support aircraft used in the Colonial Army.

ale: Slang for "alien"; applied to any nonhuman.

anfangen: German (Laut Besar Uro dialect) for "begin." Used to order the start of a fencing engagement.

anteilzucht: German (Laut Besar Uro dialect) for "part-breed," a child of mixed Uro and Indomay blood.

arbebaril: French (Devereaux dialect) for "barrel tree," the multi-trunked tree cultivated in the Archipel d'Aurore for its sap.

aristo: slang for "aristocrat." On Laut Besar, a complimentary term. In the Legion, it generally denotes one too soft and pampered to have much future with the Legion.

Asjyai: Military title in Dryienjaiyeel; roughly translates as "chief of staff."

Battalion: Military formation which, in Commonwealth usage, fields

6-9 companies under the command of a commandant or major. Three or more battalions form a regiment.

battledress: the combat uniform of the twenty-ninth century soldier. The typical battledress uniform, as worn by the Foreign Le-gion, consists of a duraweave coverall, boots, and a combat helmet. The coverall is not only resistant to shrapnel and small arms fire, but also contains a net of microcircuits which provide environ-mental control, plus a "chameleon cloth" weave which detects patterns and shades of light and matches the uniform to various backgrounds. Web gear may be worn to hold a variety of items, and a backpack may be provided for extended marches. Many sold-iers augment the basic uniforms with plasteel armor segments covering chest and back, arms, or legs; there is little uniformity in the extent and use of armor. Onager gunners wear full body armor over their regular battledress. Light gloves and a hostile environ-ment version of the combat helmet may convert the outfit into a lightweight spacesuit, and other adaptations allow it to be used in a variety of environs.

Batu: outer satellite of Laut Besar, a planetoid holding a small as-tronomical observatory but no other facilities. The name means "Rock" in Indomay.

bhourrkh: Native name for the fierce storms on Polypheme.

blunderbuss: Bazooka-like rocket launcher employed by the hannies, so named for its bell-shaped muzzle.

binatanganas: "wildbeast," a savage predator native to wilderness regions of Laut Besar.

C^3: Command, control, and communication; used in referring to specialist technicians, to the computer/commo packs they carry and operate, or the larger control centers in bases or vehicles where these operations are performed. Also "C-cubed."

Camerone-class lighters: Standard unarmed battalion-level tran-sports employed by the Fifth Foreign Legion. Names are based on famous Legion battles (Camerone, Ganymede, Devereaux, Tuyen Quang, Somme, Ankh'Qwar, etc.).

cafarde: originally a French term (literally: "the cockroach") with close associations with the Legion. "The bug" is the madness caused by boredom and stress common to Legion forces on garrison duty.

cargomod: "Cargo module," a standard shipping container used for transporting shipboard cargos. Also slang, the equivalent of "crate."

carriership: Generic term for the multi-million-ton FTL ships used by the Commonwealth and other interstellar cultures, so called because they are used to carry large numbers of interplanetary vessels from one system to another. Requiring the computing power of a full artificially intelligent computer to handle the intricacies of interstellar navigation, carrierships are imbued with distinctive computer personalities. These carry the names of famous philo-sophers or wise counselors from history and mythology. Breaking with usual navy traditions, the computers and the ships are both referred to by using masculine pronouns.

CEK: *(Cannon d'Energie Kinetique)* Vehicle mounted auto-cannon.

C-cubed: the C^3 center of an HQ or vehicle.

chief sergeant: NCO equivalent in rank to US master sergeant; found as battalion-level NCO.

chip: Short for adchip; used as a verb, "to chip" means to take computer-induced instruction in a subject such as language.

Citizen: Citizenship in the Terran Commonwealth is universal on Terra but highly prized off-planet, and the title "Citizen" is commonly used on Colonial and frontier worlds to denote someone who has inherited or been awarded citizenship. Legionnaires who have served for at least one five-year term receive Commonwealth citizenship as a reward for service.

Colonial Army: The military arm of the Commonwealth employed to defend and extend the Colonies. Unlike the regular Terran Army, the Colonial Army is raised entirely from the Colonies, generally as part of each planet's own Planetary Armed Forces. A few designated regiments of each of these PAFs will then be assigned to Colonial Army service, seeing duty on worlds other than their home planet (usually in the Conclave Sphere or along the frontier of Commonwealth space).

commandant: Commonwealth military officer commanding a battalion; equivalent to the rank of major.

commlink: Radio with a range of roughly 250 km, mounted in combat helmets or on vehicles.

company: Smallest independently fielded fighting unit of the Terran Commonwealth. A standard Light Infantry company of the Fifth Foreign Legion comprises three platoons plus a command lance of five (CO, Exec, Company NCO, and two C^3 technicians), as well as any attached personnel such as warrant officers, transport units, sappers, etc. Typically a company will contain 109 officers and men.

compboard: A self-contained minicomputer used like a clipboard.

compols: short for "Commonwealth Police", the chief law enforcement arm of the Terran Commonwealth.

ConRig: Control harness which governs onager aiming in conjunction with helmet HUD sights.

CSN: Commonwealth Space Navy, the arm of the Commonwealth armed forces charged with interplanetary and interstellar transport and combat missions.

demi-battalion: An ad hoc formation of two or more companies, usually commanded by the senior company commander present. Demi-battalions are frequently fielded for long-term detached operations where a full battalion may not be appropriate or available.

detpack: A programmable detonator system used with PX-90 explosives. The operator may select remote, timed, or conditional detonation; without programming, the detpack/explosive combination is completely safe.

Devereaux: Frontier world, attacked 2729 by a Semti invasion fleet.

Site of the heroic Fourth Foreign Legion resistance to an eight-month siege, which saw the destruction of that Legion as an effective fighting force. Now the homeworld of the Fifth Foreign Legion and site of its extensive training facilities.

dreamchip: Originally a trade name, now generic, for ad-chips designed to impart game or fantasy sequences. Also used loosely for the similar programs run on implants.

dreamland: slang for the withdrawn state of someone using an ad-chip or implant.

dwyk: Unit of time on Hanuman. Ten dwyk is roughly fifteen minutes.

Fabrique Europa: Prominent Terran manufacturer of small arms, headquartered in Brussels. The company supplies such well-known weapons systems as the FE-FEK/27 kinetic energy rifle, the FE-MEK/15 kinetic energy assault gun, and the FE-PLF rocket pistol, all in use with the Fifth Foreign Legion.

Fafnir: Man-portable rocket launcher issued on a section level to the Fifth Foreign Legion. The Fafnir rocket is "smart" (able to discriminate various target silhouettes preprogrammed by the opera-tor) and is equally proficient in antitank and air-defense roles.

FE-FEK/24 (*Fusil d'energie Kinetique* Model 24): kinetic energy rifle manufactured by Fabrique Europa, now considered obsolete but still found in local militias, security forces, and private collec-tions. The model lacks the grenade launcher found on the FEK/27.

FE-FEK/27 (Fusil d'Energie Kinetique Model 27): Kinetic energy rifle manufactured by Fabrique Europa, standard longarm of the Fifth Foreign Legion.

FE-MEK/15 (Mitrailleuse d'Energie Kinetique Model 15): Kinetic energy assault gun manufactured by Fabrique Europa, the standard lance-level support weapon used by the Fifth Foreign Legion.

FE-PLF (Pistolet Lance-Fusee): 10mm rocket pistol manufactured by Fabrique Europa, a popular sidearm with officers of the Fifth Foreign Legion.

FLB: Free Laut Besar; the designation of the Besaran forces who fled the planet after the Ubrenfar invasion and accompanied the Commonwealth counterattack.

floatcar: An open-topped magnetic suspension vehicle used in both civilian and military applications. A staff car or jeep.

Freiheit Stern: German for "Liberty Star," the Germanic version of *Soleil Liberté*. Also a liner of Laut Besaran registry.

Freiherr: honorific on Laut Besar between Uro aristocrats.

FSV: acronym for Fire Support Vehicle.

FTL: Faster-Than-Light. The term has entered slang usage as an expression describing any sort of great speed.

fusand: Derived from "fused sand"; a process developed by the Toels and used in the construction of their bases on Polypheme.

fusion airjets: propulsion system used in magrep and other vehicle types. Air is superheated and expelled by small fusion reactors in the system's intake ducts. The Commonwealth prefers turbofans when vehicles are to be used in conjunction with troops due to safety considerations, but other races, notably the Ubrenfars, are less fussy.

Fwynzei: Island enclave ceded by Vyujiid to the Commonwealth. The enclave is garrisoned by a reinforced battalion of the Fifth Foreign Legion (two companies were later detached to develop the trading post at Monkeyville) plus native auxiliary regiments, and is home to the Commonwealth's resident-general, diplomatic and Colonial Administration personnel, and several large trading concerns.

Galahad: M46 anti-personnel mine. The open-topped tube con-tains ten separate egg-shaped bomblets loaded with shrapnel, and sensor gear that triggers the mine when a living creature comes within 10 meters—unless it is wearing a Legion helmet with wor-king IFF gear. Galahads are safe to friendly personnel, but lethal to anyone else.

Gorgon: Commonwealth designation for a Magrep Assault Ve-hicle built by the Toeljuk Autarchy.

Graff: a major landholder on Laut Besar.

Grendel: Large vehicle-mounted missile found on the Sabertooth FSV.

gunnery sergeant: NCO in Commonwealth forces, equivalent in rank to a US Army staff sergeant. Employed as a company-level NCO. Frequently addressed as "Gunny."

Gwyrran: Native of Gwyrr (Lywstryn IV) or any of the colonies planted under the auspices of the Semti. The typical Gwyrran is a bipedal, furred, homeothermic sophont standing roughly 1.9 meters in height. Their culture is highly feudalistic, with similarities to that of Medieval Japan on Terra. Humans and Gwyrrans find it very hard to understand one another's languages and underlying philo-sophies even with the aid of the adchip instruction.

The Gwyrrans, like the Ubrenfars, were favored by the Semti Con-clave as soldiers, but Gwyrr never chose to rebel from Conclave rule.

H & F stamp: Legion slang for an honorable discharge, derived from the phrase "Served with Honor and Fidelity" stamped on the discharge papers of the legionnaire.

hauptmann: rank in the Army of Laut Besar corresponding to Commonwealth captain.

hannie: Slang term for the natives of Hanuman, applied by Terr-ans. Considered derogatory, but by no means as bad as "monkey," the other popular label.

Hanuman: Fourth planet of Morrison's Star, a former Semti sub-ject. Now a client of the Commonwealth.

holetter: message using a holocube to send 3D sound-and-video data.

holo: slang for a holographic image.

holocube: a small, flat projector which can store and image 3D still or moving pictures. Very inexpensive models simply project an un-moving, silent image. Advanced types can carry up to half an hour or more of sound and video.

holopic: a holographic image in a wall or frame mount, the lineal descendent of a painting, poster, or photograph.

holovid: a 3D holographic projection using full sight, sound, and motion.

HUD: Heads Up Display. Found in many vehicles and craft, this type of display system is also used in combat helmets by individual infantrymen.

ident disk: a derivative of chip technology worn by most people within the Commonwealth and associated regions. The ident disk contains retinal scan and DNA trace for unique identification of the owner. It also contains a record of professional, financial, edu-cational, and other background. The ident disk is considered the most reliable method of recording information available, and is an individual's most important single possession.

implant: Computer link surgically placed directly in the brain. Most upper-class Terrans and a few exceptionally wealthy Colon-ials have implants, as do certain military officers whose duties re-quire their use.

Indomay: person of Indonesian/Malaysian descent; member of Laut Besar's lower class.

kajudjati: a dark hardwood grown on Laut Besar.

kapitan: rank and position in the Navy of Laut Besar, usually de-noting the commanding officer of a ship.

KEC: A heavy kinetic-energy weapon found in a vehicle mount aboard Sabertooth and Sandray class vehicles. It is the kinetic-energy weapon equivalent of a contemporary Vulcan Gatling can-non, with an extremely high rate of fire and muzzle velocities that will defeat almost any type of conventional armor.

kepi: the traditional headgear of the Foreign Legion dress uniform. Enlisted personnel wear a white kepi, officers black. Much mys-tique is built around the award of the kepi to the Legion trainee.

kopral: rank in the Army of Laut Besar corresponding to the Commonwealth's corporal.

lance: Designation of the Commonwealth's basic military unit, either five infantrymen or a single tank or aircraft.

last march: Legion slang for death.

Lebensraum Bergbau und Ingenieurwesen Korporation: Lebensraum Mining and Engineering Corporation, a now-defunct resource exploitation firm originally based on the colony world of Lebensraum which provided the first Uro technical experts who took over economic and later political control of Laut Besar shortly before the Semti War.

legionnaire: Loosely, a member of the Fifth Foreign Legion (or any other "Legion" in the army, if there are such). Specifically, an enlisted soldier holding the rank of legionnaire first class, legion-naire second class, or legionnaire third class. Non-Legion units use the designation "soldier" instead of legionnaire.

leutnant: rank in the Army of Laut Besar corresponding to the Commonwealth rank of subaltern.

life-support chair: powered wheelchair used for extreme injuries and geriatric cases who no longer respond to regen or bionic therapy. The chair is enclosed around the legs and lower torso, and houses a variety of life support equipment. It is powered and can be steered by voice command or keyboard input.

lighter: Generic name applied to the small transports used for the bulk of ground-to-orbit transport. Lighters are grav-powered ships with a fair-sized cargo capacity, and generally run in the five to ten-thousand-ton displacement range. They are slower and less maneuverable than scramjet shuttles and other boats, but compensate for this by their superior loads. In Legion parlance, a "lighter" almost invariably refers to the 10,000-ton transports which can carry several companies of legionnaires and their equip-ment from ground to orbit or between any two ground bases. Lighters are usually unarmed, though this is not always true.

linnax: naval or planetary defense gun; the name derives from "linear accelerator." It fires projectiles at very high velocities, using the same principles as the kinetic energy rifle but on a much larger scale.

loke: Slang for "local"; applied to a native nonhuman.

magger: Anyone who operates an MSV; a tank or APC crewman.

mag: Slang derived from magnetic suspension technology, mean-ing "move." To "mag out" is to "move out" or "bug out"; a "mag-out" is a hasty departure.

magger: anyone who operates an MSV; a tank or APC crewman.

maglev tube: fixed transport system commonly used around large Commonwealth cities and installations. By mounting magrep modules in the tubes themselves and in the cars traversing them, manipulation of magnetic fields allows high speeds to be reached. The tubes are in a vacuum to reduce friction problems.

magrep module: Small semicircular projection unit (linked to a generator) that produces a magnetic suspension cushion.

magnetic: suspension cushion: Effect produced by the interplay of a magnetic repulsion generator and a planetary magnetic field. The cushion allows a vehicle to float up to a meter away from any semi-solid surface, providing a magnetic field is present to interact with the vehicle-mounted generator. The effect is much more powerful (and infinitely quieter) than an air cushion, allowing really massive vehicles to be moved fairly easily by turbofans (or, occasionally, fusion airjets). However, the cushion does not function effectively over extremely rugged terrain or allow the vehicle to "fly."

magnetic suspension vehicle (MSV): Official designation of any vehicle operating on a magnetic suspension cushion.

major: rank in the Army of Laut Besar corresponding to the Commonwealth ranks of commandant or major. It is pronounced "mai-yor" when used by or for Besarans.

marchman: Legion slang for the common soldier; doughboy; grognard; grunt.

Mark 18 Mjollnir KEC: A heavy kinetic energy weapon found in a vehicle mount aboard Sabertooth and Sandray class vehicles. It is the kinetic energy weapon equivalent of a contemporary Vulcan Gatling cannon, with an extremely high rate of fire and muzzle velocities that will defeat almost any type of conventional armor.

MAV: acronym for Magrep Assault Vehicle.

messtalk: slang for rumor or scuttlebutt.

MSV: Magnetic Suspension Vehicle, official designation of any vehicle operating on a Magnetic Suspension Cushion.

murphy: Any unforeseen and potentially catastrophic occurrence.

Milky Way Magician: figure from a popular children's entertainment series of the Reclamation Era. The Milky Way Magician stories have become classics in the past two hundred years. "I be-lieve in the Milky Way Magician" is on par with belief in Santa Claus or the Easter Bunny.

narcostick: a nonaddictive, mildly narcotic cigarette.

nube: A newcomer or rookie.

oberleutnant: rank in the Army of Laut Besar corresponding to the Commonwealth rank of lieutenant.

oberst: rank in the Army of Laut Besar corresponding to the Commonwealth rank of colonel.

Onager; *fusil d'onage;* **storm rifle:** Plasma gun, originally invent-ed during the French Imperial period (hence the French-derived name). The onager is one of the standard section-level heavy weap-ons used by the Fifth Foreign Legion (the other is the Fafnir rocket launcher).

Onagers require soldiers to wear fairly cumbersome body armor to protect them from heat effects, but are devastatingly powerful on the battlefield. A larger version of the weapon, the onager cannon, is found in a turret mount on the Sabertooth FSV.

onnesium: a trans-100 element existing in an "island of stability" beyond the short-lived radioactives on the periodic table. Onnesium is used to plate field coils in Reynier-Kessler FTL drive units. It is rare and extremely valuable, both monetarily and strategically.

Ortwaffen: German (Laut Besaran Uro dialect) for "Place of Arms," a training area devoted to weapons practice found in insti-tutions and some private homes.

Pegasus (TH-39): hypersonic shuttle used by the Commonwealth military for rapid deployment of small units over continental distances or to and from orbit.

penal battalions: auxiliary units of the Colonial Army, employed for dirty jobs involving heavy labor, including construction, colon -ization projects, Terraforming preparation, and similar tasks. The penal battalions are filled by criminals facing short-term punish-ment, often as an alternative to regular military service.

platoon: Basic tactical unit of the Commonwealth's ground forces, containing either six tanks, thirteen APCs, or two infantry sections plus a sublieutenant as platoon leader and a platoon sergeant as unit NCO (for a total of 34 men).

platoon sergeant: NCO rank equivalent to the contemporary USA rank of staff sergeant. Serves as platoon XO.

primmie: Commonwealth slang for "primitive."

PX-90: Explosive compound, packaged in 1-kg blocks. The explosive is a high-tech version of plastique used with a detpack programmable detonator. PX-90 has both military and engineering applications.

ra-pack: Ration pack; the twenty-ninth century equivalent to a MRE.

regen therapy: Advanced medical technique for re-growth of damaged tissue.

rembot: labor-saving device, a robot controlled by a master computer system in a household, factory, etc. This approach to robotics was found to be far more efficient than the use of numerous independent machines.

repbay: maintenance and storage facility for vehicles, aircraft, and so forth. A hangar or garage.

Republic Trisystem: name given by Captain Francois Robespierre of the *ISS TALLEYRAND* to the loose trinary system surveyed by his expedition in 2362 AD. The three stars he dubbed *Liberté*, *Ega-lité* and *Fraternité* in honor of the French Revolution, which was an especial interest of his due to his famous name. The Trisystem was never settled as a single entity. The planet bearing Robespierre's name was colonized by Imperial France, while Laut Besar was sett-led under the Clearance Edicts by Indomalaysian troublemakers; it later became an unaligned neutral outside the Commonwealth. Two planets orbiting Soleil Fraternity were claimed by the Ubrenfars during the Shadow Centuries.

resident-general: Colonial Administration official appointed as administrative head of Terran interests on a Client World. Unlike governors, resident-generals have little direct influence over local governmental affairs; their job is to administer and look after the Terrans who live or work on the planet. In fact, though, the resident-general's control of Commonwealth trade and Colonial Army garrisons gives him a tremendous ability to influence native rulers.

Reynier Industries: Giant corporation in Commonwealth space that retains a monopoly on the manufacture of interstellar drive systems. The company's political influence is very extensive, and Reynier has been called "the forty-sixth Member" in the Com-monwealth's forty-five member-worlds.

rezplex: A residential complex.

Sabertooth (M-980 FSV): Company-level Fire Support Vehicle employed by the Fifth Foreign Legion, mounting 2 Grendel mis-siles, an onager cannon in a turret, and a fixed-forward kinetic energy cannon. It can carry up to 6 men plus a crew of two. Typic-ally, a company mounted on 13 vehicles will include two Saber-tooths.

Sandray (M-786 series): Generic name for an entire family of armored personnel carriers and specialty variants used by the Fifth Foreign Legion. Typical vehicles include an APC, a command van, an engineering vehicle, a supply carrier, a medical van, and so on. They carry six men plus a specialty compartment (except the APC, which carries twelve men). Many of them mount kinetic energy cannons in a remote-controlled turret; the engineering vehicle mounts a low-power laser cannon and various types of engineering hardware such as bulldozer blades or cranes.

Also, the life-form native to the Great Desert of Devereaux, a burrowing carnivore trapper which subdues its prey with a muscle-paralyzing poison.

savkey: A retreat, derived from French *"sauve qui peut."*

section: Designation for an infantry unit containing three lances, plus a sergeant as section leader. The section thus contains sixteen men.

Semti: An alien race, formerly rulers of the Semti Conclave but now subject (for the most part) to the Terran Commonwealth. Evol-ved from scavenger stock, they are bilaterally symmetrical, upright bipeds, basically humanoid in appearance but with dry, leathery skins and large eyes. They apparently evolved in desert conditions under a K or M class star, and frequently shroud themselves in dark robes when visiting planets around more energetic stars. Their voices are soft and whispery.

The Semti have been civilized for many thousands of years, and have a rich civilization full of tradition and high culture. Unfor-tunately, they also are rather disgusting to humans (thanks to a carrion stink on their breaths and their cold, clammy skin), fre-quently earning such appellations as "ghoul" or "zombie." Their ruthless pragmatism brought them into direct conflict with Terra during the Semti War, in which they lost control of the two hun-dred-world empire known as the Semti Conclave.

An aptitude for administration has made them an invaluable part of the post-war Commonwealth administrative system, despite their place as former enemies, and despite the distaste they generate on a personal level. Having a Semti mandarin on one's staff is con-sidered to be the height of status within the Colonial Admin-istration; they can do the work it would take a hundred human bur-eaucrats to accomplish.

Semti philosophy is extremely alien to human thought. They are very long-lived, and "taking the long view" can, for a Semti, in-volve many centuries. For example, the Semti showed no particular ill feeling at the loss of their empire, and they work tirelessly at their jobs helping humans govern the same territory "because that is our function in life." Once humans could accept this attitude, they welcomed the Semti with open arms.

Semti Conclave: Interstellar state, now disbanded, lying to core-ward of the Terran Commonwealth. The Semti Conclave was dominated by the Semti, who were able to administer approx-imately 200 planets and perhaps 125 separate races in a stable government which had survived almost unchanged over a span of several thousand years at least. Semti policy was to discourage technological or social change and maintain an iron grip over individual civilizations through the manipulation of local reli-gions, rulers, and institutions. Though they had a reputation for excellent government, the Semti proved quite capable of taking whatever measures they deemed necessary—even genocide—to maintain control over members of the Conclave.

The Conclave collapsed after the destruction of the Semti capital at the hands of the Terran Commonwealth in 2744. Since that time the Conclave Sphere has been a wide-open colonial frontier over which the Commonwealth and other interstellar powers have ex-tended their control.

Semti War: conflict fought between the Terran Commonwealth and the Semti Conclave (2725-2745 AD). The initial Semti pene-tration of Terran space was slowed down by the Fourth Foreign Legion's heroic stand on Devereaux, giving the unprepared Com-monwealth time to gather military forces and make several crucial diplomatic alliances with other interstellar powers bordering on the Conclave. The final Terran offensive deep into Conclave space ended with the surrender of the last Semti military forces in 2745.

serdadu: rank in the Army of Laut Besar corresponding to the Commonwealth ranks of legionnaire or soldier.

sersan: rank in the Army of Laut Besar corresponding to the Commonwealth rank of sergeant.

sersan peloten: rank in the Army of Laut Besar corresponding to the Commonwealth rank of platoon sergeant.

Shadow Centuries, the: term applied to the period of 2425-2590 AD, a period of anarchy on Terra. The Shadow Centuries were marked by a lapse of some Terran technologies. Although existing carrierships continued to operate on an irregular basis, there was no new ship construction and no organized effort to stay in touch with the bulk of the human colony worlds. Mankind's return to interstellar space was put on hold until Terrestrial affairs could be set in order, leaving the colonial worlds to survive—or perish—on their own.

Sky Guard: military organization on Laut Besar. A largely ceremonial formation.

softsnake: a large but primitive animal native to Laut Besar, snake-like in appearance but lacking an endoskeleton and possessing many characteristics of Terran gastropods.

sol: basic unit of Commonwealth currency, buying power roughly equivalent to one dollar in 1990 US funds.

Soleil Egalité: G3V star, part of the "Republic Trisystem." Robespierre, a Commonwealth colony world, circles this star.

Soleil Fraternité: F8V star, part of the "Republic Trisystem." The system's two habitable planets are controlled by the Ubrenfars.

Soleil Liberté: K2V star, part of the "Republic Trisystem." The system supports two habitable planets, Laut Besar (I) and Danton (Vb).

strakk: (1) a small, nasty, ill-tempered, rodentlike species native to Devereaux which congregates in large swarms. They are smelly, dirty, stupid beasts that combine the worst behavioral charac-teristics of rats, cockroaches, and lemmings. (2) swear word, der-ived from the creature. The word has entered the language, es-pecially in the Legion, in a number of ways: as a noun, "you filthy strakk" (very insulting); as a verb, "strakking" (i.e. behaving like a strakk), etc.

subaltern: Lowest officer rank, commanding a platoon. Com-monly "sub."

synthol: a synthetic alcohol beverage much favored in the Legion.

systerm: "System Terminal," the major port facilities used for car-riership operations near the fringe of a star system.

Systerm Liberty: name of the system terminal in the Laut Besaran system, administered by Commonwealth authorities.

tacdata: tactical database. Before a mission or during transport, all soldiers are given a tacdata feed from HQ or vehicle computers to their individual wristpieces or other personal computers. Tacdata includes maps, last known dispositions of friendly and enemy units, radio frequencies, mission profiles, etc.

Telok: inner satellite of Laut Besar, housing planetary port facilities and a military installation. The word, in Indomay, means "port."

Terran Commonwealth: The human interstellar state that fields the Fifth Foreign Legion. Following the Semti War, the Common-wealth acquired virtual control over most of the Conclave Sphere, and thus became a colonial power in the old (nineteenth century) sense of the term.

Terranglic: the common tongue of modern humanity, especially the Commonwealth, derived from English with many borrowings from other tongues, especially French.

Toeljuk: Alien race, another of the colonial powers exploiting for-mer Semti space. The Toeljuks are a squat, low-grav race with tentacles. They have a reputation for brutality and greed.

Topheth: Planet of the Procyon star system noted for rich metal deposits and hellish conditions. The name has passed into Commonwealth usage as a common synonym for Hell.

Tuan: Indomay term of respect, the equivalent of "sir" or "my lord," usually (but not always) reserved for Uros.

Ubrenfars: alien starfaring race, a serious rival with the Terran Commonwealth for interstellar power. The typical Ubrenfar is a two-meter tall, warm-blooded biped with a powerful tail, highly mobile and expressive ear-folds, and thick scales. The gross ap-pearance suggests a Terran dinosaur, but the actual biology is to-tally alien. They are known pejoratively among humans as "scalies."

The Ubrenfars, like Mankind, were involved in hostilities against the Semti when the Conclave collapsed, and indeed were perceived by the Semti as the more dangerous opponent. They are aggressive, territorial, and warlike.

Uro: person of Germanic/European descent; member of Laut Be-sar's upper class.

veeter: A small VTOL aircraft used for recon work.

vidmagazine: A holovid entertainment device worn like glasses, which allows the user to experience the contents as if at first hand. Becoming largely obsolete as adchips spread, the vidmagazine is primarily found now in the role of 20th-century newspapers or infotainment magazines or programs.

Vyujiid: Nation dominating the northern hemisphere of Hanuman. Remnant of a former empire, Vyujiid is the most civilized of the nations on Hanuman and the main point of Commonwealth pene-tration on the world.

warrant officer: A specialist officer in the Colonial Army, not in the regular chain of command but with many of the privileges and responsibilities of regular officers. There are four grades (WO/1 through WO/4); a WO/4 is equivalent to a sublieutenant and is found on a company staff. Ability as a warrant officer frequently leads to a full officer's commission. Typical specialties include me-dical, chaplain, sciences, intel/alien technologies, combat engi-neering, and others. Note that other branches of the armed forces do not use this system.

Whitney-Sykes HPLR-55 (High-Power Laser Rifle Mark 55): A laser rifle manufactured by the Australian small-arms company Whitney-Sykes, commonly used as a sniper's rifle by the Fifth For-eign Legion.

wog: Derogatory slang term (derived from "polliwog") for the na-tives of Polypheme. Though not originally based on the pejorative "wog" of 19th-century Terra, usage is quite similar.

wristpiece: A computer terminal worn on the wrist and forearm. The wristpiece is now becoming largely obsolete on Terra (where computer implants are the cutting edge of technology), but are still quite common off Terra. They can perform a wide variety of func-tions, including calculation, data storage/retrieval, translation, and other jobs. Some are designed to link to implants or adchips worn by the operator, while others are voice-activated with a remote radio receiver worn behind the ear.

Commonly known as a "piece."

Wynsarrysa: "the Lost," descendants of the original Gwyrran col-onists on Devereaux, or, more specifically, those who have not been assimilated into colonial life. They are regarded as brigands and rebels.

yiiz: Standard kyendyp unit of measurement, equal to about 1.76 kilograms.

Yzyeel: *Kyendyp* word, translated roughly as "king." The ruler of Dryienjaiyeel.

zymlat: Beast of burden used on Hanuman.

About the Authors

J. Andrew Keith and William H. Keith, Jr., are prolific game designers and authors of adventure science fiction novels. The two brothers worked together for FASA on the Traveller game and then expanded to other gaming universes. As novelists, they wrote for Wing Commander, BattleTech, as well as the Fifth Foreign Legion series. Andrew Keith passed away in 1999.

William H. Keith, Jr. produced an enormous number of novels under his own name and various pseudonyms, working with colla-borators Stephen Coonts, and Peter Jurasik and Bruce Boxleitner (both from the TV show *Babylon 5*). Three of his novels have been *New York Times* bestsellers and his gaming work has won several prominent industry awards.

IF YOU LIKED ...

If you liked *The Fifth Foreign Legion Omnibus*, you might also enjoy:

Strong Arm Tactics
Five by Five
The Outpost

Other WordFire Press Titles by Andrew Keith & William Keith, Jr.

March or Die

Honor and Fidelity

Cohort of the Damned

Our list of other WordFire Press authors and titles is always growing. To find out more and to see our selection of titles, visit us at:

wordfirepress.com